I0602190

THE RISE OF THE GODDESS

by E A CARTER

Transcendence Series
The Lost Valor of Love
The Call of Eternity
The Rise of the Goddess

THE RISE OF THE GODDESS

E A CARTER

Copyright © 2019 by E A CARTER

The moral right of the author is hereby asserted in accordance
with the Copyright, Designs and Patents Act 1988

*All characters and events in this publication,
other than those clearly in the public domain,
are fictitious and any resemblance to actual persons,
living or dead, is purely coincidental.*

All rights reserved. No part of this publication may be
reproduced, stored in a retrieval system, or transmitted, in any
form or by any means without the prior written permission of
the publisher, nor be otherwise circulated in any form of binding
or cover other than that in which it is published and without a
similar condition being imposed on the subsequent buyer.

First Edition

Printed in the United States of America

First Printing, 2020

ISBN: 978-1-64184-275-4 (paperback)

Arundel House Press
www.arundelhousepress.com

Interior Print Design Jetlaunch LLC www.jetlaunch.net
Cover Art Michał Karcz www.michalkarcz.com
Cover Design & Map ©Debbie O'Byrne

For you, the goddesses who surrounded me with your light
I will never forget you, in this life, or any other

KIUM
PRES
CHAUS
THOLIS
SARITOVA
SERDE
SENAS
VINAY
LAUCA
NIMIDIA
AURIANDE SEA
ANKI
SURRU
TYRATU
CHERN
ENION
QATU
SERI
RZHEV
PIR
SENICHIN ISLES
N
E
S
W

PROLOGUE

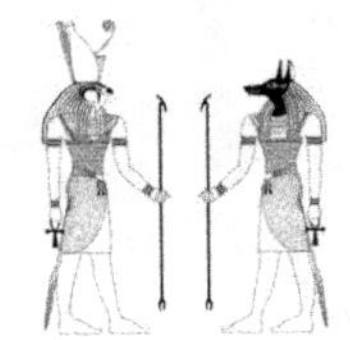

Sethi slammed his way through a glut of warriors, his arms and chest bloody, his double-bladed jihn thrumming, hungry for the essence of the living. He looked up, breathing hard, the burning air searing his lungs.

There. He had her. Istara stood alone and undefended, surrounded by smoke and fire. In the heated updrafts, her star-clad, tangled hair whipped around her face. Her golden eyes raked over the scores of Elati's dead and dying, her healing light pulsing across the battlefield, brilliant haloes of gold. He stood still. Waited until she found him. Caught the parting of her lips. The tremor of her heart. The quiet hope. He smiled at her, cold, the god of war, and tread over the carpet of her fallen warriors, never taking his eyes from her, his soul scorched with hate. No one could stop him now. Not even the one who called himself her protector—

A blade, from behind, delved into his heart, the pain brutal, agonizing. He turned. Urhi-Teshub twisted the weapon, his eyes hard, hatred bleeding from him. With a roar, Sethi yanked himself free and slammed his fist into Urhi-Teshub's skull, once, twice, three times. Istara's protector collapsed, senseless. Sethi staggered, blinded by pain. His left pectoral lay torn open, muscle and bone sundered, his heart riven in two. The jihn slid from his grip. He cursed as his light ignited, slow, unsteady, working to heal him. He sank into a crouch, blackened by fury. By the time he was strong enough to stand, his quarry would have fled.

Hands came to his face and cradled his jaw, tender. He looked up. Istara's golden eyes, bright with tears, met his. She spoke, her words stolen by the thunder of an explosion. Light exploded out of her heart into his, brilliant, a nova, blinding. In its wake, tendrils of her healing light wove around him, a multitude, closing the rent in his heart, making him whole again.

His nemesis—the one who had rallied the armies of men and gods against him—granted him her healing light, the stars limning her hair dimming as she brought him back to his full power: Sethi, god of war, Commander of Elati, second only to Marduk, Lord of All, Giver of Life, Taker of Life.

Rejuvenated, he rose and hefted the jihn, the heat of battle still hot in his veins. In his grip, the jihn's curved blades awakened. Its lethal hunger coursed through him, hardening him. He looked down at his once-consort, filled with abhorrence for her weakness, scorning her gift to him. He would never have done the same for her. She remained on her knees, her eyes on his. A tear slid free and tracked a path through the fine coating of soot dusting her face.

Her lips moved again. He couldn't hear anything over the scream of the ships as they tore across the burning sky, but he read her lips, words enslaved queens had whispered as he rode them, desperate for his favor.

I love you.

He lifted his weapon. The jihn's black blades glinted, blue-white, slavering for her light, her annihilation. She was a fool. Love meant nothing. And soon she would be nothing, her light consumed by the jihn. He smiled, cold, triumphant. At last. Victory.

He thrust the glowing blades toward her heart.

Sethi sat up, abrupt, panting. He touched the back of his neck, the agony of the device Marduk had driven into the base of his skull unforgettable, the shear of its bite hot and sharp as it dug its way through flesh and bone and burrowed deep into his brain. Its malevolent presence had poisoned his thoughts, corrupted his memories—had made him into a weapon.

It hadn't taken long for the device to betray Sethi's awareness of Istara's presence in Elati. Marduk had listened, impassive, then showed Sethi images of Istara with Urhi-Teshub in the Etemen'anki. The once-king of Hatti had taken her, willing, to his bed. Sethi had destroyed everything in the suite. It hadn't been enough.

Blinded by the hateful thing controlling his mind, Sethi dined on his rage, his hunger for revenge. And yet, despite his descent into evil, his god-light remained. Each morning, during the ephemeral heartbeats of dawn, golden tendrils of his light would overcome the device's control. Fragments of his true self would slip from their bond, would force him to face the horror of what he had become, of the crimes he had committed, and of the lie he believed against the one he loved—and his helplessness to stop it.

He carved messages into his flesh: *It is a lie. Istara was not unfaithful. Protect her at all costs.* But no matter how deep he cut, his warnings would last no more than a few hours, his light erasing every desperate, bloody symbol. He clenched his fists, the dream returning, haunting him. To think he might do it, might drive his blade into the heart of the one he loved beyond all reason—

He caught a glimpse of his bleak reflection in the enormous mirror facing the bed. The tyranny of his acts seared his mind, damned him for his brutality. Everything he had once stood for had become perverted, his power used to oppress those who dared resist Marduk's conquest of Elati .

The air in the room oppressed him. He lunged from the bed and shoved aside the shutters leading to the terrace. The lavender hue of dawn sliced its way along the mountain's ridge to the east. At the edge of the terrace, he eyed the sheer drop into an enormous lake, more than half a short iter distant.

From an outcropping in the mountains, a waterfall thundered into the lake, shrouded in pre-dawn mist. The night before, he had flung a king from this terrace—for entertainment—then dragged the dead king's queen to his bed before throwing her to her death after him. Anguished, he clawed at the back of his head, desperate to dig the vile device out, to end what he had become. How many times had tried to cut it out with his dagger before the device reignited? More than he could count. There was never enough time.

The warmth of the sun's rays slid over him. He glanced at the golden disk as it ascended, fast, recalling a smaller, statelier sun which had risen over the desert sands of an empire that had once been his home. The memories of his mortal life had almost vanished. Soon there would be nothing left of the commander he used to be, or of the princess he loved beyond all reason.

His fingers bloody, he pressed his palm over his heart, sensing his light reawakening his bond with Istara. For a beat, joy. Then, the agony of her grief for his crimes slammed into him, followed by her yearning, her loneliness; her determination to free him from Marduk's grip. Shame engulfed him. Somewhere out there, beyond the mountains, beyond the sea, beyond the desert, she gathered allies—to save him from himself. His goddess. His consort. His everything.

A shear of blue-white light tore through his mind, washed her presence away. He sank to his knees and gripped the edge of the terrace, his muscles straining, resisting the device as it dragged him back, unwilling, to its filth, its lies. Nausea boiled, rancid and bitter. Hate sawed through him, ugly and familiar.

He clung, stubborn, to the last images he had of Istara, of when he had lived with her in another world, his love for her endless, overwhelming. The device's light screamed through the images, scoured his mind, its heat blistering, blinding. He fought its brutal onslaught, vomiting over the edge of the terrace, his heart aching, bitterness saturating him as his memories dissolved and slipped through his fingers, grains of sand. Gone. For eternity.

The god of war fell back on his haunches. He blinked, disoriented, unable to recall when he had come to the terrace from his bed. The images of his dream crept into the corridors of his mind, of the mysterious weapon which could consume a god's light, a weapon which had called to him. With such a powerful artifact, none could stand against him, not even the gods. He would search for this weapon, and once he possessed it . . . he smiled, cold, as he considered his faithless consort and the agonies he would inflict on her for betraying him. Yes. He glared at the sun as it soared into the sky. For what she had done with Urhi-Teshub, he would make her suffer. Forever.

PART I

JIHN

CHAPTER 1

The thunderous downpour ended, abrupt. In its wake, a rush of rich, rain-cleansed air. The quiet ripple of potted bamboo. A shear of silence. The plaintive cry of a night heron, far-off. Thoth picked up his wine, left the chaos of his desk and pushed past the silken hangings separating his apartment from the terrace. Barefoot, he went to its edge, skirting the pots overflowing with geraniums, their soft leaves laden with water droplets.

He sipped his wine, once more turning over Istara's request to create a sanctuary for the gods when none of his powers remained. Her words, said so quiet almost a month earlier, still kept him awake at night: *We cannot remain in Imaru. We must find a location separate from the kingdoms where we can gather allies and prepare to face our enemy. There must be a way you can grant us the protection we need.*

A warm breeze slid past, languid and damp. Below his apartment, the golden lights of the city of Imaru skirted the shore of a vast lake. The clouds parted. Two crescent moons hovered just over the horizon—one pink, one white, both breathtaking. Across the lake's dark surface, the moons' light danced and shimmered, a starry canopy to match the profusion of glittering lights spanning the heavens.

A sweet, earthy scent swept over the terrace. Thoth inhaled, deep, savoring the fresh air denied to him after almost two years of captivity, buried deep beneath the Etemen'anki of Babylon—the enormous stepped pyramid Thoth's presence had destroyed, along with half of Istara's world. If Istara and Baalat's sacrifice hadn't ensured his escape through the portal at Surru to Elati—the world he now called home—nothing would have been left of Istara's world on the other side of the portal's ephemeral, churning wall.

Surru. His greatest achievement. A portal which traversed the distance between two universes. The amount of energy it had taken to power it up had been immense, had required the building of—

He caught his breath.

Of course. It was so simple.

He turned and hurried back to his desk, uncaring of the wine sloshing over the rim of his cup and onto his hand. The answer he had been seeking for weeks had come in the blink of an eye. How had he not thought of it before? Surru held the answer. It always had. But—his hands stilled against his notes—Surru led to not one but two worlds, neither of them safe. He sank onto his chair. When he last traversed Surru from Elati to Istara's world how long had he had before her world robbed him of his powers as a god and rendered him mortal? Hours, at most.

But they would still be there—the pyramids he had created in the long distant past, their cores once used to power up the portals, later modified to protect themselves from destruction— he had given up a fair portion of his own light to ensure they would never fail. They would have stood against the worst of the unraveling in Egypt while the rest of the world succumbed, torn apart by his presence. They had also granted an unexpected barrier against Marduk's devices, although he had discovered *that* advantage far too late. He would not make the same mistake twice.

Could it be done in time? A trip to Istara's world, all the way to Egypt and back? He exhaled. Of course not. He was mad to even consider it. It was too far and would take too long, even with a fast ship—and what of the instability he would bring back to her world? No. He had no choice. He would have to return to the parallel world he and Arinna had fled, the one still caught in the *other* Marduk's brutal grip.

Thoth sighed, so many worlds, so many outcomes, yet all with one constant—Marduk and the endless worlds-spanning war to overcome him. A fight which, right now, the gods were losing as one kingdom of Elati after another pledged allegiance to Marduk, their unwilling submission forced upon them by the brutality of the god of war, no longer Horus, but another, the once-commander of Egypt, Sethi, Istara's consort.

Thoth dried his wine-soaked hand against his kilt, his usual pleasure at considering the complex abandoning him. From among the piles of pages and scrolls, a map protruded. He pulled it out and followed the familiar lines and contours of the world he had fled with Arinna more than two years before. His gaze came to rest on the delta of Egypt, long made into a barren wasteland, its boundaries guarded by Marduk's malevolent, patrolling devices.

Beyond the open doors of the terrace, a white star fell from the heavens. Thoth eyed its descent, grim, thinking of the price three of the gods from his world had paid to free the others from Marduk's tyranny. In a final, desperate act, they had evaded the patrols and entered the hearts of the pyramids where, as one, they had sacrificed their light to the pyramids' cores in the hopes of increasing the radius of the pyramids' defenses. It had worked. Their combined energies had, for a brief time, forced Marduk to flee to the heavens, his devices and weapons useless to him while the others escaped.

A red star slid from the sky's indigo canopy, followed by another, haloed in a brilliant blue. Thoth's heart clenched. Remorse, raw and jagged, cut deep. His portals had caused more harm than he could ever have anticipated. He looked down into his cup, morose. The trio of gods from his pantheon who had sacrificed their light would have suffered unimaginable anguish. The cores would have burned them from the inside out. Though the gods of Istara's world had lived on, the gods of *his* world—Teshub, Horus, and Baalat—were gone. Obliterated.

His grip tightened on his cup. No. Their sacrifice would not be for nothing. If the survivors in Elati from his and Istara's worlds were to have any chance against Marduk, Thoth needed the cores. With them he could construct the pyramids again and grant the gods an impenetrable refuge from Marduk. He might have gained immortality by traversing the portal with Istara, but his godly powers—just like Teshub's and Arinna's—were long gone. He would never be able to make such powerful artifacts again.

A rustle of material. He looked up.

"Lady Istara." He rose. "I did not hear you come in."

"You were deep in thought," Istara said. Her golden eyes met his, shrouded with grief. "I did not wish to disturb you."

Thoth moved around his desk and took her hands in his. "I might have a plan."

The stars in her hair brightened, a shear of hope against her sorrow.

"I have to go back," he said.

"Back?" Istara's brow furrowed. "Where?"

"To the world Arinna and I left. I must retrieve artifacts of great power which could save us all."

"A dangerous decision," Istara murmured. "The enemy of your world still controls it. If he finds you, he will enslave you again."

Thoth smiled, dry. "Then I had best ensure I am not found." A cool wind sliced through the apartment. The silken hangings of the terrace billowed inward. A profusion of geranium petals skidded across the damp terrace. "However, I cannot go alone since I am no longer a god—the portal will not open for me."

Istara's grip tightened against his fingers. "I will come with you."

"As will I."

An immortal, his powerful body clad in a gold-gilt leather tunic and kilt stepped from the shadows of the doorway. A pair of Marduk's appropriated weapons hung from his belt. From over his shoulders, two more of the once-god of Babylon's stolen weapons reared up.

Thoth met Urhi-Teshub's eyes and nodded. "Tomorrow then," he said, "we will leave for Surru at dawn. May the Creator—"

A scream split the skies. Marduk's warship sundered the night's canopy with blue fire. Thoth eyed it, bleak. It was the first time he had seen it since their arrival. He had heard Marduk's reach was growing. The god of war would be seeking out new kingdoms to conquer, while Marduk remained with his consort, Meresamun, in a location still unknown.

Istara pressed her hand against her heart, her eyes fixed on the ship, her longing for the one within tangible. "My love," she whispered, "I beg you. Fight this. Fight him. Come back to me."

Her hand fell to her side. Desolate, she met Thoth's look and shook her head. The ship ascended into the stars. A burst of blue and it was gone. In the silence of its wake, the broken cry of a goddess.

❋　❋　❋

In the hushed silence of Rzhev's deepest night, the halls, vaults, and corridors of Imaru's royal armory slept. Pale moonlight pierced the metal latticework of the armory's narrow windows, and washed the stone-flagged floor in watery light. Beyond the city's walls, the cry of a nightbird rose, plaintive, lonely. Close by, a watchman tolled the fourth hour. Outside, a loose shutter ricocheted against the wall, captive to the prowling wind.

In just a few hours, they would depart. Urhi-Teshub was not ready.

His hands on his hips, he pondered the assortment of seamless, silvery weapons and devices he had liberated along with Teshub, Thoth, and Ahmen from Marduk's armory in the Etemen'anki. Each item bore unique, appealing merits. Even so, an immortal could only carry so much. A prickle of uncertainty glided through him as his gaze lingered on the largest weapon, one he had discovered with a single shot could consume an entire building in a vortex of white heat. Even if it was heavy and cumbersome, it felt wrong to leave it behind. Thoth had said the pyramid complex was large, and to expect to have to run. A weapon of this size would be certain to slow him down. And yet . . . No. He could not leave it behind.

With a grunt, he hefted it from the table and threw its strap over his shoulder. Its weight bore down on him, dense as an ashlar. He rolled his shoulder, fighting the thing's drag, its length unwieldy and its balance pulling him to one side. Knots tightened in his neck, screaming this was not a weapon to be carried by any other than Marduk, whose armor granted him strength beyond what was natural. And yet, during their escape from the Etemen'anki, the once-god Teshub had borne its weight through the wreckage of the collapsing *ziqquratu*, while also carrying his fallen consort, Arinna. A shot of admiration rippled through Urhi-Teshub. If Teshub could do it, so could he. It would be madness to face Marduk's patrols with anything less.

"If you take that one," a quiet voice said from beyond the vault's open door, "you will regret it." A slim woman emerged from the shadows, her skin flawless, a midnight marble burnished by the torchlight. "Urhi-Teshub," she said, "I am Sekhmet." A greeting, of sorts.

Clad from neck to toe in fitted black leather, she glided over to him, her movements sleek, mesmerizing, graceful. She came to a halt behind him and ran her hand along the weapon's enormous barrel. "I like the way you think." Her words washed over him, rich, luxurious, a fountain of dark, red wine. "When it comes to Marduk, bigger usually is better. But perhaps, not this time."

He turned, unwilling to leave his back exposed to her. Teshub had once confided Sekhmet was wild and unpredictable. She met his eyes, hers a dark, molten gold, fathomless, unreadable. He did not look away, refused to let her think him afraid. A faint smile touched her lips.

"Thoth tells me you were once the king of a great empire." Her gaze slid over him, impassive. She took his hand and turned his palm upward, exposed the lines marking the path of his life. "It appears you are an honorable man," she said. "Of pure heart. A great warrior. Noble. Just. At times, stubborn." She paused to trace her forefinger over his scar of binding. "Hmmm." She let go of his hand and turned to examine his chosen array of weapons. "I have decided to aid Thoth." She shot an enigmatic look at Urhi-Teshub. "Osiris took it upon himself to point out my ship is the fastest."

"I am in your debt," Urhi-Teshub said, hoping he sounded more grateful than he felt. When she lifted one of Marduk's devices, Urhi-Teshub cut an oblique look at her, his curiosity getting the better of him. After the tales he had heard of the goddess of war, he had expected her to be savage, bloodthirsty, brutal; her visage disfigured, ugly from glorying in violence. Teshub had said she was a loner, friendless, her rage during battle terrifying, legendary. Known as the queen of revenge, death, and destruction—she was a goddess to be feared and avoided. Urhi-Teshub had heard the stories, what she was capable of in battle, her brutality far beyond anything his father had done. After the things he had heard, he never could have expected a woman like this, clad in beauty, elegance, and grace, her features even, perfect, as though carved by a master sculptor. She turned, caught his frank appraisal. He turned away, but there was nothing to look at it except the wall.

She laughed, soft. It washed over him, honeyed and warm. "You have heard the stories about me."

"Who hasn't," he said, hauling the strap away from his shoulder. He dropped the weapon back onto the table. It landed between them, hitting the wood with a dense thud. He met her eyes again. "I admit you are not who I expected."

"I am never what anyone expects," Sekhmet returned. She reached past him to pick up a slim pair of blunt-nosed weapons, their polished metal reflecting the flames of the torches. "Take these." She held the weapons out to him. "Where we are going, we will not have much room to maneuver."

He took them with a murmur of thanks and waited for her to select more. Though she picked up several pieces and set them down again, she gave him nothing else. With only two weapons, he felt exposed. Unprepared. Even escorting Istara along the palace's corridors, he carried twice as much. His gaze slid back to the largest weapon. He could stow it in the ship—

"Not that one," Sekhmet said, following his look. "There is a better one." She went to where the weapons of the gods were set out, and opened a metal case. From within its depths she retrieved a long-barreled weapon along with a leather harness. "Wear this on your thigh," she said, handing him the harness, before letting him take the weapon. "This is only to be used when there are no other options left."

Urhi-Teshub took the weapon. Made of black metal, it looked similar to the design of Marduk's weapons, although unlike them, this one had a pleasing, reassuring heft. He took hold of its grip and held it up, admiring its simple design, liking it already. "What does it do?"

"It is one of Set's," Sekhmet answered. "Those targeted by it will turn against their own. But the effect is brief, and once they return to their senses, they will come back with a vengeance." She touched it, reverent. "Be sure not to lose it. Set dismembers those who offend him."

He sensed she hoped for a reaction; he gave her none. Instead: "Will it work on Marduk's patrols?" he asked, eyeing the length of the weapon, nearer to that of a short sword, imagining what it could have wrought in his world—what he could have done with it at Kadesh.

Sekhmet nodded. "Patrols. Ships' weapons. It is the only thing we possess apart from the pyramids' cores which can overcome Marduk's devices."

Urhi-Teshub lifted a brow, impressed. He turned the weapon over in his hands, appreciating anew the balance and weight of it. "I could do a lot of damage with this."

"You could, but you won't," Sekhmet said. Her gaze drifted once more to the weapons taken from the Etemen'anki. She eyed them, cool, her expression tightening. "It is regrettable there is only the one or we could have escaped without the loss of my sister and brothers." She fell silent, though sorrow tainted the curve of her lips. "This time we must be quiet. But the next time, we fight."

She went to the door. Her eyes touched his. A flicker of her fury scorched him, a furnace of hate, buried alive. "You have my word." The heat faded. Sorrow returned. She cut a look at the windows. "A storm is coming."

A fresh gust rattled the vault's latticed windows. The loose shutter banged against the wall. The wind surged past him, catching at the panels of his kilt. All but one of the torches guttered. The dry, acrid tang of smoke soaked the air. Another gust swept through the vault, thick with the slap of rain.

He went to the corridor, his skin prickling. He had not seen Sekhmet leave. Faint, on the edge of his hearing he caught the whisper of leather. He turned. One heartbeat. Two. Thunder tore a chasm through the skies and rolled over the citadel. Underfoot, the stone trembled. A burst of lightning sliced through the darkness. Further down, along the open walkway, he found her. She stood in the midst of the storm's fury, her small fists clenched at her sides, her face raised to the heavens, her profile soaked in anguish. In the space between heartbeats, her image seared his mind, raw, vulnerable, broken, her sorrow frozen in the staccato beat of the jagged, savaged skies.

Darkness returned, thick, furious at having been usurped. Rain sluiced from the heavens, and pounded against the walkway, violent, deafening. His heart thudded, awakening, skidding between terror and anticipation, fuelled by the rage of the storm. He waited. Lightning sheeted across the walkway, drowning it in a world of black and white. Her dark outline slipped to the opposite end of the walkway, and then she was gone, lost in the tumult of the storm.

❆ ❆ ❆

Ahmen paced the length of his rain-swept terrace locked in futility. Above, the splendor of Elati's shimmering canopy of stars and two crescent moons emerged from behind the storm clouds, their reflections spreading across Imaru's vast lake. Though he knew he shouldn't, he let his thoughts wander forbidden corridors, imagining other lives, and other outcomes. Meresamun would have loved Imaru with its wild, chaotic storms and endless skies. To be here, with her, in this beautiful, pristine world, his terrible crime uncommitted, never having led to what she had become, the enslaved consort of a tyrant. No. He forced his thoughts away. He had no right to think such things. None.

He went to the edge of the terrace, unseeing, agitated. He needed to do something. If only he could work with horses again, feel the pull of their reins against his forearms, sense the revolutions of a chariot's axel under his feet. A day in the royal stables working himself to exhaustion was what he needed to clear his mind. Not this. Not waiting, simmering in guilt and indolence, doing nothing. The lack of physical activity over the last weeks had left him caged, confining not only his body, but his mind. Without any way to relieve the pent-up energy within him, without purpose, or employment, his world had collapsed to a single focused point: Meresamun.

The day they had arrived to Elati, he learned Meresamun had cried she no longer wished to be Marduk's consort when he refused to aid her people during Babylon's destruction. Within Ahmen's breast, fury had burned. Marduk had stolen Meresamun's memories, and taken what little she had shared with Ahmen, leaving her mind empty of the love she had once had for him—a love he had destroyed, consumed by bitterness and jealousy. He looked down at his hands clenched into fists, hating himself. What a fool he had been. If only he could turn back time. He pressed his lips together, enduring a punishing wave of regret. And now, it turned out, time was all he had.

He came to a stop, eyeing one of the brighter constellations of Elati's heavens, certain of at least one thing in this place of near-eternal uncertainty: His estranged wife no longer wished to be with the one who had stolen her heart and memories. And if Marduk would not let her go, that made her Marduk's prisoner.

Somewhere out there, in this vast, new world, the woman Ahmen still loved, suffered, and considering what Istara and the others spent their time discussing—the building of a sanctuary from which they could launch their war against Marduk, and the liberation of Sethi from Marduk's clutches—it was clear Meresamun was of little to no importance. If Ahmen didn't help her, no one would.

When he had pressed Thoth to consider Meresamun's plight, the once-god of wisdom had suggested when Marduk was subdued and Sethi had been returned to them, perhaps Meresamun could be considered. Ahmen asked to join the search for Marduk's stronghold, but Thoth had looked away, uneasy, muttering it was a job better suited to his brothers and sisters. Ahmen knew what Thoth wasn't saying: Ahmen was a liability, as was Meresamun.

Even if she were liberated, she would never be welcome among the pantheon of refugee gods, not while Marduk remained. Thoth had told Ahmen of the love Marduk had harbored for his first consort, Zarpanitu, the one Horus had beheaded in cold blood during the wars of gods and men—Horus's act the reason for Sethi's enslavement. No, Thoth had said, Meresamun was best where she was, where if she had any influence over Marduk as Zarpanitu had once done, she might be best placed to aid the gods.

Thoth had departed soon after, murmuring he still had to solve the question of the creation of a sanctuary, leaving Ahmen to face his bitter truth: In Elati, Lord Ahmen-om-onet, Pharaoh Ramesses II's Royal Charioteer and Chief of the Archers was no one. As the weeks passed, the connection to his life in Egypt faded—of its orderly, precise seasons measured by the brief span of one's mortality.

He thought of Ramesses, wondering how the pharaoh would have reacted to being flung into another world where he could walk among those he once worshiped. Ahmen lifted his brow. No, far from balking at his fate, Ramesses would waste no time in building his empire. But Ahmen wasn't Ramesses, and never would be. He had been content in the role of a soldier, happy to leave the greater responsibilities of running an empire to others.

He turned his back to the sky. He was on his own, his destiny no longer directed by the gods or the pharaoh. It unnerved him. In Egypt, everyone had their place and behaved according to their station. But now, he had no such constraints. It was time to discover of what he was capable.

He glanced at the tangled sheets of his bed, where sleep eluded him and thoughts of Meresamun and of his failings tormented him. In Elati, there was only one constant which remained from his mortal life: The one he still loved, beyond all reason. He would free her with or without the help of the gods. Had he not survived the odds at the battle at Kadesh, and walked across Thamud Desert to Babylon without their aid?

Even after he learned she had become the consort of Marduk, he had gone to her father, the king of Babylon to face his crimes. Beaten, but not broken, he had followed Marduk into the depths of the Etemen'anki, where he had almost been buried alive in its collapse. With the others, he had escaped by boarding one of Marduk's ships which Thoth had flown across the skies to a distant underground cavern where an ancient, vast, glowing wall of cerulean light led to another world—and to her—the journey through the void between their world and Elati granting him the unexpected gift of immortality. Now he existed in a place between mortals and gods. He wasn't alone. As they had crossed into Elati, Urhi-Teshub, Thoth, Teshub, Arinna, Marduk, and Meresamun had also become immortal.

He crossed his arms over his chest. A strange thing to face— the loss of one's mortality. But if he couldn't die, neither did he have anything to lose. With his crossing into Elati, everything had changed, and he was tired of waiting, of letting others decide his and Meresamun's fate—of being the least priority. He had been someone in Egypt. He could be someone here. He just had to find out who.

He eyed the skies, at the strange constellations of the stars. He couldn't just fling himself out into an unknown world. First, a visit to the palace library, and a map. He didn't even know if Imaru lay to the north, south, east, or west, was an island, or part of a continent. He had no idea what other countries and empires existed in Elati, or what their histories, alliances and loyalties were. Neither did he know who had succumbed to Marduk's control and who still remained free. He had much to learn. As a man who could not die he could take risks, and slip in and out of cities unremarked. He would learn everything he could, and follow the trail he was certain would lead to her. He had no currency, and nothing of value, apart from the blade he had taken from Marduk's armory. He had always been a man of the sword, now he would also need to be a man who used his wits. So be it.

He would find her. He would not fail. Let the others fight their battles. He would fight his, alone.

❅   ❅   ❅

Horus rolled onto his back and pulled Baalat up against him, cradling her head against his shoulder.

Her fingers traced the outline of his pectorals. "Do you ever feel guilty?" she asked, soft.

He lifted his head to meet her eyes. "Guilty?" he asked, glancing down at their naked bodies glistening with perspiration. "For making love to you? Never."

Baalat smiled and kissed him, slow, arousing him anew.

He pulled back, breaking off the kiss. "I can tell you have something on your mind, better to say it before you entice me again."

With a quiet smile, Baalat slipped out from under his arm and left him alone on the bed. She went to the table and lifted their new wine pitcher, crafted in gold and chased with silver—payment for her ensuring the safe delivery of a high nobleman's son—and poured the ruby liquid into the jug's matching goblets, deft, elegant. Horus eyed her, appreciative, his woman, his only love. He wasn't done. Next, he would take her, slow, steady, and watch her as she crested hidden waves of pleasure, her eyes dark with her private ecstasies.

She returned to him, no longer the goddess of healing, or the one who had fallen from the Immortal Realm to remain with him in Egypt, still bearing a remnant of her immortal light. No. All their light was gone. Nothing had been left of their scintillating past except their memories. Now, just like him, Baalat was as mortal as their neighbors in the well-off trade quarter of Serde's capital of Ikalur, granted a second chance by the Creator to live again on Elati—a chance Horus had no intention of squandering.

He ran a reverent hand down the side of her breast, along the indentation of her waist and over her hip before taking the proffered wine and moving to join her on the edge of the bed. They drank together, quiet, companionable. The wine pleased him, its notes rich, full-bodied, sensual. A perfect finish to the love they'd just shared.

Baalat lowered her goblet and tucked its stem between her bare thighs. She trailed her forefinger around the goblet's silvered rim. Horus watched her, trying and failing not to be aroused by her guileless actions.

"I do," she said, low. She glanced up at him.

He blinked, his thoughts still on the cup nestled between her thighs. "Do what?"

"Feel guilty."

"For what?" he asked, a sinking part of him sensing wherever she was going with this was going to affect him too, in ways he didn't want to face—at least, not yet. Baalat could never rest easy when there was work to be done. And she always found work to do. Always. It both drove him mad and made him love her beyond all reason.

She sighed and returned her attention to her goblet. She dipped her fingertip into the wine and traced the rim anew. He put his hand over her fingers, stopping her. "You have no idea how arousing that is," he murmured.

"Oh." A tiny flare of pink touched her cheekbones. She set the goblet onto the floor, out of harm's way.

"My love," Horus said, soft. "Tell me. What troubles you?"

She got to her feet and went back to the table. Her fingers followed its outline. Horus forced himself to look at her fingers and not her buttocks.

She turned. He lifted his gaze to her face. She bit her lip. "I want us to have a child."

Horus blinked, taken aback. "You feel guilty for wishing to have a baby?"

Baalat nodded. A glint came to her eyes. She turned her back to him and brushed at her eyes. Horus went after her, gathered her into his arms.

"There is nothing wrong with wishing for a child of our own." He cupped her chin, gentle. "Now we can finally have one I think we should—"

Baalat crumpled. Her beautiful mouth turned downward. One, then another tear slipped free. Horus floundered, uncertain what he had said wrong. He waited, stroking her hair, kissing her brow, whispering quiet reassurances, giving her time. She quieted, and sighed, desolate.

"How can we sit here and pretend to make a life," she murmured, pushing her tears away, "when we know Marduk is here and what his intentions are—how this will end if he is not overcome." She pulled free, putting as much distance from him as their sleeping room would allow. He went after her. She backed away until her legs pressed against a chair. "Please. Don't touch me—"

"My love," Horus pleaded, "I beg you, talk to me. Tell me how I can alleviate your pain."

"You can't," she said, miserable. "Now I have said it, I have made it real. I am selfish to think of raising a family when I know what this world is facing, and what we still must do. I want to believe we will be safe, that we have done our part and can do as we please, but—" she touched the spot over her heart "—in here, I know he will come. Eventually he will come to Ikalur, and we will be enslaved, like everyone else." She lifted a trembling hand to her mouth. "It's not over. With him it's never over." She sank onto the chair and pressed her face into her hands, weeping in earnest.

Horus knelt beside her, his heart aching. Since the day the Creator had granted them a second chance, one beautiful, precious month ago, he had refused to think of Marduk and of the part he would eventually have to play in the fight against him. After all they had been through, after everything they had sacrificed, how could it be wrong to wish for a quiet life with the woman he loved, spending his evenings drinking, eating, and making love. And his serendipitous employment—arranged via one of Baalat's wealthy clients—at the royal falconry training messenger falcons had given him more satisfaction than he had anticipated. They weren't wealthy, but they had done well enough for themselves, considering they had had nothing but the clothes on their backs a month ago. Life was good. He had never wanted it to end.

He went back to the bed and picked up Baalat's goblet, thinking of the desperate messages which had been arriving hourly over the last days begging for aid, warning of a new and powerful invader with weapons beyond anyone's comprehension; the messenger a brutal, vicious god who meted out cruelties beyond one's worst nightmares.

He had kept his misgivings from Baalat, not wishing to bring their brief idyll to its end. On the map pinned to the wall of the falconry's office, Horus had taken in the breadth of Elati. It was bigger than the world they had left behind, perhaps twice as large, vast enough for him to harbor the hope of at least another month of peace. Two continents, three large islands, and many smaller ones encircled by a vast ocean. The messages pleading for aid had arrived from all over their continent, which meant Marduk could be anywhere.

Horus knew what Sethi was doing. He would have done the same—conquering cities at random, the misdirection leaving no obvious path to Marduk's stronghold. Elati was vast and Sethi, although a god, was still only one. It would take time to conquer every kingdom. Horus let out a heavy breath. Once the messages began to arrive, he knew Ikalur's days were numbered. He eyed Baalat, locked in silent sorrow. Ever the canny one, she had hastened the end of their reprieve, simply by wishing for a child. She looked up, tearstained and unhappy. He held out the wine. She drank it all.

"We will have our child," he said, pressing his forehead to hers. "I swear it." She shuddered and succumbed to a fresh onslaught of tears. He collected her into his arms and carried her back to the bed where he made slow, tender love to her, kissing her tears away, swearing to finish this fight once and for all—for her, and for the child he too longed to have.

❋   ❋   ❋

"Lady Ninsunu. I have brought a woman to serve you. She did not please me."

Meresamun woke. Disorientation swarmed over her. She had been dreaming of Ahmen, of the night he had found her in the rain at Kadesh. He had just begun to kiss her. Her lips still tingled from the memory. Beyond the closed shutters leading to the terrace, thin gray light heralded the approach of dawn. The dream faded. The present coalesced. Ahmen had broken her heart. She belonged to another now. Marduk. Once her god, now her consort, he had left her father and her people to their brutal deaths when he took her beyond the boundary of her disintegrating world and into another, stranger one—to a place where she could never die. To where she walked the lonely corridors of her new, opulent home, adrift, lost, and purposeless.

Sethi stood in the middle of her sleeping room, his golden eyes cold and distant in the dying flames of the brazier's heat, gripping the upper arm of a beautiful, quivering woman. A golden circlet hung in the tangles of her unbound hair. He flung her away from him. She collided into the back of a divan.

"*Meresamun*," Meresamun said, leaving the bed, eyeing the one she had once known as the commander of Egypt's army, the third most powerful man in the empire. And now . . . she looked away, sickened. Nothing was left of Sethi, of the one who had lived with honor and integrity—who had loved Istara more than his own eternal soul. "My name is Meresamun, not Ninsunu."

Sethi glared at her, baleful, the golden fractals on his chest stuttered, jagged, angry. "I will call you what Lord Marduk calls you, *Ninsunu*."

"Don't you have another kingdom to oppress?" she snapped, going to the woman huddled by the divan. "Perhaps another unwilling queen to rape?"

He took a step toward her, his eyes churning. "I am the god of war. To be chosen to share my bed is a great honor."

The woman behind Meresamun failed to suppress a shudder. Meresamun crossed her arms over her chest, realizing too late her transparent night dress did nothing to conceal her nakedness. "I suspect not all of your conquests agree."

"The women here are ungrateful." Sethi sniffed. "You, at least, know my worth."

"Meaning?"

"I had you at Kadesh—many times—" He blinked. A sliver of confusion rippled over his features. Meresamun caught her breath.

"You remember," she whispered. She unfolded her arms. "Sethi." He looked at her, sharp, wary. "Tell me you remember who you are."

"I—" The rancor surrounding him melted away. "Meresamun," he said. "Where—" he looked around, disoriented. His gaze fell to the woman. She glared back at him, riven between hate and fear.

He took a step back. "No," he breathed, horror circling him. "The things I did to you, I remember it all. How could I—" His fingers went to the base of his skull. "Get it out," he panted. He tore into his flesh, opening a bloody, gaping hole, granting a pale glimpse of bone. "Hurry. Before the sun rises."

Meresamun gaped. Through the slick of his blood, tendrils of golden light burst free and darted into his wound. "Get *what* out?"

"The device," Sethi grunted. His eyes raked her dressing table. "I need a blade. Something. Anything. Help me. I cannot do it alone. Not before the sun rises."

"I have nothing like that. Marduk has an aversion to blades near his consort."

Faint strips of sunlight probed the gaps in the shutters, brightening with each heartbeat. Sethi roared, primal, his anguish palpable. "Augh! Why does their sun have to rise so fast?"

Meresamun scrambled through the contents of her dressing table, knocking combs and jewels onto the floor. There. Her obsidian hairpin. She held it up. "How much time do you have?"

"Not enough, not with that." He cut a look at the shutters. Sunlight clawed to get in. "In my palace, there are other women, you must—" A shudder slammed through him. He pressed his palm over his heart. "Istara," he breathed. The golden markings on his chest slid to a halt and rotated anew, smooth, seamless, mesmerizing. "I can feel her." Remorse cut a savage path through his features, stained his eyes. "She suffers. Because of me." He looked down at his hands, his fingers dark with blood. "How could I return to her, after all I have done? How shall I ever cleanse myself of my crimes?"

"Your crimes are not your own," Meresamun said, tilting her head at the ragged opening in his flesh, his golden light closing it, fast. "They are Marduk's."

A burst of brilliant sunlight streamed through the slats of the shutters and slid across the suite. Colors flared to life, the golden cover of her bed, the rubies woven into her slippers, the jeweled green of her gown thrown over the back of a dark blue upholstered chair.

"You need to leave," Sethi panted as the light crept toward his sandaled feet. His hands clenched into fists, the veins in his arms protruded, a river of torment, stark from his inner battle. He jerked his head at the woman watching them, stricken. "Take her with you." He turned his back to them, to face the rising sun. "Run! I can't last much long—" He staggered.

Meresamun held out her hand to the fallen queen. Together they fled her sleeping room, their gowns whispering against the marble floor as he bellowed, despairing, crying out Istara's name. At the far end of the suite, Meresamun drew the woman behind a privacy screen as he strode out, possessed by the device once more, his eyes hard, and his lips turned downward, a cruel, harsh line. The fractals on his chest jerked, chaotic, disconnected.

He left, clad in violence, a weapon, deadly, indestructible. Meresamun's thoughts tumbled, tumultuous, replaying Sethi's transformation from evil to good, back to evil.

The roar of Marduk's warship sheared through the morning's quiet, drowning out the cries of the birds wheeling along the cliffs. It screamed past her suite, a thing made for brutality and oppression, and shot up over the mountain range, black, malevolent, hateful, in pursuit of its next quarry. Several heartbeats passed. Its cry faded. Silence fell, heavy and accusing.

At a loss what else to do, she poured wine leftover from Marduk's visit the night before. She held out a brimming cup to the woman, who took it, vicious bruises staining her wrists and forearms.

"I am Meresamun, daughter of Kadashman-Turgu, king of Babylon, and Consort of Marduk," Meresamun said, eyeing the bruises, the memory of that final night with Ahmen salting open wounds. "Like you, I do not wish to be here."

"Marduk," the woman repeated, bleak. She sipped her wine and met Meresamun's eyes, hers hollow, empty. "I am Urah, Queen of Thes Dios. My husband refused to submit." A tear tracked a path through the remnants of her ruined cosmetics. "Now he is dead, and the one who butchered my only love has spilled his seed inside me." She sipped again, her gaze drifting to the terrace. "Elati has known peace for thousands of years. And now, in the blink of an eye, your consort has brought fear and sorrow into our world." She met Meresamun's eyes, the condemnation in hers, brutal. "Why?"

Meresamun welcomed the sting of shame, refused to soften the truth with a lie. "Marduk believes it is his destiny to rule supreme, for eternity."

Urah eyed her, cold. "You came through the wall of light on Pir's westernmost isle, didn't you?"

"Did we?" Meresamun answered. She lifted her shoulders and let them fall again. "I have no knowledge of your world, or even where I am. Perhaps you might know where we are?"

Urah set aside her wine, walked toward the terrace.

"Where are you going?"

"To see if I recognize where we are," Urah replied, dull. She pushed past the transparent curtains.

Meresamun followed her to the terrace's edge, haunted by misgiving. "Do you recognize it?" she asked, uneasy, stricken by Urah's blank expression—her desolation.

Urah shook her head. A mere breath stood between her and oblivion. Tears glistened in her eyes. Meresamun took her hand.

Urah cut a withering look at Meresamun's grip on hers. "Let go, or I will take you with me."

"No." Meresamun pulled on Urah's hand, dragged her back from the edge. "Please. Do not do this thing."

"I do not wish to live in the world your consort intends for us," Urah said. Her gaze moved to a pair of herons flying across the chasm. "Do you know what it is to love someone with all your being?"

Meresamun blinked, the memory of Ahmen holding her against him on his pallet as he made love to her during those brief nights they had had on the march back from Kadesh slammed into her. "I do," she answered, her heart tight, fighting the feelings the forgotten memory stirred. "But he is gone. Forever."

"Then you must know how much it hurts to continue to live without him," Urah continued, soft. She glanced at Meresamun, her eyes laden with tears. "What do I have to live for now, hm? Nothing."

"You must live for the fight," Meresamun pleaded. "For your people, so you can return and free them. Please." She hauled on Urah's arm, but the other woman resisted. "You call yourself a queen?" Meresamun cried as Urah moved back to the edge. "Where is your honor?"

Urah shook herself free of Meresamun's grip. "Honor? Our sages spoke of an ancient prophecy: One day a great evil would befall Elati. An invader would breach Pir's impenetrable wall of light and ravage Elati for his own ends. His darkness would leave our world in ashes. I will not remain to face what is to come. I will join my love in the light." She pulled her crown free and tossed it aside. It clattered across the terrace. "I am no longer queen of Thes Dios. I am Urah—the youngest daughter of Vreka, a fisherman—who caught the eye of a king, and lived to love and be loved in return."

She stepped out, into nothingness. Meresamun lunged after her with a cry, her fingers slipping through Urah's gown. She staggered and sank to her knees, disbelieving, clinging to the edge of the terrace, helpless, as Urah plummeted, her gown whipping around her, the broken wings of a dying bird. The queen of Thes Dios struck an outcropping and crumpled, a shattered doll, her gown a faint smear of white against the black-dark ledge. A fat blot of red spread from its center.

A hand gripped Meresamun's shoulder, hauled her back. She slammed against Marduk's chest, the heavy thudding of his heart harsh against her flesh. He dragged her away from the edge and caught her to him. His kiss came, deep and punishing.

"To see you there, so close to the edge," he said, holding her face in his hands, "I thought you would fall. Even if you are immortal, your body can still be broken. You can still feel pain. My love, you can still break my heart." He kissed her again, soft, tender, arousing her, as he always did—despite what he was. He grazed his teeth against her lower lip, slow, seductive, a private act Meresamun had no defense against. Shards of carnal need slid through her and coiled deep in her torso, hungering for his dominance—for the familiar, solid heat of him filling her. She returned his kiss with a sigh. He groaned and claimed her then, devouring her, his hands tangling in her hair, her cries echoing along the rugged cliffs as he guided her to the stars. She fell back to him, shuddering, cocooned in bliss.

He left her and gazed into her eyes, his pupils thin slits in the brilliant light of a new day. "I may have your body," he murmured as he brushed a tendril of hair from her brow, "but what must I do to hold your heart?"

"You left my father and my people to die," Meresamun answered, hating herself for having succumbed to him, addicted to the heights of pleasure he carried her to—heights Ahmen had never taken her. Guilt sawed at her, harsh. She looked at the chasm, thinking of Urah—of what Marduk drove others to do to escape him. Tears pricked her eyes. "You could have helped them but you didn't. I cannot love you."

He flinched. "I had no choice," he said, low. "Sethi would never have survived if I had remained to aid the others. Without him granting us access to the portal, we would have perished." He pulled her against him and cradled her against his chest, sunlight bathing them in its nascent warmth. "My love, I cannot bear to exist without you." His eyes met hers. "I need you, Ninsunu. Ask anything of me. For you, I will do it."

Meresamun thought of Urah's fall, her shattered body. "Let me go," she said, "I no longer wish to be your consort. You stand for everything I do not."

A flicker shimmered in Marduk's eyes. He leaned back, the markings on his chest and arms shifting, shearing into points and edges. He reached out and lifted a thick tress of her hair, let it trickle through his fingers.

"And where would my consort go?" he asked, soft. "Do you think the Elatians wouldn't find out where you came from—who you are?" He leaned forward, until his lips brushed her ear, sending a traitorous prickle of pleasure shivering along her spine. "They would torture you, to get to me. And I *would* come for you, once I have killed every single one of them."

Meresamun pulled back. "So you intend to keep me your prisoner."

"No," Marduk said. "I intend to keep you safe." He stood, his markings shifting, unsettled, reflecting his inner turmoil. He held out his hand and helped her to her feet. "If you do not wish to be my consort, I cannot force you, but I cannot let you go. At least not until Elati is mine. Then perhaps we could find you a kingdom of your own, and you would remain my consort in name only." He took a step back. Meresamun blinked, she had expected a fight. Not this. Not quiet acceptance.

"But if you do not share my bed," Meresamun began, a sudden, unexpected bolt of jealousy shearing through her, dark, "whose will you warm?"

Marduk folded his arms over his chest. His markings seethed, tumultuous. His gaze moved to the mountains in the distance. "For a time," he answered, "I will wait for you, in the hope you will return to me. But—" his markings stuttered to a halt, "—if you will not come back to me, there will be others. Elati is not short of beautiful women."

In her mind, she saw it, him mounting a willing woman, taking her in his arms, calling out her name as he reached his release. She took a step back, sickened, unable to face it, knowing she could never share him.

"What have you done to me?" she whispered, horror claiming her. "I cannot love you yet neither can I share you."

Marduk nodded, his gaze still fixed on the mountains. "Once, long ago, Zarpanitu said the same." His eyes met hers. "It seems my heart is captured only by those whose hearts are so pure they cannot love me once they know what I am." The muscles of his jaw clenched. "I have been loved, many times, but those who loved me I did not love in return. Their hearts were as dark as mine. If only I could be loved by you, I would be complete." He looked away. "But how could you? You are good, and I am not, and I never will be. I am incapable of it."

"Marduk," Meresamun breathed, stunned by his revelation, his honesty. He looked back at her, aching, raw, exposed. His markings slid, tenuous, into a symphony of whorls and swirls.

"Tell me about Zarpanitu," she said, quiet. "Tell me how she found her way with you, so I might find mine."

❋ ❋ ❋

Teshub cursed. He hated being so far out of his depth. Once, long ago, he had been a god, feared and revered, able to turn mountains to dust. But *this*. It was too much. He eyed the closed door, dithering, uncertain, before deciding to ease the cumbersome tray onto his forearm. Cautious, he shifted its weight under his arm, seeking its point of equilibrium.

He let go of the tray with his other hand and reached for the handle of the door, slow, careful. The contents of the tray tilted to a precarious angle, the laden gold and silver platters rattling as they shifted toward the edge. With a muffled curse, he grabbed onto the tray and steadied it. How in the name of all that was eternal was he supposed to get the door open *and* hold the tray at the same time. For the hundredth time, he wondered how the servants managed it. To think, Teshub, once the mighty storm god, could be bested by a breakfast tray. Biting back a curse he eyed the last hurdle standing between him and success and decided to try another approach.

He edged up to the wall beside the door. Holding the tray steady, he positioned it against his torso, and braced the hateful thing against the wall. He lifted one finger free, then another, testing its stability. He waited. Nothing happened. He let go of the tray and again reached for the door's handle. The tray wobbled. He darted a look at it, baleful, daring it to tilt. It stilled. He wrapped his fingers around the door's handle and pulled, gentle. Nothing happened.

"For the love of—" he erupted, his temper, long suppressed, threatened to free itself from its restraints. The tray jiggled. He shut his mouth and held his breath. It had been a long morning.

Hours ago, in the heavy darkness before dawn he had risen sleepy-eyed and surly to spend far too long wandering Imaru palace's torchlit maze of corridors, elegant wings, and courtyards in search of the kitchens. When he finally arrived, irritable and frustrated, he ordered the bemused servants to make space for him at the large work table where he cracked eggs into a bowl until it was full of broken yolks and eggshells. After an eternity spent picking out every treacherous shell fragment, he rummaged through the baskets of cheeses, searching for the right one to add to the eggs as they fried in a slab of creamy butter.

One of the cooks held out a wooden platter bearing round patties of soft cheese made from goat's milk. Teshub took two and crumbled them on top of the eggs, sprinkling a handful of thin green herbs over them. He had no idea what the herbs were, but they smelled nice—warm, spicy, yet lively and invigorating. Atragon, the cook said as Teshub took more and scattered it over the eggs and cheese, bubbling in the hot pan. At first, he worried he had made a mistake, his creation looked terrible—a sticky, unappealing mess—but he kept stirring it, coaxing it along, a linen hand towel tossed over his shoulder. Once it cooked through, it looked better and smelled delicious. He tasted it.

"Salt," he muttered. He wasted an age searching the cupboards and worktops for it only to find it had been sitting on a shelf in a bowl above the stove all along, white flakes of it, piled into a soft point. He jabbed his thumb and forefinger into its peak and sprinkled a generous amount over the food with a flourish. He tasted it again. It was good. Really good.

As the eggs rested in their pan, fluffy and glistening, he found a tray, and lay several gold and silver platters onto it, piling an assortment of breads, a selection of cubed fruit, and cold slices of roast boar, venison, and pheasant onto them. He found another platter of smoked fish seasoned with pepper and stuffed it onto the side of the bulging tray. Some eating utensils, linen napkins, a pot of butter, and another of honey with a fat piece of honeycomb found their way into the cracks and crevices remaining. One of the servants wedged two cups and a crystal jug of fresh-squeezed fruit juice between the platters. Another added a little dish of bite-sized pastries, still warm from the oven. Teshub loaded the eggs into a golden bowl and covered it with a dish to keep them warm. A young serving girl came forward, diffident, and lay a little bouquet of pink and white wildflowers tied with a yellow ribbon atop the platter covering the eggs. Teshub smiled at her, making her blush a furious shade of red.

"Thank you," Teshub said, hefting the tray from the table and making his way, unsteady, up the stone steps and out into the early morning sun of the lower courtyard. The servants and cooks bowed as he departed, respectful, but as he crossed the courtyard their chatter swept after him, filled with excitement and laughter. He realized they had probably never watched a noble work in their kitchen, much less one like him, an immortal who had come from another world in a ship which could soar across Elati's pristine blue skies, flames jetting from its tail.

But his nascent moment of triumph and anticipation in delivering his gift had long since soured. It had been a long walk back, and in the intervening two hours since he had left his bed the palace had become congested with servants, guards, courtiers, courtesans, and merchants. He fretted for the eggs, willing them to remain warm, biting back foul oaths every time the way became barred by endless entourages of nobility. Thoth had warned him to treat the noble families of Imaru with respect, their stay granted by the king on the slightest thread of trust, so Teshub pressed his lips together and waited, impatient and seething, longing for the past, when he had been a god and none had dared bar his way.

He let out his breath, slow, and tried the door handle again, pulling it just a fraction harder, one eye on the tray, willing its contents to remain steady.

The door slipped free, just enough for him to wedge his foot into the opening. With an exhalation of relief, he slid the door open. He glanced at the nosegay of wildflowers. They had wilted a little from the heat of the eggs. He swallowed his curse. He had tried. He really had. He entered the apartment and tugged the door closed behind him, half-fearing his consort had already broken her fast, but the reception room lay shrouded in shadow. He crept across the suite to the sleeping room, its shuttered terrace faced west, away from the rising sun. Through the slats, he could see the cerulean blue of the sky, brightening with each heartbeat.

Under the silken sheet, caught in the realm of dreams, Arinna lay on her side, her golden hair spilling over her cushion, her chest rising and falling, slow. Teshub set the tray onto a low table and knelt beside her, his heart aching, as it always did whenever he was alone with her. He leaned over and kissed her, soft.

She stirred and smiled, lazy, without opening her eyes. "Mm," she murmured, husky. "Let me sleep, just a little longer."

He kissed her again, longer, deeper. She opened her eyes and blinked, taking in his leather tunic studded with gold oblongs.

"You are already dressed." Her brow furrowed as she brought herself up onto her elbow. "Is something amiss?"

"No," Teshub smiled, filled with pleasurable anticipation. "I wanted to surprise you. I have been up since before the sun rose." He edged to one side so she could see the tray, piled with their morning meal.

A quiet smile touched her lips. He collected the tray and slid it onto the middle of the bed, joining her as she sat up against the cushions.

He waited, nervous, as she gazed at his offering. She reached out and picked up the wilted bouquet, her fingers trailing over its fragile blossoms. "You did this?" she asked, quiet, tilting up the dish covering the bowl of eggs. Steam slid out, followed by the enticing scent of atragon.

He nodded, drinking in her soft expression, the slight upward tilt of her mouth, the warmth of pleasure in her eyes. Everything he had endured, every frustration, every setback, was worth it. Happiness saturated her.

"You cooked for me." She met his eyes, hers bright. "After an eternity of waiting, you have at last granted my wish."

He lifted the dish from the eggs. "Better late than never." The eggs still looked edible. He dipped the utensil in, and held a portion of the herbed eggs up to her lips. She opened her mouth. He slid the eggs in. Her eyes lit up.

"It's delicious." She leaned forward, eager. "More, please."

He obliged and fed her, savoring the morning, and her. When they were done, he let her pull apart the fastenings of his tunic and draw away his leather kilt. He pushed her nightgown up to her hips and carried her down into the cushions, finding her as he always did, as he always would. He made love to her, steady and slow, until she trembled in his arms, lost to him. He waited for her to return to him, worshiping her anew with each gentle thrust until he followed her to oblivion, her name on his lips, his consort, his only love. His everything.

He descended back from the heights. The one he thought he had forever lost lay in his arms, content, satiated, languid. After a million years without her, his silenced heart had once more burst to life. With her by his side, he could do anything. He would defeat the one who had stolen her from him—the one who had left him lost, broken, and empty. He tightened his hold on her, fierce, thinking of Marduk, and the agonies he intended for the one who had torn his existence apart. He would make him suffer for an eternity. He glanced at Arinna, succumbing to the pull of sleep, his heart tight. Still holding her, he rolled onto his back and stared at the elaborate mosaic on the ceiling, a hunt scene, dissatisfaction gnawing at his contentment, knowing for Marduk, even an eternity of suffering would never be enough.

A knock, quiet, came to Istara's door. She turned from her unhappy reflection in the dressing table's silver mirror. Since they had arrived in Elati she had not once seen herself smile.

"Enter."

The door opened and closed again, soft. A heavy tread crossed the reception room. Urhi-Teshub came to a stop at the open double doors leading to her sleeping room. He had changed from his usual attire of a gold-gilt leather kilt and tunic to a close-fitting pair of dark leather leggings and tunic. His legs, arms and hips gleamed with an assortment of weapons, snub-nosed and compact, strapped close to his powerful body.

He looked at her, enigmatic. She waited, wondering what the once-king of an empire was thinking. A little while after their arrival, he had admitted to a shared history between them, although it was one she could not recall. Despite her questions, he refused to say anything more, claiming what was in the past would remain there. And yet, the way he looked at her—Istara looked away, uneasy. No matter how hard she tried to recall the emptiness beyond the wall between the Immortal Realm and Elati, she only found darkness.

Since she had arrived in Imaru she felt as if she had wakened from a deep sleep, her heart reeling with loss, aching for her lost, corrupted consort. She could remember Marduk, but from another world, riven by endless wars and destruction, brought to an end by the gods' flight to a hidden realm, where Sethi had made love to her on a silken bed, and golden fractals rotated on the ceiling. Now, Sethi belonged to Marduk, though she could not remember how she had lost him, or why. Neither did she have any memory of the man standing before her, though within the darkened corridors of her mind she suspected much had transpired between her and her protector.

Once, she had asked if she had been unfaithful to Sethi with him. Her protector had held her gaze, an unreadable look in his eyes. He had crossed his arms and shook his head, though not before she glimpsed his battle-hardened features darkening with a cleave of regret.

Urhi-Teshub came to her, his presence, as always, protective, reassuring. "We are ready to depart for Surru." He held out his hand. She took it. As she rose, his thumb slid over the indelible scar which marred her palm, a faint caress. A memory triggered, visceral. The scent of soap, leather, horses. She caught her breath and looked down at his strong hand cradling hers, at his thick calluses, somehow both familiar, yet not. Shadows flickered against her soul, roused by the scent of a lost past. The weight of his presence rushed into her. It called to her from the gap between the memories of her life with the god of war in the Immortal Realm, and her reawakening in Elati.

"You . . . loved me," she whispered, stunned.

"I still do," he murmured. He let go of her hand and backed away. She met his eyes. A veil dropped over his. "But you belong to Sethi," he continued, low. "You always have, and you always will. It took a long time to understand who you truly are." He looked away and swallowed. "Too long."

"I—" Istara clung to the fading memory, unwilling to let it go. She sensed it meant something—would answer the questions which haunted her. Another knock came to the door, a quick staccato.

Urhi-Teshub left, abrupt, to answer it. A quiet conversation. He came back, Sekhmet gliding after him, her slim body clad in black leather, a variety of blades and throwing stars strapped to her legs, torso, and arms.

"Sekhmet will be joining us." Urhi-Teshub nodded at the goddess, who eyed Istara's opulent suite with a hint of disdain. Her gaze moved to the unmade bed and lingered there a heartbeat longer than necessary. A look fleeted through her dark eyes, unreadable. She turned to Istara and nodded at her, regal, cold.

"If you do not wish to travel with us," Sekhmet smiled, showing her teeth, even and white, "you may remain here, safe in Imaru. Thoth informed me Surru only requires one god to access the portal." She gestured, elegant, at her weapon-clad body. "I rather think I should be sufficient to the task."

"It has already been arranged." Istara glanced at Urhi-Teshub. He met her eyes, revealing nothing of his thoughts, though he folded his arms over his chest. "Unless *you* think I should remain behind?"

Expressionless, Sekhmet followed Istara's look.

Urhi-Teshub nodded. "Though it makes sense to risk no more than one god on this mission, I prefer to have you near me. I would rather not leave you alone in Elati while Sethi roams free."

A shear of silence slid through the room.

"Of course," Sekhmet's smile was ice. "Shall we?" She strode through Istara's rooms, her presence screaming of suppressed violence.

"Why is she—" Istara began, wondering why the goddess of war would wish to return to the world she had just escaped.

"Hers is the fastest ship," Urhi-Teshub said. He lowered his voice. "Thoth told me she was with them."

"With who?"

"With Baalat, Horus, and Teshub when they activated the cores. Sekhmet was there when they sacrificed their light so the others could escape."

"Ah," Istara said. Thoth had explained the gods which had arrived in Elati had not come from her world, but another, a parallel one with an identical pantheon of gods to her own—a world which had once been his home. A world where, unlike her own, an identical Marduk had ruled, immortal and supreme, the gods enslaved for two million years. They had only escaped his tyranny when three of their pantheon sacrificed everything. Their names replayed through her mind. Teshub she knew, but the others were unfamiliar: *Horus. Baalat.* She blinked. *Her* pantheon had never had gods with those names. Another question for Thoth.

As her protector led her through Imaru's summer palace toward the ships, Istara considered anew her plan to create a sanctuary. If Thoth's idea to use the cores worked, it would change everything.

The greatest threat the gods faced was their vulnerability. If they were to have any hope of standing against Marduk, or of gathering mortal allies to their cause, they needed to be somewhere Marduk's devices and weapons could not function. It was much to ask of Thoth, deprived as he was of his godly powers, but just when she had begun to lose hope, he had found a way. Now all they need do was return to the world the other gods had fled, slip past Marduk's protectors around the pyramids, retrieve the cores and make it back to Elati without being detected. The odds against them couldn't be worse.

They reached Sekhmet's ship. Istara entered the cabin and nodded at Thoth, who remained oblivious to her, occupied with rearranging a clutter of notes. The door to the cabin slid closed with a quiet hiss. Istara took a seat on the divan across from Thoth. Urhi-Teshub turned to join her.

"I could use a little help," Sekhmet called, her fingers moving, deft, over the lighted instruments of the console. "Thoth?"

"Have Urhi-Teshub assist you," Thoth answered, holding up a page covered with mathematical formulas. He tutted and set it aside. "I need more time to factor in the permutations of the internal resonance scale so we don't upset the balance when we break the connection between the pyramids. If I don't redirect the . . ." He picked up another page and examined it. He blinked, his harried expression lightening. "Ah! I see I already triangulated the energy currents to divert into the pyramids' structures, in case I ever needed to remove one of the cores." He made a sound of approval. "Typical me, thinking of everything."

Urhi-Teshub eyed the console at the front of the ship. Disappointment surrounded him. "Then you don't need me?"

Thoth gestured toward the flight deck. "Go," he muttered, "I still have to decide in which order to remove the cores. It's quite complicated. We can't just barge in and yank them out any which way. We will only have one chance to get this right." He looked up, his gaze unfocusing. "Largest to smallest or the other way round? There are benefits and dangers to both. Perhaps if I were to first disable the beacons to the other portals, it might just be enough to mitigate the sudden release of entropic force. . . hmmm." He turned and rifled through the pages on the seat beside him, lost in thought.

Urhi-Teshub hastened to the front of the ship and settled into the seat beside Sekhmet. He leaned forward, eyeing the levers, switches, and lights of the ship's instrument panel, hungry, eager to begin. Sekhmet pointed at the topography screen which would record the features of the land and coasts beneath the ship as they flew to their destination.

"I want you to do the mapping," she said. "Ensure this does not go black, or worse, changes suddenly from land to sea without any continuity. If it does, tell me." She glanced at him, her elegant profile severe against the morning light glinting against the window. "The only one with the ability to block mapping sensors is Marduk. If we are close to him, his beacon will scramble the readings."

"Or," Urhi-Teshub said, meeting her eyes, "he has beacons scattered across Elati to mislead and confuse us."

Sekhmet's lips curved into an approving smile. "I knew you were no fool." She punched a button on the console and the door separating the front of the ship from the cabin slid closed, separating the pair from Istara and Thoth.

Istara leaned back and rested her head against the headrest, Urhi-Teshub's pleasure to be at the ship's controls palpable, even through the closed door. The once-king had often stood on her terrace watching the ships of the gods take off and land, his fists clenched at his sides, naked with longing. She rearranged the folds of her gown over her legs, gratified by the thought at least one of them was happy.

The ship roared to life and shot into the sky toward the far reaches of Pir's island chain, where, In the center of an isolated, uninhabited island, Surru's churning portal of cerulean light awaited.

The walls and floor of the ship shimmered and turned translucent. The sprawl of Imaru's royal city fell away, its golden spires, crystal cupolas, and white towers glinting in the light of the rising sun. Rzhev's capital city hugged the bay of a great lake, set within the basin of a long dead volcano. The lake's dark waters bobbed, choppy and uneven, its peaks and troughs sparkling against the depths beneath. Another shimmer, and the cloaking device engaged as they shot over the bamboo-forested rim of the crater. A thundering came from the rear. The ship ascended, heading for Rzhev's coastline, the white ribbon of its verdant shores paying homage to the endless expanse of the Adriande Sea.

For the thousandth time since her arrival in Elati, Istara wandered the fallow fields of her mind, searching for the answers which eluded her, finding none.

Though Thoth had advised her to let things take their course, his guarded answers had troubled her, and despite his reassurances to trust in the Creator's wisdom, she sought to recall what had happened before she came to Elati. She longed to understand Urhi-Teshub's enigmatic melancholy, and why she could not remember Horus and Baalat, the gods who had given up their light alongside another Teshub. No matter which way she turned the questions in her mind, unbreachable, silent walls enclosed her in a narrow, hollow place of alienation and loneliness.

And so, each morning, though she knew what it would cost her, she stood on her terrace and waited for the dawn. Her brief connection to Sethi always came fast. It slammed into her and dragged her deep into the viscous depths of Sethi's confusion, misery, guilt, and sorrow. The magnitude of his suffering in those brief heartbeats would send her to her knees, bombarding her with the onslaught of his anguish for his brutality and the dread he bore for his overpowering hunger to uncover a brutal, malevolent weapon which had the power to sever his bond to her, the one he loved more than his own existence.

Fatigue circled her. She hadn't slept much the night before, and Sethi's awakening at dawn had been particularly grim. He had called out her name, despairing, his suffering visceral, cleaving her heart in two. She pressed her hands over her heart, thinking of when he had still been hers, how he had always been by her side, protecting her, as Urhi-Teshub wished to do now.

Her eyelids drifted down. The harrowing memory of the last time her consort had protected her crept forward. She fought it, her heart aching, but it saturated her mind, vivid, brilliant, clear. She had been tending the flowers of her garden, a litter of two-month old white kittens exploring the flowerbeds beside her, their tiny paws speckled with the humid soil, their discovery of a pair of blue butterflies a delight. Her consort had burst into the idyllic scene, his face hard, desperate. Without saying a word, he had thrown her over his shoulder and carried her away, screaming and struggling, forcing her to leave her companions, guards, servants—even her kittens behind.

Once in his ship, he had dragged her, weeping and angry to the flight deck, punched its ignition and flew them one-handed into the skies, the ship's walls and floors shimmering, cloaking even as they swept past the roofs of the city's villas.

Outraged, she had swung her hand back to strike him when she saw them hurtling toward her city—dozens of ships, the allies of Marduk, in attack formation. Stunned, she watched, helpless, as they fired into her city, its villas, markets, squares, and stables erupting in flames, her people and the animals fleeing, terrified. As she clawed at the panel, trying to gain control of his locked ship, it came from the heavens—a sleek black tube with fire blazing from its tail—falling faster than a star. It slammed into her palace gardens—where her kittens had just been playing, innocent, happy, and filled with the wonder of life—ten thousand times more powerful than all the weapons the gods possessed combined. Stricken, she stumbled out into the cabin and fell to her knees, devastated, screaming until her throat bled, powerless against the fiery cloud spreading over the ruins of her city and across the molten skies. Sethi had held her in his arms, silent, furious, cold, clothed in vengeance. When she could weep no more, he carried her to his bed and made fierce love to her as her city succumbed to the firestorm, vowing he would never forget—promising to do whatever it would take to end Marduk. Forever.

❋   ❋   ❋

A hand touched Istara's. She opened her eyes. Ahead, Surru's misty, ephemeral wall sparked and churned. Its cerulean light lapped over the ship's interior, gentle, like water. The ship stood silent and still. Waves of heated air slid from its wings, distorting the view. Urhi-Teshub looked down at her, his arms folded over his chest.

"Thoth wanted to speak with you before we go through," he said. He stepped back. Behind him, Sekhmet sat before the console, her fingers moving over its switches and buttons, preparing for their departure.

Thoth stood, set aside his notes onto the divan and cleared his throat. He glanced at her, then at the portal. He took a breath, began to speak, thought better of it and closed his mouth. Istara waited, uneasy. It wasn't like Thoth to hesitate.

"Lady Istara," he began, then fell silent. He sat down again. His hands moved back and forth over his thighs, rucking up the material of his kilt. He stopped, abrupt, and looked up at her. "There is a chance the portal might not take us where we intend to go."

Istara folded her eyebrows together. "I don't understand," she said. "I thought the portal leads straight through."

"It could," Thoth said. "However, when Arinna vanished during the wars of gods and men, the world split into an identical copy of itself. From that point, each world followed a different path and reached a different outcome, neither aware of the existence of the other." He sighed. "This means from the other side of the portal, the destination will always be Elati, but from this side, Surru's pathway is branched. It will either lead us out to the world where I and the other gods came from, where the cores are, or—" he paused to brush away a smudge of dust on his kilt, "—the one you, Sethi, Marduk, Urhi-Teshub, Ahmen, and Teshub originated from. A world my presence almost destroyed."

A sliver of hope touched Istara. "If we return to my world, might I recover my memories?"

Thoth poked at the pile of his notes. Unhappiness saturated him. "For the brief time we might be there, I suspect not."

Istara cut a look to the front of the ship. Sekhmet had leaned back in her seat. Her booted feet rested on the console, crossed at the ankles. In the reflection of the ship's window, the goddess of war eyed the streamers of light darting over the surface of the portal.

Istara turned back to Thoth. "Who was Baalat?"

Thoth pressed the heels of his palms against his eyes. "In my world, she was—" he cleared his throat, glanced up at her, "—the goddess of healing."

"And Horus?" Istara asked, her heart tight.

Hesitation. A flicker behind Thoth's eyes. "The god of war."

"How is that possible?" Istara asked. "Sethi and I are the gods of war and healing. I have never before heard of Baalat or Horus. Who am I if not the goddess of healing? You told me the pantheon was *identical.*"

Thoth shot Urhi-Teshub a troubled look. Urhi-Teshub returned his glance, impassive. Sekhmet pulled her legs down from the console and glided around in her seat to face them, her eyes on Thoth, dark, intent.

"Yes," she said, soft. "If Istara is not the goddess of healing, who *is* she?"

"This is not the time for this," Thoth snapped. "Is it not enough to accept the Creator moves in mysterious ways? What matters is Istara is the goddess of healing, and Sethi is the god war. Horus and Baalat are gone, forever—from both worlds."

"From *both* worlds?" Istara repeated. She looked down at her hands. Tiny tendrils of her golden light darted along her fingers. "My memories of the Immortal Realm," she whispered, "and the destruction of my city." She looked up, fierce. "They are mine. I was *there.*"

"This is not the time," Thoth repeated, severe. "We must focus on getting the cores—"

"No," Istara cut in. "Now is exactly the time."

"It is better to forget what came before and press forward, nothing good will come of asking these questions," Thoth said, his hands curling into fists, tension oozing from him. "The Creator took your memories for a reason. That should be enough for you."

"So you refuse to tell me."

Thoth nodded, terse, his narrow jaw hardening into a definite, stubborn line.

Istara glared at him, furious, trembling. "You began all this by saying the portal might not lead where you wanted. And you told me this, why?"

"I have no control over what happens once we are inside the portal," he answered, "but if we do emerge in the world you came from, both you and Sekhmet will be in grave danger."

"What kind of danger?"

He cut a look at the portal, then back to her. "Grave danger," he repeated, holding her eyes. "You must trust me in this matter. Urhi-Teshub will watch over you, and I will join Sekhmet, should I need to take control of the ship."

He strode to the front of the ship. The door slid closed, final, an impassable gulf. Silence surrounded Istara.

Urhi-Teshub lowered his bulk onto the seat opposite her. Thoth's neat pile of notes slid toward him. He caught them and set them out of the way, further down the divan. The ship rumbled, its nose easing toward the improbable doorway to another world. Her protector leaned forward, his elbows on his thighs, and folded his fingers together.

"I think Thoth is right," he said, gentle. "You should trust in the Creator's wisdom."

She opened her mouth to disagree, but the ship slid into the soft, watery light of the portal. A heartbeat later she fell with her protector into the silence of the void.

After the darkness and disconnection of her body from her mind—pale, gray light. By degrees, pure, clean, cerulean light washed over Istara. Her senses sharpened, raw with clarity. While still lost in the cocoon of light, the crunch of stone came from under the ship. Istara blinked. An image fleeted through her mind, sharp, visceral, of an enormous black ship, its pointed nose facing a portal, and two women, locked in a cage made of light set a little distance away. The dark ship moved toward the portal, the flat, black stones breaking under its wheels as it slid into the doorway embraced by tendrils of blue-white light. It shot through the churning wall and vanished, leaving the weeping women in their cage, shivering with cold, destined to die.

The light surrounding Sekhmet's ship faded. Istara looked at Urhi-Teshub, seeking answers. He leaned forward and eyed her, enigmatic, revealing nothing.

The ship's wings cleared the massive engraved ashlars of the portal and emerged onto a bleak, barren island, its surface clad in flat, black rocks. Dark, inky water lapped its uneven shoreline. Above, a roof of living rock glinted with the sparkle of frost. The ship slid out from the portal into an underground cavern bathed in blue-white light. Istara stood up, blinking, drinking in the sight of it, her senses resonating. Though she could not remember being here, it *felt* familiar. She had been here once before, she was certain of it. Something important had happened in this dark, hidden place—something connected to the black ship, the cage, and the two women trapped within it.

She clutched at her tendril of certainty as new fragments of images tumbled through her mind: a ragged, starving child huddling in the shadows beside a golden statue of herself; a brown puppy playing in a verdant garden, chasing peacocks; a woman dressed in finery fleeing a stone-walled city, running through a damp, dripping wood; a great, bloody battle, the eyes of the dead lit by the flames of a raging fire; two women hiding in a tent, one of them blue-eyed, a dagger lying on the ground between them; endless rows of wounded, dying soldiers lined up alongside blazing pits of fire, the skies bearing down on them, cold and cruel; a needle against flesh, its thin thread pulling muscle and skin back together; a journey through a great wood; a vile, filthy man primed to rape a woman, felled by a spear; a battle between two men in the blazing heat of the sun; a journey across a desert;

a terrible earthquake; a stepped pyramid; a luxurious suite deep underground, Urhi-Teshub upon a divan, looking at a woman asleep on a bed, filled with longing.

She caught her breath and looked at her protector.

"You were there." She moved toward him. "In the suite under the stepped pyramid. There was a woman. You loved her."

Urhi-Teshub blinked. His lips parted. "I—"

The ship turned on itself, sharp. Istara staggered. It swung back around to face the portal. Tendrils of light slid from it to embrace the ship. The walls of the ship shimmered and the view of the cavern faded. From the front of the ship, Thoth's voice rang out, sharp, urgent, giving commands.

Istara sank onto the divan beside Urhi-Teshub. "Was she the woman in the cage?" She tilted her head toward the wall of the ship. "Out there? Is that where you lost her?"

Urhi-Teshub took a ragged breath as they slid back into the portal. She caught the glint of tears in his eyes. He nodded, tight. She took his hand and squeezed it. "I sense she is still with you, in spirit."

Urhi-Teshub choked and looked away. Darkness came again, but in Istara's heart—light. It was a beginning. Though they made no sense to her, the images had come to her for a reason. She needed to return to this place to learn more. Here was where her questions would be answered, where her lost memories would be found. And she *would* uncover them—with or without Thoth's help.

CHAPTER 3

It was a beautiful afternoon. From Horus's vantage on the balcony of the palace's western tower, clear, deep blue skies arced over Ikalur's turquoise bay toward the endless expanse of the Adriande Sea. Where the waters of the bay and sea merged, the sea's waves glittered, studded by thousands of miniature reflective suns, brilliant white globes, so blinding, Horus had to shade his eyes.

To the north, a dark speck pierced the darker blue of the heavens. Faint, it came—the sound he had been waiting for—the piercing cry of a falcon announcing her return home. Horus lifted his gauntleted arm, bracing himself for the oncoming rush of the bird's landing. She arrived, her talons encircling his arm, gripping him hard, the weight of her sudden and reassuring. He carried her into the mews, freeing the leather scroll case from around her leg as he walked. Once settled onto her perch, she ruffled her feathers and eyed him as he set aside the tiny scroll case and collected a fat morsel of raw rabbit flesh from a covered bowl.

With a quiet word of affection, he tossed it to her, enduring a stab of envy. Once, long ago, he too could soar across the skies, unfettered by the pull of the land. As she worked her way through the sinews of flesh, he glanced at the map tacked to the wall of the office, reflecting on how far she had flown—all the way from Chaus's capital city of Itin—and in how little time she had accomplished the return trip. Two days. He had begun to suspect Elati possessed more enhancements than just the speed of the sun's rise and fall and the near-everlasting youthfulness of its people. He sensed the power of the Creator was stronger here, though why he couldn't guess.

Horus left the falcon to her meal and returned to the balcony. Putting his back to the sun so it would warm his shoulders, he pulled the message from the scroll case.

We are with Serde. Chaus is prepared to stand against the invader. We have begun preparations for war.

Beckoning one of the mews' runners to him, he handed her the note. With a quick bow, she sprinted away to make her way down the three hundred thirty-three steps of the tower's stairs and through the maze of the palace's corridors to the office of the king.

Horus glanced back at the falcon, already halfway through her breakfast. He had been taught to tether the birds as soon as they were set upon their perch, but he liked giving Yryn the freedom to eat, she deserved as much after her grueling journey. Midway through tearing a length of sinew free, she lifted her head, alert, and tilted her head, listening, a glistening strip of flesh hanging from her beak.

"What is it, Yryn?" Horus asked, eyeing her, wary. The bird lowered her talon, slow. The meat hit the stone-flagged floor with a soft slap. Her feathers flattened and she hunched down. Too late, Horus realized what she was about to do. He lunged for her just as she surged past him in a rush of feathers.

"Yryn!" he cried. She shot out over the bay, heading south, her keening cry fading in her wake. Horus bit back a curse. He cut a look at her empty perch, regret clawing at him. Yryn was one of the queen's favorites. He wondered how would he explain the falcon's sudden departure. Yryn had never done anything like this before, and to leave her breakfast unfinished, it was—

In the distance, just on the edge of his hearing, a deep, throaty roar. He turned, his spine prickling. The roar deepened, surrounding him, holding him captive to its heavy, seductive thrill. From over the forested hills north of the city, it came: black dark, hulking, massive. A ship he knew far too well. It thundered over the bay and screamed past the tower, circling the city in a wide arc, searching for a place to land. Through the haze of his despair, a memory jangled, urgent, calling to him. Over breakfast, Baalat had said she would be in the palace for the day, attending the queen who had as yet been unable to conceive. A bittersweet task, after Baalat's broken confession the night before—His thoughts shuddered to a halt. Dread touched him. No. Not the palace.

He ran, taking the stairs three at a time. Of all the places Baalat could have been today, why did she have to be with the queen? He stumbled and caught hold of a niche in the wall. He would be no good to her with a broken ankle. Forcing himself to slow down, he continued, steady, taking the steps two at a time instead of three, frustration tearing at him.

Outside, the ship continued to scream past in regular circuits, its high-pitched whine blistering his ears. Halfway down the stairs, he began to nurse the hope Sethi might not land after all. He might merely fly overhead to let the king know of his awareness of Ikalur, and return another day.

The steps fled from under Horus's feet. He eyed the markers as he went. Two-thirds of the way down. Almost there. Outside, one last deafening sky-shattering scream, followed by the gushing roar of the ship's engines cutting out as it came to rest. Blinded by the windowless interior of the endless staircase Horus bellowed a curse, desperate to reach Baalat, to not be too late.

He burst out of the tower's lower rooms and into the courtyard, unprepared for the sudden onslaught of pandemonium. Everywhere, chaos. Courtiers ran, directionless, their decorum lost, and their elaborate garments and headdresses askew; servants cowered in alcoves, weeping; soldiers pushed their way through the milling mess, torn between trying to keep order, and shoving their way through the press.

Horus shouldered his way past a huddled group of white-robed sages bunched up against a cart. One of them climbed into it and raised her arms to the heavens.

"It is the ancient prophecy," she cried, her voice rising, high and shrill over the noise of the crowd, "the invader has come through the impenetrable wall of light. Without the protection of the gods we will be cut down like wheat to the sickle."

In the wake of her proclamation the courtyard erupted in renewed wails. Misery sloshed back and forth in the confined space, gaining momentum, suffocating, oppressive. Grinding his teeth, Horus shoved his way through, rough, uncaring of those who fell in his path. There was only Baalat.

He reached the courtyard's gate. Hulking over the crushed oyster shells of the black and white squares of the garden's game board—meant to be populated by tokens of horses and costumed men and women—thin tendrils of exhaust trickling from the ship's tail, Marduk's warship cooled in all its powerful, malevolent, brutal glory.

Under the ship's curved wing, a door slid open. A heartbeat later, he came, the resurrected god of war, clad in a white kilt etched with golden symbols. In utter silence, he descended the ship's floating steps and emerged from the wing's shadow into the sunlight, the golden fractals on his chest jerking, stuttering, suppressed, broken. On his hips, a pair of Marduk's weapons glinted in the afternoon light.

Dispassionate, cold, Sethi's golden eyes raked over the ruined gardens, lingering, impassive, on the once-verdant flowering bushes blackened from his landing.

"Bring me your king," he called to a young palace guard standing alone at the edge of the board, holding his spear out, defiant. The youth shook his head and lifted his spear higher. A challenge.

Sethi strode to the youth. He took the spear from him and tossed it aside. It sailed over the scorched garden and smacked against the courtyard wall. "Tell him Sethi, god of war, Commander of Marduk's armies, Mighty, Lord of All, Giver of Life, and Taker of Life demands Serde's allegiance."

The guard shook his head again, his jaw set, stubborn. "I will not," he cried, though the glint of tears glistened in his eyes. "I will die before I kneel to the enemy of Elati."

Sethi's brow twitched. "How old are you, boy?"

"Sixteen," he answered, though he held his ground as Sethi stepped closer and towered over him.

"So young," Sethi said. "And have you yet known the pleasure of a woman?"

The youth blanched. He nodded, uncertain.

Sethi laughed. "You are a terrible liar. Last night I bedded the queen of Thes Dios after her husband refused to kneel." He glanced at the curved flight of a dozen marble steps leading up from the game board to the palace. "Do you think tonight I will be taking Ikalur's queen to my palace to savor her delights?"

"You will not," a voice rang out, imperious, hostile. From the shadows of the palace, the king of Ikalur stepped onto the terrace, clad in a purple robe edged in gold, a crown of golden leaves upon his brow.

Sethi turned, his golden eyes hardened. "Ah, at last."

Horus eyed the group following King Rhewyn down the steps to Sethi—four royal guard and a half dozen members of the high council. The queen was not among them. Horus breathed his thanks to the Creator. Baalat was safe. For now. He edged his way along the shadows of the courtyard wall, drawn to the god he once had been, fascinated by the transformation of Egypt's once-commander into an immortal god. Sethi had taken on the attributes of the god of war: the clothing, the golden fractals, and blazing eyes, yet he was nothing like Horus in his bearing or demeanor. The essence of Sethi's mortal personality and physique persisted in a bizarre juxtaposition of man and god. The stink of Marduk's corruption permeated him, violence saturated him, and malevolent power suffused him. Whatever good Sethi possessed, Horus could see no trace of it in the hard features of the being eyeing the king with cold contempt.

"You have come to us from beyond the impenetrable wall of light," King Rhewyn said, meeting Sethi's baleful look. "The prophecy has foretold it. And now you have come to Ikalur." The king lifted his chin. "Let us not waste time. What are your terms?"

"Only this:" Sethi said, "Serde's allegiance to Lord Marduk, a quarterly payment of tribute, and Serde's army will be mine to control. If you fulfill these conditions, you will be allowed to remain on Serde's throne and know a certain degree of authority."

Rhewyn glared at him. "So I will be powerless while you force my men to oppress our allies in the name of your overlord." He looked across the devastation of his gardens. The muscles in his jaw thinned. "And if I refuse?"

Sethi rested his hands on the handles of his weapons. "You die, your queen becomes my concubine, and your kingdom will be enslaved to Lord Marduk's allies." He tilted his head to the north. "This morning, Chaus's king pledged allegiance to Elati's one true lord. He is prepared to sack the cities of Serde on my command and has been ordered not to spare a soul, mortal or beast until you kneel to him."

Rhewyn said nothing for a long time. Sethi pulled the weapon from his belt, and pressed an indentation on its handle. The thing gave off a quiet chirp and several blue lights gleamed along the handle's edge. It began to hum, quiet. He pointed it at the youthful guard still standing close by, listening, pale.

"You said you would not kneel to the enemy of Elati," he said as the guard stepped back, his courage waning. "This is what happens to those who don't."

The boy didn't even have a chance to cry out. A beam of blue light shot out from the nose of the weapon, and in less than a heartbeat, he was gone, obliterated into a smear of blue particles, the faint outline of his form lingering, ephemeral, before fading away as though he had never been.

Horrified cries came from the councilors surrounding the king. The group shrank back, leaving Rhewyn to stand alone before the monster Sethi had become. Within the gardens, fearful murmurs filled the air. Horus knew what the people were thinking, without a body to inter, there could be no soul—the boy would never know any kind of afterlife. Sethi carried total annihilation in a weapon small enough to hold in his hand. He pointed it at the king and lifted an eyebrow, a question.

Rhewyn knelt. He lifted his face to Sethi, his eyes filled with hate. "Serde is yours."

Sethi tucked the weapon into its holder. "It appears you are not a fool after all." He looked over the palace, proprietary. "I am hungry. While I dine you will prepare Serde's tribute." He strode up the steps into the palace—its new owner, arrogant, hostile, indomitable. He stopped at the top, and eyed the still-kneeling king. "My share shall be a dozen of your most beautiful women. If they do not please me—" he tilted his head to the yawning gap where the boy had once stood, defiant, with his spear, "—they will not be returned to you. Only your most beautiful women will suffice. I care not whether they are married or maids, they belong to me now."

He turned and entered the palace. "And bring me a sage," he called as he disappeared into its shadows. "Your most learned one."

Rhewyn rose and ascended the steps, following after his new master, a dog, beaten into submission. When the king was gone, silence swallowed the garden, blanketed by the quiet of dread, and of death.

Horus wasted no time. He slipped into the palace to begin the search for Baalat, a new fear sawing into him, leaving him raw and aching. Baalat was not safe, not with a face like hers. The perfection of a goddess still lingered on her features. He pushed his way through the chaos spreading through the palace, past the frightened screams of women caught in the grip of the soldiers once sworn to protect them, pleading for their husbands to save them. Dread circled him, black serpents, their fangs glistening. They coiled around him, hungry, seeking his despair. No. He would not lose her. Not today. He ran.

✳ ✳ ✳

Sethi ate and drank, quick. He wasn't interested in the elegant women serving him, or the gentle stringed melody filtering through the jasmine-scented air from one of the upper balconies. He had done his work for today, now it was time for him to continue his search for the elusive double-bladed jihn. He pushed his platter aside, and waited for the sage to arrive. If everything he had heard was true, Serde's sages were the most knowledgeable of the legends and history of Elati's long-vanished ancient race. If he were ever to have the answers he sought, he would have them here.

He took a sip of wine and grunted with appreciation. It was a very good, robust red. He was glad Rhewyn had knelt; Ikalur appealed to Sethi. The temperature was perfect, every structure soaked in pillared beauty. Perhaps when Elati was conquered, he would ask Marduk to allow him to make Ikalur his home. He could live well here, surrounded by white towers overlooking a clear, turquoise sea, the mosaic-tiled courtyards surrounded by waterfalls and gardens drenched in color. He would spend his days seeking out and savoring the pleasures of beautiful, willing women—

Last night had been . . . unpleasant. He had been far too merciful. He should have thrown Thes Dios's queen off his terrace, how dare she curse him to never know love. After he had been so patient with her, too, enduring her weeping, offering her wine, promising her a better life with him than with her dead king. But her tongue—the woman had been a viper, stinging and striking, provoking him, daring him to do what he did to her. And yet, if he had thrown her into the chasm perhaps her curse—breathed from the depths of a broken heart—might have come true. He had come to learn Elati vibrated with an energy more powerful than even the one which granted him the powers of a god. It surrounded him; clean, pure, suffused with an ancient, nameless sentience which slid past him, refusing to touch him. It unnerved him. He might be the god of war and the commander of Marduk's armies, but to live an eternity without love—

No, he had done the right thing sparing her, even if he had had to spend two hours flying to Marduk's stronghold to get rid of her. Marduk, at least would be happy. He had mentioned more than once Ninsunu needed a companion.

Sethi swirled the cup's ruby contents, his thoughts turning to the progress of his campaign. With the kingdoms of Serde and Chaus he had secured a large section of the eastern coast of Tholis. Marduk would be pleased.

In the province where Marduk had taken his residence—an abandoned palace perched on Kium's rugged north coast—no overlord ruled. Over time, the ruling families had died out, the remote mountainous land given over to bearded, ax-wielding tribesmen who congregated in small, primitive settlements in the valleys, their villages surrounded by vast banks of mounded earth, buried within small hills. They lived by hunting, raiding each other's villages, and drinking. They could be ignored, for now.

However, the verdant, forested kingdoms of Nimidia and Vinay to the south, and the wheat drenched plains of Pres to the west where Urah had once ruled, had refused to kneel. Even their lesser cities preferred death to submission. They would be a problem. If Saritova also refused to yield, he would have his work cut out to bring the whole of the western half of the continent to heel using only the armies of Chaus and Serde. He rubbed a hand over his eyes and considered the other unresolved issue: Lauca. Like Kium, Lauca was an outlier. Occupied by artisan guilds and merchants, Tholis's southwestern province was Elati's sole supplier of luxury goods. Lauca kept no army, preferring to settle disputes with sanctions. Neither did they have a king, instead elected citizens collaborated in what they termed a democratic process.

In Ningwu, Lauca's capital, the senate members had listened, unimpressed, to Sethi's terms, replying they would discuss the matter and take a vote in a month, their patronizing tone trying Sethi's patience to its limit. Instead he let them appease him with samples of their goods: a dozen bolts of silk, a pallet of luxurious furs, ten crates of wine, and jewels for Ninsunu. Let Lauca have their pathetic vote, they had no army, and had grown indolent with wealth. He could wait.

Once he secured Tholis, he would move to Chern, the continent across the ocean, then to Rzhev and Pir. He finished his wine, dwelling on the magnitude of work he had yet to do. A young serving woman slipped forward and refilled his cup from a gold-chased silver jug. He watched her, indifferent to her tremulous smile. He was one god, with one ship: Elati was vast, and filled with resilient, stubborn men and women. Marduk asked much of him, and progress was slow. He might have full access to Marduk's cache of devices and weapons, but Marduk had commanded him to keep those in reserve, in anticipation of what he suspected would come if Sethi did not find Istara. However, after what he had learned today from Chaus's king—of sea merchants' reports of ships plying the skies over the ocean he was certain Istara wasn't the only other god in Elati. He pressed the heels of his palms against his eyes. More complications.

He set his cup on the table, impatient for the sage to arrive. Ever since he had dreamed of the double-bladed jihn he could think of nothing else, his focus narrowing to a single, determined point. He had to possess it. With a weapon like that, he would be invincible. None could challenge him. It was real, he was certain of it. Since his dream it had continued to call to him. A beacon, hidden away in this vast, near-endless world. A thought slipped though his mind, unbidden: What if one of the others found the jihn first? What if Istara did? He clenched his jaw, and looked down at his hands as they curled into fists. To be on the receiving end of that. . . no. He had to find it first. He *would* find it first.

"Great Lord," a voice, as faint and fragile as ancient vellum broached the walls of his solitude. "I am Zherei, Master of the Ages. How may I serve you?"

Sethi looked up. A bony, wizened man, holding an ebony staff and wearing a plain white robe tied over his thin shoulder, bowed, stiff with age.

"I have heard there are legends," Sethi said, eyeing the sage, weighing his worthiness, "of Elati's first race. Are you able to tell me all I wish to know?"

The sage nodded, slow. "I am."

"I seek the most learned of all the Masters. I will not tolerate half-truths and speculation."

Zherei pressed a blue-veined hand to his chest and lowered his head. "Mighty One, I am the last living master who carries the true knowledge of Elati's tragic history. If I cannot answer your questions, no one can."

Sethi said nothing. Instead he gestured to have his cup refilled. He waited while the serving woman tilted the pitcher and the ruby liquid poured out, the last drops reflecting the afternoon light. He lifted his cup and took a slow measure of the sage, debating whether he could trust him. Zherei waited, patient, his head lowered. He eased his weight onto the staff, his knuckles whitening.

"Bring Master Zherei a chair," Sethi said to the withdrawing servant. Zherei's eyes flicked up to Sethi's, for a heartbeat his gratitude plain. Another servant emerged from the colonnaded vestibule and ran across the marble-tiled courtyard, carrying an elegant, fine-carved chair, gilt in gold and bearing a thin crimson cushion upon its seat.

"I would know more of the double-bladed jihn which consumes the light of the gods," Sethi said as Zherei relinquished the staff to the servant and sank onto the chair.

The old man cut a look at Sethi from under his brow, his gray eyes bright despite the ravages of his years. "The double-bladed jihn," he murmured, shooting a wary glance at the retreating back of the servant. "Hidden for eons, the blade is one of Elati's deepest, darkest secrets, and the cause of the annihilation of the ancient ones. It is dangerous to even speak of it."

"I dreamed of it," Sethi said, leaning forward, elbowing aside the platters still laden with roasted meat. He folded his fingers together. "It was mine."

The sage blanched. "By the fullness of the twin moons, the Creator truly *has* abandoned us. I had hoped—" He looked down at his robe and busied himself straightening it over his knees, unease seeping from him.

Sethi waited. His senses prickled. Zherei's reaction had been spontaneous, unaffected. Raw, stark fear bled from the Master of the Ages.

Zherei looked up at Sethi, his expression hollow, defeated—a rabbit in a snare. "Great Lord," he whispered, "forgive me. I had hoped I would not to live long enough to see this day."

"And what day *is* this?" Sethi demanded, tired of the circuitous, vague responses of the Elatians regarding their hateful prophecy, and of his supposed part in it.

"For that, the answer must be given in the whole," Zherei answered with a resigned sigh. He tilted his head in the direction of the waiting wine bearer in the vestibule. "Perhaps I might be permitted a little restoration before I begin?"

Sethi waved the woman over. Zherei took the offered cup; his hand trembling as he lifted it to his lips. He drank, deep, settling the near-empty cup onto his lap, his hand steadier than before. "You have my thanks," he murmured.

Sethi said nothing. Impatience stalked him. He leaned back in his seat and folded his arms over his chest, willing the sage to go on.

Zherei began. "Long before Elati was ruled by mortals, gods walked among us, and were the stewards of the world. It was an age of knowledge, peace, and perfection. None fell to disease, nor did mortals age as they do now. Then, men and women lived ten thousand years, yet appeared to age no more than thirty, enduring in an attractive, unblemished state until their final sleep when they were welcomed into the bosom of the Creator's realm. In those long lost times, it is said the Creator often walked in the gardens and cities of Elati, a being of pure light, visiting both the wisest of men, and his children, the gods. A more wondrous existence could not be imagined.

"Then, after almost twelve million years of peace, a breach tore into the fabric of our world. From that breach emerged the one who possessed the double-bladed jihn. It was he who overcame the gods using his tainted, insatiable weapon. Though the gods pleaded for the aid of the Creator, he did not come. They were indefensible against the weapon. One by one they were annihilated."

"And who was this one who possessed the weapon?" Sethi asked into the heavy silence. "Is he still in Elati?"

Zherei shook his head. "Yes and no," he said, quiet, his eyes falling to his cup.

"More riddles," Sethi muttered, lifting his wine. He sipped. "You will speak plain. I command it."

"Great One," Zherei said, meeting Sethi's eyes again, though the sage's had become immeasurably sad, "in the aftermath of the loss of the gods, the Creator returned to us, just once. He gathered the wisest of mortals, and commanded them to commit to memory the truth of what had happened and to hear the prophecy of what was to come . . . though perhaps it might have been better if he hadn't, since there is nothing any mortal could ever have done to prevent it."

Zherei lifted the cup again and finished the last of his wine. He shivered, though in the dappled shade of the potted palms, the air was almost too warm. "The one who came to Elati, his form unutterable darkness, black as the bleakest pit, bearing that awful weapon—was also the Creator."

Sethi blinked. "How can that be possible?"

"The Creator," Zherei began, cautious, "told our ancient ancestors he is comprised of both the most malevolent of darkness and the purest of light. Soon after his awakening the dark and light in him wrestled for supremacy. The light managed to trap the dark in an empty, lifeless world, but the dark, being clever and resourceful, created the jihn with a portion of its essence and pierced the walls of its imprisonment. Elati was where the breach led. Once here, the dark fed the jihn the light of the gods, increasing its power so it could continue to cross the boundaries separating the worlds. It had no desire to rule, or to be served, its only goal to steal the light of the gods until it became powerful enough to consume the boundless light of the Creator."

Zherei's eyes met his, faint with reproach. Sethi dropped his gaze to his cup. He turned it round in his hands, watching the wine within swirl, disturbed a weapon with such a purpose would call to him. He wondered who that made him. "But the jihn is still here, in Elati," he mused. "The dark must have failed."

"The Creator captured the darkness as it traveled through the boundaries between the worlds," Zherei said. He looked as though he would say more, but he fell silent and eyed the wine bearer, his expression taut. Sethi didn't call her back. Zherei could have all the wine he wished, later, when he had told all.

"And?"

Zherei shook his head, bleak. "And then the wise ones were given the prophecy—the one I hoped was only a legend and would never come to be."

"The prophecy of the impassable wall of light and an invader who would arrive from another world and leave Elati in flames and ruin?" Sethi asked, unable to keep the contempt from his voice. He knew better. Marduk had no intention of destroying Elati, and for that matter, neither did he. The prophecy was nonsense.

"Not that one," Zherei said, misery emanating from him. He fiddled with the cup, tracing the curlicues of its chased design. "The Creator could not destroy the jihn without destroying a part of himself which would bring chaos, so he sealed it away in Elati. The dark side of himself, he did not attempt to cage again. Instead, he broke it apart and deposited a single fragment of his darkness into each world. Though weakened, each fragment remained powerful enough to manifest great evil. In some worlds, the darkness would touch every sentient thing, growing in power over time, feeding on hate, war, and greed. In others, it would attach itself to a single being who would rise to great power and cause the downfall of its world. In each of those worlds, the Creator left a pantheon of gods, who bore his light against his darkness. He predicted all of the worlds would fail to stand against the dark, and it would be here, where it all began, the darkness would return, inexorably drawn to the call of the jihn.

"The impassable wall of light appeared soon after these events. The wise men and women believed it had been placed there by the Creator, and predicted once it was breached the end of our world would soon follow. Great Lord, forgive me, but with your arrival darkness has once more come to the peaceful existence of Elati. If the jihn is indeed calling to you—that darkness is you."

Sethi set aside his cup. He had asked about the jihn, and instead he had been subject to the darkest of accusations. How dare anyone, even a Master of the Ages, speak so to the god of war. The Elatians were stubborn, ignorant, superstitious fools who believed nonsense and legends. The Creator was light, nothing more. This was just another tale of dark and light, a fabrication of mortal minds. His hand went to the weapon at his hip. He pulled it free, his finger moving, automatic, over its lighted indentations. The weapon hummed, ready to strike. He lifted his arm and aimed, his heart cold.

Zherei slid from the chair, pale and unsteady. His head bowed, he knelt, his chest lifting and falling in tight, shallow breaths, prepared—no, willing to die.

"Ah," Sethi said, perceiving the slipperiness of the other man's mind, "you hoped to provoke me into granting you your wish. You shall not have it. Instead, you will reside with me until I have found the jihn. Prepare what you need to bring with you. Once the tribute is loaded, we depart."

He picked up his wine and gulped it down, furious. When there was nothing left, he hurled the empty cup across the courtyard. It slammed against a pillar and clattered away, ugly, discordant.

Locked in silent fury, he strode back through the halls of the palace to his ship, unseeing. He was not the darkness. Marduk had told him he would *liberate* Elati from the darkness. One day, they would know the truth. Sethi was their savior, not their enemy. But first, the jihn. If anyone knew where to begin looking for it, Zherei would. And when he found the weapon, he would reward the sage—with death.

❋   ❋   ❋

In the ensuing chaos unfolding across the palace, Horus managed to get as far as the inner courtyard leading to the queen's apartments before a pair of royal guards prevented him from going any further. They crossed their spears before him and glared at him from under their vermillion-plumed golden helmets.

"My woman, the healer Baalat, is in the queen's presence," Horus said, "I must see her."

"The healer cannot leave the queen's presence without Queen Welyn's permission," the taller of the guards said.

"Then," Horus retorted, bridling at the guard's condescending tone, "I would ask Baalat be advised Horus is waiting without, and carries a message of great importance for her."

"We cannot leave our post," the shorter guard replied, bland. "If you wish to send a message, you must write it down and give it to a palace messenger. It is protocol."

"Protocol? Now?" Horus cried, his patience shot. "I am not going to fetch a messenger. I am right here! Have you no idea what is unfolding? How much danger Baalat is—"

From behind, a shout. "Make way by order of the king."

The guards snapped their spears back and stood to attention, their eyes fixed straight ahead, blank. A shove, and Horus stumbled, shouldered aside by a phalanx of soldiers wearing full armor, their hips bristling with daggers and short swords.

One strode ahead of the group, the plume of his helmet higher and fuller than the rest. He pulled it off and rested it in the crook of his arm before pushing open the double doors to the queen's apartment.

"My lady queen," he called as he entered, "I come by the order of the king. You are to remain in your residence, but your companions and serving women must leave with me." He moved deeper into the apartment, gesturing and calling out orders, his words lost in a clamor of armor and weapons as the soldiers trotted past Horus, their eyes hard.

From further within, feminine cries of distress rippled out, crescendoing, sharp, pungent with terror. Terror slithered into the courtyard and wrapped itself around Horus. Once more barred by the guards, he eyed the corridor leading to the one he loved, panting, furious. Baalat was in there, alone. Defenseless.

He threw himself at the guards, grunting through the pain of their vicious retaliations, cursing the loss of his once-superior strength and enhancements, determined not to fall. Caught in a choking grip of one of the guards, his shoved his knee once, twice, deep into the groin of the other guard. The guard staggered and fell to his knees. One down. Throwing his head back, a shear of blinding pain scoured his vision, followed by the satisfying crunch of the guard's nose breaking. Freed by the bloodied, bellowing guard, he spun around and rammed his elbow into his oppressor's throat. Not waiting to see if the guards stayed down, he threw himself past the double doors, down the corridor and into the pandemonium of the queen's suite, his eyes raking over the bedlam, searching, frantic, for the one who possessed his heart.

More than a two dozen scantily-clad women fled from the soldiers, exotic creatures draped in gold, jewels, feathers, and silk. The queen had risen from her golden seat and cried her resistance, her refusal to obey, demanding the soldiers leave her and her women in peace. None heeded her.

A raven-haired woman in a near-transparent gown of violet draped over a golden undergarment collided with Horus. She stumbled away and clung to one of the gold and white pillars. A soldier lunged after her and caught her around her waist. He tugged on her and pulled her free, her shrieks of panic claws against Horus's ears.

"Baalat!" Her name skidded over the screams of the women and bellows of the soldiers.

Horus.

He spun around, cut between hope and dread he had imagined her voice. Desperate, he pushed through the melee, toward where he sensed she had called to him. There. Behind a screen, deeper in the apartment, a door, concealed to those who didn't know where to look. He cast a quick look if any regarded him. No one did. Before the queen's seat, several soldiers pinned three women to the floor, where they struggled and wept, helpless against the soldiers' implacable, unforgiving grips. Numb, Queen Welyn surveyed the wreckage of her once-elegant reception—the toppled divans and overturned tables; the spilled wine; strewn cups; shattered plant pots, bleeding soil and trampled palms; the torn cushions, their feathers drifting, innocent of the brutality surrounding them—her eyes bright with tears, and her fists clenched at her sides.

Keeping his head down, Horus worked his way around a pair of soldiers preoccupied with restraining a clawing and kicking woman, desperate to escape her fate—and slipped behind the screen into an airy, marble-walled room. A dozen pastel-colored tapestries graced its heights from floor to ceiling. He hauled back the nearest one, the next, and the next. Nothing but marble glared back at him. He yanked aside six more. Cold, white walls greeted him. At the opposite end, he reached a blue and gold-tiled bathing pool overlooking the sea, surrounded on three sides by pillars and silken hangings. The pool's surface lay quiet and still, dotted with floating basins of pink flowers. With a cry of frustration, he stormed past a thick curtain into the queen's privy. The quiet burble of running water reached him, soothing as a fountain. Behind a low wall of marble, a glimpse of the top of a golden chair. He leaned over the wall, aching with hope. Nothing.

His heart tight, he returned to the main room and called Baalat's name. One heartbeat. Two. Three. He cut a look over his shoulder, back toward the reception. Dread lanced a scathing path through him. He had been wrong. Past the screen, soldiers shouted their readiness to leave. Rage slammed into him. He had been a god. If he had to kill every one of them with his bare hands, he would, they would never have her—

Movement whispered against one of the tapestries he had not checked. He held his breath, hope shredding him. Please. He waited. Willed it to be her. She emerged, cautious, defensive, her incision knife held up before her. Her eyes met his, wet with fear. His name painted her lips, scored his heart. The blade fell from her fingers, clattered against the floor.

He crossed the space in two strides and caught her face in his hands, his mouth found hers, savage, fierce.

"My love," he stroked her cheeks with his thumbs, reverent, "I thought I had lost you."

"We saw it all." Her eyes darkened. A tear slid free. He kissed it away. "He's you," she breathed, horror coating her features. "But not you. He's an abomination of everything you once were."

Out in the hall, the desperate cries of the women ebbed. The heavy tread of the soldiers retreated. A dull boom as the doors closed. Silence.

Horus went to the screen, wary. The guards would have roused and would be looking for him. He eyed the hall. It lay in ruins, ransacked. Apart from the queen's chair, almost everything else had been broken, overturned, or stained. The emptiness of the vast, pillared hall bore down on him, oppressive. A space like this was meant to be filled with society, laughter, music, and poetry. Now, there was nothing, only a yawning, barren cavern tainted by the darkness of what had just unfolded.

Alone, her face in her hands, the queen huddled into herself, weeping hard. Baalat slipped through the hall's wreckage and knelt before her.

"My lady queen, how may I aid you?"

The queen lifted her head, her fine, even features blotchy with tears. She stared at Baalat, astonished. "How are you still here?"

"I hid in your privy," Baalat answered. She gestured to Horus. "My husband, Horus. He came to protect me."

Queen Welyn nodded, vague. She looked over the hall, her hollow gaze pausing on the fragile silver links of a trampled waist-chain, lost in the fracas by one of her companions. "My husband the king knows the prophecy as well as any of us, and yet he has knelt to the one who will destroy Elati. How could he betray his people? How could he betray me? Why did he not stand against the invader and fight?"

"My lady," Horus said, bowing his head, "the king has bought Serde time, and saved countless lives. The enemy is not the one who has come today, but another, the one who controls him—Marduk. It is he whom all of Elati must stand against."

The queen cut a sharp look at Horus. "And who is this . . . Marduk?"

"A very dangerous, very patient and persistent enemy," Horus answered, folding his arms over his chest. His gaze moved to the terrace, from where, below, the weeping of the captured women rose and fell, a susurration of fear and desolation.

"And how could *you* possibly know this?" Queen Welyn demanded. "The mere husband of a healer?"

"I was not always thus," Horus met the queen's eyes. "Once, I was more powerful than all the kings of the world. To save my consort, I sacrificed my immortal light to another. While I was weak, Marduk defeated me. Baalat followed me soon after."

The queen paled. She rose and took a step toward him, eyeing him, suspicious. "Though what you say challenges everything I know, let us assume you speak the truth. Tell me, if you have been defeated by Marduk, how is it you are both alive?"

"The Creator granted us another chance to live," Horus replied, "though no longer as gods, but as mortals. The Creator said those who would stand against Marduk would need all the help they could get."

Queen Welyn said nothing for a long time. She folded her hands over her waist, her fingers laden with jewels.

"And you were gods of what?" she asked, low.

"I, of war," Horus said, holding her gaze, "and Baalat of healing."

When the queen fell silent again. He continued, "The one who has come today was once a mortal, the commander of an army. He was good, honorable, just, and willing to sacrifice everything for the woman he loved. Whatever he has been twisted into by Marduk is the opposite of the man I returned to life."

The queen's eyes moved to Baalat, then returned to him. Her gaze drifted once more to the ruins of her apartment. "Although what you say stretches the limits of what I am willing to believe, if the Creator *has* sent you to us, who am I to stand in his way? If you have already faced the one called Marduk, you will know things. Many things. Therefore, you must aid us."

"I would be honored." Anticipation rippled through Horus. Baalat's fingers touched his arm. He caught her look, her acceptance their reprieve was at its end, the fight begun once more. He covered her fingers with his hand, and gave them a gentle squeeze. Purpose surged through him. This time Marduk would fall. He would not fail a second time. "If I may," he said, "I would like to send one of the falcons with the tribute."

Queen Welyn's eyebrows folded together, though her gaze lingered on the fragments of a shattered mirror spread over a rug, its jagged pieces glittering in the light of the sun. "Why?"

"Because if one of Ikalur's captives learns where they have been taken, they can send the bird back to me with a message. From them we will know where Marduk's stronghold is."

The queen nodded. "You may send Tyrn. She is the fastest." She met his eyes, hers veiled. "I pray you will not fail us, Horus, once-god of war."

Horus crouched in the shadow of the ship's rear, Tyrn hooded and perched on his gauntlet, searching for the one to whom he would entrust the dangerous task of revealing Marduk's stronghold. He eyed the group of quaking, sobbing women, surrounded by a wall of soldiers to prevent their escape, the king's unhappiness plain as he winnowed the women down one by one into the unfortunate dozen who would be doomed to satisfy Sethi's lust. No. It could not be one of them. They would have more than enough to endure.

Further up, on the terrace, Sethi stood with his back to the scene, looking out over the gardens, his hands on his hips, ignoring the servants offering him wine and sweets. Close by, Serde's tribute stood in open crates ready to be loaded onto the ship. A fortune lay spread out in the shade of the ship's wing: gold and silver ingots, jewels, bolts of silk organza, white linen, wool, jars of wine, spices, incense, fragrant oils, silk blankets, fine woven rugs, even furniture, chairs, tables, chests with drawers, gilt in gold. A group of twenty palace servants huddled beside the tribute, frightened and miserable, also under guard. Horus cursed, wondering how he would even have a chance to speak to any of the captives with so many soldiers present. He hadn't really thought his plan through as well as he should have.

"So, even our falcons are not safe from our oppressor's predations."

Horus turned, wary. An old man approached from behind, lugging a bulging satchel stuffed with scrolls. "I know this one," the wizened man said, nodding at the peregrine, her white breast feathers speckled with warm spots of brown. "Tyrn. A clever bird. Shame it has to be her."

"And you are?" Horus asked, sharp, annoyed by the intrusion.

"Zherei, Master of the Ages," the old man answered, lowering his burden with a heavy sigh. He sank down beside Horus onto the charcoal-dyed oyster shells of one of the black squares of the game board, uncaring of the dark powder staining the pristine white of his robe. He gestured at the ship, resigned. "I am destined for wherever this is going. I am certain I will never come back. Not after what I said."

Horus took the bait. "And what was that?"

Zherei fiddled with his staff. "Ah, nothing. Pay me no mind." He cast a furtive look at Sethi, who still stood with his back to them, his bearing shrouded in contained anger. "Well, I suppose it does not matter now," he muttered, rubbing his forefinger under his nose, "and perhaps I ought to warn someone what he's after before it's too late . . . unless you are destined to travel with me?"

"I am not," Horus paused. "What do you mean warn—?"

"And Tyrn?" Zherei interrupted.

"She has to go," Horus said, eyeing Zherei in a new light. Perhaps the old man might—

"Shame," Zherei murmured. "She's a fine bird. Deserves a better fate than this." He gestured, vague, at the tribute, captive servants, and shrinking group of women.

Horus tried again. "What do you mean warn someone?"

"Yes, that," Zherei said. He adjusted several of the scrolls in his satchel until they lay in a neat bundle. "He's looking for the jihn, an ancient, hidden artifact of great power. It consumes the light of the gods and obliterates them. He says he dreamed of it—that it was his. Although why he would want it is beyond me, since apart from him there are no other gods on Elati."

Horus digested Zherei's words. A tendril of dread circled the pit of his torso. "And . . . now he's taking you with him."

Zherei nodded, morose. "I should not have told him he was the darkness. As usual, I got carried away."

"The darkness?" Horus repeated. "You *meant* to insult him?"

"No, not at all, the darkness is real. An entity," Zherei said, tilting his head back to examine the ship, his gaze following its dark contours, the curve of its wings, and the floating steps as he revealed the tale of the Creator, of the separation of himself between darkness and light, and of the weapon the darkness had made which consumed the light of the gods. "Since the jihn was made with part of his essence he could not destroy it, so he hid it in Elati, foretelling one day the fragments of darkness would gather once more, and its vessel would arrive, drawn to the jihn— and when that happened," Zherei waved his hand, encompassing the city, the sky, and the sea, its waves crashing against the white shore far below, "all this would end."

His heart heavy, Horus looked at Tyrn. A bird. He had thought he might overcome Marduk with a bird, when Sethi was seeking a weapon which had once belonged the dark aspect of the Creator. A weapon which consumed the light of the gods. Baalat had shared—just once—of her end and Istara's transition into a goddess at the threshold of Surru. Istara *had* to be in Elati. Even through his hateful possession, Sethi would know it; his bond to his consort was indestructible. Horus let out a thin breath. Sethi was far gone if he sought a weapon which would annihilate his own consort.

"Do you know where the jihn is?"

"I have an idea," Zherei muttered, unhappiness seeping from him. "More of a logical conclusion, since there is only one place in Elati which has remained uninhabited since the time of the gods." He paused, bleakness surrounding him. "However, the region is vast. It will take time, unless of course, he can sense the jihn's presence once he is near enough to it, then it will take no time at all."

"Where is it?" Horus repeated, swiveling to face the sage. "Sethi is not the only god in Elati—there is another here, a goddess, his consort. If he finds her, he will use it to destroy her. She could aid us."

Zherei caught his breath. "If you know such things, who are—?"

"It's better for your sake if you don't know," Horus interrupted, cutting a look at Sethi, considering him in a new light. Perhaps the influence over him wasn't only Marduk's doing after all, perhaps there was more to this than met the eye. Horus felt far out of his depth. He longed for the chance to speak with Thoth about what Zherei had revealed. The Creator was both dark and light. He had always believed the Creator to be good, and yet, why not? What else could explain the darkness in the hearts of men? He loosened the straps of the gauntlet. "Tell me where it is."

"I suspect if it is anywhere, it will be in Anki," Zherei said. When Horus looked at him, blank, Zherei jerked his head toward the east. "It's an island in the middle of the Adriande Sea. It was once the home of the gods. None go there, not even the seafaring clans of Kium's savages. All nations believe the isle to be cursed."

"If that *thing* is there, Anki must be an unpleasant place."

Zherei nodded, bleak. "I once met a bankrupted merchant who claimed a raging storm surrounds the island. Every one of the boats in his fleet apart from his own were driven toward the island by strong winds and smashed against its cliffs."

"You must not tell Sethi where you think it is," Horus said. He hefted the gauntlet with the falcon from his arm onto Zherei's and retied the straps, "It is vital he does not find it."

"But the prophecy," Zherei muttered, lifting his arm to admire Tyrn. "One cannot stop what is meant to be."

"We can try," Horus said. "Just send him on wild chases, play the fool. Do what you must to buy us time."

"I'll try," Zherei sighed. He eyed Marduk's ship again, wary. "However, I imagine if he is able to traverse the skies in a wonder like this, he also has things which can persuade a man to speak the truth against his will." He ran a reverent finger along Tyrn's breast. "And why have you given me Tyrn?"

"The queen requires a task of you," Horus said. He fished out Tyrn's scroll case from his pouch and handed it to Zherei. "This ties to Tyrn's leg, make sure it's secure before you set her free."

"And why am I taking her with me, if only to set her free?"

"Because you are going to send the queen a message."

Zherei lifted an eyebrow. "Indeed? And what shall this message be?"

"Where he has delivered the tribute."

"Ah," Zherei nodded. He shot a look of triumph at Sethi's back and tucked the scroll case in amongst his satchel of scrolls. "It is fortunate I am able to navigate by the constellations. Inform our good queen I shall not let her down."

Horus clasped Zherei's thin shoulder. "May the Creator protect you."

Zherei met Horus's eyes, then dropped his gaze to Horus's hand on his shoulder. "Perhaps he already does," he said, soft.

Horus backed into the gardens, watching, grim, as the captive servants loaded the ship. When the last of it had been stowed inside, twelve tear-stained, disheveled women crept up the steps, silent and broken, into the dark interior. Zherei went in last, stroking Tyrn's feathers as though she were his own companion. In the numb, thick silence of the gardens, Sethi turned and strode down the steps of the terrace, across the ruined game board and up the steps into the ship. The steps retracted and the door slid closed.

A blast of heat and fire. The ship lifted into the deep blue of the sky until it loomed over the tallest towers. It turned toward the east and shot away in a cone of brilliance, in its wake, a deep thunder. Then, nothing. Zherei, the women, the servants, Tyrn, gone.

That night, as Baalat slept in his arms, Horus lay awake and thought of the jihn, of Anki, and of Istara, and of what he must endure to stop the one his light had become.

Through the haze of the portal's cerulean mist, beams of white light pierced the translucent walls of the ship, a rippling curtain of sunlight through water. They drifted over Istara and her protector, lingering against his weapons, tracing the metallic outlines of their curves.

The door to the flight deck slid open. Silhouetted against the glare, Thoth and Sekhmet worked the ship's controls. Istara leaned forward, half-expecting to see the cold, shale-strewn cavern where images of another world had come to her, the first she had had since her awakening in Elati. Beyond the ship's clear walls a yellow, desiccated plain slid past, blistered by a white-hot sun.

A shimmer rippled over the ship.

"Cloaking enabled," Thoth said. He pressed another series of switches as they rolled out into the world from which he, Arinna, Sekhmet, and the other gods had escaped. "Shields up." He scanned the cloudless sky, wary. "Let's go."

Sekhmet punched the ignition and a roar burst from the ship's rear. They tore up into the heavens, toward the dazzling white disc of the sun. The vast edifice of Surru's portal plummeted away, its blackened ashlars bearing witness to a purge of immense heat. It stood there, alone, a wounded, crippled thing, lost in a barren wasteland of scorched earth.

The ruined land merged with a fragile, blue sea, the blackened coast caressed by gentle breakers edged in ribbons of white. Above, the emptiness of a deep blue sky. Far beneath, the endless reach of the turquoise sea. Sekhmet's ship climbed higher. They pierced roof of the heavens. The roar cut out. Silence tore through the ship. Below, a thin strip of atmosphere gleamed in a layer of blue and pale orange above the curve of the world. Above, nothingness. Darkness. Far in the distance, the cold pinpricks of stars beckoned. Istara stood up transfixed, and turned, slow, locked in wonder, caught between heaven and earth.

"Never before have I flown this high," she breathed. "Sethi's ship could never breach the final barrier." She pressed her hand against the ship's clear wall, longing to touch the stars, so near, yet so far. "Somewhere out there is our Creator. He is watching us. I can sense it."

Urhi-Teshub rose and stood beside her. His gaze fell to his feet, drawn to the weight of a blue and white sphere hanging suspended in the infinite dark. "I had no idea the world could be so vast," he murmured. "To think I thought I ruled an empire. All my kingdoms together were nothing but a drop compared to this. Even Ramesses's mighty Egypt is but a feeble patch. How vain we were." He sank onto the seat, and stared, bleak, into the starry void. "How vain I was."

"Engaging ion drive," Sekhmet called over her shoulder. "Hold on."

A explosion of blue fire erupted from the ship's tail. A savage force slammed into Istara. It lifted her from her feet and threw her toward the flight deck, helpless as a doll. Urhi-Teshub lunged after her and caught her arm, the bruising pain of his grip lost in the wall of pressure determined to separate flesh from bone. Against the ship's mind-shearing thrust, he hauled her back to him and shielded her from the acceleration, his feet planted against the floor, his body rigid, the veins in the backs of his hands proud, enraged rivers of agony.

They blistered a path across the heavens, trailed by a brilliant column of blue and white light. It was impossible to speak, to think. Istara willed it to end. Just a handful of heartbeats passed, but in the vice of such immense force, it felt an eternity. The ion drive cut out. In its wake, epochal silence cut a swathe through the ship.

Istara sagged against Urhi-Teshub, her arm aching where he had caught her. Sekhmet's ship continued to hurtle over the sky's canopy, skimming along the arc of the world, a star shooting across the heavens.

Thoth came to them. A pair of fat, red weals from the seat's restraints criss-crossed his torso. Along their edges, blood oozed. He ran his hand along one of the weals, leaving behind a trail of smeared blood. "All well here?" he asked, looking around for something on which to clean his hand.

"Well enough," Urhi-Teshub answered. He tilted his head at the bright red lines marring Thoth's chest. "And you?"

"It's nothing." Thoth said, eyeing his scattered notes as he cleaned his hand, absent, against his kilt. "Better this than plastered across the console."

"Since when do the gods' ships have an ion drive?" Istara asked. "I thought only Marduk's ships have them."

"They do," Thoth answered. A whisper of pride flickered over his bony features. "However, before she went to the pyramids, Sekhmet modified her ship with equipment she, ah, shall we say 'liberated' from one of Marduk's kings."

"She upgraded her ship by herself?" Urhi-Teshub's gaze slid to Sekhmet, frank with admiration.

Thoth nodded. "She did. When she puts her mind to it, the goddess of war can be quite resourceful." He turned to Istara and eyed her, shrewd. "I trust you suffered no ill effects from our little detour?"

Istara turned her attention to the front of the ship, feigning interest in the view. "Nothing of consequence."

She sensed his gaze on her for a heartbeat longer. "Excellent," he said and bent to gather his notes. "Right now we are coasting over the world as we make our descent. Sekhmet used enough thrust to bring us to the pyramids or as near as she can manage. She has done this once before, when she brought the others here so we must have faith in her abilities. However, do be prepared for eventualities."

"Such as?" Urhi-Teshub picked up a sheaf of stray pages near him and handed them to Thoth.

"Oh, unpleasant things I should imagine," Thoth shrugged, sorting the pages into order. "Marduk was never one to do things halfway. Just be on your guard. The cores should protect us from Marduk's weapons and devices once we have them on the ship. Even deactivated, they will retain latent power, however—" he reached past Istara to collect a page, "—considering what Marduk has done to the portal at Surru, I suspect he has been busy trying to wipe out everything which might remind men we escaped his tyranny. He was never one to accept failure with grace."

"And yet, Surru still stands," Istara murmured.

"Indeed," Thoth muttered. "Though it is my most powerful portal, I did have misgivings whether it would still be standing since Teshub was able to destroy the portals in your world, and his weapons were far less powerful than Marduk's." His hands stilled, and his gaze drifted out to the numinous ribbon of light surrounding the planet. "It might have to do with the split, perhaps the portals must be destroyed at the same time, or—" he tilted his head as though hearing a voice inside his head. "Hm." His attention fell, blank, to the notes in his hand, his presence drifting away from them. "Perhaps Surru cannot be destroyed because of Elati's connection—but to withstand such power—Elati must be unlike any other world. Although, I have noted despite there being no gods, Elati's mortals possess extended life spans. It is as though the world itself is enhanced, its power coming from another source—but what could it—"

Sekhmet called for Thoth, sharp, impatient. He left, deep in thought, the question unanswered.

They descended, steady, sliding from the darkness and the cold glint of the stars into the nebulous mantle of blue-orange light, the ship's shield blazing as they hurtled back into the skies, screaming down from the heavens like a bird of prey. Istara could see nothing through the burning shield, its glow molten white. The ship juddered, rough, buffeted by the resistance of the world's boundary as if resenting the hubris of those who would challenge its might.

She glanced at Urhi-Teshub. Invigoration surrounded him. His eyes glinted, hungry for more, the raw power of their descent awakening him, bringing him to life. His hands curled into fists and he smiled, ecstatic. Istara watched him, fascinated, wondering at this once-mortal, who should be afraid, but instead reminded her of Teshub—passionate, fearless, reckless even. She wondered anew at their history. *Had* she strayed from her consort and loved this man, this powerful, passionate, yet restrained once-king of an empire? Urhi-Teshub was attractive, there was no doubt, with his rugged features, long, dark hair, charismatic presence, and aura of power. Others of her brothers and sisters often dallied with mortals, their flings nothing more than a passing diversion. But she and Sethi had ever been committed to each other, never tiring of their love.

And yet . . . Sethi was gone and Urhi-Teshub was with her. A dark thought circled her: What if Sethi had gone to Marduk because she had been unfaithful? She blinked, troubled, and searched the corridors of her mind, finding, as usual, nothing but empty, silent halls. If Urhi-Teshub had been her lover, Sethi would never forgive her. Could her consort's endless torment be her fault? No. She closed her eyes. It was unbearable. To think she could have done such a thing to him. She had to find a way to remember, to know the truth.

Only in that bleak, underground cavern had she pierced the seamless, impenetrable barrier of her mind and been granted a sense of what had once passed. None of it had made any sense. Still, it was better than being locked in a wasteland of nothing, of having to ask others for answers they refused to give. She blinked back the tears burning in her eyes, thinking of Sethi's anguish as each morning he suffered for his crimes, her guilt paralyzing her—the agony of her heart drowning out the thunder of the ship as it pierced the sky of a desert world riven by a verdant, sinuous river. In the far distance, three massive pyramids reared out of the sands—sentinels, ancient, sentient.

"We've been spotted," Sekhmet shouted over the roar of the ship screaming over the surface of the river, its passage shoving troughs of waves into the reed-choked riverbanks. "Sensors indicate twelve patrol ships incoming from the south, another four from the north. Thoth, are the cores are still active?"

"It's difficult to say—the readings are unstable." Thoth hunched over the console's screen. "There's some kind of field interfering with their output. No . . . By the Creator's light, Marduk has created a non-local field around the complex." He rubbed his forehead. Agitation bled from him. "He must have deciphered my notes . . . it will be alright, so long as he has not found the ones—" The once-god of wisdom bellowed a curse.

Alarmed, Istara went to the flight deck. Urhi-Teshub followed her, his bulk crowding the confined space.

Thoth's fingers moved over the screen. Complicated mathematical formulas swept across its surface at a dizzying speed.

"Has not found *which* ones?" Urhi-Teshub asked.

"Ones I should have destroyed," Thoth answered without taking his eyes from the screen.

"*Meaning?*"

"Meaning we might leave with the cores, but then again, depending on *when* we exit the field, we might not—*if* we ever exit it at all."

"How is that possible?" Urhi-Teshub demanded. "Either we have them or we do not."

"Because," Thoth muttered, "he is creating a naked singularity."

"Plain words, I beg you," Urhi-Teshub cried.

"It means once the field reaches a critical point, the cores will no longer be able to withstand the immense gravitational forces tearing at them and everything within the field will be obliterated as if it never was." He caught Urhi-Teshub's blank look. "Beside the fact we might be torn to shreds, time will also be unstable. Within a field like this, outside the realm of the laws which prevent chaos, there is no way to predict if we will get out with the cores, or even if we *will* get out. It will also affect whether we will see each other, and make our experiences individual, not shared. It is very dangerous."

"But I can see the pyramids," Istara said, tilting her head at them. "They are right there."

"That's because we are *outside* the field!" Thoth thumped his fist against the arm of his seat, his patience spent. "Time is linear here, so the pyramids won't vanish until the field has collapsed, then—" he snapped his fingers, "—nothing, not even a memory of them. It's quite thorough. Final. Even gods cannot escape."

"Thoth," Sekhmet said, swerving to avoid a pod of hippopotamuses, "now is not the time to explain your theories. Either I pull up and we leave in one piece or we're going in—we are fast approaching the point of no return."

"We need the cores," Thoth muttered.

"So we are going in?" Istara asked, uneasy. "You are certain there is no other way to create a sanctuary in Elati?"

Thoth's gaze moved to the pyramids. They beckoned, solid, massive. Real. He shook his head, miserable. "This is all I have to offer to withstand Marduk's devices and weapons. The cores are our last and only hope."

"I say we go in," Urhi-Teshub said. "If we succeed, we will still have a chance against Marduk. If we fail," he shrugged, "at least we tried everything we could."

"I agree," Sekhmet said, cutting a look up at Urhi-Teshub. "Although we will not fail. Thoth worries too much. He always has."

In the distance, hulking low over the horizon, four sleek, black ships approached, fast, deadly.

An alarm blared from the console. Sekhmet flipped several switches. The alarm cut out. "I recall the core's range reaching further out than this," she said. "We should have crossed the boundary of their protection by now."

Thoth's attention went back to the screen. Formulas and symbols sped across its face. He jabbed his forefinger at a result, working, brisk, through another series of calculations. Another result slid onto the screen. It blinked at him, red. "No," he breathed. "The perimeter is shrinking, and it's gaining speed. It's—" he paled, and looked up again at the mountainous complex looming over the river, coming at them fast, "—already at the outer edges of the pyramids. Aim for the middle, just south of the central pyramid. And lock these coordinates into the system. Our landing position."

From out of the desert sands, the trio of pyramids reared up, vast, monumental, their gold-sheathed capstones glinting in the brilliant light, wonders of mathematical perfection, erected eons ago by Thoth in just a matter of days.

"We aren't going to make it before the patrols reach us. Hold on." Sekhmet hit the thrusters. The ship screamed down the center of the river toward an ashlar-paved avenue leading to the complex.

"Incoming," Sekhmet said, her fingers moving, fast, over the console.

Istara tore her gaze from the pyramids. A pair of Marduk's ships broke rank. From their curved wings, two pairs of missiles launched, blue flame igniting their tails A heartbeat later a pair of dense thuds boomed through the ship, from the opposite side two more rocked the fuselage, sending Istara stumbling into the back of Thoth's seat. Blossoms of fire erupted across the shields, red-hot. They shimmered, viscous, barely holding under the searing heat. Blue fire swept over the ship's exterior, hungry, clawing, searching for a breach.

"By Anubis's balls," Sekhmet shouted, swiping through the damage reports streaming down her screen, "my shields won't survive many more hits like that."

"We are almost in," Thoth bellowed from his screen as another thud slammed against the ship's tail and a blinding sheet of blue-white flames swept over the ship's rear.

"How will we know when we have gone into the field?" Urhi-Teshub asked, his eyes raking over the complex. "I can't see anything."

"You'll know," Thoth cried, clinging to the console as the ship juddered through another blistering blow. "Because the limits of your sanity will be stretched beyond anything you could imagine."

It happened in an instant. In one heartbeat they were under heavy assault, in the next, a fat, rubbery ripple undulated through the flight deck, similar to when engaging cloaking, but heavier, denser, as though stepping out of a seamless, smooth place and into one which was not. Silence, thick as syrup pressed down onto Istara, claustrophobic, suffocating. She turned, still clinging to the top of Thoth's seat. The ships were gone. Above, a black sky hung heavy with a full white moon, its radiance blotting out the stars. The shadows of the pyramids hung over the river as its waters flowed north, quiet, peaceful.

"Auto pilot," Thoth said, his voice flat in the heaviness of the unnatural air.

A faint beep came from the console as Sekhmet switched control to the ship. She eased back into her seat, still scanning the readouts as the ship slowed, swiveled and came to rest atop the paved plaza, dead center in the triad of pyramids, which flickered, faded to nothing, and returned like the beating of a heart.

"Shields are near critical," Sekhmet muttered, tapping her finger against the console. She eyed the diagonal row of pyramids as they reformed, their oblique, smooth sides washed pale in the white light of the moon. They flickered again, shifting and wavering in the dense, heavy air, caught in the throes of their silent, subtle destruction. "Looks like Marduk was expecting us to return," she continued. "His patrols have been upgraded since I was last here. They hit us with weapons powerful enough to wipe out entire cities."

Thoth stood and rubbed his hands together. "Time is short. Although it pains me to do so, we must separate. Istara and I will go into the largest pyramid, where I will break the connection between the cores and redistribute the latent energy into the complex. That should protect us from the worst of the effects of the field a little while longer, but once it fades, we must be fast, lest we are caught in the impending collapse." He met Sekhmet's eyes and nodded at the middle pyramid. "You will take the second pyramid. Urhi-Teshub, you will be responsible for the smallest pyramid." He crouched on the floor and gestured for Urhi-Teshub to join him. With his finger he traced out a diagram. "A third of the way up the pyramid there is an opening to the east. Pass through it and descend the slope. You will need to crouch, it is a low-ceilinged corridor. Keep going straight until it opens into a high-ceilinged incline. Follow that until it terminates in a large chamber. At the chamber's far end, there is a rectangular stone plinth. The core hangs suspended above it. It will be glowing white. You must not touch it while it is glows. If you do it will obliterate you, as it did my brothers and sister."

Sekhmet looked away from Thoth's phantom diagram toward the middle pyramid, blinking hard, her golden eyes glistening. "There will be no more loss," she said, tight. "The next one to fall will be Marduk."

"Indeed," Thoth murmured. "Now," he said, rising, "when the core's light dims, and it pulses a pale blue, only then will it be safe to take it. We must do the retrieval sequentially. Istara and I will go first, then Sekhmet, and finally you, Urhi-Teshub. Smallest to largest." At Urhi-Teshub's surprised look, Thoth smiled. "Ah, you thought you were going to be carrying the smallest one? Not everything is at is appears. Symmetry is the secret. Once the first blue beat of the core completes, count to sixty, when it will be safe for you, Sekhmet, to take your core. At the count of one-hundred-twenty, it will be safe for you, Urhi-Teshub, to take yours. Are we understood?"

Everyone nodded. Istara glanced out the window. The pyramids were gone. Their ship stood in the midst of barren undulating waves of sand. She turned. The river had vanished. "Thoth?"

He turned. His expression tightened. "Not good."

"How much time do we have?" Sekhmet asked.

"It's hard to say," Thoth muttered. "Just move fast. Run when you can. Remember we are part of this field now, and can be eliminated as though we never were. If the field shrinks enough to reach us we will simply cease to exist. Gone, just like that."

Urhi-Teshub met Istara's eyes. "If anything goes wrong, do not come for me. Leave me behind. I am the least of you."

Before Istara could answer, Sekhmet jabbed a lighted button on the console and the door slid open. Stale, cold air seeped in, sharp, acrid, metallic. "No one gets left behind," she said. "Let's go." She strode out, leonine and sleek in her armor, her skin burnished by the moon's white light. Istara followed the others down the ship's steps onto the desert sands, her feet sinking ankle-deep. The pyramids were still gone. A flickering, and they slipped back into existence, ephemeral, transparent.

"What happens if they disappear while we are inside?" Istara asked as the complex firmed, solid once more.

"I really don't know," Thoth answered. "My advice is to remain still until they reappear and then continue your work. Do not move, unless you wish to end up inside the walls or floor."

"And how shall we see once we are inside?" Urhi-Teshub wondered, casting a look over his shoulder at his destination.

"There are lights along the corridor's floor," Thoth said, a glimmer of pride touching his tone. "I created them to siphon off the excess energy circulating through the pyramids. It is a shame they will be lost. Though minor, they were one of my greatest triumphs—"

Sekhmet sprinted away, her long legs eating up the distance to the middle pyramid. Urhi-Teshub shot Istara one last, long look. "Be safe," he murmured and bolted away.

"Shall we?" Thoth asked, nodding at the largest pyramid. An opening yawned at its base. Faint light flickered within. "Keep your eyes on the opening." He rolled his kilt up at his waist until its length shortened to his knees. "If it disappears, stop and wait."

Istara gathered up her gown. Its endless starlight cascaded over her hands and tumbled onto the plaza's ancient ashlars, a waterfall of light in a lonely, dying place.

Thoth gave her one last shuttered look touched with apprehension, drew a deep breath and lurched off, his strides jerky and uncoordinated, like a day-old colt running for the first time. Istara went after him, matching her pace to his, starlight trailing after her, her gaze fixed on the opening, its girth growing until it loomed before them as wide and high as a courtyard.

A shimmer rippled over the pyramid, distorting the razor sharp outline of its edges and sides. She glanced at Thoth. He wavered, fluid, and vanished mid-stride with a quiet pop. With a cry, she stumbled to a halt and stared at the space he had just possessed. The distortion slid over her, cool, a current of static sparking in her hair. Blistering sunlight slammed into her. Heat blasted up from the plaza's stone ashlars.

She turned, terror circling her. This wasn't what she expected. She had thought whatever would happen would affect them all, that they would stay together just like when the pyramids vanished. This time, however, the pyramids remained, bathed in the brilliance of a sweltering mid-afternoon sun. She turned, Sekhmet's ship stood further down on the avenue, skidded to one side, reckless, nowhere near where they had left it.

"It is not real," Istara murmured, seeking courage, despite her heart fluttering, wild within her breast, her senses betraying her mind, screaming their denial, telling her what she was seeing was very much real and her mind was lying. She closed her eyes, waiting for the heat to vanish, for the cool of the night to return. "It will pass. I will return to Thoth and the others, and we will retrieve the cores."

The heat remained. Voices. Wary, she opened her eyes. Four figures stood outside Sekhmet's ship, their upper halves hidden by the ship's nose. She waited, a slick of dread sliding against her skin.

Sekhmet stepped out first, encased in black leather, her body gilded with knives and throwing stars. The storm god Teshub followed her, the weapon in his hand a double-headed ax, alive with jagged bursts of cerulean lightning. Together, they ran toward the middle pyramid, past her, unseeing, Sekhmet's eyes glittering in the sunlight, hot with tears, her gaze moving to Teshub's harsh, determined profile, her anguish palpable.

From around the side of the ship, the other pair emerged. Istara staggered.

"Sethi," she whispered. Tears cut into her eyes. She pushed them away, desperate to see her consort, the way she remembered him before her memories were stolen from her. No, she realized, her heart aching anew, the one she saw was not Sethi, but Horus. Golden fractals rotated on the god of war's chest, and his immaculate white kilt edged in gold gleamed in the light. Heavy gold-embossed armbands sheathed his forearms. Tall, elegant, lean, muscled, he bore all the traits of Sethi, yet he was not Sethi.

The god of war took the goddess of healing into his arms and kissed her, savage, passionate, his hands on her face. She clung to him, weeping, sagging in his grip. They pulled apart, shuddering from the weight of their grief. They shared a long, hard look. She glanced at the pyramids and nodded. Taking her hand in his, they bolted down the avenue into the plaza, the goddess's gown trailing behind her as she fled with him, her starlight following her, mournful, the sight of them hurtling to their demise beautiful, terrible, stunning. They stopped before the entrance to the largest pyramid—Istara's destination—and embraced, their passion violent, bleeding with torment.

"My love," the god of war said, his voice harsh, rough, ragged, his golden eyes raking over her, memorizing her, "I will find you. This isn't over. We are not over."

She pulled back, tears slid down her face, silent sentinels of her agony. "Horus," she whispered, "it was always you. To the end, it will only be you. I will wait for you."

Istara quivered, caught in the thrall of their parting. The goddess, so like her in every way, yet different, disentangled herself from Horus's embrace and backed into the pyramid, her lips breathing her love for him, her eyes locked on her consort's who choked as she slipped out of sight into the shadows. He stood for a heartbeat longer, his fists clenched at his sides, his chest rising and falling, grief carving him, ruthless, into an edifice of misery.

He backed away, slow, hesitant, his longing to go after her palpable. He murmured her name, once, reverent, and ran, transforming into a falcon, his sorrowful keening piercing Istara's heart as he soared into the opening of the smallest pyramid and plunged into its depths.

Istara sank to her knees, panting, her thoughts reeling. Confusion clawed at her. She dug her nails into her palms, desperate to feel something real. Blood trickled from her clenched fists. She let them bleed, a tsunami of uncertainty washing over her—understanding at once the suspiciousness of the other gods who had never welcomed her, of their harbored belief she and Sethi were these other two, somehow changed and tainted by Marduk. She would have thought the same in their position.

A thought tore into her, harsh, dangerous, complete. What if they were right—what if Thoth had kept the truth from her and she *had* been the other goddess, but instead of being obliterated by the core, she had been remade—which made her nothing more than a simulacrum of the true goddess. She shivered, cold despite the raging, relentless heat. Panic touched her, even as her thoughts reorganized, as the broken pieces gathered and remade themselves into a patched whole.

An iridescent blast of white light exploded from the smallest pyramid. One after the other, the other two followed. Three waves of light slammed through her, ferocious, consuming her in their blinding, aching grip, burning her to her core. She screamed, clawing at her flesh, longing to rid herself of its constraints, desperate to escape. Heat sheared, jagged, through her mind—far beyond the agony she had suffered when she had watched her city burn. It ripped through her, tearing her apart, obliterating her essence. It shredded through her light, delved deep into the core of her existence.

The light parted. She blinked and sat up, her breathing ragged. Darkness circled her. She eyed her changed surroundings, untrusting, wondering if she had returned inside the pyramid. A pale puddle of light granted by the dying flame of a crude lamp perched on the stone flags beside her. She wore a ragged, dirty robe, and her small thin arms were wrapped around her knees. She caught her breath. No longer was she a goddess, but a starving child. Her stomach clawed at her, clamped hard with hunger. She huddled closer to the base of a stone altar, making out the shape of a golden statue, the folds of its gown wreathed in thick tendrils of opium incense. Silence bore down on her. The light pierced her again and she hurtled free of the child with a tearing, brutal wrench.

The child looked up, her dark eyes huge in her emaciated face. "Lady Baalat, is it you?" she called, her voice sweet and uncertain, laden with hope.

Istara closed her eyes and fell, tumbling, quaking with relief, away from the place. An abyss of darkness cocooned her, sheltering her from the light's bitter, brutal excising. Images flitted past, fleeting, a blur of color, far too fast for her to see. They slowed. One unfolded, slow, like a rose lifting its face to the sun. She lay in a mortal's bed, bathed in lamplight, unclothed, and shivering with anticipation. Urhi-Teshub's hard body covered hers, naked, primed to take her, his member grazed her inner thigh, awakening her. He gazed at her as he caressed her face, tender, love drenching his eyes.

"Istara," he murmured against her ear, "my love, my queen." He kissed her, deep, passionate, his need for her searing her soul—

"Lady Istara!" Thin hands took hold of her shoulders, hurting her. They shook her, hard. "Please, I beg you, return to me."

Istara stirred, the image of Urhi-Teshub lingered as she opened her eyes. Urhi-Teshub's features shifted, slid into Thoth's. The once-god of wisdom let out an exhalation, relief freeing the taut, anxious slant of his jaw. "Thank the light," he cried. "Finally, you return. I had begun to fear—"

Istara sat up, abrupt, and looked around, wary, fearing another delusion. The heat was gone, and so was the day. Night bore down on her. Sekhmet's ship stood where they had left it. The stink of burnt metal assailed her, stronger than before, acrid, sharp, setting her teeth on edge.

"Who am I?" she cried, pushing Thoth's hands away, claustrophobic, the image of Urhi-Teshub's passionate kiss returning, vivid. Real. They had been together. She had loved him, once, long ago, not as a goddess—as a mortal. She shot a look at the smallest pyramid, thinking of the one waiting within to claim the core—the one who, at times regarded her with a secret, haunted look. No. It could not be true. It was not possible.

It had to be a lie, manifested by the shifting corridors of this foul place. She would never betray her consort. She was a god. It was impossible to be mortal.

"You are the goddess of healing," Thoth said, meeting her eyes, his boring into hers, reassuring, holding her steady as she returned to her senses. He turned, agitation soaking him as he eyed the pyramid awaiting their arrival. "We must hurry. It took a long time for you to return. The field is shrinking fast."

Her legs trembling, Istara rose, her thoughts splintering, fragmented. Too much had passed. She couldn't think straight. She took an unsteady step, half-expecting the ground to open up and swallow her, to send her plummeting into another horror. Deep within her heart she wandered, lost, searching for something to cling to, away from the storm-tossed waves crashing against the blackened shores of her mind.

Her lost memories clamored, ferocious, awakening to the hidden bonds buried deep within her. They pounded against the bars caging them, longing to be freed. She dug her fingers into her temples, desiring nothing more than to escape, dreading another passage into another reality. Chaos ruled her mind. No longer did she know what was real, what was true, what she could trust. Who she could trust. Thoth had said not to believe what she would see. But the things she had seen and felt, had felt real. Perhaps they were all lies, false memories her broken mind had fabricated in the aftermath of the brutal light's onslaught, and yet, a part of her, deep, silent, buried, *remembered*. She walked on, quickening her steps, Thoth encouraging her to run, fretting about the cores.

As they crossed the threshold into the vast corridor of the pyramid, an image of Sethi came to her, of him looking into her eyes as he made love to her on the day her city burned, the fires of her home reflecting in the golden flecks of his eyes. She lunged for it. Sethi. He was all who mattered. Her mind cleared, her hold on the memory strengthening. She clung to him, just as she had done that day on his ship as he moved over her, taking her, swearing his revenge. She looked into the depths of the pyramid, the blue lights along the edges of the corridor flickered, tremulous, shivering under the onslaught of the field, trapped in their death throes. She remembered why she was here, and how little time they had. The cores. Sanctuary. Sethi. She ran.

❋   ❋   ❋

Urhi-Teshub eased into the chamber housing the core. Perhaps this place was making him fanciful, after its having disappeared and reappeared two times more before he reached his destination, but he sensed an awareness emanating from the pyramid, as though it were taking its measure of him. An ancient sentience saturated the ashlars, reeking of incomprehensible age. He thought of the gods giving up their light to the cores, then wished he hadn't. It unnerved him.

In the center of the empty chamber, a large rectangular ashlar faced him, sheathed in a smooth, reflective metal. It sat within a deep recess in the floor, surrounded by a thick trough of gold an arm span wide. He kept back from it, sensing its latent power. The metal coating the ashlar gleamed in the white light of the core, granting him a perfect reflection of the room, the core, and himself.

The core itself hung suspended a handspan over the ashlar. It rotated, steady, mesmerizing, its precise contours glinting with dormant power. He had expected the core to be in the shape of a gem, or some kind of sigil. Instead, a perfect pyramid hung suspended before him—a miniature version of the structure which housed it. He watched it, transfixed, his respect for Thoth's abilities deepening. The once-god of wisdom was no distracted academic after all, rather a being of utter brilliance, hidden in an unassuming, plain form. Urhi-Teshub eyed the soaring roof of the chamber, bare of engravings, each ashlar fitted together with near-seamless precision. Thoth had said he had created these structures merely through the manipulation of sound. Urhi-Teshub would have liked to have seen that.

He peered into the core, squinting against its light. Within its center, another smaller pyramid turned in the opposite direction. He edged nearer the golden trough surrounding the base of the ashlar, wondering if another, tinier core existed within that one. He glanced down. The toe of his boot almost touched the edge of the trough. He pulled back, sharp, remonstrating himself, ashamed his curiosity had almost cost them the mission. Thoth had said to stay back until the glow faded and the core began to blink the color blue. After the first pulse he was to count to one-hundred-twenty. Only then would he dare risk his existence and move closer.

He fell back several paces and folded his arms over his chest, occupying his thoughts with examining the chamber, marveling at the math which would have been required to build such a thing. The weight of the structure alone would be boggling. He tried to work out how thick the foundation would have needed to be to support so much pressure. Several calculations filled his time, the numbers becoming too vast for him to proceed. Thoth certainly was a dark horse. Out of all the gods, none could compare to him. The others might be great warriors, but Thoth's intellectual abilities far exceeded them all.

If any of the gods were nearest to the mind of the Creator, Urhi-Teshub suspected Thoth had been granted the greatest, though perhaps, loneliest gift. Thoth had no one, no consort whom he loved, who loved him in return, only his theories kept him company. An eternity with no one. Urhi-Teshub shuddered. How could Thoth do it? Even this last month had been brutal for Urhi-Teshub, almost unbearable, as he struggled to accept who Istara was—and who she belonged to. He had forced himself to let her go, though his traitorous heart still thought of her when she had been mortal, when she had once, long ago, loved him; when he had held her in his arms and she had returned his kisses.

His own immortality stretched before him. Who would there be for him, he wondered, morose, in a world of mortals? Was he doomed to search for her replacement, over and over, watching, helpless, as his lovers aged and succumbed to death? He shoved the depressing thought aside. Now was not the time to dwell on his private troubles. The core continued to glow white and process through its endless hypnotic cycle of rotation. He eyed it, a quiver of trepidation rippling through him. Thoth and Istara should have reached their destination. By now the core should have faded and begun to pulse. Perhaps something had waylaid them—or, his heart chilled at the thought—perhaps this hateful place had taken them elsewhere and they had not returned.

He turned, dithering, debating whether he should go back and check, caught between his need to protect Istara and his duty to remain to collect the core. If he missed the first pulse, he would have the count wrong. He let out an agitated breath, fretting, his thoughts growing more restless with each passing heartbeat. The walls shimmered. He braced himself, biting back an oath. Not again. Not now.

The chamber vanished.

A beat later he found himself standing suspended mid-air in a verdant forest just as a pale yellow sun filtered by an overcast sky the color of milk rose from the horizon. Dense, humid heat bore down on him, heavy and oppressive. His chest constricted, his lungs aching in the thin air. Pressure slammed into his temples.

A little distance away, a grainy shore slipped into a pale blue sea, its placid surface coated in patches of feathery tendrils of vegetation. A heavy thud shook the earth, thick as thunder. Urhi-Teshub cut a wary look over his shoulder.

Another thud, followed by another, slow, stately, reverberated through the air. The palms trembled, nervous as lambs before a wolf. From out of the forest's gloom, an enormous creature materialized. Urhi-Teshub's senses boggled, rebelled. No. It couldn't be real. He tried and failed to make sense of it, a thing composed of the parts of other creatures, all of them thirty times larger than they should be: the head of a lizard, the body and legs of a hippopotamus, and the tail of a crocodile. It lifted its long, sinuous neck, opened its vast mouth and tore free the spiky fronds of a tree.

Urhi-Teshub gaped as the creature denuded the massive tree in two bites. It left behind a pitiable, shorn crown. As it continued to destroy all the trees within its range, Urhi-Teshub tried to make sense of it. Its legs were thicker than the circumference of a temple pillar, and more than twice his height. With its neck fully raised to reach the highest fronds of the fern-like trees, it towered almost as high as Teshub's golden pillar, the tallest structure in all of Hatti. Its body bore a thin armor of overlapping scales which rippled as it moved, a jeweled mosaic of yellow-greens—the pale green of an unripe melon speckled with scales of deeper malachite, and a brownish-yellow similar to topaz. It turned from the tree, slow, laborious. Its massive, bronze, reptilian eye lowered. Urhi-Teshub moved his hand to Set's weapon.

Their eyes met. Urhi-Teshub's heart thudded. He waited, both exhilarated and horrified by the immensity of the creature's eye, as big as a serving platter. The creature continued to turn, its gaze sliding past him, unseeing, oblivious of the leather-clad two-legged creature hovering mid-air, one hand primed to seize the weapon strapped to his thigh.

With each laborious step the creature took, the trunks of the stoic trees juddered. Several palm fronds snapped free. They tumbled past Urhi-Teshub and crashed into the dense undergrowth.

Despite his mind jagging at the improbability of what he was witnessing, he held himself steady, forcing himself to drink in every detail, his curiosity sudden, visceral. Though it felt real— from his short, shallows breaths snatched from the thin air to the deepening headache drilling into the back of his eyes—he knew it was nothing more than a delusion caused by the field surrounding the complex. Thoth had said so, and yet . . . as a swarm of leathery-winged creatures hurtled up from a rotting carcass at the edge of the sea and glided past him, their long, pointed teeth and vicious talons more than able to make a meal of him, he had to concede everything about this lush, primal place felt as real as the rest of his existence.

The creature rumbled to a halt, lifted its tail and let out a deafening blast of flatulence. It washed over Urhi-Teshub, fetid, ripe, and fat with the stink of fecal fermentation. He gagged, his eyes watering as the moist heat of it slid over his face. Clenching his teeth, he vowed if they survived this wild mission to collect the cores, he would demand answers. He suspected what Thoth had told them had not been the whole truth, but a partial one to keep them from losing their minds, because *this*, he thought, as the vile stink of the monstrosity's guts permeated his nose and entered his mouth, was very real. In sick fascination, he eyed the creature as it unloaded its bowels, depositing enormous loose patties onto the forest floor, its filth splattering against its hind legs. The creature groaned, a deep, satisfied bass, and lumbered off, languid, toward the sea, a steaming pile of dung the size of a bathing pool its parting gift to the once-king of an empire.

A shimmer and the world of giant reptiles faded. Darkness suffused Urhi-Teshub's vision, and then—the luxury of air. He gulped at it, grateful, greedy for its sudden bounty, the throbbing pain behind his eyes receding with each deep, restoring breath.

The glow of white returned. The walls and floors firmed. A wave of relief washed through him. The core still glowed white. He hadn't missed its changeover to the pulse. He took a step closer. The core glimmered and stuttered in its rotation. He held still, fearing another shift, willing the field to hold, desperate to leave and be free of the hateful, unstable place.

"Please," he breathed, dreading another trip to a mind-bending world, perhaps one with no air at all. His hands curled into fists.

A sliver of anger kindled, his helplessness in the face of the power obliterating the complex infuriating him. "Please," he repeated, his voice hardening, "it is enough."

The core glided to a halt. The light within it flickered and dimmed. A heartbeat later it winked out. Pitch dark blanketed Urhi-Teshub. He waited, riven between relief Istara and Thoth had reached their destination and an agony of hope Thoth would complete his task before he was hit with another shift.

Several long, slow heartbeats passed. He counted to ten, then twenty. Thirty approached. The darkness bore down on him, heavy and oppressive. A pulse of blue erupted from the core. It wavered and brightened. He held his breath and waited for it to fade before he began the long, slow count to one-hundred-twenty.

❋   ❋   ❋

Sekhmet reached the number sixty. Knowing firsthand what the core was capable of doing to a god, she held her breath and slid her gloved hands under the core's base. It settled its weight against her palms, calm, quiet. Though no bigger than a scroll chest, the weight of it was substantial. She pulled it away from the base, deft, and cradled it against her heart as it continued to pulse its mournful song—the song of Teshub's light.

She hurried through the narrow corridors, haunted by the memory of when she had last fled this place. A wall of tears piled up in her eyes. *Teshub.* No. She would not mourn him here, not when so much was at stake. And yet, her heart wept, reminding her, ruthless, this was where she had lost him, forever, the one who had possessed her heart—though he had never known it, not even at the end. It had been her secret, her deepest, darkest one, never shared, not even when he took her to his bed in an agony of loneliness for his lost consort, and made love to her, seeking comfort in her arms, unaware of how much he meant to her.

One heartbeat he had been there, powerful, dangerous, the god of storms, then with a harsh, parting kiss, he left her, reached out for the core and whispered Arinna's name, the one he truly loved, the one he could not exist without—the one who had vanished without a trace along with Thoth more than two years before.

He hadn't looked back as he touched the core. He roared, his body juddering—snared by the forces he had unleashed—as his light tore free and burned his flesh away, leaving nothing but an outline of his form before it gathered and plunged into the core. An explosion of blistering white light had poured through her, scathing, brutal, stripping her of her senses. When she came to, she was alone. Of Teshub nothing remained, although the core blazed a brilliant, blinding white, energized by the sacrifice he had made.

She hugged the core closer, her arms aching under its dense weight, seeking to connect with what might remain of him. "Teshub," she whispered, her throat aching, raw, her confession buried within the sacred dark of the dying sentinel, "I love you." She shuddered, devastated, vulnerable, the hallowed words finally freed after an eternity of bondage. A tear slipped free. She let it fall. It slid over the core, bathing it in the anguish of her broken, lonely heart.

In the distance, the pale light of the moon glimmered through the opening to the plaza. She ran on, alone, and unloved—as she always was. As she always would be.

❋　❋　❋

Istara followed Thoth up the steps of the ship, her arms aching under the burden of the core's weight. Within the cabin, they set it down, cautious, Thoth filling the air with warnings and admonitions. It sat there, looking far too small to be able to weigh so much, and continued to pulse, bathing the cabin in soft iterations of cool, cerulean blue.

With a last fretful look at the core, Thoth hurried to the console and began to punch in codes and flick switches, preparing the ship for its departure.

Istara followed him, glad to have at last returned to the ship. Their progress out of the pyramid had been slow, and the burden of sharing the core's weight between them cumbersome. Throughout, Thoth had been fractious and fretful, though now as his eyes moved to the middle pyramid, it was plain his concerns had moved to the next core. He stood before the console, drumming his fingers against it, a staccato of impatience.

Sekhmet bolted out onto the plaza, the core hugged against her, its weight borne by her far better than Istara and Thoth had managed theirs. The goddess of war ascended the ship's steps, quick and light. A soft thump filled the quiet as she set the core down on the cabin's floor. Without saying a word, she slipped past Istara and settled into her seat, her movements over the console focused and precise. With the other two occupied, Istara waited in an agony of anticipation, her gaze fixed on the smallest pyramid, willing her protector to emerge, the core in his arms. A steep staircase descended from the pyramid's opening. It would take time for Urhi-Teshub to clamber down burdened by the weight of the core. If the core she had lugged out with Thoth was the 'lightest' of the three, and Urhi-Teshub's the heaviest, its weight would be staggering.

A ripple of distortion shimmered against the northern boundary of the largest pyramid all the way up to the night sky. A heartbeat later, a wall of sunlight slammed down from the sky, shearing the nightscape in two. On the other side of the viscous, shimmering wall, Marduk's patrol ships darted back and forth along the boundary, impatient, hungry for their prey.

"It's begun," Thoth cried, "the field is collapsing."

Her heart thundering, Istara tore her gaze from the patrols. At the smallest pyramid, nothing.

One heartbeat. Two. Three. Ten. "Please," Istara breathed.

Urhi-Teshub lunged out of the opening, cast one look at the stairs and threw himself onto the slope alongside them, the core hugged against his chest. He slid, tumbling and reckless down its length, dust billowing behind him and hit the plaza at speed.

From out of the wall of sundered time, a wall of distortion rippled free, fat and viscous. It juddered through the ship, the drag of it clawing at Istara's senses. She staggered and caught hold of the back of Thoth's seat in time to see it ram through Urhi-Teshub. He stumbled like a drunkard, but kept his feet. He ran again. Nothing happened. He remained fixed to the spot, though the ground slid away beneath him.

"Thoth?" Sekhmet asked, her eyes cutting to the encroaching wall of sundered time as it churned into the largest pyramid, obliterating its existence and back to Urhi-Teshub straining to free himself from the field's hold. "How much time is left?"

Thoth looked up from the screen where rows of calculations streamed past. He shook his head, bleak, his lips compressed into a thin line.

"Then we don't have time to wait," Sekhmet muttered. She hit the ignition. Thunder erupted from the back of ship.

"You will not leave him behind," Istara cried. "I forbid it."

"Who said anything about leaving him behind?" Sekhmet fired the forward thrusters. The ship hurtled backward across the plaza, away from Urhi-Teshub, a paradox.

"Cut the power," Thoth bellowed, "it's drawn to the force of the field."

Sekhmet slammed her palm against the console. The ship skidded to a halt. They stood twice as far from Urhi-Teshub as before. A thick silence tore through the cabin. Istara looked over her shoulder. The distortion churned through the last of the largest pyramid, steady, malevolent, an insatiable thing. As it crossed the distance to the middle pyramid, the ashlars of the plaza tore free and sailed into the barrier where they folded into themselves and dissolved into nothingness, their destruction incalculable, breathtaking, complete.

Istara cut a look at Urhi-Teshub. Exhaustion coated his features. He continued to run though he made no progress. Istara caught the shared look between Sekhmet and Thoth. Urhi-Teshub would never make it in time.

"I'm going out," Sekhmet rose. "If we don't make it back, the route is mapped. Keep an eye on the shields when you break the atmosphere. I hope you can make do with two cores."

"I can't," Thoth said, catching hold of her arm. "Either we stay and be annihilated, or leave and live. He won't make it back," he gestured at the screen, bleak, "the calculations prove it."

"No," Istara said, unwilling to accept the dull beat of resignation in her protector's eyes. Her light erupted, riotous. It sharpened her senses, stripped them raw. "He will make it." Urhi-Teshub would not fall. Not this day. Never before had she used her light this way, but desperation clawed at her. Her light churned, its power fed by the image of leaving him behind in a vortex of annihilation that would shred his existence into silence. She lifted her arms. Hundreds of tendrils streamed to her fingertips, alive, sentient, laden with her essence. Her arms aching in the drag of the field, she willed her light to reach him. It exploded from her fingers, slid through the walls of the ship, and wove its way toward Urhi-Teshub, its outermost tendrils whipped by the silent storm. They twisted and writhed, chaotic, caught in the field's collapse. Several tore free and hurtled into the encroaching wall, their silent, visceral cries as they suffered their extinction searing her. They winked out, pieces of her lost, forever. She shuddered, trembling, endured the anguish of her light mourning its loss, her eyes burning with tears as Urhi-Teshub cradled the core in one arm and reached out to her light, his arm quaking in the crushing force of the field.

A single tendril burst free of the shrinking spiral of light. It touched his gloved fingertip, curled around it and clung to him. Her tendrils gathered, poured into him, a tumult of glittering, golden light. It slid down his hand and wrapped itself around him, a thin barrier of light. It wasn't enough. Istara called to her light again, staggering as she called to the last of her resources and dipped into her own precious store of light. Hundreds more tendrils slipped free. She watched them flee to him, enduring the brutal strafes against her being as one by one tendrils were torn away and obliterated, her sacrifice worth the price. Half of the tendrils reached him. They wove around him with aching slowness, a grid of golden light. He looked up, panting, gratitude bleeding from him, and ran, streamers of golden, radiant light trailing after him. He reached the steps, his tread heavy, loud, reassuring.

Istara turned, weak, trembling, trapped in the immense drag of the oncoming field. The door slid closed. The middle pyramid was already gone—in its wake, soft, undulating dunes of sand. In the distance, patrols darted past, avoiding the pyramids which still stood for them, unaware of the destruction happening within the field—or how soon the pyramids would vanish as though they had never been.

Clothed in a shimmering cocoon of gold, Urhi-Teshub knelt by the first two cores. A deep thud reverberated under Istara's feet, betraying both the core's brutal heft and the indomitable, stubborn strength of her protector. It rested, quiet and calm beside its companions, their individual pulses synchronizing into a single, steady, cerulean heartbeat. Latent energy seeped from them, and a faint blue tinge crept away from them across the floor, over the divans, and across the ship's walls until it clothed the entire ship.

He came to her, her cocoon of light melting away, its tendrils circling him before darting back to her, those irreplaceable pieces of herself she had given to him, restored. He regarded her, his dark eyes fathomless, burning with loyalty—and something else, fierce, primal. He took her hand and pressed his lips to her fingers, fervent.

A powerful surge erupted from beneath the ship. It held Istara in its grip as it shot straight up into the canopy of black alongside the field of burning daylight, the line between existence and obliteration. The ship juddered, violent, its engines screaming their resistance. The shields blistered, white-hot. Alarms blared.

"The shields are melting," Sekhmet cried. "We are not going to make it."

A blinding flash of cerulean light erupted from the cores and washed over the shields. One by one, the alarms quieted.

The ship ripped free of the field with a sickening lurch. The viscous, hateful drag released its oppressive grip. Daylight tore a line through the ship. Freed of the field's hold, the ship slingshotted into the skies. With barely a shouted warning from Sekhmet, the leg numbing thrust from beneath cut out and re-ignited at the rear. It slammed into Istara, vicious. Urhi-Teshub's hands found her. He pulled her back into the cabin, his grip solid, reassuring. Istara sank onto the divan and looked down. Far below, the pyramids still stood, just as they had when they went in. She blinked, incredulous, wondering how they could both exist and *not* exist at the same time. Marduk's patrols swarmed up after them, swinging together into formation, closing fast. There were more now than before, she counted at least twenty, sleek, focused, determined.

A shimmer rippled over the pyramid complex. A blink and they ceased to exist. Sand blew across a wasteland of nothing. She caught Urhi-Teshub looking down, the muscles in his jaw clenched, his gaze raking over the emptiness. She took his hand in hers. He met her eyes, neither of them saying what she knew preyed on their minds—how close their annihilation had been. They had almost failed.

They reached the stars. Her protector sheltered her as the ship trailed blue fire over the arc of the world and stole her breath from her. Marduk's patrols followed them, relentless, their weapons useless in this hallowed space between heaven and earth. They fell once more, hurtling, afire, seething from the detonations scouring the ship's shield, the gouges glowing blue, protected by the cores' power. They plummeted back to the savaged, ruined land surrounding Surru. At the last heartbeat, Sekhmet pulled up and tore a blazing trail toward the portal's ethereal opening, its cerulean tendrils swarming toward the ship, welcoming the presence of a god. They slammed through the wall of light and tumbled into the brutal, crushing silence of the void, surrounded by the fading glow of the cores.

Istara fell into the void's oblivion, her self nothing more than a thought. From the depths of her heart, the memory of Urhi-Teshub holding her in his arms returned, when the private contours of his muscled body pressed against her, gentle, intimate, protective. His mouth brushed against her ear, and he breathed her name, a sigh, reverent, naming her his love, his queen. His lips touched hers and in his tightening, hungry embrace, she trembled. *This*, she knew, like the beating of her heart. This, she remembered. Guilt scoured her, tore her into jagged ribbons. She might have forgotten the rest, why and how she had ended up in the bed of a mortal, pretending to be his queen, but none of it mattered anymore, she had reached the heart of it. She had betrayed her consort—had made him into what he had become.

They emerged into the gentle, palm-speckled late afternoon light of Surru's verdant glade, the ship's body and wings scorched and blistered. In the quiet calm of the glade, Thoth knelt and ran his hands over the cores, examining them for damage. Urhi-Teshub returned to the flight deck to assist Sekhmet. The door to the flight deck closed.

Istara turned her face toward the cloudless, vast expanse of Elati's indigo canopy, aching for the one she had lost. Cradling her broken heart in her hands, she retreated to the darkness of her sorrow. A tear slid down her face. She let it fall. She had sought the truth, and found it.

From over the rim of her wine cup, Meresamun eyed Marduk as he finished their late afternoon meal, his presence shuttered and withdrawn. That morning, in the wake of her request to know more of his first consort, he had pulled away from her, his departure abrupt, the distance in his demeanor as vast as the skies. The day had passed in stark isolation. He had not sent for her to share their morning meal, nor the afternoon refreshments. His silence stalked her, tortured her. She had kept to her suite, waiting for her reprieve, fearing the anguish of her past had once more found the threshold of her heart. The corridors of the palace had lain shrouded in silence. No guards passed. Not even the servants had come to her. No, she had begged the heavens. Not this. Not again.

Her consort set aside his platter and tossed his napkin on top of it. Its starched white folds slid into the bloody gravy of his unfinished venison and bled death. He rose, the gold-embossed panels on his leather tunic and kilt catching in the brazier's firelight. Meresamun lowered her eyes to her cup, to her unfinished wine. The weight of his gaze fell on her, dense as an ashlar.

"Come with me." Cold. The command of a god. He lowered his hand to her. The markings on his arm seethed, discordant, unsettled. She met his look. His impaled her, harsh, enigmatic, unreadable.

Meresamun set aside her wine and touched her fingers to his. He pulled her to him, capturing her against the hardened panels of his gilded tunic. His eyes moved over her face, came to a halt on her mouth. A flicker of torment sliced through his features. He caught her chin, held her still as he brushed his lips against hers, tender, reverent, tasting of red wine, rare meat, torment and longing. His grip tightened and his kiss deepened, fierce, possessive, the violence of his passion consuming her, robbing her of her senses. He tore himself free. She swayed, overcome by his unexpected ardor. His hand found hers, warm, strong. He turned and led her across the firelit suite, the heavy golden panels of his kilt clacking, quiet.

Before the closed doors, he cut her a dark look. "Though I have resisted this decision and may one day come to regret it," he said, "I find I can deny you nothing. Not even this." He hauled the door open. A cold draft swept in from the corridor. The flames of the braziers snapped back at it.

Another flicker of anguish sheared through his carnelian eyes. "You shall have your wish."

Meresamun caught her breath.

Zarpanitu.

Riven between fear and anticipation, Meresamun followed him through the halls and corridors of the citadel to the furthest reaches of his stronghold. Her consort said nothing more. He kept his eyes ahead, fixed on the distance, locked within the impenetrable corridors of his mind.

At the edge of a barren, windswept terrace, he came to a halt. Ahead, a thin span constructed of filigreed stone arced over a vast chasm between the terrace and the gray wall of a bleak cliff.

Her gown and hair buffeted by the sea-stained wind, Meresamun eyed the narrow crossing, haunted by misgiving. It appeared an artifice, a whim. It possessed no supports, and appeared so fragile it looked as though it might shatter from the merest touch. At the far side of the improbable bridge, a small platform met a staircase hewn from the cliff's face. It followed the curve of the cliff's wall up to its heights, the precipitous steps a breath away from a staggering drop into the chasm.

Marduk stepped onto the bridge. "It will hold," he said, catching her look of terror, "though it is too narrow for both of us to cross side by side." A gust of wind skittered through the embossed panels of his kilt. They flapped, wild, against his thigh—golden birds desperate to take flight. "I will go first. Whatever you do, do not look down."

Meresamun edged closer to him. Her gaze lowered, treacherous, to the forbidden depths.

He caught her chin and brought her eyes back up to his, heavy with warning. "Ninsunu," he said. "I command it. You must trust me. I will never let any harm come to you, but you must not look down. This place is not what it seems. It plays tricks on the mind to keep trespassers away. It is why I have hidden my greatest treasure here, in the safest place in all of Elati."

"I will not look down," she promised, and meant it.

He placed her hand against the unforgiving leather covering his shoulder. "Keep your eyes on me and only me."

Halfway across, a brutal gust shoved her away from Marduk. Her gown tangled between her legs. Terror scythed a molten path through her. Her gaze veered to the abyss's haul. Madness skirted her. Vertigo enslaved her. Her legs abandoned their purpose.

Pressed against the faint existence of the bridge, she clung to its stone lacings, trapped in the grip of nausea. Between the openings of the filigreed surface, the chasm's maw plummeted away from her, endless, washed in an ephemeral white light, devoid of the darkness which should collapse it. The depths screamed back at her, its sheer walls pierced by sharp outcroppings, ugly as crocodile teeth. Her consort's voice circled her terror, faint, incoherent. Through the haze, a single word came to her. Once. Twice. Three times.

Ninsunu.

Panting, terrified, she tore her gaze from the enormity of the emptiness beneath the thin barrier of white stone and met Marduk's carnelian eyes. Without looking down, he caught her arm, his grip firm, real, solid. He tugged on her, gentle, persistent, promising her he would not let her fall. One finger at a time, she let go of the bridge and let him help her to her feet. She followed after him, trembling, step by step as he backed across the walkway, never taking his eyes from her.

At the base of the cliff's stairs, she clung to him, quaking, shivering. He gave her time, murmuring quiet reassurances, then pressed on, placing himself between her and the stairway's edge.

Her heart thundering, she kept her eyes fixed on the cliff wall, her fingers locked tight against his, willing their hateful journey to end. The stairs came to an abrupt end before a dark metal door. It glared back at them, imperious, its surface embossed with symbols similar to the ones on Sethi's chest. The door yielded to Marduk without a sound. Inside, utter darkness. Silence.

Marduk pulled a flat device from within the folds of his leather kilt and powered it up. Across its face, an eruption of cerulean light. He tilted it toward the gloom. Ahead, a smooth-walled tunnel bored through the rock, etched in epochal silence. He led her onward. They reached another metal door. He pulled it open and stepped aside.

Meresamun caught her breath. A wonder, sudden, perfect, filled her vision. Late afternoon light poured from a blood-orange sky into a massive basin encircled by carved rock walls. Sheltered within the basin's lee, and bathed in the day's dying light, three wings of an elegant white palace framed an enormous garden, its crushed shell walkways laid out in a symmetrical pattern of triangles and squares. Along the walkways' edges, rows of sculpted evergreen bushes stood still as sentinels, their rich, resinous fragrance saturating the sheltered, damp air.

Marduk led her through the gardens, the quiet crunch of the shells underfoot loud in the courtyard's muted, ageless quiet.

Past the palace's white, silver-embossed double doors, he led her down a cavernous corridor, the blazing heat of the braziers making Meresamun's skin prickle. Above, between ancient, carved pillars, shadows danced in the vaulted stone-arched gaps.

Deep within the palace, he came to a halt before a plain wooden door bearing an unembellished iron handle. He nodded at her to open the door. Within, a study, small and comfortable. A thick rug and elegant furnishings stood arranged throughout the space in perfect symmetry. Opposite the door, a series of glazed windows overlooked a towering range of mountains, their peaks brushed in shifting patches of sunset shadows. In the center of the room, anomalous amongst the beautiful furnishings: a black metal box the size of a travel coffer. In its top right corner, a panel of three blue lights blinked, slow, like the beat of a heart.

Meresamun turned and caught her consort's look, shielded, enigmatic. The markings on his arms shifted, slow, broken whorls soaked with sorrow.

"My first love may have returned to the stars," he murmured, his markings easing into a symphony of gentle curlicues, "but within her journals, her words live on. She made me swear if I ever lost her I would not read her writings, yet neither could I bear to destroy them so I preserved them, in memory of her. You asked what she did to reconcile herself to me. I do not know. Perhaps you will find the answer you seek from her." Marduk retrieved the device he had used to light the way through the tunnel. "Her language will be indecipherable to you, but this—" he paused to power it up "—will overcome that."

Meresamun took it. It was light, pleasing to the touch and fit within the palm of her hand. Another wonder.

"Whatever you learn from her writings—" Marduk said as he demonstrated how to use it, "—you must swear to keep from me. I will not break my promise to her. Her words must forever remain her secret from me." She met his eyes and nodded. He cut a look at the box. A look flickered in the depths of his eyes, complex, unreadable.

He left with a promise to return later. The door closed. His footsteps retreated. She turned. A fire had been lit. She went to it and let its warmth soothe her and chase away her uncertainties. On a side table, a tray bore a pitcher of wine and a silver-chased goblet alongside a platter of cold meats, breads, and a hard, sweet cheese—one of her favorites, a delicacy made by the artisans of Lauca. Despite what she suspected it had cost him to share this with her, her consort had considered her every comfort.

Meresamun ran her fingers along the box's lid, reverent, tingling with anticipation. Within, the secret writings of the one who had been loved by Marduk so passionately, so completely, he had waited a million years for his brutal, infinite revenge. Who could she ever be in comparison to such a one as the fabled Zarpanitu who had followed a path of high esotericism and divined the secrets of the cosmos? Meresamun looked down at herself, self-conscious, aware of her limited knowledge of lofty matters, her only apparent purpose to belong to the darkest of all beings. She was no one, the mere daughter of a dead king—a princess who had spent almost all her life in slavery, and later, a broken woman who had fallen to the seduction of the one she had believed to be her god. She ran her fingers over the panel of lights, rehearsing the sequence Marduk had given her.

Prescience assaulted her. Her instincts wailed, ominous. She took a step back, defensive, her grip tightening on the slim translation device. Uncertainty clobbered her. Perhaps she should not breach the sanctity of Zarpanitu's long-closed volumes; perhaps there was a reason Zarpanitu made Marduk swear never to read her words. Perhaps it would be better not to know.

She went to the door. Her fingers touched the handle. And yet, what choice did she have? Without Zarpanitu's secrets, her darkening path as Marduk's consort would go on forever, an exquisite, endless betrayal of her existence. She turned from the door. No. She must do this thing, no matter the cost. It might be her only chance.

She entered the sequence. A quiet hum and a click. The lock slid free and the lid disconnected with a soft hiss. From within the slim opening, air escaped, stale, ancient, bearing the weight of eons.

Her heart thudding, she lifted the lid. It eased up, light as a feather, its gracefulness belying the staggering weight of its age. She leaned forward, torn between curiosity and foreboding. Within, neat piles of slim volumes unlike anything she could have imagined.

Intrigued, she reached in and pulled one of the topmost ones out and turned it over. She had expected scrolls, sheaves of papyrus, perhaps even a stack of engraved tablets—not this. Turning it over, she caught her breath as the thing fell open, revealing thin sheets of vellum bound together, the pages finer and smoother than anything she had ever seen, even among the sacred writings she had carried as a temple slave to be offered to Sekhmet. She leafed through Zarpanitu's journal, fascinated, drinking in the simple beauty of it, admiring its neat, green silk cover; searching for the invisible stitches holding the sheets together—every page filled with vertical lines of strange, elegant symbols written in an artful script.

She glanced back into the box. Dozens of journals just like the one in her hand awaited her, some smaller, many of them much larger. It would take a long time to go through them all. She reached into the box and pulled another volume out, larger than the rest. On its maroon silken cover, several darker blotches marred its perfection. She lifted it to the light of the fire and examined its tainted beauty. Her heart clenched. She had left similar markings on her gowns during the long, lonely days she had endured during her year-long alienation from Ahmen. She tilted the journal's cover from side to side, wondering whose tears had clothed the material, Zarpanitu's or Marduk's. Or, she blinked—a stab of unexpected envy impaling her—perhaps it bore the heartache of both.

Lowering the volume to the rug, she got up, poured herself wine and sipped, eyeing the coffer, considering whether she ought to unpack the entire box first. Her gaze slid back to the tearstained volume. It had been placed at the top of the box. A shear of jealousy sliced through her as she imagined Marduk, no longer indomitable but broken and weeping, Zarpanitu's silken volume pressed against his chest, preparing himself to lay the last of Zarpanitu's words to rest—to seal them away for eternity. Unable to resist its tragic call, Meresamun collected the journal, snatched up the translation device, and sank into the seat nearest the fire.

Soaked in warmth, she opened the journal's front cover and ran the translation device over the first lines, as Marduk had instructed her. A shimmer and the device awakened. The window in its center flickered through the symbols of Egypt's hieroglyphs as it worked, the passage assembling, rapid, into coherence. Zarpanitu's quiet voice filled Meresamun's mind, her clear, elegant words riven with sorrow and regret.

I have failed in my task. I am now completely certain of it. The Well of Life is not here. May the Creator forgive me, despite having had the greatest hope of purpose, it is impossible for me to go on. I refuse to abandon the last shred of my light to the one who claims to love me. I must find a way out. He shall not have me. I will not fall to him.

Meresamun blinked, perplexed, wondering if the translation device had failed to do its task. She read the text again, trying to make sense of it. What a strange way to begin a journal. She plucked the device from the page, shook it, and ran it over the first lines again. The same hieroglyphs appeared. Meresamun bit her lip, wondering if she was doing something wrong. She flipped through the pages, absent, hesitating at the inscription written on the page facing the back cover. If what she had just read was the beginning, then perhaps Zarpanitu's final words would make more sense. She ran the device over the lines, more hieroglyphs filled the screen.

I am drawn to him. I am repelled by him. I cannot live without him. He is undoing me. I cannot concentrate on my work. Every time he touches me, I awaken, come alive. It is wrong. How can my heart betray the light and be drawn to such evil, such malevolence? He is a liar and a murderer, addicted to power. What have I become? I must understand before he consumes me, before my light is lost. Within these pages, I will seek to understand why he found me; why he brought me back from the edge of death; why he loves me as he does, and what my purpose is in all of this. I must understand, or I will go mad. There must be a reason our paths crossed against such powerful odds. There must be—

He is coming for me. My traitorous heart beats faster. Creator help me, I beg you. Show me the way . . . before it is too late.

Meresamun stared at Zarpanitu's graceful symbols, inked in ages past, another who had also been reprieved from death by Marduk—the intervening fathomless shear of time unable to diminish the solidarity of their shared experiences. She ran her fingertips over the page, longing to connect with the one whose words warned of her own impending fate, clarion and fatal. A blanket of gloom shrouded her. So, her conflict of heart would not be endless after all. In time, Marduk's darkness would overcome her resistance. Meresamun shuddered. He *knew*. Despite his anguish of her not loving him, he knew in time she would break, the reach of his power unassailable, indefensible. Eventually, he would have her heart, though it would not be her own, but a tainted, corrupted one, possessed by him. She leaned back in the chair and followed the flickering shadows the fire made across the ceiling, understanding at least this much: He wanted her heart before his broke her will. He needed it. So long as she stood against him, she still held a margin of power over him, and she would cling to that scrap for as long as her heart could hold.

She lowered her gaze back to the volume and turned the page, intending to work her way backward through the pages to the front. So, the end was the beginning. Somehow it seemed fitting. With a quiet sigh, she set the device against the page, and read.

Far into the night, when the fire had sunk to a dull orange glow, its faint heat no longer able to keep the room's chill at bay, Meresamun set aside the final volume. Her legs tingled, numb from kneeling. Pulling her legs out from under her, she massaged them, enduring the sharp prickles of invisible needles digging into her flesh.

Around her, Zarpanitu's volumes fanned out across the rug, organized into piles by subject. There was no doubt, Marduk's first consort possessed vast knowledge and a monumental well of intelligence, her insight far outstripping even the hallowed, arcane writings of Egypt's ancient sages.

But this, what Meresamun had learned today, would take weeks to digest, perhaps even months. Everything she had learned during her time in Egypt amounted to nothing more than a shadow of what Zarpanitu knew. Marduk's first consort's understanding of the secrets of life soared far beyond the shallow perspectives of mortals to the deepest mysteries of the cosmos.

According to Zarpanitu, thousands of worlds existed within the universe, but there were also *other* universes, each with their own worlds, all of them unaware of the multitudes of other universes existing a mere breath away from their own. She claimed this collection of universes—called the multiverse—could be imagined as spheres attached to an undulating, flat surface as vast as the expanse of the ocean, comparing its appearance to beads of rain clinging to a spider's web. In each universe, darkness and light wrestled to gain supremacy, but, she had found, at least in her own universe, the darkness possessed an advantage in the material world, where exploitation and violence would reward those who chose that path. As the ages passed, the light—already weak where the pleasures of the body took precedent over the esoteric pursuits of the mind—became sequestered into sacred enclaves, fenced in by the darkness's corruption as it fed on the hate, greed, and violence of mortals.

The battle between dark and light seemed destined to end with the dark's ultimate triumph when Zarpanitu uncovered an anomaly—her calculations revealed the presence of another solitary world, separate from the multiverse—the math frustrating her. It shifted, nebulous, as though even the calculations flickered in and out of existence. She suspected this world might be the source from which all life in the multiverse had sprung. If so, perhaps there was still a chance to overcome the darkness and fill the multiverse with light. It was at this point in her research when her world began to crumble and she wondered if the cause of it lay with her, having probed too far, her calculations unraveling the fabric of reality itself. With her last breaths she had begged for forgiveness, for a reprieve, a second chance, to find a way to overcome the darkness. When she woke, held in Marduk's arms, she learned the awful truth. Her reprieve had come, not by the hand of light, but of darkness. The Creator had abandoned her to the very thing she sought to defeat.

Meresamun rubbed her eyes and let out a heavy breath. Zarpanitu's writings encompassed vast, oppressive matters, far removed from the smallness of Meresamun's own existence. Yet, even after the wealth of knowledge she had accessed, her question of how to live with Marduk and not be corrupted by him remained unanswered. Apart from the first volume which only spoke of Zarpanitu's suffering, and her research into how to find the so-called Well of Life, Meresamun was none the wiser—

A heavy knock came to the door. Meresamun started. A primal, incandescent bolt of fear shot through her. She cut a look at the closed door, her sudden awareness of the bleakness of the night hour and her being alone in an empty, dark palace paralyzing her. Outside, the black canopy of a moonless sky riven by the sweep of a milky band of stars bore down on her, heavy with the weight of night. Over the shadowed cliffs, green and red curtains of light danced in the heavens, numinous, ephemeral.

"Ninsunu," Marduk called, quiet. "It is time. Come to me."

She let out a quivering breath and got to her feet. The remaining fuel in the fire collapsed with a soft shudder. The shadows in the room eased closer, encroaching her shrinking cocoon of light. Casting one last look at the empty box, she lingered, disappointment shearing her. She had learned both much—and nothing.

With a sigh, she turned from the box. A faint gleam of blue caught her eye. She blinked and looked back. It was gone. It must have been her imagination. Turning, she caught it again. Slow, she turned back. This time she saw it. She stopped and held still. The palest of blue, no wider than the span of a thread sat concealed in the upper lip of the lid's edge. Her heart clenched. A hidden compartment. Holding her breath, she pressed her fingers against the spot, searching for a niche or a lever. There. A quiet click, and a thin section of the lid's beveled edge slid back.

Within, tucked in the narrow space, a single, slim volume, bound in black leather, its pages numbering no more than five. With trembling fingers she placed the device on it and read through its brief pages, her breath shortening as the horror of Zarpanitu's desperate words seeped into her soul. She slid the volume back into its hiding place, her heart pounding as she secreted Zarpanitu's words once more. Finally, the answer she had sought, but it was an awful, terrible thing. Realization slammed into her. Marduk had hidden that volume, *knew* its contents. Only by sheer fortune had she seen the concealed light. He couldn't know she knew. It would be the end of everything.

"Ninsunu?" The door's handle lifted, stealthy.

"Coming." Nausea slammed into her. The weight of Zarpanitu's confession and the magnitude of Marduk's deception impaled her. He had broken his promise—the one he had made *her* swear to uphold. Despite his guileless words to the contrary, he *had* read his first consort's words, because he had packed this box and purposely secreted the most damning volume away from the others, where only he would find it. Meresamun shuddered, her eyes straying back to the near-invisible hiding place. The truth was more terrible than she could ever have imagined.

The door opened. Cold air swept in. Marduk waited at the threshold in his black armor, his eyes shadowed, and his weapons glinting in the waning firelight. His dark gaze swept over her to the empty box, then to the volumes spread across the rug. He held out his gloved hand.

"Come to me, my love," he whispered, gentle.

She went, shivering in her thin gown, loathing him for his lies, his falseness—yet needing him to comfort her, she, adrift in a sea of chaos, and he, the sole, poisonous island to save her from drowning. He caught her to him and held her fast against his chest, his possessiveness saturating her, awakening her, conflicting her.

"You are overcome," he murmured, as she suppressed as shudder. "Zarpanitu's knowledge was unlike any other's. Even I struggled to keep up."

He led her back through the dark, silent palace, past the sleeping gardens, through the tunnel, and down the stairs. At the bridge, he swept her up against him and carried her over the improbable span, starlight glittering against the obsidian walls of his armor.

Within the sanctuary of his suite, a steaming, jasmine-scented bath awaited them. Surrounded by the heat of four braziers, he pulled apart the ties of her gown. Dull, she stepped into the bath and welcomed the scorching heat of the water against her flesh.

His markings shifting and swirling, dense with anticipation, Marduk joined her, the water lapping, soft, against the bathing pool's edges as he came to her. He caught her chin and kissed her, tender, gentle, his love for her palpable, heartbreaking. She closed her eyes and dined on her sorrow as the black-bound volume's words burned into the darkest corners of her mind, laden with the depth of her responsibility, and of her true purpose, its long wait at last at an end.

Alone upon her terrace, Istara gazed at Imaru's night-dark lake. Its shallow waves undulated under the carpet of stars processing across the heavens, locked in their stately, slow dance. During the five hour flight back to Imaru, as her grief solidified and encased her heart in silence, Thoth had fussed over the cores, made notes, and muttered over his calculations. In the flight deck, Sekhmet had answered Urhi-Teshub's endless questions about the construction and inner workings of her ship, his hunger to learn insatiable. The goddess of war had indulged him, sharing its secrets as her ship tore across the empty skies of Elati, wounded, yet proud, laden with its precious, hard-won cargo.

Footsteps approached. Istara turned.

"My lady," Urhi-Teshub said. "The apartment is secure. I will leave you to your rest."

Her protector had changed out of his leather armor which had borne deep, ragged abrasions from his wild slide down the side of the pyramid. Now he stood, washed and scented in the sweet, earthy scent of cyprinum, wearing his usual attire: a gold-gilt leather tunic and kilt, its fitted cut enhancing his powerful physique. He folded his arms over his chest, the hard contours of his muscles catching in the terrace's torchlight. His presence dominated her, reminding her of when he had held her in his arms, naked, and primed to love her.

Istara nodded. Dullness lapped against her. She had meant to ask him, had been determined to find out all—how she had come to him, wondering if she had been a slave girl who had caught his eye, or a princess—longing to piece together what had driven her to leave her beloved consort's side and take the form of a mortal. To have become his queen, she would have had to plan her seduction. To capture the heart of a king would require deft maneuvering. However, whatever they had shared had been no stolen night between god and mortal, it had been something much larger—she had loved him, heart and soul. She had become his queen. She closed her eyes. How could she have abandoned Sethi—for a passing infatuation? And now, her once-lover stood before her, an immortal and her protector. The evidence damned her. He had followed her to Elati, and left his empire behind. Her betrayal would have torn Sethi apart. It was unbearable.

"Why—" she began, meaning to ask him why he had left his people for her. No. It was impossible. She looked up at the stars, heartsick, unable to frame the question, condemned by the magnitude of her crime.

The soft clack of the leather panels of his kilt filled the quiet. He came to a halt beside her. "Why what?" he asked, low.

When she didn't answer. He continued, cautious, "You haven't been yourself since we returned. Did something happen while we were inside the pyramids' field?"

"What didn't happen?" she asked, unhappiness saturating her. She lifted her shoulders and let them fall again. "I am sure we all suffered equally."

"Will you not tell me what is troubling you?" She caught his look, his concern, his willingness to ease her pain.

"It is nothing more than I can manage," she said. She looked down at her hands folded over her torso. Glimmers of her golden light sparkled along them. "It is the guilt I must bear which burdens me."

"Guilt?" Urhi-Teshub repeated. His brow furrowed. "For what?"

She flashed him a reproachful look. "Of course *you* would not see it so."

He took a step back. "I do not understand your meaning. You have no guilt. In everything you are blameless."

"Ah, so you would try to convince me the guilt is *yours*?"

He stared at her, uncomprehending. "*What* guilt?" he cried. "You are speaking in riddles."

She took a step toward him, the banked fires within stirring, awakening, scorching her. "You took me to your bed," she said, her hands clenching into fists, helpless against the need to blame someone for her downfall. "We lay together, naked, as lovers. I loved you. We were in *love*."

"Istara," Urhi-Teshub took hold of her shoulders, "that was a long time ago. You moved on to another. You broke my heart."

"To another?" she cried, anguished, impaled by the depth of her faithlessness to her consort. "Where is *he*? Why did he not follow me as you have done? Perhaps I did not break his heart as I did yours."

Urhi-Teshub's grip tightened. "You do not know what you are saying," he muttered. He let her go and backed away. "You must speak with Thoth. I am sworn to silence in this matter."

"Thoth," Istara repeated, dull. "He will tell me nothing."

Urhi-Teshub looked over the city. The muscles in his jaw clenched. Silence stretched between them. Istara waited, willing him to speak the truth.

"You have nothing to be guilty of," he said at last, dogged. "Take some rest. We have endured a difficult day. Whatever you saw, do not believe it was the whole of it. Trust in the Creator. He took your memories for a reason."

Istara caught his glance in the direction of her door, his desperation to get away, to untangle himself from her predicament.

"And yet, the Creator has allowed Sethi to remember," she whispered as her protector strode from the terrace and through her rooms, eager to depart, "else why would he stand against me?"

From within the depths of her apartment, Urhi-Teshub opened the door. It closed behind him, soft. The latch clicked into place. She turned again to look at the stars, but saw nothing except darkness.

❋ ❋ ❋

Urhi-Teshub passed the guards flanking Istara's door and turned toward his own across the corridor. He longed to grant Istara the truth, but Thoth had forbidden it, insisting they must not undo what the Creator had done. Perhaps he should warn Thoth Istara's memories had begun to return. He understood well enough the story she had crafted to fit her perception of having always been a goddess: she had left Sethi to be with Urhi-Teshub, her 'affair' having driven Sethi to ally himself with Marduk. Urhi-Teshub lifted an eyebrow, amazed at how a mind, given only fragments could create such a plausible whole.

He rubbed his hand against his jaw. Perhaps after today's events he might be able to sway the once-god of wisdom's mind. Sekhmet had said Thoth worried too much. Istara was suffering. Needlessly. What possible harm could come from Istara knowing the truth? He turned.

From the depths of the corridor, a black-clad figure approached carrying a rustic-looking gourd, a rude cork jammed into its neck. Sekhmet lifted the yellowish gourd as she approached. A sloshing sound came from within.

"I hoped you might be in the mood to celebrate today's success," she smiled. "It's a local spirit, a burned liquor they call 'friend for life'. Despite its off-putting description, it's quite pleasant." She held out the gourd.

Urhi-Teshub took it, thinking only to take a sip to be polite before excusing himself to speak with Thoth. He sipped, then took a deeper swig. "It's good." He handed back the gourd.

"Nice and clean, with just enough sweetness to take the edge off its bitterness." Sekhmet took a swig, then swiped the back of her hand over her mouth, like a man. Urhi-Teshub bit back a smile and eyed the gourd, thinking he wouldn't mind another shot at it.

He tilted his head at the door of his apartment. "Would you like to come in?" He reasoned once the gourd was empty he could go to Thoth. Sekhmet *had* gone out of her way to get the drink and find him. It would be rude to send her off.

She nodded. He let her go in first.

"You want cups for this?" she asked as he closed the door.

"How do the locals drink it?"

Sekhmet waggled the gourd.

"Let's be heathens then," Urhi-Teshub said and moved to join her. She sank onto one of the divans. Her gaze went to the open doors to the terrace. "It's a private garden," he said, catching her wary look. "No one here but you and me."

She handed him the gourd. He settled onto the divan opposite hers. The cork came out with a satisfying pop. He raised the gourd and toasted her before he drank, deep. The liquid washed down his throat, smooth, satisfying, both bitter and sweet.

"Easy, there," Sekhmet said, putting her slim fingers on the gourd and pushing it down, "it's stronger than you'd expect. I don't want you incapacitated before I find out all your dark secrets."

"I don't have any dark secrets," Urhi-Teshub said, handing the gourd back. She took it, and sipped, but didn't hand it back. Neither did she put the cork back, which pleased him. "It's *your* dark secrets I am interested in," he said, the drink starting to hit him, buoying him up, melting his troubles away—though a stern voice in his mind reminded him he still needed to speak to Thoth.

"The one who brings the drink gets their answers first," Sekhmet replied with a dry look. She eased forward and rested her elbows on her leather-clad thighs, the gourd dangling in the space between her legs. Urhi-Teshub cut a surreptitious look at her fingers around the neck of the gourd. He had never seen a women clad in leggings before, nor had he seen one sit like that, oozing the easy confidence of a warrior. He looked up and caught her watching him, a sardonic look in her eye.

"When you sit like that, dressed like that, you can't expect a man not to look," he said, leaning back against the divan and spreading his arms out over the back of it. He lifted his leg and lay his ankle over the knee of his other leg, the panels of his kilt fell in the gap between.

"Hm," Sekhmet said, her gaze drifting over him as she took another slow sip of the liquor. She pushed herself up from the divan and wandered around the room, trailing her fingers over the items of virtue displayed on the tables. "Is any of this yours?"

"Not a single thing," Urhi-Teshub said, watching her, intrigued by her sudden change of mood, sensing her withdrawing from him, her earlier banter fading. "Apart from my ruined armor, I arrived in Elati carrying nothing more than the weapons I brought from Marduk's armory."

"Nothing to be ashamed of," Sekhmet said, sliding a sidewise look at him. "I heard you carried the largest ones, along with Teshub."

"I did," Urhi-Teshub said. Languidness poured through him, lowered his defenses. He glanced at the gourd with grudging admiration. Imaru's local drink was potent.

"And before," Sekhmet said, opening the lid of a jewel-encrusted box and peeking inside, "who were you?"

He shrugged. "A prince. A warrior. A king."

"And Istara was your queen?"

He blinked at her blunt question, asked in a soft, blameless tone. "I—" he floundered, the drink had dulled his thoughts, made it hard to think. "She—" He stood up, and shook himself, trying to rid himself of the tranquilizing effect of the drink. "Let us talk of other things."

"No," Sekhmet said, closing the jeweled box with a snap, "not yet."

"What does it matter who was my queen?" Urhi-Teshub demanded, the drink's effect shifting, turning dark, hardening him.

"Because I won't be second to another, ever again," Sekhmet said, her dark eyes, flecked with gold, met his. From within their depths, anguish. She blinked and it was gone, silenced, obliterated.

Urhi-Teshub let out a slow breath. "Second?" he asked, stunned by her vulnerability, glimpsed within the space of a heartbeat. "Who could make *you* second to anyone?"

"It seems we both have our dark secrets," she said, though a faint look of pleasure touched her features. She crossed the room until she stood before him, her slim, leather-encased body within arm's reach. She brought the gourd to her lips, closed her eyes and took three long gulps. Again, the back of her hand against her lips, the gesture both sensual and innocent, maddening him. She held out the gourd. "Just a little sip," she murmured as Urhi-Teshub took it, his fingers brushing against hers, "then neither of us will have the advantage of the other."

"I will never answer your question," Urhi-Teshub said, bringing the mouth of the gourd to his lips, tasting the scent of her upon its edge. He sipped, just a little as she suggested, and handed the thing back to her.

"And I will never answer yours," she said, taking the gourd and corking it. She tossed it onto the opposite divan. It bounced twice before rolling to an uneven stop, the liquid within washing back and forth within its shell.

"Now we have that out of the way, shall we play a game?" she asked, going back to the jeweled box. She carried it back and set it on the floor between the divans. From within, she retrieved a small pair of cubes with different symbols on each side. She sank onto the floor and patted the space beside her. "You coming?"

He lifted a brow. "You want me to sit on the floor?"

"The game doesn't work if you don't," Sekhmet said, cradling the cubes in her upturned palm. She shook her hand, and the cubes rattled together, the sound not unpleasant. She tossed them away from her. They rolled across the floor until they hit the side of the box. She leaned forward. "A pair of stars," she smiled, triumphant. "I win, already."

Curious, Urhi-Teshub knelt beside her. He picked up the cubes and examined them. On each of their six sides, a marking. A star; a crescent moon; a flower; a goblet; a crown; a dagger. Both of the cubes had the same markings, so if thrown at the same time one could get two of the same markings at once, as Sekhmet had just done.

"They are called dice," Sekhmet said, taking them from him and shaking them again within her cupped palm, her fingers curled over so the dice wouldn't fall out. She tossed them again. They clattered against the side of the box. A flower and a dagger showed their faces. Disappointment sliced over her features.

"To win we need to throw a matching pair?" Urhi-Teshub asked.

"Roll, not throw," Sekhmet corrected. "You roll the dice. And yes. Although, not all pairs are equal. A pair of stars is the strongest roll, followed in descending order by crowns, moons, daggers, goblets, and finally flowers."

"Sounds easy enough," Urhi-Teshub said, rubbing his hands together. It had been a long time since he had played a game, and the simplicity of this one appealed. "I'm ready."

"I wasn't done," Sekhmet continued, cutting a wry look at him. "You also need to avoid rolling four combinations, which not only loses that toss, but also gives the winner an extra turn to win." She reached up onto the divan and tugged on the frayed remains of an old rope still clinging to the gourd's neck. The gourd wobbled its way across the divan to her. She caught it, deft, as it fell off the seat. He waited for her to uncork it. Instead she settled it beside her, resting its neck against her thigh. "The losing combinations are: moon and dagger; goblet and dagger; flower and dagger, and crown and dagger."

"Daggers—bad," Urhi-Teshub said, nodding.

"Not always," Sekhmet said, her fingers falling to brush against one of the daggers strapped in its holder to her thigh. "Sometimes they are very good." She cut a look at him, and smiled, slow. "But not tonight." She uncorked the gourd. "One sip," she said handing it to him. He obliged and she followed suit.

"And the wager?" Urhi-Teshub asked.

"Ah," Sekhmet said, holding up the gourd, "the loser must take a sip and answer the question put to them."

Urhi-Teshub drew back. "I will not answer your question, so do not ask."

"I wasn't planning on it, since you can't ask me mine, either. We have established what is off limits. However," she bit back a secret smile, "everything else is fair game."

A tingling of anticipation spread through Urhi-Teshub. Sekhmet was unlike any other woman he had ever known, and he had known a lot of them. He found himself determined to win, to have the advantage of her, to ask her things he would never dare ask otherwise. She handed him one of the dice.

"We roll to see who goes first. Same as the order of pairs. Star is the highest roll, flower the lowest."

Urhi-Teshub tossed his die. It tumbled up against the box. A crown, only a star could beat it. He shot her a triumphant look. Her die came to a stop beside his. A star. He ignored her smirk. The night was still young. He would have the better of her yet.

The night progressed, though despite having an occasional edge over her, Sekhmet always rallied until neither of them ever had the advantage of the other. Despite his desire to ask deeper questions, his manners got the better of him, instead he asked useless things: What is your favorite food? Who is your least favorite god in the pantheon? Do you have names for your weapons? Most embarrassing memory. But as the gourd emptied, and they relaxed—the dice throwing becoming chaotic, their tosses forcing them to search, laughing and inebriated for dice lost under the divans, their words slurring—the questions deepened. She asked him what he thought of becoming immortal. Who he worshiped when he had been mortal. What was his weapon of choice. What he missed the most about the world he had left behind. He had to admit her questions were far better than his.

Urhi-Teshub handed the gourd to Sekhmet who had just rolled one of the losing pairs, something and a dagger, he couldn't remember. She sipped, languid, and sank back against the edge of the divan, pulling her legs out from under her with a sigh.

"Why don' you have a consor'?" he asked, weaving a little as he reached out to take the gourd back from her. He sipped, even though it wasn't his turn to drink. He liked the taste of it, and it made him feel good. He hadn't felt this way for as long as he could remember. Maybe forever.

She shrugged and lifted her hand to wipe away a stray drop of the clear liquor from her chest. She missed by a lot. "The Creat'r didn' give me any."

"Don' you wan' one?" Urhi-Teshub asked, falling back against the opposite divan. He unfolded his legs and stretched them out in front of him. It felt really good to do it. He wondered why he didn't sit on the floor like this more often.

She shrugged again and looked down at her lap. She sniffed. "Sometimes." She let out a deep exhalation. "Wha' can I do 'bout it? 'S not like there's any gods goin' spare." She held out her hand and waggled her fingers, uncoordinated. "More."

He eased himself away from his divan and hauled himself across the floor over to her, the open gourd in his other hand, its dregs sloshing in the bottom of it. He leaned back against the divan beside her, huffing from the effort of his crossing, his breath hot and sticky in his mouth. She took the gourd from him and drank the last of it, noisy, like a man. The gourd landed on her lap and the weight of her head hit his shoulder. He rolled his eyes to her. She sagged against him, unconscious, her legs and arms sprawled out like a doll's.

He plucked the empty gourd from her lap and shoved it aside. "E'rybuddy sh' hav'a consor'," he said as the room began to spin. He leaned his head against the divan and closed his eyes. "E'rybuddy."

Urhi-Teshub woke desperate to relieve his bladder. Easing himself away from Sekhmet, he got up, slow, his head aching and his mouth dry as a desert. He went to the water closet, where an opening in the floor led to a channel which coursed with running water. He spread his legs, reached under his kilt and pulled himself free of his loincloth. He went, swaying a little, struggling to keep his aim straight. The drink's earlier pleasantness had left him, slept off in oblivion. In its place, a brutal, thundering headache.

On his way back he lingered at the open doors to the garden. Elati's pair of crescent moons hung low in the indigo canopy. Taking a deep, restorative breath of the cool, humid air, Urhi-Teshub went to the little fountain in the center of the garden. He cupped his hands under the quiet burble of running water and drank until his mouth no longer felt like a desiccated wasteland. He eyed the stars, calculating at least two hours of night remained before the abrupt eruption of day. Fatigue pulled at him. He went back into the room where he and Sekhmet had whiled away the evening together in easy camaraderie. The goddess of war sagged against the divan, her body slumped at wrong angles. He couldn't leave her like that. It looked uncomfortable.

He knelt, gathered her into his arms and lifted her. She weighed more than he expected. Her slim form betrayed a vulnerability she did not possess. He bit back a smile, pleased—she was probably solid muscle under her tight sheath of dark leather. He looked down at her, fast asleep in his arms, her full lips slightly parted, her thick lashes brushing against the ebony finish of her beautiful skin. Something inside him shifted, quiet, like a key turning in a hidden lock, revealing a silent, dormant place within him he had not known existed. He realized he was attracted to her—not just her exotic, beautiful looks, which had caught his attention the first time she had spoken to him in the armory—but *her*. She intrigued him, challenged him, kept him sharp. Sekhmet was utterly unlike any other. He moved through his apartment, the goddess of war's arms and legs dangling, her body open and vulnerable in his grip, careful not to knock her against the furniture.

He reached his bed and lowered her onto the cushions, gentle, so as not to wake her. She settled onto them with a sigh, her features softening. He found a blanket and lay it over her. Unable to stop himself, he watched her sleep, unashamed when he knew he should be. There was no doubt Sekhmet was proud, and the walls she had erected around herself were high, near unbreachable, but deep within, he sensed there beat a lonely heart no one had ever known. She had given up enough for him to deduce the goddess's agony of being second to the one she had once loved cut close to his alienation from Istara. The pain in his head deepened. He turned to leave. Sleep would not be his friend this night. Behind, a moan. The quiet rustle of the blanket.

"Where is your water closet," Sekhmet asked, her words thick with sleep.

He told her. She pulled herself from the bed with a groan, shooting him a dark, unreadable look as she passed, pain etching her features. While she was gone, at a loss what else to do, he found a cup and filled it with water from the fountain and put it by the bed. Awkwardness surrounded him. He wondered if he should send to the kitchens for a night platter. She came out before he had made up his mind. He turned and she smiled, looking as fresh as when he had met her the night before. A trickle of golden light shimmered in her eyes. He scoffed. Of course gods would not have to suffer the consequences for drinking.

She crossed the room and came to him. Her eyes met his. "Kicks like a mule, doesn't it?" Her fingers brushed against his brow. "Close your eyes," she whispered.

He did. If only because the lamplight hurt them. Warmth slid into his temple. It washed through him, eradicating the heaviness of the drink, the poison lodged in his blood. A rush of invigoration slid through him followed by calm. The warmth faded. The pain was . . . gone.

"Now there is a little part of me in you," she murmured, her gaze falling to her hand as her golden tendrils slid back. "Take good care of it." She turned to go. "I'll leave you to your rest."

Her poignant gift impaled him. He had learned the gods could give up their light to aid others, but their gift was not like Istara's light which ran in surplus and regenerated. Their gift of light was their own, and once given, never regained. Sekhmet had sacrificed her light to him for something as inconsequential as a drink-soaked skull. A door inside him opened, revealing a world he wanted to explore—with her. He caught her wrist, though he kept his grip gentle. "I would have you stay. I am not the kind of man who sends a woman from his rooms in the dead of the night."

"Why does that not surprise me," Sekhmet said, dry, though when her eyes met his, he glimpsed her longing to remain with him—perceived her quiet dread of the emptiness of her lonely apartment—sensing what she said and what she felt were often not aligned. The goddess of war looked up at him, complicated, wounded, valiant. She would be a challenge, would perhaps drive him mad at times. A bolt of realization shot through him. He didn't want an easy life; he wanted to feel pain, anger, passion. Everything. With her. It was time to let the past go. He had suffered enough. He stepped toward her. She caught her breath, her stance opening, yielding, waiting, betraying her hope he would not stop.

"I have not been with a woman in a long time," he murmured, reaching out to draw her into the circle of his embrace, the contours of her body fitting against him as though they were two lost pieces of a puzzle put back together after an eon apart. His heart thudded, the last tendrils of his uncertainty dimming. In his arms, she felt right. More than right. She felt perfect. "Perhaps I will not please you."

"Perhaps," Sekhmet breathed as he caught her chin and tilted her face up to his, "but we will never know until you try."

"I am only an immortal," he whispered, lowering his mouth to her upturned one, "I will never be your equal."

"Just don't make me second to her," Sekhmet murmured. She closed her eyes, but not before he witnessed her look of uncertainty, felt her faint trembling, fearing he would be the author of past sorrows revisiting her anew.

His heart ached. Her trust in him threatened to undo him. In her wariness he felt a sameness, sensed her pain mirrored his. He tightened his hold on her. Together they would heal, would find solace in the other. Her vulnerability drew her to him, awakening deep, protective instincts. He would never hurt her. Never.

"I will not," he said. "I swear it. Where we go this night, I will not turn back." He brushed his lips against hers, tasting her, a thrill of possession coursing through him. The goddess of war wanted him, Urhi-Teshub, once a mere mortal king of a dusty empire. Their kiss deepened. Raw, sexual hunger seared through him, freed of its long imprisonment. In his arms, she swayed, overcome, caught in the thrall of his sudden, savage passion.

He picked her up, this time, she did not hang limp in his arms, she clung to him, her arms around his neck, her body pressed into his, her lips against his, harsh, desperate, aching with need, fuelling his desire to take her, over and over, and make her his. He reached the bed and carried her down with him, resting his weight on his forearms, sheltering her body with his. He touched her beautiful, exquisite face. Together they were complete. A perfect whole.

"Where have you been all my life," he murmured as he marveled at the wonder of her in his bed, wanting him as much as he realized he had been wanting her ever since she had come to the armory.

She didn't answer. Instead she pulled apart the leather straps of her armor, slow. He sat back on his haunches, watching, aroused, as she sat up and slid her open tunic off her shoulders and down her arms, seductive, revealing nothing but bare skin beneath. His gaze dropped to her breasts, each full enough to fill the cup of his hand and tipped by dark, erect nipples aching to be worshiped by him.

She pushed her leggings past her hips and down her thighs, granting him an indulgent look at her secret place. It was bare of the usual triangle of hair. He allowed himself to take his fill of it, drinking in the details of her hairless, smooth mound, longing to spend time there, pleasuring her. Her leather leggings and boots fell onto the floor with a heavy thud. She leaned back onto her elbows, one knee up, and let him survey her.

He raked his eyes over her, aching with approval. Her honed body gleamed in the lamplight, every muscle toned and defined. Never in his life had he seen a woman like her. Without ever having been aware of it, he discerned a part of him had longed for a female warrior to share his bed, who drove her body to its limits, just as he did to his. He trailed his fingers over the planes of her body, reverent.

His member called to him, swollen within its constraints. He dragged his fingers away from her to pull his own tunic and kilt away, his armor following hers until he knelt over her as naked as she, his member proud and erect, betraying his hunger for her.

"Come to me," she whispered.

He lowered himself over her, his mouth catching hers, hot, possessive. He pulled her against him until he could no longer tell where she ended and he began, her naked body sliding against his. The scented heat of her secret place called to him, a lodestone.

She opened her legs and with a low groan pressed herself against the tip of his member, signaling to him she was not interested in the lengthy foreplay other women needed. She wanted him inside her. Now. He pulled back and caught her chin in his hand, the question in his eyes clear. The hunger in hers slayed him.

He entered her, slow, taking his time as he eased the length of his member in to her depths, each thrust scouring him, cleansing him of the past, opening the way to the future, with her by his side, his warrior goddess. She clenched and held him captive in her grip. Carnality pounded through him, hot, powerful, driving him mad with the need of her. He wanted to ride her hard, to grind the root of his member against her mound, to possess her utterly, but he held back, determined to let her control the pace.

She clung to him, forcing him to take her slow, steady. He sat up and drew her against him, longing to please her. She quivered with pleasure, lost in him, her hips meeting his thrusts, her body moving with his as though they had bedded each other a hundred thousand times before. She began to increase the pace, her sheath tightening around him, warning him she was closing in on her release. He held her face in his hands, his thumb caught between her teeth, his body continuing to love her even as his heart lost itself in her rapture. Her fingers dug into his shoulders. She cried out. The strength of her release slaughtered him. One thrust. Two. He juddered and filled her with the heat of his passion. Euphoria seared his soul. He clutched her to him, his goddess of war, as she shuddered, satiated, limp, and lost in his arms.

He carried her back down onto the bed, panting, invigorated, every part of him alive, aware. Perspective beckoned, darkness diminished. Joy surrounded him. He turned to look at her and found her watching him. He kissed her, soft, tender, his heart raw with gratitude for the wonder of her until the drag of sleep called and he drifted away to dream of nothing, at long last liberated of the burden of a broken heart.

Joy suffused Meresamun. She gazed at her hand bound in a silken cord with Ahmen's, his grip firm, reassuring. *Husband.* It was done. The priestess departed. They stood alone in the courtyard of the inner temple of Isis. Ahmen whispered her name and her heart erupted anew, aching with love. She met his eyes as Re-Atum's barque breached the courtyard's pillars and mantled Ahmen's shoulders, bathing him in the golden light of a new day.

"My beloved wife," he whispered, "I am yours until the light of Re-Atum ends." He caught her to him, the one who had found her against all the odds—the one who had brought her home. His arm tightened around her, pressing their bound hands between their bodies, making them one. She waited, trembling with anticipation, for his kiss—for the beginning of forever, with him, the only man she had ever loved.

Thunder tore through the temple's quiet. It persisted, crescendoed. The ground trembled. From the pinnacle of the heavens, darkness poured. It scythed through the courtyard, devouring all in its path, the pillars, the ground, the sky, the light of Re-Atum. It reached Ahmen and robbed him of the ground beneath his feet. He fell away from her, his hand held out to hers, their binding cord torn free. It became a black serpent, its carnelian eyes cold and seared with hate, a thing of darkness, and struck Ahmen's heart.

Meresamun screamed. She sat up, her heart pounding. Brilliant sunlight flooded Marduk's suite. The thunder from her dream followed her. It deepened, reverberating against the walls of the cliffs, its throaty roar blistering her senses as it neared the palace. Past the open doors to the terrace, the smooth exterior of Marduk's warship circled, blotting out the light of the morning sun.

Her heart sinking, she eyed the ship as it descended, jets of steam hissing from its wings. Sethi. Though she was loathe to admit it, the god of war frightened her, even more than the dark moods of her consort. Marduk's enslaved god was far removed from the man she remembered from Egypt, whose honor and integrity had been legendary. Suppressed by the power of the device, he reeked of tyranny, arrogance, and heartlessness.

Life meant nothing to Sethi. Mercy was unknown. Brutality shrouded him. Whatever Marduk had buried into Sethi's head was powerful if it could overcome the will of a god—and the god of war was no lesser god. Horus, the god Sethi had superseded had been one of the greatest gods of the Egyptian pantheon. The protector of pharaohs.

Meresamun shivered as a blast of cold mountain air washed through the room, drawn in by the ship's wake. She fell back against the cushions and stared at the scene painted on the ceiling—images of white-winged horses battled against black horses bearing equally stunning wings of night—the dream haunting her. Ahmen. No. Marduk could never hurt him. Her once-husband was gone, lost in the ruins of the Etemen'anki. It was just a dream.

Hungry for a distraction, she let her gaze move over the mural. A pair of winged horses, their muscular bodies straining, faced her, frozen in violence. One, a black, bit deep into the throat of a white. The white horse's eyes rolled in pain. A fountain of dark blood stained its neck. She stared at the dying creature, stricken, thinking of Zarpanitu's writings: of the darkness Marduk's first consort had claimed would spread across every world.

Meresamun's thoughts moved, cautious, to the hidden volume, secreted there by Marduk, his intention for it never to be found by any other than he. Zarpanitu had addressed those notes to Marduk's next consort—in them she had revealed her deep regret she had failed to stop him. Soon she would fall to Marduk's thrall; his darkness clawed at her, tainted her. It had begun to change her. In a desperate bid to stop the inevitable, she wrote she would put herself in harm's way on purpose. She would tempt fate over and over until her life became forfeit. She would not let Marduk's darkness consume her heart—could not use her knowledge to aid him in his hunger to rule, alone, forever. Horus, unaware of her design, had done her a kindness by granting her the escape she sought. And now, Sethi paid the price for it.

Meresamun closed her eyes and shut out the grisly image of the suffering horse. Marduk *knew* Zarpanitu had wanted to die, had chosen death to escape him, yet, despite this, he had waited an eon feeding on thoughts of revenge, unable, or unwilling to accept the truth: *He* had been the true cause of his consort's demise. Horus had merely provided the blade.

Near the end of her hidden notes, Zarpanitu had reiterated her belief the Well of Life existed in a special world, one she termed as the first world. It would be in this *first* world where Marduk could be cleansed of the darkness within the Well of Light. And this task, Zarpanitu wrote, must now fall to her successor. If Marduk were not cleansed, the darkness would spread until no light remained. Meresamun opened her eyes. The image of the savaged horse bled into her mind, its suffering visceral. How was she—a once-enslaved priestess—to ever find this so-called Well if her illustrious predecessor had failed? How was she even to begin? Who could she ask? She was powerless, and Marduk knew it.

And yet, if she did nothing, she was destined to become as black-hearted and dangerous as her consort. No. She would not go down without a fight. She still had the translation device, and in her wanderings through the palace, she had discovered a vast library hidden behind a plain door. At first she had been delighted, her love of learning and discovery reawakened, but when she opened the scrolls she had found the language impossible to comprehend. The elegant, complex symbols alienated her despite her enhanced abilities to pick up the various languages of Elati. When she had asked a passing servant what language was written upon the scrolls, she learned it was an archaic one, long lost to the deepest of time. She had left, disappointment and loneliness deepening her isolation. But now, with Marduk's device, nothing stood in her way.

The sharp, roasted scent of coffee beckoned. On the low table beside the bed, a silver pot rested on a stand over a burning flame. The first time she had tried it, she had recoiled, unable to bear its exotic, rich, bitter heat. But when it could be adapted to suit her taste with something called sugar, a pale brown crystal from the Senichin Isles, and cream, she found it quite pleasant after all. Coffee was perhaps the only thing she and Marduk agreed on—it truly was the drink of the gods.

She poured out a generous measure, vapors of steam rising from within the smooth-glazed ceramic of her cup. From the little pots beside the warmed pot of coffee, she added sugar and cream, the familiar ritual soothing her. The coffee slid down her throat, hot, comforting, just a little too sweet. Slipping out of the bed, she pulled on a silken robe and ventured onto the terrace, the warmth of the sun against her back staving off the worst of the morning's chill. At the edge, she wrapped her arms around herself and eyed the terrace further below.

Marduk's warship hulked over it, a dark bird of prey. Greasy vapors leaked from its rear, distorting the cool morning air. Beneath the monstrosity, the terrace's once-beautiful mosaic lay scorched and blackened by the flames of the ship's many arrivals and departures.

Sethi was nowhere to be seen. Servants in Marduk's livery piled the latest offering of tribute into neat stacks, their movements discreet, quiet and precise. Meresamun watched them, idle, sipping her coffee, considering anew her plans to go to the library with the translation device.

An old man eased down the steps of the ship, a long white robe tied over his bony shoulder and a bulging leather satchel slung across his chest. He limped past the servants to the edge of the terrace where he surveyed the cliffs and palace, his gaze sharp, intelligent. On his arm, a hooded falcon perched on an elegant gauntlet. Meresamun leaned forward, intrigued. None like him had ever arrived before. She wondered who he was, and why Sethi had brought him here. The old man stroked the bird's back as his eyes moved over the sky. His gaze paused on the twin moons, pale crescents in the quiet blue. From out of the citadel, Marduk's steward approached. He bowed and gestured for his guest to follow. The old man limped after him through the growing pile of goods under the ship's wing. A heartbeat later, he entered the palace and was lost within its shadows.

Meresamun hurried back into the suite and dressed. There was something about that man, something different, something good. She sensed he could tell her much about the world Marduk had brought her to, though she also suspected Marduk would not approve of her meeting him. Her heart thudded, urgency stamping itself into her, forcing her to hurry, warning her time was short. Clasping the translation device against her torso, she left Marduk's suite to the quiet work of his silent, black-clad servants and slipped along the corridors of the palace toward her destination, aching with hope she was right, and raw with fear she was not.

Apart from the crackle of flames burning in the braziers, the library lay shrouded in shadowed silence. Meresamun walked along the rows of wooden stacks packed tight with scrolls, as pristine as the day they were written despite—at least according to a servant—the passage of tens of thousands of years since the language went extinct.

In the center of the library, a rectangle of open space stood arrayed with several massive tables and an assortment of chairs. She leaned against one of the stacks, dejected. Amongst all these scrolls, she was quite alone. The old man was not here. Her hopes had been unfounded. It had been that satchel he bore, packed tight with scrolls which had made her think he would come here. She had thought—No. She felt her cheeks darken, embarrassed by her fanciful hope the man with the falcon had arrived just when she had need of answers the most, as if it had been all about her. She had been foolish. Childish even. Sethi had brought him to meet Marduk. One such as he would possess great knowledge of this world.

She sank onto one of the chairs and set the translation device on the table, morose. Tilting her head back, she gazed at the upper galleries. Three more floors rose above her, each level reached by narrow wooden steps without any railings. The looming central gallery was only one small part of the whole. The sprawl of the library beyond the gallery was enormous, as vast as the hypostyle hall of the Temple of Sekhmet—each floor a copy of the other— four floors of equal measure. Despondence touched her, deflating her earlier hopes and mocking her expectations. It would take her years to get through just a fraction of the scrolls contained within the library's walls.

Marduk would never allow her unlimited access to so much information. He would take the device away from her. Where Zarpanitu had had the freedom to learn, Meresamun sensed she would be restrained, her leash kept much shorter and tighter than her predecessor's. She wondered anew why her consort had allowed her to read Zarpanitu's journals. Perhaps to frighten her, to teach her the pursuit of knowledge only led to more uncertainty. If he knew she had found the hidden one—

A thud as the library's door came to. Voices, low and intent, moved along the library's corridor toward her. For a panicked heartbeat, she imagined she heard Sethi's voice. But no, it was another, Marduk's steward. The voices neared. The other bore a strong accent, his voice as dry as the desert, and as fragile as ancient papyrus. Her hopes flared. The old man, the one she had longed to meet had come to the library after all. She turned, filled with anticipation before another thought struck her: The steward might inform Marduk he had found her in the library. She had only just read Zarpanitu's journals. Marduk would ask questions, ones she did not wish to answer. Better for him not to know. She retrieved the translation device, and although she had never done such a thing since she was a child, she slipped under the table to crouch beneath its immense girth. The footsteps came to a halt. She held her breath.

"I will come for you once Lord Sethi is ready to depart," the steward said. A quiet clack against the table. "A lamp should you wish to use the stacks in the upper levels. A tray of refreshment will be sent up shortly. There is a water closet near the entrance." He hesitated. "Shall I take your falcon to the mews?"

"No," the old man answered. "She remains with me—although if it will not be too much trouble, some raw meat, and perhaps a basin of water could be provided? It has been a long time since she last had any nourishment."

"Of course," the steward said. The soft swish of his robes faded as he hurried to return to his master, a loyal dog. His devotion disturbed Meresamun. Perhaps the steward bore a device like Sethi. She blocked out the thought, unwilling to imagine the agony of being possessed by such a vile thing. The door closed. A low boom reverberated through the library. The scrape of the key against the lock. Silence.

"So," the accented voice of the old man said, soft, "will you come out, or will you force my old bones to bend down to face you?"

Meresamun started. She was certain she had kept quiet. "I will come out." She crawled, inelegant and encumbered by her gown from under the table.

"Are you not too old to be playing hide and seek?" he asked, amused. He set his falcon onto the back of one of the chairs. His gaze moved over her expensive attire; his amusement faded, turned somber. "Or, are you hiding from another?"

"Perhaps a little," Meresamun admitted as she looked over her sudden companion, curious. He was by far the most aged person she had ever seen. His face in the lamplight was a map of lines, his skin as thin as the finest vellum. Light patches of brown mottled his cheeks, and underneath, a skein of blue veins.

"Who are you?" she breathed, fascinated. His fragility deceived; an aura fortitude surrounded him.

He bowed his head, though he held her eyes, his, gray, sharp, and inquisitive. "I am Zherei," he answered, "Master of the Ages. My home lies far to the south in the land of Serde. I lived in a white city beside a turquoise sea. Perhaps you can guess its name?"

Meresamun looked at him, blank. She shook her head, disappointed she would not be able to participate in his little game.

"Ah," he said, settling himself into one of the chairs with an exhalation of relief. He pulled off the leather gauntlet. "Well no matter. Not everyone enjoys examining maps, or memorizing place names."

"I would, if I could," Meresamun said, looking down at her fingers, wrapped around the translation device, embarrassed by the depth of her ignorance. She had always prided herself on her learning—and here, before her was a sage of great age and wisdom. "Once, long ago, I was a priestess who studied many of the writings of our most erudite thinkers."

Zherei looked up at her, curious. "A priestess," he repeated. A shadow of uncertainty touched his eyes. "And, which god did you serve?"

"Sekhmet," Meresamun whispered, thinking of her crime against the goddess and the long, horrible path to reach her atonement, forever lost.

Zherei blinked. A pall of confusion passed over his features. "Sekhmet? No one—How old are you, young lady?"

"I was twenty-four," Meresamun answered, wondering at his non-sequitur.

"*Was?*"

"I was twenty-four when we passed through Surru, but I became immortal because Sethi was with us," Meresamun answered, hoping he would understand, since she didn't understand much more than that, herself.

Zherei leaned back, slow. "You came through the impenetrable wall of light." He glanced at the falcon, who sat, quiet on her perch. "And apart from Sethi, who else traveled with you through . . . Surru?"

"Marduk." She looked away from him at the rows of scrolls, disappointment penetrating her. She hadn't wanted him to know, had hoped to keep her connection to Elati's oppressor a secret— had hoped the old man might teach her things about the world she lived in, but now, it would be too late. She was the enemy; he would tell her nothing.

Silence came. Meresamun waited. At last Zherei asked, quiet, "Who also became immortal because of Sethi?"

She nodded. He eyed her, sharp. He was no fool. She stood. "I suppose you would prefer if I left now you know to whom I belong."

He caught her arm, his touch gentle. "I would rather you stayed," he said, nodding for her to take a seat. "I would like to hear more about you and where you came from."

From the depths of the library, the metallic probing of a key in the door's lock. A click. The latch lifted. The scrape of one tray, then another slid across the flagged stone floor. A quiet boom as the door closed again. Another turn of a key. Quiet fell.

"Let me fetch your refreshment first."

The size of the trays required Meresamun to make two trips, granting her time to compose herself, and to realize Zherei did not hate her for her connections. Hope swelled anew. She set the trays before the sage and lifted the lids. Marduk's steward had been generous: three kinds of roasted meat, an array of breads and cheeses, even a bowl of stewed plums for the final course. She eyed Zherei anew, her curiosity deepening. To be fed so well, he must be important.

The second tray held two bowls, one with water and in the other, chunks of red, raw flesh, sinewy with tendons basked in a sheen of blood. The bird perked up, drawn to the scent of fresh kill.

"At long last," Zherei said, putting the gauntlet back on, "dinner, my darling."

He set the bird onto the table, and placed several pieces of the flesh before it, murmuring he dare not try to offer a piece with his fingers. Meresamun watched, captivated, as the hooded falcon captured a chunk in its talons and used its beak to tear strips free, its feeding both savage and beautiful.

"Does your falcon have a name?" Meresamun asked, admiring the bird's near-snowy breast speckled by rich, dark flecks of brown.

"Tyrn," Zherei answered, pulling the gauntlet off again and setting it aside. He rubbed his hands together as he looked over his meal, pleasure emanating from him. She reached for the jug and poured him wine, her troubles forgotten for the time being. Happiness touched her, the novelty of being in the company of someone learned filled her heart. She hoped he would stay at the palace for a long time.

He nodded at her as she set the jug aside. "This is far more than I can eat, please do help yourself."

Despite not having had anything except coffee since she woke, Meresamun wasn't hungry. However, it would be rude to sit and watch him eat. She plucked a piece of the honeyed sweetbread from the tray and nibbled at it, polite, while he ate, almost as ravenous as the bird.

"How long has it been since you last dined?" she asked once he turned his attention to the plums, dusted with cinnamon, and still warm from the cook pot.

His gray gaze met hers from under the wrinkles of his brow. "When I took my morning meal yesterday, although I am accustomed to fasting. Tyrn, however, is not used to being kept without nourishment. When we stopped for the night at the god of war's palace, I asked for food for her—pleaded in fact—but the one you call Sethi is a heartless being. He left me locked in his ship while he took his women away, to do what to them I cannot bear to imagine, although I heard their terrified cries. One, at least, must be dead. She screamed as she fell from a great height. It lasted a long time." At Meresamun's stricken look, he cleared his throat, picked up the napkin and dabbed the corners of his mouth. His attention moved to the galleries above, the highest levels lost in shadow. "I thought I might be next. Instead, I find myself here, where it appears the god of war's master is far more amenable to the comfort of his captives."

"Marduk is dangerous, too," Meresamun said. "Do not be fooled. Underneath his charming exterior, his heart is as black as night."

Zherei didn't say anything, although he kept his eyes on her as he finished the plums, examining her, his gaze incisive. He settled back in his seat, cradling his half-empty cup of wine. "Now, where were we?" he mused. "Ah yes," he caught her eyes, "you were going to tell me about you and the world you came from."

"What would you know?" Meresamun asked.

"Whatever you wish to tell me."

Meresamun began, hesitant, encouraged by the kindness in Zherei's eyes; his lack of judgment, and his empathy as she shared the details of her life from its beginning to her escape from the devastation of Babylon and her arrival at the threshold of Surru. He nodded as she described her caged existence in Elati, the blindness of her location, her ignorance of Elati's history, its peoples and kingdoms, and her deep regret for having succumbed to Marduk in Babylon—her terrible choice dooming her to be the consort of the oppressor of Elati's people.

Zherei refilled his cup with wine and handed it to her. She drank, realizing she might have been foolish to trust him. She knew nothing about him. Nothing at all. He possessed every advantage.

He took her hand in his, his palm warm and dry, and as fragile as the thinnest alabaster dish. "And so you wish to escape once more," he said.

"Once more?" Meresamun repeated, not understanding his meaning.

"In Elati," Zherei continued, "the wise ones talk of unpleasant experiences which occur throughout one's life. They believe these experiences are manifestations of lessons the Creator wishes us to learn as we journey through the gift of our existence. Until we learn what we must about our failings, the experiences will continue." He lifted his near non-existent eyebrows. "It appears *your* lesson is clear."

"Perhaps to one such as you, but not to me," Meresamun said. "All I see is hopelessness. Marduk is too strong, too powerful. I am nothing against him. He will win. He always does." She drank the last of her wine, morose.

"His path is not yours," Zherei said. "Only you can decide how you will react to what is unfolding in your life. You are stronger than you perceive. Perhaps if you saw yourself in that light, you might be able to find your answer."

Meresamun stared at him. The man spoke in riddles. "I beg you, speak plain. What use is a lesson to me when I cannot change anything? Marduk has told me I will always be his." Tears burned against her eyes, deepened the ache in her heart. "In time, when he has possessed me long enough, my heart will be corrupted by his. The woman I am now will cease to exist and I will become as heartless as Sethi. And unlike Zarpanitu, I cannot die. I will never be able to escape. Ever." The truth of Zarpanitu's words impaled her. She had lost. No one and nothing could help her now. She would never be able to find the Well of Life. It was hopeless.

"Did I hear you correctly?' Zherei poured more wine for her. "Are you referring to Zarpanitu, the great and learned one?"

Meresamun blinked and took the wine. His face wavered in the sheen of her tears. "What?"

"Was Zarpanitu Marduk's consort?" Zherei asked.

"Yes." Meresamun sipped. The wine's heat poured into her, soaked her regrets. She drank the rest, handed the empty cup back. "Why?"

Zherei took the cup and set it aside. "So the circle closes, after all this time."

Meresamun sensed something of great importance hung in the air between them. She brushed aside the tears clinging to her lashes. When he continued to remain silent, lost in thought, she ventured, "How is it you know of Zarpanitu? Was she from Elati?"

Zherei looked uneasy. "Not as far as I know." He looked down at the table. "Until you said her name, I believed her existence to be a legend, nothing more." He poured out the last of the wine and sipped. "To think she was the consort of the one who intends to enslave Elati," he muttered, staring into his cup. "Of all the possible outcomes—" He glanced up, catching Meresamun watching him, her confusion giving him pause. He cleared his throat. "Forgive me, I shall explain: Almost a millennia ago, while still a young sage, I traveled the length and breadth of Elati searching for reclusive ancient sages.

"High in the remote mountain chain of Qatu, I found Elati's most venerated sage. He told me a tale: during the age when the gods still walked among us, one of the high priests of Thoth fell into a trance for days. As he sat, neither eating nor drinking, he transcribed a vast message from one who called herself Zarpanitu, her message coming to him from across an unimaginable distance—carried to him past the heaven's immutable physical barriers by the power of her consciousness. I could scarce believe his words until he showed me the proof—aging scrolls filled with knowledge I could not read let alone comprehend. He instructed me to copy all of it onto fresh scrolls.

"Over the next months, as I worked through my task, ignorant of the symbols my brush so faithfully replicated, he told me when he was young an ancient sage had chosen him to do what he had instructed me to do, just as *that* sage had been chosen when he was young by another—the knowledge before me claimed to have been first transcribed two million years ago." He lifted his brow and sipped again. "A sacred task, indeed, which I bore with deep humility and honor. As I departed, I was instructed to guard this knowledge until the time would come for me to pass it on, unless of course it could be deciphered."

As Zherei finished his wine, Meresamun's gaze slid to the translation device sitting, innocuous, on the table, then fell to the satchel on the floor. "If you were meant to guard it, does that mean those are—?"

Zherei nodded. "They are."

"I wonder," she began, diffident, "if you might let me look at one? I have seen Zarpanitu's writings and know her symbols. If it truly was Zarpanitu who contacted one of your priests, I should be able to confirm it."

Zherei pulled one of the scrolls free. He set it before her, watching, intent, as she unrolled it. She glanced down, and caught her breath. She looked up at Zherei, hope scouring her. "It is her language," she breathed. Taking up the translation device, she woke it from its slumber and unrolled the scroll to the end.

"You read it from the end to the beginning," she murmured as she lay the device atop the symbols and waited for it to begin the translation.

Zherei leaned closer, intrigued. "What does this thing do?" he asked.

"It takes her words and translates them into my language," Meresamun said, pointing to the screen as it lit up. A stream of blue hieroglyphs assembled into coherence.

"How fascinating," Zherei murmured, reaching out to touch the corner of the device. "A wonder."

"It belongs to Marduk," Meresamun said, "he possesses many wonders like this, though most are weapons. Some are powerful enough to control those who would otherwise never serve him."

"Like Sethi?" Zherei asked, soft, his eyes meeting hers, clear, honest.

"Yes," Meresamun whispered. "Once, Sethi was valiant, noble, and honorable, until Marduk enslaved him."

"I heard him," Zherei said, as Meresamun slid the device along the first lines of the scroll. "Not long before we departed from his palace, he cried out in agony, begging the Creator for mercy, to be freed from what he has become."

Meresamun paused in her work. "Every dawn, just before the sun rises, he returns to his true self and remembers all he has wrought before the device claims him again," she shuddered. "His suffering must be unimaginable."

"So," Zherei murmured, "the question begs to be asked: is the jihn calling to *him*, or to the *device* controlling him?"

Meresamun didn't know what Zherei was talking about, but she didn't ask, the translation device occupied her full attention; she had forgotten how complicated Zarpanitu's thoughts were. She closed the scroll with a sigh.

"And?" Zherei asked.

"It is much the same as what I have read before," Meresamun said, condensing the message within. "Zarpanitu was sending out a message, asking those who heard her if they knew where she might find the origin of all creation, what she calls the Well of Life. She believed if the embodiment of darkness could be cast into it, every world would be cleansed of its taint. At least, that was her theory." She rolled up the scroll, handed it back, and waited for him to pass her another.

"The Well of Life," Zherei repeated, thoughtful. "I have never heard of such a thing, although, now I think of it, there is a place . . . hmmm." He rummaged through his satchel and pulled out another scroll, larger than the others, tied together with a leather strap. Pushing aside the platters, he unfurled it. A map.

Meresamun leaned closer, her fascination with Zherei's scrolls superseded by her desire to find her place in Elati, to lose her sense of rootlessness. "Is this Elati?" she breathed. She looked up at him. "Where are we?"

Zherei's forefinger came down on an empty spot at the far north of the largest of the map's two continents, among the cliffs overlooking a large bay. A vast mountain range surrounded the bay. Its peaks stretched deep into the land, far removed from civilization. Her heart sank. She was as isolated as she could possibly be.

"Perev," Zherei said. "When we landed, the twin moons and three great stars of the north were still bright enough for me to make rudimentary calculations." He glanced at her and confessed, "The constellations and movements of the heavenly bodies are somewhat of a passion of mine."

Meresamun's gaze returned to the place he had indicated. The bay soared out to the north toward a narrow, mountainous isthmus. Beyond that thin strip of land—nothing, just water, endless water. To the south, east, and west: mountains. She gazed up at the galleries of the upper floors of the library, at the elegance of her enormous gilded cage, endured the suffocating grip of claustrophobia. Without a ship, she would never escape, and the only ship in Elati was Marduk's. Her thoughts moved back to Zarpanitu's hidden message, charging her successor to find the Well of Life, to do what must be done. No. It was impossible.

She would never succeed. Not while trapped in this immutable fortress.

"I came upon this citadel while lost in a snowstorm," Zherei continued, breaking into Meresamun's bleak thoughts. "Even then, a thousand years ago, it had already lain abandoned for an age. Having come into the palace today from quite another way, I had forgotten about Perev until I entered the library, and recalled the three days I passed waiting for the storm to end, surrounded by a wealth of knowledge I could not read." He shook his head, eyeing the stacks laden with scrolls. "It was most exasperating."

Meresamun said nothing. She pulled the translation device to her and pressed the blue-lit indentation. The screen darkened.

Zherei leaned forward. "Have I said something amiss?"

Meresamun shook her head. "I am tired," she said. "Tired of seeking answers only to find I am still powerless." She pushed the device aside.

Zherei said nothing for a while. He sat back and considered her. She let him, uncaring of his perusal. He could not help her, no one could. Desolation surrounded her. A sudden longing for the past overwhelmed her. If only she could go back to when she had been granted her freedom. She would never have left Ahmen, would have remained with him. Even if they had succumbed to the world's unfolding destruction, it would have been better to have died in his arms, than this endless fall into darkness, lost and alone, forever.

Zherei shifted in his seat and pulled the map to him; with a heave he flipped it over. It slapped against the table, startling Tyrn. "I would like to show you something," he said. "It is the reason I brought out the map in the first place." Across the face of the map nothing but the wave tipped markings of a vast sea. In its center, a vortex had been inked. He pointed at it. "This is what I wanted you to see."

Meresamun eyed it. It was just a swirled marking. It meant nothing. "What am I supposed to be seeing?"

"One of the greatest mysteries Elati possesses." Zherei folded his hands together. "This is, to the best of our knowledge what the other side of Elati looks like. There is no land at all beyond the coasts of the continents and since the age of the gods, no boat has ever successfully traversed its girth."

"Because of the distance between the land?" Meresamun asked, despite her desire to retreat to her rooms and drown her despair in a pitcher of wine.

"Not necessarily, since crossings were possible before the gods disappeared. There are those of us who have calculated from the growing distortions in the constellations that this," he pointed again at the vortex, "has grown considerably larger since the gods vanished. During the time of the gods, it was noted in the center of the great sea there was an anomaly, described in various translations as both a 'golden sphere' and a 'thin, endless, black pillar' that breached the world itself." He glanced up at her, his eyes bright, warming to the subject. "Baffling, isn't it? How can whatever this is, be golden, black, a pillar, *and* a sphere all at the same time? It must be a mistake in our translation." He sighed and shook his head. "The texts we have regarding it are fragmentary, and were only discovered during my lifetime, buried deep in the caves of Pir, written in an ancient dialect of the sages. From them, we know this much: Whatever the anomaly is, it was considered to be more powerful than the gods. Much of the text was lost to us, but this much was decipherable—it warped time and space. Any who drew near to it vanished, never to return."

"And why would you show me this?" Meresamun asked, wondering why he would bother to share this with her. Mysteries such as these were far above her station.

Zherei shot her a warm look as he hauled the map back over, revealing once more the outlines of the continents and islands of Elati. He lowered his finger onto an island in the middle of the sea. "Anki," he said, reverent. "I have calculated it over and over, and am quite certain the vortex in the center of the sea aligns precisely with the center of Anki."

Meresamun looked up at him. "If that is so, why has no one found it? The distance to it from the continents is not insurmountable."

"Ah," Zherei continued, holding up a bony forefinger, "because Anki was the home of the gods. Since they vanished, Anki has been surrounded by violent storms. Only death awaits those who try to reach its shores. In the past, many did try." He lifted a brow. "I cannot blame them. Considering some of the wonders others have discovered scattered around Elati, it is tempting to imagine what other wonders still remain hidden within the walls of their citadels." He blinked. The animation slid from his face. He rolled up the map, abrupt.

Meresamun waited, wondering at his sudden change of mood. He tucked the map back into his satchel, his attention drifted to Tyrn, roosting, content.

He cut a look at Meresamun. "You say Zarpanitu sought out something called the Well of Life?"

She nodded.

"Everything points to Anki," he murmured. He rubbed his chin. "The 'origin of all creation' I believe you said she called it." He sniffed and scratched the side of his face. "If the anomaly *is* this Well of Life, then I suspect Anki is also where the jihn will be found." He let out a troubled sigh. "How dense of me not to see it. Anki is where it all began, where the Creator wrestled with himself. Everything came after."

"You have mentioned this word before," Meresamun said, her curiosity getting the better of her. "Jihn—what is it?"

His expression tightened. "Only a weapon of the darkest malevolence. It feeds on the light of the gods until it annihilates them."

Meresamun blinked. "But who could create such a thing, if even the gods are powerless against it?"

Zherei met her eyes. "The Creator."

"Re-Atum?" Meresamun floundered. "Why would he . . ." She couldn't finish the question. Could not comprehend it.

"Everything which lives," Zherei said, brushing the crumbs from the table, "possesses within them the traits of darkness and light. Why would the Creator not possess them, also? It is known to us when he came to life, he waged a war within himself and separated the darkness from his light, although he did not manage to contain it. The jihn belongs to the dark part of him. It created it with its own essence, in order to destroy the Creator we know and worship."

Meresamun stared at Zherei. Fragments of what she had read the night before drifted down and settled within her, coalescing into a horrible, terrifying whole. "Zarpanitu wrote she believed Marduk is the embodiment of the darkness which must be destroyed in the Well of Life," she breathed. "I didn't understand the magnitude of it then, but if she is correct . . . Are you saying the one who possesses me is the manifestation of the Creator's darkness?"

"I am saying the reason I am traveling with the god of war is because he intends to use my knowledge to find the jihn. That foul thing, hidden eons ago by the Creator, is calling to him," Zherei muttered. "I confess, when he told me that, I believed *he* was the darkness, but with all I have learned today I have no choice but to reconsider my assumption."

Dread sank its talons into Meresamun. "Meaning?"

"Meaning, I am convinced the one who controls the thing in Sethi's head is the true darkness. Marduk is using Sethi to find the jihn, and will use the weapon through him to finish what the darkness began so long ago—to feed the jihn until it becomes powerful enough to draw the Creator from his realm and consume his light. Nothing but darkness would be left to us. Nothing."

Meresamun sagged. Unlike Zherei's bald explanation, Zarpanitu had been careful, clever even, couching her words in euphemisms, focusing all her concerns on her changing heart, but between the lines, the warning was clear. Marduk was the darkness—drawn to the perfection of Zarpanitu's light, destined only to destroy it, as he was destined to destroy all light. And now, Meresamun stood in Zarpanitu's place, another light Marduk would extinguish—unless she stopped him first. Her responsibility bore down on her, onerous, devastating. She gagged, the burning heat of the contents of her stomach rebelling, unwilling to remain a part of her any longer.

She bolted from the table, clutching Tyrn's empty meat bowl, rank with the stink of stale blood. Behind one of the stacks, and out of sight of Zherei, she sank to her knees and vomited her meager meal of sweetbread, wine, and coffee. Burning bile followed. She continued to heave, wretched, desolation lapping over her in dark, fetid waves. Against her shins, the cold flagstones seeped an ancient, epochal chill. Footsteps approached. A hand, warm, dry, gentle, touched her shoulder.

"I have no doubt the days left to me are short," Zherei murmured. "The scrolls containing the writings of Zarpanitu are on my chair. When you are done your translations, hide them among these sacred scrolls. Perev was once the summer home of Thoth. I suspect the citadel's agelessness has been granted by the contents of this library, where, though the god of wisdom is long gone, the power imbued in his words have carried on. I cannot think of a better resting place for Zarpanitu's sacred message."

He squeezed her shoulder. "For doing me this favor, I will grant you a secret: There is another way out of this palace, apart from the use of a ship."

She glanced up, naked with hope.

"There is second palace in the citadel. It stands on the other side of a filigreed walkway which spans a bottomless chasm."

Meresamun's heart sank. Not the bridge. Not again. She nodded, dull. "I know it."

"Follow the staircase up the cliff that leads to a metal door, and through a tunnel. On the other side, the palace. Upon entering the great hall," Zherei continued, his eyes unfocusing as he mentally retraced his steps, "turn left and make your way into the southernmost wing. At its furthest reach, there is a room. On its far wall is a large mirror. I have no idea how it works, but you can step through it. On its opposite side, there is a circular stairway, hewed from out of the living rock of the mountain, illuminated by lights which never die. It is a very long walk down, so be prepared. At the bottom you will reach another mirror. Hold your breath and walk through it. You will emerge at the bottom of a pool within a cavern. When you leave the cavern you will no longer be anywhere near the palace, but in the mountains of Tyratu, which lies across the sea. I had taken shelter there during a fierce storm, but when a wild boar came in I fled into the cavern's depths, stumbled and fell into the pool, where I discovered the mirror." He smiled. "The rest was history."

Zherei offered her his hand. "Let me show you where Tyratu is." He led her back and unrolled the map. It was far. Very far. She gazed at the place. Freedom. Escape. She closed her eyes. No. It was a fantasy. There was no escaping Marduk.

"I suspect," Zherei said, lowering his voice, "there may be other mirrors hidden throughout this citadel which lead to other places in Elati, perhaps even to other worlds. I always intended to come back when I had more provisions, but my adventures always kept me from returning, and then, one day, it was too late. I had become an old man." He looked up at the galleries, a flicker of regret in his eyes. "Despite Perev's prestige, there is no question its lack of inhabitation over the ages means Thoth ensured even in his absence it would remain isolated from the encroach of mortals, although now, with Marduk as its new master, I can sense its protective power fading. Whether he is aware of what he is doing or not, I suspect your consort is feeding off the power which has enshrined Perev for eons."

The heavy click of a key turned in the door's lock.

Zherei bent and pulled a small wax tablet and stylus from his satchel. He wrote out a short word on it, its symbols the same as the ones used on the map. "I need to ask for your help," he said, going back to his satchel and rummaging again. "Copy this word, precisely as you see it onto a sliver of vellum, roll it up, and place it in this." He handed her a tiny scroll case bearing two leather ties. "Once Sethi has left, tie this to Tyrn's leg and set her free."

Zherei glanced at her as the door thudded closed and footsteps approached. He held out the gauntlet. She eyed it, aware he had given her no details, or what danger she might be putting herself into, and yet as his look of urgency deepened, she accepted he had been kind to her, and had shared many profound and perhaps even useful secrets with her. She nodded. "I will do it."

Gratitude flooded his eyes. The footsteps neared. "May I have the map?" she asked, her heart aching at the thought of losing it. She longed to learn the language written upon it, to memorize the names and places of the world in which she had become imprisoned.

"Of course. I doubt it will be of any use where I am going."

Marduk's steward approached. He caught sight of Meresamun. Uncertainty slid over his features. He bowed low. "Great Lady, I did not realize I had locked you in here with Lord Sethi's advisor. I beg you, forgive me."

"Lord Marduk shall decide whether you will be forgiven or not," she said, pleased to see the steward's color blanch, the stark fear tainting his eyes. Even so, she did not trust the steward to keep his mouth shut. Sooner or later Marduk would know the truth, as he always did. "Leave the bird," she continued, as Zherei feigned his intention to put on the gauntlet. "I would have it for myself."

The steward escorted Zherei from Meresamun, ignoring the old man's cries of outrage over having to relinquish Tyrn. The door opened and thudded closed again. No key this time. Zherei's shouts of protest faded. Silence washed over her. She shivered, alone once more, already missing her learned companion.

The scrolls peeked up at her from within the depths of Zherei's chair, both innocent and damning. She wasted no time. Marduk would seek her out once Sethi departed, bearing gifts stolen from the lands Sethi had conquered. She would need to be quick.

Gathering up the map and scrolls, she hunted through the stacks of the library for a place to hide them. In one of the far corners, she found a little space locked deep in shadow. Making certain to remember where she had secreted them, she retraced her steps back to the table, collected the wax tablet and tiny scroll case and tucked them into her gown. She eyed the gauntlet. Never before had she used one. After several failed attempts, at last she secured its ties against her arm.

Tyrn stepped onto the gauntlet, docile, a quiet trill rippling in her throat, endearing herself to her new mistress. For a heartbeat, as Meresamun stroked the soft feathers of the falcon's breast, she flirted with the thought of keeping the bird and not setting her free with the mysterious message tied to her leg. It was only one word. How could it hold so much importance that she would need to relinquish such a fine companion? No. She would keep Tyrn for herself. This fine falcon would ease her loneliness. Perhaps she could learn to hunt with her—

Meresamun blinked, taken aback by the direction of her thoughts, by their utter lack of honor. She had given Zherei her word. His look of gratitude had told her all she needed to know: His message, though simple, would mean everything to someone. She eyed the falcon, morose. So this was what Zarpanitu had meant when she wrote about the seductive encroach of Marduk's darkness. Meresamun shuddered, horrified by its insidious creep. She had believed it would come from without, something she could see and resist. Instead, it came from within. It slid into her thoughts, hijacking them, until she didn't know where her thoughts ended and her consort's influence began.

She wasn't like Zarpanitu, *her* inner strength wasn't comparable to Marduk's first consort's, who had been capable of holding out against him for an extraordinary period of time. How could one such as she resist a darkness so powerful, its mere presence stripped the deep, ancient power from Thoth's once-citadel? Her thoughts tormenting her, she fled from the place where she had shared her story with a total stranger, realizing she was no wiser to her path than when she entered. Forcing her troubled thoughts to silence, she opened the library's door, and peeked into the empty corridor. For now, it was enough for her to keep her promise. Her senses prickling with dread, she ran.

Marduk's warship tore a line of smoke and fire across the chasm. Within her suite, Meresamun's fingers trembled as she strove to copy the bizarre symbols from Zherei's wax tablet, sacrificing precious heartbeats to double-check she had not made any mistakes before smoothing over the wax impressions and tucking the missive into the minuscule scroll case. The falcon waited, patient, as she fumbled to tie the scroll case's straps against its leg, her fingers clumsy with haste, dogged by the looming sensation of Marduk's impending arrival.

At the terrace's edge, she pulled away the jesses. The bird hunched down, her body taut, prepared to launch. Cautious, Meresamun pulled the braces, plucked the top knot, and struck the hood. For the briefest heartbeat she glimpsed the keen, diurnal blink of the falcon's gaze as it adapted to the light. Downward pressure slammed against her arm, followed by a startling burst of air. Its wake washed over her, cold and crisp. Her heart pounding, Meresamun shaded her eyes against the glare of the sun. Tyrn soared into the blue depths of Perev's sky and wheeled in a slow arc, toward the vast mountain chain Meresamun now knew barricaded Perev from the rest of the world. She envied the falcon, her heart aching as the bird diminished with distance, wondering where she would go, and to whom she would carry

Zherei's message. Tyrn shrank to a blur, then a speck, then a dot. Then, nothing. Emptiness poured into Meresamun.

A heartbeat of hesitation as Meresamun eyed the intricate, artisanal beauty of the falcon's hood. Though she would have liked to have kept it as a memento, it would be too dangerous. With a stab of regret, she tossed the falcon's hood over the edge of the terrace. It tumbled into the chasm's savage depths, forsaken, forlorn.

She turned her attention to the ties of the gauntlet. Its knots tangled and tightened. A pounding came to her door. Guards announced Marduk's arrival. She hauled at the snarled ties, frantic, desperate to free herself from the heavy glove. Her door opened. Footsteps echoed. Marduk called her name. Her heart thudded, his voice a lodestone to her soul, betraying her, drawing her to him, even now, even after knowing what he was. The gauntlet jerked free. She let it fall into the chasm and turned to face her oppressor, her lover, her consort. Her enemy.

He emerged onto the terrace clad in his black armor, exuding wealth and power, trailed by a convoy of servants laden with the most desirable of spoils from Sethi's conquests. Her consort gave her a private look which devastated her defenses. He strode across the terrace, eyeing her, dominant, possessive, soaked in charisma, charm, elegance. Though she hated herself for it, she let him take her in his arms, let him press his lips to hers, let him claim her anew—losing her battle to him before she had even begun, sensing her light succumbing as always to his ardor, her heart unable, no—unwilling to stop her fall.

Horus eyed the sun as it plunged into the horizon. The gloaming deepened. Across the city, dark windows awakened in the flickering warmth of lamplight. Within a few more heartbeats, the stars would erupt, a glitter of white against a canopy of obsidian. Horus still wasn't used to it. He turned his back to the fleeing sun and gazed at the purple and pink hues of the darkling skies. Five days ago Zherei had left with Tyrn. Five long days of watching, waiting, hoping. Horus raked his eyes over the heavens, vigilant, his grip tight against the terrace's rail. *Come home.*

Over the last days, he had examined Elati's map until his head ached, had spent hours calculating distances and flying times until he was able to estimate Tyrn's arrival from every corner of the world. He had asked whether Elati's falcons could cross the Adriande Sea without sustenance. The mews master had confirmed it, adding each nation was bound by an ancient Elatian decree to feed those falcons which landed on their boats. Tyrn would come home. Eventually. And yet, doubt prevailed. Questions piled up in Horus's mind, tormented him, antagonized him.

At night, dark dreams thrust him from sleep, leaving him to pace the rooms and corridors of his luxurious villa in an anguish of uncertainty. The day after Sethi departed, the queen had offered Horus the keys to a sumptuous three-storied villa, admitting she hoped Serde might gain the Creator's protection if it bestowed favor to the once-gods of war and healing. Horus had thanked her, but promised nothing. How could he? He was as mortal as she—the Creator as far removed from him as the stars.

Never before had he felt this vulnerable, or as dependent on the passage of external events out of his control. Apart from the choice to retreat to the Immortal Realm—a choice he and the other gods had made to protect their world from Marduk's annihilation—he had remained untouched by the travails of mortals, his position immune to the horrors of their existence. He shuddered. How could they bear it? He hated everything about mortality, longed for the return of his power, his immutability. Baalat had come to terms with her fate far better than he, her wealth of knowledge and skills a sop to her lost light. But him? No, he had had his wings clipped hard. He had been the god of war, of blood, heroism, and death. No longer could he face an adversary knowing he would survive no matter how grave the blows against his body. Now he could fall, just like any man, and leave Baalat alone, and unprotected. It was unthinkable, unbearable.

As he had walked, unseeing, through his new home, the long nights had proved a cruel mistress, shredding his hopes his plan would work. What if Zherei had not had a chance to see the sky, or Tyrn had been taken from him? What if Zherei was already dead? What if the plan had been uncovered, what would befall Serde for her treachery? There were too many variables, too many ways to fail.

His heart heavy, he continued to scan the noctilucent clouds, bleak, his hopes for Tyrn's arrival fading fast. Below, the city barely stirred even though the hour was still early. Quiet despair seeped from Ikalur's walls. Hopelessness and defeat plagued the hearts of men. Fear preyed on their thoughts, just as it did to his. He had seen this before—during the wars of gods and men—as one nation after another succumbed to Marduk's dark sway. Wherever he went, he sowed doubt, created chaos, then devastation, blaming innocents for what his weapons had wrought, only to turn around and offer mercy, a dark savior—the price for his reprieve, brutal, crippling. His greatest weapon was fear. He planted conspiracies, uncertainty, lies, and suspicions. He divided and conquered, letting others do his dirty work while he sat back and waited, watching, amused, as men poisoned themselves on hate and tribalism. They would go to him to arbitrate their disputes, unaware they had been warring over nothing more than whispers, rumors, fakery, and deceptions, all started by him. In those dark years, truth curled up and died, along with hundreds of thousands of innocent lives. And now, it had begun again. This time, Marduk could not be killed, and Horus could, and there would be no escape to an Immortal Realm. Horus ground his teeth. He needed Tyrn to come home. Just to know where Marduk was. It would be a start. He waited. The stars blossomed. Darkness reigned.

With a low curse, Horus tore his gaze from the night sky and glanced at the city, sensing Marduk's foul taint already spreading, of men turning against each other, father against son, wife against husband, friend against friend.

He made his way back into the mews, eyeing Tyrn's empty perch, his heart tight, a new fear rising to torment him, of Zherei being forced to admit the truth—Tyrn's life taken from her in revenge for Horus's half-baked plan. Guilt cascaded through him. Not the falcon. Not her.

He picked up the covered bowl, and checked its contents. The meat was still fresh, a runner had brought it up only a little while before, replacing the previous bowl, as had been done over and over for the last days, and would continue to be done until she returned.

If she returned.

Horus silenced the traitorous thought, refused to entertain it. With the bowl of meat still held in his hand, he returned to the rail, drawn to the place of his vigil, a moth to a flame.

He ran his eyes over the sky again, the sweep of his search familiar, automatic. Against the starlight to the north, a flicker of darkness eclipsed the brightest star. Horus held his breath, raw with hope. Another star dimmed and brightened, then another, then two stars, three. Let it be Tyrn, he willed, clenching the base of the wooden bowl so hard it cracked.

The faint beat of wings. A far-off piercing cry. A greeting. Horus knew that cry. Relief poured through him, his heart pounded, escaped its long restraint, fierce, exultant.

"Tyrn," he breathed as she swept closer, ephemeral, the starry glint of the heavens illuminating her pale feathers. "Tyrn!" he cried, raising his gauntleted arm, triumphant, as she tore down from the skies to him, her talons outstretched. She hit his arm, heavy, reassuring, and let out another keening cry, tainted with urgency, tilting her head toward the covered bowl.

With soft words of praise, Horus carried Tyrn into the mews and settled her on her perch. Fastening her jesses, he slipped on her hood and let her select one of the morsels in the bowl. She attacked it, ravenous. Though he longed to removed the scroll case, he waited, giving her time to eat, examining her for injury. She looked thinner, but otherwise herself. He let out a quiet exhalation. She was home. Safe. His vigil was over. And now, he would learn where his nemesis kept his lair. He pulled the scroll case free and opened it. Inside, written in a crude hand, one word. He furrowed his brow. Perev? He had never seen that name before. He went to the map and scanned it, searching through the northern kingdoms, from where Tyrn had arrived.

No location called Perev existed in the north of Tholis. He checked the west, then the island of Senas to the east. Nothing. He eyed the scrap of thin vellum between his fingers, the script written not in the hand of a sage, but what looked like the hand of a child, the curves overly rounded. Splatters of ink stained the edges of the letters. He eyed the map, sour. Perev didn't exist. His gaze moved across the sea to the continent of Chaus. Even though he already knew Tyrn could never have flown all the way from Chaus in such a short time, he persisted, stubborn, poring over the valleys, plains, and mountains of its kingdoms, though he was not surprised when his search turned up fruitless.

He pressed his lips together, bitterness assailing him. He had been sent a meaningless answer. Sethi must have learned of his intent. But why would Sethi have bothered to return the bird, and with a nonsense message? The answer slammed into him like the drop of an anchor. Because Sethi didn't send the bird back. Marduk did—the message clear in his cryptic response. *You will never find me.*

Sickened, Horus turned his back to the map and offered Tyrn some water. There was nothing left for him to do but face the queen. He had failed. Bleak, furious, he began the long descent through the tower, Marduk's mocking message buried deep within his fist.

Within the empty reception of the queen's apartment, Horus waited. He eyed the space, noting its return to opulence, the memory of its destruction denied by the quiet beauty reflected in the hall's gold-gilt mirrors. Soft lamplight imbued the reception with warmth, yet despite its orderly calm, a quiet despair permeated the space. He glanced at the pillar where one of the queen's women had clung to it, resisting the grip of a soldier, intent on sacrificing her to Sethi. She had not escaped the twelve. Horus had seen her ascend the steps of the ship quaking with terror, her gown torn and disheveled, her face swollen and stained from weeping.

He pulled his gaze from the pillar, sickened. Her presence may have been erased from this room but somewhere her life went on, trapped in the merciless grip of a corrupted god, as he, Horus, stood waiting—the once-immutable god of war, mortal and powerless—to reveal his useless information to the queen.

Footsteps whispered against the marble tiles. Queen Welyn ascended the two steps to her seat, though she remained standing, a loose robe tied at the waist, her long hair unbound and hanging to her hips. She folded her hands before her.

"Tyrn has returned?"

Horus nodded and opened his fist. He plucked out the scrap of vellum and handed it to her, silent.

She took it and gazed at it. "Perev," she breathed. She glanced at Horus. Her look flickered toward disbelief. He waited, bracing himself for her ire. It did not come. Instead, after a long silence she called one of her guards. He came to her and knelt.

"Send for Master Iyun," she said. "And," she continued as the guard rose and pressed his fist to his chest, "send a message to the king, requesting our permission to see him."

As her guard departed, the queen looked back down at the piece of vellum between her elegant fingers. She stroked its inked letters, reverent. Horus waited, wondering what he was missing.

While they waited for Iyun to arrive, the queen said nothing, her eyes remained distant, turned inward, traveling paths known only to her.

Hurried footsteps approached. An elderly, gray-haired man clad in a white robe tied over his shoulder approached the queen and knelt.

"My queen," he said, his voice elegant, yet warm. "How may I serve you?"

She held out the message to him. He rose and took it with both hands, quick, despite the evidence of his age.

"Perev," he read. He looked up at her, bland. "What is it you wish of me, my lady?"

"Now that Master Zherei has left us," she answered, folding her hands before her once more, "you are Serde's most learned of sages. Tonight, the fate of Elati may well rest upon your shoulders."

Iyun made a gesture of humility, though a hint of color touched his cheeks, betraying his pleasure at her words.

"We know your order keeps many secrets," the queen continued, "and for good reasons, but in this instance, we must ask you to consider breaching your oath for the sake of Elati's survival."

The color slid from Iyun's face. "My lady," he dithered, "the order's oaths are sacred. I—"

"We command it."

Consternation billowed from him. She waited. He bowed his head. "As my queen commands."

"Do you recognize that name?" she asked, nodding at the piece of vellum in the sage's fingers.

He hesitated, feigning consideration, but Horus caught Iyun's look, that of an animal trapped, desperate, afraid.

"Answer your queen," Horus said, moving closer.

Iyun shot him a cold look, filled with resentment. Horus narrowed his eyes, sensing the sage searched for a middle way between obeying the queen and keeping his oath.

"My lady," Iyun began, "Perev is known to me only from conversations with Master Zherei. There is nothing I am aware of which has been written about it."

Horus glared at Iyun. The man was a coward.

The sage ignored him, continuing, "Once, over a flask of wine, Master Zherei regaled me with tales of when he was a young sage and had traveled the length and breadth of Elati in search of the most learned sages." He rubbed the back of his neck, and glanced at the queen, uncertain. "He mentioned a palace he found which had been preserved from the time of the gods, locked in the northernmost mountains of Kium, inaccessible by either land or sea."

The queen's brow lifted. "Then . . . how did he manage to find it?"

Iyun let out a nervous chuckle. "He, ah, well—he said he fell into a pool in a cavern in Tyratu and at the bottom of it there was, ehm, a mirror?"

"There was a mirror in a pool?" Queen Welyn repeated, dubious.

Iyun nodded. "So he claimed. And then he said the most remarkable thing happened, he went to the mirror, because, well he was curious. And then—forgive me, but this part struck me as very odd—he said he was able to go *through* the mirror which led all the way across the sea to Kium, to the fabled summer palace of the god of wisdom known as Perev."

"Good old Thoth," Horus erupted, jubilant. Perev was real after all. "He does love his portals."

Silence greeted him. Iyun glared at him. "Did you just utter the god of wisdom's sacred name?"

"I did," Horus answered, folding his arms over his chest. "I take it you have heard of him?"

"Heard of—?" Iyun erupted, bristling with indignation. "It is *he* whom our order venerates. And you, you heathen, toss his name around as if he were your *drinking* companion." He turned to the queen. "My lady, I beg you, I cannot bear to be in this man's presence." He sniffed and put his back to Horus, rigid, his affront tangible.

The queen suppressed a smile. "I suggest you do not judge a man by his cover, there is more to Lord Horus than meets the eye. It is because of him we have the information you hold in your hand."

Iyun eyed Horus over his shoulder, baleful, offence bleeding from him. "*Horus?* Even your name is sacrilege. You youngsters these days," he ranted, "you have no respect, society has gone to the dogs. How dare you name yourself after Lord Horakhti."

Horus blinked. "Never heard of him."

"How could you never—" Iyun gaped, incredulous. "Have you been living under a rock your whole life?"

Horus glanced at the queen, wondering when she might intervene. "Something like that," he muttered.

"You will show us where Perev is," the queen said, drawing Iyun's attention back to the matter at hand. She went to a desk set against the wall and opened the top drawer. From within, she extracted a large scroll held closed with a red-tasseled cord. She carried it back and handed it to Iyun. He knelt and unfurled it.

An elegant, detailed map of Tholis lettered in gold shimmered in the lamplight. Iyun rubbed his jaw, contemplating the vast mountainous range girdling all of Kium's northern coast.

"It was quite some time ago when we had this conversation," he said. "I do recall him giving me the location, since he had calculated its position using the stars and spent a great deal of time explaining his methodology. Hmmm." He glanced at the queen's empty terrace, its braziers unlit in mourning for her lost women. "May I?"

Queen Welyn nodded. Iyun slipped onto the darkened terrace and gazed up at the glittering canopy of constellations, muttering to himself as he held his thumb up to the heavens, measuring. After a short while, he returned and stared at the map. He held out his forefinger, and lowered it, slow, onto a spot on the south side of a bay in Kium, at the edge of the mountains. "To the best of my knowledge," he said, "it should be there, or very nearly. I have had to take into account the stars' precession, since he told me this more than eight hundred years ago."

The queen nodded, pleased. "You have done well," she said. "And now, where in Tyratu is the cavern with its mirror which leads into the palace?"

A pained look crossed Iyun's face. "That I cannot say, my lady," he said.

"Cannot," Horus demanded, "or will not?"

"Cannot," Iyun repeated. "Master Zherei refused to tell me. He said those who were meant to find it, would. He refused to risk the pillaging of the sacred library of the once-home of the god of wisdom. He thought it better to leave it hidden, as intended." He looked back down at the map, and continued, diffident, "May I ask why Perev is important to our queen? I cannot comprehend how the god of wisdom's once-home could be connected with

Elati's survival. Perhaps my lady seeks an ancient text?" He cut a look at her, hopeful.

"Not at this time," the queen answered, taking the scrap of vellum from him. "You have served us well. You will not speak of this meeting to anyone, on pain of death."

Iyun paled. "Of course," he said, bowing his head, "you may be assured of my utmost discretion." He backed three steps, shot an uncertain look at Horus and left.

When the quiet thud of her door echoed from the corridor, the queen looked at Horus.

"Tell me," she said, soft, "do you believe in miracles?"

Horus didn't believe in miracles, but he had been spared the trouble of replying. The queen had left, bidding him wait while she prepared to meet with the king. Now, Horus stood just inside the closed door of the private study of the king, waiting as the king and queen conferred, quiet, at the opposite end of the dark, wood-paneled room. The queen held out the message carried south by Tyrn. The king's reaction revealed he had known nothing of their plan. Horus wondered if she had expected it to fail.

The king gazed at the letters written on the vellum, silent. His wife spoke again, fervent, gesturing toward the floor, then at Horus. King Rhewyn glanced up, sharp, at Horus, then back at the vellum. The muscles of his jaw worked. Tension bled from him. The queen touched her husband's hand, her tone changing, becoming urgent, persuasive. Fragments of her entreaty reached Horus. *Choice. Try. Sign.*

The king shook his head. She stepped closer, and whispered into her husband's ear. He looked again at Horus, taking his time examining him, considering him. He exhaled, and murmured a few words. The queen's face softened. Whatever she had requested, she had gotten it. Perhaps this was the miracle, Horus mused, a queen's ability to change a king's mind.

Impassive, King Rhewyn motioned for Horus to approach.

"Our queen has revealed to us the successful conclusion of your plan to learn the location of the enemy of Elati," he said as Horus neared them and bowed his head. "We congratulate you on your quick thinking." Horus looked up. King Rhewyn's gaze dropped to the scrap bearing the solitary, momentous word. "And now, we have a choice," he continued, low, as if to himself, "do we trust you, and risk our meager hold on stability, or do we cower here, and do nothing?"

He handed the note to the queen. She took it, subdued, uncertain.

"I was a coward," the king said, meeting his wife's eyes. "I knelt when one of my guards would not. I should have defied Marduk's demands and died that day, but I could not bear to leave my queen alone and defenseless. When the king of Thes Dios refused to kneel, Lord Sethi killed him and took Queen Urah for himself. She vowed to take her life, swore he would never have her." He reached out and touched Welyn's cheek, tender, the dark circles surrounding his eyes accentuated by the flickering flames of the lamps. "I could not sacrifice you to such a fate. But now—" he dropped his hand and turned to Horus, abrupt, his expression hardening "—the time for cowardice is over. Follow me." He turned and went to one of the panels along the wall. He ran his fingers along its edge. A click and the panel eased from the wall.

The king cut a look at Horus, cold, calculating. "Queen Welyn has vouched for you, claims you are more than who you appear to be. What lies below is Serde's most powerful relic, not even the sages know of its existence. It is a secret which has been passed down from king to king since time immemorial. A secret which must be kept at any cost, *unless* a miracle happens. Below, you will face a test. If you are able to pass it, the miracle will have been confirmed. If not, your life shall be taken, regardless of the aid you have given Serde thus far. Do you understand?"

Horus eyed the panel, open no more than a finger's span. It revealed nothing except a thick, inky darkness. Within the study, the lamps' flames wavered, caught in a cold draft, a rare thing in the continual warmth of Ikalur. An epochal silence seeped from the depths, oppressive, weighing of eons.

"I would prefer to know what the test is before I commit my life against it," he said, his senses awakening, tingling in the presence of something *other*. It called to him, like a buried memory, longing to resurrect.

Rhewyn narrowed his eyes. "The queen says you claim to have been the god of war. Have you told the truth?"

Horus nodded, slow. "I have."

Rhewyn pulled the panel open. A gust of cold, stale air washed over Horus. "Then you have nothing to fear." He picked up a lamp, its flame bobbing as he entered the corridor and glanced back at Welyn, who hung back, uncertain. Rhewyn held out his hand to her. A shimmer of pleasure rippled over her fine features as she went to him and took it.

Horus held back one heartbeat. Two. With a curse he followed them, hoping he wasn't making the worst mistake of his existence.

Rhewyn led them down a long, circular, stone stairway, his tiny flame the only light in a well of black. Claustrophobia skidded around Horus, oppressing him with the sensation he was walking into his tomb.

They continued on until he thought he could hear the faint crash of waves against the shore. He strained to hear over their quiet footsteps; beyond the soft breathing of the queen, his own rasping breaths, and those of Rhewyn. There. A low boom, dulled by the weight of the stone, followed by the familiar roar of waves slamming against a rocky shore.

The stairs ended. Rhewyn and the queen came to a halt. Neither spoke, though reverence suffused them. The king turned and lifted his lamp to the stone wall and moved along its length. Massive ashlars greeted him, easily the width of two men, their height impossible to gauge in the weak light of a single flame.

He continued, his eyes moving over the smooth stone wall. He stopped and lifted the lamp higher. Horus edged closer, curious. A metal covering lay flush against the stone. The king pressed his fingers against it. The cover opened without a sound. Inside, cerulean blue light poured into a sigil. Its form took shape, slow, stately. Horus stared, incredulous. No. It couldn't be.

The king pressed his hand against the lit sigil. White light shattered the darkness. Horus shielded his eyes, impatient for them to adapt to the clean, clear light. Beside him, the wall soared up as high as a four story villa. He turned. A massive stone chamber faced him, constructed of fine-cut ashlars as large as a villa. And there, in the center of the space, silent, and alone—a memory returned to life.

"How can it be?" he breathed. He tore his eyes from it and cut a look at Rhewyn, his heart pounding so hard, it hurt. "I never thought—" He ran to it, crying out, tears burning his eyes. He touched it, reveling in the feel of it, real again, no longer a thought, but resurrected from the ephemeral fragments of his lost existence. He ran his hands along its side, worshipful. It was as beautiful, as perfect as he remembered. He pressed his hand against the sigil beside the door. It slid open and the stairs unfolded, seamless, just as they had always done. Within the cabin, the lights flickered on, white, and soft, welcoming him just like he remembered. He caught sight of the metal gate leading out of the chamber toward the sea, as familiar to him as the one he had once had in his city, long ago, before Marduk had arrived to tear his world apart—

Realization slammed into him. In Elati, Ikalur had been his city. Of all the places the Creator could have sent them—

He shouted, triumphant, longing to once more cross the skies with Baalat by his side. To think all this had unfolded simply because he had had the wit to send a falcon along with Zherei. He clenched his fists, invigorated, renewed. With his ship restored to him, he was no longer powerless. It was not over yet. Not by a long shot.

He turned. Serde's king and queen regarded him, pale, trembling.

Rhewyn sank to his knees. "Forgive me," he breathed, tears glinting in his eyes. "I dared not allow myself to hope my queen had spoken true when she said: '*The Creator has sent Lord Horakhti to us in our greatest hour of need.*'" He lowered his head, his chest rising and falling, his composure lost.

"Since the gods were vanquished two million years ago," Welyn whispered, "this ship has remained locked in utter silence." Tears slipped from her eyes as she gazed, awestruck, at Horus and his ship, resurrected after its slumber of eons. "It is a miracle." She sank to her knees. Another tear slipped free. "*You* are the miracle."

✳   ✳   ✳

A low boom woke Baalat. She sat up, abrupt, startled, disoriented. A pile of medical notes tumbled from her desk, carpeting the marble tiles around her in a sea of parchment. She blinked, struggling to regain her bearings. Gathering up the notes still left on the desk, she scanned her mind for her most recent memory. Ah, yes. In the midst of making notes about a treatment for burns, an overwhelming need for sleep had overcome her, leading her straight into a vivid, profound dream. She had found herself back in the Creator's realm, walking hand in hand with him across the starry disk, under a glittering canopy of stars and planets, his presence reassuring, calming, peaceful.

Heavy footsteps hastened through the courtyard, she ignored their approach, seeking to grasp the fading tendrils of her dream. What was it the Creator had said just before she had been torn away from her dream? It had been important.

Fragments glimmered, like the silver fish in the courtyard's pool, darting up to her, flashing between her fingers, only to slip away, elusive. The footsteps neared, echoing along the colonnaded

corridor, quickening, urgent. She closed her eyes, willing herself
to recall the Creator's parting words before it was too late. More
flickers, remnants, shadows. A glimpse. She held still. It came,
like a sunburst through a raincloud.

For the darkness to fall, the goddess must rise.

Baalat shivered. Her skin prickled, prescience surrounding her
as the power of the Creator's words imprinted themselves into her
heart, indelible. His message, like everything else about him, was
cryptic. But if he had taken the trouble to send her into a deep
sleep to give her a message, it meant much, but, she wondered,
humbled, as she bent to collect her fallen notes, what could it—

Horus burst into her study, his eyes afire, and his body
quivering with energy, alive, fierce, as though he has just returned
from the battlefield. He crossed the room in two strides and
pulled her from her chair.

"My love," he breathed, "just wait until you see this."

Baalat let go of Horus's hand, and stared, disbelieving, at a lost
piece of her past. It stood, proud, fierce and beautiful upon a
massive ashlar floor far beneath the palace of Ikalur. Its presence
filled her mind, solid, real. The king and queen knelt, their diadems glinting in the sconces' brilliant white light, its illumination
a remnant of an age long gone, vanished amongst the ashes of
another life, one she believed forever lost.

She approached the ship, rapt. Its golden contours gleamed,
brilliant. Awakened by Horus's presence, it thrummed, ready to
depart. A streamer of white light pulsed along its hull.

She touched it, reverent. Tears burned her eyes. Horus came
up behind her.

"The Creator left us outside Ikalur on purpose," he said, low.
"Again, he has aided us in our fight, although the key which
turned the lock was a humble one—a mere falcon."

Baalat said nothing. Her heart overflowed. Gratitude poured
through her. How she missed the power of flight. To leave the

ground—to fly free. Horus moved in front of her and held out his hand, his eyes dark, unreadable. She touched her fingers to his, trembling with anticipation and followed him into his ship—into the past. Present. Future.

The gate slid back into the wall. Horus guided the ship through the opening onto a massive, crumbling, mossy platform, jutting out a quarter of the way up the cliff wall. Baalat leaned forward and peered out the window. Below, Ikalur's starlit turquoise sea seethed against the sheer northern face of Ikalur's ancient foundations, gobbets of white foam speckling the mollusk-encrusted rocks.

"Are you ready, my love?" Horus asked, his attention fixed on the console, his fingers moving over the controls, confident, as though more than one million years had not separated him from the last time his fingers had guided his ship through the heavens.

"Yes," Baalat breathed, turning her face up to the star-clad skies, longing to feel its embrace. "Oh, yes."

He punched the ignition. A familiar roar filled her senses, laden with nostalgia. They shot away from the platform, the thrust pinning Baalat to her seat. The ship's walls rippled as Horus engaged the cloaking device, then shimmered as its walls and floor turned translucent. Far below, Ikalur dwindled, its torchlit gold and white sprawl shrinking, the importance of their lives played out within its walls paling against the scope of the continent's shadowed bulk spreading away to the north, west, and south.

Horus veered toward the endless reach of the sea.

"Where are we going?" she asked.

He enabled one of the screens on the console. A map appeared. He pointed to a spot far to the north of Ikalur, nestled at the southern edge of a bay. "Eventually, Perev. Once Thoth's summer palace, now Marduk's stronghold," he said. "It is only accessible by air, however we know there is at least one way in via a hidden portal in Tyratu. Knowing Thoth, I suspect there are other portals into it as well." Her consort then pointed at an island in the middle of the map. "And this is Anki. Long ago, it was the home of the gods. Since they were vanquished, a violent storm has raged around it, making it impossible to reach, at least by sea. No one has been there in two million years. We are going there first."

"And what do you hope to find in Anki?" Baalat asked, eyeing the map, curious what the once-home of her Elatian counterparts would be like.

"A weapon Sethi wants which I intend to find first," Horus said, his voice hard. "And hopefully, another portal into Marduk's stronghold. If I can find a way in he doesn't know about it would grant us a great advantage." He punched a few more buttons, flicked several switches. He stood and held out his hand.

"It's a long flight," he said, his voice low. He glanced into the cabin, toward the divan, where, as they had flown across the heavens of another world he had made love to her more times than she could count.

She stood and took his hand, her body awakening, quivering with anticipation, recognizing in his eyes the promise of what was to come. He led her from the flight deck and across the clear floor, the faint ridges and ripples of the dark sea an endless, shifting carpet. At the divan, he paused. She sensed his thoughts. It could never be the same now they were no longer gods.

His dark eyes moved over her face, erased of their golden light. Horus, but not Horus. The fractals had long since vanished, but to Baalat, he was still a god. Her god. He kissed her, deep, his hands cradling her face, reverent, as he whispered how much he loved her, how she was everything to him, and how at last, they would defeat Marduk. She sighed and sank onto the divan and let him love her, the stars their sole companions, just as they once were, long, long ago.

It was an elaborate yet beautiful ritual. From atop a golden tray, the once-god of wisdom opened various ceramic pots filled with the warmth of herbs and spices and placed a scant measure of each into a little alabaster bowl. From other pots, he added minuscule dried leaves and tiny blossoms of roses. He mixed them together, their floral, spiced scent reaching Istara, warm and appealing. With a quick look to see if she was watching, he lifted a small silver ball pierced with minute star-shaped holes and cracked it open. It split into two perfect halves held together by a delicate hinge. In one half, he tipped in the mixture. He closed the ball with a little snap.

Catching her look of curiosity, he smiled as he lifted the lid of a ceramic pot perched atop a burner and dropped the ball in. "It's called a diffuser. The boiled water can steep in the concoction without the water becoming full of little bits. It's quite clever." He replaced the lid and lowered the burner's flame.

He leaned back, his bony elbows stark against the wooden arms of his chair. "There now." He folded his hands together and tilted his head at the pot. "All there is left for us to do is wait until the water has brewed, and then you shall be in for a treat." His gaze moved over her, seeking a way past her silent walls.

Istara was not ready. Not yet. She turned her attention to the profusion of his geraniums clothing his terrace in a riot of reds, pinks, whites, and purples. Fat bees drifted between them, languid in the heat of Imaru's late-afternoon sun.

"My lady," Thoth broached, the quiet between them soothed by the gentle hum of the bees, "it has been six days since we returned with the cores. Since then you have come to visit me every afternoon, yet have said very little."

"Must one always have a reason to visit a friend?" Istara countered with a faint smile.

"With me," Thoth said, dry, "as a rule, yes." His gaze flicked to his desk, overflowing with scrolls and maps. For a heartbeat his mien thinned with worry. After all they had endured retrieving the cores, it had been a bitter pill to realize sourcing a location for their sanctuary had turned out to be much more difficult than expected. Thoth fretted as the gods returned unable to find what he required: An isolated, remote location with an abundance of granite, and a plateau large enough to bear three new pyramids to house the cores. Each day he complained a little louder about the time it would take to construct them, even with the help of the gods.

The once-god of wisdom blinked, cleared his throat, and continued, "You are, of course, a rare exception," he said. She turned her attention back to the geraniums, unwilling to take the bait.

A quiet exhalation. "Lady Istara, anyone with eyes can see you bear a great burden. You need not carry your pain alone. Perhaps I might be able to grant you some clarity?"

"Hm," Istara murmured, non-committal, lowering her gaze to the brew pot and its little flame, noting the warm, sweet, spiced scent of cloves, and something else, sharp, peppery—what she recognized as ginger. The Imarians made a sweet bread of it, which she had discovered she loved.

Thoth waited, patient, but Istara said no more. Each day since their return she had come to him, determined to find out the truth, to wrest from him the missing pieces of her past, and each time she had left, unable to bring herself to begin—to throw open the doors to her condemnation.

Outside the bulwark of her isolation, Thoth busied himself with selecting two ceramic cups and setting them before him. He lifted the pot from the stand and poured a bronze-tinted brew. He handed her one of the cups. She held it at the top, the sides too hot to touch, and breathed in the content's aroma. It smelled delicious, a little like Imaru's ginger sweetbread she had come to love.

She sipped. Warm, aromatic spices caressed her throat, soothed her. She sighed, content. It was perfect, just like everything else Thoth created.

"It's called *téy*," Thoth said, smacking his lips and setting his cup back down onto the tray. He rubbed his hands together. "The people of Imaru may be a little wary of outsiders, but this humble beverage appears to be the bridge which can span the divide." He reached out to straighten the pot on its holder, continuing, "In the lower town, there is a museum. Yesterday, while the gods searched for our new home, I took the tour. It was quite fascinating. Apart from its various healing properties, I learned there is a *téy* for every occasion and reason." He took another sip and sighed. "Its walls are covered from floor to ceiling with little drawers, each filled with a different herb, leaf, flower, or spice, imported from every corner of Elati. It is a wonderful place. I was quite enchanted by it. Perhaps Urhi-Teshub could escort you there—"

Tears cut into her eyes. Istara blinked and looked away. Unable to suppress her anguish, she shuddered. A tear slid free. She brushed it away, hoping to be discreet.

"No," Thoth breathed, "my lady, forgive me. Please, I cannot bear to see you like this. What ails you?"

She said nothing. She didn't know where to begin—how to begin.

Thoth cleared his throat. "Is it . . . to do with what has transpired between Urhi-Teshub and Sekhmet?"

Startled by his non-sequitur, Istara looked back at him. "What do mean? *What* has transpired?"

"Ah." Thoth's gaze fell back to his cup. He adjusted it so it lined up with the little containers of herbs. "Never mind. It is not my place to speak of it."

"It is now," Istara said, unable to keep the tartness from her tone.

"Perhaps," he said, "it is a matter best taken up with Urhi-Teshub. I rather thought he would have mentioned it to you considering—" He cut her a look from under his narrow brow, and asked, quiet, "Surely you are aware Sekhmet has been teaching him how to fly her ship?"

Istara nodded and took another sip of her *téy*. "He has mentioned *that*, at least," she said. "I have noticed he has been in a lighter mood since we returned from the pyramids, although I had credited it to his learning how to pilot a ship." She set her cup onto the tray. "But I have been mistaken, haven't I? This is not the true cause of his happiness, is it?"

Thoth pressed his lips together. Stubbornness radiated from him. He picked up his cup and sipped his drink. "What would you have me say?" he asked at last.

"The truth," Istara answered. Unpleasant sensations pooled in the pit of her torso as she recalled the goddess of war's nascent territoriality toward Urhi-Teshub as they flew back with the cores. Sekhmet was dangerous, an outlier, loyal to none but herself. Over the course of the Golden Age, mortal kings had ended their lives when she had tired of them, none of them able to go on, their lives empty and meaningless without the intoxication of her dangerous games and forbidden glamour. A host of raw emotions welled up—dread, jealousy, anger, betrayal—their ugly weight dragged against the walls of her resistance.

"Only if you will tell me what troubles you," countered Thoth, quiet. "Perhaps together we might be able to make the pieces fit."

Istara looked back at the bees busying themselves amongst the geraniums. She wished for their oblivion, their simple existence, their freedom. "When we traveled through Surru," she began, low, "vivid images came to me. Memories." She glanced at Thoth, hoping to see a reaction.

He gave her none. Instead, he set his cup down, calm, perfunctory and sat back, his hands once more folded together. "Of?" he asked into the lengthening silence.

"Sethi went to Marduk because of me." Istara reached out to cradle her cup, its comforting warmth feeble against the guilt engulfing her, the weight of it threatening to drag her into the depths of its bleak tide. "And now we are forced to stand against him because of something I have done. You told me the Creator took my memories for a reason and to let things take their course. I know now what I have done. The Creator showed me."

Thoth blinked. "He did?" He went to collect his *téy*, thought better of it and sat back again. "May I ask what he showed you?"

Istara gazed into the recess of her cup. Vapors of steam curled toward her, rich with the spice of ginger, making her nose tingle. "I left him for a mortal." She cut a look at Thoth, humiliation enveloping her. "I left him to have an affair with Urhi-Teshub, and for my betrayal, my consort brought Marduk to Elati. After all we endured to contain Marduk, *Sethi* granted Marduk his immortality." Her eyes welled, once more heavy with tears. One, then another slipped free, hot with her shame. "All of what has unfolded in Elati is my fault, and I cannot think how to remedy it. Despite my pleas for guidance, the Creator is silent." Several more tears slipped free. She swept them away, riven between anger at herself and guilt for the innocent men and women Sethi had murdered. She looked up at Thoth, broken, anguished.

Thoth looked down and rubbed his hands over his kilt. "My lady," he began, "I—" he looked up at her, his expression conflicted, troubled.

"No," Istara set aside her cup and stood, unwilling to force him to condemn her. "Don't say anything. I am what I am—have done what I have done." She turned her back to him and pushed the last of her tears away. "You were right to refuse to speak to me of this. Forgive me for having demanded more from you. I committed a terrible, selfish act. There is only one way forward: I must find my way through this. Alone."

From behind, the quiet scrape of Thoth's chair against the marble floor. A rustle of starched linen. The gentle, soothing scent of cloves and ginger. He held out her abandoned cup of *téy*. "Please," he said, soft. "Drink it. I created this infusion just for you."

She shuddered, stricken by his unending kindness to her—a wretch, a fallen goddess—the cause of the horrors unleashed upon the people of Elati. A wrenching sob shook her. She took the cup and cradled it against her chest, defensive. "Why are you so good to me," she asked, her throat aching, tight, "even after all I have done?"

"Lady Istara," Thoth answered, pausing to take a sip of his own *téy*, "the Creator moves in mysterious ways. I trust in his wisdom."

Istara said nothing. She drank her *téy* in silence while the bees drifted from flower to flower, busy, happy, and drunk with life.

Night thrust itself upon Imaru. Across its multitude of terraces, torches flared, dotting the city in a twinkling carpet of firelight. A knock came to the door. Urhi-Teshub joined them clad in his gold-gilt leather tunic and kilt, ready to escort Istara back to her apartment. Thoth had said nothing more of the affair between her protector and the goddess of war—neither had Istara asked.

Instead, as he had poured more *téy* and spoke of his plans for the cores, a glimmer of clarity touched her. Perhaps the Creator's silence was intentional. Since they had arrived in Elati, apart from her initial request for Thoth to create a sanctuary for the gods—when, she realized in hindsight, she had been far stronger in mind and spirit—she had done little else to aid in the fight against Marduk. Instead, she had spent her days languishing in her apartment, spending her time correcting Imaru's texts on healing, while the other gods crossed the heavens in search of Marduk's stronghold, or in seeking out allies and gathering information on Sethi's movements.

She could have found things to do, ways to help—more than once Thoth had suggested how she could aid him, but she had declined every time, murmuring excuses to return to the solitude of her apartment where she cocooned herself in her misery. For the last five weeks, she had done nothing, had allowed herself the luxury of seclusion, of wandering paths long gone, and counting down the hours until her heart would awaken during those brief, brutal pre-dawn connections.

But it was enough. She had wasted far too much time wallowing in self-pity. She was the goddess of healing, and the consort of the fallen god of war. No one knew her consort better than she. In those morning connections, she could find ways to learn things from him. There was more she could do. Much more.

She bid Thoth farewell and waited in the corridor as Urhi-Teshub closed the door. Within, the scrape of Thoth's chair as he pulled it back up to his desk, followed by the rustle of notes and a stream of incomprehensible mutters.

With a quiet smile, Istara followed Urhi-Teshub down a pillared walkway. As they passed one of the pillars clad in a profusion of bright purple flowers, Istara paused to inhale their scent. Nothing. Strange. She tried again. Only the fading heat of the sun touched by the dry pumice of volcanic dust greeted her. Of the flower itself, its song had long since been silenced.

"I wonder why the Creator did not grant this flower its perfume," she mused. "What could it have ever done to offend?"

Urhi-Teshub leaned against one of the pillars and eyed her, enigmatic.

"It might be," he said, as she reached up to caress another cluster of flowers, "these are his favorite."

Istara considered. "But . . . if he loved them best, why would he take something from them? Why not grant them more gifts?"

"Perhaps," Urhi-Teshub answered, low, as she turned and met the golden flecks of his dark green eyes, "those he loves the most must work the hardest, else it would be unfair to the others." A flicker of compassion touched her protector's features. He blinked and it was gone. Since their return from the pyramids, he had hardened. Melancholy no longer shrouded him, instead he girded himself with strength, purpose, focus. There was something else, too. Peace. He had found peace. So, hers had not been the only turning point at the pyramids. She wondered—

Footsteps approached quick, light.

Urhi-Teshub pushed away from the pillar and turned. The hard edges and planes of his face softened. Istara waited. From the shadows further down the walkway, Sekhmet's slim, leather-clad figure emerged. She approached, her dark eyes first going to Urhi-Teshub, warm with affection, then to Istara. She nodded at Istara, her warmth cooling.

"Lady Istara," she said.

Istara tilted her head to her. "Sekhmet."

An awkward silence slid between them. Istara waited.

"Do you wish to see Thoth?" Urhi-Teshub asked at last.

"No," Sekhmet answered, eyeing Istara, the tension tangible. "I came in search of the goddess of healing."

Istara folded her hands before her. She had never liked Sekhmet, had never trusted her. The goddess of war was a law unto herself. The tension between her and the other goddess thickened.

Sekhmet jerked her head at the adjacent terrace laid into a camellia garden. "Shall we?" She didn't wait for Istara to accept.

She strode away, lithe, elegant, and waited a little further in, her back to Istara, her gloved hands on her hips, oozing defiance.

Istara looked at Urhi-Teshub to gauge his reaction but his attention remained on Sekhmet, tense, uneasy. She swept after the goddess of war, her starlight tumbling over the twilit camellias. At the edge of the garden's terrace, a servant lit a row of lamps imbedded into the flagstones. They flared alight, one by one, casting flickering shadows along the path. He finished his task and departed, leaving them alone, between the lamplit camellias and a blossoming canopy of stars.

Sekhmet turned, abrupt. "I am sleeping with him," she said. "I am only telling you this out of courtesy, goddess to goddess, since he is your protector."

"I note your courtesy," Istara replied, cold, "but my protector belongs to me. He is not like the others you have dallied with. I will not allow him to be your toy."

Sekhmet's eyes darkened. "It seems to me the only one who has treated him like a toy has been you."

Istara stepped closer. She would not be rebuked by Sekhmet. "Meaning?"

Sekhmet scoffed. "Any fool can see he loved you once, perhaps even now he loves you still. You, a goddess and he, a mortal king? He left his empire to follow you here. That tells us all we need to know. It means you of all people are not in a position to cast judgment."

Istara bristled. "You dare speak to me thus—*you*, a cold-hearted whore?"

"Perhaps, but it does not do for you to accuse another of what you, yourself are guilty."

Fury tore through Istara. She struck Sekhmet's mouth, hard. A drop of blood bloomed against the goddess of war's lower lip, a brilliant liquid garnet. She smiled, cold as death.

"If violence is what you want," a tendril of Sekhmet's light rippled over her split lip, "violence you shall have." She lifted her hand, her leather-clad fingers curled into a small, hard fist.

Urhi-Teshub pushed his way past Istara and caught Sekhmet's wrist in his grip. "Enough," he said. "Both of you." He turned to Istara. "I assume this is about me. I will not have you come to blows over a trivial matter—"

"Trivial?" Sekhmet erupted. "I thought we—"

"Trivial?" Istara echoed, scorched in rage. "You don't know what she is, what she has done to—"

"I don't care what she has done," Urhi-Teshub interrupted. "I have committed enough crimes of my own to last for an eternity. Lady Istara, I have chosen to share my bed with Sekhmet, and will continue to do so with or without your permission. However, this should have been for me to reveal." He shot a harsh look at Sekhmet, who looked away, chastened. Istara caught her breath, incredulous—Urhi-Teshub had the power to subdue the goddess of war. "Whatever we once shared," he continued, gentling his tone as he turned back to Istara, "is over. For you, it ended years ago. But for me, it ended at Surru when I drove a dagger into your heart and killed you."

"Killed her?" Sekhmet breathed. "But what weapon could possibly . . . ?"

"What do you mean, killed me?" Istara pressed her fingers to her breast. She had no memory of a dagger. She met Urhi-Teshub's eyes. He returned her look, veiled, distant.

The muscles in his jaw clenched. Silence stretched. He looked up at the heavens as if seeking the answer amongst its starry lights. "It's . . . a metaphor," he muttered. "Nothing more." He turned and left.

Sekhmet moved to leave. Istara ignored her, willed her to go.

"It's not the same with him as the others," Sekhmet said, low. "I swear I will not hurt him."

"All you do is hurt," Istara snapped. "You are incapable of anything else."

Sekhmet gazed over the twinkling city. "Maybe this cold-hearted whore has finally found out what a broken heart feels like." She turned. A sheen of tears glinted in her eyes. "Let's just say what happened at the pyramids stays at the pyramids."

"Wait."

Sekhmet waited, the lamplight enhancing the elegant contours of her features. Istara eyed her, tried to see her as her protector would. There was no doubt the goddess of war was beautiful, perhaps the most beautiful of all the goddesses. Within the pillared walkway, Urhi-Teshub moved further away, trusting them to work out their differences. Perhaps *she* had stolen *him* from another and after all she had taken from him—his throne, his empire, his heart, his life—he deserved to be happy. If the goddess of war was the one he wanted, it was not her place to decide.

"Love him with all your heart," Istara whispered. "As I once did."

Sekhmet glanced at Urhi-Teshub. Her eyes softened. Tenderness surrounded her. "I already do." She met Istara's eyes, hers frank, sincere. "I understand why you did what you did. He is no ordinary mortal. I am honored to have been chosen by him."

Istara blinked, stunned by Sekhmet's unexpected solidarity. With a quiet smile, the goddess of war left, her leather-clad legs brushing the camellia blossoms. A trail of white petals drifted to the flagstones, dusting it with scented flakes of silken snow. In the shadows of the walkway, a few quiet words, a stolen, passionate kiss, and then, with a whisper, the goddess of war departed. Quiet fell.

Urhi-Teshub returned to Istara. His scent surrounded her, cyprinum, earthy, sun-warmed grass, cinnamon, and sandalwood. The heat of him made her miss Sethi. If only *he* stood there instead of her protector—No. She would not go down that path again.

She went to the edge of the terrace, closed her eyes and inhaled deep, seeking to cleanse her mind of her sordid past, and of the development between Sekhmet and Urhi-Teshub. Dense, humid evening air filled her lungs. It washed through her, carrying the rich alkaline scent of the lake. She exhaled. Better.

"I have heard there is a *téy* museum in the lower city," she said, opening her eyes to take in the view once more. The sky hung barren of its moons. Instead, the stars bore down on them, fierce, brilliant, hard, burning with vengeance. "Tomorrow morning I would like to see what I can learn in the art of healing brews." She looked back at Urhi-Teshub, who eyed her, a hint of approval gilding his expression.

Her protector held out his arm. She took it. Together, they walked back to her apartment along the walkways and corridors of the palace, companionable, peaceful. He was right. It was over. And now, it was time to begin again. Alone.

❊ ❊ ❊

Ahmen leaned back in his chair and stared at the map spread across the width of the table, its edges dangling over the sides. He had never seen a map which comprised not only an empire, but an entire world. The distance he had traveled from Egypt to Babylon had been overwhelming enough, the seventy-five day journey so daunting only seasoned caravan traders dared make the brutal desert crossing with any regularity.

But *this*.

He glared at the map, hating it. Elati was enormous. His mind reeled at the scope of it: Two large continents, Chern and Tholis, dominated the map. Chern boasted four kingdoms and occupied a large swathe to the north of the Senichin Isles of Pir and Rzhev. On the other side of the Adriande Sea, Tholis straddled the world from the north to the south and possessed eight kingdoms. Close questioning of one of the library's cartographers revealed the journey from Rzhev, where Imaru nestled in a long-dead volcanic crater, to the island of Senas off the coast of Tholis took four months on a trading vessel, more if the weather was bad. From Senas, the crossing to Tholis took another month. Ahmen rubbed his eyes, sick of staring at the map, of willing it not to be what it was. Five months on a boat to reach the easternmost coast of Tholis. And that wasn't all: Rzhev alone was at least five times larger than the whole of the Egyptian empire, and Imaru lay a month's ride from the nearest seaport.

He had asked if it might be faster to travel east from Rzhev across the sea to the western coast of Tholis. The cartographer had given him an unreadable look, cleared his throat and confided though many had tried, none had survived the journey, and after hundreds of years of failure, no amount of gold would convince even the most avaricious trader to try. When Ahmen pressed him for more information, the cartographer suggested perhaps it might be best if the foreigner did not ask so many questions. A warning look had flickered in his eyes, and Ahmen, aware it had taken him a week to be granted access to the palace's library and of his delicate position as Imaru's guest, nodded and murmured his understanding.

His heart heavy, he turned his attention away from the map to the library's interior. Clad in honey-colored carved wood, the library housed an open central hall, its bottom floor arranged with large tables and chairs. He looked up. High above, a cupola of brilliant colored glass bore images of an idyllic river scene populated by herons, fish, butterflies, and flowers. Between him and the cupola, six floors of identical balconies surrounded the central hall, lined with shelves the height of two men, each shelf packed with scrolls and something the Imarians called books. Bound in leather, their interiors contained sheaves of the local plant, bamboo, made into a kind of papyrus the locals called paper, far smoother and lighter in color than papyrus.

His gaze fell back to the map. He didn't care about books or paper, all he wanted was to find Meresamun. It was going to be far more difficult than his worst expectations. Elati was vast. Meresamun could be anywhere. It would take him years to find her. He might never find her.

He closed his eyes. He was going to need the help of the gods after all. They had ships which could cross vast distances in mere hours. But Thoth had made his position clear: Meresamun was a liability. No help would come from that quarter. Ahmen regarded the map once more. Morning light filtered from the glazed dome, speckling the map's continents and seas in a riot of pinks, greens, blues, and purples. He needed to ask someone who was not a god—someone like him, an immortal. Someone who could fly a ship, had access to a ship, and would understand his need.

His gaze drifted over an island, much smaller than the others, though still far bigger than Egypt, alone in the midst of a vast oceanic sea. He drummed his fingers against the tabletop, considering the remoteness of it. If he were Marduk where would he go? Somewhere isolated and hard to reach. His attention firmed on the spot. He would chose a place just like that island, far beyond the reach of the other islands and continents. He waved the nearest of the librarians over and pointed at the spot, grateful for his innate ability to understand the spoken language of the locals, suspecting it to be a perk of his immortality.

"What is this island called?"

The librarian cut a look to the island then back at Ahmen. He shook his head, dour. "Anki. A forbidden place."

Ahmen lifted his brow, intrigued. "Forbidden? And why is that?"

The librarian glanced around, wary, before answering, low, "Eons ago, it was the home of the gods. It is a place where a great evil transpired. All the gods vanished, never to return."

Ahmen ran his finger along the island's outline. An abandoned island of gods, isolated, dangerous, and forbidden. It sounded exactly the sort of place Marduk would want to live while he sent his dog out to snap at the heels of his quarry. A tendril of certainty caught at his heart. Perhaps his search for Meresamun would not be so difficult after all. He just needed to find someone to take him to this forbidden island. He got up, nodded his thanks to the librarian and left the studious quiet of the hall.

In the dappled sunlight of the library's courtyard, he thought of her, the one he had violated, in heart and body. *Meresamun.* A spear of guilt probed the unhealed lesion of his crime. His heart tightened, aching from the memory of how it had all begun, how she had looked the night their paths collided—so long ago, and so far away—at the banquet in Waset, when she stood, trembling before Ramesses and recounted the Creation Myth in her beautiful, captivating voice. It was his fault she had fallen to the seductive power of Babylon's god; his cruel, vengeful jealousy had driven her away from their home, and back to the land of her childhood straight into the armor-clad arms of the one who had been waiting for her.

Despite her having persisted in loving him far longer than he had deserved, Ahmen knew his estranged wife would never love him again. But, he was not seeking to redeem himself, or to win back her heart, rather to do just one thing right in an endless chorus of wrongs. That he still loved her, he had no doubt, but he would not be so selfish as to hope for anything more than for her to be safe, free, and able to choose the course of her life unencumbered by the will of another. This much at least she deserved, and no matter the suffering, torment, or hardship he might endure, he would not stop until she was the mistress of her own destiny, no longer trapped in the grip of another's will—his or any other's.

He considered Meresamun, the one whose beauty and gifts drew those to her who only sought to possess her, a trinket, while she wilted in the dying glow of her inner fire—Ramesses; Sethi, once; Marduk; even, Ahmen admitted, ashamed, himself—yet perhaps of all the women Ahmen had known, Meresamun had shown strength and courage far beyond others of her sex, her independence, tenacity, and clearness of heart confirmed her qualities reached beyond the scope of the ordinary into the extraordinary. Her wings should not be clipped, the tether binding her ankles demanded to be torn away. He longed to unlatch the door of her cage so she might soar away and fly free.

He struck out, determined to find the one who might aid him. Once, they had been enemies, had fought on opposite sides of a brutal, dishonorable battle. But after the chaos of their desperate escape from Babylon and their journey to Elati, they had found a common ground, and had, not long after their arrival to Imaru, even shared a pitcher of wine and spoken, quiet, of the ones they still loved. Together, they wandered the pathways of those golden days when the fire of their love had burned bright—the wine dulling the pain in their hearts as they drank their fill, aware they could never go back, and the ones they loved were gone, as forever lost to them as the dying world they had left behind.

Urhi-Teshub collected the last of his weapons from the table in the armory and slid them into the holders on his hips and across his back.

"You ask much of me," he said, turning to meet Ahmen's gaze. "Beside the fact I would not leave Istara unprotected, I am nowhere near ready to pilot a ship, alone. I am unable to help you, although even if I could, I doubt I would." He lifted an eyebrow. "A forbidden island of vanquished gods." He folded his arms over his chest, his leather armor, although cleaned and oiled, still bore the scores and abrasions from his journey to retrieve the cores. "I can understand your desire to go after your wife, but your heart is ruling your head. It is a fool's mission. If Marduk *is* there, you would not last an hour before he or Sethi found you, and what good would you be to Meresamun then, a prisoner?"

Ahmen looked away, determined to contain his disappointment. Urhi-Teshub's words had robbed him of his last hope. "I don't know what else to do," he muttered, morose, reaching out to pick up one of the silvery weapons taken from the Etemen'anki during their escape from Babylon. He turned it over in his hands, admiring the perfection of its balance, the handle which curved against the palm of his hand; the slim, elongated tube, and the weapon's slight, satisfying heft, thinking how good a pair would feel hanging from the belt on his hips. "I cannot think of anything else apart from trying to find her." He set the weapon back down in the exact position it had lain in. "At least if I knew where she was, I could plan what to do next, but without a ship I will never find her, this world, it's—"

"Enormous," Teshub said, sauntering into the room, eyeing Urhi-Teshub's savaged armor. "I'm still put out no one asked me to come on your little jaunt. However there is still time for me to be the one who finds the location for our sanctuary." He cut an oblique look at Ahmen. "You were talking about a forbidden island of vanquished gods? Call me interested."

Ahmen blinked. "I doubt you would want to have your sanctuary there."

Teshub sniffed and wandered along the row of arranged weapons. He stopped in front of one of the largest ones. "Oh? And why would that be?"

Ahmen didn't want to point out the obvious, that perhaps gods might not want to live where other gods had been annihilated. When Teshub continued to look at him, blank, Ahmen answered, "I suspect it might be where Marduk resides."

"Well," Teshub said, shooting a roguish smirk at Urhi-Teshub as he hefted the massive weapon up onto his shoulder, "I suggest we find out."

In the ship from which they had fled the Etemen'anki, Ahmen eyed the pile of weapons spread over the floor and across the opposite divan. Considering the only passengers were himself, Teshub, and Arinna, the assortment felt excessive—between the three of them, they could never carry them all, but Teshub had been adamant. It was good to have a selection because one never knew what to expect, he'd said, and since none of them were gods, it was best to be prepared. The ship tore up over the gardens into the heavens, screaming past the citizens in the lower city, who ducked, despite the ship already being far above the tops of the buildings. They looked up, frightened, unused to the devastating thunder of the ships of the gods.

The door to the flight deck slid closed. Ahmen leaned forward, anticipation shimmering through him as the cloaking system shivered over the ship and the walls and floor turned translucent. Only a few hours ago he had been in the palace library staring at the map of Elati, despairing at the odds of finding the woman he loved, and now he was headed to the very place he suspected where she might be. Beneath, the verdant, wild, green land of Rzhev retreated.

He leaned back. He could get used to this life, being immortal and soaring through the heavens on the ships of the gods. Once he had liberated Meresamun, he would force himself to find his way in this vast world—alone, without her—and learn to live again as he had once done, in the quiet time before his heart had been ravaged by the chaos of his passion for a forbidden priestess. His thoughts drifted as he admired the artful beauty of Rzhev's sinuous rice fields clothing the volcano's mountainside.

Horses. He would have horses. Dozens of them, and he would breed them to perfection. He rubbed his hand along his kilt, realizing he missed the snug feel of reins wrapped around his forearms and the rattle of a chariot's box under his feet more than he thought. They had been his sole passion until Meresamun happened. Perhaps he could begin there—

The ship tilted and ascended toward the sun. The land shrank, its mountains and coasts settling into the distinct contours of a map. He wished he could have the freedom of flight as the gods did. He wondered if Teshub would teach him the control of a ship, as Sekhmet now taught Urhi-Teshub. Somehow he doubted it. He hadn't ingratiated himself with the gods, was nothing more than an outlier who had been swept up in their net. He imagined none of them, perhaps apart from Urhi-Teshub, his once-enemy, would be sorry if Ahmen-om-onet disappeared and never returned.

Far below, a fleet of boats, their colorful sails full and billowing, cut their way through the sea toward the far distant shore of Pir, the white crests of their wakes spreading behind them. He wondered how long they would spend at sea before seeing land again. Weeks, at least. A surge of gratitude swept through him, grateful he had escaped the rigors of a sea crossing.

They soared higher, above a thin veneer of clouds. The boats plummeted into the distance. Ahmen eyed the smooth, elegant interior of Marduk's ship, the white divans no longer pristine but marred with bloodstains—the memory of his desperate flight from the Etemen'anki, and Istara's sacrificial death at the threshold of the portal still fresh in his mind. He let out an unsteady breath and looked down. His hands had clenched into fists, the muscles and veins of his forearms stood proud, defined. He could never do what Urhi-Teshub had done, drive a blade into his wife's heart. Perhaps that was why Urhi-Teshub had been a king, and he, nothing more than a—

A glint caught his eye, brilliant white, pure as starlight. He leaned forward, curious. Tucked in a crack between the divan and the wall separating the cabin from the front of the ship, a thin strip of gold protruded. Strange. It glinted again, a quiet shimmer, as though its light came from within. Ahmen scoffed. What nonsense. Elati was making him fanciful. He looked up, thinking whatever it was might be catching the light of the sun. A shaft of sunlight cut through the rear of the ship and wandered over the edges of the furthest weapons. Ahmen looked back at the anomalous item, a tremor of uncertainty touching him. Perhaps it was one of Marduk's vile things . . . although—he considered as he knelt to examine it—Marduk's weapons and devices were never wrought of gold, but of something *other*, a silver metal, its reflection purer than even the rarest of mirrors.

He reached out, tentative, and tugged on it. It slid free, as if it longed to escape its confinement. He lay it across his palm and tilted it, admiring its detailed workmanship. This was not one of Marduk's. Although whatever it was, it was beautiful. Cradling it in his hand, he returned to his seat and examined it. A staff, entwined by a pair of serpents. They faced each other at the staff's crown, their mouths open, ready to strike. A burst of white starlight shimmered along the staff's length. He cried out, horrified, and threw it onto the divan. It bounced against the seat, its light dimming. He glared at it, uneasy, willing whatever he thought he had seen to be a figment of his imagination.

When it shimmered a third time, awakening like the beat of a heart, he pounded on the panel separating him from the front of the ship. A thick silence greeted him. He pounded again, harder. After several heartbeats, it slid open. Teshub turned, a hint of annoyance tightening his jaw. Her eyes averted, Arinna busied herself pinning her hair back into place, a faint stain of color gracing her cheeks.

Ahmen went to Teshub and held his hand out, heavy with its burden, longing to rid himself of it.

Teshub leaned forward. "Istara's pendant?" he breathed, his annoyance melting away. "How is it possible?" He took it and turned it over in his hand. "I thought nothing of her possessions had survived her transition." He lifted it up to show Arinna, who eyed it, curious. "While we journeyed across Thamud to Babylon, Urhi-Teshub told me the story behind it. Bought by the Hittite Chief Surgeon from a Babylonian trader, it had been a gift to Istara to mark the completion of her education as a surgeon. On the brink of his death, Urhi-Teshub managed to reclaim it from the thief who had stolen it. He returned it to Istara during the desert crossing." Teshub traced its outline, reverent. "But it should have been consumed along with everything else she possessed when she became the goddess of healing. If it still exists, it means this is no ordinary pendant." A whisper of its inner starlight sighed across it, like the wash of a storm tide.

Arinna caught her breath. "A relic." She reached out to touch it, her fingers trembling. "I haven't seen one of these since before the wars of gods and men. Didn't they all vanish when the Creator departed?"

Teshub held it out to her. She took it and cradled it against her breast, tears glinting in her eyes. A look of quiet satisfaction touched Teshub's lips. "Apparently not. To think, after all this time, this one managed to survive, and right under my nose." He looked up at Ahmen, his eyes alight. "Relics are gifts of the Creator which have been imbued with his light. They only awaken once they are near to their source of power." He met Arinna's eyes, anticipation bleeding from him. "Now all we have to do is follow the light, and we will find him, the father of us all."

Ahmen left the once-gods and returned to his seat. This time they left the door open, their quiet conversation drifting back to him, their excitement simmering, threatening to boil over. Ahmen wanted to care about his discovery, but he couldn't. Relics meant nothing to him. And anyway, even if the pendant led them to the Creator, it wouldn't matter. Re-Atum wouldn't see them. He could only see the gods—the ones he had created with his secret word. Ahmen didn't want to remind them neither of them bore the light of the gods, it wasn't his place.

Teshub pushed the ship higher, their flight no longer languid, but filled with urgency. Ahmen let out a bleak sigh. Unless the pendant led them to Anki, he doubted he would get to see the island they had set out to explore. He turned his eyes up to the heavens as the ship slid through another thin, ephemeral layer of clouds, sensing, despite all he had already endured, his path had only just begun. He closed his eyes, shutting out the roar of the ship, and Arinna's melodic laughter, her joy euphoric, tangible. So long as Meresamun was out there and needed him, nothing else mattered. He would endure anything for her. Anything. The rest could come later, once he had set her free.

With Baalat's hand clasped in his, Horus crossed the expanse of the top tier of one of the stepped pyramids surrounding the vast city dominating the heart of Anki, the pyramid's height and girth double that of Babylon's Etemen'anki. They had had to rest several times on their way up the steep staircase, but as Horus reached the tier's edge and took in the view he knew their effort had been worth it.

Baalat came to a halt beside him, her eyes alight with wonder. Anki's once-city of the gods spread into the horizon, its symmetry breathtaking. Even the refined grace of Ikalur's verdant terraces and slender gold-pinnacled towers paled in comparison to the elegance of the lost city of the gods. Hidden in the shadows of its former glory, Horus recognized many of the hallmarks of Thoth's designs: towering obelisks, sunken temples, wide avenues, vast plazas and deep pools, long abandoned and overgrown with vegetation. Further out, between the sentinels of stepped pyramids and the sprawl of the city: walled estates and palaces, each enclave a small city to itself.

Within most of the estates Horus had discovered ships—some housed three ships, others two, many, just one. They stood where they had been left, eons ago, dormant and meaningless without their masters and mistresses, each bearing the characteristic sigil of its owner—like the one belonging to Horus's Elatian counterpart in Ikalur—only those who possessed a sigil could awaken the ships' power. But there were no gods in Elati apart from Istara and Sethi, which meant there was only one ship left for Horus to find: Baalat's. Despite being dogged by continual failure, he had tried to open each ship he found, desperation driving him, fostering the vain hope he might find even one ship he could salvage, but they all stood shrouded in ageless silence, locked in their wait for those long gone, never to return.

Over the last day and a half, he had counted more than thirty ships, but from this vantage, as he looked out over the vastness of the city, at least four times larger than Pi-Ramesses, he realized he had only just scratched the surface, dozens more estates spread into the distance, as far as he could see. He chafed anew against the paradox of the ships, of their potential usefulness and their utter uselessness, aware if only he could activate them, he could have brought Ikalur's men to Anki and trained them to use the ships in their fight against Marduk. But it was impossible. Without the gods, the ships were nothing more than beautiful piles of scrap.

He eyed the nearest estate, which had held three ships bearing the sigil of Set. Horus bit back a bitter curse. Of all the gods, Set's ships were equipped with the deadliest weapons—appropriate for the god of violence. Horus turned away, sickened. Another silent victory for Marduk. At times, Horus felt, the odds tilted much too far in the favor of his nemesis. Just once, he would like to seize the upper hand. But no, despite the Creator having given him his ship back, the odds had reverted back to their usual position. With every step Horus took, he lost two more.

He eyed the city, scrutinizing it, searching for something, anything which might indicate the presence of the jihn, but nothing stood out. Apart from the creep of vines, the buildings of Anki's gods remained as they had once stood in ages past, preserved by whatever energy enhanced Elati. Almost every temple, library, and pleasure villa contained a multitude of rooms, and knowing Thoth, hidden doorways and false walls—none of which Horus had yet found. Horus clenched his fists. And it wasn't Thoth who had hidden the jihn, but the Creator. Another level altogether. He raked his gaze over the city, his heart sinking at the scope of it. The jihn could be anywhere. It hadn't taken him long to come to the conclusion that without any leads, it would take years to search every room of the city. Although, if it was going to be difficult for him to find the jihn, he hoped—despite Zherei's fear Sethi might be able to sense its presence—it would be just as difficult for Sethi to find as well. It was a faint hope, but he clung to it.

Lifting her hand to shade her eyes, Baalat moved to the far side of the tier to face the dense jungle surrounding the city. In the distance, a fierce wall of storm clouds churned and roiled. Violent flashes of lightning cut jagged swathes through the curtain of darkness. A burst of fire erupted at the edge of the jungle, drenched almost immediately by a downpour. Further along, another lightning strike, and another flash of flames followed by a thick gout of black smoke.

Zherei hadn't exaggerated the strength of the storm surrounding the enormous island. Horus had had to fly his ship as high as it could go to rise above the fierce barrier of wind, lightning, and hail. He had expected the storm to comprise a thin band surrounding the isle. He had been wrong. The storm raged far inland, and as he had cut across the roof of the heavens, his engines screaming their resistance, he began to fear he might not be able to breach the near-endless boundary. Just as his control panel lit up, warning him the engines were about to shut down— he fell through the buffeting winds, his engines whining, into a well of blazing sunlight.

Horus turned his attention to the center of the city. Three massive pyramids surrounded a tower as though kneeling in homage to its improbability.

The tower defied gravity. It reached up to the heavens—to the stars. He had circled it as high as he dared, yet even as the ship's engines began to protest anew, the tower soared away, appearing to have no end. Unwilling to test his ship further, Horus gave up on the mystery of the tower and landed in the shadow of one of the tower's buttresses. Leaving the ship cloaked, they had emerged onto the plaza to begin their exploration.

It had taken two hours to circumnavigate the tower's base, its girth supported by a complex of vast buttresses, their lowest point more than five stories high. Neither the tower nor the buttresses bore any openings. Nothing but impassable, sheer walls fitted together with unprecedented precision greeted them. Alongside one buttress, Baalat had paced out the length of its smallest ashlar. It dwarfed the dimensions of a temple courtyard.

As far as he could recall, apart from Thoth's manifestation of the dimension of the Immortal Realm, the pyramids of the Golden Age were Thoth's greatest accomplishment. But *this* precinct—its design anomalous amongst the structures of the rest of the city— stood pristine and untouched by the creep of the jungle, defying Horus's impression of what even Thoth could manage.

He narrowed his eyes, suspicion touching him. If the structures had not been constructed by Thoth, the only architect more powerful was the Creator. Zherei had said the Creator had hidden the jihn and suspected it had been secreted somewhere in Anki. Which meant if the jihn was anywhere, it was going to be there. It had to be there.

Horus rubbed his hand against his jaw, his stubble rasping against his fingers as he considered the pyramids. Maybe there would be a way in to the tower through one of them, or perhaps there was a hidden underground entrance. He had been wasting time, searching the city, distracting himself in his search for ships. The answer had been right in front of him from the heartbeat they landed. At last, direction, purpose. This was why they had climbed all the way up here, to gain perspective. He had not wasted their time after all.

His mood lifting, he glanced at Baalat, standing at the opposite edge of the tier. His consort wrapped her arms around her torso and hugged herself. She cut a look back at him and offered a wan smile. A shimmer of pain tightened the fine features of her profile. A wave of guilt washed over Horus. He crossed the distance and pulled her against him, her sun-warmed skin soft against the hardened slabs of his chest. Against his arms he felt the contractions of her stomach as it groaned, pleading for sustenance. He tightened his hold on her, murmuring against her ear once they were back on the ground he would find her more food. She nodded, quiet, patient, good. Guilt sliced through him, harder this time. In its wake: shame.

In his haste to reach Anki he had not thought of carrying supplies, and considering how difficult the crossing through the storm's barrier had been, he was in no hurry make the return trip to Ikalur for provisions. The possibility his ship might not be able to transcend the storm a second time was real. He couldn't leave. Not until he found the jihn.

He considered returning to the orchard grove they had found laden with ripe citrus fruit, where the trees surrounded a spring bubbling with clear, cold water. No. It wouldn't be enough. His consort needed more nourishment than that. If only he could find Thoth's estate, from where he had hoped to uncover portals traversing the whole of Elati. When they had arrived the night before last, finding an easy way in and out of Anki had been a lower priority, but now, as the wrenching, gnawing ache of his own hunger cramps echoed Baalat's, it was fast becoming his first. He longed to return to the central complex, but they both needed food, and in that colossal, barren place, he knew he would find none.

He held out his hand and led Baalat back across the tier to the top of the steps. He looked down, then wished he hadn't.

The steps fell away, the steepness of them dizzying, it looked more like a ladder than a staircase. Baalat let out a little cry and wilted against him. He caught her, noting the paleness of her complexion.

"It's so steep," she whispered. "I didn't realize on the way up it—"

A deep thundering tore through the sky. Horus looked up, dread scaling his spine. He knew that sound—the roar of Marduk's powerful ion thrusters. From out of the heavens, a black ship fell like a meteor. It screamed into the well of sunlight bathing the city, the ship's shadowy wings gilded with molten heat. The thunder eased, and the ship slid into a slow, arcing spiral, toward the stepped pyramids at the edge of the city. Soon it would fly right over them.

His eyes locked on the approaching ship, Horus eased Baalat across the tier into the shadows of the white-colonnaded cupola, hoping they hadn't already been spotted.

The ship approached. Horus's heart clenched. He willed the thing to keep going. It slowed, its high pitched whine slicing through his bones as it neared and circled the top tier, the scream of its existence blistering his senses. Baalat met Horus's eyes and reached out to caress his face, sorrow cloaking her. Horus pulled her against him, fierce, and kissed her, refusing to believe after all they had gone through it would end here, like this. It felt pointless, wasteful. He would not fall. Not today.

The roar escalated as the ship lowered its bulk onto the expanse of the top tier. The engines cut out, abrupt. A chorus of harsh hisses filled the vacuum. Horus led Baalat through the colonnaded expanse of the deserted cupola to its opposite side, and took up position behind one of the pillars. The ship hulked over the scorched marble, confident, calm, patient, a spider waiting for the folly of its prey. From the undersides of the ship's wings, jets of steam hissed and pulsed. Intense heat rolled away from it in blistering waves.

"I know this ship," Baalat whispered.

"As do I," muttered Horus. He gripped the hilt of his dagger, wishing he possessed something far more powerful than a mere blade, longing to level the field between him and the one his light had become. If only he had found the jihn, he could have used it against Sethi. Why had he wasted his time searching for more ships? He had been unfocused. The Creator had granted him a chance to find the jihn, and now, it was too late.

"There is something about that ship," Baalat said, easing out from behind the shelter of the column, curious, "something familiar. I can feel it."

Horus pulled Baalat back. "Have you lost your senses?" he demanded. "It's one of Marduk's ships." He caught her look of bewilderment, her gaze straying back in the direction of the ship. He softened his tone. "My love, hunger has robbed you of reason. We are in grave danger. I beg you, stay behind me."

He eased around the pillar. The door slid open and the steps emerged from their casing, floating midair. Movement came from within. One, no two, shadowed forms moved back and forth past the door. One edged toward the opening, his silhouette powerful: Sethi. In his hands, the nose of a massive weapon pointed toward the pillar where Horus and Baalat waited. He stepped down, arrogant, invincible. The weapon's metal glared in the light, blinding Horus. His eyes watering, he lifted his hand to shade his eyes, desperate to see.

"I know you're here," the one descending the steps called. A malevolent hum came from the weapon as it prepared to fire. "The sensors don't lie."

Horus blinked. That wasn't Sethi's voice. His heart thundered, bolting to life, riotous with unbridled hope. He glanced at Baalat, incredulous.

She smiled back at him, soft. "I knew I knew that ship."

He kissed her brow, tender. He should have trusted her. Baalat was no fool.

"Teshub?" he called.

The weapon's hum cut out. Silence. Footsteps approached, slow, cautious. They stopped.

"Tell me something only you could know about me," Teshub said, low.

"You gave up your light to save a mortal," Horus answered, quiet. "As did I."

The silence deepened. Several more hisses of steam erupted from the ship, followed by dissonant clicks of cooling metal.

"Come out," Teshub said, his voice thick. "Let me see you."

Horus stepped out. Teshub stood only a few paces away, just as Horus remembered him from their reunion in the Etemen'anki. He moved toward him, to embrace him, his comrade, his friend, his oldest ally.

Teshub paled and took a step back. "Aren't you supposed to be . . . gone?" He glanced back at the open door of the ship, from where Arinna and Ahmen looked out. "Are you seeing what I'm seeing?" he called. "Or have I lost my mind?"

Ahmen came down the steps, his eyes fixed on Horus. He came to him, slow, and sank to his knees. "Lord Horus," he breathed, reverent. "You live again."

A cry came from the ship.

"Baalat!" Arinna hurried down the steps, her gown caught up in her hands, and ran across the tier, her eyes brilliant with tears. She crashed into Baalat and clung to her. "Oh my sister, to have you back, it is a gift, a wondrous gift." She took Baalat's face in her hands, and gazed at her, worshipful. "How can it be?" she breathed. "How are you here?"

"The Creator," Baalat answered, gentle, reaching out to wipe a tear from Arinna's face, "chose to give us another chance."

"How?" Teshub demanded.

"As mortals," Horus answered, "although, the next time we fall, it will be forever." He cut a look at Marduk's ship. "I thought today might have been that day."

Teshub sniffed. "It's our ship now, even if it is less elegant than the one I used to have." He hefted the weapon's support strap from his shoulder and tossed the thing to Ahmen, who caught it with an annoyed look and propped it against a nearby pillar. Teshub folded his arms over his chest and eyed Horus. "I saw you vanish when the last of your light merged with Sethi," he said. "And yet here you are, alive again." He looked away, the muscles of his jaw tightening. "Stick around for awhile this time, hm?"

"I intend to," Horus said. His stomach growled, loud. Teshub looked back at him.

"We haven't eaten much in the last two days," Horus admitted. He cut an oblique look at the open door of the ship. "You wouldn't happen to have brought any provisions with you?"

Arinna took Baalat's hand. "Come with me," she said, her pale lashes dense with unshed tears. "I made sure to pack plenty." She shot a quavering smile at Teshub. "Teshub brought too many weapons, and I, too much food."

Within the shadows of the cupola's pillared hall, Horus waited for Baalat to take her fill before taking just enough to stave off the worst of his hunger. He caught Teshub watching him from under his brow. As Horus wiped his hands on a napkin, Teshub crumpled up the paper around his roasted fowl.

"Eat my share," he said, gruff, handing it to Horus. "I'm not hungry anyway." He picked up the wineskin and tilted it back, drinking deep, his eyes moving over of the expanse of the city. "So this is the forbidden island of fallen gods," he said as he wiped his hand over the back of his mouth. He tilted his head at the central complex. "Impressive. Those make Thoth's pyramids look like toys. He's going to lose his mind when he sees them."

"We forgot to tell them Ahmen found Istara's pendant," Arinna murmured as she gathered up the empty papers and tucked them into a leather satchel.

Baalat's brow creased. "In the Etemen'anki?"

"No, in the ship, on our way here," Arinna said, bestowing the Egyptian an indulgent smile. Ahmen made a dismissive gesture and turned his attention back to the vista. He sipped from his cup, a tinge of disappointment shadowing his dark eyes.

"It survived her transition," Baalat breathed. "That must mean—" she looked at Horus, hope bleeding from her.

Arinna smiled and nodded. "All this time, right under our noses, Istara possessed a relic." Her gaze moved to the central complex, bathed in sunlight, radiant, golden, a beacon. "It led us here." She pointed at the tower, its heights melting into the depths of the skies. "To that."

Horus eyed the tower. Only an hour ago everything had seemed so bleak, and now— "If it led you to Anki, it can only mean one thing. The Creator is *here*."

"It's how the relics worked before," Teshub said, stoppering the wineskin and handing it to Arinna who packed it away with the rest of the things. "I say we go and find out."

"But we already searched for a way into the tower," Baalat said. The others turned to her. Her shoulders lifted and fell. "If he is there, we will not be able to reach him. There is no way in."

"You are sure?" Teshub asked. "What about higher up?"

Horus shook his head. "Nothing. We flew as high as the engines would allow. If there is a way into it, it will not be via the tower. Before your arrival, my intention was to search for a way in through the pyramids."

"So you have a ship," Ahmen said, turning his back to the view, intrigued. "But you are mortal. How?"

The others eyed him, curious. It was a good question. He told them: of their weeks spent in Ikalur rising in favor; of Sethi's arrival, and his mercilessness terms; of what he had learned from Zherei of the jihn and its history; of his hopes to find the weapon before Sethi did; of his discovery of Marduk's location in Perev, and of its portal, and the possibility there might be another portal to Perev hidden in Anki, and finally, of the discovery of Horakhti's ship in Ikalur and the other ships he had found throughout the city.

A heavy silence stretched in the wake of his words. Teshub pushed away from the pillar and paced to the tier's edge. He turned. "So, you're saying spread out all over the city, we have ships. Lots of ships."

"Yes and no. Only those of us who possess a sigil can awaken them," Horus said, oppressed anew by their limitations. "We can claim three ships more: yours, Arinna's, and Baalat's, but against Marduk, it will not be enough."

"We'll be claiming far more than three ships," Teshub said, his expression hardening as he rejoined them. Horus listened, his hopes soaring as he learned his brothers and sisters had escaped to Elati from a parallel world ruled by an immortal Marduk, and of Thoth's retrieval of the pyramids' powerful cores from that world to provide a sanctuary on Elati for the gods, immortals, and their mortal allies.

Teshub folded his arms over his chest. "Between our relic and your jihn, securing Anki is critical." He tossed a look back at the complex of pyramids. "Ever since he returned with the cores, Thoth has been fretting about the time it will take to build new pyramids. I can't wait to see the look on his face when I tell him not only have I found our new home but I have three pyramids ready and waiting." He chuckled. "That should shut him up—for a day." He sobered and continued, "Since we are here, let's take an hour to see if there is any way into the tower via the pyramids. We might also find this jihn of yours. If nothing turns up, I'll head back to Imaru to collect Thoth and the cores." He raked his eyes over the clear, innocuous blue sky. "An hour should be safe enough, although the sooner we lock this place down, the better."

Teshub was firm. One hour. No more. A pittance of time to search the vast structures. They agreed to split up.

Horus scanned the vast opening of the largest pyramid, anticipation rippling through him. Too far distant for him to see across the enormity of the plaza, Arinna and Teshub would be approaching the middle pyramid, and Ahmen the smallest. Unlike the implacable face of the tower, the pyramids bore identical entrances to the ones Thoth had constructed during the Golden Age. He hoped the layout inside was the same, it would make their search easier.

Taking Baalat's hand in his, he led his consort under the golden lintel of the entrance, the way ahead lit by clear lights recessed into the floor and walls

"This is big enough to fly a ship into," Baalat murmured, her eyes moving over the interior's white walls, their pristine surfaces covered in engravings of golden symbols. She pointed at them. "Do you recognize any of these?" In the barrenness of the stone corridor, her question flew ahead of her, echoing into the depths of the pyramid's cavity.

Horus shook his head. It had been a long time since he had felt wonder—not since the day he had traversed the glittering disk of the Creator's realm had he felt so small, so insignificant. "Those are not the symbols of the Creator," he said as he tightened his grip on her hand and led her deeper within. "At least not the ones he used to communicate with *us*."

They walked on, quiet, reverent, the way ahead lighting as they approached. As they processed, the golden symbols flared to life in the white light, laden with knowledge meaningless to them.

"These pyramids," Baalat whispered as the corridor narrowed, easing from its downward slant into an upward angle. "Thoth didn't build them, did he?"

"I don't think so, no."

"But he built the pyramids during the Golden Age," Baalat persisted, "he was obsessed with planning that project, do you remember?"

Horus nodded, uneasiness stealing over him. "I remember."

"This pyramid is the same design as the one he built, inside and out," Baalat said, "but he came to Elati *after* he built the pyramids, so how could he—"

The corridor came to an abrupt end. A sheer wall of white faced them. Over its surface, the golden symbols shimmered and began to move, reassembling into different patterns, their motions stately, intimidating.

"*That's* not the same," Baalat whispered, backing away. The lights behind them flickered out. Only the wall ahead remained illuminated.

"No," said Horus. He pulled his dagger free. "It's not."

The symbols slid back, exposing the outline of an opening in the center of the wall. It rippled and liquefied, stone turned to water. Beyond it, another chamber. Horus edged closer, wary.

Down a short tunnel, a bleak chamber of gray stone. In its center, suspended in midair, a black, circular weapon, its blades carved with the same symbols as those on the pyramid's walls. It rotated in a slow, stately circuit until its blades faced him. It stopped. Its symbols ignited in cold flames of blue-white light. A shimmer rippled over it, raw with hunger. Malevolence bled from it.

Horus backed up, horror crawling over him. The thing seeped pure evil. It was the jihn. It had to be.

"We need to leave," he said, reaching behind him to take hold of Baalat. "It's too dangerous." His hand met with nothing. He turned, alarmed. "Baalat?" Her name echoed down the darkened corridor. The light extinguished. Impenetrable, suffocating darkness bore down on him.

He called her name again. Silence, thick and damning. Panic reached for him, cold, tenebrous. He resisted its call. She was just here, she would be here. He groped along the floor. Nothing.

Horus. His consort's voice came to him, faint, as though from a great distance.

He turned, slow, his spine prickling, dread shredding him. On the opposite side of the barrier, bathed in pale blue-white light, his consort beat against the liquid wall separating them. Ripples of water billowed from the blows of her fists.

"Baalat!" He threw himself against the barrier. It repelled him, stone against flesh and bone. He punched it until his knuckles bled. "My love," he roared, desperate, as she faded, her fingers clawing at the barrier, waves of terror pounding from her. Behind her, the jihn vanished in a blinding glare of blue-white light. The wall solidified. Behind him, the corridor's lights reignited, welcoming his departure.

"No!" he bellowed, horrified, anguished. "No!"

The symbols slid back into place, imperious, disdainful. Frantic, he ran his hands over where she had last been. The wall glared at him, implacable, solid. A lie. Rage boiled into him. He backed away, quaking. If the jihn thought it could take her from him, it was mistaken. He wasn't giving up. He would never give up. His ship had weapons powerful enough to disintegrate stone. He would get her back, nothing would take her from him. Nothing. Bloody and bruised, he drank of his rage and ran.

❋　❋　❋

Resentment washed over Ahmen as he made his way along the vast corridor leading to the center of the pyramid. Dark thoughts plagued him, and with each step, his mood soured. He had left Imaru to find Marduk's stronghold, not become entangled in the pursuits of the once-gods. Their problems were not his problem. Certainly none of them were interested in helping *him* liberate his wife from Marduk, so why should he have to—

Ahead, at the top of the incline, the lights illuminated. He stopped, breathing hard from the steep climb and eyed the way ahead. A solid wall loomed over him, covered with more of the strange golden symbols which plastered every wall and ceiling of the structure. A dead end. Of course. What a waste of his time. He turned, relieved to have completed his task, free to return to his own objective. Horus had said Marduk was holed up in a palace called Perev, the fabled summer palace of Thoth, reachable only by ship or via portals which looked like mirrors. Horus had mentioned he intended to find Thoth's estate on Anki, where he suspected there might be a way in to Perev. Ahmen hurried back down the corridor, eager to begin his search. Once he found Teshub, he would make his excuses and—

The lights cut out. A wall of darkness slammed into him. From behind, a sheen of golden light shifted and glimmered, like sunlight piercing water. His flesh crawling, he turned, his hand going to his dagger.

Against the wall, the golden symbols *moved*, slow, hypnotic, sliding into a new formation: the outline of a doorway. The empty space shivered. He stepped closer, transfixed, as the stone morphed into liquid, becoming an impossible, vertical wall of water, held in place by surface tension. He went to it, filled with wonder. He had seen some strange things since coming to Elati, but this was something else altogether. He paused, hope igniting in his breast. What if this was one of those portals Horus had spoken of? It wasn't a mirror, but then, who was he to question how Horus described a portal? He edged closer, pulling his dagger free. He brought its point up to the surface expecting the blade to slide into the opening. It didn't. The liquid wall deceived. It was as solid and unforgiving as stone.

Low voices drifted through the barrier. He leaned closer. A ripple and an opulent, firelit room coalesced on the other side of the wall. It sprawled away, filled with luxurious divans, gilded furnishings, and sumptuous cushions and rugs. At the far end, two massive arches opened out onto a torchlit terrace, the wooden panels folded back to reveal a black sky, glittering with a canopy of stars. A shadow, powerful, male, holding a golden cup moved from the terrace into the opening, clad in black leather armor, reeking of power and domination.

Ahmen blinked, incredulous, recognizing in a heartbeat the unforgettable, arrogant stance of the one he sought. He clenched his fists, and leaned closer. Marduk sipped and gazed at something beyond Ahmen's view. Another shadow moved toward the opening, elegant, graceful. A woman. She came to a halt and sipped from her cup, clad in a near-transparent silken gown of black, her throat and bare arms glittering in the torchlight, laden with a fortune of gold and jewels. Marduk took her cup from her, set them both aside, and held out his hand, as elegant as a courtier. She took it and followed him into the suite. They passed one of the flaming braziers, and the shadow's surrounding the woman's face melted away. Ahmen's heart slammed to a standstill.

Meresamun. He raked his eyes over her, drinking in the sight of her. She walked away from Marduk straight toward Ahmen, unaware her husband could see her through an impenetrable wall of water. He searched her for signs of injury or harm. Nothing. She was just as beautiful as he remembered, though she had remained thin, only a fraction of the weight she had lost since he had turned his back on her filled the deepest hollows of her frame. Marduk came after her, leaned toward her, and said something against her ear. She walked away from him, expressionless, and faced Ahmen, into what must have been for her, a mirror, looking at herself as she adjusted her jeweled collar, her blue eyes brilliant against the silvery-black powder dusting her eyelids and smudged under her eyes. Marduk came up behind her and unpinned her hair, taking his time, every movement screaming brutal sensuality.

A faint hardness touched the contours of Meresamun's features as Marduk brushed aside the drape of her hair, exposing the soft skin of her neck. He bent to drag his lips against the skin behind her ear. In the depths of her eyes, a flicker of revulsion. He bared his teeth and slid them along the back of her neck. A broiling snap of heat shattered the ice in her eyes. She closed her eyes and leaned back, her lips parting, her breasts rising and falling, her breath quickening.

Marduk's hand slid up her arm, his fingers catching at the ties of her gown at her shoulder. With several deft movements, the ties fell away, and her gown slipped free of her breasts, cascading like a whisper over her hips, leaving her naked apart from the wealth of jewels coating her arms and throat. His irises almost fully dilated, Marduk stripped, the slabs of his muscles inked in elegant abstract designs. Around one of his legs, the sinuous curve of a serpent's coils circled its way up to his lower abdomen. Its outline continued toward the thickening girth of Marduk's member. Unable to stop himself, Ahmen followed the design to its end. At the end of Marduk's member, the serpent's mouth opened, awakened by Marduk's lust. Revolted, disturbed, Ahmen looked away.

Tossing his armor onto a divan, Marduk's gaze went to Meresamun, hot, hungry as she watched him in the mirror, unmoving, caught by his dark look, broiling with intent.

Ahmen backed away, nauseous, aware of what was to come. He couldn't look—couldn't watch *this*. "Cease," he cried to the wall. "I have seen enough. I cannot bear to see that abomination take my wife."

The wall ignored him. Unable to stop himself, he returned to the liquid wall—to his wife—and pressed his palm against the barrier, his heart aching, raw, readying itself for its worst nightmare.

"Meresamun," he said, his throat tight. He looked straight into the blue fire of her eyes—hers, unaware, oblivious to him, "I am with you. You are not alone. I am coming for you."

Marduk moved up behind Meresamun and ran his hands over her, worshiping her, watching himself in their reflection as he worked. Her jewels and gold glinting in the torchlight, Meresamun arched her back and succumbed to him, letting his fingers roam as they pleased, his attention, slow, sensual, controlled.

She turned toward Marduk, panting, ready and willing, but he turned her back to face the mirror and entered her, slow, from behind, and rode her, tender, their bodies moving in perfect rhythm. It was a dance, a hypnotic, poetic dance, one to which only they knew the moves.

Fascinated, sickened, unable to tear his eyes from them, Ahmen watched, tasting bile as Marduk pulled Meresamun back against him and cradled her, the markings on his arms shifting into beautiful, sentient designs, mirroring the quiet passion of their act of love. Whorls and spirals slid from Marduk's flesh and spread across Meresamun's skin, his dark taint claiming her, encircling her, making her one with him. He caught her jaw and turned her face to his to kiss her, deep, slow, his hips moving, gentle, his restrained pace owning her more completely than the even the most passionate nights Ahmen had shared with her. Humiliated, shamed, Ahmen sagged against the wall, decimated by Marduk's prowess, his confidence, his power.

Meresamun shuddered and cried out, her ecstasy piercing the barrier, pinioning Ahmen's soul. Marduk followed soon after, clutching Meresamun to him, his release powerful, harsh, primal.

In the wake of their climaxes, Marduk pulled himself free and caught Meresamun as she wilted against him, his markings sliding from her skin back onto his. He lifted her up, her jewel-clad body languid in his arms, and walked out of Ahmen's view.

The wall shimmered, solidifying, turning opaque. At the edge of Ahmen's hearing, he heard Marduk murmur: "Ninsunu, my love, you slay me."

Ahmen backed away, quaking. All those nights he had tormented himself thinking of her with Sethi, imagining them together, gorging himself on a feast of outrage and jealousy—He deserved to see this, had brought it upon himself.

But still, to see her loved by another—a near-god—her body pliant and willing in his grip. No. It was too much. The images tormented him, tore through him, savage, devastating.

He shuddered, his heart clenching so hard he couldn't breathe. The memory of her crying out from her release slammed through him, vivid, visceral. He heaved, and his gorge opened, foul with the burning heat of bile.

Against the hateful wall, he emptied the contents of his stomach, the stink of it sickening him, making him retch long after he had anything left to give. He wiped the back of his forearm against his mouth, desperate to think of anything but what he had just witnessed. Another image rose over the miasma polluting his mind. Before Marduk had begun his seduction, there had been a flicker of revulsion in Meresamun's eyes. Ahmen lifted his head. Why would she let him take her if he repulsed her?

Realization hit him. Without being able to escape her oppressor, she had no choice but to submit. Ahmen shuddered, a searing point of guilt speared him afresh. It was he who had condemned her to her fate.

His resolve hardened. He turned toward the corridor's darkened slope, his heart condemning him anew for what he had done to her while enslaved to jealousy and hate—for the destiny his act had bestowed on her. All her life she had been enslaved to others. No more. No matter what it cost him, she would be free. The lights flared to life. Bathed in the brilliance of the pyramid's white light, he bolted away, determination tearing through him. He was immortal. He would never stop. Even if it took him forever, he would not quit until the door to Meresamun's cage opened and she flew free.

✳   ✳   ✳

Teshub came to a halt at the top of the incline. He let go of Arinna's hand and ran his fingers over the wall blocking their way.

"Did you see any other passages leading away from this one?" he asked as he searched for a niche, or an indentation, something, anything to deny what his eyes were telling him: A dead end stood before them, when there should have been an opening and a chamber ahead.

Arinna shook her head. "Nothing." She edged closer, watching his fingers as they slid over the engraved symbols, written in a language she had never seen. "In Thoth's pyramid, wasn't there a chamber at the end of this incline, where he kept one of the cores?"

"There was," Teshub muttered. He stepped back, annoyed, feeling cheated. The pyramid was keeping something from them, he could feel it. He continued to prod at the wall, determined. Nothing. The barrier with its asymmetrical golden symbols remained silent, obstinate, unwilling to give up its secrets. Behind, the corridor glowed, bathing his shoulders in bright white light.

"Teshub. Look at this."

He turned. Arinna unfolded her fingers. In her hand, the relic brightened, its inner light pulsing with a quiet beat. He lifted his brow, caught his consort's eye and shot her a look loaded with vindication. He knew there had to be more. A place like this didn't finish with dead ends. Arinna eyes widened. She caught her breath and tilted her head at the wall.

He cut a look over his shoulder. The wall shimmered, reminding him of the flicker of fish scales under sunlit water. In total silence, a massive section collapsed inward, morphing from a white wall into a floor, black as polished obsidian. In the blink of an eye, the opening unfolded itself in complete silence, revealing a vast corridor which sloped downward, deep into the pyramid's heart.

Teshub edged closer and examined the opening. The floor and ceiling mirrored each other, a dense, glossy black, while the walls gleamed with their own inner light, granting the corridor a dull internal illumination—

"Those walls are solid gold," Arinna breathed.

His flesh prickled. Something was wrong. He couldn't get his bearings. In one heartbeat, he felt both peaceful and euphoric, as he once did in the presence of the Creator, and in the next, the deepest, starkest despair stripped him of hope.

"Are you feeling this too?" he asked.

"Feel what?" Arinna murmured, reaching out to run her fingers over the wall, wondrous. "My love, the wall . . . it's warm." She knelt and touched the floor. "And the floor it's . . . cold. I have never seen anything like this before. There is something about this place. I cannot tell if it is dangerous or a blessing. Perhaps we should find Horus and Baalat so if anything happens . . ."

Her words slipped past him, tendrils of smoke, ephemeral. Teshub endured a fresh avalanche of conflicting emotions. They slammed through him, jagged icicles of love and bleak stones of hate.

"My love," he cried. "Do you not feel it?"

His consort tore her attention from the corridor and looked back at him, calm, composed, the relic glowing in her palm. Through the chaos of his heart, a flicker of understanding, brief, bright. He held out his hand to her. "Take my hand," he said as hope fleeted from him and another savage roil of despair scoured him of purpose. He need only lay down. Succumb. Eventually the dark would consume him, and he would be free. Yes, it would be a relief, to escape, to no longer feel the pointlessness of his existence—

Arinna's fingers slid between his. Calm washed through him, a tide of serenity, the cacophonic disorder of his existence vanished as fast as it had arrived. He leaned back against the opening. "Thank the Creator's light," he said. "That was . . . unpleasant. Whatever happens," he said, eyeing her from under his brow, "do not let go of the relic or my hand."

"What happened?"

"Something I never want you to experience," Teshub answered. He turned his attention to the corridor, and eyed it, wary. It could swallow them whole—refold itself back together with them inside, crushed in its implacable grip for eternity. The relic's pulse deepened, as though answering a call from deeper within the structure, its light reflecting against the glossy dark of the floor and ceiling, the dull gold of the walls. No, he reasoned, they would be safe so long as they had the relic. Hadn't it opened the way for them? The miseries of his earlier despair yielded, as mists of dawn fall to the pure light of a new day, and hope touched him anew. Somewhere down there, the Creator awaited them. He had given them the key, now they need only use it. His hand tight against Arinna's, he stepped into the glistening gold-dark and didn't look back.

The corridor plunged far below the foundation of the pyramid. At last, it leveled off and stretched away, a perfect, straight line. Far in the distance, just visible, a pinprick of warm golden light beckoned. Teshub's heart hammered so hard it hurt. He tossed a look at Arinna, but she didn't need any encouragement. She bolted ahead of him, pulling him with her. They ran, reckless, ecstatic, like children returning from the fields to find their father home after years spent at war. The black floor fled away, the distance shortening with every heartbeat.

Soon, he would see the one who had left the message emblazoned on his arm, the one who had sent him to reprieve Urhi-Teshub from death, and who had granted him a second chance to defeat his nemesis. He had so many questions he wished to ask, they piled up inside him, clamoring against the walls of his mind, aching for their liberty.

Halfway to the end of the corridor, a burst of light erupted from within Arinna's hand. Between her fingers, the relic glowed a dazzling white, its pulse, steady, strong, sentient, guiding them to their goal, encouraging them.

They ran faster. Teshub's lungs ached, but he ignored the pain. In mere heartbeats he would be in the Creator's presence. Ahead, the golden light took shape. It didn't come from the Creator, but from another chamber, further in, down another golden tunnel. The Creator's warm light poured out of the opening, its edges sparkling, limned with tendrils of golden light.

Arinna staggered to a halt just before its threshold, her chest heaving, and her face flushed. Teshub looked back along the length of the corridor. Without the brilliance of the light beckoning them he realized the distance of the long, dim corridor. They had run far, at least half an iter.

He waited for Arinna to catch her breath. She stood on her toes and pressed her lips to his, breathless and giddy with joy. He kissed her back, hard, triumphant. They would win. This was it. Marduk was finished if they had the Creator on their side. He had thought telling Thoth about the pyramids would shut him up. But *this*. *This* would silence that annoying pedant for a week, perhaps even a month.

He tilted his head at the opening. Its light washed over Arinna's delicate features, illuminating her pale skin from within, just as it had done when she had been the goddess of the sun, her light endless, perfect. His.

Her eyes alight, Arinna nodded her agreement to continue onward, and together, side by side, reverent, they entered the brilliance of the tunnel. Teshub tightened his grip on Arinna, his heart tumbling, riotous. Soon now.

They emerged from the tunnel into an obsidian-floored chamber so vast Teshub couldn't see its end. To either side, towering golden walls curved into the distance. He looked up. The chamber's endless reaches screamed back at him, dizzying, punishing, humiliating. He staggered.

Ahead, the source of the light. He lifted his hand to shield his eyes, the glare almost blinding him. Through the gaps of his fingers, he tried to make sense of it. His mind clawed at its edges, recoiling from what his eyes claimed to see. He couldn't look at it as a whole, but only in its parts. Together, it burned his thoughts, seared his soul.

Far-off, in the center of the chamber, a sphere of golden light rotated, its depths too vast to comprehend, as though a mere drop of it could contain a billion universes. It rotated, stately, and so overwhelming it seemed impossible for it to remain within the constraints of the chamber, yet at the same time, it pulsed at a frightening speed, a fragile, tiny thing, no bigger than a toy, lost within the depths of the yawning void. Golden tendrils of light swarmed over it, streamed away from it, bathing the barren golden walls with the Creator's life-light. Within the sphere's interior, an endless array of sparkling, blistering pinpoints of light washed the chamber's floor in a shower of starlight. With each passing instant the span of a cosmos ignited and died.

It processed, haughty, playful, deadly, a friend. Both massive and minuscule, wild and tame, dangerous and sheltering. His eyes aching, Teshub looked up, seeking relief from its blinding, boggling light. The sphere greeted him. He gaped. It had moved without moving at all, as though it had always been there, yet he was sure it hadn't been. He tilted further back and pulled his hand away. He was certain darkness had clouded the chamber's heights. Brilliant light erupted into his eyes. The sphere continuing to rotate, ambivalent to his creeping insanity. Quick as he could, he looked back down again. The sphere greeted him again, implacable, unforgiving, it light streaming over the obsidian floor, as though it had always been there, for eternity, and he had only imagined it elsewhere.

"My love," he whispered, his senses raw, screaming in rebellion, begging him to flee. He kept his attention fixed on the sphere hovering over the floor, daring it to move. "Do you see the sphere?"

"Yes," Arinna answered, awed. "It's beautiful."

"Where are you looking at it?"

At the edge of his vision, she pointed to the heights. "As high as I can see." She paused, continuing, uncertain: "Why does it not get smaller with distance?"

He didn't answer. Something new had taken his attention hostage. Perhaps he had begun to adjust to the sphere's brilliance or perhaps his mind had reached the final limits of its sanity, but as the sphere turned, something other skimmed against his peripheral vision. He narrowed his eyes, looking but not looking. There. A thin sheath of darkness surrounded the sphere, cradling its outer surface. He followed its contours, careful, willing himself only to see the large sphere, refusing to allow it to collapse into the small one. He dared not even blink as he traced the darkness to the top of the sphere. The darkness slid up into a point, resembling an invisible thread, pulled taut—He looked up, eager. The sphere moved. He bit back a curse and started over, cautious, careful, following the thin line of darkness, edged in white light, its elegance drawing him in, sinuous and glossy in the heat of the light. At the top, he concentrated his will on focusing on the edge of the sphere, so it would not shift again. Keeping his gaze fixed on it, he sensed rather than saw the darkness slide free of the sphere. It soared up, lost in the heights, an endless thread of liquid obsidian. His eyes began to water. It was enough. He pulled his gaze from the impossible thing and looked at the floor under his feet, his skull aching.

"We're in the tower," he said. His voice echoed, lost in the infinite space. And then, the light died.

Only the light of the relic continued to beat its siren song, blinding now in the sudden well of black. It faded, gentle, then it too, winked out.

"Teshub?" Arinna whispered, her breathing turned ragged, bearing the taint of terror. He reached out and drew her against him, encircling her in his arms. He turned. Utter darkness, as thick as a tomb bore down on him.

"We'll go back," he said. "The way was straight. It will not be difficult."

"But the walls," Arinna panted. "Won't they close in on us?"

"No," Teshub answered, taut. "The relic will protect us." He turned, pulling her with him, reaching behind him for the opening of the tunnel out of the chamber. Nothing but emptiness greeted him. A thump of fear beat into him. They had only just stepped past the threshold when they entered the chamber. The opening should have been right behind them. He took a tentative step, his arm outstretched, expectant. His fingers swept against nothing.

"My love," Arinna whispered. "Someone is coming."

Teshub held still, cursing the pounding of his heart drumming against his ears. In the distance, a man pleaded, faint, his words too low to make out. The relic flared again. His eyes watering, Teshub tightened his hold on Arinna. The voice grew louder, closer. Teshub blinked. The relic's glow winked out. He turned. They stood at the top of the walkway, facing the wall which had opened into the gold-black tunnel, its surface once more solid and clad in golden symbols. Arinna staggered, overcome.

The pleading voice continued. Another voice spoke, cold, harsh, demanding silence. Teshub's senses slewed to a halt. His flesh crawled with prescience. Sethi. Arinna looked at him, fearful.

"Give me the relic," he murmured. He tucked it into his loincloth, his haste making it a poor job. One of the relic's points dug into his right testicle. He bore the discomfort—whatever it took to keep it from Marduk's dog. He hoped the Creator would forgive him for his sacrilege.

The voice began again, desperation etching his words. "Great lord, greatest of all, I have learned much at Perev. The jihn is a thing of pure darkness, of insatiable evil. Once it has consumed all the others, it will consume you. It has loyalty to none but its true master."

"*I* am its true master," Sethi bellowed. In the wake of his proclamation, a thick silence saturated the corridor, oppressive, soaked in tyranny. Heavy footsteps ascended the inclined, determined, followed by another pair, hesitant, unwilling. Along the walls, the golden symbols glinted. Teshub took Arinna's hand and held her eyes.

He cannot kill us, he mouthed. He lifted his eyebrows at her. She nodded, though terror coated her features. Like him, she had heard what Sethi was capable of—the crimes he had committed against innocents. His ruthlessness preceded him, a dark legend. He might not be able to kill them, but he could bestow grievous injuries to them, leaving them to suffer until help arrived. Teshub thought back to what he knew of Sethi of the brief time he had seen him in the Etemen'anki. An honorable man, just, good, a warrior, his love for Istara tangible. So, everything he wasn't now.

"But, my lord, are you not also a god?" Sethi's companion asked, his words thin with exertion.

The footsteps stopped. Silence thundered. The crunch of a fist against bone. A broken cry. The footsteps continued.

Movement against the wall caught Teshub's eye. He cut a look over his shoulder. He blinked, incredulous, as the golden symbols embedded on the wall eased out of their positions and slid, gleaming, along the surface, as though driven by an inner sentience. Arinna glanced at Teshub's loincloth. He followed her look, the last thing he needed was for a brilliant white light to erupt from his groin. No glow emanated from under his kilt. So, it was not the relic's doing, whatever *this* was. The golden symbols on the wall continued to shift, reassembling into the outline of a doorway. Teshub eyed it, wary. It might be a way out, or it might be a trap. Without the reassuring glow of the relic, he wasn't sure he wanted to walk into any more walls, but at the same time, as Sethi's relentless tread ascended the incline—

Cold, blue-white light silvered the opening. He leaned toward the incline, listening, gauging how much time he had left, resenting the choice thrust upon him, between uncertainty and certainty, aching to protect Arinna. Sethi's footfalls neared.

In heartbeats he would find them. Teshub dithered, cursing himself for having carried nothing more than a pair of blunt-nosed weapons. Yet, even if he had carried the largest weapon, he knew Marduk's devices could not vanquish a god, only slow them down. Enslaving Sethi had been a brilliant strategy. To get to Marduk, the gods would have to contain the god of war. Teshub's fingers circled the handle of one of the weapons belted to his hip, thinking to buy time until they got back to the ship. He let it go. No. It was a fool's plan. Sethi would come after them and shoot them out of the sky. Just beyond the edge of the landing, the heavy rasp of Sethi's breathing.

With a suppressed curse, Teshub chose uncertainty and slipped into the opening, Arinna following after, her hand clinging to his. His heart tight, he led her down a short corridor into a dim chamber. An ephemeral shadow hung suspended over the floor. Cold, blue light swarmed over it from beneath. He stepped closer, his instincts screaming their resistance. The shadow rotated. He gaped. The source of the light came from no lamp, but—

Arinna let out a strangled cry. She sagged against Teshub, and rammed her fist into her mouth, the air quivering with her silent scream.

Horror crawled up Teshub's spine and clawed its way into his mind. He backed up, nausea roiling through him. It was an abomination. Something no god should ever see. Even facing Sethi would have been better than this.

Her eyes churning with anguish, Baalat convulsed within the crushing constraints of the sickly tethers of light, her barren screams sleeting along the edge of Teshub's hearing, ragged with despair. More tethers shot up out of the thing embedded in the floor beneath her, hungry, insatiable.

Teshub forced his eyes from hers, to the thing whose darkness climbed over the once-goddess of healing. It lay flush to the floor within a block of black obsidian, a massive, circular weapon, its double blades black-dark, immutable, etched with the same symbols which coated the interior of the pyramid. Outlined within the obsidian's shadows the weapon's edges glinted, feeding, awakened, pale blue death-light slithering over its blades, malicious, sentient.

Teshub shuddered. So this was what Sethi was after. The jihn. A weapon of pure evil which could consume the light of the gods. Now he understood Horus's desire to find it first, and why he could never succeed. Only one could liberate such a thing from its dark grave.

Footsteps moved down the corridor. They halted. Teshub turned.

Sethi's presence consumed the chamber, reeking of power, violence, danger. He stood at the edge of the chamber, his golden eyes burning, fixed on the weapon silvering the darkness of its prison. On his chest, the golden fractals staggered out their rotations, broken, jagged. From behind him, a thin, old man emerged, his mouth bloodied, his jaw stained deep purple, macabre in the dead light. His gaze went first to the jihn, then to Baalat hanging above it, writhing in the seething tendrils, locked in her silent agonies, oblivious to any of them. Regret ravaged the old man's features. He sank to his knees.

"It is the end of all things," he whispered. A single tear slipped free, its path carved by the hollow light of the jihn.

Sethi paced to the jihn and knelt to touch the engraved haft set between the two semi-circular blades, their honed edges aflame, quivering with expectation. He ran his fingers over the blades' etched symbols, reverent, his eyes hard, drinking in the weapon's promise, his profile darkening with cold anticipation. The symbols shimmered where he touched it, pulsing with an inner light, luring him, like a lover on a sultry night.

"At last," he breathed, "you are mine."

A mind-searing hum came from the jihn, of razors slicing through light, death siphoning life. Baalat's shadowy form faded, though the torment in her eyes remained. A breath later, she vanished with a hollow, bleak cry. Teshub backed against the chamber's wall, Arinna behind him, desperate to shield her from the unfolding horror. The stone encasing the jihn rippled. Cold fire erupted from its heart, fuelled by eons of repressed hate, revenge, anger, rage. Against the jihn's ravening blades, its obsidian prison boiled, the stone liquefying, viscous, heavy. Evil poured from the weapon, consuming Teshub's thoughts, poisoning them.

Sethi grasped the weapon, lying atop solidifying rivulets of cooling obsidian. He hefted it with a grunt and held it out before him, drinking in its power. The blades rippled, humming anew, filling the chamber with its hideous slavering call. Sethi turned to Teshub.

"Where is Istara?" Hatred sleeted from him. It saturated the chamber, the pyramid, the complex. Soon it would encompass Anki, then—the world. Teshub shuddered, impaled by the oppressive weight of Sethi's baleful glare.

Teshub shook his head. The jihn's cold hum deepened. *Tell him*, a voice whispered within him, seductive, persuasive. A voice not his own. He clenched his fists, fighting its presence with every scrap of resistance he possessed.

Sethi stepped closer. The jihn's black blades glinted in cold anticipation. "I ask you again," he said, tyranny shrouding him. "Where is my faithless consort?"

"Faithless?" Teshub snapped, the jihn's darkness contaminating him, hijacking his thoughts, making him wild with the need to fight. He faced Sethi, reckless, defiant. "Istara was never unfaithful to you. Whatever you think you know, it is a lie. Istara loves you." He glared at Sethi, revulsion splitting him in two. "Even now."

Sethi blinked. A flickering, deep in his eyes. Uncertainty. Suppressed. He turned to Arinna.

"Your consort refuses to answer."

Death swept out from him and caught Arinna in its teeth. It cleaved deep into her breast and soaked up her immortal light, as if it were no more than a sip of wine. Arinna staggered, her hands catching Teshub's, giving him what little strength she had to aid him in his fight to free the weapon from her, but the jihn clung to her, a living thing, hungry, feasting on her essence, driving itself deeper until the outer curve of its blade protruded from her back. Her blood gouted onto Teshub's armor, slick, hot, the metallic taint of it imprinting the memory of her into Teshub's aching throat.

"My love," Teshub wept as her cries weakened, the jihn's darkness supping of the last of her light, until her immortality vanished, and mortality shrouded her, her inner light fading until only a whisper remained. Sethi jerked the jihn free, vicious, yanking pieces of her entrails from the ravaged cocoon of her flesh. Teshub caught her as she crumpled to the floor, her beautiful face ashen, a shell, her life stolen, embedded in the satiated weapon, steaming with her blood.

She opened her eyes, a fluttering, the final beat of a dying bird's wings. "I will find you," she rasped. Blood stained her teeth, wetted her lips. He kissed her, deep, shuddering, disbelieving. Not again. He would not lose her again. He pulled back. Her eyes met his, empty, mortal. Dead.

He rose, trembling, numb. Arinna, his love, his only love was gone. Again. Teshub looked at the ruins of his consort, his soul awash with grief, loneliness, loss.

Sethi turned and strode across the room to where the old man sagged, broken, defeated, hopelessness carving his features. His eyes rolled over the jihn, like a beast awaiting its slaughter. Its symbols, ignited anew, expectant.

"Please," he whispered, ragged, desolate, lifting his shattered face to Sethi. "It will destroy us all."

"Know that I am a merciful god," Sethi lifted the jihn. Blue-white light swept over the bloodstained blades, absorbing the last of Arinna's essence. "You wished to die, so you shall. You have served me well." Sethi spun the blade onto its side and sliced the man's head from his shoulders. Blood splattered over his kilt and chest. The old man sank to his knees and toppled over. His head rolled away, a trail of gore in its wake. It bumped against the mass of melted obsidian, and tottered to a stop, for a heartbeat a remnant of light still flickered in his eyes, haunted by sorrow. Then, nothing.

The blade rippled, satisfaction oozing from it. Sethi sniffed and turned back to Teshub, his golden eyes dark, iced vengeance.

"Where is Istara?" In his hate-slanted mouth, her name emerged tainted, ugly, foul.

Rage infused Teshub, ignited him to madness. He lunged at Sethi, the weapons freed from his hips, their hum filling the air. Nothing mattered anymore. Without Arinna he was nothing. He would not go on, trapped in immortality, his heart silenced for eternity. Today he would fall beside his consort; his blood would mingle with hers. He would not leave her. Could not leave her. He needed to die. Wanted to die. That thing was the only way. Fury shredded him. Grief blinded him. Sethi hauled the jihn up. The blades shivered, waiting, cold. Teshub pointed the weapons. The jihn swept toward him, hungry, glinting—

Brilliant light exploded from his groin.

❃　❃　❃

In the quiet of his ship's flight deck, Horus sat and stared at the middle pyramid, torn. Heartbeats after he had seated himself at the console to fly back and free Baalat from her prison, Marduk's warship arrived and Sethi had emerged, trailed by a subdued, stricken Zherei.

Sethi had headed straight into the middle pyramid, his steps direct, purposeful, his eyes dark with intent. He knew he should do something, but what? What could he do against a god who sought to liberate a weapon which had once belonged to the source of all evil? He bit back a curse, chafing against the cutting bonds of his newfound futility. He had been a god, unstoppable.

Now he was a mortal, a frail creature encased in skin, enslaved to the willing beat of his heart. Nothing. He could do nothing.

He eyed Marduk's warship, hulking over the plaza beside the middle pyramid. A glint rippled across it from head to tail. Sethi was no fool, even here where he would suspect no others, he had left his ship shielded. Horus couldn't even take out the ship. He pounded his fist against the console, frustration clawing at him, knowing he couldn't do anything until Sethi left, and while he waited, Baalat remained trapped. His heart clenched. She needed him and he was doing *nothing*. But, a quiet voice cut through the roil of his emotions, you are better alive, than dead. He cursed, then succumbed to reason, detesting the limits of his mortality with all his soul. He cut a fresh look at the middle pyramid. Guilt sluiced through him. Teshub and Arinna were in there, facing Sethi, alone. At least they were immortal. They would survive.

He shot another look over the plaza, in the far distance the smallest pyramid loomed against the horizon. Since he had returned, he had seen nothing of Ahmen, although, in truth, he hadn't been watching for him, his attention having been consumed by Sethi's arrival and the agonizing wait for him to leave.

Movement came from the entrance of the middle pyramid. Horus leaned forward. Sethi emerged, the haft of a massive circular weapon caught in his grip. Horus sat back, slow, trepidation sliding over him. The jihn. Dark patches stained Sethi's kilt and chest. Horus paled. Blood. A sinister thought touched him. Baalat had vanished, and the jihn had followed after. In his anguish he had been determined to return to free her, but what if what he had seen had not been inside their pyramid but the middle one—No. His blood turned cold. His throat tight, he waited for the others to come out, tension knotting his muscles, making his jaw ache. No one else emerged, not even Zherei. Uncertainty hauled at him, coiled into a sickening knot.

The weapon's black blades glinted, blue-white, malevolent. A sheen of darkness surrounded it, the light of the sun slid around it, avoiding it, leaving it in perpetual shadow. Sethi neared the warship and disappeared down its far side. Horus waited, holding his breath, dread slicing through him. *Baalat.* He had left her to die. He had made the wrong choice.

Thunder stormed his senses. From the midst of flame and smoke, Marduk's ship ascended along the length of the tower until it was nothing more than a blot of darkness against the sky's blue. A faint burst of fire erupted from its rear and the ship shot into the heavens, its path of flame a wound across the sky.

Horus leapt from his seat and went to the cabin's door. A burst of white light exploded from behind him. He turned, his hand on his dagger's hilt.

A heavy thump. Teshub staggered against the opening to the flight deck, his arms stretched out, pointing a pair of blunt-nosed weapons. They hummed, primed to fire. White light poured from under his kilt, bathing the cabin in starry brilliance.

"Brother," Horus cried, "you are in my ship. Do not fire."

The brilliance emanating from between Teshub's legs eased. Teshub lowered his hands and looked around, blank, uncomprehending, his breathing ragged. Cautious, Horus took the weapons from him and set them aside, careful not to touch any of the illuminated lights along their handles. He had no idea how to turn them off. He hoped they would shut down on their own.

"Arinna!" Teshub screamed, gouts of blood smeared his tunic and kilt, and coated his hands, arms, and face. He paced the confines of the ship, sightless, panting, lost. A wild animal, caged.

Horus blinked. Arinna's blood. "Please tell me she still lives—"

Teshub stopped. He came at Horus, savage, unseeing, and shoved him against the cabin's wall, his grip brutal, screaming of death. "Let me out of here," he rasped.

Horus punched the panel. The door slid open. Teshub stormed across the plaza and back into the pyramid. Horus followed, dread nocked against his spine. If Arinna was gone, then Baalat would be, too. He bolted through the pyramid's corridor, hard on Teshub's heels, his lungs burning as he scaled the steep incline after his brother.

A wall graced with golden symbols greeted him, just like the one he had faced in the pyramid where he had lost Baalat. Teshub rushed at the wall, fury pounding from him. He slammed into it, leaving a stain of blood against its pristine white. He pulled back, and glared at the wall, quivering. With a roar, he laid he fists against it. The wall ignored him, implacable. Uncaring.

"The jihn took Baalat," Horus said as Teshub's fury abated, hating the taste of the words in his mouth. "Did you see her here?"

Teshub said nothing. Horus looked over his shoulder. The corridor was too small, he wouldn't be able to fly his ship in this far. "We can use one of those weapons you brought. We'll blast our way in."

Teshub continued to stare at the wall, his eyes glazed. Blood dripped from his knuckles.

"Teshub," Horus said, touching his brother's shoulder. Teshub flinched. "Let's get the weapons. Our women need us."

A single tear cut a track through the blood on Teshub's face. "There's no point," he said, his voice taut as a skin on rack. "She's gone."

Horus stilled. *Who's gone?* he wanted to cry, but his throat closed over. His heart stuttered, darkening, the memory of his consort vanishing replayed, visceral, of the jihn's hungry light washing over the one he loved. No. Let it not be Baalat. Please, let it not be her.

Teshub reached up under his kilt and fished between his legs. He tugged something free. "Here," he said, holding out a golden pendant. "It is Istara's relic. Take it. I want nothing to do with it. It robbed me of my chance to stay with Arinna."

Numb, Horus took it. It looked an ordinary thing. No light emanated from it. It lay in his palm, a quiet thing of gold.

Teshub turned, avoiding Horus's look. He still hadn't answered his question. It hung between them, oppressive.

"That weapon—" he began, then stopped and swallowed. He looked away, his eyes burning with tears. "It stole her immortality, and her life." He shuddered, grief shrouding him. "Arinna died in my arms, a mortal."

Horus absorbed the weight of Teshub's words. Arinna. Gone. Forever. His sister, the light of the sun. His heart aching, he reached out to Teshub, but Teshub backed away defensive, raw, desolate. The once-god of storms jerked his head at the wall, hostile. "That opened up. The jihn was in there, feeding on Baalat. She was still alive when she vanished."

Horus's heart juddered to life, awakening anew. He let out a slow exhalation, cautious, concealing his kindling hopes, unwilling to add to the pain of Teshub's brutal loss. He nodded.

"Give that to Istara," Teshub muttered. His eyes flicked to the relic and away, as though he could not bear the sight of it. He turned. "I will return to Imaru and inform Thoth I have found his sanctuary. After that—" he stared down the corridor. Emptiness saturated him. After a long silence, he cut a look back over his shoulder, his eyes brittle with tears. "Will you remain here or come with me?"

Horus met his look. He took a step back, toward the wall— toward where Baalat had last been.

Teshub nodded, bleak. He left, shrouded in despair. A funereal silence fell into his wake.

Horus eyed the wall, willing the symbols to move, for the way in to open. It loomed over him, ambivalent, disdainful, as though he were no longer of any use. In the distance, the muffled scream of a ship seared into the heavens. He sank to the floor and ran his forefinger along the pendant's outline. Two serpents entwined along a staff. A relic, carried over from their world into Elati. Its light had led Teshub and Arinna to this complex, had reprieved

Teshub from Arinna's fate, but of the Creator's presence, there was no sign. Strange.

"Baalat," he whispered, desperate to find her, to protect her, to end her suffering, "where are you?"

A tear slipped free. Loneliness etched his soul. He was lost without her. He stood up and faced the corridor's steep descent, thinking to return to his ship. Perhaps there might be weapons stowed in it he could use—Warmth touched his palm, soft, comforting. He looked down, startled. The pendant shimmered, starlight limning its edges. It pulsed, like the beat of a heart. He took a step forward. The pulse dimmed just a fraction. He furrowed his brow. He took a step backward, and the light brightened. He turned and caught his breath. A wonder.

The wall's face slid inward and fell back on itself, no longer a wall but a floor. Further in, the ashlars unfolded, seamless, silent. A tunnel stood before Horus, its walls gleaming, golden, their sheen igniting the darkness of the obsidian floor as it rolled away, plumbing into the depths of the pyramid. He stepped toward it, cautious, fearing another trap.

"Will this lead me to Baalat?" he called into the passage.

Brilliant white light exploded from the pendant.

He took that as a yes. His heart pounding, he gripped the blazing relic and stepped into the gloom.

Thunder slammed into Ahmen, a living thing, relentless, insatiable. It soaked his flesh and tore through his mind. Trapped in its crushing grip, it shoved him back against a metal crate and dug into his eyes, drove them into the backs of their sockets. Stars shot through his vision, their pinpoints drilling into his brain, sharp, excruciating. He ground his teeth and endured, determined to suppress the anguished bellow hauling at his chest, clawing for its release.

After what felt an eternity—although it could have been no more than a handful of heartbeats—the agony of the warship's violent thrust eased. A quiet, steady rumble took its place. Ahmen sagged against the crate, panting, and rubbed his streaming, aching eyes, wondering if he had just made the worst mistake of his existence. He suppressed the thought. It was far too late for regrets—the heartbeat he had seen Sethi leave the ship and enter the pyramid, Ahmen knew the depth of the risk, yet he had taken it anyway. It was this or spend days searching for Thoth's residence in the hopes of a portal into Perev. No. It would always be this. A guaranteed way in to the heart of Marduk's fortress—and to Meresamun.

Keeping to the deepest shadows of the ship's cargo hold, he edged his way out from his hiding place between two towering stacks of crates. Faint blue strips of light illuminated the central corridor, barely enough to banish the well of darkness entombing the space. Near the front of the hold, a spiral staircase cut through the ceiling and continued upward. A faint glow filtered down from above. He crept closer, cautious, and looked up.

Sethi had gone up there, alone, covered in blood and carrying a fearsome weapon bearing strange, etched symbols, its black blades glinting with a sickly blue-white light. He suspected it was the jihn Horus had spoken of. Whatever it was, it was more than a blade. Evil emanated from it.

Even before Sethi had reached the ship, Ahmen had felt a subtle change in the air, like the tempting, deceptive scour of low tide. It had saturated his heart in a miasma of doubt, driving him to question his desire to go to Meresamun, mocking his intentions, suggesting there was nothing noble in them—he only sought to vindicate himself. No. Not again. He clenched his fists and walled up the thoughts, entombing the lies.

It had to be the jihn which poisoned his mind. Certainly, the nearer he drew to the steps, the stronger the oppressive thoughts, and the chaotic siphoning of the neat, orderly lines of his mind. He backed away from the light filtering from above, edgy, claustrophobic, and returned to his hiding place at the rear of the ship—the furthest he could put himself from Sethi's weapon—where the rumble was loudest and the floor's vibration made the soles of his feet tingle. He concentrated on the feel of it. He had no idea how long it would take to get to Perev or if Sethi was even going there. Ahmen had no provisions, and had eaten little at lunch, his appetite stolen by his disappointment at finding Anki empty of his objective.

Though he longed to sit, he remained on his feet, welcoming the creep of fatigue clawing at his legs and the twitch of his calf muscles protesting his cruelty as the hours passed, begging for respite, for mercy. He gave himself none, his suffering his only weapon against the darkness encroaching his mind. Each time his thoughts strayed to Meresamun he cut them off and forced himself to think of barren desert sands, of cloudless blue skies, of the blank sheet of an empty papyrus. Of nothing.

✳ ✳ ✳

The relic's light arced ahead of Horus, bathing the tunnel's obsidian floor in a path of white stars. Its light pulsed like the beat of his heart, steady, certain, guiding him down a long, straight tunnel toward an opening drenched in golden light. Lifting his arm to shield his eyes against the glare, he pressed on and passed through the opening into a smaller tunnel, bathed in tendrils of golden light. As he eased his way toward the end of the tunnel a sensation of enormity, of the profound, imposed itself upon him.

He hesitated. No longer was he a god, or even immortal. Whatever lay ahead, if it truly were linked to the awakened relic, it belonged to a realm far removed from the one he now occupied. He knew well enough what awaited mortals who were arrogant enough to attempt to trespass into the realm of the sublime. As though sensing his thoughts, the relic flared brighter, encouraging him, step by wary step. He had asked where Baalat was, and the relic had answered—had opened the way to this place. If not for her, he would leave and never return.

He felt his way forward, his fingers following the smooth length of the golden wall, sparkling with bursts of the relic's starlight. He met the end of the tunnel. Cautious, he leaned toward its edge, golden light streaming past him. He looked down. Just in front of his feet, a sheer line of dark cleaved its way through the glare. It slid up the side of the opening, across the lintel and back down the other side, the outline of a doorway.

A vast chamber poured away from it. To either side, golden walls curved to heights unseen. The magnitude of the space bore down on him, laden with the weight of a world—no, hundreds, thousands of worlds—unbearable, suffocating. Ahead, surrounded by a well of darkness—the source of the golden light—a sphere, glittering with stars regarded him, sentient, aloof. Its profundity stretched the limitations of his senses. It was there, yet it was not. It rotated. No, it was immobile. It was both vast and minuscule. And yet, despite the multitude of contradictions, the raging brilliance of its golden tendrils never faded. They washed over the obsidian floor's fathomless dark, swirled against the confines of the golden walls, and bathed Horus's feet, gentle waves of starry light. Shielding his view from the mind-shattering entity, he gilded his hopes and searched the barren space for his consort, but of the one he sought: nothing. Silence greeted him.

The relic pulsed anew. A beam of its light suggested a path along the slow, stately curve of the wall toward the chamber's furthest reaches. Uneasiness clawed at Horus. He would have to cross the threshold into a place where even when he had been a god he would have hesitated to breach. The relic brightened, its light reassuring, promising. A surge of hope cut through him. Maybe his consort *was* here, beyond the girth of the sphere, where he could not see. Blocking out the sphere with the brilliance of the relic's light, he took another look around the space. He looked up, then wished he hadn't. Far above, the sphere rotated, igniting the once-dark heights. He looked higher. The sphere turned there too, infinite, endless, its perspective unchanged, though it should have been much smaller. A wave of nausea slid through him. The rules of reality did not apply in this place. If he went in, he could fall out of time, out of space. He might never return, and if Baalat were not here, he might lose his chance to find her, forever.

Horus.

His misgivings fled. From across the span of the impossible space, he sensed her, the one for whom he existed. She called again, his name a mere breath. In the brutal, shearing silence of the chamber, her whisper was a roar. It awakened him, his love for her primal, fearless.

Holding the relic out before him, he stepped into the chamber and followed his heart.

How long passed as he put one foot in front of the other, as he crossed the endless distance? An hour? A year? A day? Horus could not tell. Time had become non-existent. It made no sense even to try to measure anything by it. He could do nothing other than follow the relic's light as it cut a path alongside the endless golden wall, streamers of living light sliding over the relic's brilliance, the sphere's light at once warm, cold, friendly, dangerous. He dared not look back. Insidious thoughts suggested the opening into the pyramid had vanished, or, it remained, yet after a thousand steps he had not progressed at all, it still stood right behind him. The essence of the place clawed at him, ravaged his mind, pulled at the threads of his sanity. Shards of hope cut through him, cross-hatched with feelings of despair, of failure, of having fallen into a trap. And still, he pressed on, for Baalat, for her, he would endure anything, even this. Even the shattering of reality.

A thousand more steps, followed by ten thousand more. The obsidian floor's sameness maddening, devastating. He fought the rising tide of despair—to sit down, to give up, to succumb.

The relic's light angled away from the floor. Horus waited, numb, his thoughts chaotic, faithless, as the light shifted toward the smooth golden wall and settled against it, a pool of light, warm, reassuring.

He looked at the wall, dull, seeing, yet not seeing. He shook himself, fighting to understand what he was supposed to be looking at. It was just more wall. There was nothing to see. It had been a trap after all. Desolation soaked him. He had failed.

The relic's light moved, sliding back and forth across the illuminated space. Within its center, a series of subtle shadows rotated. Horus stepped closer, his thoughts thick, viscous. There *was* something here. Fighting the hopelessness infusing his thoughts, he stared at the place of shadows, seeking to make sense of what the light had revealed. Then, through the murk of his confusion, he saw it, an elegant impression engraved into the wall's solid gold.

He lifted the relic's light closer and examined the design, his thoughts clogged by a bleak, endless circuit of defeat. Unable to trust his sight, he pressed his fingers against the wall and worked his way along the engraving's contours. It felt like the impression of a seal upon wax, but the inverted design eluded him, its image difficult to envision. He pushed his palm against his eyes, one after the other, fighting to see, to understand, a sliver of his senses bellowing for him to go on, to persist. The relic's brilliance dimmed to a quiet cadence, soft, gentle. He looked down at it, a staff with two serpents entwined around it. He stared at it, confusion dogging him—

Wait. He lifted his gaze back to the wall. The impression shivered back at him, its existence faint in the chamber's shifting golden light. He narrowed his eyes, the ephemeral light making the impression appear to be many different things at once. Beyond the boundary of his traitorous thoughts telling him to lie down and wait for the death he deserved, instinct slammed into him. Using the last of his will, he suppressed his thoughts and slid the relic along the wall, knowing without knowing what he must do. Just on the edge of his hearing, a quiet clink as the relic's contours slinked into the impression. He pressed his weight against the thing, holding it steady. One heartbeat. Two.

The wall fell away. Before him: the Creator's disk, or what was left of it. Gray shadows saturated the space. No starlight glittered along the disk's floor, and above and below the disk, the heavens no longer hung radiant with processing stars and planets, instead, a bleak, endless dark pressed in against the Creator's realm, its illumination extinguished. In the disk's center, Horus recognized the hulking outline of a massive game board. It flickered. He moved toward it, slow, wary, eyeing the changes wrought to it since he had last seen it. He knew this world. Elati. From Perev, dense tendrils of darkness slid, sinuous, across the continent. In their wake, death, chaos, despair. Gray shrouded two-thirds of Tholis, its taint crept over it, steady, certain, claiming the lands of the north, east, and west.

A faint gleam of golden light shimmered from beyond the game board. Horus edged his way around the towering tiers, a finger of dread touching him.

On a raised platform, a bed. And upon it, as silent as death— his heart stilled. No.

He crossed the distance in a heartbeat, his throat tight. Tendrils of darkness swarmed over his consort, living things, the opposite of the light of the gods. He reached out to touch her face.

"I would not do that if I were you."

Horus turned, his spine prickling. An old man limped up the steps of the platform. A faint sheen of starlight glimmered over his features.

Horus knelt, his heart pounding. "Father, I beg you, save her."

The Creator touched Baalat's brow. A trickle of his light left him, cleansing the rising dark contaminating her. It fell back, and began to gather again. "I cannot overcome the power of my darkness," he said, "but for a time, at least, I can contain it."

His heart bleak, Horus gazed at his consort. Her eyes were closed, but they flickered, rapid, as though she dreamed. "She was right there, behind me," he said, his throat aching, "and then she wasn't. It took her."

The Creator said nothing.

"It took Arinna, too."

"I know," the Creator said, quiet.

"Why did it take Baalat?" Horus erupted. "If the jihn is part of you, you must know."

"It wants Istara. It searches Baalat's mind for Istara's weaknesses. It is why Baalat still lives." The Creator cut a look at Horus. "But your consort is strong. She stands against it."

Horus got to his feet. The relic was still in his hand. "And this?" he asked, unfolding his fingers to show it to the one who had once granted him the powers of a god. "Does it have any purpose other than to open the way here?"

"It does not open the way here," the Creator answered, mild. "I brought you here. You and the relic would have been lost to the darkness otherwise."

"You could have saved the relic, and left me to die."

"I could have."

Horus didn't understand. Why would he—a mere mortal—receive greater favor from the Creator than Arinna, an immortal?

"Because Baalat needs you alive," the Creator said, laying bare Horus's thoughts. He turned to descend the steps of the platform. "Come, it is time to leave."

"And my consort?" Horus asked, longing to press his lips to her brow, to take hold of her hand and cradle it against his heart. "What will become of her?"

"I will aid her for as long as I am able, but with the jihn liberated, my powers will wane as the darkness grows." The Creator gestured for Horus to follow him, back to the double doors at the edge of the disk.

Horus gazed at Baalat, tears burning his eyes. It was unbearable to leave her. "*Can* she be saved from the darkness?"

The Creator turned. A shimmer of sorrow touched the depths of his eyes. "She can, but she must overcome it herself, as must every one of you. Each path will be different, all will be painful." They reached the double doors, dusty and dull, no longer gleaming with the traceries of stars. He opened it. The hall stretched away, shadowed, barren, devoid of the panoply of doors it had once possessed. Only one remained. A thick stone door, made of a single ashlar. He stopped before it. "And so, we arrive at the beginning which is also the end. Soon we will learn which force shall triumph in the final confrontation: The darkness or the light."

"*How* do we overcome the darkness?" Horus asked, despairing, wishing the Creator would not speak in riddles, not when his consort lay at the brink of her destruction.

"You are used to fighting, to war, to the use of violence to defeat your enemy." The Creator glanced back up the stairs leading toward the disk, to where Baalat endured her solitary battle. "But to defeat the darkness, the goddess must rise. Baalat engages the darkness even now."

"But Baalat is not a goddess," Horus said. Frustration lapped over him, cold, sharp. The Creator's answers meant nothing. Violence was the only way to defeat Marduk.

The Creator smiled, quiet, as though he knew a secret. He nodded at the relic. "Give that to Istara. When the time is right, it will lead her back to the seal. It is why the jihn seeks her. I made the jihn, but I also made the relic." He pursed his lips, a defiant look hardening his features. "It is my final gift. Whether it will be enough remains to be seen."

The stone ashlar slid aside and retracted into the wall. Horus faced the spot from where his journey had begun—at the top of the incline of the middle pyramid. Straight ahead, the corridor's vaulted ceiling diminished, lowering with distance. Now the time had come, he balked, unwilling to abandon Baalat. He braced his hand against the door's frame, resisting the weight of a world pulling him home, thinking to ask more questions, to learn, to understand, to stall for time.

A burst of white light exploded from the relic. He cried Baalat's name, a desperate prayer. A heartbeat later, he stood alone, bereft, powerless, the relic's glow fading. Its light flickered out. He eyed it, thinking of his consort, fighting her lonely battle, his only consolation the Creator's abstract, meaningless words. It wasn't enough. Loneliness clawed at him. How could he go on, never knowing if she would return. How could he exist and carry on the fight without her? Broiling tears stung his eyes. *Baalat.* He sank to his knees, and wept.

❋ ❋ ❋

Fire and thunder scorched into Imaru from the stars, burning with chaos and rage. Istara looked up from her notes, her heart tight. A black-dark ship hurtled past Thoth's torchlit terrace and came to a brutal, flaming halt on one of the adjacent terraces, its ragged sideways skid sending the elegant divans and potted plants hurtling over the edge. Screams rose from the lower terraces, cries for help, wails laced with anguish.

Thoth joined Istara by the lattice-covered window, his ink-spattered fingers gripping a piece of papyrus so tight the bones of his knuckles stood out pale and white.

"You should leave," he said, his eyes riveted on the ship. A pall of dread shadowed his features. "I fear the worst. Go. I will buy you time."

The door of the ship opened. Istara knew she should leave, and yet, if it were Sethi—her heart rebelled. Just to catch a glimpse of him. To see him. Just once. Within the lit interior—the outline of the powerful bulk of a warrior. Her heart stuttered, laced between hope and fear. *Sethi.*

"Lady Istara," Thoth murmured, urgency staining his tone. "I beg you. Leave."

"Thoth," a voice bellowed from the ship. "Get out here."

Istara caught Thoth's astonished look. He edged toward the silk hangings leading to the terrace, the ruined papyrus still clutched in his fist. "Teshub?" His voice cracked, uncertain.

"Who else?" came the taut answer. Teshub emerged from the ship and made his way through the wreckage to the edge of the torchlit terrace. He kicked aside a stray bench, vicious.

"Are you alone?" Thoth asked, still keeping out of sight.

Teshub came to a halt. The set of his jaw hardened. "As you can see."

"He is covered in blood," Istara whispered. She looked back at the ship, wondering where Arinna was, or Ahmen for that matter. He would not have left them behind. Ahmen perhaps, but not Arinna. Never Arinna.

Thoth stepped onto the terrace. Istara followed, dread circling her. Teshub crossed his arms over his chest as he waited for them to reach the edge. He stood bathed in the light of the burning debris, poised for battle, glaring at them, angry, vengeful, hostile. From within the apartment, Thoth's door slammed open. Two pairs of footsteps hurried through the suite, one heavy, the other light. They came to a wary halt.

"Istara," Urhi-Teshub said, low, from behind. "Come to me."

"Spare the heroics," Teshub snapped, "I am not Sethi in disguise."

"And yet," Thoth nodded at the destruction wrought by Teshub's savage landing, "what you have done has put our fragile accord with our hosts into grave danger."

"If only I could bring myself to care," Teshub muttered.

Below: shouts and cries for assistance, the rising of a hidden tide, a susurration riven with anger and despair. A wail, high and thin cut across the clamor as a mother shrieked, incoherent, over her dead child. Several voices rose, strident, demanding justice, for the king to rid Imaru of her reckless, unwanted guests. Thoth let out a resigned breath.

Sekhmet eased forward, her gaze seizing on the dried blood coating Teshub's tunic and kilt, its dark ink staining his arms and face. "Where is Arinna?" she asked, low.

Teshub shuddered. His jaw tightened. Over the crackle of the flames the grind of his teeth cut the air. His eyes glittered, ferocious, like an animal cornered, desperate. Dangerous.

He cut a bitter look at Istara. "*He* took her from me. Forever."

Istara caught her breath. Sethi. Teshub had seen Sethi.

Urhi-Teshub paced closer, his hands went to the handles of his belted weapons. "Then we will find her and bring her back."

Sekhmet nodded at Teshub. "My blade is yours, brother."

Teshub looked away. His chest rose and fell, ragged. "Only the Creator can overcome death."

A stunned silence sliced through the group.

"But," Thoth rallied, "how?"

"Get in the ship," Teshub answered. "I will tell you everything on the way."

"On the way . . . where?" Urhi-Teshub asked, tight.

"Just get in," Teshub muttered. His gaze slid across the terraced row of suites, pausing to linger on the one which belonged to him and Arinna. Anguish bled from him. "I need to be anywhere but here." His eyes glittering, he shoved his way back through the shattered detritus, his gold-embossed sandals treading on shards of broken pots and torched plants.

Thoth cut a severe look at Istara. "Sekhmet and I will go with him."

"My consort murdered my sister," Istara said, bristling at Thoth's presumption, "I will not be kept apart while you talk of his ability to strip an immortal of their existence."

"My lady," Thoth said, "you have just witnessed what Teshub has done to innocents. He is possessed by rage, and in his current state is unreasonable, even danger—"

"Enough. I am tired of being coddled and fussed over as though I were an infant. I am the goddess of healing. My consort is the god of war. I am finished with cowardice. It is time to fight." She turned and swept past Thoth. "Your warning is noted, however, no one shall convince me not to go. No," she held her hand up to Urhi-Teshub, and faced down his consternation, "not even you."

As they tore across the skies, Teshub did not tell them anything, nor would he allow any of them to sit in the seat beside him, where a single strand of Arinna's golden hair still clung to the seat's headrest. It glimmered in the console's light, filled with her quiet joy, her life going on without her. Whether Teshub was aware of this last vestige of her existence or not, Istara could not tell. He remained locked in grief, silent tears coating his face, staining his kilt and tunic, bathing her blood in his love.

No one spoke. Heaviness filled the cabin. Beside her, Urhi-Teshub checked and rechecked his weapons. Across from him, Sekhmet perched on the edge of the divan, her gaze raking the skies, vigilant, calm, watchful. Thoth alone remained silent and withdrawn. He sat staring straight ahead, lost to the depths of his thoughts, his eyes moving, yet unseeing, traveling paths known only to him.

Teshub had used the ion drive, had given no warning, though the brief trip over the canopy of the world had been worth every brutal heartbeat spent caught in the thrust's vicious grip.

They had descended, fast, reckless, through a thick layer of clouds, the world opening itself up to them again. Against the endless dark of the sea, the glint of starlight shimmered, undulating against the wave caps. The ship leveled off. In the distance, a dark blot rose out of the sea's soft carpet. An island.

"Why would he bring us here?" Sekhmet asked Thoth, quiet. She nudged him with her elbow, breaking into his deliberation. "Look." She pointed.

Thoth eyed the spot, grim, though he said nothing, neither did he look at any of them, instead he looked down at his hands, clenching into thin fists. The ink stains on his skin stretched, distorting into evocations of creatures and men.

Against Thoth disapproving silence, Sekhmet said no more. Curious, Istara raked her gaze over the island, seeking to uncover its secrets. Darkness hulked over its steep cliffs, a rugged barrier against the sea. No illumination apart from starlight pierced its cliff tops. As she searched the island's empty contours, she glimpsed a flicker in the distance, a mere pinprick of light, so faint it might have been a trick of the starlight. She narrowed her eyes, keeping her gaze on it as the ship drew toward the cliffs and soared over them. There. Another flicker, stronger this time. Urhi-Teshub leaned forward and rested his elbows on his knees, his attention fixed on the same spot.

They raced over the tops of palms, a verdant, tropical oasis, straight toward the light, brightening with each passing heartbeat, a beacon of pale, cerulean blue, shot with shifting streamers of white. Realization hit Istara like the cold slap of water. Her heart tumbled, plummeting with the ship's descent as it angled toward the vast clearing—toward the towering structure of ashlars framing an ephemeral wall of light. No. Not again. She didn't want to remember anything more. Too late she understood Thoth's foresight, he *knew* this would be where Teshub would go. She cut a look at him, but he continued to look down at his lap, his hands clenching and unclenching, his body withdrawn, coiled tight, defensive.

"He's taking us to Surru," Urhi-Teshub said. He came to his feet. "How dare he put Istara and Sekhmet in danger." He eyed the back of Teshub's seat, dark. "He has gone mad with grief, seeks to even the score and make me suffer with him." He pulled one of the weapons from his hip and lifted it up, priming it to fire. "He will not harm the women I love."

Thoth yanked Urhi-Teshub's arm down. "It is not what you think," he said, his bony features pinched, angry, sharp. "Calm yourself."

Urhi-Teshub lowered the weapon though his finger still hovered near the weapon's trigger. Agitation pounded from him, tangible, volatile. Istara caught Sekhmet looking at her, the goddess of war's expression unreadable. A flicker shunted through her dark eyes, followed by a faint tightening of her jaw, then nothing—her blank look deafening, baleful. Istara looked away, uneasy, wishing Urhi-Teshub had not spoken so plain. The truce between her and Sekhmet fragile enough without him pouring oil upon still-glowing embers.

Teshub brought the ship down into the glade a little distance from the shimmering portal. Cerulean light rippled through the cabin's interior, blue moonlight against water. Teshub punched several buttons on the console—the blue-lit panel highlighting the ragged contours of his grief-ravaged profile. The ship shut down. The cabin lights dimmed. Teshub remained in his seat for several long heartbeats, his eyes fixed on the wall of churning light. He let out a heavy, shuddering breath. Tendrils swept out from the portal, awakening, sensing the presence of gods. Sinuous streamers curled toward the ship, gentle, inquisitive, the faint blue light eerie against the deep black of night.

A creak of leather as Urhi-Teshub shifted his weight. The weapons strapped against his leather-clad thighs glinted in the portal's light. "Why have you brought us here?" he asked, his words sharp as fresh-quarried rocks.

Teshub dragged his gaze from the portal. He rose, pausing to touch Arinna's headrest. He found the strand of her golden hair. He lifted it up, his eyes glittering, glaciers of frozen pain, and tucked it into his bloodstained tunic, against his heart.

"I promised to tell you everything," he said, his voice raw, all angles and edges. He met Urhi-Teshub's challenging pose and cut a look at the divan. "Sit, this could take some time."

"Not until you tell me why you have brought us here," Urhi-Teshub bristled. "There is nothing for any of us beyond that wall. Nothing."

"Nothing is enough," Teshub said, flat.

Istara caught the tightening of Thoth's expression, the hollowing of his skin over his thin cheeks. Thoth, Teshub, and Urhi-Teshub eyed each other, saying nothing, though volumes passed between them, locked within the weighted walls of their stand-off.

Teshub held Urhi-Teshub's look, his own, hard, unrelenting. "Sekhmet can take us through and come straight back so no harm comes to her. When it is done," he jerked his head toward the shimmering portal, "you'll know where you'll need to be, if only to escape your agony."

"And the price?" Urhi-Teshub answered, his lips thinning. "I would carry your memories. Your suffering. I would forget who I was—the ones I love. Instead, I would be doomed to grieve for Arinna for an eternity, a woman I barely know."

"You would be a god," Teshub erupted, his eyes sharpening, glittering in the portal's light. "Do you not yet see? We were destined for this all along." He lifted up his blood-spattered arms. Against the ephemeral light, the faint outlines of golden symbols glinted. "This is the message the Creator gave me before I fell from the Immortal Realm: *You are next.* I thought it meant I was destined to reprieve a mortal with my light, just as my brother and sister had done. But, a tendril remained in me, just as in the end, a tendril remained in Baalat and Horus." He thrust the markings at Urhi-Teshub, pointed, angry, "What this means is I am the next *god* to be replaced. Once, you wanted this, to spare Istara. But I refused because I wasn't ready. Now, I am ready. This fight needs gods, not immortals. Think of the damage you could do, the power you would wield." He cut a look at Istara. "The protection you could offer."

A heated silence swarmed over the cabin. Urhi-Teshub said nothing, though his eyes strayed to the portal, the cut of his profile hard, impassive.

Uncertainty trailed an icy finger along the length of Istara's spine. Too much had been said, all of it aimed at the heart of what she believed irrevocable. Her mind, razored sharp with fear raked over the scraps Teshub had laid bare: He knew Baalat and Horus, yet he had never lived in Sekhmet's world. Another piece clicked. Thoth had said: *Horus and Baalat are gone, forever—from both worlds.* From the corner of her mind, Urhi-Teshub's words replayed from the night before: *Whatever we once shared is over. For you, it ended years ago. But for me, it ended at the portal when I drove a dagger into your heart and killed you.* His words had been no metaphor after all. There was more to who she was. Much more. The air thickened. A breath held. Dread assailed her.

Teshub had told Urhi-Teshub he would return a god, the storm god. She swallowed, catching Thoth eyeing her, oblique, his expression shuttered. All this time, she had been existing around half-truths. The last piece slammed into place. *I would forget who I was—the ones I love.* Horror pounded into her as the weave of her existence slid into a new design, the warp and weft flawless, perfect. Sickened, she read her truth in its threads. Once, she had been mortal and died. Teshub had said Baalat and Horus had given up their light, just as he was about to do for Urhi-Teshub, which meant she had been mortal, and had been reborn a god, her mortal memories lost, Baalat's past becoming her own. She reached a new pattern in the tapestry. A king on his throne, who loved a woman. No. Her heart folded. Shame enveloped her. Urhi-Teshub had not been her lover—but her husband and king. She looked at him with new eyes, confounded by the depth of his love, his sacrifice.

The tapestry flowed away, dragging her in its relentless current, revealing a new history, the details subtle in their differences. She had not been a goddess who had cheated on her consort with a mortal king, but had been a queen and had left her husband for Sethi, another mortal, and yet, after all she had done, her husband had stood by her, had remained with her, her protector— had watched her mourn for another. Her heart thudded, heavy, anchored to an abyss of remorse. Tears cut into her eyes. He couldn't leave, not now just when she had at last, uncovered the truth in all its ugliness. The one who had stood by her, who held the answers to their shared past would soon leave, forever, and on his return would forget her just as she had forgotten him. She wanted to stop him, to hold him back, to tell him she knew the truth, and yet, as he glanced at Sekhmet, sorrow and longing in his eyes, she knew she could not. He had moved on, had survived his love for her and found another. It was time for her to give him what he had given her. Wounded, broken, she pulled her burden to her, and cradled it against her aching heart, determined to do for him what he had done for her.

Thoth continued to eye her, watchful, wary. She looked away, and caught Sekhmet's weighted look. Trapped under the goddess of war's cold appraisal, she brushed the tears from her eyes, Sekhmet's piercing, calculating gaze unnerving.

"With both of you immortal," Thoth said, choosing his words with care, "the situation is no longer the same. It may not work."

Teshub kept his attention on Urhi-Teshub; stubbornness gilded him. "It will work."

"Grief has blinded you, has made you desperate to make the pieces fit."

Teshub rounded on Thoth, fierce. "The pieces fit! This is my decision, not yours."

Sekhmet came to her feet. "No. It is also Urhi-Teshub's."

"I saved his life," Teshub cried. "Now all I ask in return is to be released from mine." He shuddered and sank onto the divan, his face in his hands. "Arinna is alone. I must go to her. If Urhi-Teshub will not come. I will go without him."

No one spoke. Teshub grieved, quiet, his anger spent, sorrow following hard in its wake.

"I will do it." Urhi-Teshub set the weapon back into its holder, the act decisive, final. He nodded, as though answering a question posed within himself. "To lose this opportunity would be foolish. There is no other choice."

Sekhmet sank onto the divan. "No," she whispered, her eyes finding his, their shared look at once saying both everything, and nothing, "as usual, there is not."

Teshub stilled. He pressed the heels of his palms against his eyes. "Then—" he took a ragged breath, "—it is time to tell you all I know."

His words sparing, almost anemic, he described his journey to the storm-encased island of Anki; his discovery of the city of the lost gods, and of its colossal central complex with its trio of pyramids identical to the ones Thoth had built; the endless tower, and the way into it revealed by a relic Ahmen had discovered in the ship, carried from the world they fled. He carried on, dogged, his words dry, dull, telling them of Creator's fight between darkness and light, of the jihn, and of Sethi's arrival, and how Sethi had freed the jihn from its prison and used it against Arinna, feeding it with her immortal life. He began to say something else. Tears clogged his words. No one pressed him to continue. It was enough. He had suffered enough.

Istara sat back, shaken by Teshub's account. He had said Sethi's eyes had bled cold, malevolent hate as he demanded to know where his consort was. Through the murk of her tumult, she comprehended this much: Sethi did not want her back despite his cries each dawn as he called her name, his voice ragged with anguish. He intended to feed her to his hateful weapon, to do to her what he had done to Arinna. Silent, bleak walls towered over her, looming, dark, closing her off from the others. There was no sense to her existence, and no time to understand. Soon Urhi-Teshub would be gone, and with him, the last vestige of the one she had once been.

Urhi-Teshub cleared his throat and breached the uncomfortable silence. "What relic did Ahmen discover?"

"A pendant," Teshub answered, dull, looking at the bloodstains on the backs of his hands. He ran his fingers over a faded streak, his longing for his consort palpable.

"Of a staff with two serpents entwined around it?"

Teshub nodded, vague.

"Not much wonder Rhoha wanted it," Urhi-Teshub muttered, the corners of his lips turning downward. "Although, how could such a thing whose purpose is meant to be fulfilled here, end up in Tarhuntassa? The Chief Surgeon said he purchased it from a Babylonian trader."

Thoth stirred, uncoiling just a fraction. "When it comes to the Creator, there are many mysteries, things we will never understand; things we are not meant to understand. What matters is a relic made its way across a near-impossible divide to Istara—" He glanced at her, a layer of hope flickering through the slats of his shuttered thoughts. He looked at Teshub again. "If it led you through the pyramid into the interior of the tower, just imagine what it could do in the hands of the one meant to possess it."

Istara felt Thoth's eyes on her, thoughtful, speculative. She roused from under the weight of what Sethi had done to Arinna, and of what her consort, once a mortal like she, intended to do to her. "It is not mine. I have never possessed a relic."

"Hmm," Thoth said, continuing as though Istara had not spoken. "And how did you learn about the jihn and the Creator's internal battle? Was it written in one of the pyramids?"

"No," Teshub answered after a pregnant pause. He fell silent. His gaze slid to the portal, his desire to go through it, tangible. "We were not the first to reach Anki."

An expectant hush trailed after him, but he said no more.

"And?" Sekhmet prodded.

"And nothing," Teshub muttered. His gaze flicked to Istara, then to Thoth. Istara read the message. *There is more, but not in front of her. Too complicated.*

Thoth stood, brusque. "We must make our way to Anki as soon as possible. Teshub, if you are determined to do this thing, I will wait here with Istara." He met Sekhmet's cool gaze. "They need to return to the cavern. Although it took an hour for me to suffer the consequences of being where I should not, do not remain there, your presence will begin to unravel the threads holding that world together, as mine did. Waste no time with goodbyes." Sekhmet nodded, expressionless, avoiding Urhi-Teshub's aching look. "Urhi-Teshub, if you might grant me one of those weapons of yours for the time being." He held out his hand.

Uneasy, Urhi-Teshub obliged. He placed the one he had raised against Teshub into Thoth's upturned palm, tentative, as though it might explode.

"And what does this button do?" Thoth asked as he settled his fingers around the weapon's grip and eyed a small blinking light on its handle.

"Disintegration," Urhi-Teshub answered, unapologetic.

"Ah," Thoth murmured, his lips tightening, "I remember this one. Marduk would often entertain his guests at my expense. It's quite painful to break into a billion pieces and reform once more."

No one said anything. Teshub got up and punched the code to open the door. He stepped back, his eyes distant, hard. Warm, jasmine-scented air bathed the staleness from the cabin, cleansing it of its layers of anger, sorrow, resignation, and despair.

Thoth nodded at Urhi-Teshub, a terse farewell, then went to Teshub. He reached out and patted Teshub's shoulder, awkward. "Find her," he said, his words tight, mangled, "may the Creator grant you peace."

Teshub shuddered. A fresh coating of tears glazed his eyes.

Thoth backed away, and with a last, warning look at Sekhmet, he left, the soft tread of his steps retreating into the filtered wash of cerulean light.

Sensing Sekhmet's dark regard on her, Istara held out her hand to Urhi-Teshub. He took it, his, warm and callused, a warrior's grip, strong. Even just to have had a day, to talk, to learn. Regret piled onto her, as her mind raced over the dozens of days wasted, the looks he had given her before he had found Sekhmet, laden with loss. Her heart quavered. *Farewell, husband, king.* She rallied, determined not to fall to weakness when he needed her most. A multitude of words washed over her, yet from among their heaving swells she could not divine the right thing to say. She lifted her eyes to his, the golden flecks in his green ones catching in the portal's light. Soon those beautiful flecks would be gone. She would miss them.

"I will forget you," he said. A bright glint of sorrow gilded the dark blades of his words.

"I will not forget you," she whispered, willing her heart not to break, not yet.

With a groan he pulled her against him and held her fast. She drank in the scent of him, memorizing it, warm, resinous, earthy cyprinum, the oiled leather of his armor, the heat of his maleness, his strength, and valor, the scent of a warrior, the scent of the man who had been her husband. He let her go. She backed away, her throat aching, closing over, locking her final words within her, shrouding her anguish in silence. At the top of the steps, she nodded at Teshub. He nodded back, though his gaze was turned inward, to the future. To his end.

She descended and backed across the damp grass, never taking her eyes from Urhi-Teshub. He reached out and pulled Sekhmet against him, holding her face in his hands, his mouth finding hers, his passion desperate, unquenchable. The door slid closed.

"Lady Istara," Thoth murmured. He held out the crook of his arm to her. Numb, she took it and followed him to the edge of the glade. The ship rolled away, its dark weight crushing a patch of wildflowers. Their fragrance swept over Istara; life, existing beyond death. The nose of the ship turned and touched the churning wall of light. The portal thrummed, its inner light spreading, searching. Bursts of starlight swarmed over its surface, and from within its core, a deep reverberation emanated, hypnotic. It held Istara in its thrall, a captive to her loss, engraving Urhi-Teshub's departure in her heart, indelible. Eternal.

Tendrils wrapped around the ship, cradling it, protecting it against the fall to come. A tug, and the ship shot through the portal's massive ashlar frame. Brilliance slammed into the glade, white as the hottest star. It swept past her, streaming into the distance, a beacon of light in a world of dark. It hung, suspended for a tantalizing heartbeat, before it surged back, scything over the trees, the bushes, the flowers, and her. In its wake, nothing. Silence.

In the soft light of the quiescent portal, a single golden tendril emerged from her finger and settled over the white scar across her palm—the one she had never been able to erase. The one she could never explain. Her light rippled over it. An image sheared through her, of a child and a much younger Urhi-Teshub standing before an altar, the pair bathed in the light of a white moon, his blade deft against her upturned palm, a sear of blood in its wake. The scar faded—vanishing as though it had never been.

Stricken, she sank to her knees. All this time she had carried Urhi-Teshub's mark, his love so powerful it had remained with her even through her transition. She traced her fingers over her unblemished flesh, wishing she might have her imperfection back. But it was too late. Nothing between them remained. Her husband was gone. A god would return.

Bathed in the cerulean light of eternity, she wept. Where her tears touched the earth, Thoth later told her, roses lifted their faces to the portal, though their scent was silenced, drowned in the wake of her sorrow.

※　　※　　※

Baalat and Horus were alive, returned to Elati by the Creator. It had been they whom Teshub had found in Anki—how he had learned of the jihn's origin and purpose. As Teshub gave the scant details of his message for Thoth to Sekhmet, Urhi-Teshub eyed the empty ship before the portal, bathed in pale, cold, cerulean light, its nose pointed at the wall of churning light, poised to leave them there to die. Teshub fell silent, his message to Thoth complete. Without another word, he turned and walked to the edge of the dark island's inky shore and put his back to them.

Sekhmet watched him go, her look unreadable. Urhi-Teshub touched her arm, tugged her toward him, gentle. For a beat, she held firm, resisting him, stubborn. Angry.

"Please," Urhi-Teshub whispered, his heart aching, unwilling to part this way.

She met his eyes, hers dark with bitterness. He tugged again, let her see his anguish, his longing to hold her one last time. She blinked. Sorrow tainted the contours of her mouth. Her dark armor glinting with frost, she came to him, and let him enfold her in his embrace. He stroked her face, his fingers numb with cold, raking his gaze over her, drinking in her fierce beauty, her power, her passion. His throat tight, he tightened his hold and drew her to him, memorizing the feel of her—the perfect fit of her—against him.

"For a brief time," he said against her ear, "I will remember the man I once was. We will have a little time yet."

She pulled back, her eyes hard, sharp with tears. "The one I loved and lost, the one I was second to . . ." She blinked and looked away.

"It is not important," he said, pressing a kiss against her brow. "I do not need to know."

"You do," she said, forlorn, misery bleeding from her. "It was the storm god," she whispered, her expression anguished. "Teshub."

The name slammed into him. Of all the gods he could have become . . . He had promised her she would never be second to anyone, and now—

"No," he said, defiant against his fate, his loss. "I will not be him. His past is not mine. It will not be the same."

"You will be the storm god whose consort is gone." Sekhmet slipped free of his hold, her expression shuttered. "Perhaps the connection you share with him is why I was drawn to you from the first heartbeat I saw you—you bore so much of his light." She turned away, her profile taut in the wan light. "I must go. Thoth warned me not to tarry."

Urhi-Teshub lunged after her, caught her arm. She stopped, tense, defensive, her back to him.

"I *will* overcome this. I will love you," he murmured. He would not lose his past, or her, not after all he had endured, after everything he had lost. "When I return, I will write of my life before I became a god. I will not disregard my own words. I refuse to lose you."

She glanced at him, then at the portal leading back to Elati, her golden irises glistening, her lashes spiked with unshed tears. Her bleak silence slayed him.

He dragged her back into his arms and kissed her, deep, fervent, desperate, tasting the metallic tang of the tears of a goddess. With her, the colors of his life had sharpened, his existence had deepened, and the passion of his warrior's heart had awakened. He would find a way to come back to her, no matter how long it would take.

She backed away. One step, two steps, her eyes never leaving his, her soul bared to his, aching, lost, tumbling toward an eternity of lonely solitude.

"You will be my consort," he said, ragged. "We will be together again."

Giving him a final, broken look, she turned, her booted feet skimming over the loose surface of the shale-clad island, soundless, light as a cat. She slipped up the steps into the ship. The door slid closed. A beat later she took her seat in the flight deck—her profile hollow, etched with restrained grief, the raw beauty of her sorrow haunting him.

The ship's engines awakened, and a low rumble echoed over the cavern's barren, frost-rimed walls. A thud came from the undercarriage as the brakes released and the wheels lurched free. The ship rolled forward, stones snapping under its weight. He clenched his fists, willing her to look at him one last time. Tendrils from the portal swept over the ship and tugged it into its embrace. At the last heartbeat, she turned. Her eyes met his, soaking his heart with her love, her farewell. Brilliance erupted from the portal, blinding him. A dense silence surged over him, held him suspended in its grip. The beat of his heart came first, then the gentle lap of water touching the shore. The portal dimmed. He looked, but he knew the truth. The one who had stolen his heart, who had breathed life back into the shadowed remains of his world, was gone.

Deep cold gnawed Urhi-Teshub's flesh. He huddled into himself, his hands tucked under his arms, enduring the burning cut of freezing fire. Behind him, the portal pulsed soft, dim, dormant, its light reflecting against the cavern's dark waters. In such an unchanging space, time lost all relevance; he had no idea if an hour or a morning had passed. A little distance away, Teshub remained locked within himself, clad in silent, impenetrable walls.

Urhi-Teshub paced the length of the island, focusing his attention on the stones beneath his booted feet, counting the largest ones to combat the lethargy stealing over him. Dark thoughts flickered at the edge of his mind, suggesting there might be no transition after all, that Teshub was wrong and Thoth was right. Once, in this very place, Urhi-Teshub had been prepared to become the storm god, had held a dagger to his heart, oblivious to the depth of the price he would pay.

He sifted through his memories, sorting through the pieces of his life he had secreted into the deepest corridors of his heart— pieces he would not allow himself to forget: The day he gave Anash to Istara; the afternoon his father stripped him of his right to the throne; the night he forever lost Istara to Egypt in the royal enclosure at Kadesh; his crowning as King of Hatti; his return to life from the brink of death in Karchemish; his journey across Thamud Desert; his escape from the Etemen'anki; the dagger he plunged into Istara's heart, her blood coating his tunic, her legs giving out—her resurrection as a goddess; Elati; the strange beasts he had seen while collecting the cores from the pyramids; *Sekhmet*. He swallowed, his throat tight, his thoughts dwelling on her, morose. It couldn't be over. They had hardly even begun. Seven days glinted back at him, brilliant, alive, his heart had once more beat with purpose, and now—this. He kicked one of the loose stones. It skittered into the water, and sank with a quiet burble. Perhaps he was destined to be just like Sekhmet, starved of love, and alone, for eternity. No. He would fight it. The alternative was unbearable. He looked up, catching Teshub's gaze on him, cold, implacable, the portal's pale light rippling over his grief-ravaged features.

The once-storm god bore down on him.

"Don't mourn her."

"Who? Sekhmet?"

"No, *Arinna*. She is not yours to mourn. She is mine."

"Considering what has happened to Istara," Urhi-Teshub returned, stamping his feet, enduring the frigid splinters of cold crackling up his legs, "I doubt I will have much choice in the matter."

Teshub said nothing. He looked away, stricken anew. The muscles in his jaw clenched.

Urhi-Teshub stamped his feet again. More pain. He welcomed it. "As much as it is in my power to do so, I intend to remain with Sekhmet."

"I would suggest you reconsider," Teshub muttered.

Urhi-Teshub's heart thudded. Anger pooled.

Teshub folded his arms over his chest. The symbols left by the Creator gleamed, pale, in the wan light. "After I lost Arinna, Sekhmet warmed my bed for a time. I sensed she wanted more." He gave Urhi-Teshub a heavy look. "She is not consort material."

"I think she is."

"Sekhmet is blood, violence, darkness, war. It is her purpose. It is her *only* purpose."

Urhi-Teshub stilled. Blades of ice and fire sawed through him. "I see her differently."

"Perhaps," Teshub said, "but you will be the storm god. She is the goddess of war." Teshub eyed the portal, his eyes dark with grief. "In this match, there can be no balance between light and dark. All the pairs are balanced. The Creator made it so. You cannot unmake it."

Urhi-Teshub endured the deepening chill digging into his bones, damping down the nascent embers of his outrage. "So I must be alone for eternity?"

"There will be plenty of others to warm your bed."

"No," Urhi-Teshub said, his thoughts congealing, the cold pulling them away from him, one by one, taking them hostage. "I lost one woman. I will not lose another."

Silence. Teshub let out a grunt of pain. Then, low, harsh with suffering: "You remind me of me."

A shard of agony sliced through Urhi-Teshub. It skittered away into a hundred directions, a shattering erupted from within. He roared, tearing at his skin, desperate to free himself of the jagged blades shearing him of his immortal existence.

Images tore through his mind: Istara dressed in the Egyptian style; his throne in Hattusa protected by the pillars of Teshub; his crown torn from his fingers by Rhoha, smiling, cold, clad in a shimmering gown of black. Istara's pendant in his grip; the broiling heat of Karchemish stealing his last choking breaths. Light. Golden light.

He opened his eyes. The pain was gone. Light encased him within a perfect cube. He reached out, longing to touch it. Stars glided along its walls, laden with sentience. They called to him, whispering the secrets of eternity. He brushed his fingertips against them. The light rippled, the stars brightening where his touch alighted. Awareness suffused him. Euphoria found him. It lasted a single, blissful, unforgettable heartbeat, then, the light shivered and collapsed, a relentless, perfect enfolding, descending into smaller and smaller cubes until nothing more than a speck remained. Emptiness poured into him. He lunged after the remains of the light, seeking to capture it in his hand. It slid free and hurtled away, absorbed by the vast dark. A starless, dead void slid into its wake. Isolation impaled him.

A kick—rough, hard—against his leg. He opened his eyes. A roof of black stone hung over him, its frosted surface glinting in the portal's pale light. Spikes of icy cold slammed into him, pinning him to the chill, bleak stone of the cavern's forlorn isle. Violent shivers shouldered their way through him. Pain soaked his body—the deep, grinding pain of a fragile, dying existence—the kind of pain he had forgotten about in Elati. The grip of mortality dragged its brutal weight against him, relentless, vengeful. Everything hurt. Breathing hurt.

"Took you long enough." Teshub held out his hand. Urhi-Teshub took it and hauled himself to his feet. Teshub's fingers were ice, colder even than his own. "Thought I might meet my end before you got back. If the others are anything to go by, I think you have to die first for this to work." He eyed Urhi-Teshub's thigh. "It took a few tries to rouse you. I wasn't gentle."

Urhi-Teshub grunted. He didn't care about his leg. The pain of his very existence blinded him. He felt worse than he could ever remember feeling. Agony strafed him, alternating its torturous journey between his mind and body. After the perspective he had gained from far above the canopy of the skies, and of the revelations he had experienced as an immortal, the abrupt, rude, insignificance of his mortal self stunned him. How could he have lived like this for so long and never glimpsed the occlusion of his brief existence against the canopy of forever? Yet, if he had, how could he have borne it? To be mortal, then immortal, and mortal again was too much to bear. It was time to finish what he and Teshub had begun with courage and without hesitation.

His fingers clumsy with cold, he fumbled to unfasten the strap securing one of Marduk's weapons in its holder.

"No," Teshub panted, his face pale, shadowed by his own agonies. "Not disintegration. Use the blade."

Urhi-Teshub nodded, dull. Teshub was the god after all. Or had been. He freed the dagger from the scabbard strapped to his thigh, grateful he had decided to carry one at the last heartbeat. The blade's edge glinted in the chill light, cold, hungry, as if aware of its profound purpose. Urhi-Teshub lifted it to his chest and met Teshub's eyes. Hollowness eroded him. Once, he had stood in this place, ready to die to protect the woman he loved, when purpose had clothed him, ennobling his sacrifice. But this, he glanced at the blade—*this* was nothing. His end would not be borne out of sacrifice, only duty, and the hope he might resurrect as the storm god to aid the others in their fight against Marduk—a fight which had nothing to do with him. Bitterness shrouded him. His death would be nothing more than a repetition of the theme of his entire existence thus far. Dutiful. Selfless.

He eyed the quiet susurrations of the portal's light. On its opposite side, a bleak eternity awaited, where his heart, lonely and lost would be doomed to mourn a woman he had never known. He lifted the weapon to his chest, slow, reverent, allowing himself his final heartbeats, to grant himself time to recall the man he had been. With one push, he would usher in the end of Urhi-Teshub, King of Hatti, husband of Istara, Princess of Kadesh, and forever cut-off his nascent affair with Sekhmet, goddess of war. He tightened his grip on the dagger's hilt; only this morning he had wakened with her in his arms and whispered his heart would be hers until the end of time.

"Do it," Teshub breathed, his gaze on the blade primed to delve Urhi-Teshub's heart. He lifted his eyes to Urhi-Teshub's, his, aching, desperate, dark; a caged, suffering beast. "Let me go to her. Let this end."

Urhi-Teshub drew a final breath, savoring the ugly tang of the cavern's raw, damp air, his thoughts lingering on the one who had liberated his heart from its lifelong bindings, willing himself not to forget her, and to have the strength to overcome the claws of his cruel destiny. He closed his eyes, readying himself for the thrust of the blade into his heart. One heartbeat. Two. *Sekhmet.* Searing heat screamed through his breast. His breath caught, shocked, silenced by his savagery. He yanked the blade out and sank to his knees. Metallic heat saturated the razor-iced edges of his frosted tunic, stealing away the cold, warming him from the outside in. He looked up at Teshub, who fell to his knees before him. The once-god took him by his shoulders, firm, yet gentle. A glimmer of golden light swirled in Teshub's torso, awakening, scenting the final stage of its journey.

"The Creator chose well." Tears glinted in Teshub's eyes. "Already you are a better god than I."

Urhi-Teshub sagged. The dagger slipped from his fingers, its clatter abrasive in the portal's thickening, expectant silence. He lifted his palm to his chest, morbid, fascinated, as the heat of his life slipped through his fingers, his slowing pulse strafing his senses, at once both cold and hot as it fled, exquisite, raw, liberating— the pain of his existence subsumed by the pain of death. The scorching, icy fire within his breast lessened. Relief beckoned. Teshub's arms came around him, enclosed him in the embrace of a warrior. Numb, Urhi-Teshub slumped against the one who had once reprieved him, whom he now sought to reprieve. As the light of the portal brightened against the bleak stones, he closed his eyes, clinging to fading images of Sekhmet, and of Istara, even as his heart succumbed to his will, and stuttered to its final, broken beat.

Darkness surrounded Urhi-Teshub. He had expected a cocoon of golden light. Not this, a barren wasteland of nothing. In the distance, a faint glimmer of pale starlight pierced the gray, bleak expanse. It moved nearer, its form outlined by a tracery of constellations. It stopped a few paces from him, folded its hands in front of itself and surveyed him, as though weighing Urhi-Teshub's worth.

"Urhi-Teshub," it said, quiet. "You must continue to protect Istara. She, among all of us, faces the gravest of danger. If she falls, we all fall."

Wary, Urhi-Teshub stepped closer. Darkness surrounded them, imprisoning them within the other's tiny pool of starlight. "And who are you to instruct me?"

A tendril of golden light flickered over the speaker's features. An old man, worn, haggard, met his gaze. Astonished, Urhi-Teshub took a step back. "I know you. You arrived with Sethi during our imprisonment in the Etemen'anki." He searched his mind. "Imhotep. You wore an unsightly assortment of ornaments, like a sorcerer." He eyed him, sharp, suspicious. "You vanished when we crossed into Elati."

The old man smiled, soft, pleased. "You remember. How rare. Imhotep was only one of my many mortal manifestations." The golden light faded until only a dusting of pale starlight remained, a mere whisper. "I am known to mortals and gods as the Creator, although that is not my true name."

"So Teshub was right," Urhi-Teshub breathed, looking at the one who had fled the collapsing Etemen'anki with him—who had never once fretted or complained despite his injuries—seeing him with new eyes. "And he called you—"

The Creator nodded, a faint smile touched his lips. "He did. He always was a hothead. I liked him."

"Then why did you not protect his consort? I have lost everything because of it." The accusation came out before he could stop it. Urhi-Teshub shut his mouth, mortified.

The Creator said nothing for a long time. Fear glazed Urhi-Teshub's spine. He had been a king, then an immortal, and the chosen love of a goddess. He was not accustomed to others being able to command or question him, or having to watch his words. Far out of his depth, he knelt.

"I beg you, forgive me," he said, and meant it.

A touch came to his brow, soft. Warmth suffused him, comforting, reassuring, a feeling of home, of security, certainty. Shelter. A shimmer of gold rippled over his flesh, highlighting the traceries of his veins. Breathless, he looked up into the Creator's eyes. Sorrow touched them.

"A gift," the Creator said. "You will retain full possession of your memories. Teshub's memories will not become your own. I should have done so with the others, although as my power wanes their memories will return—" He let out a heavy breath. "Perhaps it is for the best. Istara has suffered much. Too much. As has Sethi." He lifted his fingers from Urhi-Teshub's brow, abrupt, ending their connection. A wave of loss swept through Urhi-Teshub, in its wake: longing for a home he had never known. "It appears the caution I exercised over the eons to protect my children has, in these final days, turned against me." The Creator continued, as though speaking to himself, "In my adherence to habit, I have granted Marduk a powerful advantage." He looked up into the darkness, his eyes moving over the desolate void, searching, finding nothing. "Or perhaps, it was not unwitting, perhaps I did it on purpose—a seed I planted long ago to sabotage myself in these final days. I cannot see the future anymore. I am as blind as my creation."

Despite his longing to thank the Creator for his gift, Urhi-Teshub found himself unwilling to break into the thoughts of the father of all life. Teshub had said many strange things about the Creator being both dark and light. He suppressed a shiver—to accept the Creator could be evil was too dark, too disturbing. He shut out the thought, uncomfortable. Dark and light were separate, as were good and evil. Even the gods were one or the other. Both could not exist together at once. It was impossible. Madness would follow.

"Come," the Creator murmured. He turned away, weary. "I must return to the one who needs me, and you must return to the one who needs you." He looked back, his eyes sharpening, glinting with the brilliance of stars seething in their death throes. "As storm god, your power is enormous. Use it only to protect her. In what is to come, nothing, and no one else matters." He stepped closer, his eyes ignited, brilliant white. A warning. "No one."

Urhi-Teshub understood. He bowed his head, dread impaling him. He would be able to remain with Sekhmet, but might lose her yet. It was not over. The light within the Creator's eyes brightened, so bright the backs of Urhi-Teshub's eyes ached. He lifted his arm to shield himself from the glare. An explosion of stars, then—nothing. Crushing silence. The crunch of his boot against stone. He opened his eyes. Water lapped, quiet, against the cavern's inky shore.

Close by, Teshub's tunic, kilt, and gold-embossed sandals lay in a heap, shed like the skin of snake. Urhi-Teshub looked himself over. Not only had he retained his memories, he had retained his armor, even Marduk's weapons remained. The Creator had done more than leave his memories intact, he had left him unchanged, unlike Sethi, or Istara, who were the same yet not, saturated by the past of those who had lived for eons before them. Urhi-Teshub continued to survey himself, cautious, careful. Everything about him—at least as far as he could see—had remained the same. Only now, he had been remade into a god—the very one he had worshiped; the one he had been named after. The circle of his existence glared back at him, impassive. So be it. This was who he was now. The Creator had spared him an eternity of loneliness. In return, he would protect Istara from Sethi, would finally be able to face his nemesis as an equal.

From against his back, an unfamiliar yet familiar weight called to him. He reached over his shoulder and hefted the weapon free of its holder, knowing without knowing what he would find. Marduk's weapon was gone, replaced by the storm god's double-headed ax. It glinted in the portal's churning light, awakening after its long dormancy, its silvered, blackened metal forged in the fires of creation and etched with the Creator's symbols. Along its two curved blades, one longer, the other shorter, bolts of cerulean lightning streaked, alive, sentient. Urhi-Teshub held the weapon out at arm's length, admiring it, letting its power invigorate him, one of the most powerful weapons of the gods. A smile, cold, found him. It cut through the haze of his turmoil, liberated his soul. This. *This* made the years of suffering his mortal life worthwhile.

The portal awakened, its tendrils reached out, caressing him, welcoming him. He cast one last look at Teshub's bloodstained armor—willing his predecessor to have found his consort, and his peace—and walked into the light toward the goddess he loved, the god he hated, and the one he was destined to protect, no matter how grave the cost.

CHAPTER 12

It was the shift in the vibration underfoot which pulled Ahmen from his trance. He blinked, for a heartbeat, disoriented. He had been lost in a shallow sea of blue, drifting atop the clear water, watching the rippled lines of white sand slide past in perfect, hypnotic repetition.

Dullness shrouded him for beat, then: burning, stinging pain slashed through his legs, reminding him afresh of his crime against them. He gritted his teeth, listening for what had changed. There. The roar had ceased from the rear and had erupted further ahead, from under the wings, just as it had done when they left Anki.

He sank onto the cramped, narrow space between the crates and focused his attention on working through his abused muscles, enduring the hot spikes and dagger cuts of their protestations. The roar heightened. Several thunks came from beneath the ship, followed by grinding whirrs as the wheels unfolded from their resting place.

The thunder quieted as the ship touched ground. Silence sheared through it, utter, deafening. Long heartbeats passed. Ahmen counted them. Ten. Twelve. Fifteen. A heavy tread came down the steps, steady, purposeful, arrogant. In its wake, an aura of raw, barren hate swept over Ahmen. He gritted his teeth, enduring the foul wash of the jihn's presence, toxic, yet perversely enticing.

His darkest thoughts reared, taunting, battering the walls of his resistance, a flood. *Come to the lion's den, have you? Remember what happened last time? An innocent was eaten alive, and all you did was watch. How will it be any different here? You only make things worse. You always make things worse.*

The image of Haran's brutal end washed over him, vivid, visceral, hot with the metallic stink of blood. Ahmen clenched his fists, enduring the scythes of guilt flaying his soul, savaging him to his core. Sethi's footfalls came to a halt. Heaviness soaked the space, oppressive, dark, tainted with hostility. A series of quiet chirps. The door to the outside world slid open with a soft hiss, oblivious to the malevolence of the being it obeyed. A warm glow of firelight flickered against the ship's darkened interior—the humble, ordinary crackle of the fire's flames ambrosia to Ahmen's deprived senses. Sethi descended the ship's steps and strode away, calling for a guard to take him to Marduk.

The agonizing, brutal grip of the jihn's mental assault faded. Ahmen leaned back against the crate as the memory of Haran's suffering slid back into the crevices of his mind, though the stain of guilt remained.

Apart from the pinging of the cooling ship, a dense quiet shrouded the space beyond the open door. Only the quiet crackle of the brazier's fire greeted Ahmen. No voices or footfalls touched his ears, not even the creak of leather from a guard shifting position. Nothing but the occasional distant cry of a far-off bird, and fainter still, the susurration of a sea rising and falling, sacrificing its ancient umbra against a rocky shore. He rose, stealthy, and eased out from between the crates and along the cramped corridor toward the opening.

At the edge of the door, he peered out. Fortune greeted him. From under the ship's wing, across the blackened scars of what must have been a once-beautiful mosaic, a clear view into the torchlit entrance of the citadel. Above, glittering constellations punctured the sky's black canopy. Ahead, the vast basin of the metal brazier whose flames had first lit the ship's interior. Along the perimeter of the enormous platform, another half-dozen braziers. He suspected there would be more of them on the opposite side of the ship. He looked up, along the rugged cliff walls supporting the citadel. Above, several more terraces jutted out over the rock wall, their precipices also warmed by the light of lighted braziers.

He fell back into the ship's shadows and considered. No guards, nor even servants moved without. He glanced again at the brazier. The fuel was two-thirds spent, which meant the hour was late. It would explain the lack of servants, most would be abed. But guards would remain a problem. In his crossing of the platform, anyone who happened to look down from one of the terraces above would see him. He eyed the distance, uneasy. Eventually he would have to sprint into the citadel where he had no idea what awaited him. It was madness. Suicide. All he had was a dagger. The odds towered against him.

He eyed the terraces anew, gauging his risk. Movement at the edge of the middle one caught his eye. A slim woman in a diaphanous black gown moved to stand beside one of the braziers. Flame-light lapped over her, though her face remained in shadow. She tilted her head back and gazed at the skies, her dark, unbound hair cascading down her back. The fuel in the brazier beside her collapsed, its flames erupted, caught her in its fiery light. Ahmen staggered.

Meresamun.

The banked, forbidden heat of his love erupted, molten. It scoured him, a living thing. He endured its onslaught, resisting the urge to cry out her name, even as her chest rose and fell in a deep, ragged sigh.

From the black-dark shadows of her eye, a tear slid free, and tracked its way over the curve of her cheekbone, staining it the inky black of her cosmetics. Her gaze moved from the heavens to the chasm below. For a long time she eyed the abyss, bleak. Ahmen tightened his grip against the door's frame, willing her to move back from the edge, fearing her thoughts, her intention. If she fell, he would follow her. Eventually they would wake again. She glanced over her shoulder, furtive, then held her fist over the depths. From between her fingers a glint of gold slipped free. It uncoiled, a necklace, its length betraying its worth—a king's ransom. It fell, writhing like a snake, struggling against its fate, swallowed a heartbeat later in the chasm's dark embrace.

She remained for a long time after, continuing to gaze into the abyss, as still as a gazelle caught in the predator's sight, her gaze turned inward, the bauble long gone, forgotten. The brazier's flames guttered, buffeted by a cold blast of sea air. Sparks erupted, showering her in brilliance. One alighted on the ephemeral material of her gown and smoldered. A heartbeat later it ignited, glowing bright against her breast. Dull, she pulled her gown free and dropped it over the side where it erupted into flames, its brief existence outlined against the desolate cliff wall.

Naked, Meresamun stared after it, her hair billowing around her, a living thing. On her breast, the evidence of her injury, raw, red and angry. She turned. A gust of wind exposed her back. Markings, just like the ones Ahmen had seen on Marduk covered her from waist to shoulder. They shifted, slow, mournful, mesmerizing—aching with the imprint of her raw, tragic beauty.

Ahmen had seen enough. He glanced one last time across the deserted expanse of the terrace, left the shelter of the ship, and bolted into the citadel of the enemy of the gods, armed with nothing more than his dagger, his immortality, and his determination to end the suffering of the woman he still loved.

The citadel lay deep in shadow, its vaulted corridors drenched in beauty unlike anything Ahmen had ever seen or even could imagine. Mirrors of unfathomable purity lined the corridor, unsettling him, their reflections made to catch one another so each appeared to lead down an endless corridor of mirrors. Keeping his eyes away from them—and his own unnerving reflection as he crept along—he reached a hall, its floors, walls, and ceiling soaked in gold and onyx. Dozens of black pillars spread away, their shafts embedded with golden symbols, each pillar emblazoned by a unique sigil, yet together, they formed a symphony, a whole, a lexicon. Ahmen hesitated, lingering in the darkened space between two braziers and eyed the nearest pillar, intrigued. Abstract, yet beautiful, the symbols circled the pillar's circumference, each iteration at a slight angle to the previous so as he passed the pillar, the symbols seemed to move. One of the symbols looked familiar. A memory unfolded. The Etemen'anki. Sethi's transformation. On Sethi's resurrection, there had been similar markings on his chest to those upon the pillar, although they had moved against his flesh, living things.

Uneasy, Ahmen averted his gaze and pressed on, wary, cautious, surrounded by eldritch silence, sensing the very walls watched him, laden with sentience, though not of the imposter who now resided within, but of another—the one to whom this palace had once belonged. He slipped from the hall into another, a circular one supported by a dozen more of the onyx pillars, the hall empty apart from a vast, curved double staircase in its center. The staircases encircled each other in a perfect spiral, one black and one white, bound in an eternal dance, poised a heartbeat apart, reaching, longing for the other, yet never touching. Ahmen followed their elegant, sinuous curve to the floor above. He blinked, taken aback. The ceiling was not stone, but clear. Every now and then a shimmer of gold pulsed along its length, as though the palace itself possessed a heartbeat. His flesh prickled. Perev might have been the home of Elati's version of Thoth, but it was a terrible place for one to pass unnoticed. Although—he cast his eyes along the length of the upper corridor into its distant reaches—Marduk did not seem interested in having guards keep watch. Apart from the side tables and chairs gracing the corridor, its hall stood as empty and lifeless as every other.

To reach Meresamun's terrace, he needed to go up, but the spiral stairs lay utterly bare and exposed. They might be beautiful to look at, but as he ascended them, he would have no place to hide. He dithered, debating his options, unwilling to give up his sheltered spot in the lee of a pillar—he could keep looking for another way up or take one of the stairways before him. He was certain he had already overshot the distance to Meresamun's terrace by a considerable distance. No, he would not continue looking for another way up and risk losing his way. He eyed the stairs, unhappy. They would have to do.

Gritting his teeth, he pulled his dagger free and made his way to the stairs, stealthy, and ascended, quick, listening for the brisk footfall of patrolling guards, the quiet whisper of a servant's movements as they attended the braziers. Nothing. Only his own measured breaths touched his ears. He reached the top of the stairs, aware of his exposure and hating it. Further down the corridor, a door opened. He flattened himself against the steps and held his breath. A shadow slipped into the corridor and hurried away from him, toward one of the glowing braziers. Meresamun.

Ahmen's heart snagged anew, his feelings reawakening, thunderous, imprisoning him in their treacherous grip. He shoved them aside, brutal, reminding himself he had no right to relive what he had once felt for her. Not anymore. Not after what he had done. He waited as long as he dared, then followed her, making his way, cautious, past the dying braziers into the deepest shadows, his breath tight, willing her not to be going to Marduk. She came to a stop at a plain door, glanced up and down the corridor one last time, then lifted the handle and disappeared within, silent as a cloud sliding over the moon.

He decided to wait, to give her time to come out again. Long heartbeats passed. The door remained closed, impassive. Ahmen eased forward, his senses taut with their probing of the darkened corridor, searching for the presence of another. He halted in the last vestige of shadow between him and the door. Utter silence surrounded him. He had no idea what he would find on its opposite side, and yet, he could not remain where he was, standing on a floor where anyone who cared to look up from below could see him. He reached for the latch and lifted it. It yielded to him without a sound. Tightening his grip on his dagger, he drew a stealthy breath and slipped through the opening, hoping with all his heart he had not just walked into a trap.

Darkness impaled him. He held still, wretched with misgiving, for his eyes to adjust to the gloom. It came, but in staggered, agonizing increments. The dark shifted, slow, into deeper shadows atop thinner ones. The sensation of vaulted space reared over him, dwarfing him, making his flesh tingle. He backed up. Behind, the solidness of the wall. He pressed his back against it, grateful for its bulk. He crouched and ran his fingertips over the floor. The smooth, reassuring weight of flagged stone greeted him. Satisfaction slid through him. This, at least, was an improvement. A faint gleam of light, far ahead, a mere pinprick. He narrowed his eyes. It taunted him from the end of a dense tunnel of black. He crept toward it, slow, steady, listening for voices. None came. Cautious, he edged along the flagstones, drawn to the pool of light—to her—his heart betraying him, resurrecting old feelings, ones he believed long buried and laid to rest.

Meresamun sat at a table within a large gallery, a small pile of scrolls beside her, her hair piled onto the top of her head in a messy, yet beguiling style Ahmen had never seen before. Her gaze was fixed on a small device she slid over the face of an open scroll, its blue light the sole illumination in this vast place—what Ahmen realized was a repository of vast knowledge. Thoth's library. He eyed the gallery's darkened heights, uneasy. The weight of the arcane pressed down on him, oppressive, forbidding. He was a soldier, not a priest. The writings of the sages were beyond his understanding. But for Meresamun . . . He slid his dagger back into its scabbard in total silence, letting himself drink in the sight of her bent to her task, her focus absolute, her comprehension etched in the sorrowful, downward turn of her lips. His heart aching, he took a step toward her, let the faint light of her device touch him.

"Meresamun," he whispered, so low it was no more than a breath, a tendril of hope.

She lifted her head, slow. The device came to a halt. She stared straight ahead, into the shadows, seeing nothing. Tears glistened in her eyes. She lowered her gaze back to the scroll and ran her fingers over its markings. "And now I imagine your voice," she said. "How lonely I must be."

Ahmen waited, his heart thudding, heavy, aching with regret, guilt, sorrow, and love—the love he had felt the first time he had held her in his arms—the love he had imprisoned in hate, jealousy, and bitterness. He knelt. His kilt rustled, quiet.

She turned. He met her eyes, hers as blue as lapis, just as he remembered. Her lips parted. She stood, abrupt, the transparency of her gown hiding nothing. Ahmen let his gaze fall. She stood before him, as fragile and vulnerable as a young gazelle, as thin as she had been in Waset all those long, long months ago when she sat in Sethi's garden and refused him a second chance.

"Am I dreaming?" she breathed. She stepped toward him, her chest rising and falling. A tear slipped free. "Ahmen?"

His heart aching, he lifted his hand to her, striving to contain the firestorm within his breast. "I am here. You are not alone."

A faint cry bled from her depths, soaked in regret and sorrow. She staggered and caught the back of the chair. "No," she breathed. "It is impossible." She cast her gaze away from him into the darkness, fear sliding through her. "I am going mad. It is too much. I cannot—" She hurried to gather the scrolls together, her haste sending several tumbling from the table.

One rolled toward Ahmen. He picked it up. She fell utterly still, watching him, horrified, as he carried it to her.

"You are not going mad," he said, holding the scroll out to her. "I followed you into Elati and have found a way in to Perev. No one knows I am here. No one but you."

Without taking the scroll, she sank onto the chair, her eyes moving over him, hungry, as though seeing him for the first time. Her lips parted. A faint flicker of hope shivered through her. It bloomed and died within the shuttered brilliance of her eyes. She rose, her look hardening, her vulnerability shifting in a heartbeat to the imperiousness of a queen.

"You must leave before Marduk finds you."

Ahmen set the scroll onto the table, pleased by the steadiness of his hand, at direct odds with the turmoil roiling within him—to be with her again, alone, after so long. She was changed, of that there could be no doubt. His once-gentle wife was harder, colder, darker, yet something of the woman he had loved still remained, just out of reach, as yet untouched by Marduk's poisonous taint. "Not without you," he answered. "I know of a place where you will be safe from all this. Once you are free, I swear I will stay away from you, forever. You will never see me again."

Meresamun drew a ragged breath. One tear, then another slipped free. Silence yawned, an abyss. Then, low: "You should not have come. I will not leave."

Ahmen blinked. He had not expected that. The memory of what he had witnessed between her and Marduk seared his thoughts. Jealousy drew its icy finger along the contours of his heart. He shoved it aside. No. Not that again. Never again. "Is that your choice or his?" he asked, winning the battle to keep his tone neutral.

She met his eyes, steadfast, unwavering. "Mine."

He took a cautious step toward her. "I swear I have not made this journey in the hope of restoring myself to you. I only wish to do one thing right—one honorable thing among the multitude of dishonorable ones done to you." He lifted his hand to her, gentle, as though seeking to reassure a skittish foal. "A blind man could see you are suffering. Come with me. Take this opportunity to set yourself free. It may be the only one you shall have."

She retreated from him, taut, defensive, until the backs of her legs pressed against the table's edge. "Even so," she answered, so low he had to strain to hear her, "I will remain. It is my wish." Her gaze dropped to the heap of scrolls gathered on the table. Ahmen picked one of them up and unrolled it, seeking to buy time, to find a way through the barrier encasing her. Across the parchment's aged skin, incomprehensible symbols glared back at him.

"Do you love him?" The question came out before he could stop himself. He kept his eyes on the meaningless markings piled into neat rows, willing her to say no.

"Yes," she whispered.

He cut a look at her. Despair, resignation, and grief surrounded her. It made no sense. Her unhappiness was palpable. Whatever she felt for Marduk, it could not be love.

"Does he love you?" he asked, his throat tight, seeking to find a breach in the smooth walls gilding her, his fingers sliding against their frictionless shear, desperate for an opening, a way past her elusive words. He would not leave her here, locked in misery, as the darkest of all evil crept into her soul.

"As far as he is capable." Her answer came soft, quiet, matter of fact.

His heart tight, Ahmen waited. She returned to gathering the scrolls, piling them up into the crook of her arm. "Although," she halted in her work, holding one of the scrolls halfway to the bundle, continuing, pensive, "for you to come here and face grave danger, knowing we could never be reconciled . . ." A sheen of fresh tears glinted in her eyes. She blinked and let out a tremulous breath. "It is too late. You are too late."

"*Why* am I too late?" Her words made no sense. She was miserable, thin, wan, her existence slipping away, as though Marduk dined upon her very soul. Desperation touched him.

He set the scroll aside and turned to her, though she avoided his look, her attention once more upon her work. "I ask nothing of you except to allow me to help you escape. I swear on Haran's soul I will never come near you again. I only want you to be free and happy. I have vowed I will not rest until you are the mistress of your own destiny."

She fell still. So still Ahmen wondered if she had heard him. A shudder tore through her. Her eyes came to his, wide, hollow, hopeless. The scrolls tumbled from her grip and rolled away, their clattering rude in the library's sacred silence. Her chest rising and falling, she sank to her knees heaving great, heartbreaking sobs. Her anguish washed over him in bleak, cold waves. Her suffering tore through him, a tempest, fierce, devastating. He knelt and took hold of her shoulders, gentle, and tugged her to him, aching to protect her from herself. She resisted for a heartbeat, then crumpled against him, as faint as a whisper, weeping in earnest, bathing his chest with her sorrow. He stroked her hair and rocked her, whispering quiet reassurances, willing her to relent, to come with him, to flee this tainted, wretched place—to save herself.

A thud as the door to the library came to. Ahmen held still, his instincts screaming for him to retreat. Meresamun continued to weep, her senses lost. A tread approached, rapid, far too quick for Ahmen to depart without being seen. He tightened his hold on Meresamun, who quaked in his arms, her grief riding her hard, blinding her. Ahmen closed his eyes, savoring the feel of her against him, sensing it would be the last time he would ever touch her. He pressed a kiss against the crown of her head, tender, aching with the love he had lost. The footfalls came to a halt. Cold, precise fury bled over him.

A voice, elegant, disdainful. "Remove your hands from my consort."

In Ahmen's arms, Meresamun stilled, a quaver whispered through her. She looked up, not at him but at the one who had stolen her away with him to Elati, her tear-stained face gaunt in the pale light of the device. She slipped out of Ahmen's hold, and rose, trembling, uncertain. Clad in nothing more than an elegant leather kilt embossed with golden panels, Marduk pulled her to him, firm, possessive, cradling her against his chest, the markings upon it moving into jagged, pointed, vicious designs.

Ahmen came to his feet, his heart cold, rimed with hate. Marduk eyed him, impassive. He caught Meresamun's chin in his hand and tilted her face up to his. His carnelian eyes moved from Ahmen to her.

"Ninsunu, my love," he asked, his voice no longer hard, but gentle. He traced his forefinger along the track of one of her tears, "has he hurt you?"

Meresamun took a tremulous breath. "He has not."

"And yet you weep. Your grief is so powerful it called me from my work." Marduk kept his gaze on Meresamun, and waited, patient, tenderness sheathing him as he held her, fragile and trembling against him. "Tell me, what happened to cause you such unhappiness?" Meresamun gave a near imperceptible shake of her head. Silence stretched, thick, taut. Marduk cut a hostile look at Ahmen. "You told me he imprisoned you with his hate—that he raped you. How could you grieve for one such as he?"

"I—" Meresamun faltered, her pallor stark against the black of her cosmetics.

"I asked her to leave with me," Ahmen said. "She refused."

A ripple of gratification shimmered over the oppressor of Elati's dark features. A smile, faint, suppressed. He bent to kiss Meresamun, lingering, sensual. In his grip, Meresamun wilted, pliant, her eyes closing, lost to the once-god of Babylon's glamour.

"Of course you did," Marduk murmured as he pulled back, approval emanating from him. "Because you are mine." He kissed her brow, reverent. "You will always be mine. You would never leave me."

He let go of Meresamun and turned his attention to Ahmen, his pupils almost fully dilated in the near dark—the cold, dead gaze of a crocodile. Ahmen suppressed a shudder.

"You have breached my home, and attempted to abduct my consort. I wonder, what shall we do with you?" Marduk moved toward Ahmen, the markings on his flesh sliding into new designs, screaming of anticipation, cold, sadistic. Supremacy bled from the once-god of Babylon, his cold-blooded gaze assuring Ahmen the most exquisite of torture would follow; that Marduk intended to make him pay for his crimes against Meresamun.

Ahmen gritted his teeth. So be it. He would suffer, and well. In this, they were agreed, he deserved to pay for what he had done to the only woman he had ever loved. He kept his gaze on the once-god of Babylon, defiant, careful not to look at Meresamun, whose stricken silence clawed at him.

Marduk smiled, his teeth white and even in the pale blue light. "I wish to understand how a mere mortal could sustain so much hate for so long, and with so much passion, against one whose heart is so pure." His gaze fell to the dagger on Ahmen's hip. His expression hardened. "I know that blade."

Ahmen took a step back. Marduk lunged after him and swept the dagger free of its scabbard. He lifted it up and examined it, his eyes glittering, cold.

"I had this made for Zarpanitu during the wars so she might defend herself should the need arise." The muscles in his jaw clenched. He looked up at Ahmen, revulsion bleeding from him. "How dare you—a mortal worm—touch it."

A flash of metal. Scathing heat tore through Ahmen's triceps. He grunted and wrapped his hand around his savaged flesh, seeking to staunch the blood, to contain the pain.

Marduk took a step back, impassive once more. "After you," he said, tilting his head a fraction toward the distant door and the corridor beyond it with its pulses of golden light.

Ahmen shot a cold look at his oppressor. The pain in his arm screamed at him, a scorching fury. He gritted his teeth and walked on. He might be immortal, but the familiar burning scour of the blade's deep furrow felt no different to when he had been mortal. He wondered how long it would take him to heal, or if he could suffer endless injuries without the reprieve of death.

From behind, Marduk murmured something too low for Ahmen to hear. A heartbeat later, the whisper of Meresamun's gown against the ashlars joined Marduk's ominous tread. Another scour of molten fire sheared through Ahmen's arm. He tightened his grip and forced his thoughts to the heat of battle—the metallic stink of his blood resurrecting long-buried memories of rage and savagery. He sensed Marduk's gaze boring into the back of his head, soaked with hate, promising suffering beyond Ahmen's wildest imaginings. There would be more. So much more to come. He pulled his hand from his ravaged flesh and opened the door, uncaring of the slippery imprint he left smeared across the elegant handle. Rebellion coursed through him. He would never give Marduk the satisfaction he sought. Never. But he *would* suffer. For her, he would pay for what he had done. As he stepped out onto the corridor's clear floor, he realized he longed to face his punishment, to pay for his cruelties in blood.

He turned. Meresamun took a step back, her eyes fleeted to his for the merest heartbeat, raw, bleak, hollow. Wretchedness shrouded her. She backed away, her thin, black-clad form melding with the shadows. Ahmen's heart folded. He caught Marduk eyeing him, narrow, calculating. Ahmen walked on, the pain in his arm gone, drowned by a new agony. Her look told him everything. She wanted to leave, but could not. Defeat tore through him, devastating him. He had failed. Right to the very end he had failed her. Nothing Marduk could do to him could compare to the devastation washing through him as he imagined her returning to her gilded cage, sorrowful and broken, bearing the additional, gruesome responsibility for Ahmen's impetuous act.

Marduk stopped at a plain wooden door. He nodded at Ahmen to open it.

"Do what you will to me," Ahmen said, as he left a fresh imprint of his lifeblood against the handle, "but if you truly love her, allow her the freedom to leave."

Marduk said nothing, though one, then another muscle in his clenched jaw spasmed. He tilted his head toward the door, tight.

Ahmen entered and looked around. He had expected a place of torture, but apart from a massive, rectangular, silver-polished metal box resting in the center of a windowless room, the chamber was empty. He eyed the enormous thing hulking over the stone-flagged floor, the size of a sarcophagus. It reminded him of the ruined one he had passed during their escape from the Etemen'anki, half-swallowed by the collapsing foundation. He had heard enough since arriving in Elati to suspect he was looking at one of Marduk's regeneration devices. It seemed a strange place to conduct an act of vengeance.

The door closed. A quiet click betrayed the locking mechanism. Ahmen cut a look behind him, expecting to find Marduk standing there, but there was no one. Ahmen stared, bleeding and alone at the blank, shadowed door, finding himself unprepared for this change of direction. He tried the door. Nothing. A bitter laugh threatened to escape. So this was how it was to be. At least in this, Marduk was consistent with his locked doors, and the power it conferred to him.

Ahmen paced the narrow confines of the chamber, wondering what Marduk intended. His arm continued to bleed out in heavy, thick gouts. He examined the blade's work in the sole, faint light of the regeneration device's control panel. The muscle of his upper arm had been near severed in two, the blade's bite lay far too deep to heal without sutures. He tore a strip of linen from his kilt and tied it around his arm, as tight as he could manage. Within heartbeats, the material became drenched, the seep of his blood trickling down his arm, thin rivulets of his life, draining away.

Pain ground into him, deep, hot, and dense with the throb of his heartbeat. He had had enough experience of battle to know the pain would last a long time.

He continued to wait, enduring, his thoughts shifting from the searing ache in his arm to his despair for Meresamun; of his regret for his haste, and for his longing for Marduk to return and finish what had been started. He paced until his legs ached, then crouched against the wall. He paced again, then sat on top of the regeneration device and faced the door, defiant, blood leaching into his kilt and smearing over the device's smooth metallic surface. Time wore a path through his soul, slow, agonizing. Thirst assailed him, then fatigue. He fought both. More hours passed. He began to wonder if Marduk meant to torture him simply by leaving him alone and locked in solitary confinement until he went mad. Fatigue dragged on him, as heavy as the weight of the river pulling a stricken barge into its watery embrace. His back once more against the wall, he allowed himself to close his eyes just for a heartbeat. Silence washed over him. Oblivion beckoned. He followed.

❋   ❋   ❋

Alone in Marduk's suite, Meresamun leaned against a pillar and pressed her palms against her torso, longing to suppress the dark waves of nausea rippling through her. It helped, a little. Drawing a quavering breath, she sank onto one of the divans near the brazier. Images of her time with Ahmen cascaded through her, resurrecting the familiar feel of his arms around her, the solidness of his chest, the smooth warmth of his voice—

She rose, agitated, abrupt, and went to an elegant, slim-legged side table, set before a gold-gilt mirror to pour herself a cup of wine. Her fingers trembling, she lifted the silver-chased goblet. Framed by the golden glow of the brazier's flames, she caught her stricken, tear-stained reflection. In its contours, the vestige of the woman she had once been—before Elati, before Babylon, before Marduk—haunted her. If only—No. There was no looking back. Nothing would have happened differently. *This* was her destiny: to be the consort of the one chosen to carry the taint of great evil; to finish what Zarpanitu could not. There was no purpose in questioning it, or wondering why. For whatever reason, this role had fallen to her. It was her task to make sense of it, find her way through it, and perhaps in the end, find freedom. She could not allow another man to intercept her path, no matter how fine his words. She sensed she would only end up imprisoned again.

Once, during the march back from Kadesh, while still Hatti's queen-in-waiting, Istara had spoken of women being tokens on the game board of kings and men, her decision to warn the pharaoh of the Hittite ambush had been her attempt to break free of her constraints. Meresamun, too, longed for the same opportunity, even as she lay in the arms of her sleeping consort, sated by his lovemaking, certain his love for her the only pure trait he possessed. And yet: *Ahmen.*

A fresh surge of tears cut into her eyes. She fought them, suppressing her feelings, her regrets, the unwelcome tide of buried sorrow, heartbreak, and longing for a life which could never have been. Out of the impossible dark, he had come for her, had risked everything for no other purpose than to set her free—had sworn on Haran's soul he had no other motive. In his eyes: naked, raw sincerity, desperation to aid her, to free her of her oppressor. And beneath that: regret, grief, guilt—the weight of a brutal burden he would bear for an eternity, and willingly. He blamed himself for her fate. He had driven her from their home in Pi-Ramesses, heart-broken and betrayed, straight into the arms of the one who now possessed her body and soul. She never even had a chance to refuse. Marduk had found her on the brink of death and brought her back to life as though her destiny had always been to be the once-god of Babylon's consort—Ahmen nothing more than the slingshot which had sent her hurtling across the blistering iters of Thamud's desert sands back to Babylon. To Marduk.

Movement along the top of her shoulder drew her attention away from her hollow contemplations. Thin, delicate markings, inky black and sinuous, just like the ones which covered Marduk's flesh from neck to toe, curled toward her collarbone, slow, the encroachment over her untainted flesh steady, relentless, a rising tide. She watched its glacial creep, morbid, the markings binding her to her consort as permanent as the brand of a captive slave. Marduk had traced his fingers along her new markings, reveling in their beauty—in the gift of her feelings laid bare before him. *Now we are one*, he had whispered against her ear, *never again will your heart be hidden from mine.*

And now, with the secrets of her heart exposed in the markings sliding across her skin, her once-husband who had devastated her, brutalized her, and imprisoned her in hate, had crossed an infinite distance to reach Perev in a misplaced heroic attempt to set her free, unaware she already knew a way out of Perev into Tyratu via Zherei's mirror. Bitterness touched her thoughts. Ahmen had accomplished nothing apart from his own downfall, reopening wounds she would rather have left in the past.

A gust of cold sea air swept through the open doors of the terrace. The transparent silk hangings snapped, twisted and turned, tormented by the remorseless snap of the brackish air. If only she hadn't fallen prey to the tumult of her startled emotions and drawn Marduk to her. If only Ahmen hadn't come to her, hoping to rescue her and undo his crimes. And now. She set the wine aside, untouched. And now, her consort was going to do terrible things to Ahmen, because of her.

A door closed at the other end of the suite. The familiar tread of her lover approached along the length of the outer corridor. His footsteps slowed in the antechamber. The quiet slide of a drawer opening and closing. Silence. A soft beep. Meresamun waited, a slick of dread touching her. She knew Marduk kept his most precious devices close to him, locked in the cupboard in the antechamber. Before she could begin to contemplate what he intended to use it for, he appeared in the doorway. She cut a look at him, expecting to see blood. There was none.

Marduk approached, slow, his eyes finding hers. A flicker of uncertainty whispered over his features. She held her breath, wary. Marduk was never uncertain. Perhaps he intended to hurt her, to make Ahmen suffer.

He lifted his hand, closed in a fist. "I wish to show you something." He opened his hand and revealed a long, flat, rectangle of black metal, a device she had never seen before. It bore a variety of scuff marks, and in several places its edges had deep dents. Not a single light blinked on it.

Fear leaped over her dread. She took a step back and shook her head, eyeing the anomalous thing. Another secret kept from her, another lie. "No, I—"

"Ninsunu," he said, gentle. "You cannot think I intend to hurt you? I would rather drive a blade into my heart than see harm come to you." He looked down at the device cradled in his palm. His lips curved downward, betraying a hidden well of regret. "These are my memories. All of them. Every time I regenerated, I saved them." He took a step closer. The device almost touched her. She wavered, but held still. "I want to share them with you," he said, low. "Even Zarpanitu never crossed this boundary."

She met his eyes. He waited, patient.

"Why now?" she whispered. She glanced at the doorway, glad her markings were on her back, out of Marduk's sight, thinking of Ahmen, wondering what had been done to him, or if, even now, he suffered incalculable agonies. Her heart clenched, unable to face the thought of his suffering, his flesh sacrificed needlessly—for her.

Marduk eased closer, until his hips were just a breath away from hers. A chill gust of wind cut through the thin material of her gown. She shivered. Marduk's heat called to her, promising respite. She held still, willing herself to resist the loaded weight of his dark charisma.

"Because," he answered, low, "I will not do anything to your once-husband until you know all of me. I cannot let his attempt to take you from me drive a wedge between us. He came to my citadel, imposed himself upon you, and caused you terrible grief. He deserves justice."

"Justice, or *torture?*" The words came before she could stop them. They hung in the air, acrid, accusing.

An annoyed flick of an eyebrow, smoothed in a heartbeat. "He knows where the others are—where Istara is. If he will not answer my questions, then . . . he will be encouraged to talk."

"He will never talk." Meresamun caught the glimmer of agreement in Marduk's carnelian eyes—the cold lack of concern.

"There are other ways the truth can be obtained from him," he replied, his look hardening. "Despite my caution, Istara has arrived in Elati, transformed into a goddess, and has so far eluded Sethi. With our *guest's* arrival, I have been granted the opportunity to finish what should have ended at Surru." The markings on her consort's chest stuttered, seizing into hard angles and edges, seething hatred. Meresamun averted her eyes from its ugliness. Marduk turned away to pour himself a little wine. He sipped. "I have had enough of the gods and what they have cost me to last an eternity. Istara and her lot must be eradicated before what happened on your world happens here. I refuse to destroy another world." He finished his wine and returned the empty goblet onto the tray, perfunctory, deliberate. "I will not be thwarted again. Elati is mine."

Meresamun absorbed his words, sensed the implacable weight of his intention to destroy her once-confidante and friend. "What other ways?" she asked, tight.

"A device which compels the speaker to give up the truth, whether they wish to or not."

Meresamun turned away, sickened. Ahmen would talk, and Istara would be destroyed by the very one she loved—who, when not blinded by the device controlling him, still loved her, and ached for her. When Sethi realized what he had done, he would go mad, perhaps even destroy himself. She wondered if that was what Marduk intended, his final, brutal strike in return for Zarpanitu's death, the death *he* had driven her to. The depth of her consort's insidious, cold machinations crept into her, souring her. She heard the soft intake of Marduk's breath. Too late she realized, she had exposed her deepest feelings to him, her revulsion. She turned. Marduk stood behind her, still, watchful.

"Your markings betray you," he said, low, reaching out to caress one of the nascent tendrils claiming her shoulder. A flicker of genuine disappointment sheared across the angles and planes of his features. "It begins again. Just as with Zarpanitu, I must face your judgment—your distaste." He slid his fingers down the length of her arm and caught her wrist, his grip firm yet gentle. "I have lived for eons. You: mere years, your mind unable to comprehend how an immense span of time changes one's perspective. Lives played out over a handful of decades become insignificant, meaningless. Even great dynasties are soon forgotten, their once-powerful empires crumbled to dust. I have learned there is only one purpose to existence: to achieve immutable, endless supremacy. In my fight to attain it, many have suffered and died. I have learned to accept the cost."

Meresamun blinked. "What you strive for is meant for just one. Re-Atum, the Creator. Only he can be immutable, eternal."

Resignation touched the slant of Marduk's lips. "Zarpanitu once said the same. How utterly alike you are." He held up his palm, once more revealing the scuffed black device. "Let us overcome the barrier of time which separates us. Before you condemn me, my love, first know me."

His frank words delved into her, shamed her. Meresamun touched the device, tentative. Its smooth surface slid under her fingertips. It felt a little rough in places, and old, very old. "I—How does it work?"

He took a step back, her wrist still caught in his grip. "Follow me. I will show you."

He led her through his suite past a series of unused rooms far from his sleeping quarters and into a small room, accessed via a hidden door behind a tapestry. Within the austere, windowless, unfurnished space, a massive regeneration device made of dull, black metal awaited them. He crouched before it and pressed his fingertips against an indentation, the panels of his kilt splayed against the stone-flagged floor. A control panel slid out. Under the deft movements of his fingers, the panel lit up, a familiar cerulean blue. He pressed several symbols and the lid eased open. From its depths, pale white lights flickered on. Meresamun hesitated.

"Must I go in?" she whispered. She glanced at the door, longing to leave.

"We will go in together," he answered, continuing to scroll through the illuminated symbols, punching in different combinations. Another panel slid out, bearing a deep recess. Marduk set the device into the indentation. Blue light lit its perimeter, pulsed along its length. A quiet hum emanated from it. His eyes lost in shadow and the lines of his jaw stark against the upwelling of the light, Marduk waited. After several long heartbeats, he nodded to himself, satisfied. Several more presses followed, quick, efficient. The panels slid back into the regeneration device, the small metal box departing with them.

He rose, his eyes still hidden by the gloom, and held out his hand to her, palm upward. "Come to me," he whispered. "I want you to know me. All of me."

One heartbeat slammed through her. Two. Three. He waited, motionless, patience saturating him. "Ninsunu," he said, low, "it is not easy for me to offer you this. There are things I would rather you not see, yet it is in those parts you will find the whole. I need you to understand who I am. What I am—what I must be." He stepped toward her, his eyes escaping the shadows. Vulnerability crept over his features, altering him, betraying a hidden, barricaded, silenced soul. He stood before her, no longer an oppressor of worlds, but alone, alienated, vilified, misunderstood. "Please, my love," he breathed, "do not deny us this."

Her heart aching, she went to him, unable to resist, a moth to a flame. He caught her hand and drew her against him. "Ninsunu," he murmured, taking her face in his hands and pressing his mouth to hers, tender, reverent, "my brave, beautiful love."

He led her to the foot of the device, up a small flight steps and into the device's cavity. Meresamun knelt beside him, eyeing their soon-confinement. It was spacious and comfortable, its base soft, like a bed, with plenty of room for both of them to lie down. He pulled her down beside him. A soft cushion cradled their heads. Beside them, in the interior's wall, another panel scrolled various symbols. Meresamun took a quavering breath, torn between dread and anticipation. He pressed several of the lit indentations beneath the screen.

The lid closed over them and the lights dimmed. A heartbeat of stark terror juddered through her. Then, a wave of languid heaviness, peaceful, soothing. "Soon," her consort murmured against her brow, "we will sleep. You will experience my memories as though you are me."

"And you?" Meresamun whispered as Marduk pulled her closer to him, settling her within the warmth of his protective embrace.

"I will experience them, too." His body tensed, at odds with the soporific effect of the device. "All of them—even the ones I would rather forget. I have left nothing out. I will be laid bare to you."

Her eyelids drifted down. Sleep dragged on her. "No matter what happens," his words drifted into her heart, as though coming from a great distance, "I am right here with you. I will never leave you. Never."

Meresamun tumbled away from him. Brutal shards of cold sheared through her, thin, precise blades of sharp, icy fire. Agony slammed into her core, angry, vengeful. She screamed. No sound came. She opened her eyes. Nothing. Utter silence bore into her, oppressive, claustrophobic. Impenetrable dark saturated her vision. Another onslaught of frozen heat tore through her, shattering her into a multitude of pieces. They spiraled away, disconnected, chaotic.

In the distance, a breach in the endless dark. A glimmer of light. Escape. She surged toward it, formless, nothing more than a thought, desperate to flee the brutal forces working to negate her existence. Panic fueled her, drove her, panting, yet not panting, to excise herself of the horror of her impending nothingness.

The light bloomed, beckoning, brightening, as though sensing her presence, offering respite. She tumbled again, the weight of the light's churning vortex overpowering her desperate flight, capturing her, anchoring her. Again, she fell, powerless, hurtling at an impossible speed. She slammed into the light. An explosion of stars.

The quiet chirp of insects. A cool breeze. Damp, soft earth against her back. She opened her eyes. Above, within the sky's black canopy, a multitude of unfamiliar constellations. She sat up, slow, and folded her legs under her. She caught her breath. How small they felt. She unfolded them again, and pressed her hand to her mouth, catching her scream. Her legs were not her own, but those of a boy. Marduk's words came back to her: *You will experience my memories as though you are me.* She looked down at herself, at *him.* She held out her hands and examined her arms. Strange. No markings. She had assumed the designs covering his flesh were a mark of his race.

Her arms moved again, back down to her sides. She tried to move them. Nothing happened.

"What am I doing looking at my arms like an addled *rhevn?*" a child's voice asked, incredulous. "What a dream!" he continued. "I hardly know myself." He stood, and the few heartbeats of control Meresamun had had over him ended. She tried to speak. A wall of silence slammed into her. A tide of panic threatened to overwhelm her. She fought it, seeking to calm herself, reminding herself she wasn't here, but asleep with Marduk in Perev. He had allowed her presence into his memories, granting her the role of a passive watcher. She realized somewhere within this child Marduk, her consort, would be watching too. The thought comforted her, eased her fears, her loneliness. She forced herself to relax, to accept what was to unfold. The child's thoughts slid through her, sweet, innocent, endearing: *I wonder what will be my bedtime treat. I hope it is jukip. I haven't had that in a whole sar.*

He sniffed and rubbed his fist under his nose as he regarded a tall, windowless, silver structure, similar in shape to an obelisk, its bulk blocking out a sizeable section of the starry canopy. It perched atop a moss-covered, rocky hill. Further away, the soft lap of waves bathed a quiet shore. The structure gleamed in the starlight, its familiar, mirror-like surface reminding Meresamun of the metal encasing Marduk's weapons. Along the structure's circumference, pulses of cerulean blue swept past, washing the hillside in a wake of pale, ephemeral light.

"Marduk," a feminine voice called, faint with worry. "Where are you, my son?"

"Here!" He cried in his high, childish voice. "Coming!" He ran, pushing his way through the damp, waist-high grass, his little legs pumping hard to eat up the distance between him and his strange, metallic home, his thoughts straying between his reading lessons, to reminding himself to feed his pet *akana*, to wondering if there had been any messages from his father, to returning to linger on his hopes for *jukip*, his favorite savory sweet.

He reached the structure and surged up a wide, dark metal ramp into a soft-lit white room furnished with a half-dozen divans and several pieces of austere, dark metallic furniture. In the center of the large suite, a circular stairway, the same as the one in Marduk's warship, only larger and much more elaborate, the white metal railings depicting a panoply of exotic, impossible creatures, intertwined as one into a beautiful work of art. A regal, shaven-headed woman, tall, elegant, and dressed in a fragile gown of blue shot with hundreds of tiny green gems, rose from the divan nearest the opening. A quiet hiss, and the door slid closed, blocking out the stars—the night of another world.

The child ran to her, happy, expectant, into her embrace. Her gown was soft, even with the gems. She smelled of good things, flowers, the sea, sunshine. "I have news," she said, in her soft, regal-accented voice, "it is time to go home."

Marduk, the child, pulled back and met his mother's gaze, her cerulean eyes warm and doting.

"Father has summoned us back?"

She nodded, pleasure emanating from her. "He has. A message arrived saying he has taken the High Seat. The wars are over. Uribi is ours." She smiled. "Finally, Enlil and his warmongering brood have knelt to your father."

"At last, you will be the Highest Consort, Lady of All." Marduk knelt.

She smiled, gentle, and brushed a lock of his hair from his forehead. "And you will be the Highest Prince, who will spend the next thousand *sars* learning the arts of a warrior under the greatest instructors the empire possesses. Under your command, you shall lead the army out into the Deep, to find new worlds, and bring the resources we need home. You are our people's greatest hope. One day you will save us all, I can feel it here." She pressed her palm to her chest, over her heart.

"I will not fail you, my lady," the child said, solemn.

"You could never fail me," she whispered, as the walls of the suite shimmered and turned translucent, their home rising, making its slow and stately ascent over the empty reaches of Dseum's uninhabited moon, its swathes of volcanic soil, black lakes, and humid meadows diminishing.

Marduk went to the wall and pressed his hands against its clear surface, watching the only place he had known for five *sars* slip away. He would be the highest prince. That would show Dumuzi, his father's preferred second-born son, born of a favored companion and not his mother, eldest daughter of Lord Anu, over whose empty seat the wars had raged since before Marduk was born. He looked up, into the vast sprawl of the stars. Out there was home. Uribi, the capital of the greatest empire of the Deep. A world beyond imagining. At last, their exile was over.

His mother came to him and held out her hand, her fingertips tattooed with golden curlicues—the mark of the empire's purest blood. He took it, his heart aching with joy. He would make her so proud. His father would soon see *he* was the best son, and his mother the best woman. Never again would she weep for the man who, once Dumuzi was born, had commanded his consort to live halfway across the star system with the excuse of it being for her protection. Content, happy, he closed his eyes, imagining when, at last, he would prove his worth.

Marduk woke and stared at the ceiling. It glared back at him in the pale cerulean light of the lamps, stark, gray, bleak. He liked his surroundings austere, plain, ascetic—a warrior's abode. It helped to focus his mind on what was important. Thirst called to him. He left his bed and crossed the room to pour himself refreshment. He drank, deep, letting the *hikira* ambrosia's slightly sour tang wash the staleness from his mouth. He had been dreaming of when he left Dseum's lesser moon more than five thousand *sars* ago, when he had been a mere child, innocent, and blind to the depravity and corruption of the royal house.

Compared to what he had experienced since his return home, those brief *sars* had been the best of his life, spent alone with his mother, learning from her, free to do and think as he wished. And now. He glanced back at his bed, where a pale-skinned woman sighed in her sleep, lost to her dreams. What was her name again?

He couldn't remember. Her gown, a diaphanous silver, and coated with diamonds lay in a puddled heap upon the slate floor.

He went to it and picked it up. It was wrinkled. Shaking it out, he lay it over the back of one of the divans and smoothed it down, the quiet act soothing him. He disliked disorder, despite his existence having been spent drenched in battle, and his armor coated in blood. He preferred the quiet solitude of his rooms, his books, and his near-feral companion, Easar, a wounded mountain cat he had rescued during one of his campaigns. It was enough, he needed nothing more. None of Uribi's women appealed with their cunning looks, their capricious natures, and their grasping, shallow fixation on baubles and vanity. He longed for something other, someone pure, good, a woman of learning. Apart from his mother, who kept herself in near solitude far outside the capital, and with learning scorned by his father, no women like that existed anymore. They dared not.

He ran his finger along the material of his guest's gown. Very expensive. Silver was even more precious than gold. He suspected the dress had been made just to gain his favor, the cost crippling. His guest had arrived deep in the night, the virgin daughter of some noble, seeking to allocate a greater share of rations for her family by offering herself to the heir of the high seat, willing to enslave herself as his concubine, giving up her chance to choose a partner and home of her own. She had stripped before him, beautiful, yet terrified, quaking, the bones of her neck, ribs, and hips protruding, sharp with hunger.

He had said nothing, careful to hide his annoyance at having been pulled from his meditations. While she waited, naked and uncertain, her garish cosmetics stark against her skin, he prepared her a drink laced with sleep root and led her to his bed where he lay down beside her until she slipped into unconsciousness. He found an extra blanket and covered her cooling body before returning to his book to meditate on the words of one the ancient sages from the reign of his grandfather, Anu, who had ruled in peace, wisdom, and prosperity—a world he longed for. He glanced at the woman, so small in his bed, and so young. She could be his daughter. Sickened, he turned away. He would aid her, but only her. Her family, who had so cruelly used her—for them, there would be nothing.

He drank again, bitterness tainting his thoughts. In his dying world, everything had become a transaction, even a daughter's chastity could be whored to the highest bidder. Over the ages, his father had abused his power, consuming the empire's scant resources to near total depletion. How many times had Marduk taken his legions with him into the Deep to secure more gold, more food, more building material? A hundred times? He swallowed the ambrosia, tasting nothing but regret. If only it had been a hundred. In his heart he knew the number was much higher. Guilt slinked along his spine, sharp, precise, his brutalities haunting him.

He purveyed death, destruction, and despair in the name of greater good, and each time, on his return: celebration, accolades, followed by an immediate return to the same wasteful existence, his people plowing through those resources paid for with the lives and worlds of innocents. And once the gorging and gluttony ended, he would be commanded to return back to the Deep, knowing the screams of his armies' ships hurtling down from the heavens would herald the beginning of the end of the existence for those whose only crime had been not to waste what they had. Soon, nothing would be left, nothing but a wasteland of ruined planets stretching as far as the furthest reaches of the known Deep—because of him. His home was dying, and he was doing nothing to stop it, apart from destroying more worlds to delay the inevitable.

It was enough. No more would he go out into the Deep. No more would he kill innocents. Long ago, his father had cast out the sages and closed the temples so none could question him. He had made Dumuzi his vizier and together they had exploited everything Anu had worked so hard to create. His father was a despot, unfit to rule, but to overcome him—to commit the act he knew he must—Marduk would need the blessing of the exiled sages. He glanced out the crystal wall of his suite. Night bore hard upon the capital, its towering, triangular, clear-walled structures, dark, quiet. Marduk turned to look at the woman in his bed, debating what to do with her. He went to his desk and pulled out a tablet, powered it up and typed in a brief message:

You are to remain in my household as Easar's caretaker. She has become too old to accompany me on campaign. My steward will arrange your accommodation. Do not come to my bed again. Save yourself for the one who will love you.

He set the tablet onto his cushion beside her, dressed, and left. No more would men sell their daughters for food. No more would the sages be silenced. Purpose gilded him. He strode from the room, lifted his weapons from the rack by the door, and slid them into their holders on his hips. He was the Highest Prince, Commander of the Legions, a harbinger of death. Now, death would come to those who deserved it, and after the long, hard climb back to balance: order, wisdom. Peace.

Even using his fastest ship at near the speed of light, it still took ninety-six hours to reach the distant, barren moon where Uribi's sages endured their brutal, isolated existence. Under a starless, leaden night lit by the faint red glow of Ishev's twin moons, Marduk eased his ship down a short distance from the ruined city where a once-glorious shrine had sparkled from atop the city's stepped terraces.

He powered the ship down, lingering in his seat on the flight deck, surveying what was left of what had once been the jewel in Uribi's crown. During their long return trip from their exile, Marduk's mother had stopped at Ishev to pay homage to the most sacred site of their people, where, within an enormous grid of pure light, a fragment of immense, primordial power had been contained eons ago. From where it came no one knew, she had said, but this darkness had possessed one of the sacred *pegagi*, turned its snowy coat black and its golden eyes amber, like the lava from the volcanoes of Dseum. Its peaceful, quiet nature became violent, and it rampaged, unstoppable, unquenchable. A creature of darkness and destruction.

As his mother recounted Uribi's beloved legend of the winged-sphinx's capture by a being of brilliant starlight, and of the creature's imprisonment within a brilliant globe of light, Marduk had walked beside her, filled with wonder, by turns drinking in the chaotic profusion of lush gardens drenched in color, and gaping at the mythical white *pegagi* as they processed along Ishev's silver-gilt avenues, their golden eyes heavy with the weight of their forebear's crimes; their fate to sacrifice their lives to the sphere of light to prevent the dark *pegagi* from ever being able to darken the Deep with its presence again.

And now, more than five thousand *sars* later, Marduk, himself a destroyer of worlds, eyed the outline of the broken, shadowed remains of the once-glorious city. All the fabled opalescent *hepset*—a rare gift from the mines of the *pegagi*—which had once sheathed Ishev's walls had been stripped away by his father to embellish a new palace for the mother of Dumuzi, who had ever remained his father's favorite. His jaw tight, Marduk left his vantage point and pressed the sequence to open the ship's outer door. It slid open with a quiet hiss. Hot, dry, iron-tinged air leached the moisture from his skin and dried his mouth. Fine, red-hued particles settled into the grooves of his armor. Pulling on his gloves, he stepped down the steps of his ship onto a dusty, cracked lake bed. He scuffed the toe of his metal-encased boot against the hardened earth. Pieces flaked off, flinty, hard as stone. When he had last been here as a child, the city had perched beside the shore of an enormous lake whose rippled surface had sparked and fizzed with minuscule beads of cerulean light. His mother had let him run into the shallows, smiling and indulgent, as he chased the bursts of light, longing to capture one for himself.

In the distance, a pinprick of torchlight bobbed at the outer edge of the ruined city. It slowed, cautious. Hope seeped across the distance. Marduk reached back into the ship and hauled out the two metal supply crates he had brought with him—taken from his own personal stores—bearing the equipment and materials to print food and medicine for an entire *sar*. The crates hit the ground with dense thuds, stirring up clouds of choking dust. On their panels, he activated transport mode. The crates lifted with a quiet hum and levitated beside him at knee height. Satisfied, Marduk touched the control screen on his metal-gloved wrist, and activated the illumination beam in his shoulder piece. Brilliant white light scoured the way ahead, revealing among the rocks, the pitted skeletal remains of the creatures who had once lived in the depths of the lake.

He crossed the distance, the air hot, desiccated, and difficult to breathe. At irregular intervals, the weight of his armor bore down on him, heavier than usual, then lightened again. Readings flashed up on his glove's control screen, reporting air quality, mineral compounds in the soil, the usual array of data. One reading pulsed a warning. He eyed it. Strange. Ishev's gravity fluctuated, just a fraction of a percent, back and forth like a pendulum. He ran more readings, seeking a cause but found none. Apart from the fluctuations, all else appeared normal.

He drew close to the shorn walls of the city and came to a halt. Whoever had shown initial interest at his arrival had withdrawn deeper into the shadowed citadel. He pulled one of his weapons free and primed it. He lifted it up. "Show yourself," he called.

A faint shuffling of feet. He listened. Just one. If there were others, they were not giving themselves away. A glimpse of a firelight reflected against the edge of the gate's gaping opening.

"My lord," a feeble voice called. "I am alone. I beg you, lower your weapon. I am defenseless."

"And you are?" Marduk demanded.

"Ukaru."

Marduk blinked. It couldn't be. Ukaru had been Anu's closest confidant and advisor, revered as the wisest of all sages. He had vanished without a trace when Anu returned to the light. Despite his father's ban on ancient knowledge, Marduk had managed to find and devour every meditation, treatise, and volume of instruction Ukaru had written. He had longed to meet him, to speak with him, to learn from him. At times he even dreamed of him.

"Impossible," Marduk said, unwilling to let the nascent hope within his breast flourish. "The Grand Sage Ukaru disappeared five-and-a-half thousand *sars* ago. None have seen him since."

"Yes," came the answer, thin with fatigue and hunger, "I did. I had seen what was to come so I hid until your father stripped everything from Ishev, and exiled the order. It was only then I joined the others, here, in exile." He coughed, reedy, hollow, its ragged barks echoed against the stark walls, bled of their life. "I knew no one would come back except you, Marduk, my son."

"So you know who I am," Marduk said, quiet. He powered down his weapon, his heart quavering at being called Ukaru's son. *If only.* He half-turned, the beam of light on his shoulder moving along the jagged crevices of the wall where the *hepset* had been torn free more than four thousand *sars* before.

He gestured at the crates waiting, patient, behind him, their sensors locked to the location of his control screen. "I have supplies. Enough food, medicine, and condensation equipment to support twenty for a full *sar*."

A quiet sound. "Twenty." Resignation soaked that single word.

"There are more?" Marduk asked. He had suspected twenty would be optimistic.

"There is only me, and I shall not last another week."

Marduk moved toward the darkened gate, his beam of light cut a grim path through a maze of fallen ashlars crowding the once-pristine central avenue. He found Ukaru slumped on a broken stairway, wearing nothing but a filthy loincloth, his dusty wrinkled skin hung thin and loose on his frame, dragged down by the vacillating pull of Ishev's gravity.

Marduk knelt, reverent. "All my life, I have longed to meet you. My lord, the honor is mine." He held out a gloved hand. "Let me help you back to your abode. I will prepare food for you. There is medicine—"

Ukaru shot him a sharp look, as piercing and intelligent as a wild *rhevn*. "I knew you would come before I returned to the light." He lifted his hand and let Marduk help him up. "You have come for one thing, but will leave with another."

Intrigued, Marduk waited for Ukaru to say more, but the sage remained silent. Granting him his support, Marduk followed the ancient sage up into the city, their going slow, hampered by both the old man's condition and the ruined state of the avenue.

"Earthquakes," Ukaru panted, making a feeble gesture at pile of ashlars, fallen from the supporting wall of the terrace above them. "Every day now."

He returned his attention to his footing on the uneven, broken ground, its foundation stones ugly and scarred, their grim existence eroding Marduk's memory of the smooth, silver-white avenue which had basked in the rippling shade of violet-leafed trees. They continued onward and upward, Ukaru wheezing hard in the heated, brittle air.

Though Marduk could have carried him with ease, he dared not offend the sage's dignity, so he measured his steps to Ukaru's, mulling over the sage's enigmatic words about coming for one thing but leaving with another. Perhaps Ukaru would not give his blessing for Marduk to rise up against his father and free Uribi of it descent into annihilation. Perhaps there was another path meant for him. He pressed his lips together and fought back a wave of displeasure. He had expected no resistance from the sages, thinking his trip to Ishev would be nothing more than a formality baked with a promise to return them to their rightful places.

But this . . . he eyed the way ahead, cut into sharp relief by his armor's garish, unforgiving beam of light. Ishev was in its death throes with Ukaru the only sage left of the thousands stripped of their power and banished from the Highest One's sight. Inwardly, he remonstrated with himself. He should have come sooner. He had waited too long. It was already too late. Ukaru would never approve of Marduk committing regicide. He knew the sage's mind well enough from studying his philosophies, of his teaching to let the light guide one's destiny, and to float like a leaf upon a river, free of control, and accept what is to be with grace. *That,* according to Uribi's greatest sage was the true path to wisdom— and to oneness with the light. Perhaps, Marduk thought with a slash of envy, for a sage, floating along like a hapless leaf was an option, but not for a warrior who was determined to save his people from destruction.

They came to the base of a shattered semi-circular stairway. Above, a vast edifice loomed, bleak and stark, its bare walls glowing a faint red in the twin moons' light. Marduk pulled himself from his musings and looked behind him. The ruined city fell away beneath them, the ravaged central avenue splitting in half the hulking remains of five tiers of collapsed temples, toppled pillars, and shattered courtyards. He had thought Ishev was dying, but it was already gone. Marduk blinked. A thought struck him, cold, hard.

He turned back to Ukaru who continued to pant, his thin chest rising and falling, his flesh etched by the fragile lines of his ribcage. The sage looked up at him and met his eyes—a knowing look, keen, incisive despite his desperate state. It sliced through the horror rising inside Marduk.

"Where are the *pegagi?*"

"Gone," Ukaru turned to look at the edifice, mournful. "They were dying of starvation. The last ones made their sacrifice a *sar* ago. Thirty of them went in together, even the yearlings."

"And the dark one within?" Marduk demanded, fury rising up over his fear. His father had made a grave mistake abandoning Ishev to its fate. If whatever was contained within were to escape . . .

Ukaru nodded, slow. "The light holds, but barely. The *pegagi's* additional sacrifices bought a little extra time."

"And how much time is left?"

Ukaru pursed his lips. He lifted a hairless eyebrow. "At best, less than a week."

"And then?" Marduk asked, tight.

"And then we shall be swept away, caught in the crosshairs of a much greater battle, none of it our making." He let out a heavy breath and began to ascend the steps, taking care to put his callused bare feet where the way was least damaged. "Come with me. I would like you to see something."

Ukaru's calm infuriated Marduk. With Ishev in ruins, the sages dead and the *pegagi* gone, the Deep's most powerful shrine would fall, and this time Marduk was certain there would be no being of light to prevent what was contained within its elaborate, blistering white prison from breaking free.

He followed Ukaru, sour. Right to the bitter end, sages always had to find purpose and meaning, even when faced with obliteration. Not him. Not this time. Where had his meditations led him, or his ambition to save his people? To this. To nothing. He had barely even begun to live. Anu had been almost five-hundred-thousand *sars* when he ascended to the light. With his father's aggressive demands fulfilled to achieve greater longevity from the regeneration devices, Marduk had expected to live to a million. His existence amounted to just over five thousand *sars*. A mere heartbeat.

Ukaru slipped into a narrow crevice in the edifice. Marduk left the crates behind and followed, cautious, realizing the sage had led him into a great rent in a massive ashlar, presumably made by one of the many earthquakes. Apart from the narrow beam of his lamp, utter darkness surrounded them, yet Ukaru's steps were certain as he made his way past various openings, leading Marduk through a maze of cuts and angles, his progress slow, yet steady, confident.

Ukaru turned and vanished into the rock wall. Marduk hastened to catch up, uneasy. Another crevice opened before him, recessed into the rock at a ninety-degree angle. Marduk pressed on, claustrophobic, longing to escape the oppressive weight of the stone bearing down on them as the way narrowed and he had to shuffle after the sage, sidewise, his armor scraping against the ashlars. By degrees, the crevice widened and a faint glow of light breached the shadows beyond the reach of his lamp.

Ukaru took another turn. Marduk followed. Brilliance slammed into him. He fell back, stunned by the abrupt presence of light after so much dark. Lifting his arm to shield his eyes from the glare, he hunched down and edged his way forward, feeling his way along the wall, cautious, waiting for his vision to adapt. The passage ended. Ahead, in the center of a circular chamber, just before the fabled prison, Ukaru's frail silhouette stood, stark, against the unforgiving onslaught of a rotating sphere, shot with flames of light. Marduk eyed it, his instincts crawling, as it pulsed and churned, alive, a cold, dying star. Between its filaments, glimpses of unutterable darkness—of a formless, shifting entity slamming itself against its weakening barrier, determined to free itself after a near-eternity of confinement.

Ukaru turned, his face lost in shadow, and gestured for Marduk to join him. Marduk hesitated. When he had last been here, none but the *pegagi* were permitted to enter this chamber, not even his mother could go in. A viewing gallery, high above, and behind a thick barrier of pure crystal had been satisfactory enough for him to witness the existence of the prison made of light. He had looked, because his mother had wished him to, but he had been glad to leave. Even then with the shrine fully protected by the *pegagi*, he could sense the evil contained within the light's brilliance. It had called to him, had later touched his dreams, offering a destiny beyond his childish understanding, its power seductive, subtle, frightening. It was what had driven him to turn to the teachings of the sages, to contain the dark thoughts which plagued him when he was alone, or when saturated in the blood of the dead—that his conquests for Uribi were only the beginning, that a destiny of absolute power and eternal rule awaited him. For a price. Now, here he was, again. And soon, it would be free.

Ukaru gestured once more, reassuring, as though coaxing a wild animal to him. Marduk eased his way across the chamber, the sphere growing until it consumed his vision. Silence saturated the chamber.

At last. I knew you would return.

He stopped. His blood ran cold. That voice. He knew it. The same one which had haunted his dreams as a child.

"Did you hear that?" he asked, low, the silence oppressive, expectant.

Ukaru shook his head, eyeing Marduk as he took the final steps toward the sphere.

"It speaks to you?" Ukaru asked, soft.

Marduk clenched his jaw, gave a tight nod. "It began when I first came here with my mother on our return from exile. It is why I studied the philosophies, to cleanse myself of its taint."

Ukaru's gaze sharpened on Marduk. "Indeed?" He turned to look back at the prison, the flames of light encircling it slicing over its girth, harsh, angry, fighting their demise. He continued, quiet. "Why did you come here, my son?"

"I want to remove my father from the High Seat to save Uribi and the remaining worlds of the Deep from his tyranny. I hoped to gain the blessings of the sages."

Ukaru said nothing, though his silence spoke volumes. Condemnation bled from him. Marduk waited, shamed, uneasy. Now he had said his intention out loud, the ugliness of it screamed back at him. How would he be any less of a tyrant if he murdered his own father and took his throne? And yet, how else could he stop the inevitable without bloodshed?

"The lives of others are not ours for the taking." Ukaru's bland statement gilded the light-laced space. It faded, blotted out by the shards of immense dark clawing their way through the light.

Marduk clenched his fists. What did it matter what a learned sage thought? Once the prison failed, everything would change. He was a warrior, killing was all he knew. All he had ever done was take lives, most of them innocent. He had not been given a choice. It had been thrust upon him—his duty to the empire and the throne. Even his mother had lavished praises on him for his successful campaigns, while pointedly ignoring the price he had had to pay, the nightmares which haunted him.

"You said there was something you wanted me to see," Marduk said. He tilted his head at the shearing undulations of the dark's cage of light. "I assume it was this?"

Ukaru didn't say anything for a long while, he stood, with his hands folded in front of him, content to watch the ebb and flow of the web of light as it wove and re-wove itself against the thick pulses of darkness. Then, just when Marduk thought to speak again, he said: "It needs something to live within. A vessel from which to achieve its ends. A half-divine *pegagi* was a bad choice. Us, however, how pliable we are with our pride, lofty ideals . . . intelligence."

Marduk cut a look at the sage, but Ukaru's attention remained fixed on the sphere. After several heartbeats of quiet, he continued: "The poor creature it corrupted has long since been consumed by the entity which once possessed it. Once the darkness breaks free, it will seek the first living creature it can find and enter it." His lips lifted in a soft smile. "I have determined that creature shall not be me."

Marduk tensed, Ukaru's words, though soft, bore into his soul, exposed his greatest fear: that all along he had been destined for this, ever since the day he had come here, full of innocence, a mere child, and was marked by whatever lurked within the light. He took a step back. "Neither will it be me. Lead me back out into the city. I will depart immediately. Let it find a rodent or insect instead."

"How I long to return to the light," Ukaru murmured. "I have done my part and waited for you, brought you here. To this." He lifted his bony hand as though to caress the sphere. Marduk yanked him back.

"Have you lost your senses?" he demanded. "You may choose to end your life if you wish, but first see me out of here. I shall not be its vessel. In this, at least, I have a choice."

Ukaru turned to face him. Resignation shrouded him. "My son," he said, gentle, "it is your destiny. It was written even before you were born, inscribed in the heavens from the beginning of time. You will be the embodiment of the greatest darkness imaginable. It is your purpose."

"My *purpose*?!" Marduk took another step backward, pulling the sage with him, out of reach of the hateful thing, which had tormented his thoughts and dreams for the last five thousand *sars*. "How could one such as you spout such nonsense? Your whole life you taught we are subject to free will, that it is our moral obligation to choose right—to be *accountable*." He jerked his head toward the sphere. "I would never choose this. Lord Ukaru, you have gone mad from solitude and hunger, and have lost your way. Come. Let us leave this accursed place. We will find—"

Ukaru succumbed to a violent spasm of coughing, the force doubling him over. "You *will* choose," he rasped as he wiped droplets of blood from his lips, "because only *you* are strong enough to control it."

"What do mean—*control* it?" Marduk cast a wary look behind him, eyeing the immense power holding the darkness within. Doubt plagued him. No mortal could control *that*.

"Soon it will be free," Ukaru said. "You can choose to flee Ishev and let it plough its way through one creature after another, traveling through the Deep leaving a swathe of ruin in its wake until it finds you and enters you against your will, or—" Ukaru glanced at the sphere and fell silent.

Ukaru's earlier opaque words replayed in Marduk's mind: *You have come for one thing, but will leave with another.* He eyed the sphere again, the darkness within called to him, soft, enticing, just as it had done when he was child. For a heartbeat, he considered the immense power he would possess, the intelligence, the near-immortality—with power like that he would easily be able to end his father's tyranny. No. He cut off the thought. The price would be too great. He met Ukaru's calm gaze. "It would destroy me within days."

"Only if you allowed it."

Marduk bit back a smile, flattered despite the incongruity of the statement. "It overcame a *pegagi*. A half-divine creature."

"The *pegagi* was taken against its will, its purity corrupted," Ukaru said. He turned and faced Marduk, intent. "My son, unlike the *pegagi*, there is in you an affinity for the dark. Did you not come here seeking to gain the blessing of the sages for the murder of your father—the rightful possessor of the high seat—with the intention to take his seat, yourself?"

Marduk blinked. "Lord Ukaru, I came in the hopes of saving my people, to return the sages to the temples, and to protect those innocents still alive in the Deep. It is my *father* who is dark, not I. If I do not intervene, everyone will die. Only I am powerful enough to stop him."

"*Only* you?" Ukaru asked, sharp. His expression hardened. "Do you believe there is no other power within the Deep which might intervene? Perhaps Uribi is *meant* to collapse, its long ages terminated so another empire might rise from its ashes. You speak as though only you possess the agency to control vast outcomes. Do you not perceive your arrogance?"

Marduk glared at Ukaru. Was the man dense? If he did nothing, *everyone* would die. Had the sage become so blinkered by his philosophies he would chastise Marduk for *not* remaining a puppet to his father, would encourage him to continue murdering innocents so his father and half-brother could feast and drape their lovers in gems for another hundred *sars*?

"It is not arrogance that drives me," Marduk answered, cold, "but necessity."

"Indeed?" Ukaru sniffed. "I tutored your father, watched him grow into adulthood. He does as he does, but without evil intent, he is short-sighted, greedy, a wastrel; a flawed, weak, vain man, but he *is* the firstborn son of Anu, and rightful heir to Uribi's power. *You*, however, possess something else, something *other*. Did you not come to Ishev for the sole purpose of seeking a blessing to commit both patricide and regicide? You present yourself as a savior, having decided the act of premeditated murder is justifiable, as though you are above the code of life which the rest of us must honor. Is that not the mark of true darkness of heart?"

Marduk said nothing, though a frost of anger sheathed him, sharp, dangerous. Ukaru ignored Marduk's narrow look and gestured toward him, continuing: "When you were born, a sample of your life code was taken to store in the Vault. During its transfer, they discovered an insidious malevolence, a taint of darkness hidden deep within the fundamental weave of your existence. It is why your father sent you and your mother away soon after you were born. He feared what you were. Then, once he gained the throne, he feared what would happen if he left you in exile. It is the only reason—"

Fury suffused Marduk. He raised his gloved hand, abrupt. "Cease."

Ukaru had the wisdom to obey. Marduk turned his back to the sage. His thoughts churned, chaotic, laced with rage. From within the gruesome tide, a memory shoved its way free, of the night he left Dseum to return to Uribi. His mother had said his future was to be the commander of the legions, to go into the Deep and secure resources for Uribi. At the time, he had been honored, yet how could she have been so certain of his ability to fulfill such a demanding role? He had only been alive for five *sars*, was barely out of infancy, far too young for anyone to yet know his strengths and weaknesses—unless she already knew what he was, what he was capable of. He turned again and stared at the sphere, the light seething, tormented, trapped in its scorching battle against the rising dark.

All his life he had been told he had been given the hateful task of murdering millions because he was the highest prince and it was his duty—instead it was because of what was buried within him, and because his father wanted him far away, doing his dirty work. He wondered if Dumuzi knew, if he laughed at Marduk's ignorance of his fatal flaw, cleverly repurposed to suit their needs.

Anger surged, a hot, flaming wave. For five thousand *sars*, he had been deceived, had been sent out devastate entire worlds because his mother and father believed that was all he was—a brutal, cold-blooded murderer, whose darkness could only be satiated by violence. Perhaps his father never intended for him to inherit the throne, perhaps he hoped his firstborn son would suffer fatal injuries during one of his distant campaigns, and conveniently relieve him of his unpleasant burden.

He clenched his fists. "When I was a child, my mother brought me here, to *this* so I would never realize the darkness in me has always been my own," he said, his throat tight with restrained rage. "She *knew* and let me suffer, alone and in darkness, never once revealing the truth so I might come to terms with myself. Instead, she let me believe it was *this* which had brought the disturbing visions to my dreams, and prompted my dark thoughts, instigating the constant battle I have waged within myself ever since." He turned back to Ukaru who waited, patient, his grime-stained fingers folded in front of him. "She witnessed my torment—the guilt of my very existence, and did nothing to help me, apart from encourage me to go out and ravage another world." He blinked back tears, her betrayal cutting him deep, emptying his soul. "She *never* loved me." He swallowed, his throat aching as realization slammed into him, and his heart spiraled into the brutal abyss of himself. "She *feared* me."

Oppressed by the weight of his awakening, he sank into a crouch, quaking, seeking to regain control of his grief, his anger. His attention fell to a deep crack in the floor, his gaze moved along its length from its beginning to end and back again, tracing its outline, over and over. Light and shadow chased one another along the rent.

Thoughts of his childhood swept through him, of when he was young; of his mother reading him stories before bed; of him leaping out at her during a game of hide and seek; of them planting a tree together in Dseum. He shoved them aside. His life with her had been a lie. She had been pretending to love him. There was nothing left for him. Not even his memories of her were true.

Ukaru coughed again, a raw, rough bark. He spat. Silence saturated the space once more, a cocoon, washed in mute brilliance.

Marduk looked up at the sphere, seeking the coil of darkness pushing its way into the crevices of light. It thrummed, calling to him, seductive, promising the power to achieve everything he sought. He had been born with an affinity for darkness, his fate written in the heavens. Despite his longing to do right, to walk in the light, he never would. Resignation saturated him. Ukaru had been right. He would choose this. He realized he *wanted* this.

He was tired of fighting himself, of trying to be someone he was not, of someone he never could be.

He rose. A thought struck him, faint, laced with hope. "If I take this upon me, will I be able to prevent worse things from unfolding in the Deep?"

"You will."

Marduk cut a look at the sage. "You said I would be able to control it."

Ukaru glanced at him. "The stronger your affinity to the dark, the greater will be your control."

Marduk absorbed Ukaru's words. "Then let us hope for everyone's sake I am as bad as everyone believes me to be."

Ukaru looked away, but not before Marduk caught the flicker of certainty in the other man's eyes. A stab of loneliness impaled him. Even Ukaru, a man he had revered his entire life was repulsed by him.

"So how must I do this thing?" he asked, seeking to change the subject, to shorten the distance between himself and the last man who would know him as he was, and not as he would be.

Ukaru rubbed the back of his hand against his cracked lips. Several pieces of skin flaked off. He nodded at the barrier between them and the unutterable darkness. "You have to go in."

"Like the *pegagi*?"

"No. This will be different."

"And what about you?"

Ukaru's gaze dropped to the weapons strapped to Marduk's armor. "You might do an old man a kindness and put him out of his misery. I would rather not be here when your transformation is complete."

"No," Marduk said. "I have enough innocent blood on my hands. Go to my ship. There is a regeneration device, if you—"

But Ukaru shook his head. "This is where my path ends, son. Yours would have been the more merciful end, but I understand I ask much of you, and will not do so again." He took hold of

Marduk's shoulder and clasped it, though Marduk felt nothing through the metal of his armor. "Find love, if you can," he said, gentle, fatherly. "It will help ease your pain."

With a quiet nod to Marduk, he turned toward the blades of white light scything the surface of the sphere. Marduk longed to stop him, to reason with him, to force him to reconsider, to ask him to remain, his advisor, but as Ukaru moved toward the light, his steps certain, calm, Marduk divined Ukaru knew there would be no place for him in a world where the darkness roamed free.

Ukaru came to a halt, his fragile form a mere hairsbreadth from annihilation. Marduk sank to his knee and bowed his head, reverent, his heart tight, as the wisest of all Uribi's sages took the final step between life and death.

A surge of light washed over him. Marduk lifted his arm as it streamed past, blinding, cold, bathing him in waves of liquid brilliance, drowning the chamber in the light of one of the greatest souls ever to have existed. He squinted into the sphere. The blades of light pulsed, feeding on Ukaru's sacrifice. He wondered if there would be an explosion of light for him—or nothing but darkness. No. There would only be darkness. Hollowness eroded him. He rose, sorrow clawing at him, tears choking him. Total alienation saturated him.

A dull rumble rolled through the silence of Ukaru's dying light, sweeping out from beneath the sphere. Beneath his boots, the colossal ashlars of the chamber's floor juddered. The crack which had earlier occupied his focus widened and deepened. A silting of dust sleeted between him and the sphere, as fine as a silken curtain. From within the passageway, the grind of an immense fracturing. A dense thud shook the chamber's foundations, followed by another. The tremor intensified, dragging Marduk sidewise into its grip. He staggered toward the sphere as the ashlar beneath him began to tilt, easing its weight into the crevice opening beside him. Another rain of pebbles and dust showered down, slamming into his head and shoulders. His eyes watering, he pushed his way toward the sphere, its light slashing hard and fast, chaotic, angry, caught in the turmoil of the shuddering chamber.

He reached the glaring curve of its seething meniscus and lifted his gloved hand toward it, as Ukaru had done, sensing the prison of light's immutable power, its existence reaching out from beyond the realm of his own reality. He hesitated, as another shear of ashlars collapsed behind him, both testing his will to follow through, and hoarding the last heartbeats of his existence to himself. The reticulated black metal sheathing his fingers glinted back at him, bearing bleak, jeweled beads of light. Beyond the hurtling, churning web of light, the dark within reached out to him, resonating with the part of himself he had never been able to overcome. A tendril moved within the light, it slithered toward him, huddling close to the barrier, calling to him, willing him to go on, to breach the distance. A shudder rippled through the sphere. Time slowed and the blistering sears of strafing light came to a halt. The chamber dimmed. The quake's tremors faded. A wall of silence surrounded him, broken only by his ragged breaths, loud in his ears. The tendril gathered its shorn remnants together, reforming into another shape, a male, wearing identical armor to his, bearing the same height and build, and its hair tied back at the nape of its neck, just like his own. His shadowy twin lifted its hand and reached toward the barrier, its fingertips only a breath away from Marduk's.

Its faceless features turned to him. The voice, familiar, seductive, the one he knew so well scathed the edges of his mind.

There is so much more for you than this.

Visions poured through him, a tsunami. Memories of a future tantalized him. He glimpsed two breathtaking women he would love beyond all reason. Their names came to him from across the abyss of time and space. Zarpanitu. Ninsunu. His heart ached with longing for them as he tasted the bliss of the love they would share. He would not be alone after all. Worlds spread away before him, thousands of them. His power would be limitless. Even gods would not withstand him. He pulled his hand back and with a roar, thrust it through the barrier and claimed his destiny.

Meresamun screamed, her voice lost within the cage of Marduk's existence. Agony sheared through her. Violence saturated her. Darkness piled onto her, layer upon layer, suffocating, dense, endless, soaking up the fragments of her, devouring her mind, her essence, her very being. The weight of dying worlds crashed into her, shattering her, breaking her heart. In the midst of her destruction, Marduk bellowed, triumphant, drawing the darkness into him, welcoming it, embracing it, cherishing it. He lifted his arms up as the cage of light collapsed and the darkness poured into him, awakening him, empowering him, changing him.

My love. Marduk's voice cut through the evisceration of her mind. *Look at me.*

She clawed her way out the abyss of him, desperate, terrified, seeking the compass of his voice, his gentle coaxing her only tether between escape and obliteration. A touch against her face, fleeting. She lunged after it, blind, weak, broken. Another touch, a caress, aching with tenderness.

"Ninsunu," Marduk whispered, "open your eyes."

She tried but it felt as though lodestones weighed her eyelids down. Fatigue plagued her. Heaviness dragged on her thoughts. From behind, the darkness beckoned, cold, silent, bleak. She turned toward it. It would be so easy to fall, to become one with him, to end the fight. Who was she compared to what he had become? She could never stop him. His power was enormous, endless, greater than that of the gods. He had been beyond even Zarpanitu's reach—thus how could Meresamun, a mere slave-priestess, ever compare? No. It was impossible. Marduk would win. The gods would fall, and she with them.

A grip against her shoulders, harsh, rough. It hurt, but not as much as the despair of her heart.

"Wake up," his words slammed into her, hard, commanding. She tried. No. It was impossible. The voice which reached her as she slipped into the abyss of him, sharpened—a voice used to being obeyed. "I command you to return to me."

No. It was too late. He had her now, locked in his dark grip. She succumbed, and fell. It would be over soon. Her battle would end. A slap against her jaw, so violent she juddered. Blood, hot, sharp, metallic, filled her mouth, soaked her throat. She choked, felt her soul tear free of the abyss. The dark weight of his possession slid away. She opened her eyes, and coughed, staining the cushion with her blood, garish and black in the cold, blue light. With a cry, Marduk took hold of her face, fear thinning his features. His eyes raked over her, his pupils almost fully black, wild with dread.

He dragged her, limp as a doll into his lap and enfolded her against his chest, pressing feverish kisses against her brow and face, bloodying his lips with hers. "I thought I had lost you. How could I have not realized the darkness would be able to reach you through my memories?" He shuddered. "To think I almost destroyed you." He wept, harsh, shuddering sobs, his grip on her fierce, desperate. "No. I could not lose you, too. It would be the end of me—the end of all things. I could no longer contain what resides within me."

Meresamun lay passive in his embrace. Darkness circled her thoughts, tainting her heart as her consort's tears bathed her brow. He lay her back down, tender, as though she were made of the finest alabaster and joined her, stricken, hollowed. He ran his fingers over her broken, swollen lips, sorrowful. "What is within me has taken enough already, it shall not have you, too."

Meresamun said nothing as he turned to the panel in the wall and pressed a new sequence of symbols. From over his shoulder, he eyed her, remorseful. "I have stopped the memory retrieval. I will never take you into my past again." He drew her into his arms as the chamber's illumination dimmed again, and somnolence suffused her. "A brief regeneration," he murmured, guilt soaking his presence. "To heal you."

Meresamun closed her eyes. Exhaustion shrouded her. She succumbed to his embrace, and in his arms dreamed of him returning to Uribi, his eyes no longer cerulean but carnelian, and his flesh marked by the sinuous designs of the dark's presence, both a gift and curse. She followed him as he strode into the high seat's vaulted hall, the brilliant light of Uribi's blue star fractured into a corridor of angled shafts by the crystal-etched buttresses. He entered, clad in immutable power, raw, uncontrolled, and hungry for vengeance, slaughtering every living creature in the room, saving his father and half-brother for last, using no other weapon than his hands to end their lives.

In his mother's palace of exile, he found her in her gardens and ended her, too. As she fell, her final words penetrated his rage. *Forgive me. I failed you.* She tumbled to the ground, lifeless, and as he stared at her, panting, furious, the image of her and him playing hide and seek in Dseum roared through his mind, of her adoring eyes upon him, loving him despite what he was. His love for her tore through the thing he had become and he knelt, quaking, sickened by what he had done to the only woman who had ever loved him. His armor stained with the guilt of his onslaught, he gathered her broken body and carried her away, his soul sundered, ravaged by regret, grief, powerlessness.

He retreated then, to wage his internal war, to begin his endless struggle to control the darkness within him. Ages passed spent in austerity, deprivation, and discipline, as he fought to bring Uribi back from the brink of its annihilation, treading a fine line between tyranny and benevolence. It took a more than a million *sars* before his home once more flourished as in the days of Anu. A brief respite followed, before his people outpaced Uribi's dwindling resources once more. Unrest tore through the cities across the world, plaguing them with riots, violence, and sabotage. Underground cells hacked into and shredded the complex systems which kept the world stable. Water supplies were pilfered, power cells destroyed, and, at last, in a final, decimating blow, Anu's control center atop a desert plateau was infiltrated and destroyed in an act of blind stupidity. The geo-grid collapsed, exposing Uribi's atmosphere to powerful magnetic waves, unleashing savage, world-circling storms. Marduk struck back with brutality. He oppressed those who stood, defiant, against him, until he learned a massive, distant star had collapsed, and Uribi would soon cross the path of its atmosphere-ravaging destruction, leaving him and those still loyal to him no choice but to evacuate and seek a new home.

He left his dying, ravaged world for the relentless reaches of the Deep, his past crimes haunting him as he returned to the worlds he had vanquished while under the command of his father, each time hoping and failing to find a regenerated world where his people could begin again. He had been thorough in his work. Nothing had survived his legions' rapacious work, even after a million *sars*. He pushed further into the Deep. Only dead, dry worlds greeted him.

Then, far beyond the reach of his previous forays, he found Zarpanitu on the brink of death, her ethereal beauty as brilliant as the sacred white star of Calirius. He cheated her of death and made her his consort, his heart lost to her as he made tender love to her, declaring he would love her for eternity. For a time, before the darkness within him began to corrupt her, his soul found refuge, and his battle with himself eased.

Ages passed. His fleet of ships pressed on into the emptiness of the void. Thousands of his people lost hope and refused to regenerate, longing for the release of death. Ships had to be abandoned and left to drift, empty and cold, lost to the Deep. When, at last he arrived to the verdant, lush world of the gods, only a fraction of his people had survived the deprivations of their exodus through the Deep. He met with the gods and was welcomed, his people granted a second chance. For a time Marduk knew vindication. He had saved his people from annihilation, and brought them to an even more beautiful world than the one they had left. Then he had discovered the secret of the gods, and despite Zarpanitu's pleas to be happy with their lot, the darkness within him stirred, more powerful than ever, longing to taste the endless power of immortality. He brought war to the world of the gods. Zarpanitu fell silent, and her heart darkened. She shunned his presence, then deep into the wars, Horus killed her. When he discovered his consort's decapitated body, devastation and betrayal consumed him. He tore into the heavens, grief-stricken, to return her ashes to the stars, vowing revenge.

He returned, no longer interested in controlling the darkness within him. He rained destruction upon the world of the gods in revenge for Zarpanitu's death, determined to strip it of all life. But the gods were clever. They fled to a place he could not find, and left him alone, without Zarpanitu, forever denied the chance of immortality. Enraged, he turned on his mortal allies, then on his own people, warring with them until only he remained, fed by the darkness within him. Maddened by hate, he retreated to the solace of his underground palace, keeping his body alive with his devices. The ages swept past. For two million years, the descendents of the men of the Golden Age wandered a broken, shattered, ruined world, barbaric and uncivilized as the era of the gods dwindled away, lost in the deepening shadows of time, reduced to myth, legends, and superstition.

At last, from the ashes of the remains of the world of the Golden Age, men once more learned to grow food, smelt metal, and build cities, their tribes assembling into empires and kingdoms. Marduk continued to wait, patient, playing god to hundreds of generations of mortal kings, determined, alone, and driven by the darkness within him to achieve what had begun all those lost ages ago in Ishev: To be immortal and rule without end.

And then, after an eon of interminable, crushing silence, Surru had awakened, leaving two fallen gods stranded on its bleak shores. Soon after, Ninsunu arrived in Babylon, her life almost extinguished, along with two more fallen gods. Then, finally, like a gift, the one Marduk had been waiting a near-eternity to avenge himself against emerged from the endless sands of the desert— Horus—his powerful wings clipped, and able to bleed like any other mortal.

With his second consort by his side, the awakening of Surru, and the arrival of the fallen gods, immortality was once more within his grasp—only this time, it was he who possessed the advantage, not the gods. And he would not—

A low hum penetrated Meresamun's hearing. It intensified, blurring the dark images in her mind. A draft of cool air whispered over her, sterile, faint with the tang of metal. She opened her eyes. In the pale cerulean glow of the chamber, the device continued to do its work, quiet, efficient. Marduk remained unconscious, his eyes darting back and forth, rapid, under his closed eyelids. On his chest and arms, designs formed and reformed, steady, rhythmic, pulsing with the beat of his tainted existence.

Meresamun lifted herself up onto her elbow and watched him dream. Though he had stopped the retrieval, his memories had still come to her, although these at least, were passive, free of the thrall of his powerful emotions.

Now, she knew all of him, just as he had wished. Her heart heavy, she leaned back against the wall, as the panel blinked its soft cadence, and the symbols of an extinct empire scrolled past, considering the unbearable length of his existence, her mind staggering under the weight of it—an impenetrable period of time spanning the epochs of worlds. The heft of his past bore down on her, oppressive. And now, with her passage through Surru, she would exist as long as he had, continuing on, forever, not a god, but an abomination, like him. Tears blurred her eyes. The symbols smeared. It was unbearable. No mortal was meant to live for an eternity. Death was a gift from Re-Atum, a reprieve from the agonies of mortality into a place of peace. Only evil wished to endure without the Creator's light, forever.

The brutal details of her consort's past returned, vivid, of his impossible weapons decimating thousands in a heartbeat, of his cold cruelty, his armor drenched in blood—of his endless, insatiable violence. And in between the horror, other memories cut through the weave of his past, of his solitary battle to contain the darkness within him, his fortitude, determination—his strength to withstand the continual war raging within him, and his fierce refusal to give in and allow the obverse of the light to rule him.

Movement along her forearm startled her. She flinched and cut a look at it, wary. Her breath caught. Her fingers trembling, she opened her gown. It slipped free of her shoulders. In the quiet light of the device, she watched, sickened, as a panoply of new markings encasing her flesh slid, sinuous, proprietary, along the canvas of her body.

Marduk stirred. Meresamun tore her gaze from her transformed self to him, unhappiness scouring her. He sat up and caught her chin in his hand, turning her face from side to side, examining her jaw and mouth where he had struck her. "Do you have any pain?" he asked, soft, as he traced his thumb over the smooth, unblemished curve of her lower lip.

Meresamun shook her head, though it was a lie. Grief saturated her, soaked with sorrow for the innocent woman she had once been, and for the contaminated immortal she had become.

Her consort nodded, his look unreadable. His eyes left hers and traveled the length of her form, moving over the whorls and spirals seething over her breasts, across the planes of her abdomen, and encircling her thighs. For a heartbeat she feared he would become aroused, would want to take her, here in this place where he had polluted her soul. She tensed, willing him to let her be, to give her time. He met her eyes again. His jaw clenched. He looked away, taut, as if divining her thoughts—her rejection.

"I will take you back," he murmured, reaching past her to gather up her fallen gown. He settled it over her shoulders "But

I will not remain." He pulled the ties together, deft, experienced, his expression hardening. "I still have work to do."

Work. Meresamun's heart folded. *Ahmen.* In the lost hours spent in Marduk's device, she had forgotten about her once-husband, but as Marduk turned and gave his attention to the panel, scrolling through the symbols and pressing complex combinations, his eyes cold, she could see *he* hadn't. Her consort would leave her—to piece herself back together after the onslaught of his past—to torture her once-husband.

The chamber's lights brightened, bathing them in a soft white glow, innocent of the horrors she had endured. A chirp came from the panel and the lid lifted free with a soft hiss. A draft, faint with the brackish tang of the sea breached the sterile, recycled atmosphere of the chamber. Marduk stood and offered Meresamun his hand, his eyes veiled. He retrieved the dark device containing his memories and led her back through his multitude of rooms, the abyss of silence widening between them. Her heart tight, she eyed the markings on his hand merging with hers, subsuming them, hungry.

They reached the entrance to his suite, where he had made love to her more times than she could remember. He let go of her hand, abrupt. Some of his markings had time to slide back onto him, the rest remained, integrating with her markings, becoming a part of her. She shuddered. He eyed her for a heartbeat, expressionless, before turning away.

"You would leave me—after *that*?" Meresamun cried, following after him. "Will you not grant me any explanation, understanding?"

He stopped, though he did not face her. Tension surrounded him, saturated his stance. "It is not often I make such a grave miscalculation. I had thought to draw you closer to me, instead—" he cut a harsh look at her from over his shoulder, eyeing the markings on her arms, "—I have driven a wedge between us."

Meresamun said nothing. Instead she lifted up her hands to him, where her markings seethed and roiled, betraying her agitation. Tears bit into her eyes. "I thought you were born this way. But I see now it is the taint of the darkness in you, and now it is upon *my* flesh, too." Terror clawed into her, visceral. At last, she understood the depth of Zarpanitu's fear, her willingness to put herself into harm's way, to escape what Marduk was through death. "And now I cannot help but wonder," she continued, low, "if Zarpanitu bore your markings, too."

A spasm of grief sliced through the cut of his features. Without answering, he took her hands in his. His markings surged onto her flesh, blending with hers, a complex dance, seeking to soothe the chaos of her despair. Through his touch, she sensed the tumult of his heart even as his markings eased their way up her arms, washing over the broken, sharp lines of her own in waves of curlicues and spirals, gentle, tender.

"I do not know where I end and you begin." She tore her gaze from her arms and met his distant look. "The darkness. You welcomed it. Wanted it."

He nodded, taut. "I did. Even though I have lost much since then, I do not regret it."

"Why?" The question escaped, no more than a breath. "Help me understand. Please."

"Because if I had not done so, nothing would have survived. The dark seeks only one thing, to consume." He tilted his head toward his suite. "Come, sit with me." She followed him, uncertain, to the end of his bed and lowered herself onto the silken cover. He eased himself down beside her, the warmth of his body blocking the errant drafts breaching the shutters to the terrace, closed by his servants for the night. Against the opposite wall, a massive gold-gilt mirror faced them, flanked by two braziers, their flame-light illuminating their reflection as they sat, clad in unhappiness, side by side, the markings on their bodies churning, a symphony of sorrow and loss.

"Who are you?" Meresamun asked his reflection. "Are you still the highest prince, the once-commander of the legions of Uribi, or are you the darkness wearing the shell of the one who was known as Marduk?" She turned to him, her heart tight with fear, dreading the question, yet needing the answer. "Who has stolen my heart? You, or *it*?"

Marduk looked down at their clasped hands, his fingers entwined with hers, at the coiling, sinuous slide of their markings fusing together, becoming one. He remained silent for so long, Meresamun feared he would not answer. Then, his voice, low, resonant, thrilling, seductive, seared her senses: "I am both the prince, and the darkness, but it is the heart of the untainted commander who longed for a woman like no other. You." He cut an oblique look at her. "The darkness is incapable of love."

Meresamun absorbed his words. The fuel in one of the braziers crackled and snapped in two. Several sparks shot up and danced against the surface of the mirror. "And the markings that began on my back?"

Marduk looked up at their reflection, met her eyes. "The same happened to Zarpanitu." He let out a heavy breath. "Although yours have begun much sooner. And now—" The muscles in his jaw clenched. Misery bled from him. "And now," he continued, ragged, "after what I have done tonight, it will only be a matter of time before the darkness will have the power to drive you away from me, too."

"Only I cannot die like she did," Meresamun said, bleak. She rose, catching Marduk's stricken look in the mirror. "You took my mortality from me, *knowing* this would happen."

"No," Marduk answered, joining her, taking hold of her shoulders, his grip on her desperate, willing her to understand. "I learned from my mistakes with Zarpanitu. I have been so careful with you. I thought I could control it, and would be able to prevent it. It is unbearable—the thought of losing you, of knowing what I harbor within me will take you away from me."

He fell silent. Anguished. "Apart from when I took the weight of the dark upon me and committed my first atrocities, and when I lost Zarpanitu, I have found the strength to control the evil within me." He cut a harsh look at her, ravaged by the torment of his failure to protect her. "I will not allow it to drive you from me. I have sacrificed everything to carry the weight of this endless, insatiable burden, willing to be the one to give it what it longs for: an immortal reign." He knelt before her, the once-god of Babylon, bearer of the greatest dark, vanquisher of worlds. His eyes held hers, unfathomable, harsh with the weight of eons spent locked in his lonely battle. "Do not let the darkness I bear take what we have from us. It may have everything else, but not this. Not you."

"I—" Meresamun sank to her knees before him, her heart aching, lost within the convoluted corridors of her consort's passionate words.

He took her face in his hands, his thumbs caressing her cheeks. "I waited so long for you," he whispered, his eyes moving over her, memorizing her. "When I lost Zarpanitu I believed I could never love like that again, but you—" he shook his head, and a faint smile touched his lips, "—are so much more. It was you I was searching for even before I went to Ishev. It was always you. You were worth the endless, agonizing, lonely wait."

His hands slid down, along her neck and over her shoulders. He murmured her name, reverent, and tugged her toward him. She succumbed with a sigh, letting him lift her up and ease her onto the bed, knowing he would worship her, would love her until she cried out his name—knowing even as she let him carry her to the stars, lost in pleasure, Ahmen was locked away, bleeding, thinking of her, waiting to be tortured by the very one who whose gentle hands caressed her.

She closed her eyes, and clung to the one who had stolen her heart and claimed her soul. Later, she would think of the cost— but in this heartbeat, she was loved, adored, cherished. After all she had endured, her consort's passion was a respite from the weight of her burden—of her inescapable destiny. She sighed as he took her, slow, steady, certain, giving her time as he guided her to their private oasis where the darkness they shared melted away, and they basked in the brilliance of their love, freed for a heartbeat from the evil which clawed at the impenetrable, blistering barrier surrounding them, snarling, slavering, relentless.

PART II

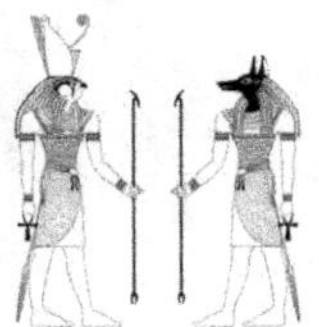

RELIC

Sethi leaned against the wall and folded his bloodstained arms over his chest, eyeing Perev's intruder from under his brow. Marduk had worked over—with methodical, cold, vengeful merciless-ness—the one who claimed to have once been the husband of Ninsunu. Yet despite the one who called himself Ahmen suffer-ing the most exquisite of agonies, he remained silent, stubborn, defiant.

Marduk turned, the dagger in his grip grisly with blood and gore, and cast a baleful look at Sethi. The muscles on his jaw spasmed, once, twice, three times. Sethi knew that tell. Despite his outward appearance of cool, Marduk was furious. Sethi pushed himself free of the wall and picked Ahmen up by his blood-soaked throat, holding him dangling, choking, mid-air. He flung him across the room. Ahmen slammed against the opposite wall and slid to the floor, leaving a thick smear of blood in his wake. He gasped for air, an ugly gurgle.

Sethi followed him and sank into a crouch. He leaned toward the broken, flayed face of the one who held the answer he sought. "Where is Istara?" he asked, conversational.

Ahmen glared at him, mutinous, burning with hate, the whites of his eyes brilliant against his exposed facial muscles gelatinous with congealed blood. He spat. A tooth bounced off Sethi's cheek. It skidded across the floor, trailing slimy tendrils of bloody tissue.

Sethi cut a look over his shoulder at Marduk. "The jihn will make him talk."

Marduk's lips thinned. "I prefer to let him suffer." He turned and headed for the door, still holding the blood-soaked dagger. "For now, you may do as you please with him. When you are done, put him in the device. Once he is sufficiently rejuvenated, he will tell us what we want to know, whether he wishes to or not." He lifted the door's handle and glanced back, fury sheathing him. "After that, the jihn may have him."

Sethi nodded. He turned back to his latest amusement. "So, what do you want to do?" he asked, casual, as the door closed behind Marduk, its quiet click promising on his return more pain would follow. Much more pain. In the ensuing silence, the ragged, wet breathing of Perev's stubborn prisoner ricocheted against the chamber's raw, bleak walls.

"Sethi," Ahmen rasped, his face ugly, contorting as his muscles moved, no longer contained within their cocoon of skin. "How can you not remember me?"

Sethi eyed the mess before him. "Why would I remember you? I am a god. You are no one."

"You were not always a god," Ahmen answered. "Before you came to Elati, you were the commander of Egypt's armies. You were mortal, and my friend." He clenched his jaw, suppressing a spasm of agony. His gaze fell to Sethi's fractals, stuttering through their rotations. "You may be a god, but *this* is not who you are meant to be."

Sethi followed his gaze to the broken fractals, their suffering plain against his flesh. Though he knew he hid it well, doubt had begun to plague him. At times, dreams of another life overlapped his own—of a world of men where he had lived, fought, and caroused. He would wake and stare at his gold-painted ceiling, picking over the details of his dreams: fragments of battles, visceral, real; memories emblazoned upon his flesh, savage with loss, pain, and blood. Even more unsettling, there were dreams of Istara, of her having lived with him in a white-washed mortal dwelling, a dog sleeping by her feet, her glorious hair piled up on her head as she plied her needle against a piece of linen—her immortal skin bare of her cascade of stars.

Sethi narrowed his eyes at Ahmen. "I was never mortal. Gods cannot be mortal."

"I saw your transformation." Ahmen winced as he leaned against the wall. Fresh blood oozed from the exposed muscles of his brutalized chest and arms. "In Babylon. You protected Istara from a falling pillar and fell in her stead. Horus, the god of war *you* worshiped, sacrificed the last of his light to bring you back. Though it nearly killed us all, you rose again, the god of war in a world where gods can no longer exist. Marduk kept you alive long enough to reach Elati, your presence as you crossed from our world into this one granting him his immortality. You might be a god, but whatever Marduk has made you into is not the Sethi I knew, who was honorable, just, and noble—who loved Istara beyond reason. Beyond death." He looked at the door, the whites of his eyes glistening in the cold, sterile light of the regeneration device. "He has remade you into everything you are not. And now, he has Meresamun." Perev's intruder slumped against the wall, the last of his fight leaving him. He gazed at the closed door, his anguish for Ninsunu palpable.

Sethi rose and put his back to the macabre thing seeping blood onto the floor, the grisly pool of flesh, blood, flayed muscle, and viscera beneath Ahmen spreading as his life diminished with each heartbeat. Marduk had been thorough, his cruelty exquisite. He knew how to make a man suffer. Even Sethi had had to look away at times. It was one thing to torture a man, another to work through it with a cold, sadistic relish. And yet, Ahmen had given nothing. Others would have relented long before having the skin of their face flayed. Marduk had taken his time with that, ensuring each incision dealt more pain than the previous. And yet, Ahmen had not cried out. Not once. He had endured his torture in stoic silence. Sethi crossed his arms over his chest. He turned back to Ahmen, abrupt.

"Why will you not tell him where Istara is?"

Ahmen flicked a look at Sethi. "Because," he said, "if you find her, you will destroy her with that vile weapon of yours, and once you realize what you have done, you will destroy yourself as well."

"And why would you care what happens to me?" Sethi demanded, intrigued despite himself. "I am your enemy."

"No. Marduk is the enemy." Ahmen swallowed. The muscles of his neck moved. Beads of blood eased out from the valleys between his tendons, viscous, near-black in the pale light. "Horus and Baalat—*gods*—extinguished themselves so you and Istara could rise again in their place. I would not be the cause of their sacrifice being for nothing." He shifted his weight, grimacing with pain. He cut a harsh look at Sethi. "Fight. Free yourself of Marduk's grip. Return to your consort. She grieves hard for what you have become."

A shear of annoyance slid through Sethi. He was wasting his time listening to this fool. "Istara was unfaithful to me." He turned, longing to leave, thinking to find a willing serving woman whose attention might silence the escalating dissonance of Ahmen's words. "I would never return to her."

"Unfaithful to *you*?" Ahmen repeated, his incredulity causing him to choke on his words. Gobbets of bloody saliva trailed from his lips. He didn't wipe them away. "When you were given the responsibility of protecting her after the battle at Kadesh, she belonged to Urhi-Teshub, the king of Hatti," he continued, his words wet, ugly, damning. "She was unfaithful to him with *you*. Despite the political chaos she caused, even after the regent queen of Hatti came to Egypt to persuade her to return, she refused to take her throne—" he glared at Sethi, "—for you."

Silence swept into Sethi, deafening, crushing. A shimmer rippled through him, heralding the approach of the awakening he dreaded, hated. He turned, seeking a window to divine the hour. He cursed. There was none.

"Dawn comes," he panted, pacing away from Ahmen, nausea taking its familiar hold. "I sense it."

"And?" Ahmen slid sideways against the wall, leaving ragged smears of himself along the ashlars.

"And something happens. Something unpleasant." He went to the regeneration device and activated it. The lid lifted with a soft hiss. "Get in," he said, as another brutal wave of nausea shoved its way through him. "Hurry."

Ahmen shifted, slow. Sethi bore down on him, grabbed his arm and hauled him up. Sections of Ahmen's muscles loosened in his grip, slick, sticky. Another onslaught of nausea assaulted Sethi, stronger than the first. He cursed again. Not long now. His heart turned, as it always did. *Istara.*

"Get in." He thrust Ahmen toward the device, desperate to escape before he said or did anything he would regret. Ahmen slammed against the device's side with a dull smack. A sickly imprint of his life stuck to its pristine surface, speckling it with pieces of flayed flesh. Bile touched Sethi's throat. Ahmen slid along the device, and sank once more to his knees. Sethi grabbed the back of Ahmen's belt and hauled him over the rim of the device, throwing him in face-first.

He went to the control panel. It was a simple code. Marduk had shown him once, in case Ninsunu would ever need to be regenerated when Marduk could not attend her. Sethi punched in the memorized code, the symbols meaningless to him.

"Sethi, I beg you," Ahmen said, struggling to turn himself over, smearing the interior with the stain of his existence. "For the commander you once were, you must fight what Marduk has done to you before it is too late. Istara loves you. You love her."

It came then. A tsunami of horror, of the wrongness of his path, of the woman he loved—who loved him—whom he was determined to destroy. Ahmen's version of the past tore through him, hot, scathing, reawakening forgotten memories: of an enormous pillar falling on him in a luxurious, underground suite, the pain excruciating, his endless love for Istara shielding him as he hurtled toward the light.

Sethi grabbed hold of the rim of the device, his knuckles white as the agony of his crimes seared his soul. Ahmen reached out to him, a bloody wreck, his *friend*. Memories of a past he had lived and forgotten coursed through him. Of dusty campaigns and perfumed courtesans, of his scarab ring of command; his horses, villas, gardens. Images washed through him, relentless. A queen, Nefertari, and her king, Ramesses, upon their thrones, regal, imperious. Edarru, his once-favored lover, her green eyes wet with tears, imploring him to stay. A bolt shot through him. He had a son. Nesu. He staggered. He was a father. *Istara*. Realization slammed into him. Ahmen had spoken the truth. Istara had never been unfaithful to him. *That* injustice belonged to her husband, the king of Hatti. The lie of his existence melted away. Another memory slammed into him. Of waking in a dark tent, a shivering, jewel-clad woman beside him. A shaft of moonlight slid over her face. It was her, the woman he had dreamed of for thirteen years. The woman he was destined to raise the jihn against and annihilate.

"No!" he bellowed. He took Ahmen's outstretched hand, slippery with blood. "Help me," he panted. "It's in my head. Get it out." He felt the spot. There, at the base of his skull, that was where Marduk had implanted the hateful device. "Here, it's here."

Ahmen rose, unsteady, quaking from the effort. "Tell me what to do."

"A blade," Sethi turned, searching. Of course, there was none. Marduk had taken it. He roared, his soul sundered by torment.

Soon it would end, and he would be tainted anew. It was torture, an endless, brutal anguish.

"He will use a device on you just as he has done to me," Sethi said, grunting with the effort to fight the tide as he felt it turn, veering back to the darkness, pouring into the abyss of hate. "You must leave before he returns and forces the truth from you. I must *not* find Istara." He shuddered, the thought of capturing her pinioning him, of what he knew he was capable of, of how much he could make her suffer. "Ahmen, do not fail me."

He pressed the last symbols of the code, and the lid lowered, slow. Ahmen sank inside the chamber, stricken, powerless. "Sethi, you can overcome this," he said. "You defied death twice and have become the god of war. You are the most powerful man I know."

Sethi said nothing. His internal battle consumed all his restraint. At the last heartbeat he jammed the barrel of one of his weapons between the rim of the lid and body of the device, preventing the device from locking Ahmen in. He had no idea if the device would still function or not. He didn't have the time to care, the rest was up to Ahmen now.

He bolted from the chamber and hastened to the warship, desperate to put as much distance between himself and the one who had opened the door to his past before what Marduk had turned him into sheathed him anew. His hands shaking, he fired the ship's engines, his final thoughts clinging to Istara, of her in his arms the last time he had made love to her, locked in the Etemen'anki, her mouth against his, their love desperate, insatiable, even as her husband pounded against the door, vowing to kill him.

The ship lifted from the terrace in a torrent of heat and flame. He punched the panel and the thrusters ignited with a deafening roar. He tore away from the citadel, his brief transition into his true self slipping away, ephemeral as a forgotten dream. He veered over the mountains, reckless, flying too low. Trees erupted into flame, tarring the cold sky in gouts of black smoke.

The mountain range fell away and the undulating forests of Kium's rugged wilds spread into the distance. Further south—the sea, and his palace, perched high up on the cliffs of Kium's southern boundary. He set course for the golden walls of his residence as the sun shot up into the sky, drenching the world in color. His memory of Istara vanished, replaced by thoughts of sending for one of his courtesans to bathe him. He recalled one of the women from Ikalur had caught his eye, the dark-haired one who had been wearing nothing more than a golden undergarment underneath a transparent violent gown. Despite her tears, her exotic beauty had been beyond compare. Anticipation touched him. His search for the jihn had left him no time to send for her. Now he had found it, he would show her she had no reason to grieve. She would be loved by a god, and perhaps, if she pleased him well enough, he might even make her his consort. His lips turned downward at the thought of his once-consort Istara, who continued to elude him. He should have replaced her long ago, it was a sign of weakness he hadn't. Every god deserved a consort.

He eyed the terrain spreading into the distance, thinking of the one he would send for. For once, he had time. He would spend the day in pleasure and return tomorrow to learn where he must go to find Istara, his thoughts turning, insidious, to the jihn, and of the one he would feed to it, relishing the thought of her suffering—of breaking her heart as she had broken his.

From within the ship, the weapon's malevolent presence called to him. He left the flight deck and went to it, to trail his fingers over its blades, flickering with its insatiable hunger, longing for the pure light of the gods.

"Soon," he whispered. It shimmered in response, drawing him to it, sultry, a lover. He picked it up, and let its presence saturate him, falling with it into the blackened, poisoned corridors of its promise, where he witnessed a world without the light of the gods—a world without Istara.

❊ ❊ ❊

Meresamun backed into the chamber and eased the door closed, her heart in her throat. Dread dragged its icy fingers through the bowl of her abdomen as she turned, slow. She shoved her fist into her mouth to silence her scream, horror slithering over her.

Her once-husband's blood coated every surface—even the ceiling's smooth ashlars were mottled with sprays of blood. She swallowed, sickened, quivering as she drank in the evidence of Marduk's calculated, patient work. Violence was in his blood, saturated the darkness of his soul. She drew a trembling breath, and immediately regretted it. The acrid, metallic taint of blood suffused her senses and left its harsh tattoo in her mouth.

Her gaze slid over the bloody smears splattered against the device, followed their path to the wall, where a shimmering pool of blood leached its way across the floor. It crept, inexorable, toward the device as though trying to return to the one it belonged. Her heart clenched. So much blood. *Ahmen.* Though she had strained to hear his cries, she had heard nothing all the long hours she had waited for her consort's return. How courageous he must have been.

An hour before, as she lay awake, riven by turmoil and fear, and the sun's rays fleeted through the cracks in the shutters and slid along the floor and walls, Marduk at last returned, long hours after he had left her satiated and sleepy, aching from his love. He came to their bed, naked, his markings seething, bleeding rage. He knelt on the bed and gathered her in his arms, his hair tied back and still damp from his bathing, and his skin warmed by his sensual, complex scent of neroli oil and black vanilla. He had kissed her with exquisite tenderness before he sank onto the cushions and glared, his eyes fully black, at the ceiling's images of the black and white winged horses fighting their endless battle, restrained fury cloaking him. She had waited, encased in his possessive hold, in a torment of terror, for her consort to succumb to sleep. And when he did—she fled, knowing what she must do, knowing what it would cost her.

In the silence of the bleak, bloodstained chamber, the cerulean light of the regeneration device slid back and forth, its rhythmic crosshatched pattern cutting a path across the bloodstained walls through a wedge cracked open by one of Marduk's weapons. She edged closer, suppressing a shudder as she lifted the hem of her gown from a puddle slippery with a ragged, viscous heap of flayed flesh.

At the device, she eased down, cautious, and peeked into the crack, averting her face from the blistering passage of the cerulean light. Blood soaked the once-pristine white interior, but of Ahmen, she could see nothing; the device was too deep, the opening too slim.

She stood and eyed the console. Dozens of symbols scrolled past, lacking both coherence and repetition. She stared at the screen, willing herself to make sense of Marduk's incomprehensible, lost language. Nothing. She moved her forefinger to the row of blinking symbols at the bottom of the console, hesitant, trying to decide which one would shut it down. She dithered, then decided on the one at the far right. No. She withdrew her finger, trembling. She dared not, Marduk's devices were far too complex.

Her attention moved to the weapon jammed between the lid and the body of the device. Strange. She wondered why Marduk would leave the lid ajar, and with a weapon, no less. She turned, cutting a look at the door. When she arrived, it had been unlocked. Prescience cut a swathe through her. There had been another. Her blood stilled. Sethi. Just before the sun rose she had heard his ship scream away from the citadel, low and hot. Her heart juddered. So, Sethi still returned to himself each morning, and in his brief heartbeat of clarity had granted Ahmen a way out. But what Sethi had begun, she would finish before Marduk returned and forced the answers he sought from him. Her love for her consort was complex and riddled with contradictions, but in this she would not waver: Marduk would not learn where Istara was, not so long as she had the power to stop it.

Her heart pounding, she grabbed onto the edge of the lid and threw all her weight against it. It resisted her desperate, feeble onslaught. Her bare feet slid in Ahmen's blood, the hem of her gown leeching up his stolen life, plastering the material against her ankles. Her arms quaking, she bit back a curse and shoved with all her might. A quiet beep came from the console. The beam of light switched off, and the lid hissed, lifting up on its own. The weapon fell into the device with a dull thud. She stepped back, her heart taut, bracing herself for what she would find inside.

Dull, gray light washed over the room, pale shadows cast by the faint light of the console. Tingling with trepidation, she leaned over the edge. Bile screamed up her throat, blistering, rancid. A bloody, skinned creature gazed up at her. The whites of Ahmen's eyes the only part of him not grisly with exposed muscle and tendon. She turned and emptied her guts against the side of the device, its vile stench making her continue to heave long after she had nothing left to give. Movement within the device dragged her from herself.

She wiped a shaking hand across her mouth and turned. He stood within the device, a macabre, horrifying thing, a monster, reeking of death, yet still alive, existing beyond the walls of his own mortality.

"Meresamun."

His voice cut through her horror—familiar, warm, the voice of the one who had once loved her body and soul, had held her in his arms and kissed her tears away, who had asked her to swear to never leave him again.

"Ahmen," she breathed. "What has he done to you?" A tear slid down her face. She let it fall. How could she love Marduk after this—after seeing what he was capable of? Ahmen had been her husband. She had loved him. For the sake of what once was, should not some things remain sacred? No. She eyed him, morbid, sick, this was more than just revenge for what Ahmen had done to her, more than just wishing to know Istara's location—it was jealousy. Her consort's calculated, brutal work screamed of envy, hate, resentment. He had sought to eradicate Ahmen piece by piece. To erase his very existence.

Ahmen did not answer. He bent down, slow, cautious, his unsheathed form bleeding afresh, wrung like a sponge. He rose again, the weapon in his skinless hand. Bloody smears stained its smooth perfection.

"I need to leave," he said, his voice the only thing still recognizable. "There is a mirror—"

"To Tyratu?"

"Where?" he asked as he dragged himself over the edge of the device, leaving behind a grisly trail. He hit the bloodstained floor with a grunt.

Meresamun forced herself to meet his eyes. He held her look, as though willing her not to see the rest of him. She took a quavering breath. "Tyratu. It lies across the great sea, on the continent to the east." She turned away, unsettled by his private look, out of place against his savaged flesh.

"No," Ahmen muttered as he checked the weapon and pressed several of the indentations. It lit up, emitting a quiet hum. "Not that one."

Meresamun blinked. "But that is the only mirror I know of."

He looked back up at her, his expression impossible to read in his ruined face. "Where did Marduk make love to you in front of a full-length mirror?"

"I—" Meresamun took a step back. The memory of their lovemaking returned. Shame flooded her. "How could you—?"

"Know?" Ahmen asked, his eyes darkening. "I watched you, though I did not enjoy it."

"What?" Meresamun whispered. "Where?"

"It is not important," Ahmen said. "Do you know where that mirror is?"

Meresamun nodded, her heart tight. Ahmen had watched her and Marduk make love, had seen her succumb, willing, to her consort's attention, and still, he had come for her. Perhaps he had spoken true when he said he only longed for her freedom. "Yes. My suite."

He went to the door, slow, the pain of his existence evident in his cautious progress. Meresamun moved aside, disturbed by the sinuous movements of his exposed muscles. He opened the door just enough to look down the corridor.

"It's clear," he turned back to her. "How far is it?"

"It's close by," Meresamun answered. She pulled the door open. "Follow me."

They progressed down the corridor, slow, steady, cautious, the braziers' fuel long since burned into ash, the way ahead instead lit by open doors leading to various rooms, speckling the corridor with precise rectangles of golden light.

Her heart pounding so hard, she feared Marduk would sense it and wake, she made her way to her suite, willing Ahmen to hurry. Beside her, Ahmen's rasping breaths, heavy with pain, punctuated the heavy, oppressive quiet.

She reached her door and pushed it open, willing it to be empty of servants. She hesitated, her heart aching with fear, listening for the quiet sounds of industry, the rattle of shutters being folded back, the snap of new sheets being unfolded over her bed. Deep silence soaked the suite, rich with shadow, the shutters still closed. Relief washed over her. They were alone. She nodded for Ahmen to follow. Once inside, she closed the door and led him through the reception into her sleeping room, where the mirror stood, flanked by two elegant, thin-legged, gold-painted side tables.

She stopped before it, thinking of the night Marduk had taken her here, of her release as he held her against him, shuddering, ecstatic, aroused by the sight of them together, moving as one. Shame saturated her. Ahmen raised his hand to his savaged reflection.

"It's just a mirror," Meresamun said. "I would have known if—"

He touched the surface. Nothing happened. Ahmen pressed harder, determination radiating from him. Against the silvered surface, his fingertips seeped, leaving the mark of him in blood. A faint shimmer of white, a mere breath, glinted under Ahmen's touch. It rippled away from his fingers like a stone tossed into a pool of water. His fingertips sank into it. Meresamun blinked, stunned, as he moved toward the mirror and eased his arm further in, up to his elbow, the ripples widening, spreading out to the edges of the mirror's frame.

He turned to her, his ravaged visage fierce, foreboding. "Marduk must never learn of this."

Meresamun shook her head, astounded something as remarkable as this had existed in front of her all this time. She stepped closer, curiosity claiming her. "Where does it go?"

"To the only place in Elati that will soon be safe from Marduk's reach," Ahmen said, easing his body toward the shimmering veil. He cut an unreadable look at her. "If you ever change your mind. This is your way out." With a last, lingering look at her, he took the final step toward the mirror. Its surface liquefied, and the reflection of Ahmen and her room rippled, becoming something else—a doorway leading to a courtyard, its sun-drenched pillars and desiccated fountain dusty with age, overgrown with vines, and overlooked by a serene blue sky. He turned and eased into the mirror as though walking through a thin wall of water. The mirror rippled, gentle, as he passed through, his body shimmering, bathed in light.

He stepped out into the courtyard and bellowed, writhing against the blistering sunlight searing his raw flesh.

Meresamun hastened after him. She stepped into the mirror. A shaft of brilliant white light suffused her senses, the passage from Perev to the ruined courtyard no more extraordinary than moving from one room to another. She caught her breath as a wall of heat, dense with the humidity of a recent downpour slammed into her. She turned. The portal back to the palace faced her, a thin, near-impossible thing, pristine and anomalous in the dust of the courtyard. It reared over her, a monolith, its surface suffused with light, its frame a filigree of clear spun material glinting in the sunlight, its existence both beautiful and unnerving. Ahmen groaned.

"Come," she coaxed, "there is shade close by." He stumbled after her out of the stunning heat of the courtyard into the deep gloom of the vestibule where he sank into a crouch, his breathing ragged.

"Will you stay?" he panted, his gaze fixed on the dusty, yellow ashlars beneath his bloodstained feet.

"No, but I will not leave you like this," Meresamun answered, looking around the strange, ancient place, somehow still intact despite the creep of vegetation. "There must be water somewhere close by."

The tendons of Ahmen's jaw tightened, though he said nothing more. She emerged back into the courtyard's heat, the sun's relentless once-familiar beat peeling back the pages of time to her mortal life in Egypt, to the day she had donned an exquisite gown and prepared to attend the pharaoh's feast to recount the Creation Myth. Unhappy memories she would rather have left buried in the past crept after her, tormenting her. She hurried away, desperate to find water, or another who would aid the one who suffered because of her.

A corridor led from the courtyard into a vast palace. Meresamun made her way past a series of silent, dust-shrouded rooms, still furnished in opulent elegance, past pillared halls, colonnaded vestibules, and overgrown gardens surrounded by empty, cracked pools—the construction of the palace so similar in design to the palace of the pharaoh she began to wonder if she had returned to

Egypt at some point far into its future. Within a grand vestibule, she came to a halt. To her left, through another great pillared hall—the sweep of a cloudless sky. She hurried toward it, riven between hope it led to a vantage point where she could search for a source of water, and fretting over the passage of time, dreading Marduk would soon wake to find both her and Ahmen gone.

She swept past enormous carved pillars, bearing designs the same as those of the pillars in Perev—several bore markings the same as those which graced Sethi's chest. Not a future Egypt then. Somewhere else. Somewhere important. And old. Very old.

The pillared hall fell away. A grand terrace sprawled before her, its once-smooth surface pitted with age. She caught her breath, rapt. Her bare feet carried her across the broiling heat of the stone ashlars, but she felt nothing. At the edge of the terrace she came to a halt. Her heart thundered. She sank to her knees, rapt.

Her mirror led to a city, a great city, filled with dozens of palaces overgrown by vegetation, and in the center: a trio of pyramids, massive, vast, and sheathed in gold. They surrounded a monumental pillar which stretched from the core of the complex up into the heavens, to the stars. To forever.

"Anki," she whispered. Tears touched her eyes. *This.* This was what Zarpanitu had been searching for, and Ahmen, seeking to help her escape had led her straight to it. She rose, reverent. Her answer, at last. To think, all this time, it had only been a heartbeat away. She turned and ran back through the palace, hastening back to where she had left Ahmen, hope coursing through her, awakening her. She fleeted across the courtyard to where the mirror stood, a sentinel, enduring, anomalous. It glinted in the sunlight, catching her reflection, a relic of an ancient world, long lost. She burst into the vestibule, panting, brimming with words to share, of what Zherei had told her, and of what Zarpanitu had written, and of her true purpose.

A faint bloodstain tainted the spot where she had left Ahmen. Several footsteps showed the dusty outline of his passage back into the courtyard. She sought in vain through the mess of her own prints for his, but found none.

"Ahmen?" Her voice echoed back, the air heavy with the desolation of eons.

Silence greeted her, purposeful, meaningful. It spoke volumes. He had done what he had said he would do. The rest was up to her. Her heart plummeted. If only she could have had the chance to explain to him, to reveal the reason for her insistence upon staying with her consort, and of her purpose, the way to it opened by Ahmen. She turned, defeated, and went to the mirror. It was time to return, but she would be back. And soon.

She pressed her fingers against the mirror and stepped into the light.

Sunlight bathed Meresamun's face as she emerged. She turned, uneasy. The shutters had been closed when she departed. If a servant had seen her come through the mirror—

She caught her breath. Movement came from just outside the edge of the opening to the terrace. Marduk's silhouette cut a harsh outline against the morning light. He came toward her, clad in his black armor, his hair tied back, his mouth set in a grim line.

"Where have you been?" He eyed her, cold, distant. In his gloved hand, a device blinked. Meresamun swallowed. She was too late. He had already gone to Ahmen.

"In here." Meresamun answered, quiet, lowering her eyes so he might not see the lie in them.

"There is dried blood and dust on your feet."

Meresamun stilled. He had not looked down. How could he—

Her consort lunged across the distance separating them, his speed startling. He took hold of her upper arm, his grip firm, verging on violence. "I ask you again," he repeated, hostile, "*where have you been?*"

Meresamun cut her eyes back to his. "In. Here."

"I woke and you were gone," Marduk continued, his hold on her arm tightening, promising pain. "And now, *he* is gone. Do not think for a heartbeat I fail to see the connection." He leaned toward her, vengeance bleeding from him. "Am I to believe despite all we have shared, you still love him?"

Meresamun glared at his hold on her. "You dare handle me thus? I am your consort."

"I dare!" He shook her arm, hard enough to make her cry out. "You will answer me," he continued, icy. "Do you still love him?"

"I do not," she answered, her arm afire within his implacable grip. "I pitied him."

"After what he did to you?" Marduk roared, incandescent. He flung her away from him, sending her sprawling into the nearest divan. He stormed away to pace the length of her room, a tide of fury cascading in his wake. "How could you betray me? Betray *us?*" He swiveled back to face her, his pupils thin, menacing, slits of rage. "You will show me where he is, or—" he held up the device in his gloved hand, meaningful, "what was meant for him, will be meant for you." He took a step toward her. Sunlight glinted along the edges of his black armor, his darkness haloed in light. "I will not lie, the pain as it burrows into your brain is unspeakable, horrifying. You will suffer much. And once it goes in, it cannot be extracted. It breaks down into a multitude of minuscule parts, which bury themselves deep within one's flesh and blood. I would own you utterly, as I own Sethi." Another step. "Tell me where he is, Ninsunu." He met her eyes, and for a heartbeat, she glimpsed his anguish through his rage. "It will destroy me to do this to you, but I cannot let what he knows slip through my fingers." Another step. "If you ever loved me, you will tell me where he is."

Meresamun pushed herself up from the divan. "I cannot." She glanced at the hateful thing, blinking, cold, malevolent, within his metal-sheathed palm. "Istara was my friend—my only friend. She gave me shelter when I left Ahmen, and brought me to Babylon. To you." Her heart tight, she approached her consort, slow, cautious. "You know I love you, but I beg you, do not force me to be a part of this."

Marduk shuddered as though she had struck him. "Ninsunu," he whispered, his anger melting away, "even if Istara protected you and is the cause of our reunion, how can you not see after all you learned of my past, if I do not defeat the gods, the same thing will happen again as before? Elati will be destroyed in the war for supremacy. Nothing will be left. I cannot—will *not* destroy another world. I vowed once I achieved immortality, things would change. *I* would change." He closed his fingers over the device and lowered his fist, shielding her from the vile thing hidden within his grip. "Whether you accept it or not, war is the very thing I wish to avoid—why else do you think I hold Sethi back?"

Meresamun came to a stop before him. "Must everything end in war? Can there not be another way? Perhaps an accord to divide Elati between you and the gods?"

"No," Marduk said, his features hardening. He turned away, his jaw tight. "I have lived long enough to know what I harbor will not share power nor will it stop until it has achieved its totality of purpose. War would be inevitable. And the brutality of war—" the muscles of his throat moved as he swallowed, "—whether I wish it so or not, is what I excel at. Once I begin, I will not cease until I have triumphed, even if it means the whole world must burn." He turned back to her, his presence blistering, intense. "Do you not see? Istara and those with her are the lesser loss. If I remove them now, Elati shall be left intact. Millions will not have to die because of what I once welcomed within me."

"Still," Meresamun breathed, her heart aching. "I will not tell you. You will have to take the answer from me." She touched the hardened back of his gloved hand, the one holding the device, and met his stricken look. "Will I forget you?"

"My love," he whispered. His anguish devoured her, palpable, excruciating. He blinked back the heat of his tears. "Your will would no longer be yours. You would love me because I commanded it." He backed away, the obsidian depths of his armor glimmering in the burning light of a new day. "No. I cannot do it. I cannot lose you—not even for the whole of Elati." He lifted his arm and hurled the device away from him. It ricocheted against the far wall, slammed into a pair of golden cups set upon a low table, and spun across the polished tiles, its metallic shell catching in the sunlight, painting the ceiling in brilliant jeweled reflections, reminding Meresamun of the wood-boring scarabs she sometimes found in the Temple of Sekhmet. It slid up against the base of the bed's frame, and came to a quiet halt. It lay there, calm, patient, its light continuing to blink, impassive, untouched, uncaring of the violence done to it.

Marduk stood with his arms at his sides, his hands clenched into fists. He stared, unseeing, at one of the golden cups tumbling across the floor, its rattling passage ugly, discordant. It smacked against the mirror. Where it had struck, a fracture marred the mirror's perfection. A sheen of opaque white slid across it the wound, closing it. It cleared, once more reflecting the perfection of Meresamun's room.

Marduk went to the mirror and sank to his knee. After a beat's hesitation, he ran his fingers over where the mirror had been damaged. He met Meresamun's eyes in his reflected ones. "It's whole again."

Meresamun looked away, but it was too late. He had caught her thoughts—butterflies in his gossamer net. He rose, elegant, effortless, and turned to face her, clad in power, dominance, once more a god. "You are not surprised. Why?" He turned again, and ran his fingers over it, just as Ahmen had done. Meresamun's heart clenched. Please. No. Not yet. Ahmen still needed time.

Marduk fell still. "You reappeared without making a sound. From here—" he pivoted back to her, abrupt. "It is a portal." He met her eyes again, his no longer remorseful, but raw, alive with hunger. "Show me how to use it, and I will forget you kept this from me."

Meresamun shook her head and backed away. He stalked back to her, a warrior, screaming violence. Terror assaulted her.

"You dare keep secrets such as this from me?" His words hit her, hard, cold things, clad in rage, betrayal, vengeance.

She quailed and fled. He came after her, his booted feet pounding a deep beat after her. He caught her at the edge of the terrace, and yanked her from the silence of the abyss, his grip around her waist punishing, brutal. He hauled her, impassive, as she struggled, panting and quaking across the terrace into the safety of her suite. He dropped her on the bed and put himself in front of her. Restrained fury sheathed him.

"You would rather smash your body against the cliffs than answer me?" The calm in his voice unraveled her. "Why?"

"I—" she shut her mouth. There was no answer as convincing as the truth—to give Ahmen time to escape—and she could never tell her consort that.

The pupils of his eyes retracted into thin, furious slits, promising retribution if she did not grant him an answer.

"There is no secret," she began, desperate to divert him. "It was Ahmen who knew of the mirror."

Her consort stilled. "*How* could he have known of it?"

Meresamun swallowed and blinked back the tears of shame burning her eyes. "He said he had watched us make love—" she cut a fearful look at her consort, who stood rigid, dangerous, towering over her, clad in death, "—in front of the mirror, the night you gave me the jeweled collar."

He glanced at the mirror. His eyes narrowed. A faint, cold smile touched his lips. "Did he?" A shimmer of satisfaction rippled through him. He turned back to Meresamun. "And until he told you, you did not know of the properties of this mirror?"

"He watched us," Meresamun whispered, humiliation sweeping through her, "If I had known I would never have done such a—"

"No more," Marduk muttered, a flicker of annoyance deepened the cut of his jaw. "I believe you." He eyed the mirror again, his mouth settling into a cruel slant. "So that was how he managed to breach my citadel." Determination hardened his features. "If someone like him could find a way to use it—" He returned to the mirror and ran his gloved fingers over the frame, searching for hidden niches. He found nothing. He stepped back and eyed its surface, his eyes moving over it, calculating, incisive. "Perhaps," he murmured, "it is as simple as touching it." He pressed his gloved palm against the silvered glass.

Meresamun brought herself to her knees, barely able to breath. She willed the mirror not to work—to refuse Marduk entry to the once-home of the gods.

Long heartbeats slid past. The mirror remained quiet, innocent of what she knew it could offer. Marduk's armored reflection filled most of the frame, mocking him. He pulled off his glove and tried again, unaware how thin the ephemeral barrier standing between him and his destruction was. He waited, patient, determined. A long time passed.

Meresamun sank onto her haunches and dared to breathe again. A tendril of hope unfolded within her breast. The mirror should have wakened by now. Perhaps it would not awaken for him, a being of the dark.

Marduk stepped back from the mirror. "He came at night and left at dawn. He was able to see us at night." He nodded, confident, certainty cloaking his words. "It must be a nocturnal device. I will try again at nightfall. It will be better if I bring Sethi with me." Meresamun shuddered. If Istara were in Anki—her thoughts raced ahead, frantic, seeking a way to stop what was unfolding.

Marduk turned. Meresamun looked down at her hands, clenched into fists against her lap, unable to hide her turmoil.

"Have your servants pack your things. You will move into my suite." He came to her, and lowered his gloveless hand, as elegant as a courtier. As she took it and rose up from her haunches, he cut a look at her bloodstained, dusty feet. "I understand why you cling to your once-mortal connections, but what must be, must be. With the passage of time you will understand." He pulled her toward him. She slid up against the unforgiving wall of his armor. He caught her chin in his gloved hand, its metal cold against her skin. "Ninsunu." Her name on his lips touched her, intimate, sensual, enticing. He tilted her face up to his, his carnelian eyes darkening, holding her captive, his look private, possessive, heated by the desperate passion of his love. "Swear you will never betray me again."

In his gentle grip, she quivered, her heart aching.

His grip tightened, just a fraction. "My love, do not torment me. You are either with me or against me."

"I am with you," she whispered, enduring the scorching shame of her weakness against the thrall of him; the silence of her lie. She succumbed to his metal-clad, cold embrace and let him lead her away from the mirror, away from her destiny—away from where she knew she must one day return to finish what Zarpanitu had begun.

A day. It felt like an eternity, and he *knew* about eternity. Existing without his consort was unbearable, meaningless. Agony. In the flight deck of his ship, Horus sat in the command seat, morose, and gazed at the relic cradled within his palm.

"Wake up," he whispered. Nothing. He rested his forearm against his thigh and followed the sinuous curves of one of the serpents wrapped around the stave. "She needs me beside her. Just for a little while, take me back to her. Let me see her—let her know I am with her." He shifted his weight. The relic's gold relief shimmered, caught in a shaft of late afternoon sunlight, the brief glint its only response. His jaw tight, he eyed the pyramid where the Creator had returned him from his crumbling realm, back to where Sethi had retrieved the jihn and annihilated Arinna—from where Baalat had vanished.

With a muttered oath, he set the relic onto Baalat's seat. "My love," he whispered, his heart tight, gripped by dread. "Hear me. I am with you, wherever you are, you are not alone. I exist only for you. Fight this. Come back to me."

The pair of serpents twined around the relic's stave gazed back at him. Their golden eyes blank, empty of light, just as they had been since the Creator sent him back with his imperative: Give the relic to Istara, and when the time was right, guide her back through the tower to the indentation. Horus leaned back in his seat and folded his arms over his chest. The Creator had given him no easy task. The tower was saturated with distortion, where time both failed and all times became one. Madness had clawed at him. He had barely made it to the indentation himself. How would he manage to lead Istara there as she suffered her own agonies, perhaps even pulled against him?

Doubt assailed him. He rubbed his hand over his jaw, the rasp of his stubble reminding him of the time he had already spent in Anki. Three days. And what had he accomplished in his reckless departure from Ikalur to pursue the jihn? Nothing. He closed his eyes as waves of guilt and regret slammed into him. He welcomed the pain. If only he had been more cautious. If only—

A pounding against the ship's outer door startled him. He leaned forward, cautious, and enabled transparency. The walls shimmered. A grotesque creature hunched by the door.

"Horus," it called, harsh.

Horus rose to his feet. That voice, he knew it . . . Ahmen. He stared at the thing which had called his name, trying to piece together the macabre mess with the one who had gone into the smallest pyramid and never returned. But how—

"For the love of the Creator," Ahmen groaned, "let me in."

Horus bolted to the door and slammed his palm against the sigil. The door slid open and the eyes of the Egyptian met his, saturated with pain and something else—despair. Ahmen eased himself up the steps and into the cabin. Horus kept out of his way, eyeing the other man's injuries. Ahmen had been skinned alive, though some time had passed since it had been done. The exposed muscles of his back and shoulders clung to his frame, pale and stiff, the blood dried out from the heat of the sun. His once-white kilt hung stiff, stained black with blood. Tucked into his belt, one of Marduk's weapons, its grip crusted with desiccated bit of gore.

Ahmen halted. Pain bled from him, visceral, raw. Horus had nothing to aid him. The Egyptian needed a healer. A fresh shaft of anguish shot through Horus as he thought of Baalat, her golden light bathing her in vibrant tendrils, as once, long ago, she had healed the fallen—had healed him. No. He clenched his fists. Not now. He turned his attention back to the suffering man. Ahmen stared at the floor, his chest rising and falling with each labored breath, his shrunken muscles taut, ready to snap.

"Where are the others?" His question rasped, harsh against the smooth contours of the cabin.

Horus couldn't bring himself to say it out loud. *Arinna is dead. Baalat is . . .*

Ahmen cut a burning look at him. "What happened?"

Horus liked that question better. He gestured toward the middle pyramid. "Sethi found the jihn."

"I know." The muscles of Ahmen's jaw tightened. Horus looked away, unsettled. It was unnatural, a man without the clothing of his skin.

"Did the pyramid do that to you?"

"No."

"Then what—"

"Sethi didn't return to Perev alone."

Horus blinked. He took a step closer, eyeing Ahmen's flayed flesh, the precision of the work. He had seen such before, during the wars of gods and men. *Marduk.* He let out a slow breath. He had underestimated the Egyptian. "You went after Meresamun?"

A flash of anguish sheathed in loss shot through Ahmen's eyes. Horus caught his breath. Even after Ahmen's incredible, insane act to aid her, Meresamun had chosen to remain.

Horus cleared his throat. An unsettling thought circled him: Within the space of one day, he, Teshub, and Ahmen had each lost their woman. What was it the Creator had said? He searched for the odd phrase. Ah, there it was: *For the darkness to fall, the goddess must rise.* What goddess? Or did he mean every female was a goddess? Horus paused. If so, perhaps it might explain why, one after another, the women had been taken from the men who loved them. Perhaps the darkness knew something the rest of them did not. Perhaps the women were the key—

"I found a way back here," Ahmen continued, his voice rough, raw. "There is a chance Marduk will follow."

Horus's thoughts juddered to a stop. No. Anki was to be the sanctuary of the gods, if Marduk were to arrive before Thoth returned with the cores, all would be lost. *Baalat would be lost.*

"What way?" he demanded. "Was it a mirror?"

Ahmen granted him the barest of nods.

"You remember where?" Horus moved past him to fire up the ship. Ahmen didn't answer. Horus cut a look over his shoulder. "For the sake of what I once was to you, answer me. *Where* is it?"

Ahmen turned, bleak, and tilted his head to the south, at a palace positioned on an outcrop, overlooking the rest of the city. "It took me all day to get here. He might already have arrived. It depends on . . . her."

Horus didn't wait. He punched the ignition. The ship roared to life, its thrum invigorating him, dulling his ache for Baalat. Ahmen picked up the relic from the seat beside Horus and set it into an indentation on the control panel. Sunlight washed over it, awakening its beauty, though its heart remained silent. The Egyptian, or what was left of him, sat, cautious.

Grateful at last to find purpose, Horus occupied himself with the controls, scanning for thermal readings, flying low over the city toward the palace, the fronds of the tallest palms quivering in his wake. He reached the palace and circled the vast structure, his weapons primed and ready to fire. The readouts showed nothing. He took the ship higher and flew over the city, crossing and re-crossing it, his heart tight. The screen remained quiescent, but he would not stop, not yet. Too much was at stake. He sailed beyond the perimeter, past the towering *ziqqurati*. Still, nothing.

"As far as I can tell, we are still alone," Horus said as he steered the ship back to the palace and brought it down onto an enormous, dusty terrace overlooking the city. Dust clouds billowed up, obscuring the view. Ahmen stared at the murk, unseeing.

Horus shut the ship down. "I need you to tell me where the mirror is." He stood. "Until the cores are activated, no one comes through. No one."

"I will take you to it." Ahmen rose, stiff, his lips pressed into a thin line, the agony of his existence etched in the grotesque mask of his face.

"When she arrives, Istara will be able to bring an end to your suffering."

"Who says I want it to end," Ahmen muttered.

Horus lifted an eyebrow. Apart from what little Baalat had said about Meresamun, he didn't know anything about Meresamun's Egyptian husband, nor did he care to. The only one who mattered was Baalat. Everyone else came a distant second.

In the cabin, Horus eyed the weapons he had taken from Teshub. Their lights had stopped blinking. He tilted his head at them. "You know how to use these?"

Ahmen nodded at his own grimy weapon tucked into his belt. "I have made some guesses. Some worked, others didn't."

"Make your guesses with these outside, then."

He opened the door. Heat radiated from the terrace's broiling ashlars into the coolness of the cabin. He followed Ahmen out from under the ship's wing and into the blistering heat of the sun. No breeze stirred. The terrace's heat, devoid of the shade of the luxurious awnings it must have once borne, bore down on him, hot as a bread oven.

Ahmen led the way toward a vast pillared hall, his gritty, dust-coated muscles creaking like unoiled reins. Horus gritted his teeth, endured the ugliness of it. Immortality was no gift. It was a curse, a perversion of what the gods had been granted. If immortality were a gift, why had the Creator not offered it to him and Baalat? No, it was not a gift. It was an abomination. The darkness's version of a god. Another distinct creak came from Ahmen. Horus suppressed a shudder, grateful such a thing could never happen to him.

He followed Ahmen deep into the shade of the palace, through halls, rooms, vestibules, and courtyards, the once-elegant furnishings laced in a creep of vines and coated in an eon of dust.

Ahmen came to a halt at the end of a corridor. It opened into the vestibule of another courtyard. He eyed the space, wary. In the center of the courtyard, a long silenced, once-elegant, three-tiered fountain overgrown with vines and lumpy with clumps of sedge occupied most of the space. Around the courtyard's circumference, a deep, pillared vestibule offered the solace of shadow.

Ahmen turned his attention to the dusty ground. A multitude of small, high-arched footprints criss-crossed the courtyard, over what Horus presumed were Ahmen's larger ones. He cut a look at Ahmen. Someone else had been here. A female by the size of the prints. Horus blinked. No. There could only be one. Marduk's consort. She had been *here*, her very presence jeopardizing the plans of the gods. How dare the Egyptian go rogue—the least one among them—and risk everything for a woman who no longer wanted him, a woman who had aligned herself with the enemy of the gods—of all life. What had *she* done to aid Istara and Baalat when they were left at the threshold of Surru, caged to die of cold? Nothing.

At last, he understood Ahmen's earlier cryptic remark about Marduk's arrival depending on Meresamun. A blazing trail of rage seared through him. He no longer pitied the once-mortal. He narrowed his eyes, thinking of all the misfortunes he would have rained upon the Egyptian if he were still a god. Let him suffer. He deserved it, after all. To think Baalat was alone, fighting for her existence at the hands of that *thing*, and Ahmen had taken it upon himself to wander, unprepared—and without informing any of the others—into the citadel of the enemy.

"No new prints," Ahmen stepped into the vestibule. "It is as I left it. She has not said anything—"

"Yet," Horus cut in, cold. He blocked Ahmen's way, examining the work Marduk had wrought against Ahmen's flesh. The Egyptian would have suffered unimaginable pain. He *would* have talked. "You have put all of us in grave danger—and for what? *Nothing.*"

A tremor rippled through Ahmen. "No," he said, low, "not nothing. I did what any man would have done to address a terrible wrong. She choose to stay. I got caught." His words, tarred in bitterness, regret, and guilt, piled up, a wall of bones. "Marduk thought his blade could entice me to give up Istara's location. I wouldn't—even when he did this." Ahmen reached down and grasped the hem of his kilt. He lifted it up. The stiff, blood-encrusted material resisted, its ugly crackles punctuating the dense, epochal silence. Ahmen turned toward the courtyard and its well of sunlight, the vestibule's shadows melting away.

Apart from a single, distended rubbery piece of flesh still attached to his groin, Ahmen's testicles were gone. Above where they should have been, nothing but the savaged, scabbed stump of the Egyptian's penis remained, the flesh at the base sawn off, rough.

"He said this was for what I did to Meresamun," Ahmen said, his voice hard. "He took his time. I welcomed the pain."

Again, Horus realized, he had underestimated the Egyptian. He swallowed back the acrid burn of bile. "You wanted to suffer?"

In the vestibule's gloom, the whites of Ahmen's eyes burned from his sunken, ruined visage. "For what I did to her, yes. A thousand times. Yes."

Horus forced himself to keep looking at him, to see the elegant, lean, muscular nobleman he remembered from their brief acquaintance in Babylon. He couldn't. This was who Ahmen was now, who he would be—would always be—the monster responsible for having driven the Babylonian princess he loved into the clutches of the being who brought darkness to everything he touched. Ahmen lowered his kilt.

An awkward silence slid between them. Horus turned his attention to the dark, waxy leaves of a vine encircling a nearby pillar. He touched one of the leaves. A thin coating of amber dust slid onto his finger. In its wake, a line of brighter green. He rubbed the rest of the leaf clean. "As a mortal, you worshiped me?"

"Always." The word cut through the air, a saw against stone, ragged with devotion. Horus shot a look at the other man. A glimmer of reverence flickered in the Egyptian's eyes. "Despite all I have witnessed since coming to Elati, to find myself in your presence once more after what happened in the Etemen'anki is nothing short of a miracle. I cannot even begin to comprehend how it must be for you."

Horus lifted his brow. He granted the Egyptian a quiet nod.

Ahmen moved on, dignified, despite the indignity of his emasculation. The Egyptian's determination to aid Meresamun revived Horus's thoughts of Baalat, and of her solitary struggle, locked away where he could never reach her—where even the Creator could not reach her. If Baalat had been caught in Marduk's thrall he knew he would have done the same as Ahmen, but much sooner—it would not have taken him a month to get to her.

They rounded the curve of the fountain. Horus slowed his steps. He had expected something similar to the portals Thoth had created during the Golden Age: a stone frame, adorned with quiet bursts of cerulean light. But this . . . this was something *other*. The Elatian version of Thoth's portal loomed over him, a stunning piece of beauty, symmetry, perfection, untouched by the dust which permeated the rest of the palace. It stood in the courtyard just outside the edge of the vestibule, opposite the dormant fountain, a thin wall of silvered glass, as though it had erupted straight up out of the ashlars. Instead of stone, the mirror bore a delicate frame of spun diamond etched with sigils of power. No bursts of cerulean light touched it. It stood inert, quiet. A mirror. Alone in a courtyard. The most anomalous thing Horus had ever seen . . . and he had seen many things.

He went to it, examining it first from the back, where a dull wall of silver faced him, twice as wide as he and half again as tall. He paced to its front and eyed its base, trying to ascertain what kept it standing. As he looked up, he caught his reflection. He blinked. A man he didn't recognize looked back at him. Stubble dusted his jaw, its growth stark in the harsh white light of the sun. Sorrow carved his lips. Anguish darkened his eyes. Emptiness cloaked him. Gone was his fire, his vigor, and the passion which had fueled him night and day. He gazed at his reflection, desolate. How could he fight for Baalat when he had lost himself?

The last image he had of her returned: she lay, alone, in the Creator's dying realm, her closed eyelids flickering, rapid, as the darkness encroached, its thin tendrils sliding over her skin, darkening her soul. Grief assailed him. *Baalat.* He reached out to touch the mirror's glass, willing it to take him to her.

"I wouldn't do that if I were you."

Horus lowered his hand. He turned. "A mere touch opens the way?"

From the shadows of the vestibule, Ahmen nodded.

Horus glanced back at his reflection again. On the other side: Marduk, Sethi, and the weapon which had taken Baalat away from him. His features hardened. "And Meresamun was able to use it."

"She was."

Horus said nothing. He wondered how long she would be able to keep a secret like this from Marduk. A day? Two? If he knew anything of Marduk, it was his ability to draw the deepest secrets from those he possessed. He backed away from the mirror and pushed aside a tangle of vines from the lowest ledge of the fountain. He sank onto it and squinted at the mirror, blinding in the glare of the late afternoon sun.

"Then," he said as he leaned forward to rest his elbows on his knees and tilted his weapon toward the portal, "all we can do is wait for Teshub to return with the others. Let us hope they arrive first. I would rather not have to aim this at Meresamun."

From the shadows, a quiet shudder.

The sun slipped lower. Its rays chased each other across the courtyard and slid past the edge of the vestibule's roof. The shadows deepened. The sky's inverted bowl raced toward twilight. A dusting of white clouds coated the sky, painted in streamers of brilliant orange and pink. Lavender hues crept up from the horizon and chased the streamers. A handful of heartbeats later, dense purple soaked the canopy, then, darkness roared across the heavens. Stars erupted by the hundreds. Ahmen limped out from the vestibule, rigid, his ruined muscles creaking, like the mast of a barge caught in a storm. He sank onto the ledge beside Horus and eyed the mirror, the whites of his eyes glittering in the gloom.

"Why are you alone?" he asked Horus's reflection.

Horus cut a look at Ahmen, but the Egyptian had dropped his attention to his weapon, checking it remained ready to fire.

He waited until he met Ahmen's eyes in the mirror. He shook his head, his jaw tight. He couldn't say it. Couldn't give it life.

Ahmen nodded, terse, and lowered his gaze to his weapon's reflection in the mirror. In the gathering dark, the weapons' cerulean indicators cast faint shadows over the footprints of the one Ahmen had lost. Horus caught Ahmen eyeing them, morose.

He turned his attention to the heavens, his heart aching for the one who existed beyond its walls—her isolation crying out to him, far beyond his reach. He tightened his grip on his weapon. No, he would not think of her with despair. Their hearts would still be connected, even if hers was silenced to him. He would be strong for her. For both of them. Shoving back the paralysis of his despondency, he forced himself to relive fragments of the eons they had shared soaked in love, of his endless desire for her, his adoration for her mind, her wit, her smile—the heartbeat he had found her on that remote Egyptian cliff top, fallen from the Immortal Realm. Her heart whispered to him, a faint skip, so weak he feared he imagined it. He pressed his palm against his chest, not even daring to breath. It came again, quiet, familiar. Tears burned his eyes. *Baalat.* He clung to their ephemeral connection. It was not over. She still fought. She would come back to him. And he would be waiting. The connection faded.

Shadows closed in on him, dense with the weight of lost ages. The mirror loomed over him, dark, impassive, ancient, a sentinel. He let out a slow breath, checked his weapon, and blinked back the heat in his eyes.

One hour passed. Two. The silence of the night slid over him, heavy, bleak.

Lonely.

✳ ✳ ✳

Bathed in the soft glow of Elati's star-glazed canopy, Istara rose from the divan and stretched, seeking to ease the dull ache in her back. The temptation to use her light to grant herself relief was visceral, but after everything the others had endured over the last night and day, it felt selfish to use her light for such a small thing. Better to conserve it for the days to come. She cut a look toward the flight deck and drank in the sight of the one who had emerged from the churning light of Surru, her heart unquiet, conflicted. He sat manning the controls, deft, experienced, exuding power and charisma—no longer Urhi-Teshub, King of Hatti, who had once been her mortal husband and king, but Urhi-Teshub, storm god, second highest in the pantheon, eclipsed only in power and rank by her consort, the corrupted god of war.

After the silent recriminations and judgments the other gods had laid at her feet for the actions of her consort and for Marduk's presence in Elati—the reborn storm god's arrival to Imaru in the early hours of the morning had changed everything, had set her free.

They had roared in from the west, Thoth cursing over the state of Imaru's once-tranquil, beautiful streets and terraces, its gardens and courtyards aflame, stained ugly by black smoke, riots, violence. They found the gods gathered in Set's suite. The king's message had been delivered: the gods were no longer welcome in Imaru and were to be gone by dawn. Set had disagreed, had threatened to take the city by force. He cared little if Teshub's destructive landing the night before had taken the lives of three Imarian nobles—one, a child of four—or if the gods were no longer welcome to remain in the capital of Rzhev. They were gods, and if the mortals would not comply, he intended to turn his weapons against them until they did. Into the chaos of the gods taking sides between concession and war, Urhi-Teshub arrived, his golden eyes afire, the storm god's double-headed ax in his grip, its blades coursing with bolts of cerulean lightning.

Silence had scythed a path through the suite as one by one the gods turned, saw what should not be. Teshub had returned, not as himself, but as another. Urhi-Teshub, the one who had been Istara's protector, a mere immortal, stood before them, transformed into the most powerful one among them.

Ptah, the leader of the peacemakers, had come to him first, and knelt. A heartbeat later, Isis followed, then Osiris, Ma'at, Bastet, Tefnut, Shu, Nisaba, Ishtar, and Ashur. One by one, the others left Set's side: Ereshkigal, Nergal, Nabu, Astarte, Shamash, Nut, Geb, and finally Set's consort Nephthys, until Set stood alone. They waited. Set scoffed, muttering he hoped Urhi-Teshub had a better plan than his.

Urhi-Teshub did. Despite Thoth's fretful, repeated admonitions to make haste, it had taken until the evening for the pantheon to pack and load their ships in preparation for their departure to their new home in Anki. And now . . . Istara looked past the transparent walls of the ship. Spread under the weight of the stars, twenty cloaked ships flanked them, following the course Thoth had set for the new home of the gods. A flicker of pleasure rippled through her. Sanctuary. At last, after so much uncertainty, a door had opened. And what a door. Eons ago, Anki had been the home of Elati's gods. After they vanished, it had lain dormant, isolated, and shielded by a powerful storm, as though waiting for their return. She shivered, prescience touching her. The Creator's hand had to be in this detail. It meant something. It meant despite the bleakness of her thoughts of late, perhaps they were not alone after all.

Her thoughts raced ahead, wild, like children freed from the claustrophobia of endless lessons. Once the cores were active, and Marduk's devices were rendered useless, there would be no limit to what the gods could do. She longed to send ships out to those countries already caught in Marduk's grip where, she suspected the generals and commanders would be amenable to sending a selection of warriors to join the gods. And yet, she pressed her palms against her abdomen, seeking to ease its ephemeral flutterings of anticipation, after so much time lost, that task alone could take weeks, if not months. Impatience wove it silver threads through her, darting, restless. She paced away from her seat, toward the back of the cabin. Thoth lay prone on the divan, his arms folded over his chest, caught in the cradle of deep sleep. A half dozen leather satchels stuffed with sheaves of bamboo paper surrounded him, with one transformed into a lumpy cushion for his head. Further down, at the back of the cabin, the cores sat upon the cabin's metal floor, patient, their cerulean hearts pulsing, quiet.

She turned to make her way back to the front of the ship. Past the open door into the flight deck, Urhi-Teshub sat alone. Sekhmet no longer occupied the seat beside him. Instead, she flew alongside them, guiding her own ship through the dark skies. Two hours earlier, Urhi-Teshub had taken the controls of Marduk's ship, Thoth beside him, translating the bizarre symbols of Marduk's language etched into the panel. Urhi-Teshub proved a quick study. Within heartbeats, the ship burst to life and they screamed back up into the stars, Urhi-Teshub's hands moving over the controls, calm, focused, the line of his jaw harsh in the control panel's illumination.

Istara had slept for a time, but now, as the distance to Anki shrank, and her hope of finding a way to liberate her consort grew, agitation gnawed. She drew closer to the open door. Urhi-Teshub kept his eyes on the controls, though she sensed he was aware of her presence. From under her lashes, she examined him, curious. He was the same and yet not. Before, he had resonated power, now his presence radiated both immutable power and authority. Quiet confidence saturated him. In many ways he reminded her of Sethi. No. She cut off the thought. Sethi was different. He possessed something, something other, something *more*. She turned and leaned against the wall, her gaze falling onto Thoth, who snored, quiet, his bony ribcage rising and falling as he traveled esoteric paths known only to him.

Over *téy* one afternoon, he had told her a tale. He claimed the storm god and god of war had been the first gods the Creator had created. One had arisen in the morning. The other in the afternoon. They had lived on the coast of a vast, primordial sea, brothers, where they spent a season together, competing one against the other in various challenges the Creator set for them. When it was done, the Creator tallied their results. The god of war had won by the merest margin and was rewarded the power of flight, a gift no other god would ever possess. The god of war chose the form of a falcon and shot up into the blue skies, triumphant, savoring his brother's jealousy.

When he returned, full of arrogance, he discovered he and his brother were no longer alone. The Creator had brought forth another, the ephemeral, beautiful sun goddess. The storm god had lost his heart to her, and all thoughts of his loss to the god of war had been forgotten.

For one month, while the storm god and his consort wandered the coast locked in their private world of love, the god of war searched the heavens, seas, and mountains in the hopes of finding his own consort, but the Creator, in his wisdom, made him wait. When at last the goddess of healing stepped out of the light and approached the god of war, gratitude and humility filled him. No longer arrogant, he was ready to lead, an equal to his brothers and sisters for eternity. But now—he was corrupted and Urhi-Teshub had taken his place.

Istara pushed away from the wall, abrupt, and paced to the back of the ship again, drawn to the calm heartbeat of the cores. It was just a tale, and had been told to cheer her. Thoth didn't know any better than the rest of them how the gods had begun, or, in truth, who the Creator intended to be first among them. In ages past, Thoth had been supreme, before that, Ptah, and even earlier, Set, but when Marduk and his people arrived, it had been the god of war who had possessed supremacy, with the storm god his second-in-command. Perhaps it had been predestined, considering how well suited he was to lead during the wars which followed. And now, the storm god had been reborn and taken Sethi's place.

Istara knelt before the row of cores. The steady pulse of the smallest one called to her. With a faint smile, she ran her fingertips along its edges and planes, thinking of the light she had sacrificed to protect Urhi-Teshub as he struggled to return with it to the ship.

Against her back, the pressure of a frank look. Suspecting her actions had roused Thoth's territoriality over his cores, she rose and turned to him, expecting to be chastened, but he remained prone, lost in the land of dreams. She turned, slow, toward the flight deck. Urhi-Teshub met her eyes, his unreadable. He tilted his head at the seat next to his, an invitation. Her heart tight, she passed Thoth as he snuffled and turned onto his side. The satchel under his head slipped to the floor with a dull thud.

She reached the door. In the dim illumination of the flight deck, Urhi-Teshub worked through several sequences, keeping his gaze on the screen. When he had emerged from the portal, he had not acknowledged her, though he had given Sekhmet a look which could have scorched lava. All through their long, silent flight back to Imaru, and throughout the day of frantic preparations he had avoided her, had not once spoken to her, or even looked at her. And now—

She perched on the edge of the empty seat.

He punched another series of buttons. "The Creator spoke to me."

Istara blinked. "When?"

"When I became the storm god." Urhi-Teshub flipped a switch beside the screen. It dimmed. In the low light of the panel's instruments he turned to her, the cut of his features outlined in shadow, softening their harsh planes. "He made clear what he wished of me," he continued, quiet. "My primary duty is to remain your protector. If so, it means the Creator wishes for you to lead us in what is to come, not me."

Istara caught hold of the seat's armrests. In the window over the panel, the canopy of stars glittered, impervious to the weight of the responsibility being handed to her. Urhi-Teshub's hand covered hers, warm, strong, familiar, reassuring. She closed her eyes, blocking out the stars—their remote happiness, their freedom. "It cannot be," she whispered. "A goddess has never led the pantheon before—and in a conflict like this? No. The others will not abide it. *I* cannot abide it."

"If I tell them what I have told you, they will have no choice."

She turned to him, fear, anger, and the scorch of resentment poured through her, a cascade. It swept her away, a leaf in a torrent. "I do not want this," she said, pulling her hand out from under his. "I beg you, take this burden from me. I know nothing of the art of war. Nothing. I am not a warrior like you or Sethi—I am everything you are not. You destroy. I *heal*." She looked down at her hands pressed against her lap, streaming with her inner starlight. She longed for Sethi, for the end of her torment, the end of her loneliness. She could not carry on like this, alone. Sorrow, long suppressed, piled up against her lashes, heavy, hot. "Sethi," she whispered. "Please. Come back. The Creator asks too much of me."

Urhi-Teshub caught one of her tears against his thumb. "Istara," he murmured, low, intimate, "you are not alone. You have me."

Istara stilled. His voice touched her soul, reawakening the memories she had lost and found again of when they had been mortal. She shuddered, her heart aching. "You still remember."

Urhi-Teshub nodded, the shadows deepening against his eyes. "The Creator did not take my memories."

"Mine," she breathed, keeping her gaze fixed on her lap, "have also returned."

He let out a ragged breath. "When?"

"When you left with Teshub." She felt the heat of his look. She turned away, her watery gaze moving over the flight deck's side panel, several rows of lights blinked, cold, remote, the ship's empty heartbeat.

"How much—" He fell silent. A creak of leather as he shifted in his seat. Uneasiness seeped from him.

"Do I remember?" She turned back to him. "Enough to know who you once were to me, and who I was to you." She shuddered. Now she had broken the impasse, she found herself unable to stop the words from escaping. "You stayed. You watched me mourn another." She met his golden eyes. "You protected me—and I forgot you."

"Istara." He reached out and wiped away her tears, gentle. "I hope, at least now you no longer blame yourself for Sethi's corruption."

Istara shook her head, numb. "I do not."

"Marduk is the enemy, not you. It was never you." A series of lights awakened on the panel. He leaned forward and punched in a sequence. They dimmed again. "The Creator has chosen you for a great purpose," he continued, "he would not have done so if he did not believe you were able to do what was needed."

Istara rested her head against the back of the seat and gazed up at the stars, resigned. "First we secure Anki, then we will see." She stood. "Say nothing of what you told me to anyone. For now, let the others believe you are in command."

Urhi-Teshub nodded. She paused at the door.

"All I want is Sethi freed of Marduk's control."

"I know."

"Can it be done?"

Urhi-Teshub met her eyes, but did not answer.

Drowning in emptiness, she left.

Anki was nothing like Istara could have imagined. She stepped out of the ship into the gray pre-dawn light, the outlines of the pyramids harsh against the canopy of waning stars.

"By the Creator's light," Thoth breathed as he came up beside her. Awe bled from him. "No god built this." He turned full circle, his gaze stalling on the central tower, its implacable, defiant presence carving a black path through the sky, blotting out the heaven's fading glow. "In theory, according to my calculations, I knew a place like this would have to exist—but to find it." He quivered, overcome, and sank to his knees. "The longevity of Elati's people, the lack of decay, the latent essence of power. Of course. How could I not see it? Without the presence of the gods, what else could have sustained Elati against the corruption of the dark for so long?" He rubbed one of his bony hands over his scalp, quick, his movements matching the rapid darting of his eyes as they drank in the brutal scope of the complex. "All this time it was *right here*, under my nose—the first world, waiting for us, ever since I made the portal to Elati millions of years ago." A bitter laugh erupted from him, sharp, nasal. He tore his attention from the tower's heights to meet the question in Istara's eyes. "It was from the first world the Creator brought forth the multiverse, it was from *here* every single living thing, every mountain, star, and sea emerged—from nothing. No, not nothing, even nothing is *something*." He shivered, delight soaking him. "Anki was not just the home of the gods, but of the *first* gods. Every pantheon in every universe would have been modeled after them. The power and knowledge of the original gods would have been staggering. To think this was where the first manifestation of Thoth once walked, it is—" He shook his head and let out a ragged breath.

Urhi-Teshub joined them. Shards of cerulean light flickered over the ashlars, ignited by the bolts of energy crackling along the blades of his ax. He sniffed. "Teshub said there were pyramids. I admit I had expected something . . . smaller."

Thoth pushed himself to his feet. "As did I. But this—" he rubbed his hands together, anticipation brightening his thin, sparse features, sharpened by the shifting light of the storm god's weapon, "—changes everything." He shot off into the night's thinning gloom toward the middle pyramid, the panels of his kilt flapping, erratic, against his thin calves. "When the others arrive," he called over his shoulder, "bring the cores. And my notes—all of them." He vanished into the darkened opening of the pyramid.

"He won't be able to see a thing," Istara said. "Perhaps—"

Brilliant white light flooded the opening.

Urhi-Teshub raised his arm to shield his eyes. "That man knows far more than he lets on."

A scream cut through the sky, followed by another, then another, until the skies roared with the arrival of the gods. He looked up, searching until he spotted Sekhmet's sleek ship coming in fast, streaming down along the length of the tower. A quiet smile touched his lips. "Now, at last. It begins."

Sethi took hold of Aiya's face and kissed her, deep. She set aside her wine cup, straddled his thighs, and sank onto his lap. She shivered, a moan of pleasure touching her lips as she took her fill of him. He stroked his thumb over her lower lip, noting its fullness, swollen from his ardor.

"I knew you would please me," he murmured, bending to drink of her again. She pulled back with a small smile and began to ride him, sensual, her green eyes half-closed, her head tilted back and her dark hair cascading over her shoulders. He leaned against the divan's cushions, savoring the sight of her as she ascended, slow—her breaths ragged, and her nipples tightening against her full, ripe breasts—to where she had shuddered with ecstasy in his arms at least a half dozen times over the last day and night. She took her time, her sheath tight against him, arousing him, blinding him with lust. He rocked her, gentle at first, then harder, matching her hungry thrusts, their bodies moving as one, driving them both to their escape. He caught her as she fell, limp and panting against him.

"I feel like I have known you before," Sethi said as he leaned back and stroked her hair. Aiya lay quiet in his embrace, her heartbeat slowing against his. He caught her chin and tilted her face up to his, so he could meet the brilliant jewel-green of her eyes. "Tell me, who were you in Ikalur?"

Aiya's shoulders lifted and fell, soft. "No one."

Sethi tucked a tendril of her hair behind her ear. "With a face like yours, I doubt that. Now, I will not ask again, who were you?"

"I was—" She looked down at one of the fractals juddering through its rotation against his pectoral. She bit her lip.

He waited.

"I was what I am to you."

"And what are you to me?"

She blinked and met his eyes. "One who gives pleasure."

A spear of jealousy touched him, faint. "And to whom did you give pleasure? The king?"

"No. The queen and her ladies."

He lifted his brow.

She bit back a quiet smile. "You are surprised. Not every woman wishes to have a man in her bed."

"And you," he asked, trailing his fingertip over the curve of her breast, "would you prefer to return to the other women, or stay here, with me?"

"What do you mean, stay here?" she asked, low.

He reached for his wine cup and handed it to her. She sipped, demure, her thick lashes lowering against her cheeks.

"I want you to be my consort," he said, taking the cup from her and finishing the last of the wine.

"How can I be your consort?" Aiya paled. "I am no goddess. One day I will age and die. And—" she looked away, abrupt, toward the terrace, eyeing the sun-drenched forested mountains in the distance.

"And?" Sethi pressed, amused by her reticence.

"Who is Istara?" she whispered, taut.

He stilled. "Where did you hear that name?"

"I—" she pulled back, fear thinned her lips, dulled the brilliance of her eyes.

He caught her. "Answer me."

She quailed. "Before dawn, I woke to you on the terrace, tearing at the back of your head until it bled. You cried out her name, and begged her to forgive you. When you came back to the bed—"

Rage slammed into him. He pulled out. Aiya huddled into herself. Terror seeped from her, visceral.

"Peace," he muttered. "I will not hurt you, but I have no memory of this." He eyed her, narrow, suspecting deception, but of malice, he could find nothing. "I want to believe you lie, yet . . . how could you know that name?"

Her gaze flicked to the fractals on his chest and back again. "Your markings," she answered, moving, cautious, to her haunches, "flowed, like music, they were breathtaking to behold. And your voice was different. You were you, yet not you. You were even more beautiful than you are now."

"What happened when I came back to the bed?" he asked, low.

"You stared at me as though the dead walked again. You called me Edarru, asked how I could be here."

"Edarru?" The name tasted familiar on his lips, like a favored wine, long forgotten, rediscovered. He searched the empty corridors of his memory. Opened one door after another. Barren rooms greeted him. Frustration clawed. He cut a low look at her. "And?"

She swallowed and continued, dogged, miserable. "Then you asked: 'How is my son?'" Her eyes claimed his, haunted. "When I couldn't answer, you whispered, 'Forgive me.'"

He searched Aiya's face for the art of duplicity. He found none. "And then?"

She blinked rapid, her expression shifting from sorrow to fear. "The sun rose. Its first light swept across the terrace. When it struck you. You . . . "

She bit her lip. A gust of warm air blew in, rich with the humid heat of the forest. She shivered.

"Tell me," he commanded, his heart tight.

"My lord," she breathed, retreating deeper into the divan, defensive, "it was terrible to behold. You bellowed in agony as though being torn apart from the inside out. At the end of your torment, you vomited, there," she flicked a shamed look at a spot in the middle of the room. "When you had purged yourself, you became yourself again." Her gaze fleeted, wary, back to his chest, over the fractals as they juddered through their ragged rotations. "You went to the side table, took some wine, then asked if I wanted food brought in as if none of what had transpired had just happened."

He eyed the place between the bed and the terrace where Aiya claimed he had emptied the contents of his stomach. He remembered nothing. The floor's black marble gleamed, warm, pristine, in the late morning sun. "There is nothing there."

"You returned to the bed and fell asleep within a heartbeat." She cut a wary look at him. "I was glad of the work. I needed to do something."

He rose and paced to the open doors of the terrace. *Edarru.* The name meant nothing, and yet—he felt something. Like the whisper of a song he once loved, a scent, a color. Malachite. He held his breath. There *was* something. Something *true*. He stilled. Waited. Silence saturated his soul. He turned.

Aiya watched him, quiet, her arms wrapped around a gold-tasseled cushion, her dark hair tangled from their lovemaking. Sunlight dappled her skin. Her beauty and presence pleased him to the depths of his being. He crossed the obsidian tiles and knelt before her.

"I will answer your question," he said, brushing aside a stray tendril of hair from her brow. "Istara was my consort. She left me for a mortal king. That is all you need to know."

Aiya nodded, though uncertainty soaked her. He sensed her thoughts, the question.

"Come," he said and held his hand out. She let go of the cushion and took it, obedient, trusting, her fingers slim and elegant against his strong ones. He rose and pulled her from out of the depths of the divan. "You witnessed a nightmare," he continued, "nothing more."

She looked away. Her profile cut through the silence of his heart, screamed of another, just like her, buried, lost. Pensiveness cloaked her. He caught her chin and lifted her face to his. "When I sent for you, you had been weeping. Why?"

"Because I was afraid," she whispered.

"Of?"

Her gaze moved to the terrace. Her jaw tightened. "Not all who leave the harem return."

He followed her gaze. "No," he said. "I would not—" He stopped, abrupt. And yet, he sensed pieces of himself were lost, their silence deafening.

He eased back from Aiya, forced himself to ask. "How many?"

Aiya let out a tremulous breath. "Since I arrived, twelve have gone to you. Three have not returned. I feared I would be the fourth." She pressed her lips together. A sheen of tears glazed her eyes. "We can hear them begging for mercy as you drag them across the terrace, their screams as they fall—though the silence which comes after is far worse."

Sethi turned away. He paced. Agitation piled up against him, oppressive, suffocating. "I have no memory of this." He turned on Aiya, fierce. "How can I not remember?" She shook her head, stricken. He sank onto his knees, and stared at the meandering rivulets of white marble breaching the depths of the floor's black surface. "I could have done the same to you." He looked up at her, sickened by the thought. "I still could." He lifted his hand to her. She went to him, cautious, and knelt.

"When does it happen?"

"Just before dawn." Aiya brushed at her eyes, discreet.

"Every time?"

Aiya nodded. "No one sleeps. We pray."

Sethi ground his teeth. "Still. I cannot remember." He rubbed his palm over his jaw. Against men he could be cruel, brutal, even. But this? This was not who the god of war was. He did not murder innocent women in cold blood. Hadn't he spared Urah, that viperine queen of Thes Dios who had cursed him to never know true love?

He rose. "You will return to the others and tell them to board the ship. I depart for Itin in an hour, where they will be free to go."

Aiya came to her feet. Gratitude bled from her. "My lord, with all my heart—"

He held up his hand. "Before you continue, know I still wish for you to be my consort."

"I—" her eyes went to the terrace, her thoughts plain. Fear gilded her.

He took her hands in his. "Not like this. Not here. I would not risk losing you. Come with me to Perev. You will remain in Marduk's stronghold, where you will be safe from me until this . . . *flaw* can be remedied. If you agree, I will give you everything you could ever dream of, and more. It is within my reach to offer you a fountain of youth and near immortality."

He waited. He would not force her. She had to come to him of her own will.

She gazed at her hands caught in his. "I wish to have children," she whispered.

"As do I," he answered.

She looked up. Hope soaked her.

He touched his brow to hers, gentle. "Aiya, let me love you."

She smiled, tremulous, and his heart soared.

Sethi brought the ship down onto the terrace in Perev. In the seat beside his, Aiya watched him work, quiet, subdued. He rose, took her hand, and led her from the ship. Though he hated to do it, he left the jihn behind in the bay with the regeneration devices. Her reaction to the weapon had disturbed him. She had paled, horror clawing her beauty, stealing her from him. He had gone after her, but she had fled, weeping, distraught, her anguish tangible, and would not come near him.

Once he had secreted the weapon and returned to her, it had taken her a long time to recover. When they landed in Itin, he had expected her to make her farewells to the women, but she had remained in the flight deck, silent, broken, as though her very soul had been savaged.

"Ninsunu is Marduk's consort," Sethi said as they entered the citadel, the braziers lining the corridor burning bright, ignited against the rampage of the oncoming night. "I will take you to her first. I am certain she will be pleased to have your companionship."

Aiya nodded, dull. Sethi stopped. He took hold of her shoulders, turned her toward him. "I will not leave you like this. Speak, tell me how to ease your suffering."

She looked up at him, bleak. Shadows touched her eyes. "That weapon you possess, it is saturated with evil. I beg you, relinquish it."

Sethi blinked, taken aback by her soft words. "*Relinquish* it? Never. It called to me. After a near eternity of silence, it chose *me*."

Aiya shuddered. Tears blotted her lashes. "No. It cannot be. The god of war would never possess such a thing." She pulled herself from his grip and backed away from him. Dread touched her look. "Tell me, who are you, truly?"

Her question gnawed, prowled at a locked door deep within. A whisper, then it was gone. "I am the god of war. The weapon is necessary to defeat those who threaten Elati's future." She retreated deeper into the shadows, eased herself between two pillars. He captured her. She looked down at his fingers encircling her wrist, bleak, resigned. "You must trust me," he continued. "With food, wine, and the pleasant company of a companion, this will pass."

He tugged her toward him, and gentled his tone. "Never again will the jihn to be near you, you have my oath."

"It is the jihn," she whispered, her words loaded with realization. She looked up at him, the green of her eyes brilliant in the heat of the firelight. "It has made you into someone you are not. It has blinded you to its darkness, its corruption. It is everything life is not."

Sethi narrowed his eyes. Her words disturbed him. He tightened his hold on her wrist. "I was thus before I found the jihn. I am who I am. Do not seek to define me."

Aiya held his gaze. "It is too late. And yet—" she bit her lower lip and looked down the length of the gilded corridor, unseeing. She cut a look back at him, tears once more blooming in her eyes. "I cannot help but hope you will overcome what is in you so you might return to the god who asked about his son, and whose markings moved over his chest, unencumbered, as they were meant to."

Sethi let go of her. He backed away. Unable to stop himself, he followed her damning gaze to his markings. They stuttered, ragged, broken, ugly. Dissonance slammed into him, visceral, hot. He turned on her, tasting fury, dining on rage. "Lest your deepest desire is to know the fate of your fallen sisters," he said, harsh, uncaring of her startled cry as he caught her arm, rough, and pulled her back to him. "You dare not speak thus to me again."

She nodded, though sorrow tainted the curve of her lips. Provoked, he hauled her the rest of the way to Ninsunu's suite, troubled by her words as they burrowed deep, boring into the foundation of his existence. He clenched his jaw. He never had a son. His markings had fallen into their shattered movements when Istara betrayed him, born from the unbearable breach she had carved into his heart when he had learned she loved another. He had nothing to overcome. Nothing.

He reached Ninsunu's suite. It lay cloaked in thick gloom, the braziers cold and white with ash. A faint flicker of lamplight shed a thin path of illumination into Ninsunu's sleeping room. He pulled one of his weapons free and primed it to fire. At the threshold of her room, the damp, alkaline chill of the sea crept over his flesh, touched his tongue. He cut a look toward the terrace. Its doors stood closed and bolted. Further in, a single lamp burned. Close by, a pair of Marduk's guards stood on either side of a full-length, gold-gilt mirror. As he approached, the guards bowed their heads. Of Marduk's consort, there was no evidence. Her suite lay shelled of life, rank with desertion.

"Where is Ninsunu?" he asked as Aiya followed after him, her gaze sweeping over the splendor of Ninsunu's shadowed suite, awed.

"Lord Sethi," one of the guards answered, "our lady has been moved to the residence of The Giver of Life, who awaits your return."

"And why are you here?"

"None are to pass either within or without."

Puzzled, Sethi looked around the silenced suite, eyed the barricaded doors to the terrace. "From?"

"The mirror, my lord."

He hadn't expected that. He stepped to the mirror, intrigued. His reflection gazed back at him, the cut of his features severe in the faint light of the lamp. So, Perev contained a portal. Anticipation tingled. It appeared much had transpired since he had left the morning before. He turned to Aiya and held out his hand. She took it, quiet.

He led her from the darkened suite. Perev was full of mirrors, perhaps the entire citadel was nothing more than a hub leading to locations all over Elati. The possibility pleased him.

As he progressed along the corridor, he paused to lift Aiya's arm toward the light of a brazier. Dark purple blotches marked her skin—the ugly silhouette of his fingers, the residue of his anger a stain upon her. Regret slammed into him. This was not who he was. He took hold of her face and cupped it in his hands. "Forgive me, if you can."

She didn't answer. Her bleakness tore through him, shaming him. There was nothing more he could say. He let her be, sensed she needed time. Her hand in his, he led her deeper into the citadel, thinking of the mirror, and of the one who eluded him, of her shrinking world, and he, its conqueror.

✳ ✳ ✳

Buried in a womb of utter, blinding darkness, Baalat ran her fingertips along the plane of a slick, rancid-smelling surface, what she presumed—hoped—was a wall. Underfoot, the way was also slimy, treacherous, and uneven. A miasma of effluent odors rose from beneath her feet as she progressed, the air thick with the acrid stink of spilled blood, rotting entrails, and bile: The stench of a battlefield—or a charnel house. She closed her eyes to blot out her thoughts. It made no difference. Darkness, palpable, insidious, relentless, saturated her existence.

How long had it been since she was taken from Horus to traverse this endless, soul-crushing path? A day? A month? A year? Time lost all meaning in this hateful, brutal place. Perhaps this was all there had ever been, and what she had thought of as her existence before had been nothing more than a construct of her mind. Perhaps Horus, the one she clung to in this dark, festering, dying place, never existed—perhaps neither had she.

Her thoughts spiraled down, heavy, bleak, hopeless. For a time she fought, but as she pressed on, her feet sinking deeper into the mire of the dead, staining her flesh with its decay, she succumbed to the despair of her thoughts. She would never escape. This was her fate, to traverse this tunnel for eternity, lost, alone, forgotten. Buried alive until she sank into the remains of the dead.

She slowed and sagged against the wall, damp heat coated her shoulder and upper arm. The metallic bite of blood filled her senses. Fresh blood. She wondered if it was her own. Exhaustion hauled on her, pulled her down until her shins sank into the carnage—until she did not know where she ended and the rot began.

She slept. Dreamed of nothing. Then, a voice, from far away, from another life, from a place of light, of hope, sliced through the murk.

Baalat, my love. Where are you?

She opened her eyes. Darkness assailed her. The violence of a butchery pit drenched her senses, soaked her throat.

"Horus?" she called, quiet, aching with hope.

Silence.

"Please," she whispered, tears slicking her eyes, setting them afire, a foil against her plummet into despair, "be real."

In the distance, the faintest glimmer of contrast breached her world of black. She caught her breath. A pale smear of light, nebulous, ephemeral, beckoned to her. She had forgotten how beautiful it was, how her soul surged toward its warmth, longing for it, seeking it. She pushed herself to her feet, the sickening pull of the morass's suction no longer nauseating, but mundane, familiar, a friend.

The light brightened, just a touch, enough for her to see the outline of another emerging from the faint glow. Her heart juddered. She knew that silhouette, it called to her like the beat of her own heart.

"Horus!" she cried, clambering through the decay, the filth, the rot of life. She surged toward him, panting, desperate. He had found her, would take her away from this place of darkness and despair back into the pyramid, back into his arms where she would be safe, protected, cherished. She sobbed, her heart aching with relief. It was over. At last.

He lunged through the depths of the dead, shoving grisly pieces aside—shattered hearts, broken limbs, severed heads—his legs, arms, and chest drenched in the fluids of the dead. He found her, caught her, held her.

"My love," he breathed, "I have you. I never stopped searching."

Baalat wept, incoherent with relief. She clung to him, relishing the solidness of his flesh, his warmth, unwilling to let go, afraid if she did he would vanish, and he would be lost to her forever. His arm tight around her shoulders, he led her back through the mire toward the faint pinprick of light, their steps slowed by the growing heap of ruined, dismembered, disemboweled bodies— past the broken, torn faces of men, women, and children, their eyes empty, bleak, hopeless.

She began to pant, the air already close, drew in, heavy, claustrophobic. The lure of the light mocked them—remained as far from them as when they had begun. Despair traced its cold finger against her heart. They would not make it. Tears piled up in her throat. It was a lie, another torment to strip her of her last hope. She huddled closer to Horus, drawing comfort from his presence. At least she was no longer alone. She could survive anything—even this—so long as his heart beat next to hers.

Her consort halted within a space almost clear of the dead. "My love," he said, his chest rising and falling from his exertion, "forgive me. I have failed you."

The light vanished. Darkness slammed into her senses. An exhalation. The whisper of a touch against her face. Then nothing. Emptiness surrounded her.

"Horus?" Baalat whispered. Hollowness clawed at her. She turned full circle, her arms outstretched, finding nothing. "Horus?" she cried, frantic, disbelieving. The dark drank in her voice, thirsty for her life, savoring her anguish.

"No," she screamed. She sank to her knees, her soul shredding into a thousand pieces as she spiraled into a chasm of loss, her free-fall peeling away the layers of her existence, of who she had been, of the one she loved, all of it gone, forever lost. She would never escape. It had been a lie. Horus had never come to her, but had been manifested by this place, where the light went to die, to torment her—to break her. She wrapped her arms around herself, and whispered his name. Silence saturated her heart. Her hope stripped, she wept, broken, lost, and waited to die.

"Baalat." A voice, quiet. Not Horus. Another. Male, soft, persuasive.

Baalat pressed her hands to her ears. Another lie. She would not listen, would not give the darkness what it sought—the ambrosia of her suffering.

"Welcome to my realm."

Baalat closed her eyes, folded into herself, willed the voice to depart, to leave her alone with her memories—to those still caught, uncontaminated, within her grasp, of her existence before it was stolen from her, of Horus holding her close as he pointed at the stars and asked where he should make love to her next.

"Perhaps this might help."

Light screamed through her eyelids, bathing her mind in a world of orange. The homely crackle of flames. A quiet breeze bathed her fouled skin. She inhaled, cautious. Jasmine. Roses.

The scrape of a chair across a smooth floor. A slink of metal against metal as the speaker took his seat.

"Look at me," the voice tore through her, soaked with dark command.

She shook her head, clinging to her resistance, even as his charismatic presence surrounded her, called to her, penetrated the last vestiges of her soul, heavy with temptation and promise.

Another slink of metal. A draft washed over her, cold, devoid of the scent of life. A gloved hand slid under her jaw, frigid, clad in metal. The fingers tightened, promising pain. "Look. At. Me."

She obeyed. From a face more perfect than should be possible, his eyes bore into her, fathomless, black. He kissed her then, deep, harsh, a punishing kiss, the kiss of possession, ownership, power, enslavement. He pulled back, abrupt, and she shuddered, consumed with revulsion. Guilt followed hard in its wake. Never before had she been touched by another, and now—the taint upon her was worse than the creep of decay.

"Do you know who I am?" he asked as he returned to his seat. He sat, elegant, powerful, exuding confidence, the black metal encasing him up to his neck so smooth he looked to be constructed of it, not wearing it.

"I can make a guess," Baalat answered, tearing her eyes from him, forcing herself to take in her surroundings, all of it black. No gilding, texture, or embossing broke the oppressive monotony of the space. The floor, walls, ceiling, furnishings, all of it closed in on her, heavy, claustrophobic. On a side table, a wine pitcher and matching pair of black diamond goblets gleamed in the low light. On another table, an obsidian vase bore an arrangement of roses, their stems, leaves, petals, hearts, soaked in darkness. Beyond a shuttered window, the depths of a starless night. Two black braziers burned with black fuel on either side of her oppressor's seat, the fiery glow bathed his armor. It slipped over it, sensual, feeding off his darkness.

He smiled, cold as death. "Amuse me. Who am I?"

"You are whatever the jihn is—incarnate."

A disdainful flick of his brow. "How dull."

Baalat came to her feet. Her gown clung to her, rank with the effluvia of the dead. "What do you want from me?"

He leaned forward, his armor glistening in the firelight. "I like that question. Very much." His eyes moved over her, drinking in the filth staining her flesh—congealing in her hair. "How beautiful," he whispered. He met her eyes, his iced with malevolence. "I look forward to destroying you."

Though her heart quailed, Baalat held his look, defiant. He still hadn't answered her question.

"I want," he continued, low, "Istara." Loathing hardened the shadows burning within his eyes.

Baalat refused to grant him a reaction, though a shaft of terror sliced through her. His hate was visceral, personal. Determined. He rose, effortless, and went to the wine pitcher. He poured out a little into each of the goblets, smooth, seductive. His presence rippled with lust, carnality, the promise of the darkest reaches of existence laced with the knowledge of forbidden depths of evil. Elegant brutality surrounded him, clothed him. He turned, catching her watching him. Satisfaction smoothed his features. "I am not what you expected." He picked up the goblets and carried them over. He handed her one, courteous. "I am never what is expected."

She took it, careful not to touch his metal-sheathed fingers. He sipped, his gaze remaining on her as he swallowed, enigmatic. He tilted his head at her cup. "Will you not taste it?"

Her skin crawling, Baalat lifted the cup, bracing herself for the acrid heat of blood. Instead, the ruby warmth of wine, rich with age and seasoned in oak filled her senses. She tipped the cup to her lips, let his cursed wine scorch her tongue. She lowered the brim. It was enough.

He watched her, amused. "It is only wine. I am not always a brute." He paced to the vase of roses, reached out to caress the petals of an open bloom. They turned to dust at his touch. He cut a look at her over his shoulder. "Did you like my impression of Horus?"

Hate soaked Baalat. She set the wine on the floor and folded her arms, rimed with the stains of the dead.

Her oppressor laughed, warm, melodic, utterly at odds with the malicious cut of his jaw. "Ah, you *are* refreshing. So much spirit. So favored. But now—" he lifted his gilded hand, palm up and closed his fist, his features hardening,"—you are mine."

A blink and the room shifted, subtle. The chair, table, vase of roses slid away into the darkness. Upon a raised platform, an opulent bed materialized. From each of its corners, slim obelisks of polished obsidian rose over the bed, impassive, cold sentinels, their faces carved with the symbols of the Creator, corrupted, bleak. Upon the bed's black silk cover, cushions, dozens of them, black as the deepest night. At each corner of the raised platform four braziers burned, low. A presence, silent, eased up behind Baalat, hungry, dark. Fear slammed into her spine. She turned, aching with terror.

He stood behind her. His metallic armor still covered his body, as supple as skin. In the dim glow of the fuel's light, she caught movement upon his shoulders. Markings slid over them, a pale silver, designs similar to the ones she had seen on Marduk's flesh, long ago, before the wars of gods and men. She caught her breath and backed away until the backs of her ankle met the lowest step of the bed's platform.

"You won't have me," Baalat said as he followed her, the markings over his armored body moving, sinuous, replete with predatory anticipation. She searched the barren, empty space for a weapon, something, anything with which to defend herself. There was only the bed and its multitude of cushions. Beyond the dim light of its boundary, an endless expanse of darkness. She met his look, sensed his triumph.

A flicker of amusement touched the depths of his eyes. He brought up his hand. A dagger manifested in it, curved, elegant, saturated with darkness. With a flick of his wrist he turned the weapon toward her, hilt first. "This is for you."

She took the blade from him, wary. Its taint clobbered her, thick with treachery, violence, hate, hungry for her betrayal of the light. Shaking with revulsion she cast it aside. It skidded to a halt beside one of the braziers and vanished.

It reappeared in his gloved hand. He ran a tender finger along its length. From under his brow, his fathomless eyes seized hers, hard with vengeance. "Get on the bed."

Baalat quailed under the torment of his look, sensing the horror he intended, the agony she would suffer in his metallic, cold grip. "No," she whispered, her heart aching with terror as his look deepened, promised unimaginable horror. She closed her eyes, forced herself to think of Horus, of his arms around her. Of the millions of nights he had taken her to the heavens. The embodiment of darkness might take her body, but he would never have her heart, her soul.

A ripple shimmered through him. Blindness slammed into her. The fleeting sensation of time melting. Beneath her back, the soft press of a mattress, the slink of silk. Her vision returned. She lay on her back on the bed, her ruined, stained gown gone, and her arms pulled taut above her head, her wrists tied to the girth of one of the obelisks, the silken ties tight, painful. The obsidian spike of her captor towered over her, seething with the corrupted symbols of the Creator. She tore her gaze from its hateful pulse to the dark, impenetrable inverted abyss of the lightless realm.

He came to her then, still wearing his armor, alive with its silvered markings, and knelt between her legs. He took her face in his gloved hands, his touch reeking of death, hopelessness. She closed her eyes, forcing herself to think of when she had been free, desperate to separate herself from what she knew was to come.

He kissed her, slow, tasting her, savoring her. He pulled back and traced a dispassionate fingertip along the space between her lips. "When I crafted the jihn, I believed to overcome *him* it would be enough to consume the light he had bestowed to the gods, but he was clever. I discovered he also gave a fragment of his light to each of you, the ones he terms *goddesses*." Her oppressor paused to trail his finger over the swell of her lower lip, down her throat, and along the line of her collarbone, his movements hinting at pain, possession. "Even with my power fragmented across thousands of worlds, I succeeded in oppressing your— his—light through men, but it was never enough. Now the jihn has been reawakened, I am whole again. My power grows, and *his* fades. At long last, his light—*your* light—is dying."

Baalat said nothing. Her heart closed in on itself, lost, alone. Annihilation pounded at the gates of her existence. *Horus.*

"Look at me."

Her eyes opened against her will. He smiled, pleased, and lifted the dagger to his chest, over where his heart would be—if he possessed one. He shoved it into his breast, a sigh of pleasure rippling through him. Horrified, Baalat shrank back against the bed. Black fluid seeped out from the rent in his armor, slid along the length of his torso, sensual, following the lines of his markings, caressing them. He pulled the blade free, slick with his essence.

His armor slid back together, the rift vanishing. He looked down at her, whole again, an aberration, a look of intense pleasure sluicing through his chiseled features. In his grip, the black blade of the dagger dripped with the fluid his being, inky, viscous, dead. He pulled the ties holding her bound to the obelisk away. A shiver of silk bathed her arms as he unleashed her and pulled her up so she sat facing him. He stroked the hair from her face, and kissed her again, hard, rough, hungry. He pulled back, abrupt, his eyes churning with desire.

"And now," he breathed, "let us begin."

He slammed the blade into her breast. Anguish sundered her soul, met her heart, carved it into two. Heat, then cold shattered her senses. In his arms, she shuddered against the onslaught of his poison, his darkness, his hate for everything she was—as his essence penetrated her, burned her, scoured her of her light.

He pulled the blade out, slow, careful not to wound her further. She sobbed, broken, lost, hope abandoning her, her inner light dimming, oppressed by the scale of his might. How could she, a mere mortal, stand against the antithesis of the light—of a dark being who possessed powers as vast as the Creator? She could not. Despair wove gossamer threads around her, drew fast, imprisoned her. She would never leave this place—would never see Horus again. She would never be herself again.

His cold, hard fingers touched her bloodied breast, drinking of her life, her warmth, chilling her, icing her bones. She sagged in his relentless, uncaring grip, fought to remain conscious, opening doors along the fading corridors of her heart, seeking Horus, desperate to retain the memory of his touch, his love, his passion, grieving as he vanished from every room, as the darkness saturated her mind, subsumed her thoughts, her will, expunged her light.

Her possessor hauled her up, carried her from the blood-soaked bed and down the steps into the depths of the dark, as her heartbeat slowed, and the reprieve of death beckoned—his metal-clad body cold against the burning heat of her flesh, a salve against the anguish of her erasure.

He lowered her onto a divan, and touched the gouge exposing her broken heart. Cold saturated her. The pain ended. A stuttering rippled through her chest, then—the quiet beat of her heart. She caught her breath. Her breast lay whole again, unmarked, as though his blade had never been.

She met the black ice of his eyes. Waited. Darkness ate through the last of her being, claimed her, made her his.

He lowered her onto the divan and joined her, his armor melting away, exposing his flesh, alive with his markings. "We are not finished," he murmured as he turned her away from him and entered her from behind, the bite of his grip on her hips possessive, cruel. She longed to fight him, to struggle, but the weakness of her obliterated existence pinioned her, crippling her as he claimed her—his supremacy inviolable, wielded in his tenebrous, inescapable, claustrophobic realm. He rode her in total silence until a spasm of cold fire lanced into her, spread deep within her. Without saying a word, he left her, as though nothing had passed between them. Droplets of his seed stained his member, black as tar. Baalat curled into herself, aching, raw, the violation of her self complete. With his final desecration, he had taken what belonged to Horus, the act cold, laced with hatred, and marked with ownership. Emptiness clawed at her. She longed for her dead heart to cease its beat.

His armor rippled back over him, his markings once more moving upon it, steady, determined, mirroring the reverse beat of his black heart.

"I know the message *he* gave you," he said, "*'For the darkness to fall, the goddess must rise.'*" A black goblet appeared in his hand. He held it out to her. She took it, numb, and drank. His wine scorched her senses, dulled the horror of her fate. He sank into a crouch and faced her, his vile presence boring into her, calling to the smear of his taint as it spread within her, a bleak, desolate wasteland.

He touched his sheathed fingers to her brow. Silence seeped from them, burrowed into her mind, encased her in despair. "Istara will fall to me, just as you have." He leaned closer and murmured into her ear, his breath cold, devoid of life. "And you will be the one to betray her."

Baalat shrank from him. Horror crawled over her, dragged her to his black abyss, cast her over its edge. He stood, eyeing her, impassive, as she bled tears, misery shrouding her. A fleeting smile touched his lips. He turned his armored back to her and walked away, melding with the emptiness of his realm. She huddled into the divan, bloodstained, alone, naked, violated, broken. One after the other, the braziers at either end of the divan vanished. A heartbeat later, the divan rippled and ceased to exist. She sank to the floor. Cold pierced her heart. Darkness soaked her soul. She wept until she could weep no more.

❋　❋　❋

Istara opened her eyes and rubbed her hand over her brow. She had dreamed of a place of unyielding darkness, and of a black-haired woman, bloodstained and broken, huddled into herself, drowning in hopelessness. Bleak, Istara sat up and looked around the quiet ship, seeking to reorient herself, but the dream's images lingered, troubling her. There had been other things: glimpses, fragments of brutality, malevolence, violence, but of the details nothing remained apart from a thickening sense of dread. It settled within the depths of her torso, visceral, a warning.

The door slid open with a quiet hiss. A shaft of sunlight slanted in from under the ship's wing and sliced its way across the floor, an elongated oblong. Urhi-Teshub came up the steps, his bulk breaching the straight lines of the light. He lay his ax on the divan opposite her and took a seat. He leaned toward her, his forearms sliding along his leather-clad thighs.

"You slept almost the whole day," he said, cutting a look over his shoulder out the open door, to where the ships of the other gods spread across the wide expanse of the central complex, their harsh outlines softened by the ripening light of the late afternoon sun. "Despite his fractiousness," Urhi-Teshub continued with a resigned lift of his brow, "Thoth has made good progress. He expects the shield to be active before the sun sets." The storm god folded his fingers together, his gaze lingering on the view beyond the open door. He cleared his throat. "There has been a development."

His tone made Istara's skin prickle. Prescience touched her. Urhi-Teshub remained silent for several heartbeats, his eyes moving over the ships, unseeing. He looked back at her, abrupt.

"Ahmen has uncovered a portal from Anki into Marduk's stronghold. He suspects Marduk will learn of it sooner rather than later."

Istara absorbed the weight of his words. "Where?"

Urhi-Teshub tilted his head toward the southern edge of the city. "It's in one of the palaces, we think it belonged to Thoth."

Fear sluiced through Istara. Her dream reared, ugly, a warning. She stood. "If Ahmen came here to tell you, who has been guarding the way? Marduk could—"

"Ahmen is still at the portal. Another has come to warn us, he—" Urhi-Teshub looked down at his hands, clasped together. The skin over his knuckles whitened.

His silence tore into her. "*Who* has come?" Istara demanded, tight. Only Teshub, Arinna, and Ahmen had gone to Anki. There could be no one else. Unless . . . her heart stuttered. *Sethi.*

The storm god met her eyes, his golden ones dark, wary. "Do you remember Horus?"

Istara blinked at his unexpected question. "I—" A memory slammed into her, of a pillar collapsing onto Sethi, decimating him, and of his resurrection, granted by the light of a fallen god. *Horus.* The one who had brought Sethi back from death. Not once, but twice. She staggered and sank onto the divan. Trepidation climbed up her spine. She cut a look to the door, at once comprehending Urhi-Teshub's focus.

"He is out there, isn't he?" Istara asked, her mouth dry. "Alive."

Urhi-Teshub nodded, terse. He stood. "He wishes to meet you." He hefted his ax and turned to the door. She caught his arm, stopped him. He waited. Gave her time.

"Is he a god?" she whispered, her throat tight. "Is Sethi—" she couldn't finish the question. *Lost.*

"Horus is mortal. The Creator gave him another chance to live. He is here to help."

Istara let out a tremulous breath. "And his consort?"

Urhi-Teshub looked back out the door, his profile taut. "He is alone." He turned again to the door and descended the steps onto the plaza's ashlars. He looked back at her, his eyes lost in the shadows cast by the ship's wing. "I will wait out here." His attention moved to the front of the ship, out of Istara's line of sight. He tilted his head at the open door and stepped back. Footsteps approached.

Istara came to her feet, her heart thudding. A burst of sunlight eclipsed the doorway. Istara shielded her eyes as the outline of a tall, powerful man ascended the steps and ducked into the cabin, sunlight ricocheting against a pair of Marduk's weapons, tucked into the belt on his hip.

He came to a halt. His eyes touched hers, brief, before they slid away to follow the cascade of her starlight. Anguish sheared his features. He lifted the back of his hand to his mouth and rubbed it against his lips. Tears glinted in his eyes.

"Istara," he said, bleak. Hollowness eroded him. He tore his gaze from her to take in the details of the flight deck. He swallowed, his throat moving, ragged, as he dined on his tears.

He reached into a fold of his kilt and pulled out a slender, golden pendant. He held it out to her, cradled in his hand. "This is yours."

She lifted her hand to him, palm upward. He tilted his hand. The slight weight of it settled against her skin, its unexpected familiar heft branding her, awakening her, exposing memories long buried under the smooth sands of the tides: A gift, from Tarhuntassa's chief surgeon for the completion of her studies as a healer; Tanu-Hepa suggesting it might be as old as the time of Gilgamesh; of Istara wearing it during her journey with Urhi-Teshub from Tarhuntassa to Kadesh; of its disappearance on the eve of the Battle of Kadesh; of its return to her on the way to Babylon, seized by Urhi-Teshub on the brink of his death in Karchemish; of her flight from the Etemen'anki with Baalat, Sethi, Marduk, and Meresamun—the others left to be buried alive in the collapsing city; of being caged and left to die on the cold shore of Surru as Marduk departed for Elati with Sethi and Meresamun; of Urhi-Teshub's dagger in her breast, and of Baalat's final embrace, the wash of her light as Istara returned to life, a goddess, her existence opening the way into Elati—

She pressed the golden, serpent-entwined stave against her breast, her heart trembling. At last, she was complete, the fullness of her memories restored. "Thank you," she murmured, lifting her eyes to Horus, who watched her, stricken.

He nodded, distant, and turned to leave. He paused, his hand braced against the door's frame. "When you have the time," he said, "Ahmen could use your light. He refuses to leave the portal." He descended the steps and strode away, as though seeking to put as much distance between them as possible.

Istara left the ship and watched him head to a sleek, golden ship. He entered it, and within heartbeats, its engines fired and he surged away in a wash of broiling, liquid heat. Its fierce wake swept over her, buffeted her hair, caught at her gown. As the roar of his ship faded, Urhi-Teshub joined her. She unfolded her fingers from the pendant.

He eyed it, quiet. "Can you remember anything?"

Istara nodded. She touched it, reverent. "All of it."

"Horus said you will know when the time will be right to use it."

Istara met his eyes. "Use it? How?"

Urhi-Teshub tilted his head in the direction of the imposing, sealed tower, its reach endless, oppressive. "It opens the way in. Within its depths, there is an impression which fits the shape of the pendant. Only you can access it."

She eyed the edifice. Uneasiness gnawed. The tower was the last place she wished to go. She forced herself to ask: "And . . . when I do?"

Urhi-Teshub lifted his brow. "The Creator did not say."

Istara's heart stilled. "The Creator?"

Urhi-Teshub folded his arms over his chest. A hint of his sun-warmed leather washed over her, mundane, familiar, reassuring. "Horus used the pendant to enter the tower. While there he was taken into the Creator's realm."

Istara cut a look back at the tower again, her trepidation deepening. "And?"

Urhi-Teshub shook his head. "And nothing. Horus is not the same as I remember. He is barely existing."

Istara thought of Horus's broken, devastated look when he met her. Though she feared the answer, she dared the question. "Where is his consort?"

Urhi-Teshub let out a heavy breath. "I do not know. I could not bring myself to ask."

In the heavy quiet, the brush of her once-husband's fingers against hers. She let him take her hand, savoring the feel of his grip—firm, solid, real, different, yet the same. They stood, alone together in the shade of the ship's wing as the sun threw itself toward the western sea, the shadows of the pyramids sliding across the plaza, paving an inexorable path toward the night.

He gestured in the direction Horus had taken. "Horus mentioned Ahmen is in desperate need of healing. Though I would rather not take you anywhere near that place, if you wish to go, I will take you there."

Numb, Istara nodded. He let go of her hand. Loneliness skirted her, cold, alienating. She returned to the ship. Urhi-Teshub followed after her and closed the door, blocking out the sight of the tower, the place she was destined to go. The place she never wished to enter.

She traced the outline of the serpents' curves, her fingers moving over their undulations, driven by memory. A glimmer of white light suffused its core. It spread along its length, faint, a promise. Her heart tightened. A *relic* Teshub had called it, a gift from the Creator. From another world—another life. Long before she had left the court of Tarhuntassa, the Creator had chosen her. The weight of her burden bore down on her. Despite all she had suffered, so much still remained uncertain. While in Imaru, she had thought her path was simple, her purpose clear: find a safe haven for the gods, aid the others as they stood against Marduk, and, her deepest desire—reprieve Sethi from the darkness.

Urhi-Teshub settled into the command seat, his fingers once more moving over the controls, deft, expert. A roar erupted from the rear, followed by a rush of speed. The walls and floor shimmered and turned translucent. Beneath her feet, the complex fell away, the ships of the gods shrinking—toys scattered across the magnificence of the complex. In the distance, the palace where Ahmen and the portal to Marduk's stronghold awaited. The palace's sprawl claimed more than half of a verdant hill, its yellowed ashlars, columns, and walls a dull orange in the heat-soaked, late afternoon light. On the largest terrace, a gleam of sunlight reflected against Horus's golden ship, in stark relief to the severity of Sekhmet's ship of night parked beside it.

Urhi-Teshub brought them down beside the other ships and cut the engine. Silence swarmed over Istara's senses. From the rear of the ship, the quiet tick of cooling metal.

In her hand, the pendant pulsed once, twice, then fell silent. She tucked it into a fold of her gown. Urhi-Teshub pressed the symbols on the door's panel. A quiet hiss. The door opened. Broiling, heated air rushed in, thick with the gritty, acrid tang of the ship's silenced fire.

He turned, his powerful silhouette filled the opening. "If Marduk arrives before the shield is activated—"

Istara nodded, quiet. Her heart tight, she rose, understanding the danger. The risk. The late afternoon light limned the storm god's leather armor, a halo. Soon the sun would set and Thoth would activate the cores. "The Creator will protect us," she said.

Urhi-Teshub blinked. An enigmatic look fleeted over his features. He turned his attention back to the blistering heat of the terrace, eyed the scorch marks left by Horus's ship. A gust heated air swept into the ship.

"Perhaps," he said, his grip on the ax's shaft tightening. He left, clad in silence, the bleakness of his response lingering, ominous, cold, despite the heat.

"So, at last you return—the prodigal god." Marduk pushed his chair away from the desk and eyed Sethi, hostile. Across the length of the desk, an array of Marduk's devices fanned out, half of them enabled, bathing the nearby walls in pale, cerulean light. On another table in the middle of the room, a heap of scrolls had been piled up, haphazard. Several lay open along the table's edge, held by the weight of inactive devices.

Marduk tilted his head toward the reception room where Sethi had left Aiya with Ninsunu. "A woman." He rose and walked around the table to face Sethi, his armor glinting in the lamplight with violent promise. "You made me wait because you were bedding a woman, and then—" he plucked a weapon from his belt, enabled it, quiet, meaningful, "—you brought her here, into my home. Why?"

Sethi eyed the weapon. "To protect her."

"You are the god of war," Marduk said, turning the weapon onto its side to examine the illuminated panel. He pressed a sequence. Sethi knew that one. Disintegration. He moved to the door. Marduk would have to go through him to get to Aiya.

Marduk cut him a look from under his brow. "How are you not fit for the task?"

"Because I am the one from whom she needs protection."

Marduk lifted an eyebrow. After a beat, he powered the weapon down and slid it back into its holder. "Indeed?"

Sethi didn't like the way Marduk's gaze slid over him, cold, impersonal, loaded with judgment. "Though I have no memory of it," he said, "I have sent three of my concubines to their deaths—"

"And the one you brought here?" Marduk interrupted, bored.

Sethi went to the point. "I would have Aiya as my consort. Until I can uncover what ails me, I thought she might provide companionship to Lady Ninsunu."

From the reception room, quiet conversation, stiff with formality.

"Hm," Marduk said. "So long as Ninsunu wishes it, your woman may stay. As to your other . . . *problem*, it will have to wait." He shot Sethi a dark look, laden with condemnation. "You chose a bad time for a liaison. Ahmen escaped before I was able to learn Istara's location."

Disbelief barreled through Sethi. "How is that even possible?"

Marduk's gaze flicked to the open door to the reception room. "I underestimated the bond between husband and wife."

Sethi said nothing, though Ninsunu's betrayal hung between them, a stain. After several thick beats of silence, Marduk continued: "The portal Ahmen used will not open for me." He gestured, vague, at the heaped piles of scrolls. "Neither have I learned where it leads."

For a heartbeat, Sethi floundered, unable to make sense of Marduk's words. Then, the image of the Ninsunu's deserted suite flooded his mind; the guards, their cryptic orders—

"The mirror," Sethi said. "Yet. . . how could he have known?"

Marduk tilted his head toward the door, his eyes black, iced with vengeance. "You are about to find out."

⁂ ⁂ ⁂

The sun slammed into the horizon. A heartbeat later, an explosion of stars erupted from the indigo canopy, bathing the way ahead in the faint glow of night. Istara followed Urhi-Teshub out of the gloom of the vestibule into a courtyard. In its center, the dark outline of a tiered fountain reared up against the starry heavens, its empty basins overgrown with vines and furred with clumps of sedge. A glint of starlight blossomed against one of the furthest clumps. Curious, Istara eased forward. Urhi-Teshub held out his arm and blocked her way. A slight shake of his head.

A shadow detached from the lee of a pillar and padded toward them, silent, clad in black leather armor, a dagger in each hand. The night sky surrounded her, embraced her. The goddess of war came to a halt. Her golden eyes touched Urhi-Teshub's, dark with fenced grief.

"Anything?" he asked. The jagged light of his ax flickered over her elegant features, caught the whisper of her suppressed longing—the weight of her loss. Istara blinked. Urhi-Teshub had not told Sekhmet he had retained his memories.

"Nothing." Sekhmet cut a look at Istara and tilted her head toward the opposite side of the fountain. "Horus is there, with Ahmen. Marduk was thorough."

Urhi-Teshub nodded. He left the goddess of war, soaked in her solitude. Istara followed him, wondering at his reason for keeping his distance from Sekhmet, why he would not—

A mirror reared up out of the courtyard's ashlars. It stood, solitary and anomalous, framed by the darkness of the vestibule, and alive with the light of the stars. She went to it, walked around it, seeking to understand. As she circled back to its face, she caught her reflection—a cascade of white stars streamed through her hair, down her gown, and pooled at her feet. Her whole being glimmered, alive with her light.

She turned to Urhi-Teshub, waiting at the mirror's side, his ax no longer on his back, but gripped in his hand. "Is *this* the portal?"

Before he could reply, another voice, from behind, rasped, "Yes."

She turned. A shadow rose from the edge of the fountain. Thick creaks emanated from it, taut with tension, reminding her of the moan of ropes straining against the weight of an obelisk hauled upright.

"Ahmen?"

He stepped closer. The fountain's shadow slid away in the reflected light of her stars. A desiccated horror met her eyes, a thing of sinew and bone, dry as dust, bloodless, skinless. "Ahmen?" she repeated, unable to piece the nightmare before her into the man she remembered.

"It is I," he answered, his words harsh as a burning desert. "This is who I am now."

Her light ignited. She lifted her hands, welcoming her power as it surrounded her and bathed the courtyard with life.

"No." He turned away. "Leave me be."

Her light surged, insistent, drawn to his pain, his torment. It soared from her fingers, arced across the space between them, a storm of stars. A tendril touched his shoulder.

He cried out, anguished, as though where her touch cleansed him, she had seared his flesh anew. He stumbled into the shadows, begged her to cease.

His distress tore through her. To harm another was against her purpose, her existence. She hauled on her light, drew it back, her soul aching from the effort. It strained against her, resisting her call, stubborn, sentient. More of her light flared from her torso, an onslaught. She staggered, struggling to contain her power.

A shout, incoherent, sliced through her senses, sharp with urgency. Horus barreled out of the darkness, straight at her, his eyes hard as stone. He tossed her aside, as though she were no more than a toy. She hurtled into the vestibule. Her hands found a pillar. She clung to it, her light churning.

The drum of booted feet. The staccato pulse of blue lightning. Urhi-Teshub's eyes found hers, harsh with intent. His fingers wrapped around her arm, pulled her from the pillar.

"Run." His command tore through her senses, the voice of a god.

Istara fled with him, buffeted by thousands of seething tendrils, aching for release. Urhi-Teshub's desperate, defiant hold on her told her all: The mirror had awakened. Marduk was coming. Dread saturated her. Bitterness clawed at her. They had been so close. How could they fail after all they had suffered, all they had endured—after all *she* had endured?

A memory cut through her, of Baalat's innocent kittens claimed by the sweeping fires of an inferno, of her city bathed in a firestorm within the beat of a heart; of Horus dragging the goddess of healing away, screaming and unwilling—a visceral memory, aching with grief. Hers, yet not hers. And now, it was Urhi-Teshub who protected her from the one who soaked everything he touched in darkness.

They reached the mouth of the corridor. The silence came first, deafening, weighted. It washed over her, numbed her senses. A beat later, a sheet of blistering white light scythed over her and sliced into the corridor's depths. The pillars awakened, reared up, bleak sentinels, washed pale in the scour of the silent light.

Urhi-Teshub's grip tightened. He ran, stirring clouds of ancient dust. Istara fleeted after him, driven by terror, her light growing, escalating, no longer purposed to heal, but to protect.

She cut a look over her shoulder. The fountain's vine-choked silhouette stood in stark contrast to the glare of the anemic, cold light of the portal as it rotated counter-clockwise, carving every vine into stark relief and sharpening each blade of grass.

Silence saturated her being, as though time had stilled—as though the courtyard and all within the portal's reach existed outside of Anki, outside of Elati, outside of reality.

A tug, fierce, against her arm. Urhi-Teshub hauled her after him, half-lifting her from her feet as they plunged down the corridor, the portal's cold light streaming past them. She ran as fast as she could, her breath ragged from willing herself to outrun what was to come. She cut a look at Urhi-Teshub. Determination bled from him as he bolted ahead—a king, a god, the one who loved her, still—his ax alive with power, crackling, vibrant, ready to cut down the enemy. But it was too late. They had failed. Without the cores—

From within the depths of her despair, a heartbeat, steady, strong. *Sethi.*

She staggered, caught her breath, slowed her steps. Hope slammed into her, saturated her dormant heart. It unfolded, a winter rose awakening, touched by the first rays of the sun. Urhi-Teshub's grip deepened. His look cut through her, severe. No. She pulled against the storm god, cried out for him to stop. Her words tumbled away, useless, muted by the portal's shearing light. Another heartbeat—heavy with the weight of her consort reverberated through her—*Sethi.* She tore herself free of her protector and raced back down the corridor, toward the courtyard, toward the one whose heart called to her, needed her, ached for her. At last Sethi had come to her, had freed himself of the poisonous taint of Marduk. Together they would rise again, would stand against the oppressor, would—

An arm came around her waist, hard with leather, brutal and unforgiving. Urhi-Teshub hauled her back. Pain seared her ribs. She screamed, her outrage consumed by the oppressive silence. Fury beat its wings against her breast. In the storm god's implacable grip, she writhed, her light billowing, tormented, conflicted, powerless against his might.

The light from the portal vanished. Darkness saturated the courtyard, poured into the corridor. Her breaths came first, loud in her ears, then her heartbeat, erratic, caught between euphoria and rage.

Then, nothing. Despair, sorrow, loss. Emptiness. The annihilation of her soul. Horror clawed its way up her spine. Whatever she had felt was gone, scoured by a tide of utter darkness. Urhi-Teshub's grip fell away. He stumbled to a halt. Blind hate scoured his eyes, tainted the cut of his lips. He turned away from her and let out of a bellow of anguished horror, trapped within the waves of malignance pulsing down the corridor.

A thick silence bled from the courtyard. A sickly blue-white light lapped the dusty ashlars. Footfalls moved away from the portal through the courtyard, toward the corridor. Toward her. From the courtyard, the quiet sound of weeping whispered against the night air. A sob. Bleak, drenched in loneliness. Sekhmet.

Istara hauled herself to the feeble shelter of a pillar, away from Urhi-Teshub who paced back and forth, unseeing, his eyes afire, battle-blind. He sliced his ax through the empty air, striking at phantoms, brutal, savage, trapped by the horrors of his mind, of battles long ended.

Sethi breached the opening of the corridor. The malevolence of his presence pinioned her, savaged her thoughts. It was impossible, she would never reprieve Sethi. He was already lost. The gods would fall and darkness would reign supreme, her consort forever enslaved to it, and she, vanquished by him. She dragged her fingers against the pillar's gritty surface, desperate to quell the ruthless siege of her bleak thoughts, welcoming the ragged burn of stone against her skin.

Her heart wavered and called to his, tentative, hopeful. Hate, anguish, suffering, and hopelessness swarmed into its secret corridors, violating the beauty of her love, ransacking her memories, mocking her existence. The source of her anguish drew closer, blinding her with misery, of her impending destruction.

Her light retreated, sought refuge within her, until only a handful of tendrils darted around her torso, furtive, lost. Pale, blue-white light slid over her ragged, bloodied fingertips.

Trembling with horror, Istara forced herself to look. Her heart stilled. No. Anguish sheared her heart in two. Her consort came to a halt over her, carved in hate, soaked with evil. The fractals on his chest juddered, erratic, ugly. He glared at her, vicious—his brutal, dispassionate regard slaughtering her soul. The one who had loved her was gone. Nothing remained of her consort's light. Darkness breathed through him, saturated his blood, his heart, his soul.

In his grip—the jihn, the weapon which had consumed Arinna's life. Its black blades glinted, ravenous, awakening, primed to gorge itself on her light. A shiver rippled through it, its poisoned waves lapping against the crumbling fortifications of her soul. Along its hate-soaked edges, the beat of sentience, of power far beyond that of mere gods. From within its heart, the hum of a thousand blades against bone. Behind it, hollow cries of anguish—of the endless suffering of its victims, of fallen gods. Of Arinna.

Istara sank to her knees. Loss scaled the walls of her being, surrounded her, lay siege to her existence. Defeat pummeled her. Sethi, the one who had loved her, and who had died for her, not once but twice—who said he would find her again, was no more. The edifice of hope she had clung to imploded. Its pieces tumbled, ephemeral, into the vortex of his darkness, crushed in a heartbeat. Clarity slammed into her, of what she stood against— the immutable, pitiless power of the dark, as vast as the Creator's light. The jihn's hunger tore into her, isolated her. The distance in Sethi's eyes slayed her. The cruel slant of his lips blurred against the walls of her sorrow.

"I might have lost you," she said between the cracks of her broken heart, "but you have never lost me. Even now, as you claim my light, my love endures."

"I care nothing for you or your love," Sethi returned, the planes of his features scoured with scorn, "I care only for the end of you." He raised the jihn. Its blades shimmered, hot with hunger and anticipation.

Istara sank into herself, devastated, his words savaging her afresh. She cradled the remains of her heart in her hands, mourning its hidden chambers laid bare, stripped, violated. Without love, there was nothing. Without the hope of Sethi, how could she—

He hefted the jihn higher, preparing to strike. Its slavering hum tore into her. She met Sethi's eyes, willing him to see her, to remember. To come back to her. He smiled, cold, hate gilding him. He let the jihn fall.

The pounding of booted feet. From out of the shadows, the lightning fire of the storm god's ax slid into the inner curve of the jihn, harsh with the fury of metal against metal. The jihn slammed to a halt. Sethi staggered, struggled to free his weapon.

His eyes virulent with hate, Urhi-Teshub yanked the jihn free of Sethi's grip, it soared away, its blue-white flames streaming end over end deep into the corridor's shadows. It slammed against a pillar and tumbled to the ashlars, a furious clatter.

"You took her from me once," Urhi-Teshub panted. "Never again." The ax glinted, its blades alive with the pulse of his power, its harsh beat aching with vengeance, long suppressed. He raised the ax. "I have waited far too long for this."

A deafening crack sundered the sky, intense, savage. It rammed into the palace and barreled down the corridor into them, a brutal wall of sound. Istara hurtled into the pillared shadows. Pain thudded into her spine, stole her breath. She tumbled to the ground face first. Ancient dust coated her gown and hair, crept into her throat.

Another shock tore through the palace's foundation. From the ceiling's ashlars, the grind of stone against stone. Bone dry dust and gravel sheeted down and pummeled Istara's flesh, ricocheted against the floor. She huddled into herself, willing her light to return. Weak sparks flared from her fingers. Her light retreated deeper into her, seeking to escape the baleful presence of the jihn.

Realization came. Sethi hadn't come alone. Marduk had followed in his ship and unleashed his weapons. Their oppressor had known all along, had waited for their arrival, and now, with the gods corralled on Anki, the final blow rained down on them, lambs to the slaughter. Before they had even begun, the gods had failed. *She* had failed. Tears, stripped of her starlight dripped down her nose and speckled the dust into a mosaic of her misery. Another rain of gravel sleeted down, cut into her flesh. Pain blossomed anew, though its spike was nothing compared to the devastation of her heart, her soul. All was lost. All.

The onslaught of thunder splintered away, its fingers reaching past the city, over the island, and up into the stars, fierce, blinding, eviscerating her senses.

A throb of silence blistered through the palace. Then, brilliance. The shear of a thousand white suns scythed past her, crackling with streamers of gold. She pulled herself to her feet, shielding her eyes as the light raced away, through the courtyard, and past the walls of the palace into the distance. It filled the sky, reached for the island's shores. A boom reverberated, faint with distance. A heartbeat later, a surge of renewed brilliance poured across the arc of the heavens back to the central complex.

From beyond the opening of the corridor, high up in the sky's canopy, beside the endless reach of the tower, it gathered, a churning vortex of light. A thin beam of white light shot up beside the tower, swirling with golden light. It connected with the vortex. A pulse of light swarmed up its length and the canopy of the heavens shimmered, golden, beautiful, alive.

By degrees, the sky's brilliance dimmed, and the quiet calm of night returned. The stars glinted anew from behind a near-transparent shield of white light.

Istara eyed the shimmering web arcing over the island. She let out a thin breath, riven between disbelief and gratitude. If Thoth had activated the cores, it meant—

A roar of anguish, primal, and harsh with suffering shattered the quiet. Sethi staggered against a pillar, clawing at the back of his skull, the act desperate, savage. Blood ran down his fingers, stained his neck and shoulders.

Urhi-Teshub edged toward him, his ax gripped in both his hands. His face hard, he lifted it to strike.

"Stay your weapon," Istara cried. Hope pinioned her, wove its gentle fragments through her broken heart. "Wait, I beg you."

Sethi lowered his hands. He turned toward her, slow. Across the pectorals of his chest, his fractals rotated, seamless, perfect, a symphony. His eyes found hers, golden, clear, the eyes of her consort, harsh with regret. His lips moved. Her name bled from him. His heartbeat collided with hers, and he shuddered. He backed away, horror stealing her from him. "No," he panted, his hands tightening into fists, the muscles of his arms standing proud. "Run. There is no time. Do not let me near you. The jihn—"

He tore his eyes from hers, raked a panicked gaze along the length of the corridor until he found the weapon. Against a pillar's base, it lay quiet, subdued. A faint beat came from its heart. A single flicker of blue-white light, then, nothing. The blades dulled, turned opaque.

He cut a look back at her, fierce, desperate. "Go!" he shouted, harsh. "The sun will soon rise."

"It is hours until sunrise," Istara whispered, her heart loaded with the suddenness of him, the weight of his existence. Her consort, the god of war, who had once been the commander of Egypt—who had sacrificed everything for her. And now, he was here, the one she remembered, the one who loved her. She took a step toward him, her arms aching to hold him, to feel him, for her lips to taste him. For her body to love him. He shook his head, his look severe, laden with warning. "I cannot stop what is within me. Once the sun breaches the—"

"What happens at sunrise?" Urhi-Teshub asked, cold. He moved in front of her, blocking her way, the ax's lightning bolts picking out the splatters of blood on Sethi's shoulders.

"The device," Sethi answered, his bloodied fingers going back to the base of his skull, digging anew, "it reawakens."

"*What* device?" Urhi-Teshub demanded.

"The one Marduk planted in me as we crossed into Elati." Sethi retorted, his eyes darkening, hard with the memory of his oppression. "How else could I have become what I have?" His gaze left the storm god's and touched hers, brutal with remorse. "Each morning, at dawn, I am myself again, and can remember all I have done, the guilt is—" he clenched his jaw and looked away, swallowed, his throat taut, then continued, low, "—once the sun rises, I forget."

"The device," Urhi-Teshub shot a tight look at Istara. "We need to get it out of him."

Istara nodded. "Can you do it?"

A look of uncertainty flickered through his eyes. A heartbeat later, it was gone. He nodded, terse, and pulled a dagger from a strap on his thigh. He turned to Sethi. "This is going to hurt."

"Just get it out." Sethi sank to his knee and tilted his head forward, exposing the bloodied spot.

Istara eased closer, her light seething, brilliant, granting Urhi-Teshub the illumination he needed.

Urhi-Teshub hesitated a heartbeat before he set his ax on the floor and moved to stand over Sethi. He settled the point of his dagger against the base of Sethi's skull. Footfalls approached, soft. Sekhmet eased nearer, her dark eyes wary. A residue of sorrow laced her features, tainted her lips. She moved in front of Sethi and positioned one of her blades close to his throat.

"Make one move I don't like," she said, quiet, tilting her blade up until it was a breath from Sethi's flesh, "just one."

"I pray you will use it if you need to," Sethi muttered. He grunted as Urhi-Teshub punched the dagger's tip into the base of his skull.

"How deep?" Urhi-Teshub asked, his eyes intent, fixed with concentration, ignoring the bright blossoming of Sethi's blood spilling over the blade.

"It's in the center," Sethi panted as Urhi-Teshub shoved the blade deeper. Sethi closed his eyes, enduring, stoic, as the storm god worked the blade from side to side, feeling for the thing which had brought so much misery upon Elati. He took his time, oblivious to Sethi's shallow breaths, and the deterrence of Sethi's light, working against him, healing the god of war even as Urhi-Teshub delved. The cut of his jaw thickened, stubborn. He pressed on, determined to find the device, his probing methodical, thorough, until the hilt lay slippery with blood.

With a tight shake of his head, he pulled the blade out. A torrent of blood and clear fluid gushed. Sethi shuddered, his chest rising and falling as several tendrils of his light swarmed out from within his wound to weave his flesh back together.

Urhi-Teshub clenched his teeth, the muscles of his jaw taut with irritation. "I cannot find it." Another look of uncertainty touched his features. He met Istara's eyes. "If the device is one of Marduk's—" he tilted his head in the direction of the central complex, meaningful. Istara understood his discretion. He did not wish Sethi to know what they had done. She nodded, recalling Thoth's words from when they retrieved the cores from the dying pyramids: *The power of the cores render Marduk's devices useless.* If Thoth was correct, it should mean as long as Sethi remained on Anki, the device could no longer control him. And yet, if Thoth were mistaken . . .

Urhi-Teshub wiped the flat of the dagger's blade against his leather-clad thigh, staining it with the god of war's essence. He eyed Sethi, his face closed in thought. Istara stepped closer, longing to answer the call of her light—to ease Sethi's suffering.

In his grim pursuit of the device, Urhi-Teshub had spared the god of war no pain.

Urhi-Teshub caught her arm, pulled her back. "No," he said, terse. "It is better for him to be like this."

"Istara's light could find it," Sekhmet said over Sethi's ragged breaths. When Urhi-Teshub kept his hold on Istara's arm and said nothing, she continued, her words sharp and precise, honed, like her daggers, "She is *his* consort, after all."

"I want to do it," Istara said, pulling herself free of the storm god's grip, for once in agreement with the goddess of war. She continued, unable to keep the reproach from her voice, "It will be better than blindly hacking into his skull."

Urhi-Teshub picked up his ax, his eyes hard on the god of war, watching as Sethi's savaged flesh knit together, slow. Silence reigned for a long time, thick, oppressive. Urhi-Teshub's grip tightened on his ax, his thoughts ambiguous, unreadable. From the courtyard, the tread of heavy footfalls. Istara turned. Horus stood at the mouth of the corridor, eyeing them, his face and shoulders highlighted by the pale illumination of the shield's canopy. A glint of silver came from the handles of his weapons, tucked into his belt, their cerulean heartbeats silenced by the empowered cores. He hesitated, taking in the strange tableau, his gaze skimming over the golden tendrils of light swarming along her torso and arms, to Urhi-Teshub gripping his ax, its blades alive, their fierce light stuttering over Sekhmet's blade at Sethi's throat, and Sethi—the one his light had become—on one knee, his face tight with endurance, tendrils of golden light flickering against the back of his neck. Horus turned and left, his footfalls retreating to his vigil at the portal with what remained of Ahmen.

"Get it out," Sethi rasped, oblivious to the one who had regarded him—the one who had once been him, "before it is too late."

Istara didn't wait for Urhi-Teshub's approval. She set her light free. It arced from her fingers and encircled her consort. Four tendrils eased into his skull, searching for the root of the darkness that fueled him, for the bitter, poisoned seed Marduk had planted the day Sethi became a god. She sensed its muted presence in the back of his brain, near the lobe which controlled his vision. Just as she began to probe the spot, another flare erupted from his frontal lobe where rationality triumphed over the fire of emotions. Two more flares erupted, one at the base of his frontal lobe where he processed speech, and another deep within his amygdala, the foundation for his emotions and memory. She sent more tendrils in, ten, then twenty, chasing the flares as they blossomed from within the corridors of his brain, a dozen eruptions, then two, then ten, until his brain glittered, afire.

Her heart clenched. Her light had to be wrong. He had said it was a single device. She sent more tendrils out. This time she searched the whole of him, delving, gentle, into his chest, torso, legs, feet, hands, groin, until every cell of him lay bared to her—bones, sinew, organs, cells, blood. The brilliance within him blinded her. She hauled her light free. Tears clogged her throat. The pillared shadows crept back, enclosed them in its embrace. Pressure, thick with grief congealed in her chest. She stared at him, the one she loved, as horror and denial clawed at the walls of her sanity. No. No. No. Please. No.

"Istara?"

The uncertainty in his voice pierced her anguish. She knelt and touched his face, uncaring of the cost. All was lost. For her, nothing was left.

"It's everywhere," she whispered, her throat burning, raw with grief. "The device has broken down into millions of fragments and meshed with you, right down to the deepest, smallest parts of your being. There is no way to remove it."

Sethi closed his eyes, shut her out. The line of his jaw, so familiar, so beloved, hardened, carved itself with hate. His hands clenched into fists. The words came, quiet, a curse. "Which means there is no escape."

Sekhmet stepped back, sheathed her dagger, its quiet hiss loud in the thunder of Sethi's silence.

No one spoke. The magnitude of his loss bore down on them, oppressive, suffocating. Istara longed to touch him, to hold him, to reach him through the walls of his alienation as they piled up around him. Instead, she took consolation from his nearness, warmth, and solidity, the weight of his tainted heartbeat in lockstep with her lonely one.

He opened his eyes, looked up at her from under his brow. "I cannot remain here," he said, his remoteness searing her soul. "While I still have time, I must return and destroy the portal in Perev." He lifted his hand and touched her face. Misery twisted his mouth, darkened his eyes, "Though that will buy no more than a handful of days, at most. It will only be a matter of time before I return." He cut a look over his shoulder at the fallen jihn. "That weapon is evil incarnate. I do not think it can be destroyed. Give it to Thoth. He will know what to do. Whatever happens, I must not find it again." He rose and took a step back. A tide of despair swept over her as she met his eyes, as they lingered on her, memorizing her. "Do not grieve for me," he said, quiet, an abyss of remorse dulling his eyes. "I ceased to be worthy of you long ago."

Istara sank onto her haunches. Nausea slid through her. It was a nightmare. A sense of unreality blanketed her, numbing her senses. He turned and strode away, his familiar, confident gait reeking of power, authority, and purpose. He paused in the courtyard, to turn and look back at her, the cut of his silhouette reviving memories of shared nights on the terrace of his villa in Waset. It was too much, she would not let him go. She would not face what was to come alone.

She bolted after him, crashed into his arms, surrendered to his passionate embrace, clung to the feel of him, his chest against hers, their hearts beating as one. He could not leave her, could not succumb to his fate without a fight. "Stay," she breathed, her heart clenching onto hope so hard, she shuddered, "do not leave. You are safe here."

He stilled. "What do you mean—safe?"

"She means nothing," Urhi-Teshub said, his approach as implacable as an avalanche. "Istara, Sethi belongs to Marduk. He cannot remain here. So long as the jihn exists, the risk is too great." He came to a halt, and caught hold of her arm. "I am duty-bound to protect you, and will do so, even if it means you will hate me for it. He leaves. Now." He tugged against her resistance, sought to tear her from the embrace of her consort, to take her from the one she loved—to separate them for eternity.

Istara yanked her arm free. Fury ignited her despair, fueled a madness within she could not harness. The words spilled free, weapons, her restraint obliterated. "Yes, you swore thus. Did you not also confide the Creator wished for me to lead the gods in what was to come?"

Her words struck true. He flinched at her betrayal. "I beg you, do not do this thing," he said. "It is a mistake. You are making a grave mistake. The jihn—"

"I make no mistake," Istara cried. "Sethi is my consort. I will not stand by, silenced, while the one I love returns to the oppressor when he could remain here, with me, the taint within him rendered useless—"

"Cease!" His eyes ablaze, Urhi-Teshub struck the metal-sheathed butt of his ax against the ground. A dozen lightning bolts exploded from its blades and struck the pillars. They raced along the lintel surrounding the courtyard's perimeter, encircling them with the might of his elemental power. "I forbid it. I will not allow it. He cannot remain here."

"You forbid nothing," Istara said, cold. Her light surged, violent, chaotic. It swirled around her, clothing her in brilliance, awakening her, a goddess, arisen. "I accept the burden placed upon me by the Creator. I will lead the gods against Marduk. Without Sethi, Marduk must leave his stronghold and expose himself to those he wishes to oppress. He might be powerful, but he is one, alone. We are many, and we have—" she lifted her hand to the sky, its arc clad in a shimmering web of translucent light "—this."

Urhi-Teshub ground his teeth. Rage flared in his eyes, hot sparks which smoldered against her gown. He knelt, stiff. "As the goddess commands," he said, his eyes and words hard as rocks, "so shall it be." He rose again, the lightning-clad blades of his ax harsh with his fury. "And may the Creator forgive you."

Thoth stared at the weapon Horus placed at his feet. It lay there, its curved blades muted, black, a quiet thing. A lie.

"No one else would touch it," Horus said. He backed away from it, wiping his hands against his kilt. It didn't help. They still felt contaminated.

"I can understand why," Thoth muttered. He walked around it, examining it from all angles, keeping his distance. "The symbols marked upon it are corrupted versions of the Creator's."

Horus nodded. He cut a look over his shoulder at the suspended core, its white light rotating against the wall covered in golden symbols—the same wall which, two days ago had turned translucent and taken his consort from him. He put his back to it.

A faint beat of blue-white light flickered in the jihn's heart. Thoth inhaled, sharp, a hiss.

"It can withstand the power of the cores. For it to do that . . ." He looked up, caught Horus's eyes. "The cores' power here is at least an order of ten magnitudes greater than the pyramids I built." He cut a wary look at the jihn, as though expecting it to rise up on its own. "You mentioned Sethi said he didn't think it could be destroyed?"

Horus folded his arms over his chest and glared at the diminished, baleful thing, hating it with all his soul. When Sethi had come through the portal, the jihn's touch had crawled over him, poisoning his thoughts, enraging him, blinding him. Then, all he could see was Baalat, encircled by a well of pure darkness, huddled naked upon a divan, her skin bloodstained, and her hair matted in filth. From the depths of her being a bleak keening arose, anguished, devoid of hope. He had screamed her name. Silence poured from him. Her cries tore through him, shredded his existence. The battle she endured was worse, far worse than his darkest fear. Her bleakness saturated him, suffocated him. His heart locked in a vice, he had pressed his weight against the immense pressure of the vile place, straining with all his might to put one foot before the other into a space as dense as tar.

With each step he took, the divan slid away, taunting him. Just before the cores ignited, the braziers beside her vanished, and darkness stole her from him. He had screamed again, tasting blood. Silence hemorrhaged from him, a bubble of impotent rage which erupted into the unnatural space and slammed back into him, vicious, sadistic. A blink, and the darkness melted away. The outline of the starlit courtyard took shape, its harsh edges brushed with the faint light of the core's shimmering shield. *Baalat.* Emptiness had clawed at him, threatened to undo him. And then—Sethi.

"I suspect Sethi is right," Horus said, "since the jihn was forged by the dark aspect of the Creator. Although," he continued, his voice hardening, "even if you could find a way to obliterate it, I wouldn't let you." He met Thoth's alarmed look. "It took Baalat. Before you activated the cores, I saw her. We have to get her back. Her suffering is—" he endured the brutal memory of her desolation, of his failure to save her. The words cut their way out, blades of fury,"—beyond comprehension."

A flicker of apprehension passed over Thoth's features, though he nodded, quiet. His gaze fell once more to the jihn, his fingers moving over his narrow jaw, his look turning inward, heavy with the weight of his thoughts. Horus turned to leave, eager to distance himself from the jihn and the hateful wall—to see open sky.

"Teshub mentioned he left the relic with you."

"He did. I gave it to Istara. It is hers after all."

"Hmm." Thoth's gaze remained on the jihn. His fingers fell from his chin. "Teshub said it opened the way into the tower. I wonder . . ." Silence trailed after him. He paced the length of the platform, tapping his bony forefinger against his lips. He blinked, rapid, as he worked through whatever calculations occupied the hidden corridors of his mind.

Horus waited, uneasy, suspecting the direction of Thoth's thinking.

"You could—"

"I'm *not* going back in there. You have no idea what it is like."

Thoth came to an abrupt stop. He cut a look at Horus over his shoulder. "*Back* in? So you—" His finger came away from his lips and pointed in the direction of the tower, his thin features losing their pinched, pensive mien. He turned, the rotating light of the core slid over him, highlighting the glint of hunger in his eyes. "What is it like?"

Horus shrugged. "It defies definition. Time does not seem to exist there, and the space is endless. Movement is slow, laborious, like struggling through a bog, but worse, much worse." He looked at the wall, its deceptive innocence an offence to his soul. He jerked his head at it. "A tunnel opens up, or rather folds inward. It is a long walk until the mouth of the tower is reached, which is vast, and empty, apart from a sphere of golden light, pierced by a thin beam of pure darkness in the center. You cannot look at it directly, the heartbeat you try, it moves, even though you can still see it. It is, augh, I cannot explain. There is nothing like it that is comparable, even for the gods. We do not belong in there. It is a place meant for—"

"The Creator," Thoth breathed, satisfaction oozing from him. He nodded, his eyes alight, as though he had just won a game of chance. "I know what to do with the jihn."

"Have you not heard anything I have said?" Horus cried. "That place is incomprehensible. It would be madness to put that in there."

"No," Thoth returned, sharp. "The jihn was made by the dark aspect of the Creator, but the *tower* was made by the Creator who made us—it is why he crafted the relic. It opens the way in." He paused, his eyes moving along the symbols along the wall. He nodded to himself and continued, "The tower is the safest place for the jihn. If we put it in there, Sethi will never be able to get his hands on it again."

"If it is the safest place for it," Horus asked, tight. "Why did the Creator not put it there in the first place?"

"I rather think he did," Thoth replied, mild.

Horus folded his arms. The man made no sense. "You just contradicted yourself."

"*How* did Sethi come upon the jihn?" Thoth asked. "Was Teshub not also there . . .with the relic?"

Horus opened his mouth. Closed it again. He eyed the wall, then the jihn. Clever, clever Thoth.

"You are absolutely certain it is our only option?"

"Absolutely. I would even say—"

A brief dimming of the core's light cut him off. The golden symbols paled. The jihn flickered, its heartbeat a shade stronger than the last.

"No," Thoth breathed, stricken. He eyed the core as it brightened again, its light a touch less brilliant than before. "The jihn is redirecting the energy from the cores into itself. If it drains their power—" He shot a horrified look at Horus. "It must be moved inside. Nothing matters more than this."

Horus backed away, revulsion crawling over him as the jihn flickered, siphoning the cores' combined energy, malevolent. "I will go in with it, alone," he said. "We need to keep that thing as far from Istara as possible—"

"Indeed." Thoth's attention returned to the weapon, his profile thinned by dread as a nascent whisper of blue-white light felt its way down the jihn's grip toward one of the blades. "Do what you must, but hurry, I beg you. If the shield falls . . ."

He didn't finish the sentence. He didn't need to. It was too awful to utter. Sethi was there, among them, corrupted to the core. If the jihn sated itself on the power of the cores—

Horus turned, and ran.

✳   ✳   ✳

It stood there, quiet, breathtaking, parked in the ship's bay underneath the palace, sleek and gleaming white, its wings tipped in gold. It had waited, patient, enduring, locked in a near-endless vigil, for the scion of the prime goddess of healing to awaken its silenced pulse. Her heart trembling, Istara pressed her hand against the glowing sigil beside the ship's door. A shimmer, and the ship opened itself to her. Three white steps emerged, bordered with traceries of gold, permitting her entry into the cabin which had lain shrouded in silence for more than two million years.

She ascended. As she crossed the threshold, the cabin's interior awakened, bathing the divans and floor in a soft, white glow. In its center—just like Horus's ship—a white divan, as large as a bed, where, long ago, she suspected the prime god of war had made love to his consort countless times. A heavy tread followed her up the steps and into the cabin. She turned, her heart aching, taut with longing. Sethi regarded her, his eyes veiled, distant, revealing nothing of his thoughts. He moved further in, taking in the details of the interior, at the silk blanket tossed, careless, over the edge of the divan, its tasseled end draped over the floor in elegant folds. He moved to the flight deck and swept his gaze over its console.

The muscles in his jaw clenched. Silence surrounded him. Istara turned to the panel beside the door, to close it.

Urhi-Teshub looked up at her from under the ship's wing. The massive blades of his ax reared over his shoulder, sparking with cerulean storm bolts. They glinted against the underside of the wing, buried his eyes in shadow. "Swear to me you will open the door the heartbeat he changes." Her protector stepped closer and lowered his voice. "Never forget, your consort has been compromised. You have bought him time, nothing more. He is still your enemy."

Istara faced his remonstration, her gratitude for his revelation of the presence of the ships of the gods garnered from his brief conversation with Horus, enormous, a debt. It hadn't taken long to find the palace of the goddess of healing. With the cores activated, it had called to her—a beacon of light guiding her home. The palace had been shrouded in dust, just like Thoth's, but this . . . she touched the pristine wall of the ship and shivered. It was perfect.

"I swear it." She glanced back at Sethi, the planes of his profile shrouded as he stared at the pair of seats in the flight deck, traveling paths known only to him—paths she sensed would forever be closed to her.

She lay her palm against the panel. The door slid closed, sliced through the storm god's harsh look, cutting her off from the weight of the warning in his golden eyes. She turned. Sethi roused, turned from the flight deck and leaned against the opening into the cabin. He folded his arms over his chest and looked down at the floor, his features packed hard, muscle tight against bone.

Silence yawned between them. Istara took a step toward him. Her gown rustled, quiet.

"Wait." Sethi cut a taut look at the closed door. "Urhi-Teshub is right. This is a mistake."

He retreated into the solitude of silence, his eyes following the smooth seams of the flooring, as though by doing so he would find the words he sought. Istara waited, would not lower herself to reiterating what she had told him about the shield—of the cores' power to overcome the curse within him. He already knew. She sank onto the divan by the door, endured the distance between them stretching with each passing heartbeat. It churned away, relentless, a ravine, a chasm, a canyon, an abyss—its walls sheer, barren, bleak.

He pushed himself away from the doorframe and sank onto the divan opposite her, eyeing the closed door as he leaned forward, his forearms on his thighs, his fingers lacing together. "It would have been better for me to leave." He looked down the length of the cabin, his gaze lingering on the central divan. The planes of his profile hardened. "I dare not return to you, not now I know what is within me—what I am." He cut a dark look up at her from under his brow, "Marduk has been thorough in his work. He has achieved his goal. He has taken you from me, forever."

His remoteness slayed her. Darkness shrouded him, his own, not Marduk's.

"All this time," he continued, his words harsh, butchered by the serrated blades of his guilt, "apart from those brief heartbeats of clarity before dawn, I believed you had been unfaithful to me in Babylon with Urhi-Teshub." He looked down at his hands. "Since then . . . there have been others. Yesterday, I chose my next consort." He came to his feet, abrupt, brittle with tension. "Her name is Aiya. She is waiting for me, in Perev." He paced away until he stood beside the central divan. "I saw it," he continued, dogged, his back to her. "I watched Urhi-Teshub make love to you." He clenched his fists. "You broke my heart. And now, even though what has controlled me is silenced, I am no longer the one you loved. My crimes, tyranny, violence, and hatred for you have all left their filthy stamps upon me." He shuddered. "Though I might try, I will never escape what I was. Never. It is a part of me. We will never be able to go back to what was. It is too late."

Numb, Istara dragged his confession into her. His ugly, hopeless words clawed at her, seared her soul, hauled her to the edge of the abyss which estranged them. Jealousy circled her, lions stalking prey: *Sethi had shared his bed with another.* No. *Many* others, and one alone had gained his favor, had been chosen to replace her. One who waited for him. His betrayal impaled her, crippled her soul. The abyss yawned before her, a void, beckoning, hungry for the shattered pieces of her heart.

"Istara?" His voice came to her, from far away.

She looked up. He stood before her. Despite the seamless flow of his fractals, misery penetrated him, darkened the slant of his mouth.

"I was *never* unfaithful to you," she whispered. A sheet of anger coursed through her, white-hot. It fenced her from her pain. She rose to face him. Rage surrounded her, sheathed her. She welcomed it. "It was a lie. While I waited for you, mourned for you, you took others to your bed, made love to—"

He caught her wrist, halted her blow, his grip scorching her, awakening the silenced corridors of her heart. Fury impaled her, screeched a searing path through her senses. She lifted her other hand to strike him. He captured her other arm and brought his hands up to his chest, pinning her wrists against him. His hold tightened.

"Istara," he said, low, intimate, her name on his lips ambrosia, tainted. "We were both deceived. The one who did so would be gratified to witness what he has accomplished."

She stilled as the poisonous layers of Marduk's machinations unfolded. Hatred for the one who had taken Sethi from her swarmed over her, savaged her. She succumbed to its harsh waves, the ferocity of its torrent, willing it to subsume her, to wash her away and free her from the gravity of her loss. It wasn't enough. It swept back through what remained of her heart, fierce, a jagged scythe. In its wake, hollowness, a heartbeat of utter emptiness, a tsunami of sorrow. She staggered, pinioned by its onslaught.

"My loss is complete," she whispered, her words salted with tears, raw with loneliness. "It is unbearable."

With a groan, his arms came around her, his embrace familiar, perfect. He sheltered her as she mourned—as she gathered up the lost fragments of her heart, silenced, broken songbirds, and buried them, one by one, deep within the wasteland of her soul.

Istara blinked. Tears soaked her face and throat, saturated the front of her gown. She had wept herself dry. Nothing was left. Sethi led her to the central divan, helped her to sit. His weight eased down beside her. He took her hand. His warmth touched her. Warmth which would never be hers again. She pulled her hand away. It was a lie. *They* were a lie. She had lost him. Marduk had won.

For a long time she sat and stared at nothing, numb, lost, bereft. Thoughts crashed through her, disjointed, chaotic. She let them rise and fall, their undulations meaningless, like the endless passage of scrabbling kings and their empires. There had only been Sethi, and now he was gone, stolen from her by the one who would not stop until he had dragged everything he touched into darkness.

From the scoured corridors of her mind, images erupted: Of Sethi, bloodied, valiant, battling against the pharaoh under the burning disk of Re-Atum, the heat of the enclosed grounds suffocating, rich with the perfume of Sethi's life, and she, forced to watch, confined to the shadows, helpless, a token; of Sethi's brutal fall and the pharaoh's dagger in her breast; of the light of the god of war closing the rift in her heart, and gifting Sethi back to her. She closed her eyes, willing the memory to cease, but it did not, it continued, clear, perfect. Sethi's return to life tore through her, visceral, triumphant with the heat of his fierce embrace, savage with his passion as he claimed her in the broiling, sanguine sand. And now—

She let out a quavering breath, humid with sorrow. "I wish Horus had let us die that day."

Quiet stretched, laden with reflection. Sethi's hand—the one she had rejected—lay against his kilt, his strong fingers curving over his thigh muscle, alone, lost without her fingers entwined among them. His chest rose and fell, once, twice, the fractals sliding along the pull of his pectorals. His voice came to her, resonant, certain. The voice she loved.

"I do not."

Bleak, Istara followed the passage of her light as it cascaded along the length of her gown and pooled at her feet. "Why?" she whispered. "We might have become gods, but we have still lost each other."

"If Horus had not intervened we would have lost each other then. On my last breath my soul was destined to be obliterated. Even if I knew our reprieve would lead to this, I would take those brief months we shared—" His hand found hers. He slid his fingers between hers, possessive, intimate. This time she did not pull away. He lifted up their enfolded hands and pressed a kiss against the backs of her fingers, gentle, "—every single time."

She bit her lip, seeking to quell the deepening ache in her breast. He pressed another soft kiss against her knuckles, tender, reverent. She breathed his name, relished its taste in her mouth, sealed it within the sacred reaches of her being. Another kiss, against the inside of her wrist, the intimacy of his touch burning through the horror of what stood between them. He pulled back, his jaw tight, his gaze fixed on where he had left the imprint of his love. His remorse cut a swathe through her, cold, precise. He met her eyes, his golden ones harsh, raw with the guilt of his crimes. Her heart clenched, though his touch was the same, a part of him was gone. Forever.

At the edge of her consciousness, a whisper: *Use your light. Ease the scars upon his mind.* Before she could consider it, a tendril of her light flared from her fingers and encircled their wrists, binding them together, lovers betrothed. She caught his indrawn breath. A surge of reckless hope ignited.

"Those brief mornings before dawn when our hearts touched," she whispered. "Your anguish became my own. You begged me to forgive you." The words tumbled out of their own volition. The buried pieces of her heart erupted from their graves and collided, violent, her light drawing them back together, a master weaver—the healer, healing herself. His eyes held hers, intense, wounded, aching with hope.

"My love," she whispered, "I forgive you."

A rush of adrenaline swept up from the base of her spine to the crown of her head. It poured from her, an endless well, resonant, expansive. It reached beyond the walls of her existence, past the boundaries of Elati, over the arc of the heavens, to a place of perfection. To the beginning. To the place of the purest light. Home. Euphoria gilded her. At last, understanding. Purpose. She tightened her grip on his hand and rose. He followed, the wonder of her transformation reflected in his eyes. White streamers of starlight swarmed around her, diffusing her form, blurring where she ended and her power began. Galaxies of stars blossomed in her hair. Starbursts erupted from her fingers.

From her torso, an explosion of light. Brilliance surrounded them, flooded the cabin, streamed from the flight deck's windows, bathing the bay in the fountain of her light. Total silence swept over them. The light retracted, surrounded them, dense, a cocoon. Alone, together, isolated outside of existence, Istara lifted her hand, afire with the flames of her light, and pressed her fingertips to his temple. A pulse, blinding, alive, jolted through her and slammed into him. He staggered, his grip tightening on their bound hands. Another pulse, fiercer this time. He panted, quaking, as her light tore through his skull, seeking his pain, his regret, his guilt.

Istara endured the weight of every one of his crimes as her light ferreted them out one by one, the burden of his guilt bearing down on her, a mountain, oppressive, suffocating. She clung to her consort, never taking her eyes from his as her light delved his darkest corridors, a healer's blade, precise, honed.

And then it came. The most heinous crime of all. A queen, her king murdered by Sethi, and she, forced to lie with the god of war against her will, struggling against his hold on her forearms, weeping, begging him to cease. Horror bled from Sethi's eyes. He shook his head, sickened, mortified, and tried to pull away from Istara. She held on, firm, unwavering, though her heart ached at how far her consort had fallen. The light binding their hands tightened. Hate surged through him. Hate—for himself. Though it took all the strength she possessed, Istara caught his eyes, mouthed the words: *I forgive you.*

He shuddered. Defeat subsumed him. His sins continued to wash over her, endless. She watched, nauseous, as he bedded his captives then hauled them, pleading and terrified, across his golden terrace and threw them to their deaths, their scant gowns fluttering, ephemeral, as they tumbled into the mists—their lives stolen, by the god meant to protect them. Still, she held on. Then—she saw her. Aiya, the one he had chosen to be his new consort. His longing for her. His proposal. Istara staggered. No. She knew those eyes, that face. The memory of another world unfolded. The scent of a garden washed over her, verdant with the weight of night, and laced with the sweetness of jasmine. The acrid scent of torch smoke came next. In a lamplit, opulent room of a high noble, she watched her mortal self go to the aid of a beautiful, green-eyed woman in the throes of labor, lay a blade against the base of her belly, cut her open, and pull her babe free. Sethi's son. *Edarru.*

She let go of Sethi. The binding around their wrists snapped away, her light streamed back into her. By degrees, the cocoon faded, and the silence enclosing them evaporated. Sethi's chest rose and fell, his ragged breaths crescendoing as the silence fled, harsh in the cabin's confined space. Her inner light cascaded over her once more, a steady stream of starlight. Her consort sank to his knee before her, his forearm on his thigh. His hand curled into a fist, the veins and muscles of his arms proud, evidence of his inner turmoil. He bowed his head. She had seen everything. Nothing had been kept from her.

Sethi lifted his head. "Can you still forgive me?" His golden eyes touched hers, cleansed by her light—though the shadow of his crimes remained between them, an eternal stain.

His heart once more beat with her own, both completing and alienating her. A wave of his remorse flooded through her, dense, oppressive. When she said nothing, he rose and turned to leave. "It is as I suspected. It is too much to ask. I fell too far. I no longer deserve your love."

He went to the door, pressed his palm against the panel. The door slid open, as she knew it would. There had never been any barriers between them—until now.

"I forgive you for all except Aiya," Istara said, quiet. Out the flight deck's window, a golden ship hurtled into the bay from out of the night. It skidded to a halt. "We both know she is Edarru," she continued, resignation cloaking her, "or at least, what Edarru once was to you. Though you hid it well, I knew you loved her in your own way. If you had never found me, it would have been her. And here we are once more, me and her, with you in the middle. I cannot face it again. It is . . . unbearable."

The arriving ship's engine cut out. The panels of Sethi's kilt rustled, stiff, just like they had done when he was the commander of Egypt. He stopped before her. A breath of quiet. Across the bay, a shout. Footfalls pounded across the bay's floor.

Sethi's hands took hers, his warmth penetrating the chill in her soul. He brushed his thumbs against the backs of her hands, just as he had once done, when they were alone, mortal, and locked in their love. Her heart quavered. "There was only you," he murmured, his golden eyes turning from hers to their enfolded hands, "even when I didn't know you, it was you." He let go of her hand and pressed his palm to his chest, against the fractal rotating, elegant, over his heart. She met his look, burning, alive, filled with promise; it sleeted over the aching beats of her broken heart. "Nothing—no one—can eclipse my love for you. My heart is yours—if you will still have it."

Voices, urgent, low, drifted through the open door. Istara closed her eyes, blocked them out. Nothing had unfolded the way she had hoped. Instead of restoring her consort to her by eliminating the power Marduk held over Sethi, her consort would never be free of the evil within him, could never again leave the sanctuary of Anki. If he did, even if they defeated Marduk, Sethi would again become the one who had found her in Thoth's palace, would not stop until he consumed her light with that hateful weapon. Their love was not the same. It would never be the same. She opened her eyes, met his, his soul bared to hers, his love for her tangible. Her heart screamed for his. She reached up, put her hand over the one covering his heart, falling to him, incapable of stopping herself—knowing his love would come at a terrible price. She said nothing, did not need to, her intentions flowed, seamless, across the conduit of their shared heartbeat.

"My love," he whispered, ragged, disbelieving. "Oh my love." He caught her to him, his embrace fierce, raw with the anguish of their brutal separation. She succumbed, willed him to go on, willed herself to never look back. Nothing mattered but this. He had found her, just as he had promised. His hands came to her face. His fingers curved around her skull, and whispered through her hair. Starlight poured over his forearms, bathed his chest, and limned his golden fractals. He tilted her face up to his, aching with tenderness, his thumb against the curve of her lips, parting them, just as he did . . . *before.* She clung to him, trembling under his worshipful gaze, in an agony of anticipation, hungering for his touch, for his warmth, for the weight of his body against hers—

Heavy footfalls came up the steps, deliberate, unapologetic. Sethi turned, though he did not relinquish his hold on her. Urhi-Teshub shouldered his way into the cabin.

"There is a problem." He cut a cold look at Sethi, a challenge, daring him to test him, just once. On his back, his ax glinted, angry, harsh. Its light stuttered over the cabin's curved walls and ceiling, washing it in the tint of his salient disapproval.

Outside, Istara caught a glimpse of Horus as he paced beneath the ship's wing, his head down and arms crossed over his chest. He shot a look into the cabin, his features taut with dread. Alarm snagged Istara. She pulled back from Sethi, left the nascent shelter of his embrace, fearing it was already too late, that the jihn had reawakened, and Horus had come to expel her consort from Anki. Urhi-Teshub halted, his eyes still on Sethi. He tilted his head toward the exit. "You need to leave."

A tremor of resistance rumbled through the cabin. Urhi-Teshub tensed, a subtle shift, a lion anticipating its kill. A flicker of expectation glinted in his eyes.

Sethi turned from the storm god's baleful glare, and traced the curve of Istara's cheek, reverent, as though he sought to embed that solitary fragment of her within his soul. She held still. He was going to leave. Forever. Dread lanced her spine, hot, harsh, barbed. Her thoughts, so carefully gathered up throughout their ordeal, skittered away, startled fawns. *Don't go. Please.*

Sethi eyes held Istara's. "I will not leave without saying goodbye—"

"Save your farewells," Urhi-Teshub said. "Time is critical."

Sethi kissed her then, harsh, ragged, deep, possessive, the kiss of a god lost and found—of a god burdened by the guilt of a thousand atrocities. Istara drank of him, drawing in the pieces she had healed, and the ones forever shattered. She cradled them against her heart, stored them away, one by one, an echo of the one whose heart beat with hers. Soon he would be her enemy again, a transformation from which there would be no reprieve. He would take Aiya as his consort, and tear Elati apart until he found her. Tears drowned her soul. No. It was unbearable. It couldn't be over. Not yet.

He pulled away, his chest heaving. Anguish tore a path through him. "My heart beats only for you," he said, defiance shearing his features. "No matter what comes between us, remember this: I love you. Only you." With a final, devastating look he descended the steps.

Urhi-Teshub moved in front of the door. Numb, she looked down at her hands, empty without Sethi's touch. A creak of leather as the storm god folded his arms over his chest. "Istara," he said, his tone gentling. "Look at me."

She lifted her eyes to his. His golden ones sparked, once, twice, strafed by the razored bolts of his cerulean power. "The jihn is draining the power from the cores, at the rate it is going, it will only be a matter of hours before it will take down the shield," he said. Vindication radiated from him. "Thoth has a theory," he continued. "He believes the jihn was originally placed in the tower by the Creator for safekeeping. Your pendant has the power to open the way. Horus is prepared to try to put the jihn back."

Dull, Istara reached into her gown, pulled the pendant free and held it out to the storm god. "And Sethi?" she asked, low, as he took the pendant from her. "If the jihn is placed within the tower and the shield remains intact, I see no reason why he should not be able to remain."

The wall of his resistance separated them. "You know he cannot stay here." Urhi-Teshub took a step toward her. "Whatever is in him resonates with what is in the jihn. It seeks to annihilate you. That weapon—" Urhi-Teshub shook his head, the lines of his jaw tightening, "—was created to feed on the light of the gods. If we cannot stop him it will vanquish us all, and then, it will consume him. We survived Sethi's arrival because of you. For whatever reason, it wanted your light first. It took all my power to overcome its evil to protect you. Another heartbeat—" he swallowed, tight, "—and I would have failed." He reached out, captured her shoulders, a friend, brother, protector. He lowered his voice. "I know how much it will cost you to relinquish him, but you must know he is no longer the one you lost. Sethi is gone. All you have gained from the shield is a reprieve—a chance to glimpse what light still remains in the god of war. Sooner or later, just as the jihn seeks to overcome the cores, what is in him will force him to return to what he has become. He cannot be here when that happens."

Istara looked away, the truth of his words bore into her, ground her soul to dust. "Then," she said, quiet, her heart taut with grief, "at least let me take him back to the portal. Alone."

The storm god's grip on her shoulders tightened. He cut a look out the open door. Horus met his look, tilted his head toward his ship, his expression laden with warning. Sethi stood with him, the pair incongruous—the fallen god of war alongside the risen one.

"I must protect you," Urhi-Teshub said, dogged. He let go of her shoulders. "How could I protect you if I am not there?"

"Sethi will not transform so long as the shield remains," Istara answered. "I would have a final hour with him. Then I will let him go. You will not deny me this."

"Much can happen in an hour," Urhi-Teshub muttered, his attention drifting back to Horus who departed for his ship. He turned back to her, abrupt. "I cannot keep Thoth waiting any longer. My duty to the Creator will not be compromised. I will take Sethi back. You can follow in your ship and say your farewells at the portal."

Clad in his conviction, he left. He veered out from under the wing and away from Sethi, meeting Horus halfway across the bay.

Istara glared at him, hating him for his certainty, his arrogance, his claim his duty to the Creator superseded her authority.

A heartbeat was all it took for her to think the thought, to realize its potential. Her consort still stood under the wing. He was so close. Defiance reared within her. Urhi-Teshub was wrong. He had ever been too rigid, too stubborn. This time he would not have his way. Her heart cried out to her consort's. *Come to me.* His heart roared in response. He bolted toward her, his legs eating up the brief distance separating them. She slammed her hand against the panel, and the door closed, an ally. In the flight deck, she caught the look Sethi gave her—the heat of his approval.

Her hands trembling, she ended the ship's eon-long silence, her fingers moving over the control panel from memory, her knowledge innate. A thrill shuddered through her. Freedom. At last. She hit another series of buttons, and the ship pivoted in total silence to face the exit. Across the bay, the door of Horus's ship slid closed.

Urhi-Teshub turned. Disbelief, then fury poured from him. He pulled his ax free and ran toward her ship. His mouth moved. She read her name on his lips, his fury turning to desperation when Sethi took the seat beside hers. Several more presses against the console, a flick of a switch, and the engines tasted fire. A quiet thunder rumbled through the ship, laden with promise.

Urhi-Teshub staggered to a halt. He rammed the butt of his ax against the ground. A shield of blue lightning exploded from it and arced over him.

"Let's get out of here," Sethi said, cutting her a dark smile. His hands moved over the controls, confident, powerful, working with her in synchrony.

Her heart aflame, she fired the thrusters. A slam of acceleration, and they hurtled out of the bay, leaving her protector hunched under his shield, awash in a torrent of liquefied heat. Her palace fell away as they screamed up into the heavens, cloaked, free, alone, and violently in love.

Far to the south of the city, Istara brought the ship down in a little glade, the ship's exhaust buffeting the fronds of the surrounding palms. She cut the power. The ship fell silent. The interior lights dimmed. The glade stilled. Beyond the translucence of the ship's fuselage, Anki's shield glimmered against the night's canopy, a rippling veil of faint, white light.

She looked under her lashes at Sethi, who occupied himself checking the console's screen. He flicked several switches—ones which didn't need changing then looked up into the glade, his eyes moving along the darkened silhouette of the palms against the night sky. The muscles in his jaw clenched, once, twice. He stood.

Istara waited, her heart thudding, caught between trepidation for her reckless act and anticipation for what she knew was to come. Soon, Sethi would love her. A god. Her consort. The one she longed for night and day would be one with her. A trembling swept over her, laced with uncertainty. Her thoughts screamed at her, reminding her he was tainted. His seed would be tainted. She should not do this thing. The risk—

He took her hand. She rose and followed him into the cabin toward the central divan, his heart thudding into hers, his uncertainty amplifying her own. He halted.

He took her face in his hands, his touch, heated with the power of a god, strafed her senses, awakening her. She shivered. His eyes met hers, seared her soul. She caught her breath, willing him to go on. His gaze slid away, followed the contours of her face. It stopped at her mouth. His lips parted, his longing tangible.

"My love," she whispered, her heart harsh with need, "take me before it is too late."

"It is already too late," Sethi murmured. His hands slid into her hair, cradled her skull. She sighed, her body ragged with need as he drew her against him, his heat surrounding her, barricading her against what he was.

His lips touched hers, tender, gentle, reverent. He kissed her slow, steady, thorough, worshiping her, taking his time. A thousand images stuttered through her as the secret corridors of his heart unfolded and its locked doors opened, exposing in raw detail the burden of his love—eternal, fathomless, a bulwark against the ravages of time. She trembled against its assault, its violence shearing her soul into a million fragments. He had always loved her, had endured the pharaoh's blade, his hate and savagery, to love her, just once. Everything he had suffered, he had done for her.

Another image roared through her, of her cradled in Urhi-Teshub's arms as he made love to her on the bed of their room in the Etemen'anki. She quailed as the image saturated her—as it had once saturated Sethi—as Urhi-Teshub traced his finger over her lips, his eyes dark with love, his hips moving in rhythm to her own as he rode her, possessing her. Tears burned her eyes. It was a lie, made to turn her consort against her. Sethi's kiss deepened, fierce, his latent heartache savaging her. His anguish tore through her, delved into her heart, left its scars behind. She staggered. Nothing of Sethi's heart remained hidden from her: The torment he suffered as he disintegrated when he entered the realm where he left his heart in a wooden cage; the grief that seared him as she died on his pallet outside Amka, leaving him alone, lost, disbelieving, cradling her limp body. He kissed her harder, his grip tightening as his past poured into her, scouring her with fresh agonies; as he left Edarru and his son behind to cross the desert after her, unwilling to let her go; of his love existing beyond the boundaries of time, his resurrection, not once, but twice, with her as his only focus—his sole, unwavering constant.

She clung to him, overcome by his passion, his sacrifices, the magnitude of his love, willing the night to never end. Without breaking their kiss, he eased her onto the divan. He sank to his knee before her, his leg sliding in between hers. His kilt parted and the heat of his inner thigh brushed against her own, intimate, sensual, hot with promise.

He pulled back, his breathing ragged, harsh in the ship's quiet. He pressed his forehead against hers. "You know what I am," he said, his chest rising and falling, ragged with the force of his restraint, "if we do this—"

"I would have this," Istara breathed, her hands going to his jaw, caressing its hardened planes, honed by the darkness, sharpened by hate. "My love, I would have nothing else but this."

He groaned. His arms captured her, sheltering her as he lowered her onto the divan, his weight easing over her, covering her, protecting her, as he once done, long ago—in another world, another life—the first time he had made love to her in his villa, their bodies bathed in the approving light of Re-Atum.

He took his time, savoring her as he undressed her, slow, worshipful. His fingers drifted over her flesh as he memorized the curve of her neck, the hollow behind her ear, the cleft of her collarbone. Whisper-light, his fingertips drifted over her breasts, breathed over the peaks of her nipples, and down her belly to her hidden place, imprinted by the seal of his multitude of possessions. His eyes held hers as he caressed her until she ached with the weight of her need, the folds of her silenced self yielding to his touch, hollow, yearning, desperate to be filled by him. His belt and kilt came off, tumbled to the floor with quiet thuds. He knelt before her naked, powerful, clad only his love and the fractals which flourished in her starlight. His golden eyes swept over her, reflecting the trails of her starlight as they shimmered over her skin.

"You are beyond beautiful," he whispered, bending down to taste her mouth anew, his absence as he had undressed suddenly unbearable. She dragged him to her, opened herself to him, a flower, seeking the sun, her womb scented with the heat of her love. With a low moan he found her and eased himself into her, slow, steady, filling her little by little until he owned her. He held still.

His lips caressed her ear. "I never want to let you go."

"Nor I you," Istara whispered, savoring the heat of him inside her, the weight of his swollen member filling her, completing her. He moved his hips, slow. His girth slid away until he was almost outside of her, until only the smooth heat of his member's head rested within the mouth of her opening. He slid himself back into her, taking his time, filling her anew. Waves of pleasure swarmed through her, jagged, hungry, dark. He withdrew again as before, tantalizing her with the promise of more. He re-entered her, his member hardening further, his arousal harsh, darkening the slant of his mouth. She lifted her hips to meet his as he penetrated her anew, each kiss of their love deeper than the last, until he no longer moved within her, but buried himself to his root, and ground himself against her, hungry, primal.

His took her face in his hands, his mouth against hers, his passion pinioning her, ravaging her. He began to ride her in earnest, his thrusts powerful, dominant, his body curving over hers, his arms cradling her as he drove himself into her, stamping his seal upon her anew, a god, and she his goddess. Istara clung to him, her senses reeling, caught in the net of his passion as it swept through her, violent, a tsunami. He knelt, his hips unceasing in their art, and dragged her up against him, until her breasts pressed against the heft of his pectorals, and his heart roared against her own, its corridors folding around hers, imprisoning her with his pain, his guilt, his sorrow, the magnitude of his loss—and of his endless, undying love.

He shifted his weight and reached the hidden spot within her only he knew, granting her the exquisite, tantalizing pressure of his member against it. She met his eyes as he watched her, his blazing with the molten heat of his love, inflaming her, singeing her senses, awakening a dark, insatiable hunger. She rocked against him, aching with need, her heart battered by the tide of his passion. Sorrow, guilt, rage, and the darkness of his crimes slammed over her in equal measures. She quaked on the brink of her release, caught in the crosshairs of his anguish, willing him to go on, willing him to invade her, willing him to ride her as hard as he could.

He rotated his hips and delved into her, deep, his act, one of mercy. She gasped as he found her one last time. The last of her resistance shattered. She tumbled from the precipice, shuddering in his grip, lost to her senses, waves of pleasure slamming into her—pleasure only a god could give. He rammed himself into her, harsh, brutal, as hard as polished granite, burying himself up to the heft of his root. She cried out as he rubbed the base of his member against the place of her greatest pleasure, granting her a second release before her first had even finished. She panted, clinging to him, raw from the savagery of his love. The heat of his seed erupted within her, full, heavy, weighted with his corruption. He tried to pull out. She clamped on to him, refusing to let him go, relishing the heat of his love soaking her, polluting her. From within her torso, her light ignited. A dozen tendrils surged toward the taint within her. They blossomed, starbursts of gold, dying as they cleansed his corruption. He tried to leave her again, his anguish palpable as her light condemned them for their crime. Still, she held on, her knuckles white with resistance. She would have him. All of him. And may the Creator forgive her.

CHAPTER 6

Urhi-Teshub brought his ship down onto the top tier of a *ziqquratu*. He killed the engines, sat back and eyed the golden beam of light anchoring the shield to the central complex. It reared up from the capstone of the largest pyramid, a glorious, liquid, coursing thing. He lowered his gaze to the screens of his console, all of them dark, mocking the long hours he had spent searching for Istara. Soon, the sun would rise. He slammed his fist against the armrest, once, twice, three times. He had done everything he could, had flown over the city and then the island, in precise, careful sweeps, scanning for the heat of her existence. Nothing but silence had glared from his screens. Istara had eluded him—the one the Creator had chosen to be her protector.

Shame tore into him, taunting him as he traveled paths he had avoided all night. Apprehension—no longer barricaded behind the fire of his rage—clawed at him. A single thought pushed through his misery. *At least Horus has the relic.*

It wasn't enough. He folded his arms, the creak of his leather tunic loud in the condemning silence of the flight deck. The Creator had stressed Istara's importance in the confrontation to come, yet at the first opportunity Urhi-Teshub had lost her to the enemy.

A fresh wave of fury seared his blood. He shoved himself free of his seat. He needed to get out of the ship, walk, and breathe fresh air; he had been cramped up in the flight deck too long. He stepped out onto the tier and paced away from the radiant heat of the ship, the tier's marble surface cool in the pre-dawn air. At the *ziqquratu's* edge he came to a halt and inhaled, deep, seeking calm, though he knew there would be none. Not until she was safe.

"Where are you?" he asked the emptiness, his gaze sliding over the shadowed outline of the city, caught in the pale web of the shield's light. The city was vast, and with the storm silenced by the shield, the island even more so. He had had to travel at brutal speeds, screaming over Anki's storm-soaked contours to cover its length and breadth. The scanners in Marduk's ship were good—even at the punishing speeds he had traveled, the invisible net he had cast had caught everything else: birds, wildlife, fish in fathomless hidden lakes, even a cluster of ancient trees ripe with sentience. But of the fugitive gods . . . nothing. The ship of the prime goddess of healing had cloaking capabilities beyond the reach of Marduk's devices. All he could do was wait for her return. And when she did . . . he pulled his ax free, his grip tightening on the shaft, its blades brightening, fed by his anger. There would be words. And Sethi would go. He would see to it, even if he had to restrain her. She had fooled him once. Never again.

In the east, a pulse of orange light fractured the horizon. It thickened, cleaving its way into the night. Urhi-Teshub glared at it. An entire night, gone. Soon her absence would be noticeable. Questions would be asked. Accusations made—

The scream of a ship, faint with distance. He turned and searched the western horizon still pressed hard by night, ragged with hope Istara had at last, chosen to return. The ship shot past him and arced into a smooth curve, cutting a line through the burning cusp of the sun's ascendance. He narrowed his eyes as it scorched a path over the *ziqquratu* and came in to land beside his ship, black, sleek. Elegant. A thing of dark beauty, the opposite of Istara's white ship, its wings tipped in gold.

A burst of disappointment pierced the depths of his futility. He clenched his fists, chafing anew against Istara's counter-move, the cut of it deep, a festering wound—one he would not cease to prod until she returned to her place under his protection, where she belonged.

Sour, he waited, his back to the sun, its heat already swarming over his back and shoulders as the door of Sekhmet's ship opened. The goddess of war's slim, leather-clad figure stepped down and crossed the tier, the sun's nascent rays racing to her, worshiping her. She came to a stop before him and met his eyes, hers, veiled.

He said nothing. Humiliation enveloped him. The goddess of war was the last god he wished to face while caught in the jaws of defeat.

She turned her attention to the rising sun. "Horus has returned from the tower."

Urhi-Teshub set his ax back into its holder, perfunctory, deliberate. When he chose not to reply, she continued, with the faintest of diffidence, "The cores have stabilized. I thought you might want to know."

Urhi-Teshub nodded, terse, and turned away, willing her to leave, shame dragging its talons over him. At least she did not know he had retained his memories so he could focus on keeping Istara safe—a sacrifice he now realized had been fruitless. He pressed his lips together and bit back a curse.

From behind, a quavering intake of breath. Sekhmet's alienation washed over him. Guilt slammed into him, harsh, ragged. He had hurt her, had broken his promise he would not forget. He turned, abrupt. She looked up. Tears coated her eyes, glinted in the brilliance of a new day.

"You should go."

Her anguished look crucified him. He walked away, left her standing alone, willing himself to hold firm, to stay true to his path. He had a sacred duty, one which superseded his needs and desires. Later, once they had won, he would tell her everything, but now—

Quiet footsteps approached. "I know you haven't forgotten us," she whispered. "I have seen it in your eyes."

He folded his arms over his chest, clad himself in silence. Sooner or later she would give up, just like the cats who would come to Tarhuntassa's stables looking for scraps. If you didn't feed them, eventually they went away, and their pitiful cries ended.

Her hand came to his forearm. He yanked free of her hold. "Leave me," he said, though his heart ached at the depth of his cruelty, at her stricken look. He tilted his head at her ship. "I will not ask again."

A heartbeat of silence. Then, "No."

He felt the muscles in his jaw tick. He was not accustomed to a woman disobeying his command, and now, in the space of one day, it had happened not once, but twice. Istara's humiliation afflicted him anew, stirred the embers of his banked fury. A quiet hiss as Sekhmet pulled her daggers free. He turned. Sekhmet tilted her blades up.

Her golden eyes snapped, cold, whip-harsh. "Only if you defeat me, will I leave."

"I will not fight you," Urhi-Teshub muttered. "You would lose."

"Do not be so certain," Sekhmet said, sliding her blades together, their metal cries betraying her hunger to begin. "I know the storm god's weaknesses. You do not know mine."

"I do not have time for this," he snapped as she circled him, preparing to strike. "Istara is—"

A slash, low, against his inner thigh, far too close for comfort to his groin. He recoiled with a grunt. Pain blossomed, hot, deep, scouring him, awakening him. The seep of blood slid down the inside of his armor.

"Have you lost your senses?" he cried as he yanked his ax free.

"Say her name one more time."

Sekhmet circled him, a lioness, deadly, focused. She lunged. He caught her blade against the shaft of his ax.

"Cease! I refuse to strike you."

"Then don't," she said, carving a fresh furrow into his forearm, her speed blinding, disorienting. He belted out an oath as another searing line of fire tore through him. More blood filled his armor. His anger mounted. He hauled it back, reined it in. He would not strike her. He could not. Golden tendrils darted over his thigh and arm, weaving his flesh back together, soothing his pain.

She came at him again, her daggers quick, precise, opening his legs, arms, shoulders, and torso to the morning's heated air. A flurry of his golden tendrils erupted, trailing after him as she drove him across the tier in a complex dance mated to hers. Pain soaked him, but he welcomed it even as she taunted him, beautiful, terrible, her armor glinting in the heat, a blaze of darkness, her blades soaked with his blood. At last, he lived again.

She pulled back, panting. The sun stalked them, its heat broiling, intense. A sheen of perspiration gilded the elegant cut of her cheekbones.

Urhi-Teshub retreated, his lungs afire. He paced back and forth in front her, gripping his ax, in an agony of pain, admiration, and arousal. Never before had he faced such an enticing sparring partner. Her breasts rose and fell within the tight sheath of her leather tunic. He longed to tear apart the fastenings, to feel her body once more against his, the firmness of her flesh under his, her hips moving as one with his own. His member stirred, trapped, straining to be freed, to find her, to fill her. Desire for her saturated him, heated his blood.

"Shall I continue?" She paced up to him, exotic, predatory, indomitable, her blades held loose at her sides, shining with the essence of a god. She stopped before him, her body a breath away from his, the heat of her swarmed into him, made him vibrate with longing. "Or," the back of her gloved fingers trailed up the length of his inner thigh, scorching his senses, driving him mad with lust, "are we done here?" Her eyes touched his, hers dark, heated by violence, and something else. Need. The scent of her arousal penetrated him, slaughtered him.

His restraint fled. Still gripping his ax, he captured her, hauled her up against him. His mouth found hers, savage, hungry. She met his passion, hers brutal, tinged with cruelty, darkened by revenge. He drank of her viciousness, he was her equal and he knew it, had, on those sultry nights they'd shared in Imaru, ridden her until she screamed, until she shuddered against him, lost in his arms, tamed—for a time.

He ground himself against her, pressed the weight of his swollen heat into her, greedy for her, needing her. A dull clatter as her daggers struck the ground. His ax followed, striking the marble tier with a heavy, resentful thud. He yanked off his gloves and sought the fastenings of her tunic, his palms grazing the swell of her breasts, pressed against their pitiless imprisonment. A wild desire to be bound and ridden by her sliced through him, opening a hidden door within him he had never known existed. He pulled her tunic free, just as she tore his from his shoulders and the heat of the sun struck his back. Their armor tumbled down and hit the marble, dense smacks.

She stood before him, glorious, beautiful, perfect, her breasts bearing the horizontal imprint of their binding. He caught her hand and led her to the edge of the terrace, to the low wall of its perimeter, the only thing between them and the well of empty space beneath. Her fingers moved to her leggings. The straps fell away. She stood before him, the firm muscles of her body sculpted in the heat of the sun. Hunger scoured him, his hands went to the fastenings of his leggings. She pushed his hands away and pulled each strap free, one by one, the hiss of leather sliding against leather searing his senses, blistering a path into his soul.

He willed her to hurry, but she took her time, her fingers brushing over his sheathed member as she worked, tantalizing him, maddening him. At last she released him, and he stood before her, the storm god, stained in blood, his body harsh with need, ready to take her, the goddess he loved to the depths of his soul—

He fell upon her breasts, favoring them, one by one, worshiping them as he had done so many times before, teasing her until her nipples peaked into fine points, defiant against the raging heat of the day. She found him, stroked him, stoking the inferno within him. He picked her up, set her on the wall's ledge.

"Don't let me fall," she breathed as he parted her legs, and positioned himself between her thighs.

"Never."

He pressed himself against her opening, long since ready for him, the scent of her dragging him to her, a lodestone. He found her. She sighed, her hips moving in synchrony with his. He drank in the sight of their union, their bodies melding as one, locked in perfection. Her caught her hips, holding her against the weight of the drop beneath them as he rode her, his blood pounding, hot with the act of their love, the heat of the day—the violence she had awakened in him.

"It's not enough," she panted. "I want you deeper in me."

Something in her eyes touched a hidden place within him. He knew that look. Carnality swept over him. Yes. He would take her there. He realized he *wanted* to go there. He pulled out, his member slick with her sex, and probed her, lower.

Her lips parted. Raw hunger rippled from her. "As deep as you can go," she breathed, the heat in her eyes a torrent of need. "I need to be as close to you as possible."

He entered her. The grip of her hauled on him, tugged at his restraint. He groaned, pacing himself even as a tsunami of desire swarmed through him and caught him in its insatiable tide.

He waited a heartbeat, giving her time to accept him, then eased his way further in. She bucked against him in an agony of anticipation, her hunger contagious, fueling his own. He hauled at the pull of his lust, against the urge to ram himself into her, to own, dominate, and violate her as he had once done, long ago in Kadesh to another. No. Never that. Tightening his grip on her, he marshaled his restraint, sought only to please her. He pressed himself deeper into her, his member so hard it ached. She moaned, shivering with ecstasy. The wall within her eased, just a fraction. It was enough. He shifted his weight and filled her to his root. Her eyes slid closed, her entire self lost to a world of bliss—a world where he was the master.

He rocked her, slow, the forbidden pleasure of their private, intimate act tearing a swathe through him. Everything about her felt so right—even this. It should be sordid, as it was before, but it was not. It was beautiful, perfect, a celebration of what they shared, their love dangerous, volatile, violent, passionate, anchored on loss, built on trust. He had never felt closer to a woman than this heartbeat. He kissed her, tender, his love for her strafing him, lashing him to her, bonds which could never be broken.

Her release came. She cried out, her fingers digging into his arms, the heat of her spasms tearing down the last of his restraint. He breathed her name and filled her with his love.

"More," she sighed, hunger flaring anew in her eyes. With a dark smile, he gathered her up and carried her back to her ship where he loved her again, and again. And again.

❋ ❋ ❋

Cloaked in the silence of the western reaches of Nisu, Horus came to a halt. He pushed his palm against a gold-embossed door. A flood of morning light streamed over him, golden, warm, laden with motes of dust.

He eased forward, past the threshold into what, eons ago, he suspected had been the private suite of Horakhti, Elati's prime god of war, from whom whose image he had been made. He looked around, disturbed by his familiarity of the god of war's rooms. He might never have lived in such an apartment, yet as he paced its corridor of golden pillars, past the dust-laden light streaming in from the terrace, he found himself knowing the way. He moved further into the suite, stirring dust from the gilded furnishings, where, as the epochal sleep of two million years melted away, he glimpsed the glittering days when the god of war's palace had breathed with life, when drinks were poured, conversations held, and opulent dinners taken.

Before a set of closed double doors, he came to a halt. A rush of adrenaline swept through him. He had gone straight to it—to the image of the falcon which had called to him as his ship surged away from the tower, weighted once more with the malevolence of the jihn. The doors loomed over him, sheathed in alabaster and emblazoned with the obsidian silhouette of a falcon, its outstretched gold-gilt wings spread across breadth of the doors.

A gentle push and they glided inward, soundless. Within, funereal silence, dense with shadow. Slivers of daylight probed the closed shutters. He went to the nearest one and hauled it open. A piece of the day claimed the darkness, slicing a path through an elegant arrangement of white divans and low tables to a massive pillared bed set on a raised platform, surrounded by opaque, golden hangings.

Drawn to the elegant relief of falcons carved into the bed's white marble frame, he went to it and circled the platform, admiring the detailed workmanship of each pillar bearing a falcon with one wing down the pillar and the other unfurled across the frame's upper panel. He followed the engravings to the far side of the bed. He came to a halt. Against the pristine hanging, a savage rent of utter black, a violent, ugly stain. Innocent of its crime, the ruined material billowed in the freshening air.

He pushed the sundered hangings aside. In the center of the bed, a silken stew of tangled sheets and cushions. From under the edge of a pair of cushions, a faint gleam of gold. He leaned in and pushed the cushions aside.

His heart stilled. No. Not this. Anything but this.

A pair of embossed golden armbands and a gold-embroidered kilt—effects he knew better than his own heartbeat. Behind them, the ephemeral material of a regal gown, its stars long silenced. They had perished together. Here, in this bed. Horakhti's kilt lay just in front of his consort's gown, proof he had sought to protect her to the very end. Horus clenched his fists, shame enveloping him—as *he* ought to have done with Baalat. Guilt scoured him, hot, scathing, merciless. He stumbled down the steps and struck his knee against the corner of a divan. Ignoring the pain, he limped away, prescience scouring his soul. To see his consort's gown empty—its eternal starlight extinguished—sheared him with horror. The calling to come here. It was a harbinger. No. It was too much. It came far too close to his fear she would be annihilated in that place of unutterable dark.

He bolted to an open door and plunged into a smaller room. It was empty, a dead end hung deep in shadow. He cursed. He could not pass that bed again, where once, the prime gods of war and healing had lived and loved—where they had been annihilated. He turned. There was no other way out. He glared at the wall, his enemy. Rage pummeled him. He rammed his fist against the wood-paneled wall, bellowing Baalat's name, futility clawing at him. Only the pain of his uncertainty and dread remained left to him. He sheathed it in the fury of his loss, the violence of his terror, the endless drag of his grief.

He punched the wall again, harder, uncaring of the damage, or the pain that ricocheted through his bones. He wished he had never come. His raised his fist again, determined not to stop until the barrier between him and his escape from the nightmare behind him lay in splinters.

He heaved his fist back and let go with a roar. The wall slid away. His punch flew into nothing. He staggered into the opening, thrown by momentum of his violence.

White light blistered his eyes. The roar died in his mouth. He blinked, the ragged tear of his breathing loud in the soft quiet of the hidden room. Through the haze of his fury, he glimpsed a man wearing a kilt, his face rough, unshaven. A heartbeat was all it took.

He edged closer. A mirror, just like the one in Thoth's courtyard, timeless, patient. A thought struck him. What if—

He pressed his fingertips to its surface. Nothing. He waited, willing it to respond, to sense the residue of the god he had once been, just as the ship had done. A faint glimmer of white resonated against his touch. It spread outward, the mirror's surface rippling like the waters of a pool. There it was.

He eased his fingertips into the surface, they slid through, as though gliding through thin air. A voice within him warned he should go back and discuss his discovery with Thoth. He hesitated, then rebelled. Baalat was in grave danger, he would not sit around trapped in endless discussions, caught in Thoth's web when there was a chance he had found something even better than the dormant ships of the gods.

He thrust his arm in up to his elbow, his misgivings fleeing. Always, he had been a god of action. Had the wooden panel not opened up for him and the room's lights ignited? *This* was why he had been called to this place. It was an invitation. One he would not refuse. He eased himself into the shimmering surface and stepped into the brilliance of its light.

A cacophony of noise sleeted through Horus's senses: the crash of metal, the shattering of alabaster, the clatter of various items rolling away, their revolutions discordant. The light faded. Horus blinked. He stood at the top of a tiered marble platform. Ahead, the torchlit shadows of a golden-pillared sanctuary greeted him.

Further down, a pair of golden double doors, closed fast. To his right, the crunch of a footfall against a piece of broken pottery. A breath inhaled, rank with terror.

Horus turned, his hand against the weapon tucked into his belt. "Come out."

An old man stepped out of the shadows of a pillar.

Horus bit back a smile of triumph. He *knew* it. Ikalur.

"Iyun," he said, thinking of the last time he had seen the sage when Tyrn had returned from the north bearing her single-worded message: *Perev*. The sage Iyun had been summoned, and upon Queen Welyn's command had shared the secret of Thoth's hidden citadel. Iyun had not troubled himself to hide his contempt for Horus's familiarity with Thoth. A sacrilege, he had said as he had glared at Horus, his scorn palpable.

The sage stumbled to his knee. He landed hard, catching the edge of the fallen golden tray. It swung upward and smacked against his shin. A pained look fleeted across his face.

"Lord Horus." He lifted his hands in supplication. His fingers trembled. "I beg you. Forgive me for the things I said. I did not know." He glanced up, furtive. Tears coated his eyes, tears of hope, of disbelief, of fear. "*How* could I know?"

Horus moved down the wide steps of the tier and joined Iyun. He held out his hand, his ravaged knuckles still seeping blood. Iyun hesitated for a heartbeat, then took it, his hand thin and warm. Horus helped him to his feet.

"Do not kneel to me," he said. "I am no longer a god." He eyed the space, clad in eternal, austere beauty, a shrine to a god long vanished.

"No longer—?" Iyun caught his breath. A tremor rippled through him. "Were you . . . Lord Horakhti?"

The memory of the violated bed of the prime god of war slashed through Horus's mind, of the fallen garments of a god and his consort long vanquished, their combined powers silenced by the darkness.

"No. I was once—" he paused to consider, "—his son."

Iyun bowed his head, reverence bleeding from him. "My lord, in this grave time of darkness, I beg you, aid us."

Horus nodded at the closed doors. "I intend to. Take me to the king."

Iyun backed away, skirting the detritus of the fallen tray. He hefted the doors open. A pillared vestibule stretched away, carved into the living stone of a cliff. At its edge, a sheer drop tumbled to the muted crash of the sea, its moon-washed whitecaps faint with distance. Horus eyed the eastern horizon, still hard with night. In less than a heartbeat, he had crossed a vast distance, had outpaced even the speed of Elati's sun. Satisfaction rolled through him. Thoth's shield was good, but this was what the gods needed. Allies. Just as in the wars of gods and men, the more men who sided with the gods, the less Marduk had.

He grasped Iyun's shoulder. The sage turned, hope saturating him. "You will tell no one what you have witnessed today."

Iyun pressed his hand against his the folds of his robe, over his heart, and bowed his head. "My lord, the sacred panel you came through has been as black as pitch for an eternity. I have lived to see it come alive with light. I seek only to serve you. Anything you ask. Anything. It is yours."

King Rhewyn eased out from between the carved double doors of his bedchamber, a dark green robe tied loose around his waist. He came toward Horus, the shadows around his eyes deeper than the last time Horus had seen him. He came to a halt. His gaze moved over the once-god's unshaven, dirty body, pausing to examine Horus's bloodied knuckles, and the weapon tucked into his belt.

A faint intake of breath came from behind him. The queen slipped out, barefoot and swathed in a robe of pale gold, her hair loose and tangled from sleep.

"Five days," she breathed, eyeing him as thoroughly as her husband had done, concern whispering over her features. "I feared we had lost you." She glanced behind him, searched the torchlit reception, emptied of its servants and guards. "Where is Baalat?"

Horus stilled. Her question, asked so plain, impaled him. He looked away, his heart tight, the ache of his loss boring into him afresh.

Silence fell, thick, heavy with dread.

Rhewyn cleared his throat. "Iyun claims he witnessed the sacred panel of Horakhti fill with light. He says it is how you returned to us." He went to one of the side tables, lifted a golden pitcher and poured out a brimming goblet of wine. He brought it to Horus, and held it out. Horus took it and drank, deep. The wine's ruby warmth slid through him, soaked through the emptiness of his stomach, heated his blood.

"It is." He set the empty goblet onto a nearby table, catching Welyn's stricken, hollow look, her eyes still searching the space behind him, seeking the one who was gone. Rhewyn took Welyn's hand, offered her a quiet, reassuring squeeze. Envy seared a path through Horus. He folded his arms over his chest.

"And the ship?" Rhewyn asked, cautious. "Is it—"

"It awaits me at the palace of the fallen god of war." Horus looked down at his feet, streaked with dried sweat and caked with yellow dust. "In Anki."

A stunned heartbeat of quiet. Then, Rhewyn continued: "I had understood you intended to travel to Perev."

Horus met the king's eyes. "I did. But there was something else I intended to do first. Something I now greatly regret." He nodded at a pair of divans. "Perhaps you would like to sit for this."

The sun shattered the horizon. Its rays slid, rapid, across the floor of the opulent reception room toward the feet of the trio. Rhewyn and Welyn sat together, their hands clasped, shrouded in silence as they absorbed the last of Horus's account of his discovery of the hidden mirror, and its reawakening after its dormancy of a near-eternity.

Horus rose. "I must return. I came here in haste. I suspect there will be other portals, leading to other cities. There is much work still to be done."

Rhewyn came to his feet. Determination gilded him, hardened the despair shadowing his features. "Whatever you need. Weapons, warriors, servants, supplies. Ikalur is yours."

"Everything you can gather in one day, do it." Horus said. "I will return tomorrow at dawn. Be ready."

Rhewyn bowed his head. "As you command."

Horus turned to leave. Welyn's whisper found him. "I will pray for her."

His heart clenched. The queen's prayers would be useless. He had told them nothing of Baalat, of what had taken her, or where she was. He swallowed the ache in his throat and walked on. Until she was freed her from her prison he would fight for her, would wage war against the agents of the dark and tear them down, one by one: the jihn, Sethi, Marduk. Baalat would not fall as the prime god of war's consort had fallen. The darkness would not have her. He would find a way to her—even if he must return to the tower and defeat the darkness, himself.

❋   ❋   ❋

Sethi woke. Beyond the translucence of the ship's fuselage, the sun-soaked, cloudless blue sky of Anki bore down on them, as drenched with the weight of its brilliance as the Egyptian one he had once loved. A fragment of alarm speared his lassitude. The sky. It was *too* clear. No. It couldn't be. Not so soon.

He lifted himself up onto his elbows. A faint glimmering erupted against the outline of the trees. He eyed it, narrow. There. Another glimmer. He sank back against the divan, the nascent thunder of his heartbeat eased. It was not too late. They still had time. Though—considering what he had seen in his dreams as he slept, not as much time as the gods expected.

Against the might of the jihn's corrosive power, he knew Anki's shield wouldn't be enough. Neither would he stand long against the call of the dark weapon which pulsed within him like the beat of his own heart. Although, for now, despite the malevolence of the past night's dreams saturated with images of his future and of the betrayal he knew he was capable, his will was stronger, the light in him bolstered by the radiant power of the shield.

He eyed the shield's faint gleam at the tree line, the rest eclipsed by the brilliance of the sun. How long would he last before he would do what the jihn commanded? Months? Weeks? No. Days—at most. Already he felt the shift within him, subtle, quiet, the jihn's darkness seeking to extinguish the last of his light.

And when it did—he would revert to what he was, and would not stop until he had fed the light of the gods to the jihn and ushered in the supremacy of the darkness. War, greed, enslavement, fear, lies, violence, oppression . . . He sat up, desperate to distance himself from the evil within him as it slid, insidious, into the cleansed corridors of his mind and infected his thoughts, feeding him subtle lies.

Istara shifted with a quiet sigh, lost to the realm of dreams, contentment seeping from her. Her skin shimmered with starlight, its pulses softened by sleep. He watched the gentle rise and fall of her chest, his heart aching, tight with love, harsh with despair. It would only ever be this for them, a brief respite, and then, he would end her.

A remnant of a dream he had had deep in the night flashed through his mind, dark with longing. He saw himself in the midst of a battlefield, strewn with the dead and dying, Istara's protector incapacitated, and she, alone, on her knees before the god of war, a lamb to the slaughter. His other self rammed the jihn into her breast, just as he had done to Arinna, his consort's obliteration soaking him in an arousal of dominance and power. Shredded of her light, her gown had fluttered to the bloodsoaked ground, depleted of its stars. He licked the blades in an orgy of triumph, his eyes black and haloed in golden fire.

Nausea slammed into him. He stood. No. It was unbearable. He paced to the flight deck, his fists clenched. If only he were not a god. If only he could die. He fell still. Of course. Surru. Thoth and Arinna had lost their god-light when they passed into his world from Elati. If he could just get to Surru, he could strand himself on the other side. Perhaps Thoth could generate a shield around Istara's ship which could last long enough for him to make the trip to the other side without the darkness within him stopping him. He glared at the sky, unseeing, imagining himself leaving Elati. Determination found him. A way out. At last. His nightmare would not be realized. He would not allow the darkness to win. He would remain with Istara as long as he dared, and then he would fly to Surru, from where, he knew, he would never return. Not even for her.

The door of the ship slid open. Humid, mid-afternoon heat surged into the cabin, tinted with the acrid taint of the ship's fumes. Istara hesitated for the barest of beats, allowed herself one last, lingering look at her consort. Sethi returned her look, his, dark, tormented, resigned.

In the afterglow of a morning spent in their love, as he cherished her, caressed her, and traced the outlines of her flesh with his fingers, he had told her of his desperate plan to finish what had been begun in him. She had listened, numb, as he detailed his hope Thoth might be able to aid him in the pursuit of his own destruction. When he asked for her aid, the rawness of his request slaying her, she had nodded, had accepted his plan was their best hope to protect the world from what he had become. What she didn't tell him was her intention to go through the barrier with him, where she would also die with him on that bleak, cold shore.

She descended the steps onto the central complex. Urhi-Teshub stood with Thoth, Horus, and Sekhmet in the shade of the yawning entrance to the largest pyramid. Her protector surveyed her as she and Sethi approached, his mien cold, implacable.

They reached the pyramid. No one spoke, though looks laden with the weight of mountains slammed into her from across the damning chasm of silence. Even Thoth, the one she had hoped would stand by her, looked into the depths of the pyramid, his longing to escape the impending altercation tangible.

Sethi glanced into the pyramid, his look unreadable, though a shiver of uncertainty whispered through Istara. An oblique message from Horus's ship had come during the early hours of the morning, while she and Sethi still slept, lost in each other's arms. *It is done. Find me. I have something of yours. Horus.*

And yet, even with the jihn safe inside the tower, and the shield intact, uneasiness circled Istara. Sethi possessed great darkness, could not be trusted. Peril traced a single, scathing talon against her spine. A warning.

She caught Urhi-Teshub eyeing her, distant. Her betrayal hung between them, rank, a festering wound. He waited, tense, coiled, gripping his ax, its lightning bolts jagged, hot with suppressed rage.

"I will not ask for your forgiveness for I am not sorry," Istara said, meeting his look. "However, you are right. Sethi cannot remain in Anki. It is too dangerous."

Urhi-Teshub uncoiled just a fraction. He met Sethi's eyes and tilted his head at his ship, his look hard, iced with vengeance. "Shall we?"

Sethi returned Urhi-Teshub's look, shrouded in a faint aura of hostility.

"Thoth," he said though his gaze remained on the storm god. "I wish to travel to Surru."

Thoth had eased a little way from the group. He cut a look at Sethi, his discomfort acute.

"Surru? I don't under—" He blinked. His gaze dropped to the stone ashlars, his eyes moved back and forth along a seam, unseeing. Sethi waited, let him work it out.

Thoth looked back up, abrupt. A shimmer of approval rippled through him. "Ah. Of course." He cut a look up at the shield, then back at Sethi, narrow, wary. "No. It won't work. You won't make it."

Sethi jutted his chin toward Istara's ship. "I will if you can you do to her ship what you did to Anki. The shield only needs to work long enough for me to reach the other side of Surru—until what happened to you, happens to me."

Thoth's look turned inward. "Without my power to create anything new, I only have the cores. Although, if I were to—" he rubbed his hand over his chin, "—no, I would need a conduit . . ." He paced away, lost to his thoughts, continuing, to himself, "But then, Anki's ships are far more enhanced than our own were." He looked up, sharp, at Istara's ship. "Perhaps if your ship has something similar to an ion drive, I might be able to partition it off and repurpose it as a conduit. So long as it isn't used in flight, it might work." He cut a look at Sekhmet. "I would need your help with the technical aspects."

Sekhmet avoided Urhi-Teshub's heavy look. "Anything you need."

"Then," Thoth continued, warming to the subject, "I would need to siphon off a little of the cores energy into . . ." he looked around the barren complex, as though the item he needed might manifest out of the air, "what . . ?"

Horus pulled the pendant out from within a fold of his kilt. "This?"

Thoth brightened. "Maybe. Yes. It might just work." He cut an oblique look at Istara. "With your permission, of course."

Everyone looked at her, Thoth with hope, Sekhmet with a hint of pity. Horus, veiled, expressionless. Urhi-Teshub shook his head, tilted his head toward Thoth's palace to where the mirror awaited—to where he wished Sethi to go.

Sethi met her eyes. A flicker of darkness whispered within his, clawed at its imprisonment. Peril pressed another scorching talon against Istara's spine, harder this time. There was no choice. If she refused, the evil within him would be unleashed and unstoppable. Her consort would bring about the end of all things—the end of her. She would not bequeath him such a fate.

She nodded. Urhi-Teshub paced away, bolts of cerulean fury striking the ground in his wake. Thoth took her pendant from Horus, reverence bleeding from him. Without another word, he departed to examine Istara's ship. Sekhmet followed after him.

"How long until it's ready?" Sethi called.

Thoth paused. He half-turned, his lips pursed in consideration. "If all goes as it should? A week." He hurried away, eager to begin, the dust-stained hem of his kilt flapping against his thin calves.

Encased in silence, Istara watched them go. As the once-god of wisdom and the goddess of war worked their way along the exterior of her ship, examining it, locked deep in discussion, a bleak scythe carved a path through Istara's soul and harvested the last of her hope. It was over. This was the end.

Sethi took her hand in his and met her eyes. The magnitude of his intended sacrifice threatened to undo her.

She caught Horus's gaze on them, laden with the eternity of his existence, of his own losses. No. It wasn't the end. It was the beginning of *their* end. But for the rest—the chance to start again.

Alone in Thoth's palace, Istara paced the length of one of its terraces, the sun's white heat cascading over her shoulders, picking out her starlight. From beyond the terrace's opened shutters—in the suite she had selected to be the war room of the gods—came the soothing sounds of industry. From within, the quiet hush of horsehair brooms, the thump of cushions liberated of dust, the swish of linen cloths drenched in lavender-scented beeswax against wooden panels.

Two more women arrived. They set down their wash buckets and tied up their skirts, sharing how they were selected from among Ikalur's palace staff to walk through the sacred panel while carrying buckets, soap, and brushes. A slap of water against stone. The rhythmic cadence of a stiff brush. One of the women broke into song, a ditty about a girl who loved a farmer's son, but he loved her best friend more, so she stole his prize pig and sold it in revenge. The song ended. Several of the servants laughed, soft. The work went on. Quiet. Reverent.

Despite her melancholy, Istara succumbed to the tug of a smile. It was a ridiculous song, although its jaunty melody had lifted her spirits. It did not last. After Sethi told her of his decision to end his existence, she had begun to collect the tiniest details, pieces of her existence she would linger over as her light faded and died: The flash of a songbird's blue wings as it surged into the sky; the sharp glint of the stars against the night's canopy; the touch of Sethi's fingers against her face, his lips against hers, tender; the heat of his body as he lay beside her, his arms around her, protective.

One day gone. Six left. Then the ship would be ready. She would fly with her consort to the place where it all began, but instead of remaining in Elati, would journey through the barrier with Sethi and never come back. This morning, after a night spent in calculations, Thoth had said he was certain he could ensure Sethi would make it to Surru, and had even found a way to disable the ship once it crossed the barrier so he would not be able to escape should the shield fail before he lost his god-light. Sethi had nodded in grim approval. Istara had turned away, tears soaking her heart.

She had woken that morning in the sleeping room of the prime goddess of healing, alone. Urhi-Teshub had come for her, though he said little, his disapproval thundering before him. She had followed him to the ship's bay where she found the panels of her ship removed and its interior workings exposed. Sekhmet and Thoth stood before the opened fuselage, laboring over the intricacies of the ship's design, by turns frustrated and exulted. Sethi had greeted her as he hauled one of the panels away. It was faint, but as she left with Urhi-Teshub, Istara had caught the quiet seed of desperation thinning Sethi's features. It tightened the slant of his mouth as he bent to remove another panel from the ship's frame. Fear touched her anew as she sensed his urgency, as he willed Thoth to work faster. Perhaps Sethi knew something the rest did not, perhaps—

The screams of a pair of ships scored the indigo sky. Istara lifted her hand to shield her eyes from the glare of sunlight against their wings. Against their tailfins, the glow of their sigils. Istara smiled. Isis and Osiris.

Yesterday, upon Urhi-Teshub's revelation of the Creator's wish for Istara to lead the pantheon, silence had mushroomed over the assembled gods. Thirty-one pairs of eyes had regarded her, assessed her. Then, with a quiet rustle of her gown, Isis had come to her, a faint smile on her lips, saying perhaps the Creator knew something the gods did not, and she, for one, was ready to follow a goddess. Into the stunned silence, she had bowed her head and with graceful elegance sank to her knee. In her wake, the other goddesses had knelt, Ma'at, Nut, Bastet, Tefnut, Nephthys, Astarte, Nisaba, Ishtar, and Ereshkigal, until only Sekhmet remained.

The goddess of war had eyed Istara, clever, dark, sharp as a night-honed blade. "Before I kneel," she had said, "I must have your vow you will do whatever is necessary to defeat our enemy. Are you prepared to sacrifice everything, or will you, in the end, become compromised?"

Istara had caught Set's dark look of deepening interest, of his ripening hope Urhi-Teshub's charade of a goddess leading them would come to an end and a worthy god would take her place. The goddesses waited, a ripple of uncertainty shimmering through their ranks. The others did not know Sethi was on Anki, or of his plan to annihilate himself—to protect them.

Though she had kept her calm, Istara had bristled at the injustice of the question. Her consort was going to end his existence, and though it had torn her apart, she had accepted it, and yet, even so, the goddess of war could not resist questioning her, casting doubt on her, adding insult to Istara's pain.

"My only purpose is to overcome the darkness which is destroying Elati," she had answered. "Whatever is required to end its presence, I shall do it . . . even if it means my own demise."

Sekhmet had blinked. A flicker of shame shunted through her eyes. "My lady." She sank, clad in perfection and beauty, to her knee. "Forgive me. I have underestimated you. The Creator has chosen well."

The gods had followed after. Urhi-Teshub had knelt first, then Osiris, Ptah, Shu, Geb, Shamash, Nabu, Ashur, Nergal, and finally, alone and alienated, Set had knelt, ungracious, resentment seeping from him, muttering madness had descended upon them all.

Osiris and Isis approached from the north, flying in formation, their silvered ships angling into a curving arc toward the great terrace, its surface blackened and pitted from so many ships coming and going. Istara left the sweltering heat of the terrace to prepare for their arrival. It had been like this all day. With Horus's discovery of the portal to Ikalur, the gods had awakened the portals in their palaces and visited the cities of men, returning with reports of those who would come—and those who would not, either through fear, internal politics, or the taint of the darkness already upon them.

The servants eyed her, shy, as she came into the welcome shade of the suite, her starlight drifting over their aquiline features, catching against their white robes, clasped together at their shoulders with golden brooches. They bowed and backed away. Once in the pillared hall, their excited whispers drifted back of their incredible fortune to have been sent to the island of the gods, and to have been selected to serve the leader of the pantheon, a goddess who possessed healing powers beyond mortal comprehension.

Istara took a seat at the central table, its gilded mahogany surface already laden with maps and notes. In its midst, a detailed map of the city of the gods, known as Nisu. Thoth had pulled the map from the palace's library—as though he himself had once placed it there in an epoch long past. She eyed it, a hint of sorrow touching her soul. She had known the city was vast, but with the creep of vegetation, many of the buildings had been obscured, deceiving one into believing only the palaces large enough and high enough to rise out of the jungle were all there were.

Not so. According to the map, many more gods and goddesses had walked among the prime pantheon, had lived in sprawling residences of their own. Some of the names she knew—those who had not survived Marduk's violence in Thoth's world: Baal. Montu. Adad. Ninhursag. Dagon. She eyed the gold-marked symbols upon the map, noting the other names: Parvati. Shiva. Kali. Lakshmi. Saraswati. Gayatri. Ganga. Yami. Vishnu. Krishna. Ahura Mazda. Shango. Orishas. Bumba. Obatala. Eshu. The list of gods went on, each marked over their residence—dozens more, brothers and sisters she and her predecessor had never known.

She leaned back, pondering who they had been, and why the pantheon had been sundered, with only a handful breathed into life in her world. Perhaps, the others had been sent to other worlds, and even now were fighting their own battles against the manifestation of the dark. A question for Thoth, though when she would have the opportunity to ask him—she closed her eyes and shut out the precise symmetrical lines of Nisu's map, recalling her departure that morning from her palace, as Thoth prodded the internal workings of her ship, his focus intense, and his mood irritable, Sethi and Sekhmet enduring in stoic silence the once-god of wisdom's fractiousness when he could not find what he was looking for.

She picked up another piece of parchment and glanced at its tallies, noted by one of the scribes sent from Ikalur.

Nine of the gods had already returned, another dozen remained. The numbers of allies who had committed to the fight against Marduk had already swelled to the thousands, with each city determined to additionally send tradesmen, cooks, servants, and supplies, both to support the gods, and to maintain their armies.

All which remained for them now was patience. It would take days to get everyone through the portals, to clear the vegetation which swarmed over the city, and to organize the armies of the various kingdoms.

As Horus's portal from Ikalur continued to pour men, women, and resources into Nisu, Istara could not help but hope the awakened portals might grant the gods the advantage which had been forever denied to them, and the darkness, at last, would fall.

❋   ❋   ❋

Meresamun stared at the dead guard Marduk deposited at her feet. Blood pooled under his opened neck and eased toward the hem of her gown.

Aiya slipped away, ashen, leaving Meresamun alone before her consort who glared at her, his lips thin, and his face a mask of rage carved in stone.

"How long," Marduk asked, icy, his pupils narrowing to vicious slits, "do you intend to remain silent while others must die in search of the answer you possess?"

"As long as it takes."

He stepped over the fallen guard, trod in the spreading pool of his blood. Meresamun held her ground. Though her consort always took great pains to lay the blame on her, it was *he* who ordered his guards to enter the mirror and face whomever stood on its opposite side. They never lasted long. Within heartbeats they returned in their death throes. No. She was not to blame. Those deaths were Marduk's guilt to bear, not hers.

"You test me." Marduk raised his metal-clad hand. Meresamun waited, willed him to hit her, to make her hate him. He caught the back of her head. His grip tightened, his armored fingertips harsh against her skull. Pain blossomed. He leaned in, slow, seductive, until his lips brushed her ear. "You will test me no longer."

He let her go. She staggered against the divan. He turned and caught hold of Aiya's arm. In his implacable, bleak grip, she wilted. Terror bled from her. Her eyes, brilliant green in the braziers' light, found Meresamun's, begged for her intervention.

"Let us hope they will be kinder to a woman." Marduk's brutal gaze bored into Meresamun. A flicker ignited in them, savage, lethal. He intended for Aiya to die, to take from Meresamun her only comfort during his campaign to uncover the portal's destination, and perhaps, to punish Sethi, who had not returned for three days.

Her consort tugged on Aiya's arm, gentle, at odds with the violence sheathing him. "Then again," he said, cutting a meaningful look at the empty eyes of the dead guard, "hope is for fools."

"My lady?" Aiya cried, fear swarming after her as she trotted to keep up, her gown billowing in their wake. "I beg you, tell him!"

Meresamun said nothing. Her consort pressed on, clad in the black fury of his armor. Aiya wept in earnest, pled for mercy, her cries wasted on the one whose heart had long become immune to such acts. Tears blistered Meresamun's eyes, her heart shaming her as she did nothing to aid her companion. She could not tell him, not even for Aiya—

"Anki!" Aiya screamed as Marduk threw the suite's door open. "My lord, it is Anki. The mirror leads to the island of the gods."

Marduk fell still, his silhouette a blister against the brazier's flames in the corridor. He cut a severe look at Aiya, hot with warning. She shrank from him, rank with fear.

"Tell me more."

Meresamun's legs folded. She sank onto the divan. She had said nothing, had given no hint to her companion of what she knew. How could the concubine of a queen know where—

"At first—" Aiya whispered, "—before I belonged to the queen, I serviced Ikalur's sages."

Marduk's look sharpened. A beat passed, broken only by the crackle of the braziers' flames and Aiya's hollow, shuddering breaths. He let go of her arm and held out a gloved hand to her, elegant, a courtier. "Indeed?" he asked as she took it, wary, her fingers quavering. He led her back to the divan opposite Meresamun. She sank onto the seat and folded her hands together, pressed them tight against her lap.

"His name was Zherei," she whispered. "A very old sage. He didn't take the usual pleasure from me the others did, he just wanted to . . ." she flicked a look at Meresamun, torn between guilt and hope, "talk."

Meresamun looked away, desolate, as Aiya recounted her tale—the same tale Zherei had shared with her in the library when he had left Tyrn behind. Although, as Aiya's version unfolded, it became clear Zherei had been far more circumspect with the consort of Marduk. He had not—as he had claimed—remained in the library waiting for the storm to end. He had wandered throughout the entire citadel and tried every mirror he had found, uncovering a network of portals which spanned all of Elati. The most scintillating discovery he had made had been the mirror which led to the city of the gods in Anki within the palace's second largest suite.

"As givers of pleasure, we are sworn to silence," Aiya finished, soft. "When I was taken from Ikalur, I saw Zherei enter the warship, a captive, like me. He looked at me and shook his head, once, the warning in his eye unmistakable." A tear slipped down her cheek. "I have broken my silence to save my life. I have proven my worth."

Marduk sank to a crouch before her. He brushed the tear from her cheek, his metal-clad fingers drinking in her misery. He caught her chin and lifted her face up to his. A quiet nod of approval. "Sethi chose his consort well."

He rose and turned to Meresamun. She met his amber eyes, afire with quiet triumph, her heart bleak. She knew what he would do, what he was capable of—had seen what he had wrought against his own people during the uprisings of Uribi. She had learned Sethi had gone to Anki, and yet, against all the odds, he had not come back. As the days passed and the mirror remained silent, her dread lessened, replaced by a fragile kindling of nascent hope. Perhaps the gods had found a way to undo what Marduk had done to Sethi. She needed only buy more time.

And now—she shot a hostile look at Aiya—it was over. Marduk would obliterate the island of the gods and every living thing on it. And of the Well of Life? His weapons would obliterate it, too. Emptiness clawed at her. Darkness was her fate. For eternity.

"Come." Marduk held out his black-clad hand to her. A sheath of ice slid over the fire in his eyes. "It is time to finish this."

※　※　※

Istara set aside her wine and leaned back against the divan. Above, the night sky glittered, riotous with its stars, its canopy still devoid of the light of Elati's twin moons. Beneath the reach of the heavens, Anki's veil shimmered, reassuring and warm, speckling the terrace of Istara's suite in ripples of white-gold light. Sethi pushed his platter aside and joined her, cradling his wine.

He caught her hand in his and lifted it to his lips. A kiss, tender, brushed against the heel of her palm. She met his eyes. A ripple of darkness shimmered within them. He blinked, and it was gone. Such glimpses of what possessed him had become more frequent of late, as if it were growing in strength despite the might of the shield.

A thought snared her. What if the jihn—even within the tower—could erode the shield's suppression over him? No. She forced the thought away. It couldn't be. Thoth said the shield was stable. Sethi still had time.

"How goes the work with my ship?" she asked, seeking to quiet the uncertainty within her.

Sethi sipped his wine. He cast a taut look to the south, toward Surru. "Slower than expected." The muscles in his jaw clenched. He looked down into his cup and turned it round, watching the wine within swirl. "Thoth says he will need at least one day more than planned." Her consort cut a tight look at her. "We need your ship to be ready sooner, not later. Despite the shield, I can sense what is within me is testing the boundaries of its restraints. Its presence touches my every thought. It questions you, and my love for you." He let go of her hand and swept an arc over the expanse of the terrace, taking in the city of Anki, the pyramids, and the shield. "And it questions this. It tells me everything here is a lie—Even our love. It pushes me to return through the mirror to Marduk, where it promises I will find peace." He lifted the cup to his lips. "It is . . . relentless."

He drank the rest of his wine, then poured more. Misery shrouded him. He drank again. "For now, I am able to withstand its insinuations, and its lies veiled as truth. But what of tomorrow, or the next day?" He finished the rest of his wine and wiped the back of his hand across his mouth. "Sooner or later, it will once more gain its power over me, and just as before, I will have no choice but to succumb." He looked at her from under his brow. "And then I will not stop until I have retrieved the jihn, until I have—" He stood, abrupt. His hands clenched into fists.

Movement on the terrace. Istara turned. Her protector moved toward them, wary, his eyes dark, lost in the evening's shadow. Over his shoulder, the blades of his ax seethed with cerulean bolts of lightning.

Istara rose. "Come." She touched Sethi's arm. "Let us retire, where we might speak of this, alone."

Sethi cut a thin look at Urhi-Teshub, but said nothing.

Istara went into the suite and began to pull the shutters together, one by one, the panels clicking into place with soft, homely clacks. From without, Urhi-Teshub regarded her as she pulled the final pair toward her, their gold-gilt edges glinting against the light of the terrace's solitary brazier.

"Let us at least have this," she said, girding herself against his look of recrimination. "So little time remains. Soon, he will be gone. Forever."

Urhi-Teshub eyed her, impassive. "From now on," he said, sliding a narrow, untrusting look at Sethi over her shoulder, "I would prefer if you do not lock yourself in."

Resigned to Urhi-Teshub's hostility, Istara closed the panels against her protector, quiet. For a heartbeat she lingered over the final latch. A creak of leather as Urhi-Teshub moved to stand outside the barrier. His misgiving poured through the carved latticework, punctuated by harsh bursts of cerulean fire. She lifted the heavy latch. The taint of darkness in Sethi's eyes filled her mind. She set the latch back down, unfastened, and walked away.

Sethi had gone to the side table and poured them both wine. He handed her a cup. She drank.

He nodded at her pendant, returned to her for the night, hanging from a gold chain around her neck. "Thoth says your pendant is a relic, crafted by the Creator, himself."

Istara sipped. "It is."

"And it came into your possession while you were in Tarhuntassa?"

"It did."

He drank, his gaze on her pendant shuttered, unreadable. She wondered at his thoughts as she sipped anew, sensing their corridors were destined to be locked to her, forever. His eyes left her pendant and moved over the opulence of her suite. Further in, through a pair of golden double doors, her silken-cocooned bed, where he had made love to her for the last two nights, over and over, and where, in between their unions they had talked of many things, of their journeys across Thamud Desert to Babylon;

of the ambush which had almost ended his life in the ravine, his rescue by Imhotep, and his discovery of Horus's true identity; of her time in Imaru, and of the gods' acrimonious departure from the capital of Rzhev, neither of them allowing themselves to waste the night's precious hours in sleep.

Yet despite the slowness of the love they made, aching with tenderness, sorrow, and regret, it was never enough. The distance between them could never be breached. They loved across a chasm—their touch brief, fleeting, tainted by what consumed him.

"And what does it do?"

His question startled her from the morosity of her musings. "What does what do?"

He tilted his head at her pendant.

She looked down at it, then back at him. Another susurration of darkness rippled against the gold of his eyes. Another blink, and he was Sethi again. She sipped, a slither of dread coiled around her. She suppressed it. Perhaps she had imagined it. No. There it was again. Darkness incarnate. She lay her palm over the pendant, sensing it was not he who asked, but his otherness. Though she had never held anything back from him before, she chose to be circumspect.

"I do not know," she lied, guilt assailing her as she met his bleak look. Her heart betrayed her, laid her deception bare.

He finished his wine and set aside his cup, perfunctory. His eyes touched hers, golden, clear, etched with turmoil. "You know you cannot hide anything from me." His gaze moved back to her pendant. Another flicker of darkness, a whisper of hunger, malevolent. He blinked and looked away. "Three days." He murmured. "We had three days." He closed his eyes, clenched his fists. The muscles of his jaw tensed. "No," he said, taut. "I will not succumb. I must leave. Take me back to the mirror."

"Not yet," Istara whispered as he took her wine from her and set it beside his. She looked at the golden pair of goblets, elegant and understated, their quiet beauty lacking the ostentation of the gaudy wealth of kings and queens. Once, they had been used by the prime goddess of healing and her consort. Now, they sat on the polished table, side by side, a memory of a heartbeat shared between those who stood in their shadow. Grief assailed her. Soon they too, would fall. But first—

"Love me," she breathed, tears filling her soul, coating her eyes. He blinked back his grief as he took her in his arms, his warmth suffusing her with hope, and his strength sowing within her the belief they could still overcome what stood between them. She closed her eyes, unwilling to risk seeing the darkness in his. His lips brushed against her brow, bathing it in the garnet warmth of the wine they had shared. She waited, her body hushed, in an agony of expectation. The reverent, gentle brush of his thumb against her lower lip. Her god, her consort. Her love. Her only love. She let out a tremulous breath, willing him to go on.

He kissed her, fierce, harsh, the cold, sharp waves of his sorrow lashed against her soul, stripped her raw. Quiet thuds as his kilt and belt landed on a nearby divan. His hands returned to her, undressed her, released her to him. He caught her buttocks, and lifted her up. He found her, impaled her, made them one. She clung to him, her hips meeting his hungry thrusts, her body drinking of his, denying their fate until the remote heat of his darkness filled her once more. His grief slammed into her, a battering ram. The walls surrounding her hope vanished, ephemeral, filthy lies. The distance between them yawned anew, a chasm of silence. Alienation prowled, hungry, at the gates of their love.

Still deep within her, he carried her to a divan. She settled onto his lap, her star-clad breasts golden in the quiet glow of his fractals. His fingers slid between hers, his grip tight, almost painful as she watched her light wipe his love away.

At last she found the courage to meet his eyes. In his, the anguish of his love, untainted by the darkness. He was going to leave her. Tears blazed a path through her soul. He drew her against him, cradling her as she wept, as she accepted what he already knew: She must let him go. There would be no Surru. For them, there would only be war.

✳   ✳   ✳

Anki's coastline rose out of the sea and stretched into the distance as far as Meresamun could see. Along its boundary, a shimmering wall of near-translucent white-gold. It sheared down from the heavens into the sea many iters from Anki's rugged, cliff-strung coast. Meresamun leaned forward to scan its height. No. It was impossible. It angled up, endless, into the heavens.

Marduk's gaze swept over the barrier, his mien cold, calculating. He pressed several switches on the console. Four slim metallic weapons erupted from the ship's wings, their tails blazing blue fire. The first one reached the barrier. A blistering eruption of white heat smeared into the perfection of the web. Total silence followed in its wake. One after another, the other three weapons struck the ephemeral wall. Meresamun averted her eyes from the glare, its intensity bathing the flight deck in stark white light, stripped of shadow. When it was over, she looked again. Marduk's weapons had done nothing. Not even a tendril of smoke remained. The shimmering wall reared away, implacable. Indestructible.

For several heartbeats, a thundering silence tore through the flight deck. Marduk glared at the barrier, his jaw a hard, determined edge. He returned his attention to the console. His fingers worked their way over its panels and sigils, resetting the flight path, arming more weapons. He hit the thrusters and they ascended, skimming the shield's periphery, leaving a glittering swathe of white in their wake. Anki's coastline fled into the distance as they pushed higher and deeper into the island's interior.

Meresamun cut a look into the cabin. Aiya clung to the edge of the divan, her gaze raking over the contours of the island beneath its veil, her curiosity tangible for the island of the gods—a near mythical place to the Elatians.

The shield spread away in every direction, endless, impenetrable. The entire island lay shrouded in its web of light. At its apex, within the center of the city of the gods, a beam of golden light emanated from the capstone of a massive pyramid. It soared up to the base of the shimmering shield, rooting it to the complex. Alongside the beam of light, the tower reared into the heavens, endless, its circumference glimmering in the shield's radiant light.

Marduk surveyed it, cold. Fury emanated from him. He exhaled, thin. "Thoth," he said, his voice granite. "I should have killed you when I had the chance."

He circled the tower's shielded girth, spiraling around it until the brilliant well of the sky's blue vanished. On and on he went, up into the silence of the endless dark, seeking a breach in the shield's wall. It persisted, implacable, a glittering sentinel.

He tore away from it, encased in fury. His fingers moved over the console again. He hit the ion thrusters. Pressure slammed into Meresamun. A yawning, deepening pain tore a path through her eyes and into the back of her brain. Blistered by the fire of her tears, she endured as the ship screamed over the arc of Elati, between the ribbons of blue and orange encasing its shell and the endless canopy of stars above.

Her consort angled the ship's nose downward. They tore free of the heavens and screamed back into the world, the ship's wings afire, blazing, a falling star. An explosion of blue sky swarmed over them. A shaft of sunlight pierced the windows, brilliant, blinding. Still, they fell. The ship roared in protest. Alarms blared.

Marduk punched a series of buttons and the violence of the ion's thrust cut out. Meresamun's restraints did not hold. She hurtled from her seat toward the unforgiving wall of the console. Her consort's armored arm slammed into her, held her back. A ripple of blue light washed over his armor, absorbing the force of her impact. She clung to him, fighting the drag of her weight as they continued to fall toward Elati, straight as an arrow, their screaming transit splitting the sky in two. Without letting her go, Marduk braced his feet against the console, hauled on the controls and brought the ship up.

Along the panel of the console, more than a dozen switches and buttons flared orange. They blinked at Marduk, plaintive, yearning for his touch. A multitude of messages streamed along the screens of the console. More warnings chirped. He continued to work, intent, calm, focused. Dangerous. One by one the alarms ceased. The dull thunder of the ship's engines filled the quiet. He glanced up at the horizon, his intensity palpable. It washed over Meresamun, a poisoned tide.

Despite her distress, and the dislocation of the ion drive, dread snared her. She eyed her consort from under her tear-soaked lashes. Dark anticipation saturated him. He flipped a lever tucked into the side of the console. A flat panel slid out. On its face, a small screen. It lit up and began scrolling symbols. He punched in a series of codes. An indentation beneath the panel lit up, outlined in a pulse of cerulean light. A quiet beep emitted from the panel, steady, like the beat of a heart.

Meresamun pulled herself up and looked out the window, overcome by a sudden need to know where they were. Marduk's ship cut a low, blistering path over a turquoise sea, its whitecaps innocent to the malevolent shadow slicing through the light of the sun.

Ahead, fast approaching, land hefted itself from the basin of the sea, a white sandy beach crowned with a fringe of palms. On one of the screens, a blinking blue light encircled by a series of rings coalesced. Along either side of it, an endless series of symbols scrolled past, far too rapid for Meresamun to register. The beep within the panel increased its tempo, its heart beating twice as fast. The blinking blue light also blinked faster. Meresamun leaned forward, dread entombing her.

"No," she breathed as the ship screamed over the beach past the line of trees and hurtled toward the white walls of a distant city cradling the banks of a wide river. She clung to the armrests of the seat, helpless, sick, numb. He was going to do it—was going to unleash his weapons against innocents.

"Please, I beg you," she cried as he circled the enormous city, granting her a view of its colonnaded perfection, its pristine symmetry and beauty. Men and women looked up, shading their eyes against the glare of the sun. Children ran after them, waving, excited. "My love," she cried, tearing her eyes from the blameless city to her consort, his profile as hard as the metal sheathing his body, "do not do this thing. I cannot bear it."

The beeping from the panel increased, threefold, fourfold. It blurred into a single, horrifying whine. The blinking light on the screen turned red. Marduk punched the indentation on the panel. A black tube streamed away from the ship's fuselage, its rear bright with liquid flame. It curved to align itself with the heart of the city. Marduk flew on, leaving the city behind, cutting a searing a path up into the heavens.

Unable to stop herself, Meresamun turned in her seat, bile burning her throat. Past the translucent walls of the ship, the tube detonated over the city. Brilliance washed over her, obliterating her senses. Her eyes streaming, aching, she forced herself to look. A raging firestorm swept over the city, its heat melting the land, evaporating the river. Nothing could survive that. Nothing.

Quivering, sick, she turned back to Marduk, who continued to work the controls, plotting his course for their next destination, as though he had not just annihilated an entire city.

"I hate you," she whispered.

He cut a look at her, impassive. "This is war. I am a warrior. I am used to being hated."

She got up and left. Aiya looked up at her, incoherent with tears, insensible with terror. She pointed at the blistering boil of molten heat Marduk's weapon had created. The city and everything within it wiped off the face of Elati within the space of a single heartbeat. At last she saw her consort as Zarpanitu had, a being possessed by utter darkness. A darkness she needed to destroy.

With a subdued Aiya beside her, Meresamun followed Marduk as he strode down a colonnaded corridor, cutting a path between shafts of brilliant, white mid-afternoon light and dense bars of pillared shadow. Ever since her consort had brought his ship down onto the massive game board in Ikalur's palace garden, silence had greeted Serde's overlord. No guards tipped their spears to him as they passed. No servants hurried to move out of his path. Not a single courtier graced the corridors. The palace glared back at them, empty, desolate, weighted with the stink of abandonment.

Marduk pressed on, impassive, the obsidian depths of his armor repelling the relentless glare of the sun, his booted tread warning of the approach of one accustomed to domination, obedience, and the right of retribution. Every now and again he slowed to check the screen at his wrist, blinking with the quiet pulse of life—of those still within the citadel. Each pause granted Meresamun and her estranged companion a brief respite before he moved on in a new direction in pursuit of his quarry, leading them at a punishing pace through a maze of empty corridors, suites, and vestibules.

They came to a halt in a deserted chamber deep in the palace, its walls and pillars clad in marble and gold. Opposite the entrance, a massive golden door bore down on them, imperious, its panels engraved with elegant sigils and the emblem of a falcon with its wings spread open.

Marduk tested the door's handle. It remained closed, locked from within. He freed one of the weapons at his hip, pressed a series of lights upon its handle and pointed. A bolt of cerulean light streamed from the weapon's nose. It encased the door in a shimmering web. A heartbeat later, it erupted into a burst of light. Meresamun blinked back the imprint of its glare. A memory of the door hung in the air, as fine as ephemeral blue powder, and then, nothing. The door vanished in total silence, as though it had never been.

Beyond the opening, darkness and the faint tang of the sea. Marduk went through. His footfalls echoed against stone, diminishing with distance.

"That door was crafted during the time of the gods," Aiya whispered. "It leads to the holy sanctuary of Horakhti."

A draft of air stirred the tendrils of Meresamun's hair. She went to the opening. Outlined in the spluttering light of ensconced torches, a narrow stone staircase spiraled upward, its steps curved into deep basins, worn by thousands of footfalls over an immense period of time.

She ascended the treacherous, uneven steps, her arms outstretched between the wall and the stairwell's spine, the going slow, monotonous. From further behind, the quiet slap of Aiya's sandals against the stairs as she followed, unwilling, just as Meresamun followed Marduk—two leaves caught in the wake of his dark torrent.

At last, her legs trembling and her lungs aching, she reached the top of the stairwell. Sunlight poured over her, and heavy gusts of salted, sea air buffeted her hair and gown. Ahead, a colonnaded vestibule crossed a short distance to another set of closed doors. To her right, a wall of solid rock carved from the face of the cliff. Opposite, barricaded by nothing more than a low wall and a series of pillars, a sheer, eye-watering drop plummeted to the faint crash of the sea.

At the other end of the vestibule, Marduk came to a halt. A silvered glint flared as he lifted his weapon before the pair of gold-paneled double doors. No guards stood without. A beam of cerulean light shot into the doors. It spread, rapid, weaving its deadly, crushing web. A heartbeat later, a puff of light and another piece of Elati's history vaporized, its existence obliterated, forever.

Aiya's quiet pants breached the crown of the stairs. Meresamun waited, dread assaulting her, hoping she had gone far enough and could remain where she was. Marduk turned. His eyes found hers, the message clear. She hadn't. He lifted his hand, the one holding his weapon, and beckoned her to him. Domination poured from him. *Come to me.*

She went, Aiya's fear-soaked presence close behind.

At the gaping maw of the entrance, Marduk held out his hand to Meresamun, regal, his sudden calm unnerving her. She slid her hand into the cold curve of his metallic palm and ascended the short flight of steps up into the chamber.

Within, lit by four braziers, a white marble chamber lined by two rows of golden pillars. Straight ahead, in the center of a marble tier, an opaque panel similar to the mirror Meresamun had emerged from in Anki reared out of the smooth, ageless floor. It stood, as fragile as alabaster and as big as a door, flat, thin, alone and unsupported, a thing of utter improbability. White light churned within its frameless sides.

A rustle of silks came from behind the nearest pillar. A man and a woman stepped out, clad in elegant finery. Both wore purple gilt in gold, and on their brows, golden diadems. Marduk eyed them, dispassionate, then turned his attention to the monolith of light, his profile stark against its soft pulsing. Silence, dense and cold mantled him, so thick it suffocated the distant susurration of the sea. It stretched, taut as a hide on a tanning rack.

He powered down his weapon, lowered it back into his belt, and walked to the pair. They faced his dark presence with quiet defiance. Neither knelt.

He paced a slow circuit around them, the light of the monolith sliding along the contours of his armour, seeking escape. His precise, metallic footfalls ceased before the king. "You sent my people to Anki." He tilted his head toward the sliver-thin sentinel. "To my enemies." He lifted his wrist and scanned the screen on the back of his glove. "One hundred and twelve of my subjects were in this citadel when I arrived. And now—" he lifted his brow at the pair, "—there is only Serde's king and queen, treacherous to the end."

The king said nothing, he looked past Marduk as though her consort did not exist. The queen's eyes met Meresamun's, then flicked past her to Aiya. A blink of recognition, smoothed in a heartbeat.

Marduk stepped back. Without taking his eyes from the king, he pulled a device from a slot in his belt. It was a small thing, innocuous. It gleamed in the light, shimmering in jeweled colors, reminding Meresamun of the beetles in the Temple of Sekhmet. A memory stirred. No. Her heart juddered to a halt. Horror clawed up her spine, sharp, urgent.

Before she could blink, Marduk's gloved hand shot out and captured the queen of Serde. He hauled her over to him and forced her to her knees, facing away from him.

"Please," Meresamun whispered as her consort gathered up the queen's hair from the nape of her neck, gentle, seductive, as a lover would. "My love. Not this."

Marduk set the device against the hollow at the base of the queen's skull, the cut of his mouth cruel, sadistic. "Yes," he answered. "This."

The queen's eyes remained on her king, brilliant with unshed tears. "I love you," she breathed. Marduk pressed against the side of the device. It awakened, a living thing, and burrowed into her flesh, sheared through bone, buried itself into her brain.

Her screams filled the chamber, brutal, endless, ragged with anguish, her cries mirrored by her husband's grief, his despair. Marduk left and ascended the tier, ignoring their distress. He inspected the monolith, his eyes raking over it, his pupils fully dilated despite its fierce glow.

By degrees, the queen's suffering slowed, then ended. Blood soaked her gown, drenched her hair, pooled on the pristine marble. The acrid, dense heat of it polluted the air. She quieted and pulled herself from the floor.

"Giver of Life," she whispered, prostrating herself before Marduk. "I am your servant. What would you have me do?"

Marduk turned. In his hand, another of the hateful devices. He held out it to her at arms' length, disdainful. She pulled herself up the wide steps of the tier, her legs trembling, weak, and took the device from him.

"For the traitor?"

"For the traitor," Marduk answered, cold. He turned back to the panel of light, a bleak shadow against its purity. The queen backed away from him, unsteady, descended the steps, and approached her husband, her silken slippers smearing a path through her own blood.

"Whatever it takes to be with you," he whispered as she placed the device against the base of his skull, her eyes empty, her existence no longer her own. A tear slid down his cheek. "Anything for you."

Meresamun fled. She hadn't even reached the yawning gap where the doors had once stood before the king's torment slammed into her. She bolted down the steps and tore across the length of the vestibule, her gown whipping against her legs, and her tears blinding her as Serde's regent paid the vicious price for having stood against the dark—for having chosen to send everyone else through first, a true king. She sank to her knees, and clung to the ledge of the low wall, drinking in the fresh sea air, seeking to cleanse her lungs of the acrid taint of the queen's blood, of the memory of the gaping, ragged hole in the back of her skull, the device worming its way in, a metallic nightmare.

In the distance, the hollow cries of the king persisted, relentless with his suffering, with the erasure of his memories and of his soul, until he quieted, enslaved to Marduk's will, doomed to exist beside the woman he once loved, while his heart beat on, neither dead, nor alive.

✳ ✳ ✳

His flesh prickling with misgiving, Horus waited by the mirror in Horakhti's palace. The king and queen of Serde should have come through long ago. Though his instincts warned him not to, he stepped through the mirror. A gust of wind slammed into him, dense with the tang of fresh-spilled blood. He pulled his weapon free and powered it up by feel. A blink and his vision cleared.

The chamber glared back at him, a wounded thing, shorn of its doors, its pristine white marble floor soaked with the essence of life. Of the king and queen, only the evidence of the violence done to them remained where they should have been. Horus knelt by one of the sanguine pools and sank his fingertips into it. Its fading heat cried out to him, screaming of the darkest of violations. He stood, his senses tingling. The taint of fear should have saturated the space. It did not. Rather, a peculiar, distant calm suffused the chamber. A tendril of prescience whispered over him. Death had not walked here. Though much blood had been lost, he sensed Rhewyn and Welyn were still alive.

Cautious, he edged along the pillars to the opening, acutely aware of both his mortality and of the depth of his disadvantage. He paused at the final pillar to consider what he hoped to achieve. Him, against Marduk, with a single weapon. It was a fool's mission. His instincts hauled at him to return to Anki, to save this fight for another day.

A distant thunder rumbled from beyond the cliff's wall. He eased out from the pillar, just enough to cut a look up into the cloudless blue sky. The thunder's intensity increased, reverberating through the floor and the pillar. A heartbeat later, Marduk's massive warship reared over the cliff and shot away to the north.

Horus moved to the opening and watched Marduk's departure. He powered down his weapon, thinking to search for Rhewyn and Welyn when a brilliant flare erupted from the ship's undercarriage.

From out of its heat, a long, dark tube sped toward Ikalur, a stain against the sky. A thin, high scream found Horus. It impaled the heavens, soaked with the promise of death. He backed away, horrified. He knew that cry. The overture to annihilation.

He turned and ran, splattering his legs with the blood of the king and queen of Ikalur as the scream crescendoed, scouring the air with its promise, its shriek pummeling his senses with its brutal descent. He reached the threshold of the top tier. A deep boom tore through him, sent him staggering sideways. Warmth trickled from his ears and down his throat, acrid, metallic.

A wall of blinding white light scythed through the cliff's wall toward the sanctuary, obliterating everything in its path. He threw himself into the mirror just as the light enveloped him. Blistering heat pursued him, singed his flesh, even within the transition of the portal. He hurtled out of the mirror and crashed into the paneled wall in Horakhti's hidden room in Anki, his kilt smoldering. He slapped at the incandescent sparks, the horror of what Marduk had wrought slamming into him. Images of Baalat's burning city replayed, her devastation haunting him, vivid, brutal, igniting anew the depth of his hate.

The glow of the mirror died, abrupt. He turned. Its surface turned black as obsidian. In total silence, an explosion of pressure distorted its surface. At its center, as though it had been punched from within, a ring of jagged fractures rippled out. Heat radiated from its black-dark ruins, hot as a blacksmith's furnace. Horus backed away, his chest rising and falling, his flesh cauterized by the incinerating heat radiating from the mirror.

He stared at the destroyed mirror, numb. Ikalur was gone, and with it, the last home he and Baalat had shared. Nothing had been left of her to him. Nothing.

Marduk had taken all.

✳   ✳   ✳

Sethi drank deep. It wasn't enough. He poured more wine, banging the golden pitcher against the cup's rim, willing his consort to wake, to stop him from what he knew he was about to do. But Istara slept on through the depths of the night, naked, beautiful, glittering with starlight, perfect in heart and soul. Against her throat, the relic shimmered, alive with her light. He eyed it from under his brow as he sipped the wine, resisting its pull, continuing, by sheer will to hold out against the siege which raged on, relentless, within him.

He let his gaze drift over her, seeking the feelings he had felt only a few hours before. But of his passion, love, desperation and sorrow, he found nothing. His heart glared back at him, cold, sheathed in silence, and open to the slow creep of his growing hatred for her and everything for which she stood. He drank again, deeper. He swallowed and looked down into his cup, turning it round and round, seeking to find himself in the wine's gentle swirl.

Yesterday, Horus delivered the news of Ikalur's destruction, and of its missing king and queen, their blood bathing the floor of the sanctuary. Sethi had once again said he wanted to leave, but Thoth had made good progress, and Istara insisted he remain just a little longer. Despite his deepening misgivings, he had stayed and endured his inner battle, holding on, for her, for him. For Elati.

Then, the portals to Chaus, Thes Dios, Saritova, Vinay, and Nimidia also turned black, their ancient power extinguished, forever. Sorties of gods flew out. All returned with the same report. Tholis's great cities were gone, its lesser cities, too. Even Ningwu had been obliterated, a city, like Imaru, which had no portal, or patron god. And thus it was, in the space of a day, half of Elati lay in ruins.

The goddesses wept, and the gods raged, their hatred and longing for revenge a festering wound. Only Istara remained steadfast, never wavering in her belief Thoth would come through as he had with the shield, and Sethi would be reprieved from what he had become. His departure would cripple Marduk and strengthen the gods. They could not stop now, she had insisted, not when they were so close.

He finished his wine and set the cup back onto the table with a thud. But she was wrong. It was over. The line had been crossed. There was no going back. It was time to leave. He ascended the steps of the bed's platform, his tread heavy with the weight of what he would do. His consort stirred and rolled onto her back, her star-clad hair spreading across the cushion. Her breasts rose and fell, quiet, rhythmic. Calm suffused her. Soon there would be no calm for her. Soon—

He clenched his fists. No. He would not allow his darkness to relish the anguish he would give her. Later, when he was safely away, he would ease back on the reins he had been hauling against for the past two days. But with the last of his will, he would leave her, safe, she who was still sacred to the one who was fast sinking into the depths of his lost, poisoned self. He had taken her for the last time this night, savoring what was left of their bond, even as it faded away, subsumed by the taint within him. Though she had not wished to sleep, she had succumbed after so many nights spent awake. He had left her only heartbeats later to drink, to endure, and to resist what called to him, its whispers insistent, insidious, seductive.

He gazed down at her, longing to feel something for her, anything, even a shaft of guilt, but all he felt was numb. Instead, he freed the pendant from her neck, tucked it into the folds of his kilt, went to the door, and opened it.

Urhi-Teshub was there, as always. He looked up, narrow. Suspicion bled from him. His hand went to the haft of his ax, to heft it free of its holder.

"Peace," Sethi muttered, holding up his hand, forestalling the storm god. "I only need to get some air."

Urhi-Teshub said nothing. He fell into step beside him. Distrust poured from him. "It is only out of love for Istara I tolerate you," he said, cutting a dark look at Sethi, his golden eyes harsh with restraint, "I would have torn you limb from limb for the things you have done."

"Things in Elati," Sethi asked, dry, "or elsewhere?"

A baleful silence slammed into him, salted with fury. They paced on. Sethi eyed the way ahead. He turned toward the perimeter of the palace, processing past a series of lit and extinguished braziers, his steps taking him through patches of light and shadow.

"You never loved her as much as I," Urhi-Teshub said.

"I did not realize we were in a competition."

Jagged light exploded from the ax's blades. They walked on in a silence as taut as a drum's skin, then, "I understand you have chosen another to replace her."

Sethi emerged from the corridor and turned along a colonnade at the edge of the palace, its height granting a view of the golden beam of light bathing the central complex. "As have you."

"Five weeks," Urhi-Teshub retorted, ignoring Sethi's taunt, "was all it took before you replaced her. It proves how little Istara meant to you."

Sethi halted, the storm god's accusation struck true, flint against stone. A spark touched the residue of his love. Sethi nourished its embers, willing it to thrive. There. The faintest tremor of regret. It ripened into a tsunami of guilt. His hand strayed to the fold in his kilt where he had secreted Istara's pendant. He had meant to deprive her of it. If he could not have the jihn, she would not have the pendant.

"It proves nothing," Sethi returned. "I was not myself. I *am* not myself." He met Urhi-Teshub's golden eyes, faced her protector's hatred. "You will never know how much I loved her," he continued, "the years I waited for her, searched for her, longed for her, never even certain if she existed. I sacrificed everything for her. I gave up my position, my life, my heart. My soul." He looked past Urhi-Teshub's hostile glare into the sleeping quiet of the city. "Even this—though I cannot understand why—I sense, is a sacrifice I must make for her."

Urhi-Teshub said nothing for several heartbeats. The heat of his gaze slid away. The storm god sniffed. He rolled one of his shoulders, easing the weight of the ax on his back. "*This?*" he repeated.

"What I have become."

"Hm." Urhi-Teshub folded his arms over his chest. He shifted his weight, the creak of his leather armor loud in the night's silence. He leaned his hip against the wall, eyeing the lower levels of the palace watered by the faint light of the shield. Three floors beneath them, the opening to the ship bay yawned, a dark rectangle against the pale illumination of the palace's walls. He cut a narrow look back at him. "You have not come out to take the night air."

"I cannot wait any longer for Thoth. I have already stayed too long."

"And Istara?"

"It will be easier for her to find me gone."

Urhi-Teshub said nothing for a long time, his profile cut a harsh line of disapproval against the sky's canopy. "You knew I would take you to the portal, even if it meant hurting her anew."

Sethi waited, as each heartbeat cost him another fragment of his soul, as he bled back into what he was. Darkness soaked his thoughts, a relentless, seductive creep. It scoured away the brief taste of his regret and guilt. His gaze slid to the central complex, drawn by the bleak heartbeat buried within the largest pyramid, as always, seeking to realign with his own. Despite her denial of what the relic could do, Istara's heart had shown him all. Hunger scorched a path through his soul. To have it again, to feel its power. To finish the gods once and for all. He saw it all, what he needed to do. The final barrier within him crumbled.

"So be it," Urhi-Teshub muttered. "Though I am bound by duty to protect Istara, her needs must come second to this." He turned and strode to the stairs which would lead them to the bay.

Sethi followed after him. He pulled the relic from his kilt and rammed its coiled length into the hollow at the base of Urhi-Teshub's skull and twisted it, vicious, seeking to sever the connection between Urhi-Teshub's spine and brain. He yanked it free, splattering his arm and chest with the storm god's blood. Istara's protector sank to his knees and tumbled to his side, caught in the brutal grip of his paralysis. He tried to speak. A gurgle, nothing more. Gouts of blood coated his teeth. His eyes ignited with golden fire, seething with the eternal gift of a god's living light. A handful of tendrils ignited within his torso and wove their way up into the gaping hole, working to close it, to piece him back together.

Sethi eyed the incapacitated god, his heart cold, assessing the speed of the storm god's return, and how much time he would have before Istara's protector would be recovered enough to raise the alarm and come after him. More tendrils shot out of Urhi-Teshub's torso and slid into his throat. It wasn't fast, but neither was it slow. Enough time to do what needed to be done. With one last look at the stricken god, Sethi descended the stairs, Istara's blood-soaked relic still in his hand.

❈   ❈   ❈

His heart thundering and his lungs afire, Thoth hauled himself up the steep incline within the great pyramid willing his instincts to be wrong and Istara to be right. She had woken him in her guest suite, and with quiet, urgent words had told him of being roused by the roar of a ship leaving her palace. Within heartbeats she discovered both Sethi and her pendant were gone, and after a frantic search, had found Urhi-Teshub wrapped in his light, still locked in the grip of paralysis. She had brought him back, only to learn the terrible truth. The darkness in Sethi had overcome him. Now, he was loose in Anki.

With her ship in pieces and Urhi-Teshub's ship from the Etemen'anki taken by Sethi, Urhi-Teshub had had no choice but to run to the next nearest palace to gain access to another ship. Thoth had listened, uneasy, as Istara confessed she had persuaded Sethi not to leave for the last three nights, despite his warnings he was losing control, so blinded had she been by her desperate hope Thoth would finish the ship's shield in time.

A mountain of guilt crushed Thoth as he pressed on, his legs quivering with exhaustion. He had run the entire way from her palace to the complex, the weight of the dread within him equal to the guilt compressing him without. Despite Istara's hopes her consort had gone back through the portal, Thoth had deep misgivings. He had to know, to see for himself. He couldn't wait for the gods to be roused, to organize themselves. The distance to the complex turned out to be further than he had anticipated. The city's size deceived.

He should have worked faster, thought things through more quickly. It was his fault it had come to this. He could not bring himself to blame Istara for wanting to hold out until the last heartbeat. No. The only one responsible for this was him. He had taken too long studying the schematics, his tendency to perfection slowing things down. *It only needs to work for a few hours*, Sekhmet had said, but he hadn't listened.

He had been insistent, unwilling to bend from his ways. He had clung to his defense, though now he was caught in the harsh light of failure, the truth bore down on him, ugly, damning. He could have cut corners, but he did not, he hated to leave a task half-finished. It would irk him if he did, would keep him awake at night—for years. So he had proceeded at the speed which pleased him, repeating to Sekhmet each time she tried to hurry him along if it wasn't perfect, the shield might fail, though in his heart he knew the risk would be almost non-existent. And now—shame slammed into him, raw, visceral—look what his pride, and his adherence to habit had wrought.

He pressed his palm against his chest. His heart pounded, erratic, far too fast for comfort. Thirst clobbered him. He wasn't made for running, he was made for thinking. He pressed on, putting one foot in front of the other, enduring the protests of his body, his breathing ragged and harsh in the pyramid's epochal silence. *Please*, he beseeched the Creator from behind the wall of his mind, *let Sethi not be here. Let Istara be right.*

Ahead, against the glow of the pyramid's internal light, the blue-white light of the rotating core streamed down the incline, a shifting, glorious thing. Hope spiraled in his breast, granting him a final spurt of energy. He clambered up the rest of the incline, keeping his eyes on the suspended core, his hopes galloping away, wild, like beasts freed from captivity. Istara had been right, after all. He knew he should have trusted her. He crested the top of the incline. The tunnel completed its in-folding, became a wall.

Sethi turned, the jihn in his hand. A pale shimmer swept over the weapon's bleak blades, highlighting its symbols, weakened, seeking sustenance. The core dimmed just a fraction, caught anew in the dance between light and dark, between life and annihilation.

Sethi eyed the core. Malignance swarmed through his eyes. A blink. It faded, and he was Sethi again. He turned to Thoth, a shear of regret slid over his features.

"You are too late."

"I failed you," Thoth said. Defeat washed over him, bleak, cold. "I could have had the ship ready sooner, yet I did not. I *chose* this."

Sethi dropped his gaze to the jihn and eyed its edges as they awakened, drinking of the core's power, soaking themselves anew with hate. "You underestimated its power." He tilted his head at the wall, where the gold-obsidian corridor had been. "Even in there."

Thoth blinked. A dark suspicion slammed through the agony of his guilt. "Within the tower, the jihn's power must be contained, unless . . . no." He cut a look back up at Sethi, who regarded him, impassive, waiting while he worked it out. "You knew. All this time, you knew." He staggered, dumbfounded by the depth of Sethi's deception. "You never intended to go to Surru."

A wash of darkness rippled through his eyes, hardening the lines of his jaw and mouth, altering him. Another blink, and Sethi—the one Thoth knew—looked back at him. The harshness of his profile faded. "I—" Sethi looked down at the jihn in his hand. Confusion sheared his features. "No. *I* intended to go. I *wanted* to go."

"Urhi-Teshub was right," Thoth breathed. "So long as you remained here. We were *never* safe." Horror crawled over him. He eyed the core, weakening by the heartbeat. He had not come back to check on the cores since the day Sethi had asked him to refit Istara's ship. All of his attention had been fixed on that pointless project, which had kept him away from where he should have been. "*You* have been empowering the jihn," he said, backing away, seeking to distance himself from himself, from the magnitude of his error—from the fate he had bequeathed the gods. "And in return," Thoth went on, dogged, unable to stop himself from unraveling the terrible threads of his destiny, "the jihn fed the darkness within you until you could overcome the suppression of the shield." He sagged against the wall, overwhelmed by the enormity of his responsibility. "A perfect feedback loop." He cut a look at the fading light of the core, as it endured, valiant against the onslaught of the jihn's hunger. "And now—the shield will fall, just as you intended."

He felt Sethi's eyes on him. He met his look. Malevolence coursed through the corrupted god, cold, brutal.

The core's rotation slowed to a crawl. Its cerulean light dimmed, then brightened, calling for sustenance from its siblings. A surge of brilliance erupted from its heart. It washed over Thoth, pure, clean, white, soaked in perfection, and slammed into the jihn.

A piercing cry, faint with distance came from the weapon. Its rising dark faded. One beat. Two. The core began to rotate again. Thoth held his breath, willing the cores and the power of the complex to overcome the thing. A surge of blue-white light swarmed down the blades of the jihn into its heart. It darkened and fell silent. Hope saturated Thoth. A beat later, the jihn's corrupted symbols ignited. A blinding flash soaked Thoth's vision, imprinting perfect copies of them against the walls of his mind.

His vision dancing with the imprints of the hateful markings, he pushed himself free of the wall as the core stuttered to a halt. Its light dimmed, rapid, until only half its power remained. Its beat went on, weakened, subdued. The shield remained, just. Thoth stared at the diminished core, at the monumental power the jihn possessed. The jihn's blades erupted in a wash of silvered light.

An aura of violence swam over the god of war, reshaping his features and tainting the slant of his lips. He glared at Thoth, baleful. Hatred soaked him. He swept the jihn down.

Thoth cried out, fell back against the wall. The silence of the jihn's obsidian blade clove a molten path through his heart and into his soul. Anguish saturated him. The metallic, heated burn of blood filled his senses, soaked his throat, slid over his teeth.

The jihn left him. A pull tugged at him, yanked him free of his body. He looked back at himself, a ruined, broken, bloodied thing, his torso torn open, a grisly furrow of bone and viscera bathed in the faint light of the dying core. He watched a tear escape, track through the blood on his face. Grief assailed him. The cores. The shield. No.

Suffocating under the weight of his guilt he hurtled into the jihn's heart, tumbled past barren cliffs of misery and hopelessness into a pit of darkness. The horror of non-existence slammed into him. With his light trapped within the jihn, he would remain aware, condemned to a living death, locked within a weapon crafted of the deepest of evil. The torment of the souls trapped inside the jihn bled through him, became a part of him. Darkness surrounded him, impenetrable. Endless.

Thoth?

A voice. Soft, feminine, soaked in despair. A void bereft of hope pressed down on him. He reached out. Nothing. He had no hands. No eyes. No voice. He only had his awareness. He tried again, enduring the hunger of the jihn's evil, its oppression. Its eternity.

Arinna?

The agony of her sorrow, her loneliness, her brutal fate rammed into him.

Help me.

I am here, he cried. But she was gone. Her existence slipped away from him as quick as it had arrived, subsumed by the seething dark, roiling with the endless beat of awareness without escape. Its grip crushed him. A thousand thoughts coursed through him, circled him, accused him. He screamed and bled silence. No. It would be unbearable to go on this way forever, a prisoner of his mind, trapped within a miasma of eternal, inescapable suffering. He begged for the Creator's light. Darkness answered.

❋   ❋   ❋

The distant roar of a ship's engine cut out. Ahmen slipped deeper into the shadow of a pillar, his attention fixed on the opening leading from the corridor into the courtyard to where the mirror stood, innocent, quiet.

Since Sethi's arrival, the mirror had become Ahmen's sole occupation. As his flesh work to knit itself back together, he sat before the mirror through the scorching days and lonely nights, waiting, patient, vigilant, dispatching Marduk's warriors before they even knew where they were. Then, two nights ago, the mirror fell silent. Its abrupt somnolence unnerved Ahmen. He waited as the days and nights passed, his uneasiness growing, paired with dread.

He cut a quick look up at the night sky, its stars far brighter than before. The shield remained, though only a faint glimmer coated the canopy, a shadow of its former glory. A short while ago, within the mirror's reflection, the shield had flickered and dimmed. He had stood and scanned the sky, waiting for the shield to return to its former state, willing it to have been the tinkering of Thoth. But it did not. Instead, it continued to dim. And now—

A heavy tread came from the furthest end of the corridor, determined, purposeful, heading straight for the courtyard. Ahmen tightened his hold on his weapon, his instincts hauling on him, warning him to stay back.

Sethi emerged from the corridor into the starlit courtyard, his chest and arms splattered in blood, the jihn once more in his possession. The weapon's bleak presence slammed into Ahmen. Along its dark blades, ripples of pale blue light undulated, the symbols flaring each time the light passed over them. He braced himself for its onslaught, for the despair, the rage, the guilt. It came, insidious, sliding between the cracks of his mind. He resisted, willing himself to bear it.

Sethi came to a halt just before the mirror, his chest rose and fell, his breathing ragged. He turned and scanned the courtyard, the fractals against his chest moving, seamless. A glint of tears sheared through his eyes.

He reached into the folds of his kilt and yanked something free. The dull gleam of gold caught Ahmen's eyes. Sethi set it on the ground beside the mirror. He stared at it for a heartbeat, redolent with grief and regret.

"I have lost the battle," he rasped. "It is over."

The jihn's symbols ignited. With a roar of anguish, he threw his head back, the muscles of his chest and arms taut from his inner battle. The fractals on his chest ceased their rotation, then juddered back to life, erratic. The jihn's light seethed toward the portal, seeking relief from the lingering oppression of the shield. Sethi lowered his head. Darkness poured into his eyes. He slammed his palm against the mirror. Its surface rippled. The stars' reflections faded as the portal coalesced into Meresamun's suite in—Ahmen blinked. He eased nearer the pillar, clenching his teeth, enduring the brutal, grinding accusations of the jihn's subdued presence. *That* was not Perev—

Sethi pushed his arm in up to his elbow. Light poured over him, bathing the courtyard in pale white light. He plunged into the opening, his profile streaming into a sleet of light before it surged into the portal, leaving nothing but the residue of his presence behind. A heartbeat passed, enormous, loaded with the weight of Sethi's departure. The portal's light faded. Darkness slid over the courtyard. Silence.

Ahmen eased out from behind the pillar and went to the mirror. Gone was the portal's destination. He glared at the mirror, blameless in the faint light of the stars, hating Marduk for his cunning. His reflection glared back at him, an ugly mess of half-healed flesh and half-exposed tendon and muscle. He bent to collect the item Sethi had left behind. From beneath a thick coating of congealed blood, a pair of golden serpents entwined a stave. He rubbed the blood away from their faces. Istara's pendant glinted back at him in the starlight, mournful.

The scream of another ship tore through the desolate silence and came to a skidding halt on the terrace. Ahmen wrapped his fingers around the pendant, bleak. It was too late. Sethi was gone, and with him, the jihn. He lifted his gaze to the sky, where the shield glimmered, faint, its web so thin in places he could almost see through it. Soon, very soon, he sensed Sethi would return, and when he did, there would be no reprieve. None.

✳   ✳   ✳

A thundering slammed into Sethi. Intense pressure gripped him. Disorientation assaulted him. The portal's light faded. His vision cleared. He turned. The mirror from Ninsunu's suite stood strapped against the dark gray metal of Marduk's warship. To its left, the door to the chamber with the regeneration devices. He caught hold of the edge of a crate and steadied himself. Down a corridor lined with rows of hulking crates, their faint blue heartbeats blinking in the near-darkness, a familiar pool of light beckoned.

He left the mirror and headed for the spiral stairway. Freed from the oppression of Anki's shield, the jihn's ravenous power coursed through him, rejuvenating him, reigniting his hatred for Istara and the shield she had had Thoth create to control him.

He reached the bottom of the stairwell. A thought occurred. Marduk had been decimating the cities of Tholis. He paused and cast a look over his shoulder at the mirror. Five long days ago he had passed through it. The pieces assembled, created a whole. Marduk believed he had lost his commander so he had abandoned Perev to begin his assault on the gods, had taken the mirror with him in case Sethi found a way to return. He eyed the jihn, loathe to leave it behind after their long separation, and yet, after Aiya's reaction to it, he did not relish a repeat of her trauma. He returned to the regeneration chamber, punched the code into the panel and locked the weapon inside.

Back at the stairs, he took them two at a time. He had gained considerable intelligence while he had been oppressed by the shield, Marduk would be pleased. He emerged from the stairwell. The walls of the cabin were opaque, lit in a soft white light. The door to the flight deck stood closed. Aiya sat on a divan with the king of Ikalur and another woman—the queen, he presumed from the golden diadem tangled in her hair. Both the king and queen's once-regal finery clung to them, stiff with dried blood. Neither looked at him. They sat, quiet, blank, biddable, their eyes on the closed door, reminding him of the devoted obedience of Marduk's steward.

Aiya came to her feet, her gown torn and stained, her hair disheveled, and her face swollen from weeping. A purple bruise marred her shoulder. She stood before him, trembling, broken. He took her into his arms. Wretched, she clung to him and wept, the events of the past five days unfolding between the shuddering breaths of her misery. She told of entire cities decimated with a single strike; the king and queen of Ikalur's brutal, bloody enslavement; her confession to Marduk to save her life; Anki's golden shield, impervious to the violence sweeping out from Marduk's ship. The days spent traveling across the heavens, the endless hours only punctuated by Marduk's savagery and destruction.

At last, she quieted. He gifted her a kiss and led her back to her seat. She sank onto it, numb. Exhaustion ravaged her elegant features. With a murmur of reassurance, he went to the door of the flight deck and punched in the code.

In the faint light of the console's illumination, Ninsunu turned, her eyes snagging on the blood staining his arms and chest. A wall of dread slid over her.

Marduk cut a look over his shoulder, granted him a cool look. "Whose blood is that?"

"Thoth's," Sethi muttered, catching Ninsunu's tremulous exhalation of relief, her hands knotting into fists against her lap.

Marduk pressed a series of buttons. "And the others?" he asked, bland.

Sethi folded his arms over his chest. "Alive. The shield suppressed my will, it took some time to overcome it enough to retrieve the jihn and get out."

Marduk said nothing, though disapproval oozed from him. Silence soaked the flight deck.

Sethi glanced at the screen in the center of the console, backlit against the dark of the star-clad night. "How far are we from Imaru?"

Marduk slid a look at the screen. "Imaru is of little interest to me. Rhewyn has proven useful in your absence. Rzhev is a new nation. A godless people. They do not have a portal."

"Imaru hates the gods," Sethi said. When Marduk ignored him, checking the readouts on the various screens, Sethi tried again. "They hate *these* gods."

Marduk swiped the nearest screen through several panes, disinterested. "And?"

"And they will join you if you offer them the power to avenge themselves against what the gods did to them." He tilted his head toward the back of the ship. "We have the mirror and what is contained in the crates. If you take the shield down, the gods and their allies will not be able to stand against us."

"The shield resisted my strongest weapons." Marduk's focus returned to the console. "The only way to defeat the gods is to destroy the world. If I cannot have it, neither will they. I have done this once before, with success. They take pity on the mortals, and leave. I can wait for the world to heal."

Ninsunu rose, brittle with unhappiness, the flight deck's shadows deepening those around her eyes. She slipped past Sethi and went into the cabin. Sethi took her empty seat.

"You might want to try again."

"Try *what* again?"

"Your weapons against the shield." Sethi endured Marduk's acrimonious silence. "The jihn drained a vast amount of the shield's power. It is no longer what it was anymore. And Thoth, the one who created it—"

Marduk's amber eyes flicked to Sethi, granted him a glimmer of approval. "Is gone," he finished. The slant of his mouth shifted, darkened. "Have Ninsunu return to her seat," he said, his hands moving over the controls, re-configuring the flight path, and setting the parameters to fire the ion drive.

Sethi rose, the map on the screen tilted, recalculating the route away from Chern toward Rzhev. Satisfaction shot through him. He left the flight deck to its faint illumination and joined Aiya.

After a beat's hesitation, Ninsunu returned to her consort, a shadow in the quiet cerulean light. Marduk regarded her as she sank onto the seat beside him, the sharp edges of his ruthlessness fading. He leaned over and fastened the restraints against her, gentle, his gloved fingers moving over her, a caress. The obsidian metal of his palm caught her chin and tilted her face up to his. He kissed her, soft. Trapped within the restraints, Ninsunu sagged, succumbed to him. Their kiss deepened. The door slid closed.

Sethi pulled Aiya against him and cradled her head against his chest, readying her for the grip of the drive. For them, there would be no restraints.

The ion's brutal thrust tore through the ship. Pressure rammed into him, brutal, excruciating. He bore down, concentrating all his strength on withstanding its force. In his hold, Aiya quaked, silent, enduring. He tightened his grip on her as the curve of the world fell away and they screamed into the heavens where they skimmed a path across the stars and Elati spun beneath them, stately, calm, ripe for the taking.

It began heartbeat she woke to the scream of a ship tearing out of the bay, a downward spiral of pain, regret, and sorrow. But *this*. This went beyond the agony of forever losing her consort to the darkness.

Taut with grief and ragged with guilt, Istara knelt before Thoth's savaged body. His chest had been torn asunder, his heart cleaved in two, his ribs shattered. Blood pooled beneath him, still warm from the heat of his stolen life. It touched the hem of her gown, stained it with her crime. She lifted her eyes from the brutality of his demise to his face. His eyes were still open, fixed on the faint heartbeat of the core. A single tear had tracked its way through the blood splattering his face.

She rose, gripping the bloodstained pendant so tight its points dug into her flesh and drew blood. With a quiet creak of leather, Urhi-Teshub joined her. His hand found hers. A gentle squeeze. She waited for his recriminations, his vindication, the words she deserved to hear—wanted to hear. He said nothing. He gazed at Thoth, cloaked in sorrow.

Pain sheared through her palm. She loosened her hold on the pendant. A shimmer rippled through it. Another followed, then another, each pulse stronger, like the sacred beat of a heart.

A burst of brilliance erupted from it, bathing the space in pure, white light.

The golden symbols on the wall facing her rotated and slid away. The outline of an opening took shape. In total silence, it separated from the wall and fell inward. Further in, ashlars continued to fold into themselves, seamless, improbable, opening the way into the tower, the ceiling and floor transforming into a glossy obsidian, and the walls a soft, warm gold.

The tunnel continued to stretch away, diminishing with distance. Istara turned her attention back to the pendant. Its light pulsed, alive, a star within her palm. She touched its crown, reverent. "The Creator said I would know when the right time would be to use this." She lifted her gaze to the faded core, its once-breathtaking cerulean light a mere whisper, its power barely able to sustain the shield, then down to Thoth, the one who had been her counselor, her friend, gone, forever—because of her.

Her heart clenched, harsh with its chorus of accusations. If only she had let Sethi go, Thoth would still be alive, the jihn would still be within the tower, and the shield would not be compromised. In her determination to send her consort to Surru, she had blinded herself to the evil within him, and had cost the gods everything.

She pulled free of Urhi-Teshub's grip and faced the opening of the tunnel. "*Now* is the time." She stepped toward the tunnel's threshold, determination girding her. She would remedy her error, would claw back what she had lost, would never again put her heart over the needs of others. Whatever she would face, she would face with courage, no matter the cost.

Urhi-Teshub caught hold of her arm. "Horus knows where you must go."

Istara nodded. She would make no more errors, would not fail the gods again.

"Bring him to me."

Urhi-Teshub backed away, his eyes hard on hers, seeking her pain, ready to offer consolation. She looked back at the opening, his solace refused. There was no consolation. There was only what was to come and whether she would have the strength to face it, alone. Her protector held his ground for a heartbeat, then departed, the lightning glint of his ax gilding the walls with his stormy light.

In the quiet of her solitude, she knelt beside Thoth and took his hand in hers. Ink stains marred the skin of his thumb and forefinger. She rubbed her fingers against them, seeking his voice, his reassurance, his presence. The silence of his soul clawed at her.

"To lose you . . . it is unbearable," she whispered. Tears coated her eyes. She pressed her lips against his fingers, thinking of his deft, precise movements the day he made her *téy*. "You will not have died in vain. I swear it. I will defeat him. I will conquer the darkness. Elati shall live in light." She bent her head, and against Thoth's thin shoulder, she wept, her tears staining his chest, stars against his broken, sundered heart.

The tunnel went on, endless, monotonous. Istara looked back. The opening to the pyramid was long gone, lost to the steep decline. Ahead, the passage leveled off. It cut through the foundation of the complex as straight as a spear until it vanished, lost to a dark point. Claustrophobia clawed.

Horus paced before her, leading the way, his presence distant, as always, and his words spare, as though he resented the expense of speaking to her. At her side, Urhi-Teshub. His eyes moved over the smooth gold and obsidian planes of the tunnel, distrustful. Gripped within his fist, the haft of his ax, its blades flickered, sporadic, his power suppressed in a place where gods did not belong.

They pressed on, walking in subdued silence. Within her hand, the pendant pulsed, gentle, encouraging her, the purity of its light anomalous in the dense, oppressive atmosphere of the corridor.

"At last," Horus muttered. "The tower."

Istara peered down the length of the tunnel. She saw nothing. After a few steps more, it came, sudden—a brilliant well of golden light bathed the end of the corridor with its promise. She quickened her pace, eager to be free of the tunnel, to be anywhere but within its inexplicable, suffocating confines.

They proceeded through a narrower tunnel, awash with golden light until they reached the threshold of the tower's cavernous girth. The floor sheared away from her, black, sleek, endless, humbling. She gazed into it the tower's depths, both awed and fearful, sensing it contained power far beyond anything she could comprehend—beyond anything Thoth could have comprehended.

To either side of the opening, golden walls curved away, diminishing with distance. She looked up, then wished she hadn't. An impossible height roared away, eldritch, fathomless. She averted her gaze, seeking the other side of the tower, the distance shoved her back, vast, improbable, unseeable.

Within the tower's midst, a seething sphere of golden light rotated, suspended upon a thin beam of darkness. It refused to touch her eyes, each time she tried to look at it, it reappeared elsewhere along the beam of darkness, both present and not, the whole of it a mind-numbing dichotomy.

From the corner of her eye, she caught the speed of its rotation, both dignified and rapid, its size a contradiction, all at once massive and minuscule. Golden tendrils snapped out of it, frantic. They lashed against the walls, as though seeking their escape. Within its depths, a plethora of stars blistered and burned out, their lights dying by the hundreds, thousands.

"What is it?" she breathed.

Horus shook his head, his features taut, harsh in the tower's unnerving light. "I do not know," he said. "Nor do I want to know."

"Whatever it is," Urhi-Teshub said, "it appears to be in its death throes."

Horus turned to face Istara. He tilted his head toward the vast space within. "Once we cross this threshold, we leave behind everything which orders the realms of mortals and gods. Time and space flow differently within the tower. It is . . . unpleasant."

Istara glanced back into the tower. Her eyes slid over the sphere as it slipped away and reared over them from a great height, its brilliance increasing and dimming, steady, a dying heartbeat. She met Horus's eyes. "Tell me what I need to do."

"I will guide you to where there is the impression of a seal in the wall. The relic must be placed against it."

Istara unfolded her fingers from the pendant. Its clear, white light streamed over her gown, blazed against the light of her stars. "And then?" she asked.

Horus rubbed the back of his hand against his mouth. Uneasiness seeped from him. "I do not know. The Creator only said this: *For the darkness to fall, the goddess must rise.*"

"The goddess must rise?" Urhi-Teshub repeated. He eyed his weapon, his power flickering over the blades, faint. "The only way to defeat Marduk is to destroy him, with weapons. With war. What can a single goddess do against his power? Nothing."

Horus folded his arms over his chest and looked into the tower's expanse, his gaze turned inward. Unhappiness surrounded him. "Perhaps," he said. "But who can know the mind of the Creator? He made the jihn." He gestured at the improbable sphere, which was there yet not there. "He made *that.*"

"And this," Istara murmured, her gaze following the familiar lines of the pendant, recalling the broiling day in Tarhuntassa when the chief surgeon had given it to her—a relic of the Creator. A flood of memories sleeted through her, highlighting her path from the capital of Hatti, through Kadesh, Egypt, and Babylon, to her death and resurrection at Surru. The pendant flared. Its light scythed a path through her, a sunbeam of clarity parting the storm clouds within her soul. "Once," she began, her heart quavering, awakening, "I believed I was a token on the game board of men, then of gods, always moved against my will." She looked up, met Urhi-Teshub's quiet look. "But if I could go back to the day I was gifted this, and knew all I know now, I would have done everything the same. It is who I am, who I was born to be. Though I could not see it until now, I have ever been the master of my destiny." She eyed the sphere's bursts of dying light reflecting against the obsidian floor, sensed what awaited her beyond the seal would be her darkest battle—perhaps her final one. She folded her fingers over the pendant. "And now, I choose this."

Horus eyed her, the faintest glimmer of admiration touched his eyes. He held out his hand to her. She placed hers within the warmth of his palm. He looked down at her hand in his, the steady stream of her starlight flowing over his fingers. His eyes closed. The muscles of his jaw clenched. "Do not let go until we reach the seal," he said, rough. "No matter what."

She held on, despite the disorientation, the distortion of time, and her rising fear Horus had lost his way and they would never escape the shifting, dense morass which pulled at her senses, destroyed her thoughts, and hauled on her sanity. She forced herself to concentrate on putting one foot in front of the other. A thousand steps. Ten thousand, their passage through the tower relentless, punishing in its endless, hopeless sameness. Ahead and behind, the wall's slow curve stretched into an impossible distance with no end in sight. She forced herself to keep pace with Horus, sensing the passage of time fleeting past her, a morass of hours, years, days. Exhaustion clawed at her, and her mind fragmented, savaged by the chaos of the shredded constants of time and space.

The sphere followed her, haunted her, both there and not there, its paradoxical presence tormenting her. Ever at the edge of her vision, its golden light rotated and slid along the pillar of darkness, at once both present and distant, an impossible, brutal anomaly. Against the floor's polished surface, the reflections of its implosions of starlight lessened. One by one, the golden tendrils slid back into the sphere.

The tower's chamber darkened. An unnatural dusk swarmed over the sphere's fading golden light. She dared not look at it, to see what it had become. It was enough to just walk, to endure the misery of her existence in the increasing darkness. Ahead, the seductive curve of the wall beckoned to her, taunted her, maddened her.

Behind, Urhi-Teshub met her despair, his shuttered look loaded with suffering. She pressed on, deeper into the place where no god should tread, willing herself to hold on to the last threads of her sanity, trying to recall why she was there. Darkness clouded her mind. There was only the tower. Its existence consumed her. There had never been anything else. There could be nothing else.

Horus came to a halt. Istara stumbled up against him. He held steady, his face a mask of endurance. He lifted her hand to the wall, and slid her palm up its frictionless, cool surface. He met her eyes, his loaded with meaning. He let her go and backed away, his eyes closed, grinding the heels of his palms against his temples.

Istara stared at her hand pressed against the seamless surface of the wall. Something important was meant to happen here. She tried to remember. Silence filled her mind, brutal with the weight of the tower's crushing presence. Her thoughts fleeted around her, jumbled, nonsensical, distorted. She held still, desperate to remember what she was doing there, or why she was touching a golden wall. She looked to the others, hoping they might know. Both leaned against the wall, their chests heaving, their suffering visceral, their eyes unseeing, each locked in their own silent battles.

She slid her hand higher, sweeping her palm against the wall, searching, for what, she didn't know, reaching as high as she could. Nothing. Nothing. Noth—Her fingertips dipped into a groove. A jolt shot through her. This meant something. An indentation in the wall. It was important. Her thoughts clamored, noisy, incoherent, wild. None made sense. She sagged, clinging to the indentation, willing her mind to work, to give her the answer.

From within her other hand, the quiet pulse of the pendant's light focused into a single beam. She lifted it up, her breathing shallow, struggling to make the pieces fit, her thoughts dull, sluggish. The answer flitted before her, quicksilver, an image, it blurred, too rapid to see. She grappled for it, desperate to catch it. As soon as she reached it, it slipped from her hands, and vanished, ephemeral. Darkness took its place.

The pendant blazed brighter, its light sliding up the wall to her other hand. She followed its path, the oppressiveness within her mind intensifying, warning her to stop. She pushed the relic up, her arms heavy as granite. The relic slid over the grooves, crooked. It popped out again.

She shuddered, her arms aching, and clung to the wall, panting, enduring the barrage of thoughts telling her to give up, how it was impossible, she would never succeed. Lifting herself onto her toes, her legs quaking, she tried again, fumbling with the relic until she found the engraved grooves once more. She closed her eyes, held her breath and eased the relic into the seal's engraving.

A clink resonated through her fingers. For a heartbeat, nothing happened. Istara bit her lip and held on, determined, her entire self trembling as she fought to hold the relic steady. Please. Let it end.

A burst of molten light erupted from under the relic. She staggered and clung to it, her eyes streaming, the brilliance of the relic's image searing her mind. A storm of starlight surged from the seal. It plunged past Horus and Urhi-Teshub, a tsunami, drenched with unquenchable power. It swarmed away, transforming the tower's walls into a well of pure, white light.

The indentation vanished. The relic slid back into her palm. Istara looked up, rapt, as the weight of the tower melted into light. In the distance: a pinprick of darkness. It opened, widening with each heartbeat. She stared, incredulous, as the night sky, faint with its shield and glittering with stars bore down on her. Strange. The tower reached far into the heavens. It should be impossible to see the sky. The distance shrank. The gap widened, swarmed with stars.

She turned to the others. Nothingness glared at her. Urhi-Teshub and Horus were gone, as though they had never been. The tower imploded in an explosion of white. In its wake, darkness swept in, a malignant tide. A shadow slinked over her shoulders, cold, malevolent. She turned, ragged with dread, clutching the relic, defensive, against her breast.

In the center of the tower's brilliance, the sphere continued to rotate, no longer golden, but opaque, soaked in impenetrable darkness. All which remained of the sphere's golden light was a thin vertical beam—the beam which had once been black.

Dark tendrils slid from the sphere, probing, searching. One writhed toward her, massive, sleek, its scales metallic, its presence reeking of malignance. Its tentacles probed the hem of her gown, tasted Thoth's blood. She held herself still, her heart thundering as it wrapped itself around her legs and torso, its touch sharp, icy, and pale as death. It lifted her from the ground, its touch numbing her. The obsidian depths of the sphere loomed before her, a well of nothingness. A void. She closed her eyes as the tendril slid through the wall, carrying her with it away from the light, and into a realm of infinite dark.

❋　❋　❋

An explosion of light slammed into Urhi-Teshub, sent him hurtling toward the largest pyramid. Its bulk reared up before him, implacable, unforgiving. Solid. He forced himself to go limp.

His shoulder hit the pyramid. Bones snapped. He gritted his teeth, pain screaming a path through him as he tumbled down its side, blistering waves of fire strafing his ruined shoulder. The base of the pyramid came and went. He slid to a ragged halt.

Panting, nauseous, he lay still. Brutal spears of agony prodded his shoulder. Breathing hurt. Everything hurt. He forced himself to sit, bellowing at the cost. From within his torso, golden tendrils bloomed and surged into his shoulder. He waited, focusing on his breathing, enduring his pain, knowing it would take time. He willed Istara and Horus to have fared better than he.

Light footsteps hurried across the ashlars. He looked up, locked in misery. Sekhmet knelt before him, his ax in her hand. She set it down beside him. Her golden eyes met his. A faint smile dusted her lips. "Some things never change."

Urhi-Teshub glared at her. "Meaning?"

Her gaze flicked behind him. "Wherever the storm god goes, chaos follows."

He turned to see what she meant, endured another strafe of agony. "The tower," he breathed. "It's gone. All of it." Nothing of its construction remained. A vast emptiness screamed from where its walls and vast buttresses once loomed. He picked up his ax and hefted himself to his feet, ignoring the deep shafts of pain boring through his shoulder.

He eyed what remained, subdued. At last, he said, "I didn't think things could get any worse. I was wrong."

Sekhmet came to her feet. "I do not think this is what anyone expected."

Urhi-Teshub said nothing. Foreboding consumed him. No longer did a golden sphere rotate on a thin beam of black. Now, all which remained was a liquid pillar of utter darkness. It stretched all the way up into the heavens, infinite.

"Where are the others?" Urhi-Teshub scanned the complex. Faint with distance, he caught movement near to where the tower's wall would have been. A figure staggered to their feet. Urhi-Teshub narrowed his eyes, recognized the kilt. Horus. He searched the rest of the area. Emptiness shouted at him. His uncertainty deepened to dread. "Where is Istara?" Fear lanced him, harsh. "The relic?"

"I do not know," Sekhmet answered. Her eyes touched his, soft. "Only you and Horus returned."

❋ ❋ ❋

Istara opened her eyes. Impenetrable darkness flooded her senses, impaled her eyes, poured into her mouth, and deafened her ears, its leaden weight excruciating, immutable.

Disorientation clobbered her. Beneath, a smooth, cool surface. Wary, she pulled herself to her knees, her instincts wailing, recoiling. She closed her eyes, then opened them again. Not a single glimmer of light broke the obsidian shear, not even from herself. Her hands shaking, she hung the relic around her neck and pressed her hands together, seeking to rekindle her light. Nothing.

A primal stab of fear lanced through her. Perhaps she was no longer a goddess anymore, her light extinguished by her transition into the dark. Her fear deepening into terror, she ran her hands along the length of her arms, chafing them, desperate to be wrong, to reawaken her light. Silence soaked her. Powerlessness assailed her.

In this place she was nothing, no one. Her fingers drifted to the weight of the pendant against her breastbone. She wrapped her hand around its stave, seeking its power, its connection to the Creator. It hung in her hand, quiet, meaningless, caught in the crushing silence of the void. Against the inky pressure of dark, a whisper of air stirred the tendrils of hair against her face. She stiffened. Her heart pounded, tight, aching with terror.

A flare of light slammed into her vision. She recoiled, her eyes streaming from the sudden onslaught of a red-orange glow. She peered through her fingers. A brazier, its basin black, burned with dark fuel, its glow sinister, malevolent, and devoid of warmth.

A rustle of silk. A figure moved before her, elegant, screaming of incalculable ruthlessness.

"Arise daughter," a woman said, low, commanding, seductive. "Join me."

Istara lowered her hand from her eyes. Dread circled her. She rose and met the gaze of the other. Horror sluiced over her. Clad in darkness, her eyes bleak hollows of obsidian, Baalat looked at her, arch, haughty, cold. Only the merest residue remained of the one who had sacrificed her light so Istara might live. It caught against the edge of Istara's vision, ephemeral, scouring her heart with grief.

"Are you here because you gave up your light to me?" Istara asked, guilt coruscating her soul.

A flicker of a perfect brow, a heartbeat of consideration. "Perhaps. Though it is of little importance now." She walked past the brazier and bled into the dense dark. Her voice drifted back. "Come."

Istara remained where she was, unwilling to leave the bleak pool of light.

"Ah." Baalat said, her disembodied voice unnerving Istara. "Of course. Your eyes have not yet been opened." Ahead, a dull glow erupted within a brazier, followed by another further down, then another, and another. They stretched into the endless dark, a chorus of murky lights. Baalat met Istara's eyes. In the glow of the brazier a liquid tendril of darkness slithered through her eyes. "Better now?" Her gaze fell to the relic against Istara's neck. Her lips thinned. She turned, the material of her gown transparent, hiding nothing. Raw sensuality bled from her, as though she had just left the bed of a lover, her womb still drenched in his seed.

Istara hesitated. Raw malevolence bore down on her, pressed its stain into her soul. The brazier beside her folded into non-existence in total silence, a phantom, a lie. Darkness rushed into its wake. Baalat continued her procession, a specter. As she passed, the braziers crushed themselves back into the void. In her wake, desolation.

Istara's fingers once more went to the relic. She longed for its quiet pulse in this bleak, soulless place. It slept on, silent. Another brazier shuddered into oblivion. Baalat did not look back, she did not need to. She departed with the arrogance of a tyrant, knowing Istara would follow, would flee the darkness for the wan comfort of the fires. Another brazier died. Istara fled toward the poisoned light.

Her soul aching, hollow, Istara moved along the row of braziers. The once-goddess of healing walked on, her eyes unseeing, her face a cold, empty mask. Darkness swarmed after them, a bleak tide. They passed ten, twenty, fifty braziers in their progression through the well of black. In the distance, the line of braziers came to an end. Just before the last one, Baalat came to a halt. She turned. A monolith slid up from out of the floor, as wide as two doors. Around it, nothing, open space. Istara peered behind it. Emptiness yawned. Nothing adorned its face. It loomed over her, oppressive.

Baalat pressed her palm to its center. She cut a look at Istara, her features macabre in the faint light. "My lord has granted me the power to prepare for your arrival." A vertical line slid away from her touch, separating the monolith in two. A heartbeat later, the structure parted and opened in total silence.

Within, lit by a dozen braziers glowing a dull orange, an elegant suite. Everything was black, the low tables, cushioned divans, vases, rugs, and silken bed upon its raised platform. On a black table, a pair of goblets and a wine pitcher gleamed, their metallic surfaces glinting in the bleak light. Baalat swept past her and went to the far end of the suite where she passed through a silken hanging. The brazier outside the bizarre door succumbed to the dark. The doors began to close. Again, Istara followed, powerless, a lamb to its slaughter.

"Join me, daughter." From behind the silken hangings, Istara could just make out Baalat's silhouette, the darker shade of her existence against the thin wall of material. Her back to Istara, Baalat lifted her hand and beckoned Istara to her. "You failed to cleanse what is in Sethi, and now you believe you have lost him forever." She turned, a shadow. "But there is another way. Let me show you. Let me set you free."

Her heart leaden, Istara parted the hangings. Baalat stepped aside. A table stood before her. Upon it, a large, flat basin filled with an inky liquid. The liquid stirred at Istara's approach, coalesced into an image. Under a sky of night, and surrounded by burning braziers, Sethi stood outside Marduk's ship, watching as the crates within were hefted out and arranged into long rows. Istara leaned closer, her skin prickling. Despite the shadows cast by the braziers' flames making it difficult to see, there was something familiar about the place. One of the men unloading the ship passed near her view. She blinked. A chill slivered through her. She knew that garb. Gold-embroidered, dark green silken tunics. Leather leggings, a pair of long, thin, curved swords crossed over their backs.

The livery of Imaru's palace guard.

"He is in Rzhev," she breathed. "Why?"

Baalat smiled, quiet, her profile clad in secrets. "Sethi cannot fail. With the jihn once again in his possession, and Marduk's army behind him, the gods will fall. But we—" she cut a look at Istara, her expression haughty, drowning in arrogance, "—have been chosen. We have been granted a second chance."

Istara's gaze gravitated back to Sethi, her heart betraying her. His presence hauled on her, a lodestone. Brutality seeped from him. On his chest, the fractals jerked, jagged, broken, and in his hand, the jihn's blades seethed, hungry, flaring each time one of the guards walked past. Even through the distance separating them, she could sense its evil, its desire to annihilate the light. She turned her attention back to the crates. So many. With Sethi's departure, the damage he had wrought against the shield had been critical. And without Thoth—

"It will not take much to bring down Thoth's precious shield," Baalat remarked, exposing Istara's thoughts. She lifted her hand to examine her fingernails. A dusting of ash covered her fingertips and nails. A tracery of lines darkened the length of her fingers and laced the back of her hand, veins of black. Istara looked away.

"Your thoughts are mine now, daughter, as is the greatest desire of your heart." She dipped her fingertips into the basin's pool. The image of Sethi slid away, and merged into another, of her suite in Anki.

Upon her opulent bed, Sethi held her against him, her face in his hands, his lips against her mouth, his hips moving as one with hers as they made love. She dragged her eyes over him, drinking in the sight of him, her heart aching as he kissed her, tender. It was the last time he had taken her. She lifted her eyes back to Baalat who continued to watch, expressionless. "He belongs to the dark now. He will never return to you." Her eyes slid up from the basin, paused at the relic against Istara's neck. "To the light."

Her fingers touched the basin's surface once more. The image melted away, and formed anew. Another bed, the one in Marduk's ship. Sethi made love to another, with equal passion. Edarru. No, Aiya. Nausea slammed into Istara. She turned away. Baalat's tainted fingers caught her chin, forced her to look, to watch Sethi and Aiya as they writhed, locked in their passionate embrace. "No. See the one he has been forced to take in your stead because you are stubborn and cling to what must fade—because you abandoned him."

"I have not abandoned him," Istara said, yanking Baalat's fingers away. She wiped the back of her hand over her jaw, seeking to cleanse herself from the stink of Baalat's corruption. "He was taken from *me*."

Another secret smile. Baalat's fingers returned to the basin, stirred its surface, languid. "Perhaps. Or, he has been protected, just as you are now. You could be with him again, his consort. For eternity." The surface rippled, awakened anew.

Unable to stop herself, Istara looked down. Against a bleak, dark cliff, a palace of black jutted out, it walls and pillars veined with gold. Upon its highest terrace, she stood with Sethi, diadems of obsidian crowning their brows, their eyes no longer gold, but soaked in shadow. They stood at the terrace's edge, sharing a single dark cup. Her consort's kilt was no longer white but the deepest of black, and her gown no longer shimmered with the light of the stars, but rippled with tendrils of darkness. Through its transparent material, golden disks clung to her nipples, and around her neck, a black leather collar cut into her throat. Down the back of her spine, a gold-embossed leash hung from it. Sethi held it in his hand, wrapped around his fist, possessive, dominant.

Beneath their gold sandals, a vast city sprawled into the distance, its black granite villas, walls, and towers shadowed against the dense roil of storm clouds hanging low in the sky. Everywhere she looked, life wilted on the edge of existence. Silence soaked the land.

"This is my alternative? To live in darkness, possessed like an animal?" Istara tore her gaze from the nightmare. "I would rather be alone than face such an existence."

"That is because you see with eyes which are blinded to the truth," Baalat said.

Istara turned to her, incredulous. "If anyone is blind, it is you."

Baalat lifted an elegant eyebrow, undaunted, and continued, "Are the wars of men and gods not fought over possession? They fight for kingdoms, slaves, empires, queens. Power." Her gaze flicked once more to the pendant. A curve of distaste ghosted her lips. "That thing is a lie. For far too long, *he* has suppressed the truth the darkness possesses. Instead he buried it, locked it away, allowing himself the freedom to have all the control, unchallenged and unfettered. You have only ever seen what *he* wants you to see. And now his game draws to an end, a game he could never win because the dark cannot be defeated. Soon now, *he* will fall, and the dark will rise." She met Istara's eyes. "And we will rise with it."

Istara looked down at the silenced pendant. She plucked it from her chest and held it up toward Baalat. "*This* is a lie?"

The once-goddess took a step back, distanced herself from it. She nodded, cool. "Imagine living in a world where there are no wars for possession." She turned her attention back to the basin as its surface darkened, and the image of the dark city vanished. "Where all is at peace because everyone knows their place and accepts their fate. What *he* wants you to believe is each has the power to change their existence to their favor. So men go to war. Thousands die—" she let out a soft laugh, her mockery tangible, "—for a passing thing, a kingdom, a crown. A bauble. *He* is the one who oppresses, because he gives the appearance of hope, where there is none, causing countless innocents to suffer. We are all tied to the game. To *his* game. I have seen it. We are nothing but tokens to him. Disposable. Meaningless."

Istara lowered the pendant. Its weight settled against her chest, its once-reassuring presence tainted by Baalat's disturbing words. "*He?*" she challenged, unsettled afresh at the possibility she might be nothing more than a token in a greater game, her will not her own. "The one who granted you your godhead? The one who gave you another chance to live with your consort? Why not call him by his name—the Creator?"

A tendril of darkness slid through Baalat's eyes, rancid with bitterness. "He has deceived us all. I will never say his name."

"So you choose this instead?" Istara cried. She gestured at the dark-clad suite, rank with its burden of malignance and hate. "You were the goddess of healing, of *life*. And now you extol the virtues of darkness, seeking to convert me to your twisted philosophy by offering an eternity of darkness lashed to the fist of a corrupted god?"

Baalat nodded. "I do." She turned away from the basin and pushed through the silken hangings, took a seat on the nearest divan. "Come. Sit."

Istara sat, the white of her gown a blister against the divan's impenetrable darkness. "Why am I here?"

Baalat's eyes went to the relic again. "If you remove that, you will understand."

Istara caught the pendant in her hand, defensive. "I would rather not."

"As you wish," Baalat answered. She blinked and the suite vanished. Darkness surrounded Istara, suffocating, burying her alive.

"Baalat?" she called, her courage evaporating, abandoning her to the silence of her fate.

Nothingness pressed down on her. She called again. The depth of a void glared back at her. Terror shrieked up her spine, tore her apart. Her hands went to the pendant. She clung to it, endured the fury of her isolation.

Time shuddered past, viscous, hateful. Endless. In the darkest corridors of her mind, Baalat's words took root, flourished, sowed doubt. Istara thought of her and Sethi, rulers of a dark kingdom. Anything would be better than this. Anything. Panting, her hands trembling, she lifted the pendant from her neck. She set it onto the surface beside her, her fingertips lingering against it. The oppression of the void roiled over her, its weight immense. She lifted her fingers and the dark bled away. The suite flickered back into existence as though she had never left. Baalat rose from the divan.

"And now," she said, gentle, holding out her hand, the tips of her fingers no longer black, but golden, "let me show you another way."

Elati's mid-morning sun bore down on Urhi-Teshub. Its rays blistered, relentless, against the ashlars and pyramids of Anki's central complex. Under his leather casing of armor, his flesh broiled, damp, sticky, desperate for its freedom. Ignoring his discomfort, he eyed the liquid pillar of impenetrable black, expanded to almost twice its girth from the night before. Even the brilliance of the sun's light could not escape its clutches. He glared at it, hating it, fearing it, unable to understand it, or its true purpose.

Sekhmet joined him. She gazed at the anomaly pouring into the heavens, subdued.

He cut a look at her. "How go the preparations?"

"The gods are ready," she said, tilting her head toward the line of ships glinting in the heat of the sun, "and the armies of their allies are assembled. Their commanders await your orders."

Urhi-Teshub nodded. He knew he should be pleased by the rapid response of the gods and organization of their allies, yet even as the heat of battle beckoned, his heart betrayed him. A second time he had not protected Istara. He had failed both her and the Creator. She was gone. Obliterated. He could feel it in his bones.

Even after he had taken Sekhmet into his heart, there had remained within him a secret, sheltered place for the one he had once loved beyond all reason. Istara's silence clawed at him.

Loneliness assailed him. Grief skirted his heart. He shoved it back, held it at bay. Not yet. Later. He would build the greatest temple to honor her, its fires would burn day and night. She would never be forgotten. Never.

He turned his back to the loathsome pillar and looked over the assembled armies of the Elatian kingdoms spread across the expanse of the plaza. Forty thousand warriors stood armed and ready to stand with the gods in their confrontation against Marduk. In the gentle breeze, the brilliant hued pennants of the kingdoms of Pres, Chaus, Serde, Saritova, Vinay, Lauca, Dena, Tyratu, Pir, Seri, Enion, and Qatu billowed.

He turned his gaze to the deep blue of the heated skies. Against is blameless depths, the faint glint of the shield's white-gold web rippled, no longer a glorious web of light but a savaged, weakened thing. In places, its frayed lacings strained to hold. He let out a thin exhalation. If the shield fell, Elati's armies would be helpless against Marduk's weapons. They needed to be where he couldn't see them, not out here in the open, wilting in the heat of the morning sun.

He scanned the skies. His instincts sharpened, baleful with warning: *Do not waste time. Prepare.* Throughout the long hours of the night, during his counsel with the gods, he had gleaned much of Marduk's tactics. The oppressor started slow, his strikes loaded with warning, then, when he did not accomplish his aim, he struck fast and with total ruthlessness, using his most devastating weapons. Considering the destruction he had already wrought on the kingdoms of Tholis, Urhi-Teshub had come to the conclusion their enemy wasn't in the mood to use his previous strategy. There would only be this, the gods' last stand.

Grim, Urhi-Teshub eyed the allied armies. His father had had the same number of soldiers for the Battle at Kadesh—for a mortal battle. *These* men would not face men, but Marduk, an immortal shielded in his ship, bearing weapons beyond comprehension, and the corrupted god of war, empowered by a weapon of infinite evil.

Forty thousand men. It wasn't enough. One hundred thousand would not be enough. Urhi-Teshub closed his eyes and forced the despair of his thoughts away. With Istara gone, he must lead—must believe the gods would triumph, and Marduk would at last, fall. He cut his eyes back up to the skies.

"What is he waiting for?" he muttered. "Why does he do *nothing*?" As of dawn, the portals to the kingdoms of Chern still stood, still coursed with men, women, children, and warriors seeking to aid the gods in their war against Elati's oppressor. Yet, after his frenzy of annihilation across Tholis, Marduk's sudden inactivity set Urhi-Teshub's nerves on edge. "Marduk must know by now Sethi has weakened the shield and ended Thoth. Worse," he bit back a curse, "he will know what we have been doing to prepare." He folded his arms over his chest, despite the slick of heat against his chest deepening his discomfort. "We might have more numbers, but he has every advantage." He shot an uneasy look over his shoulder at the pillar of darkness. "And *that* only complicates matters. Whatever it is, it is not on our side, and with each passing hour it grows in size. Now we must face enemies both within and without. I *knew* we should have sent Sethi back." He met Sekhmet's eyes, caught the faint look of reproach. "What?"

"Unlike your predecessor," she said, pulling one of her daggers free, "you think too much." Her golden eyes slid over the engravings along the center of one of the blades. "We are warriors. Our task is to lay our plans, and fight until we cannot fight any longer. Either we win or we lose. There is nothing more for us. We have lost Thoth, Arinna, Istara, and Sethi, a terrible thing, but we must go on. We have our wits, our weapons, our experiences of the past, and have laid our plans. I will lead a sortie against Marduk outside the shield. Five of the prime gods' ships against one. His weapons cache is not inexhaustible. We intend to keep him busy so he cannot attack the shield, and to miss us *every* time." She slid her dagger back into its sheath, its snap as the cross-guard met the scabbard, a challenge.

Her gaze moved to the line of ships, glinting in the brutal white light of the sun. A sultry smile slid over her lips. "Set has a few tricks up his sleeve, as does Nergal. I have the ion drive. Marduk won't be expecting to triangulate against *that*. We are not without our surprises. Marduk will face the dogfight of his life. We have sworn to bring him down or face obliteration trying."

Urhi-Teshub eyed her, admiration cutting a swathe through him. "Where have you been all my life?" he asked, quiet, taking her into his arms. "Once more, you have returned me to my senses, to my true purpose." He tilted her chin up and graced her beautiful mouth with a gentle kiss. "Survive this and come back to me. I am not done with you yet."

"Yet?" Sekhmet repeated, mischievous, as she backed away, avoiding him as he lunged after her, her black armor soaking the light, blinding him with her beauty.

"Ever," Urhi-Teshub shouted after her as she fleeted across the plaza to join the five who would fly with her. She had chosen well: Set, and Nergal, gods of violence and destruction, Osiris, god of death, Ereshkigal, goddess of the dead, and Astarte, goddess of warfare. Sekhmet threw a triumphant smile back at him and ran on, through the shimmering waves of heat dancing against the plaza's ashlars.

He crossed the plaza and ducked under the wing of Horus's ship, grateful for the reprieve of shade. He ascended the steps and entered the cabin. Clustered around a map of Nisu spread across the central divan, Horus, Ptah, Ashur, and Nabu moved tokens representing the armies, discussed strategy. Horus looked up, tilted his head toward the flight deck.

Ahmen stood within. Urhi-Teshub went to him. Ahmen bent his head and lowered his eyes before the storm god, sparing him the unpleasantness of having to look at a man half-clothed in flesh.

"You have news?"

Ahmen nodded. "I have been unable to destroy the mirror as you commanded. No matter what I do, it repairs itself."

Urhi-Teshub leaned against the doorframe. The pillar of darkness glared at him through the deck's window. "Marduk managed to destroy the other mirrors."

"I do not have Marduk's resources. Although," Ahmen continued after a beat of hesitation, "it might be *this* mirror is indestructible. It was Thoth's own after all."

"I suppose in this place anything is possible." Urhi-Teshub pulled his gaze from the pulsing pillar of darkness and met Ahmen's eyes. One still had no eyelid. Urhi-Teshub suppressed a shudder. "If we don't destroy it," he continued, "Sethi will use it again."

Ahmen waited, the exposed globe of his eyeball unsettling. Urhi-Teshub looked away. "You mentioned you thought Sethi did not go to Perev."

"He did not. He went into the lower deck of Marduk's ship, I am certain of it."

"And you are only telling me this *now*?"

Ahmen lifted a non-existent eyebrow. "I thought if I could destroy the mirror it would not matter."

"It matters," Urhi-Teshub muttered. "Right now, everything matters." His thoughts fleeted past him, chased loose ends down blind corridors. He looked at the others stationed around the map. "*Why* did Marduk take the mirror? He has his ship, and his weapons. He has no allies—"

His thoughts ground to a halt. He went to the pile of maps, pulled out the one of Elati and unfurled it across the floor. The answer stared back at him, sudden, brutal. He cursed the foulest oath he knew. Its filth skidded against the cabin's pristine interior. The others turned to look at him.

"Rzhev," he said, glaring at the map, angry with himself for not having seen it before. "That is why Marduk has gone silent.

He's gone to Imaru, the only kingdom left in Elati who would ally with him—" he looked up, met Ahmen's realization, his dawning horror, "—because Sethi knew they would."

He clenched his fists. Fury impaled him. Those long nights he had stood outside Istara's suite, the pair's voices a quiet burr against the susurration of the night, low, intimate, the sharing of secrets. Istara must have told Sethi what had transpired in Imaru in the wake of Arinna's death, Teshub's reckless arrival had killed four—one, a child. Imaru possessed the deadliest warriors in Elati, renowned for having perfected the art of combat over thousands of years. With her careless words, Istara had handed Marduk an army on a platter—and Sethi had a portal into Anki. An indestructible one.

He cut a look back at Ahmen. "When you were on Marduk's ship, did you see his weapons cache?"

Ahmen shook his head. "I was on the lowest deck. It was packed full of large metal crates. I had a look up the stairwell, there were two more decks above that one."

"How many crates did you see?" Urhi-Teshub asked.

Ahmen's eyes unfocused, his look turned inward. "On the lowest deck, my best guess is seventy," he said. "I cannot say for the upper decks, I dared not go up."

"And we have no way to know what is in them," Horus said, quiet. "Some of Marduk's most incapacitating weapons can be held in the palm of the hand."

"Like that one he used in Babylon," Ahmen muttered. "It brought us to our knees, nothing more than sound."

"Ah, that one," Ptah joined in, distaste coating his elegant features. "I remember it well. One of Marduk's favorites." Ashur and Nabu nodded, their expressions grim.

"So," Urhi-Teshub said, "this is what we know: Marduk has an untold amount of weapons and devices cached on his ship, and he has the mirror which means if the shield falls, he can return to Anki with an army of . . . how many?" He tossed a questioning look at Ahmen. "I recall hearing a large number, something like sixty thousand, but how is that possible? The city's population is only ninety thousand."

"In Rzhev," Ahmen answered, "I was told every citizen is trained in the skills of combat. Even the infirm and children are adept in sabotage and poisons."

Urhi-Teshub met the eyes of the others. One by one, their looks turned distant as they returned to paths they had already walked, through a failed war which had led to their enslavement for two million years. Silence soaked the cabin. He folded his arms over his chest. "So we are outnumbered and overpowered. What do we have to our advantage?"

"If Sekhmet and her sortie can take Marduk's ship down before he can destroy the shield," Nabu said, "then it will not matter how large his army is, his devices and weapons will be useless here. We can take his warriors out as they arrive, one by one."

A murmur of quiet agreement filtered through the group.

"And if they fail and the shield falls?" Horus asked.

The others looked up, blank. Ptah cut a look at the obsidian monolith. "Can *that* be used to aid us?"

Urhi-Teshub balked at the thought. He wanted nothing to do with it.

"Having been inside the tower three times," Horus said, "I am certain there is more to whatever that is than we could ever understand. I have begun to wonder if the Creator gave Istara the relic to use because he *wanted* her to go wherever she went." He slid a quiet look at Urhi-Teshub. "Even if it makes no sense to us."

"You are right, "Urhi-Teshub said, bristling at Horus's assumption. "It makes no sense the Creator would sacrifice the goddess of healing just so the tower would vanish and the sphere of light would be replaced by a pillar of darkness which grows with every passing—"

"No." Horus cut in. "*She* has not been sacrificed. She *made* a sacrifice. I believe she is in there . . . with Baalat." A hiss of indrawn breaths filled the cabin.

Urhi-Teshub blinked. Horus had never said what happened to Baalat, and he had never asked. He waited, his instincts prickling.

"Baalat was taken from me in the pyramid," Horus continued, the lines of his mouth thinning, harsh. "Later, the relic led me to the seal in the tower where I was transported to the Creator's realm. I found my consort in a trance, her flesh tainted by tendrils of darkness, kept at bay by the Creator's light. He said: *'For the darkness to fall, the goddess must rise.'*" Horus let out an unsteady breath. "I still cannot understand what he meant, and yet—" He cast a wary look at the pillar. Its presence loomed over them, ominous, baleful, "—first Baalat and now Istara have vanished, taken to a realm where we cannot protect them." He looked down at his hands clenched into fists, and continued, low, "Where even the Creator himself has no power."

"It's almost as if," Ptah began, his resonant voice halting as he considered his words, "they must fight the darkness from within whilst we confront Marduk from without."

A ripple of soft assent came from the other gods. Urhi-Teshub longed to resist Ptah's conclusion, though the longer he dwelled on it, the more sense it made. *Something* had to be driving Marduk and the jihn. Even if the gods and their allies managed to defeat Marduk and Sethi, they would never win until they reached the heart of evil itself—where Horus believed the Creator had sent Istara and Baalat. His heart thudded, heavy, as realization struck him. If Horus was right, Istara still lived.

An uncomfortable silence settled over the group. Nabu reached down and straightened the map of Nisu so it lay square against the divan's edges. He cleared his throat. "Why would the Creator choose the least powerful among us to face his darkest aspect? Why not us? We are stronger by far. I cannot help but wonder if he has primed us to fail."

"And how would you defeat the origin of evil?" Horus asked, quiet. "With weapons? Brute strength? Your powers?"

Nabu lifted his brow and shook his head. "But to send the goddess of healing and her mortal counterpart to stand against *that*?" He slid a look at the pillar, then away. "It makes no sense."

"I agree," Urhi-Teshub said. "It makes no sense, and neither do the Creator's words about goddesses rising and darkness falling. Without Thoth to give us any understanding of what that might mean all we can do is trust the Creator's wisdom, and prepare as well as we might for what is to come." He turned his attention to the map of the city.

"Ashur, I would have you take your army to the mirror. Should the shield fall, I need you to hold the Imarians back for as long as you are able. Ptah, hold your army in reserve outside the palace. Ambush those that get through, use the vegetation and buildings for cover." Ashur and Ptah nodded.

"Nabu, position the rest of the armies before the tiers leading to the complex, ready to fall back. If Istara and Baalat are facing what is within that pillar, we need to buy them as much time as we can. When we can't hold the Imarians at Thoth's palace any longer, fall back to the tiers leading to the complex and hold the line for as long as you can. Use everything your ships have to protect our allies."

"As you command," Nabu said. "It shall be done."

The gods filed out of the cabin and strode across the plaza, their golden armor and weapons glinting in the sunlight. Horus rolled up the maps and set them aside. Across one divan, an array of weapons had been laid out. He picked up a pair of curved swords and fastened their scabbards to his belt.

He looked up at them, his expression hard. "For Baalat."

Ahmen went to the divan, selected a dagger, a bow and quiver of arrows, the pink skin of his flesh puckering as he settled the quiver's strap over his chest. "For Meresamun."

Urhi-Teshub pulled his ax free and cut a look at the impenetrable black pillar, willing the one he still loved to be alive. "For Istara." At her name, the ax's blades blistered with power, drenched the cabin in an explosion of cerulean light. He met the eyes of the others. "And may the Creator protect us all."

❊　❊　❊

Sethi turned, following the sleek lines of Marduk's warship as it screamed over Imaru's lake in a deep arc, cutting a dark line across the light of a new day. Aiya had said a strange thing to him before she left. *When the dawn came you did not change.* He had no idea what she had meant, but there had been no time to speak of it so he had pressed a kiss to her lips and said he would see her soon.

He sensed her gaze on him as he regarded their departure, imagined seeing himself from her eyes as he stood in the midst of the city's massive plaza surrounded by hundreds of open crates, Imaru's warriors equipping themselves with Marduk's arsenal of armor and weapons. In the center of the plaza, a bloom of gold and red silk stood out from the bleak rectangles of crates. The king had sent his own opulent tent to house the mirror which would transport Marduk's army into Anki.

A burst of blue fire erupted from the warship's tail. A heartbeat later, nothing remained of it but a smear of white where the ion drive had engaged. Sethi turned back to the courtyard and eyed the warriors as they worked in disciplined silence, stoic, clever, men and women both, listening to their captains explain how to use their weapons, information granted to them by Marduk hours before.

Sethi turned and made his way to the tent. It had been a long night and he needed refreshment. From outside the thin barrier of silk fluttering in the lake's breeze, a variety of delicious smells assailed him.

In two hours, Marduk would be in Anki, his weapons shredding what remained of the shield. In two hours, Sethi would use the mirror. If the shield had fallen he would not come back and his warriors would follow. If the shield still stood, he would return and wait to try again. But right now, all he wanted to do was eat.

He ducked into the tent and set the jihn against the mirror's edge. It leaned against the gold-gilt frame, its blades quiet, as though preparing for the feast to come. Picking up a platter, Sethi piled it with slices of roasted duck, and pale parcels stuffed with meat and spiced vegetables. In a covered bowl, a fragrant jasmine-scented staple the servant called rice. He added that to several helpings of fried vegetables in a rich, dark sauce.

He sat. A servant poured wine, deft, elegant. Sethi eyed him from under his brow, noting the livery. One of the king's own men. Sethi drank and thought of Istara, of her lies and deceptions; of her lover, no longer mortal, but reborn a god, always watching, his eyes narrow with suspicion; of the oppression of the shield, and how it had changed him, made him someone he was not. He had made love to her, his enemy—had told her he loved her.

Anger coursed through him, cold, then hot, a living thing. He considered what he would do with the manipulative goddess of healing when he found her. Would he rid himself of her fast, as he had done to Arinna, or take his time? He sipped his wine, tasting nothing but resentment for the time he had lost in Anki. The shield had overwhelmed his mind, his will.

To think he had almost destroyed himself for her. He tore into the roasted duck with his eating knife, vicious. The answer came, abrupt as an Elatian sunrise. He would take his time and make her suffer, would revel in watching her existence wane. Her pleas for mercy would be ambrosia to his soul. The faintest smile touched his lips. Anticipation scored his senses.

Against the side of the mirror, the jihn rippled in response to his thoughts. Slivers of blue-white light sawed over its symbols. One after another they pulsed, slow, like the beat of a heart until its thirteen symbols blistered with silver light. A bleak wail emanated from it, a slavering, bone-crushing cry, ragged with hate-drenched hunger. His face pale, the servant fled, the wine pitcher still in his hand. Wine sloshed over its rim, stained his hand the color of blood.

Sethi eyed the jihn as he swallowed a mouthful of roasted duck. Two hours. He turned his attention back to his platter and let the jihn's hunger soak his soul. This time he would not fail. This time Urhi-Teshub would not stop him. This time, the one who had stood against him, who had oppressed, deceived, and controlled him would be extinguished. Today, Istara would fall and never rise again.

✳ ✳ ✳

Though it made her uneasy, Istara left the relic behind and followed Baalat. For a heartbeat she feared it would vanish. She cut a look over her shoulder. It remained on the divan, lone, small, and lost without her, surrounded by the darkness.

Baalat came to a halt beside the silken-curtained space. She placed her palm against the wall, and a section of it slid into the floor. Beyond, a circular hall, empty apart from a jagged rift yawning from a dip in the center of the floor. Baalat made her way to its edge. Istara came after her, clawed by uncertainty. Beyond its sheer drop, a well of liquid darkness churned. Within its depths, faint tendrils of golden light glimmered, their lengths truncated, shredded by the oppression of the void.

"The Well of Life," Baalat murmured. "Before you came, there were far more of those golden tendrils. But, now you are here, and the light dies." A faint smile graced her lips. "Just as my lord predicted."

"Meaning?"

"My lord has taught me many things," Baalat answered, cutting an oblique look at Istara. She tilted her head at the opening. "Everything must begin somewhere. Worlds, stars, life. Before you used the relic and freed the Well from its prison, this was the sphere in the tower. It is where everything we know of begins—and ends. Even the Well must adhere to vast, near incomprehensible cycles of collapse and renewal. And now we approach the end of this cycle. Soon, it will renew, only this time its rebirth will be different." Baalat paused to point at a pair of golden tendrils disintegrating within the darkness. "*He* knew this, so he forced the darkness from himself, and sealed it away anticipating with the Well's rebirth there would only be light, and the darkness would be destroyed, forever. But of course, he did not take into account how resilient or resourceful my master is."

Istara thought of the image she had seen in the font of her and Sethi on the terrace of a dark palace. "The one you serve wishes to do the same but with the darkness."

Baalat nodded. "He does. But it was not he who started this. It was *him*."

Istara waited for Baalat to continue, but her companion fell silent, content to observe the waning of the Creator's dying light. Istara eyed the rift, wide as a vestibule. "Why am I here?"

Baalat turned from the opening. "You possess something my lord wants."

"The relic?"

A quiet smile. "No. Not that."

"Then what?"

Baalat did not answer, instead she gestured for Istara to follow. They returned to the basin. "See what you are missing."

Its surface cleared. In it, the sprawl of the shield's white-gold net, stretched thin, large sections held together by only a handful of threads. The view soared up toward the skies. A vast ship sliced down from the heavens, its shields shimmering with heat. A pair of weapons erupted from its wings, blue fire blazing from their tails. They slammed into the shield in total silence. The shield juddered. It held. Just.

"And now they come," Baalat said, pointing to the other side of the basin where six sleek ships tore across the surface of the shield, heading straight for Marduk's ship. While still some distance away, they split apart, and veered into different directions. Five of them vanished into thin air. One remained. Istara recognized it. Sekhmet's ship. It swerved in a high arc before it too vanished. A flurry of explosives slammed into Marduk's ship's fuselage, the shields blistering under the impact.

Another blaze of fire erupted from the wing of Marduk's ship. A ball of white heat scoured the sky. From within its heart, pieces of a ship tumbled away and rammed into the shield. They skidded away, soaked in flames.

"One down," Baalat said. She flicked a look at Istara. Caught her naked hope. "They will never stop him. The shield will fall. Sethi will arrive, and the gods will be annihilated just as the cycle begins again. The darkness will rise with my master supreme, and me, by his side. You are being offered the chance to remain Sethi's consort. If you refuse, you will be returned to Anki where you will be destroyed. It is only a matter of throwing you back into the Well."

Istara said nothing. She did not need reminding of Sethi's hatred of her light, his virulent hunger to obliterate her. Within the basin's view, another of the gods' ships blistered into liquid fire.

"Two," Baalat murmured, amused. She turned. The view in the basin faded. "The gods cannot stand against Marduk. Nothing can stop him from fulfilling his destiny. Nothing. My lord has made certain of it. Marduk is the darkness incarnate." She passed through the silken hangings and returned to the suite. Istara followed her, bleak. Despite all they had done, the gods would fall, one by one and with them, the last of the Creator's light would die. Everything would be reborn in darkness. There would never be light again.

Sekhmet hit the reverse thrusters and slid underneath Marduk's ship just as an array of explosions peppered where she had just been. Damage reports poured down the console's screens, a wall of red. Alarms blared. She punched the override and took manual control. She would be damned if he shot her down. Ereshkigal's and Nergal's ships had already been lost, incinerated by the blistering heat of Marduk's weapons. Two down. Four against one. She sensed Marduk was toying with them. Another volley of fire rained onto Anki's shield.

She slapped four switches up, preparing to fire. "Set," she yelled, despite knowing he could not hear her, "it's time. Use the damn thing." She scanned her screens for his heat signature. Nothing. He was nowhere. She cursed and slapped her gloved palm against the armrest. The weapons primer bleated at her, urgent. She hit it and her weapons released. They slammed into the side of Marduk's ship, dissipating, useless, against the might of his shield. She roared up into a spiral as he returned fire. One hit. Two. Three. Five. Her shields blistered. More alarms. More red messages on the screens. She gritted her teeth and faced the chaos of her console.

Another enormous weapon offloaded from the base of Marduk's ship. Blue fire erupted from its tail. Not good.

"Set," she screamed as the thing fell toward the shield in an elegant, deadly arc. "For the love of the Creator, use your weapon."

Marduk's missile hurtled downward, a thing of annihilation, powerful enough to wipe out an entire city. Sekhmet clenched her fist, furious with futility. "Please," Sekhmet cried to shield. "Hold."

A mere arm's span over the shield's shimmering, brutalized web, the missile juddered and flew backwards as though struck by a giant fist. It tumbled end over end for several long iters, carried far across the surface of the shield by the force of its momentum. At last, it stilled. It turned, slow, until its nose pointed at Marduk's ship, a malevolent, hateful thing. Its rear blazed, a surge of brilliant blue, and tore away from the shield back to its master, now its enemy courtesy of Set's weapon.

"I love you Set," Sekhmet breathed. Already her fingers were flying over the console. She hit the thrusters, asking everything of them as she pushed her broken, wounded ship into the heavens, as high as her engines would allow. At the sky's plateau, deafened by the shrill scream of her alarms she leaned forward. A trail of blue fire swarmed toward Marduk's massive warship. The heat of its ion drive melted the sky. His ship shot away, a blur over the shield. The missile followed him relentless, unstoppable— Marduk's weapon as ruthless as its master.

"And now you will know what it feels like," Sekhmet said as the weapon, smaller, lighter, and faster closed the distance. Marduk's ship shimmered and melted into the blue as he engaged every shield he possessed. A heartbeat later the weapon struck.

Sekhmet caught her breath. Her heart held still. An explosion, blinding. A shock of brutal white tore through her senses. Her heart awakened, jolted to violence by hope. She blinked the tears from her eyes. Molten fire swept over the fuselage and wings, outlining the stricken ship's shape in liquid heat. She clung to the ends of the armrests, surrounded by the deafening agonies of her ship. Please. The fire slid away. No. Sekhmet gaped at the impossibility—at the justice denied. The shields had held. She bellowed the foulest oath she knew. Set's weapon took time to recharge. Apart from one last desperate option, she was out of moves. A dozen missiles erupted from Marduk's ship, retaliatory, vicious. A heartbeat later, two more ships tumbled from the heavens. The signatures of Astarte's and Osiris's ships vanished from her screen. Fury soaked her.

She hit the thrusters and tore back down from the heavens. It wasn't over. Not yet. Not by a long shot.

❋ ❋ ❋

Urhi-Teshub gripped the haft of his ax so hard, his fingers ached. Above the shield, after surviving a blistering attack of his own weapon against him, Marduk's weapons had just taken out two more of the gods' ships, though which two Urhi-Teshub did not know. He raked his eyes across the canopy beyond the shield's dying web, searching for the one he loved. Nothing. The only ship not cloaked was the oppressor's.

"He has launched another weapon against the shield," Horus said. He pointed.

Urhi-Teshub squinted against the glare of the midday sun. At first he couldn't see anything. Then he saw it. A falling star, a smear of blue flame sparking against the white-gold web of the shield.

"If they can't stop it like last time . . ." Ahmen said. He didn't finish. He didn't need to.

Silent explosions erupted along the missile's fuselage. It kept falling, unscathed, relentless, the desperation of the two remaining gods to destroy it, tangible. Urhi-Teshub clenched his fist. The sortie had failed. The shield would fall. He dragged his eyes from the sky, willing his consort to be one of the ones still fighting.

"It is time," he said, his heart leaden. "I must give the command."

Ahmen pressed his fist against the sinews of his chest. "I will carry it for you."

He cut a look at the row of ships waiting on the plaza, ready to join the battle. "My brothers and sisters must remain in the air, out of reach of the jihn. I have no other commands for them apart from protecting our allies. They know Marduk's strategies. They may fight as they see fit." A little distance away, the allied commanders waited outside Horus's ship for their final orders. Some sat atop horses, others stood in chariots. All of them eyed the falling weapon, bleak. "Give the order for the allied armies to hold their positions for as long as possible. If they become outnumbered, they are to fall back to the plaza where the gods can better protect them."

Grim, Ahmen backed away.

"Wait." Urhi-Teshub held out his arm to his once-enemy, a soldier's farewell. After a heartbeat, Ahmen gripped it, harsh. Urhi-Teshub ignored the unpleasant feel of the Egyptian's half-exposed muscles and tendons. "May the Creator protect you. Friend."

Ahmen nodded, terse. "And you." He turned, and with a wary look at the heavens, ran.

Urhi-Teshub turned his gaze back to the shield as Horus pulled his swords free, the quiet hiss of his blades leaving their scabbards familiar, reassuring.

The gods' ships tore away from the plaza, the roar of their engines deafening, exhilarating. Beneath his feet the ground reverberated as they swept past, the shear of their departure buffeting his turmoil.

A burst of blue mushroomed over the arc of the shield. A heartbeat later, white brilliance punched into the shield's web, the walls of its devastation swarmed over its weave in total silence, an expanding pool of liquid heat. His eyes watering, Urhi-Teshub lifted his forearm. From under its wan shelter, he forced himself to endure the punishing glare of the shield's molten demise.

A roar thundered from its boiling core into the plaza. A storm's fury followed after it, a hungering thing. It tore past Urhi-Teshub into the city, shattering columns and flattening trees. It swept on, relentless, far beyond the circumference of the city. Calm reigned for a single heartbeat before another roar reared up from the horizon, ominous, laden with promise. The storm's tide surged back, fierce, furious, carrying its detritus, flotsam in a sea of wind. Ashlars and trees hurtled past him, slammed into the pyramids, its destruction pummeling Urhi-Teshub. He crouched. Endured.

Pressure rammed into him, crushed his lungs. He hauled at the air. It hauled back, denying him sustenance. Dark spots peppered his vision. He blinked, desperate to see. Liquid fire, hot as lava, poured along the sundered weave of the shield's web. Heat radiated from it, a blistering inferno. His lungs aching, he braced himself as a wall of savage heat, ten thousand times worse than the heat of the desert, hotter than a thousand blacksmith furnaces pulled the moisture from his body, desiccated his mouth, blistered his lips, singed his eyebrows and lashes, fused his armor to his skin. He gritted his teeth, his throat raw, scorched, his eyes aching, and his flesh screaming in agony. From the depths of his disorientation, he sensed his light igniting, its tendrils sliding around him, protecting him, soothing him, easing the shriek of his agonies.

A violent crack splintered the horizon. His eyes laden with his light, he rose, enduring the tortured heat of his vision. In every direction, molten sections of the shield hung by a thread—massive, liquid droplets. One by one, they tore free and plummeted into the city, liquid fire. Past the distant perimeter of *ziqqurati*, Anki's primordial forests burst into flame. Gouts of black smoke bled from the horizon.

Horus rose, his skin blistered and raw, and his kilt blackened and smoking. His eyes went to the sky, to Marduk's ship as it cut a dark path through one the shield's ragged openings toward the plaza. The once-god of war gripped his swords, vengeance scouring his stance.

From the edge of Urhi-Teshub's vision, a distortion rippled over the city, like a stone cast against a still pond. He cut a look over his shoulder toward Thoth's palace, his instincts hollowing a cold path through his torso. Another ripple erupted from the palace, out past the massive terrace the gods had used to land their ships. It knocked several pillars down, taking part of the roof with it. Faint, like the gnawing of a dark thought in the depths of the night, the presence of the jihn settled itself over the city, laying waste to hope, savaging the order of Urhi-Teshub's thoughts. He gritted his teeth, fought the lies even as they crowded in.

He turned, cut his eyes over the expanse of the plaza, littered with the detritus of the shield's destruction, shattered ashlars, and splintered palm trees. Peppered throughout the chaos, sections of the fallen shield burned, enormous, molten fires the size of temples. He searched through the haze of white heat for Ahmen. Nothing but fire, heat, smoke, and the scream of the ships cutting across the skies filled his senses. He gave up. Only he and Horus remained on the plaza.

He tilted his head toward Horus's ship, a piece of melted shield had fallen close by it. "It's time to go—before we lose your ship."

The muscles of Horus's jaw clenched. Blood oozed from under his scorched skin. "I will not leave the pillar," he said. "Baalat might come."

"We agreed not to leave any ships on the ground," Urhi-Teshub said as Marduk's warship circled the dark pillar and headed toward Thoth's palace, his shields blooming, liquid blisters of blue, indolent against the barrage of fire the gods rained upon it. No return fire came from the ship. Marduk ignored the gods, content to circle Thoth's palace and observe the progress of Sethi and the Imarians. A cat watching another cat with a mouse.

Horus lifted his swords, inspected the bloody skin of his burnt palms seared to their hilts. "I'm staying. Teshub knew the controls.

You will, too." He turned his eyes back to the sky, narrowed them against Marduk's ship, taking fire from every direction. "Go. Aid the others. Stop him, if you can."

Urhi-Teshub slid a look at the pillar of darkness. Its girth rippled against a segment of the molten shield, consuming it as though it were nothing more than air. He looked away, uncomfortable. How Istara could survive in such a place failed him.

He nodded at Horus. "May you find her again."

Horus said nothing. Rage cloaked him. Pain shrouded him. Urhi-Teshub sensed Horus wanted to be alone. His ax at his side, its light jagged, hungry for the fight, Urhi-Teshub strode through the wreckage of the shield, went to the ship, and with a rush of heat and fire joined the gods in the skies.

※　※　※

From within what remained of her ship, Sekhmet eyed the devastation of the shield. It hung in tatters, its once-beautiful light no longer ephemeral, but molten, white-hot. Across its brutalized tapestry, huge sections slid from its tethers and tumbled end over end into the burning ruins of the city, slamming into its palaces, *ziqqurati*, and avenues already laid to waste, savaged by the violence of Marduk's weapon against the shield.

Marduk's black warship circled over Thoth's palace, where distortions in the air radiated outward from within the once-prime god of wisdom's residence. Sekhmet knew that weapon, it fired a burst of intense pressure, so powerful a direct hit could shatter an obelisk. She angled her ship as close as she dared, ignoring the blares coming from her console, the warning bleats of her proximity to Marduk's warship.

She flicked a look at the cloaking readout. Apart from her ion drive, it was the only thing which still remained intact. Everything else was done. No more fire power, no more shields. Even the atmosphere in the cabin would soon run out. Marduk might have brought her to her knees, but she was Sekhmet. It would take more than this to stop her. She kept her breathing thin, slow, saving the air.

Below, within Thoth's courtyard, a steady stream of warriors emerged from the brilliance of the mirror, clad in armor similar to Marduk's, fitted with enhanced capabilities, strength, and defenses. On their hips, and over their shoulders, silvered weapons, devices of devastation. They strode through the massive palace, arrogant, confident, disappearing under the roofs of the palace's vast colonnaded corridors and halls and out onto Thoth's scorched terrace, their armored bodies melding into a sea of black. At the forefront, the one who belonged to Marduk. Sethi stood at the edge of the terrace, the jihn in his hand, its blades' sickly light rippling with expectation. Despair slithered into her thoughts. She eased the ship back, withdrew from the jihn's poisonous reach.

Triumphant, Sethi regarded the ravaged, burning city, anticipation soaking him. Across the terrace, the bodies of the Elatians lay broken and bloody, mutilated by the power of the dislocation weapon. One must have survived. A warrior dragged the soldier to Sethi and threw him at the once-god of war's gold-sandaled feet.

Sethi turned. He eyed the suffering soldier with indifference and struck the man with the jihn, splitting his skull in two. The jihn shimmered as it consumed the soldier's soul. When it was done, Sethi jerked the curved blade free. Blood and brains splattered his chest and kilt. He turned back to the view, the jihn a living thing in his hand. He licked its blade, drank of its evil. Tendrils of darkness swept out from it onto his face and down his chest, they poured into the gold of his fractals. One by one, they turned black, and began to rotate, perfect, seamless.

Sekhmet had seen enough. She retreated to the perimeter of the city and hovered over a *ziqquratu*. One of the corners of its top tier were gone, its white marble sheared off by a fallen piece of the shield. Further down, the shield's fierce heat had left a deep trough along the side of the *ziqquratu*, a scar against its face, as though the structure itself had wept.

She looked back at the *ziqquratu*, then at the city. Caught her breath. She remembered this view. This was where she had confronted Urhi-Teshub and battled against him—where he had made love to her and made her his. Her heart clenched. The part of the wall where he had taken her was gone. She clenched her teeth and shoved her nostalgia aside. Her air was running out, fast. She eyed Marduk's ship, hovering over Thoth's palace, serene against the efforts of the gods' combined firepower. She locked onto its position, let her ship fix the co-ordinates, and allow for permutations. The screen beeped its readiness to her, faint under the riot of warnings, alarms, and notifications. She lifted her finger and held it over the ignition for the ion drive, allowed herself one final look at the ruined *ziqquratu*. She had been loved. It was enough. She punched the ignition and hurtled across the roof of the city, straight at her nemesis, her heart soaring with grief, vengeance, and violence, ready for the fall, for the pain, the suffering. For the end.

❆ ❆ ❆

Urhi-Teshub glared at Marduk's ship. The readout on his screen told him Marduk's shields were at half power, but the damage he and the other gods had rained onto the warship since Marduk had breached the shield had done almost nothing to change that. They needed another weapon like the one Set has used against Marduk. But Marduk was no fool. He would not risk *that* happening again. Set's presence, at least, granted them a small victory. So long as Set remained, the gods and their allies would be spared the deadliest of Marduk's weaponry. And yet it had led to this, a stalemate. Marduk would not use his weapons, and the gods could not get through his shields. So long as they were occupied with Marduk, none aided the allies.

He punched the weapons relay and launched another volley of explosives at the front of the warship, aiming for the flight deck's windows. The shields rippled against the impacts, as though the might of the prime god Horakhti's weapons were nothing more than pebbles tossed into a pool.

Urhi-Teshub punched the console and roared a string of oaths. Was there *nothing* he could do to stop this nightmare? Below, the armies of the allies streamed back through ruins of the city toward the burning plaza, the commanders of the kingdoms valiant despite the insurmountable odds, even as Sethi and his army pursued the armies of the gods, relentless, brutal. One Imarian could take out ten of the gods' allies at once. And still, more arrived. They poured out from Imaru through the blistering light of the mirror. Black as cockroaches. Pestilent. Evil. Their armor drinking in the light of the sun.

Sethi made his way down the central avenue, using the jihn against those caught in his path. Its blades flared, streaming trails of brilliant blue-white light, verdant with the weight of the slain. With each feeding, its oppressive reach spread, loaded with hate. It called to Urhi-Teshub. Its presence assaulted his mind, blinded his senses: *It is over. Today I will feast on Sekhmet's light, and then yours. Istara will be last. Her suffering will be exquisite. You have failed.*

Urhi-Teshub bellowed, his anger drowning out the poison seeking to take root in his mind. He would not succumb. He forced himself to focus on the console's weapons display, to prepare to fire again—this time at Sethi, even if it meant Marduk would take him out. His fall would be worth it to slow Istara's consort down, to buy the allies time.

An alarm blared, fat with warning. He cut a look at the screen, suspecting Marduk had locked onto him. No. The warning was not coming from Marduk's ship. He stared at the red streaming over the screen, the message made no sense. *Proximity alert. Collision of ion drives imminent.*

Marduk's ship roared to life, its ion drive flared, a blinding explosion of liquid heat. Urhi-Teshub grabbed onto the controls, fired the thrusters, and tore up into the heavens, his mind reeling. He eyed the message again. No. He hadn't read it wrong. Ion *drives*. His heart tight, he pulled up. The alarm quieted. Within the silence of the ship, he gripped the armrests of the seat. The only other ship which possessed an ion drive was Sekhmet's. His brave, beautiful goddess would stop at nothing to bring down their oppressor, and all he could do was watch. No. He would not watch. He punched the thrusters and plummeted back down from the skies. He would be there, waiting for her, when she fell.

❈   ❈   ❈

Amidst a flurry of deafening wails blaring from the console, Marduk hit the ion drive. Meresamun's skull slammed against the head rest, her chest compressed and her lungs screaming in protest. Blind to her suffering, her consort worked the controls, protected against the ion drive's brutal onslaught within the dark sheath of his armor.

The gods had proven more resourceful than she expected her consort had anticipated. From behind the console's reflection against his helmet, Marduk's cold silence spoke volumes. The weapon the gods had turned against them had left scorch marks across the console and along the inner walls of the flight deck. Suffocating heat, hot as a baker's oven still ravaged the space, although compared to the nightmare temperatures of the missile's detonation, it could be the chill of a desert night. As the devastation meant to destroy a city swept over the warship, the heat of an inferno had consumed the air, burned her skin, and ignited the fabric of her gown. Aiya's hair had caught fire. The acrid stink of it still filled the cabin. Meresamun clung to the armrests so hard, her fingers ached. Please. Not again. Not the blistering, punishing, drowning heat. Not the flames.

Against the intense pressure of the ion drive, Marduk veered toward the pillar of unutterable darkness, where an endless tower had once reared into the heavens. She quailed against the inexpressible magnitude of it, of the rank evil emanating from its heart. Marduk ignored it, his attention focused on the console, his fingers moving, deft, against the weapons console, preparing to unleash another series of weapons.

During their brief interlude hovering over the city, she had examined the pillar, her hopes in shreds, and her heart vanquished. Defeat had swept through her. It still clogged her throat. Hopelessness slaughtered her. She had thought what had been housed within the tower was good—if it was called the Well of Life, it would have to be—but the pillar of abyssal dark which speared the center of the city bled malevolence, destruction, oppression. Zherei's information had to be wrong, that *thing* could not be Zarpanitu's Well of Life.

She closed her eyes, hauled herself away from the chaos of alarms and warnings pouring from the ship's console and beyond the barrier of the ion drive's bone-searing roar to search her mind for what she could recall of the sage's vague descriptions. A fragment pierced the turmoil of her mind, a distant flicker of light glimpsed from the dark waves of a storm. She surged after it, desperate, sensing it was important. There. As they had sat at the table in the quiet of the library in Perev and gazed at the map of Elati, Zherei had said the Well was comprised of a contradictory combination of both light and dark. She opened her eyes and forced herself to face the pillar's bottomless dark, her existence reeling with revulsion. Nothing. The monstrosity possessed no light at all. It could not be the Well. She had failed.

It was too late. Marduk would never be stopped. The darkness had won. Soon, he would reign supreme, and she would stand by his side, a creature of the dark, a perpetrator of torment. Tears scoured her heart.

Marduk rotated the ship onto its side. The restraints bit into Meresamun's flesh. Pain sliced through her blistered skin, blade-thin, exquisite. She hung, limp, within the brutal cradle of her seat, exhausted, defeated, broken. Oblivious to her suffering, Marduk hauled the ship around the curve of the pillar, the ship's roof just beyond the pillar's obsidian reach. They tore free and leveled off, heading toward the largest pyramid. Its golden capstone glinted in the sun's light. A new alarm blared, high pitched, drowning out the lesser cries of the ship. The flight deck's interior lights turned blood red.

Within the space of a heartbeat, Marduk cut the ion drive, let go of the controls, yanked his restraints away and did the same to Meresamun's, the speed of his work startling her. He kicked away a panel under the console and pushed her into the hidden, padded space, rough, his metal clad hands harsh with haste. He came in after her, clad in silent black, his face lost to her. She caught her reflection in the red glow his visor, her eyes hollow and raw with despair, her cosmetics smeared from weeping, the singed tangles of her hair. He pulled her against him, a warrior, hot with rage. His armor wrapped around her, a cocoon. She huddled against the cold sheath of him, her heart thundering. At the edge of her hearing, the terrified screams of Aiya, thin with dread. The final alarm escalated, its tempo increasing, urgent, desperate, loaded with warning. The red light deepened, soaked Meresamun's senses. Marduk pressed the symbols on the screen against his wrist and a blister of energy snapped out from his armor, surrounding them in a field of dark light.

"I have you," Marduk cried, his voice metallic and harsh in the ship's dying light. "I will not let you go."

Caught within his savage embrace, Meresamun closed her eyes. Red-black light drenched the backs of her eyes, dragged her into a sea of blood. One heartbeat. Two. A brutal thundering tore into the rear of the ship. The alarms died. A breath of silence.

Marduk's grip tightened, his gloved hand wrapped around her skull, braced her against the unforgiving wall of his armored chest.

A wall of blue flames slammed over his back, and streamed over his shield, the heat of it scorching her anew, blinding, furious. A blistering, solid field of white radiance surrounded them, melted the console above them, twisting its metal frame. Sections of the console blew outward, exposing the sunlit world outside the dying light of the ship. Marduk grabbed onto one of the glowing metal struts of the console just as the floor caved in beneath them. With brutal efficiency, he hauled her up onto the floor of the flight deck, his grip so violent her ribs screamed against the crush of his hold.

Another explosion ripped through the fuselage of the stricken ship. A wall of raging, boiling fire roiled over Marduk's shield. He wrapped himself around her, cradling her against the death throes of his ship. A shearing, heated, hiss tore through her senses, deafened her. Terror stalked her spine as the wall of the flight deck sundered itself from the ship's cabin, slow, stately. The cabin fell away, an ugly, distorted twist of metal soaked in blue fire. Through the aching heat of her vision, Meresamun searched for Aiya, but of the other woman, there was nothing, the section where she had sat was gone, only a gaping, burning hole remained.

A vicious jolt rammed into her. Her stomach slammed into her throat, yanked away her breath. Brutal dislocation stormed through her. Marduk pulled her legs up, gathered her against him, tight as a ball, his armor surrounding her. Outside the empty space where the cabin had once been, the pillar rotated to its side. Vertigo rammed into her as they slid from the sky, tumbling within the flaming wreckage toward the sheer, golden walls of the pyramid.

Locked in Marduk's fierce embrace, surrounded by the ephemeral dark wall of his shield, Meresamun plummeted with him, lost within a well of flames toward the ruined plaza of the gods. She had believed reaching Anki would mark the culmination of her existence, would define her path, her purpose, and would grant her the chance to do what Zarpanitu could not. But, as the pyramid's girth raced toward them, beautiful and cruel, Meresamun knew there would never be a reprieve, not for her, or for the one who loved her.

❈　❈　❈

"At last we meet," a voice, dark, seductive, cold, cut through Istara. She looked up. Obsidian eyes bored into her, languid with hate. Istara took a step back, horror crawling up her spine as Baalat eased nearer the metal-clad figure, her eyes darkening with desire. "You have something I want," he said, "and I have something you want."

"You have nothing I want," Istara answered.

"Indeed?"

A shimmer and Istara stood alone in the suite.

"Istara."

Her heart thudded. *Sethi.* She turned. He stood before her, clad in an elegant, gold-embroidered black kilt, his eyes no longer golden but black as pitch. Dark fractals rotated upon the slabs of his pectorals, seamless, mesmerizing. She looked down at herself, her gown no longer white, but black, shot with threads of gold. He came to her, caught her against him, the feel of him warm, real, visceral. She clung to him, desperate in this lightless, twisted place for something familiar. He kissed her, his hands tangling in her hair, his thumbs caressing her jaw, intimate, gentle. He pulled back and let her go. She staggered, lost without him. "Give him what he wants." His voice saturated her, weakened her. His warmth left her as he retreated. "Do not cling to what is past. Come to me."

She lunged after him, willing him to remain, just a little longer. He vanished. In his place, the cold shear of oblivion. The dark aspect stepped out of the shadows, his dead gaze blistered her soul.

"Do you still believe I have nothing you want?"

Istara backed away. Her calves collided with the divan. At the edge of her vision, the faint existence of the pendant penned in by the malevolent darkness called to her, mournful, alienated. Denied.

"What could I possibly possess you would want?" Istara cried, hating herself for asking, yet the feel of Sethi's arms around her had seared her senses, assaulted her reason. The thought of losing him, of being slain by his hand overwhelmed her. Why should she fall for a mistake the Creator had made out of arrogance? For a fight which had never been hers? She thought of the fallen gods, obliterated by Marduk's weapons. Of Baalat's amusement. Defeat hauled at her. The darkness would win. She would have another chance to live on, with Sethi, forever.

A flicker of satisfaction rippled through the depths of her oppressor's eyes. In its wake, naked hunger. "Your thoughts betray you," he said. "I can give you your heart's desire for one small thing. A cleansing. You will sacrifice your light to me. Willingly."

"I have no light left," Istara answered, ashamed at the shear of her disappointment. "I lost it when I used the relic in the tower."

"No," he said, moving closer, his baleful gaze lowering to her breast. "It is still there, buried deep within your heart, hiding from me." Baalat approached, her gown a silken whisper against the floor. She carried a black dagger engraved with silver symbols. He took it from her and held out the blade hilt first to Istara. "You are no fool. You know how to use this. Find your heart, empty it. Strike the final blow against my nemesis and tonight you will sleep with Sethi, his queen, for eternity."

"Queen?" Istara drew back from the blade's hilt. "I am a goddess."

The faintest of a sneer shadowed his elegant features. "I am not *him*. The time of the gods is at an end. You will have other powers, abilities granted by the darkness. Or," he stepped aside, and gestured toward the rift boiling with darkness, "if my offer does not please, you are welcome to return to have your light taken by the jihn. Either way, your light dies."

Baalat reached out and caught Istara's hand. "Daughter," she said, soft, compelling, a mother. "You are part of me. I cannot bear to lose you. Take the blade. Free yourself. Join me in the truth."

Istara caught the merest flick of the dark aspect's eyes at the pendant, perceived the depth of his loathing. The pendant disturbed both Baalat and the dark aspect. Through the veil of darkness she grappled for the truth. The Creator had chosen her, had ensured the pendant had come into her possession long before she began her journey to Egypt. Like spent fuel collapsing in a fire pit, she sensed within the ashes of her thoughts, an ember. There had to be a reason the darkness wished her to sacrifice her light—why he had brought her here to be tempted by Baalat, someone who would be able to reach her, cause her to doubt, and sabotage her thoughts. Why had he not left her in Anki to face Sethi and the jihn?

The jihn. Her thoughts halted. The ember within the ashes glowed.

She blinked. Realization slammed into her. She had been blind. So blind. Sethi had become the darkness, and she, the light. He had the jihn and she had the pendant. The pendant possessed power equal to the jihn—power only she could wield. She had thought its only purpose was to press it against the seal in the tower. The day she had been reunited with the pendant,

Urhi-Teshub had given her the message Horus had brought from the Creator: *You will know when the time will be right to use it.*

Her heart trembled. She forced herself to keep her eyes on the dagger, still held out before her, willing her thoughts to be hidden from the entity before her, waiting, patient, the bleak weapon cradled in his metal-gloved hand. From across the silent void, the pendant's purpose hauled on her. It was not too late.

She dared not think any longer, she swept her fingers down and caught the pendant's stave into her palm. Baalat hissed and let go of her hand. She backed away, her breasts rising and falling under the transparent material. "Daughter," she said, low, "do not do this thing."

The dark aspect took a step back. He turned the dagger in his hand, deft, and caught the hilt in his grip. "If you won't give your light to me willingly, then I shall take it." He lunged at her, his speed astonishing. Istara closed her eyes to the darkness and called to the light buried within her heart. It exploded out of her, brilliant, white, a cocoon. The blade slammed against the barrier of her light. Its keening bled against the edge of her hearing, gnawed at her mind.

"Baalat." The dark aspect caught hold of the once-goddess's arm and thrust her toward Istara. "The relic. Take it from her or face an eternity of suffering."

Baalat staggered. Fear sawed her features. "Please," she breathed. "For what we once were, relinquish the relic." She tilted her head at the divan. Her entire body quaked. Terror bled from her, visceral. "I beg you," she whispered. "You cannot imagine what he is capable of doing to me."

Istara walked toward the rift, surrounded by the light of the Creator, a beacon of purity in a place of utter desolation. Against her back, the silent hatred of the dark aspect bored into her, raw, fetid, savage. Baalat trailed after her, weeping, pleading. Istara reached the edge of the rift. Baalat fell to her knees, just outside Istara's cocoon of light.

"I saved you," she cried, desperation clawing at her. "I returned you to Sethi."

Istara tightened her hold on the pendant, its light coursed around her, dripped into the silence of her soul. "Take my hand." She held hers out to Baalat. "Leave this place with me. The relic will protect you."

Baalat shrank from Istara, her eyes dark, haunted. "I cannot," she breathed, her chest rising and falling, her enslavement to her master palpable. "I belong to him now. I bear his taint. I can never go back. He will never let me go."

"And what of Horus?" Istara asked, quiet. "He is lost without you."

Baalat's gaze slid to the rift. She blinked, rapid, her eyes moving back and forth, as if searching for her consort within the churning boil. A single tear slipped free, black, poisoned. She shook her head, her features ravaged by grief. "I am the darkness now. I am lost to him. Forever."

Istara turned her eyes from Baalat's anguish to the pendant. She could save Baalat or Sethi. She could not save both.

She met Baalat's eyes. The once-goddess still knelt beside her. "Please," Baalat whispered, tremulous, a broken, lost bird, her song stolen, doomed to face an eternity in a cage of hate.

Istara stepped into the rift. The devastating cry of Baalat filled her soul. As she fell, she hurled the pendant at Baalat.

It struck Baalat's chest. With what remained of her power, Istara channeled all her light into the relic. It poured into Baalat, who screamed in agony as the light burned through the pollution of her soul. Istara closed her eyes and plummeted away. There could be no regret. She would not leave Baalat in the endless silence of the dark. Istara was the goddess of healing—even here, in this place of the greatest darkness. She fell into infinity, her light trailing after her, toward the one destined to destroy her light, her love, her soul.

❋ ❋ ❋

Everything hurt. Breathing hurt. Thinking hurt. The anguish of existence screamed through Meresamun. The horror of her fate swarmed over her. Marduk had put his back to the pyramid and taken the force of their landing, its vicious punch even through his armor and shield ramming into her bones, smashing through her skull. Then, nothing. The mercy of the dark.

"Ninsunu," Marduk's metallic voice, devoid of emotion, cut through the haze of her suffering. "Can you hear me?" Against the shear of her shattered senses, the touch of his gloved fingers against the corner of her mouth. Blood trickled down her throat, hot, salty. Heat soaked her flesh. Nearby, the spit and hiss of flames. The acrid burn of smoke scoured her lungs.

"How brave you were." The metallic whirr of his helmet came to her as it slid against its connectors. Through the fog of her mind, she sensed he was searching the plaza for their enemies—for those who had been her friends. A hiss as he pulled a weapon free, its low beeps as he readied it to fire. "Until Sethi and the Imarians arrive," he continued, his voice cold and disembodied behind the implacable wall of his helmet, "I will not leave you here unprotected." Another whirr as he turned back to face her. His fingers came to her face again, tender despite the harsh edges of his glove. "My love. Come back to me. Look at me."

His words claimed her, hauled her from the edge of oblivion. She opened her eyes. Her flame-bathed reflection in his visor glared back at her. Blood soaked her temple, matted her hair, and seeped from her mouth and nose. A dark bruise stained her jaw and cheekbone. Raw, weeping burns peppered her face, neck, and shoulders.

Her consort gazed at her, utterly still, locked behind the silence of his armor. A heartbeat later he reached up, still holding the weapon in his gloved hand, and disconnected the connectors of his helmet. With a deft movement he pulled it off and set it on the scorched ground between his legs. His carnelian eyes held hers, hard with pride. He bent and pressed his lips to hers, a lingering, quiet kiss, granted amidst the burning ruins of his ship. He pulled back and settled his helmet back in place, no longer a lover, but a warrior. The chill of calculated, controlled violence swept over him, subtle, terrifying.

He pulled his other weapon free and enabled it. Resting his forearms against his armored thighs, he scanned the carnage of his ship and the shield's remains across the plaza, the metal of his weapons glinting in the scorching heat of the fires. "I need you on your feet." He held out the crook of his arm. Her fingers trembling, she wrapped her hand around its metallic sheath. He rose and pulled her to her feet.

Fresh pain sluiced through her. Nausea roiled within her torso, rank with the heaviness of blood. It tore up her throat, metallic, thick, and splattered against the ashlars, staining them with her life.

When she finished, trembling, her eyes burning with smoke and tears, she turned. Of her consort, she could see nothing.

"Come," his clipped, metallic voice came to her from out of the haze of heat and smoke. "We need to move." Above, through the gouts of black smoke, the scream of three ships sliced through the sky, ashen whorls rippling in their wake. "They will be looking for me. My armor can cloak me, but not you." A disembodied touch came to her hand, the dominant feel of his gloved fingers slid around her palm, clasped her to him, protective. "Come with me," he said, the absence of his presence unnerving her. "Until this is finished, I know where you will be safe."

❋   ❋   ❋

Blistering heat and fire surrounded Urhi-Teshub. He cursed the acrid burn of poisoned smoke pouring from the remains of a severed thruster and pushed past its boiling well toward three enormous metal ribs. They loomed over him, scorched talons. He halted. This should be the spot, or near enough. Before he had left his ship, he had searched for her signature, for the faint beat of her existence. He was certain he had not lost his direction. He turned in a slow circle, seeking her presence, her powerful, brilliant, enigmatic immortal soul. There. A whisper. She was close.

He turned. A wall of flames blocked his way. He plunged through it, into a white-hot corridor of molten metal. The blast of a thousand furnaces scorched his flesh. He hissed and dined on agony. His light erupted, though the echo of the inferno's heat continued to strafe him, blades of fire. Within the shimmering coil of his god-light, he shoved his way through the liquid heat. Ahead, the remains of a divan's frame melted into the white-hot skeleton of a fuselage. A tremor of hope rippled through him. His eyes streaming, he searched for the remains of the wall which had once separated the cabin from the flight deck. His hopes hardened. There. It took shape, familiar, a dying, tragic thing. Sekhmet's ship. Beyond the struts, into the flight deck, another barrier of fire.

He pushed his way through the flames, his lungs bellowing for air. Black spots speckled his vision. One final shove and he erupted out of the incinerating heat into a scorched well of blackened ashlars, dense with streamers of sooty smoke. He staggered to the center of the bleak well. A gust of smoke-laden air swept over him. He hauled at it. Poison scalded his throat. The pressure in his lungs eased, though they ached anew, fouled by the toxic air. He drew another breath, endured the searing wash of the fumes.

Over a pile of charred wreckage, flames roamed, desultory, insipid, seeking the last of the fuel. A flicker of golden light glimmered from behind it. A dark jumble of twisted metal blocked his way. It reared over him, draped in a tangle of writhing cables. Their truncated ends sparked, erratic, snapping with blue fire.

A burst of golden light erupted from the depths of the debris, brighter than his own. *Sekhmet.* He drew another poisoned breath and shouldered his way between two broiling struts. The cables lunged at him, vicious, brutal. Jolts of raw power slammed into him.

He tumbled through the opening into the heated debris and endured the searing grip of the ship's power as it coursed through him, seeking escape. Hard in its wake, the sensation of a thousand needles, hot as boiling oil.

His light surged. He pulled himself to his knees and waited for his strength to return. A little distance away, within a growing cocoon of her light, Sekhmet hung upside down, caught between the charred shell of her seat and the melted console, her abdomen almost severed in two. She met Urhi-Teshub's eyes, hers, blank. He blinked back the tears burning his eyes. The flames had claimed her face, left her an unrecognizable pulp. He wondered how long she had remained conscious before the anguish of her injuries granted her an escape. He suspected far longer than she should have.

He climbed the heap of twisted metal beneath her seat and took hold of the seat's frame and tugged, hard, ignoring the metal's latent heat bleeding through his gloves. His fingers blistering, he hauled against the bars separating her from him. They defied him, stubborn. He considered his ax. No. The blade would strike her, too. Brute force was all he had. His feet sliding on the debris beneath him, he pulled. Nothing happened. He loaded the polluted space with oaths. The debris underfoot shifted. He stumbled, only caught himself just before he returned to the embrace of the cables. Clad in rage, he stormed back and attacked the seat's frame anew.

One of the bars gave, just a little. He threw all his strength against it. It held, defiant, mocking him. He glared at it. He was the god of storms. This was madness, what was a piece of metal against *him*? Gritting his teeth, he closed his eyes, tightened his grip and heaved. The memory of the last time he had wrestled against metal bars condemned him—when he had lost against those which had imprisoned him in the Etemen'anki. When he believed he had lost Istara.

The sharp edges of the frame dug into his gloves, cut his flesh. Pain seared him. He ignored it. He would not fail again. Intense focus called to him. Like the sparks of the severed cables, he sensed his power gathering. He held still, waited for the mystery which resided within him to ignite. He thought of Sekhmet, of her sacrifice, and her courage, and of his futility to pull her from the wreckage of her ship and carry her to the safety of the skies before Sethi arrived with his brutal god-eating weapon.

Sethi.

Fury pummeled him. The one who had taken Istara from him would not take Sekhmet, too. That whoreson had done enough. Vengeance, denied far too long, shattered its bonds and blistered through him. The storm of his rage gathered. Black clouds boiled within his soul, riven by bolts of blue lightning. It exploded from him and slammed into the seat, its assault so brilliant it burned the backs of his eyes. Multiple metallic snaps washed through his senses. The seat's frame shattered. He let go. Splintered pieces clattered into the wreckage, sharp, brittle rain.

Sekhmet remained hanging upside down, her body fused to the console. He eyed her torso. The pain must have been unimaginable. He took her weight against him and drew several ragged breaths of the savage air. His lungs afire, he pulled, gentle. She did not budge. He pulled harder. Nothing. He let her go.

Freed of the seat's back, she hung, pinioned to the console, her golden light wreathing around her.

In the distance, the crump of explosions. When Urhi-Teshub had landed, Sethi was already halfway to the complex. By now, he would almost be at the plaza. Urhi-Teshub had no choice, he would have to hurt the goddess of war to help her. He swore the foulest oath he knew. Another crump, closer this time. He clenched his fists. So be it. He gritted his teeth and pulled his ax free.

"My love," he said, grim, as he lined up his aim, "forgive me for what I am about to do to you."

He brought the blade down and severed the goddess of war from her ship. As gently as he could, he cut the metal from her torso, averting his eyes from the half of her he had left behind. He called to his power again, drinking of his rage, his fury, and his hunger to avenge himself—at last in possession of the hidden key within him. He turned it against the lock and the full power of the storm god poured through him.

Surrounded by the lightning-streaked cerulean shield of his storm-light, he carried her away, through the cables, through the fire, past the white heat of the ion flames to his ship. He lay her on the divan, hating himself for the crime he had been forced to commit against her. Beneath the lowest of her ribs, her severed torso lay open, her internal organs cooked dry. She did not bleed. The heat had stolen everything from her. He pressed a soft kiss to the thin, blistered gash of what had once been her lips.

"Come back to me," he whispered.

He went to the flight deck, smashed his palm against the thrusters and tore away from the ruins of the plaza. He had found her. Nothing else mattered in this heartbeat. Nothing. She was safe.

And now, as he crested the flames of the city—he drank of the revenge of the storm god, prepared his weapons, and fired.

❋ ❋ ❋

White fire burned through Baalat, seared the bleak rot of her soul. Horrified, sickened, she shunted herself back from the edge of the rift, seeking to distance herself from Istara's relic nestled against her lap, its brilliance a star against the punishing, empty dark of her gown.

Glittering white tendrils of light swarmed from its heart into her breast. She panted, wild, conflicted, as they blistered a path of aching clarity through her, scouring the lies from her heart and mind, granting her glimpses of the one she had been. Shame flooded her. Hard on its heels, guilt, oppressive as the weight of a mountain. No, an ocean, its depths unfathomable. There would be no reprieve for her. Even with Istara's relic, the dark still called to her, a lover.

The relic pulsed. More tendrils erupted from it, spiraled into her torso, helixes of light surrounded by a sea of black. Fragments of her past pierced the tainted shadows of her mind, thin, narrow shafts, reminding her of the dawns she had shared with Horus in Pi-Ramesses. A memory flared, dense with the humid heat of the delta, of pink, early morning light slipping through the closed shutters of their villa, of his arms around her as he made love to her, worshiped her, the one for whom he had sacrificed eternity. She bit back a sob, her longing for him intense, visceral. *Horus.* Her love. Her only love. And she had become *this*, a servant of the dark, soiled by hate. A betrayer of the light. No more.

She touched the relic, cautious, as though it were a viper. Against her fingertips, its purity scorched her, reminded her of the distance between her and everything she had lost—of the one she had lost. The darkness within her fled from the relic's fire. She rose and turned to face the one who had stolen her from herself.

He stood at the opening to the chamber, and smiled, seductive, pleased. A sheen of dark silver rippled over the skin of his armor.

"You have done well," he said. He stepped back, making way for her to return to the suite. He tilted his head toward the basin of liquid dark, created by her for this very purpose. "Now, destroy it."

Baalat tightened her hold on the relic, its power feeding her, conflicting her, punishing her. "No," she said, her throat tight. Waves of fear and determination struck her, sharp, cold. She lifted her chin. "I refuse."

A flicker of displeasure marred the elegance of his features. "You dare disobey me?" he asked, low.

"You took me from Horus," she answered, forcing herself to cling to the memory of her consort, of the love they had shared— of the love the darkness had taken from her. "And then made me your vessel so I would betray Istara and destroy the relic." She took a shuddering breath. Another wave of guilt sluiced through her. "Yet after all I have done, she sacrificed the only thing which can stop you—to save me." Tears came, pure, silent—an upwelling of honesty in a place of lies.

"How quaint." Contempt darkened her master's lips, hardened his mien. "These stories you tell yourselves to make the meaninglessness of your existences matter." He eyed her, cold, the bleak promise of eternal suffering clear in his look. "The only thing which matters is the end of the light. You hold her bauble and now you think you can be saved. You cannot. This is my realm, not *his*. *That* can only go so far with *you*. You belong to me. You can never return to what you were. Never." He took a step toward her, just past the threshold of the chamber, his bearing ominous, brutal. "Consider with care what your next action will be. Do as you have been commanded, or face suffering beyond your worst nightmares."

Baalat clung to the relic, even as it tormented her, as its light laid bare the depths of her depravity, her enslavement to the dark. "So long as this continues to exist," she said, "there is hope." Her heart thudded, dread choking her as his countenance hardened, turned cold. Sadistic. She pressed on, refusing to stop now she had started. "I will not be the one to destroy it."

Malevolence bled from him. His gaze bore into her, vile, soaked in hate, his thoughts became her own, allowing her to glimpse the darkest of agonies. She closed her eyes. So long as she held the relic, she knew he would not touch her. It was impossible for him to touch the relic, or its bearer—a powerful foresight of the Creator. He needed another to destroy it. And she would not do it, no matter what he did to her.

Silence thundered. She counted her poisoned heartbeats. Ten. Twenty. Thirty.

A liquid shimmer rippled through her. She clutched the relic until its edges cut into her flesh, until she felt the heat of blood. Soon, it would begin. She braced herself.

Close by, the sharp hiss of a breath drawn. The rustle of a kilt. The creak of leather. His scent reached her, harsh with sweat, reminding her of sweltering nights in Waset locked in his arms. Her heart lurched. No. Please. Not this. Anything but this.

His voice came to her, aching, raw with hope. "Baalat?"

She opened her eyes, lifted them to the one who loved her. He stood in the chamber—hauled in by the darkness, just as Istara had been—his eyes lost in the shadows, no more than an arm's span distance away, his once-perfect skin raw and blistered, and his hands bloody, his flesh seared to the hilts of his swords. He pulled his fingers free, grunting, pain ravaging his features. One sword fell to the smooth floor, then the other, their fall muted in the oppressive air of the chamber. He faced her, blood dripping from his fingertips. A warrior to the end. The god of war. How many times had she healed him, returned him to his glory? A thousand thousand times. She need only reach out to him to feel him, to be in his arms, to taste his kiss. The heat of tears scorched her eyes. Her master had not lied. He had promised suffering beyond her worst nightmares. *Horus.*

Her consort came to her, a stride which devoured the abyss between them. "My love," he breathed, a broken whisper. Lines of grief carved deep tracks against the planes of his jaw and around his eyes, turned the corners of his lips downward. His gaze raked over her, haunted, desperate, searching for the one who no longer existed. "What has been done to you?"

"Everything," Baalat answered, flat. She took a step back, distanced herself from the one who was still good, untouched by the evil which would never be cleansed from her, not even by Istara's light—perhaps not even by the Creator, himself.

His gaze fell to her hand, where Istara's relic still granted its light to her, holding the worst of the evil within her at bay. In the leaden silence, taut with brutal expectation, his eyes came back to hers. Understanding flickered. Clever, sharp Horus.

"He is going to make you suffer," Baalat said, her heart tight, hating the words, their utterance making it real. "I have the power to stop it . . . if I destroy the relic."

"But you won't," Horus said, admiration hardening his features, granting her a glimpse of the god he once was. He reached out to cup her jaw, the acrid, familiar heat of his blood filling her senses. She flinched, unwilling to let her taint touch him, but he caught her, his grip soaked with the essence of his life. His touch poured into her, captured the remains of her soul, scoured its filth with the depth of his love. A thousand memories slammed into her, their passage spanning an eternity spent in love—an endless, beautiful, perfect existence. Her heart huddled into itself, seeking refuge against the onslaught of their glittering past and this, their dark, tortured present. A keening filled her, the lament of a dying creature drenched in sorrow, riven between longing for a return to the past, and the end of their suffering.

"I am not undeserving of this fate," he said, his eyes holding hers, fierce with fenced passion. "I killed an innocent in cold blood, a being whose only crime was to have been enslaved as Marduk's consort. It is a wrong I have never ceased to regret."

His thumb stroked her cheek, his tenderness a crime in this place of cruelty. "My brave, courageous love. Be strong. We will find each other again. Our bond can never be destroyed, even in this place of utter darkness."

"Horus." His name slipped from her lips, sacred, eternal. A tear slid free. His gaze followed its track to his hand. Anguish tightened his lips. She did not need to look down—knew what he saw. Her tears, once golden, were black, saturated by the evil within her heart, her soul. She took a quavering breath. "How will I go on without the hope of you?"

His look turned inward. She waited as he traveled the paths of his mind in search of words to comfort her. A light flared within the depths of his eyes. He stepped closer, lowered his mouth to her ear. "Because you are a goddess," he said, his breath against her neck, intimate, familiar. "You no longer need me. Everything you require is within you." Her chin still caught in his grip, he turned her face to his. A heartbeat passed as he gazed at her, accepted what she had become. His sorrowful mouth touched hers, a final, parting kiss. She clung to him, sensing the dark one's observation, the amusement rippling from him, as though they were nothing more than a heartbeat's entertainment.

Horus pulled back. Tears glinted in his eyes. "Farewell my love." He let her go. A vacuum of emptiness swarmed through her. She staggered as he stepped back and turned to face the dark one.

"I am ready," he said.

"No," the dark aspect smiled, cold. "You are not."

Under Horus's feet, the floor rippled. Dark, liquid tendrils coiled up around him, caging him within a space barely enough for him to move, to breath.

Pain slammed into Baalat, tore at her eyes, her mind, shattered her soul, a thousand heated blades loaded with persecution. She fell to her knees, suffocating, struggling to breath. Fire ripped through her lungs, anguish burned her throat. Pressure rammed against her eyes.

From a distance, through the roar of her suffering, Horus's cry, laden with anguish, vowing to do anything to make her suffering cease.

Against her fingers, the icy chill of dark tendrils bit into her flesh, working to free the relic from her grip. Blinded by pain, deafened by the thunder of her silenced breaths, she tightened her grip, desperation driving her. She would never let go. Never. The pressure of a vice surrounded her, crushed her. The dull snap of bones. Pain beyond her darkest imaging swept through her. She longed for the end, for the silence of nonexistence.

Horus's cries hammered at the walls of her torment. Blood soaked her mouth, her ears, her eyes, it burst from her veins, drenched her gown. Still, she held on, against the burning ice of the tendrils, against the immutable force of the dark one's will, against the anguish of her consort.

Horus's voice came to her. Close by. "Give me the relic," he cried. "I beg you."

Through a suffocating haze of blood, she saw him. He knelt before, his blistered face ravaged by horror. His hands went to hers, pulled at her fingers, forced them open, one by one.

Through the depths of her agony, the last of her will reared up. It shredded her, splintered a jagged path through the chrysalis of her isolation. Horus would destroy the relic. To save her, he would obliterate everything.

"No." The word came out, wet, bloody. She caught hold of his wrist, and called to the power the dark one had granted her. Horus met her eyes. Read the message within hers.

"Do it," he said. A single tear slid from his eye; bathed the ruins of his flesh.

Darkness engulfed her, drank of her misery, fed on her blood and broken bones. Annihilation poured into him, shattered his life, eradicated his existence. Within a heartbeat, he was gone. A mortal life crushed as easily as one might stand on a beetle.

Inconsequential. Meaningless. An eternity of love snuffed out within the space of a breath.

Despite the coil of evil soaking her, relishing in her act of destruction, the relic's light swarmed into her, continued to heal her. Ignoring the shrieks of pain from her broken bones, she crawled to Horus, nauseous, sickened by what she had wrought against him. His pupils dilated. The last of his light fled. The one she loved gazed back at her, lifeless, empty. A shell. Her gaze drifted from the husk of his body to the swords he had shed on his arrival, to the raw pieces of his flesh stuck to the hilts. She inhaled the stench of the place, the metallic taint of blood. Of desperation. Hate. She bent over his still-warm body and pressed a bloody kiss to his dead lips. *Horus. My love. Be free.* Her body aching, wreathed in the weakening tendrils of the relic's store of light, she rose and faced the darkness.

"You will never have what you want," she said, taut with grief. "You will never destroy the light. I will stand against you until the end of time."

Her oppressor leaned against the opening's bleak jamb, boredom oozing from him. He eyed her injuries, impassive. "He lasted longer than I expected." Contempt soaked each of his precise, cutting words. "If only you could see what I have done to you, what he had to witness. I have remade you into a beautiful, broken creature. *My* creature." He pushed away from the jamb and approached her, slow, malignant. His gaze flicked to the relic. "Sooner or later, you will obey." He tilted his head toward the suite, toward the dread font waiting for its sacrifice. "You have ever been destined to be my consort. Once you shed the last of your defiance, you will rise, a being unlike any other. Your cruelty will surpass mine." He turned to Horus's body and rocked his metal-sheathed foot against her consort's hip. He pushed his weight against it. Her consort's body rolled to the edge of the rift. Another shove from the dark aspect's obsidian boot and Horus tumbled over the edge into the darkness, unceremonious, as worthless and unwanted as the leavings of a meal. Anguish clogged Baalat's soul. Guilt rammed into her, stripped her raw. He had been the god of war. His sacrifice was for nothing. No. He had not died for nothing. She still had the relic.

Her oppressor turned back to her. "Despite your tendency to disobedience, you intrigue me. You are unpredictable. A challenge. Now I remember why I waited so long for you. A once-goddess who is capable of killing her consort." A sadistic smile fleeted over his lips. "I enjoyed that. You are more than worthy to sit by my side, to share my bed, and bear the fruit of our couplings." He moved toward her, seductive, dark, sensual, the abrupt shift in his demeanor assaulting her senses, weakening her will. He eyed her, hot, hungry. The darkness within her awakened, responding to the promise of the brutal taint of his touch. His private look shredded her defenses. "Think of the enormous power you will wield," he murmured. "Apart from the one who possesses you, none could ever overcome you. Absolute power would be yours. For eternity. And you would throw it all away for—" he cut a scathing look at her hand, her bloodied fingers tight against the relic's fading light, "—a bauble?"

Baalat closed her eyes. Blinded herself to the sight of the one who offered her everything and nothing. A memory filled her mind. Horus pointing up at the stars, the scent of wine on his breath, the solidness of his arm around her shoulder. *One day, I will take you there and make love to you.*

She opened her eyes. Evil faced her. Waited for her. Tempted her. "Yes."

The floor rippled. A dozen tendrils erupted around her. The relic surged, surrounded her in a cocoon of light. The dark one retreated a step, his glare laden with virulent hate. Pain shattered her anew. More bones snapped within her chest, the pain so brutal she could not even cry out. Blood filled her mouth, soaked her throat. More tendrils piled up outside the feeble well of the relic's light, slavering malignance. The relic's light weakened. Once she no longer possessed it, he would bring her back to this place, would punish her for eternity. Pain would be her only companion. She gritted her teeth as two more bones snapped in her foot. So be it.

The rift beckoned, a mere heartbeat away. She dragged herself to it, one step, two, enduring the blistering shears within her, of splintered bone slicing through flesh. She fell into the rift's embrace, away from the lair of the dark one—from the storm of his fury.

Impenetrable darkness clobbered her. Within the thin cocoon of the relic's light she searched for Horus, but of the one she loved, there was nothing. Alone, broken, lost, she plummeted through the abyss toward the light, the relic brightening with each silenced, sundered heartbeat.

❋ ❋ ❋

His unseen grip encircling her hand, Marduk came to a halt, far closer to the pillar of obliterating darkness than Meresamun wished to be. Just beyond the reach of her arm, its boundary shifted, nebulous, distorting everything it touched, its circuitous undulations resonant of a strong tide. Its bulk reared up, a living thing which poured up into the heavens out from the plaza's ancient ashlars, its presence enormous, oppressive. Evil soaked it. Even marred by Marduk's taint, its close proximity was too much for her heart to bear. She took a step back, her soul shuddering, desperate to flee. Marduk's hold tightened. He drew her back into the darkness's shadow, its outer aura rippling around them, a poisoned panoply of silken hangings.

She cast a look over her shoulder, longing to see something other than what sought to annihilate her. Through the morass of the pillar's presence, the view of the pyramids and its shattered, shield-strewn plaza smeared and blurred, distorted by the chaotic forces within the pillar, as destructive a power as the force of Creation itself. Dense silence soaked the space, ripe with the promise of hopelessness, loss, despair.

"You must remain at this distance," her consort said, his metallic voice loud in the emptiness of the pillar's void. "The gods won't risk coming this close, not even for you. You will wait here until I return for you, it is my command." He let go of her hand. His presence faded with his retreating tread. She lunged after him. Her fingers found nothing but emptiness. She turned back to the pillar and eyed it. It rippled toward her, sentient, reeking of insatiable hunger. Tendrils slid from its recesses and slithered across the ashlars to her feet. Her shallow breaths loud in her ears, she backed away from them, razor-sharp walls of terror closing in on her. One of the tendrils reared up and extended a thin filament to one of the markings on her shoulder. Its touch came down, cold as a tomb. It followed the movement of her marking, drinking of her terror. Bereft of the protection of Marduk's affinity with the dark, the brunt of the pillar's malignance clobbered her. Pure darkness called to her, a promise. A lie.

The tendril's cold touch deepened, its vile presence seeping into her flesh, searing her soul, marking her anew. An unnamable escalation of terror swarmed through her. She sensed this was the prime font of evil from which Marduk's darkness was fed, from which the jihn had been spawned. The depths of the pillar's evil surrounded her, insidious, ancient, feeding on her anguish, searching for the last of her light, determined to erase what little of herself was left to her. She screamed her consort's name.

The pounding of booted feet neared. The firm grip of his hand found hers. She clung to her consort's touch, gibbering with horror at the tendril fastened to her flesh, a parasite, tenacious.

"Get it off me," she cried. "Make it stop."

He tore at the thing, the metal tips of his gloves opening her blistered flesh. The tendril remained, arrogant, impervious, its girth pulsing as it fed. Sorrow washed through her, a forsaken tide, leaving her alone upon a bleak, gray shore, a hollow vessel waiting to be filled. Darkness beckoned. She turned toward the pillar, her heart empty, seeking a home.

Come.

She stepped toward the churning barrier.

"No!" Marduk hauled her back. His arms came around her, the ferocity of his grip a hair's breadth from violence. "She is mine," he cried, his voice behind the visor a bronze saw against granite. "Have you not taken enough from me?"

The tendril's bite deepened, a thousand icy pincers streamed into the corridors of Meresamun's soul, penetrating rooms long shuttered. In a heartbeat, her deepest hopes and secrets lay before the master of the dark, a tiny collection of miserable, pathetic tokens. Caught in Marduk's embrace, she wilted as the dark's sear of malevolence corroded her, mocked her hopes, erased her purpose.

Marduk caught hold of her chin, shoved it up. Through the roar of the dark tide's surge, his words skidded past her. "Look at me." His voice rammed into her, ragged, raw with dread. She tried to open her eyes, but it cost too much. Exhaustion dug its talons into her, pinioned her. The pillar's weight bore down on her, called to her, offered relief. His gloved fingers bit into her jaw. Lances of pain blossomed anew, hot and red. "You will not leave me. Open your eyes. See *me*." His grip turned brutal. "Ninsunu!" She tried again. Failed again. It was too late. A wall of silence bled from him, then, low, desperate, a beacon. "Meresamun. Come back to me."

Her name on his lips shuddered through her. Egypt. Home. Her heart beat, once, twice, a bird's wings caught in a net. She opened her eyes. What remained of her existence regarded her in the dark surface of his visor. She blinked, slow, and her empty reflection blinked back. His visor slid up. From within the helmet's shell, he gazed at her, anguish ravaging the lines of his jaw. From the ruined recesses of her being she recognized the one who loved her, who had removed his cloaking and stood exposed to the gods. For her. He was here. Her love. Her enemy. The one she had hoped to reprieve—standing between her and what he was, himself.

He backed away from the pillar, pulling her with him. They emerged from the shifting, nebulous ripples of the pillar's aura, its eldritch silence shattered by the roar of the gods' ships tearing through the inflamed skies; the deep crump of distant explosions. The tendril remained. It slid deeper into her, possessive, unyielding. Its presence permeated her thoughts, sedated her against the chill of the annihilation of the last of her light. Soon now. It would have her. Through the tendril's bond, the pillar called to her, dark susurrations which washed through her—soft, sibilant whispers, offering a harbor to her battered soul.

Come.

Clarity shattered the last of her resistance. In the war between light and dark, there was *only* the dark, there had always only been the dark. The dark ruled the realm of the living. The light, intangible and abstract was for . . . the recycling of the dead. The darkness was life. Light was death. She need only give herself to the darkness and she would be free, eternal, just like her consort, her heart beating in time with his. The struggle would end. Freedom beckoned. She had been a fool. How could she, a mere mortal ever believe she could stop Marduk, the dark's chosen one? She had always been destined to fail. He belonged to the darkness. And soon, so would she. None could overcome the dark's supremacy. Not her. Not Zarpanitu. Not the gods. Not even the Creator.

It would be easier to accept her fate rather than endure a long, slow demise into the darkness. Unlike Zarpanitu, she would choose this path, would accept her destiny, rather than have it thrust upon her. There was no other choice. There never had been. Everything else had been a lie dressed in false hope.

"I must go back." She pulled against her consort. "Let me go."

"No," Marduk answered, his hold on her implacable. "Never. You would—"

A profound, ominous thrum drowned out the rest of his words, its deepening resonance deafened the chaos of her soul, vanquished the thunder of the gods' ships. It surged up from the foundations of the plaza and slammed into her feet, its brutal thrust shoving her and her consort into the air. They hung suspended before the pillar, caught in the intensity of its grip. Another reverberation joined the first, then another, each resonance as deep as the horns of war. Together, they formed an exquisite, mind-aching whole. A soul-punishing reverberation came from the pyramids, their combined power humiliating, humbling.

Around the circumference of the pillar, an eruption of glittering white light shot up into the heavens. It rotated, fast and tight, a solid, restrained thing. A heartbeat later, it erupted into a multitude of glittering stars. A second bolt of white light streamed down from above and rammed into the ground. Another multitude of stars swept through the abyss, reforming until it settled into a swirling, rotating pillar both within and without the dark's brutal, crushing depths.

Still held aloft by the field of deep resonance, Meresamun gazed at it, her flesh tingling, her senses afire. No longer a thing of pure darkness, the pillar rippled with light. Hope scored the lines of her despair. She had been wrong. The tower *had* housed the Well of Life. It called to her, a thing of endless dark and blistering light, a terrifying, beautiful, blinding thing. At last. Euphoria skidded against the edges of her existence. Marduk had saved her—so she could save him.

She eyed him in the light of the pillar, white stars glinted against his armor as he regarded the pillar's transformation. Pain lanced her breast, deep, paralyzing. She looked down. The tendril had burrowed through her breast into her heart. Darkness poured into her, saturated her, poisoned her. A tsunami of hate washed away the vestiges of her hope. Her soul staggered under its weight.

She closed her eyes, resisting the evil rising in her, its call turning her against her true purpose.

Come.

She opened her eyes, drawn once more to the darkness, pulled to the one who summoned her, his power equal to the Creator's. She struggled against Marduk's grip, desperate to obey. From within the pillar, a star tore itself free of the helix. It plummeted down the length of the tendril and slammed into Meresamun. For the briefest breath, brilliance soaked her, exposed the dark's lies in the glare of truth.

A bleak keening skidded against the edge of her hearing. Pain erupted anew from her breast. The tendril tore itself free, dripping gouts of hate from its maw. It fled back to the pillar, writhing, suffering. Its latent touch roiled through her, sickening her, spearing her hope. Another blinding shard of light eclipsed her mind and saturated her heart until she could not tell where the light began and she ended—the only constant Marduk's arms around her, holding her as they fell, never letting her go.

❈ ❈ ❈

Urhi-Teshub veered around the largest pyramid, the quiet thunder of his engines carrying him away from the smoke-soaked carnage of the destroyed ships to the center of the complex. Elati's allied armies were in full retreat. They surged up the massive tiers to the complex, avoiding the fallen shreds of the molten shield, their armor sharp glints against the broiling light.

He tilted the ship to its side and cut a dark look at the twisted, flaming wreckage of Marduk's warship spread across the plaza. Marduk might be immortal, but without any of his regeneration devices, it would take him a long time to heal. He cut a look over his shoulder at the ruins of the one his heart clung to, her light growing in strength with each heartbeat. If Sekhmet had suffered the injuries she had, and she was a god, he didn't expect Marduk to have fared much better, even with his enhanced armor. There had to be a limit, even for Marduk. The detonation of the ships' collision had shorn Urhi-Teshub of his vision, and sent his ship hurtling so fast up into the heavens, his engines had stalled. No. Marduk was down, Urhi-Teshub would wager his ax on it. He bit back a harsh smile, a scythe of pride for Sekhmet's ferocity cutting a swathe through him. One down. One to go.

He lifted his attention from the complex—seething with the allies' retreat and the oncoming tsunami of Marduk's army—to the screen on the console marked with the heat signatures of the other gods' cloaked ships. He counted the marks. Of those who had departed before the shield fell, all apart from one still remained in the air.

He turned toward Thoth's palace, thinking to stem the tide of arrivals, but he would not be needed. While he had gone after Sekhmet, the gods had laid waste to Thoth's palace. In its bleak, shattered ruins, only the mirror remained standing, and those still coming through faced a barrage of fire half did not survive. So, it had come to this. Attrition. So be it. The Imarians had chosen their fate. Let them die. Those who still lived would be cut down. He would see to it. There would be no room on Elati for those who had allied themselves to the dark.

Across the entire south eastern section of the city, fire from the cloaked ships of the gods rained into the city, soaking Nisu's once-verdant basin in flames. Smoke hung across the city in thick blankets, its layers obscuring his view and concealing the one he would not stop seeking until he had found him and severed him limb from limb.

In between the lacings of flame and smoke, a burst of silver caught his eye. He slowed the ship and circled the spot. For a heartbeat, the smoke thinned. From behind a fallen ashlar, a black-armored warrior hauled a massive tube onto his shoulder, its silvered length catching against the smoke-wreathed rays of the sun. The warrior pointed it into the sky. Urhi-Teshub checked his screen. Ptah's heat signature glared back at him from the spot.

A white star surrounded by a fierce cerulean glow burst from the weapon's nose and scorched a path over the burning city up into the sky. It exploded against thin air, and for the briefest heartbeat revealed the cloaked outline of Ptah's ship before it blossomed into a blister of white. Its glare rammed into Urhi-Teshub's skull. He recoiled, his arm going up to shield his eyes, but it was too late, white saturated his vision. His eyes watering, he blinked, frantic, desperate to see. There. In the light's wake— nothing. He checked the screen. Ptah's ship had vanished as if it had never existed. Another star shrouded in cerulean light erupted from the smoke-filled basin, a beat later, a second ship vaporized in a sheeting of brutal white.

Against the console, the indicator for the ship's cloaking winked out. The ship shimmered, and from within its flight deck, Urhi-Teshub knew Horakhti's golden ship hung over the burning city, visible to anyone who cared to look. He reset the switch. A quiet click, nothing more. He pressed his lips together, bit back an ugly oath. Another 'gift' from Marduk's arsenal. Across the skies, the other ships' translucent skins rippled, one by one revealing the location of each of the remaining ships. They hung spread out over the city, exposed, vulnerable. There was no time to retaliate. He roared away, toward the opposite side of the city, where the Imarians were not and the flames and smoke had not yet reached the ancient trees and vines. At the edge of his vision, close to Thoth's palace, a third ship succumbed to the eviscerating silence of Marduk's weaponry. He gritted his teeth. Of course there would be more than one of them.

He took a slow arc over one of the crumbling *ziqquratu* sentinels ringing the city's perimeter. The sun's rays slid over the console as he turned the ship's nose back toward the center of the city. The gods had retreated, as he had done, taking up position at the city's edge, far from the reach of the weapons. He tried the cloaking again. Nothing. Fury nailed him. He let it ride him, welcomed the power coursing through him in its wake, its blue heat sharp, acrid, powerful enough to shatter a mountain.

He flicked the switch again, willed the cloaking to turn on. Darkness shot through the ship, utter and blinding. A single heartbeat of stunned silence passed before the ship's internal lights flickered on.

Outside, a wall of black prowled the windows, dense as tar. Only the quiet thunder of the ship and its faint illumination touched his senses, reassured him he still existed. He scanned the console's screens. Silence greeted him. Every sensor peered up at him, blank, denied their purpose. He cut the thrusters and brought the ship into a holding position, somewhere still near the edge of the city—if there still *was* a city. Long heartbeats passed. The perpetual darkness persisted. Claustrophobia clawed at him. He shoved it back, and stared at the dormant console, searching for an explanation, though none were desirable. Perhaps another one of Marduk's devices, or a manifestation of the jihn's power, or the pillar had broken its restraints and consumed the entire city, perhaps even the whole of Anki. He cut a look over his shoulder at Sekhmet. Golden light surrounded her, dozens of layers deep, the seething tendrils of her cocoon obscuring her from him. A finger of envy touched him. In the short time they had been in the air, her cocoon's length had increased to her full height. The goddess of war possessed far more rapid regeneration powers than he.

The darkness surged back to the center of the city. Murky light slid into the ship, dense with shadow, and bled of color. Urhi-Teshub leaned forward, his eye on the console as the screens crackled back to life. Distorted symbols and gibberish stuttered down their faces.

A massive clap tore through the ship, its force so brutal the engines cut out, the sudden silence deafening. The ship fell, plummeting in an arc back toward the *ziqquratu* as though the god of war's ship were no more than a toy caught on the wake of a passing barge. Urhi-Teshub scrambled for the controls. Only half responded. The lights for the reverse thrusters blinked at him. He punched all four buttons at the same time and endured the surge of power against the ship's freefall. Mere heartbeats from the *ziqquratu's* topmost tier, he pulled the ship up, and brought it back into a holding position.

Darkness bled from above. The sun and its heat had vanished. The only light came from below. His flesh prickled, taut with prescience. Whatever this was, this wasn't Marduk, or even the jihn. This was something far bigger. He leaned forward, wary of another burst of sound. None came. The single source of light came from the center of the city—from the pillar. He blinked. From its entire circumference, a beautiful, clean, white light rotated. The light of the Creator. Within the pillar's core, a solid line of black remained. He followed its length up to the heavens as its core widened, until it utterly subsumed all but a narrow line of light within its center. He blinked and pulled back, disorientation churning a brutal path through him. He forced his gaze back to the console, at the screens still pouring out their nonsense, willing himself to have imagined the horror of what the darkness had brought.

Against his better instincts, he looked again. No. It was madness. His senses reeled. Again, he forced his gaze back to the console, seeking certainty, balance. A center.

A groan came from the cabin. He turned. Sekhmet lay on her side on the cabin's floor, herself once more. The last of her light slipped back into her torso. She sat up, slow, and looked around the cabin, blank. He waited, gave her time. Her eyes warmed up, shimmering with the golden fire of her god-light. Her hands went to her abdomen, exploring the once-tear where the console had wedged itself into her. So, Urhi-Teshub thought, uneasy, she remembered *that*. She looked up and caught him watching her.

"I never want to know what you did to free me," she said. She got up, a little unsteady, and went to him. As she neared his seat her gaze left him, drawn to the nightmare beyond the flight deck. Her legs folded into the seat beside his. Apprehension shrouded her eyes.

"Did I do that?"

"No," Urhi-Teshub said, flicking several switches, finding a way to work around the dead conduits of the ship's power. From the rear of the ship, the quiet boom of the thrusters ignited. "Definitely not. But I have an idea who might have."

He forced himself to sight a path to the complex, his spine ratcheted with disorientation. Far above, linked by the umbilical girth of the pillar, the sky had vanished. In its stead, an upside-down copy of Nisu hung over them, locked in shadow. No fires burned within its dead city, and no light gleamed, only darkness presided. The capstones of its pyramids pointed down to the ones beneath, a perfect, inverted mirror. He did not know if the ground beneath them had begun to rise or the dark version of Nisu above had begun to fall, but one thing was certain—the space between them had already diminished far too fast for his liking.

He guided the ship away from the *ziqquratu*, unable to stop himself from hunching down in his seat, his skin crawling under the weight of the inverted city of darkness. Beside him, Sekhmet eyed the pillar where darkness and light collided.

"I love you," she said, so low he wondered if he imagined it.

He cut a look at her. She didn't look at him.

"When this is over," Urhi-Teshub said, "I would have you as my consort—if you will have me."

For a heartbeat she said nothing, then, fraction of a nod. A single tear slipped free. It fell against the armor encasing her heart. She did not wipe it away.

❊ ❊ ❊

Ahmen circled the wreckage of the ships, his flesh raw and itching from the heat. He bit back a curse as he stumbled over a shattered piece of ashlar and sliced open his shin. Pain seared his leg, angry, red. A slick of blood erupted from the gash, coating the unhealed sheaths of his tendons. A wall of thunder roared toward him. He turned and ducked, just in time.

A pair of ships hurtled over the debris, their thunder punched through his pain, drowned it. In their wake, a scorching wash of acrid smoke and fumes. He narrowed his eyes, found their sigils. Set and Ma'at. They peeled away toward the golden capstone of the largest pyramid, readying to turn back to the front and fill the air with the fury of their missiles. He followed their ascent toward the dark city hanging over him, the weight of it unbearable, impossible, its upside-down pyramids lowering toward those beneath, their points perfectly aligned. He slid his gaze toward the pillar of darkness with its thin thread of light, its girth morphing from darkness to light as it reached the plaza, laced with a parallel thread of darkness. Vertigo assailed him. He turned his gaze back to the trio of pyramids, the space between the capstones of the pyramids had lessened. He pulled off the empty quiver, long spent of its arrows and tossed it aside, the bow followed after. It clattered against the scorched ashlars. He needed to hurry. Whatever was about to unfold, would unfold soon. He had to find her.

Meresamun. His heart clenched as he turned his attention back to the devastation strewn across the ashlars. He was no god, could not push his way past the scorched metal and flames like he had seen Urhi-Teshub do. And yet. She was in there, somewhere, fallen like a star from the blistering blue-white explosion. She would have survived, an immortal, like him, but in what state he would find—

A cry, weak, feminine, came from behind. He turned, his skin prickling. The cry came again, faint, incoherent, laced with terror and pain. His heart lurched. He plunged past a molten piece of the shield, its heat blistering. Another cry bled from the smoke. A massive pile of blackened ashlars blocked his way. He scrambled up their torn faces, their surfaces still hot and smoking from the shield's fall. At the top, he found a piece of a ship wedged in between a pair of ashlars, cradled in its vee.

Between the savage shear of torn metal, he caught sight of movement, a weak struggle. He clambered into the pit, his heart thudding so hard it hurt. He had found her. It was not too late. At last, she would be free. He reached the edge of the ship's debris and searched for a way in. A narrow opening, jagged with shorn metal, beckoned. He crawled through the ashlars toward it, scraping his shoulders and hands against the unforgiving walls of her prison. He reached the opening.

"Meres—" Her name died in his mouth. He searched the rest of the debris—what little there was. No. Please no.

A woman—not the one he sought—lay trapped within the restraints of a mutilated bench, her body streaked with blood, her hair scorched, and her gown in tatters. She lifted her face up to him, flooded with hope. Her eyes widened. She screamed, horror eclipsing her terror.

"Please," she panted, her struggle futile, hampered by a dislocated shoulder and the restraints cutting into her torso, "whatever you are, stay away from me."

Ahmen eyed her. "I wouldn't be so particular if I were you," he said, easing his way in between the opening and lowering himself down into the wreckage beside her. "No one else is coming."

She held still, quivering and wary as he pulled his blade free and worked, careful, to saw apart the belts holding her in place. "You've dislocated your shoulder," he said as he worked, keeping his eyes on his task, unwilling to see himself with her eyes—his hideousness reflected in her fearful look. "If it is your worst injury, you have been fortunate."

She said nothing. He could feel her eyes on him, terror bleeding from her in hot waves, like a wild animal, trapped and waiting to bolt.

"I am Ahmen-om-onet," he said, reaching for the last strap. He slid his forefinger behind it, easing a path between it and the charred material of her gown over her breast. He pulled the strap up so he would not nick her as he worked. "I come from the empire of Egypt."

"*You* are Ahmen?" she breathed.

The weight of her gaze deepened on him. He concentrated on the steady saw of his blade against the material of the restraint, the distant scream of the ships, and the thunder of the gods' weapons hammering the enemy's lines. On Meresamun.

"I heard what you did," she said, unable to disguise her admiration, "and how you escaped. Marduk was furious." A pause. "Did . . . Marduk do that to you?"

He cut a look at her without ceasing his work. She met his eyes, the green of hers, piercing, honest. "He did."

The last strap fell away. She slipped free of the bench with a shudder, biting back a spasm of pain. He caught her, gentle, as she stumbled past him into the wreckage.

"I can fix that for you," he said, nodding at her shoulder. "The pain will be intense, but brief. Then, it will be gone." In his grip she tensed, but held still. "Do you trust me?"

"Do it." She closed her eyes, bit her lip.

He took hold of her and shoved. She screamed, her anguish palpable. He let her go. She sagged against the side of the bench, panting. Her breathing slowed. She moved her arm and looked up at him, incredulous.

"I thought you were just saying there would be no pain as an enticement, but there truly is none at all."

"I am pleased to learn Egypt possesses at least some knowledge Elati does not," he said, offering her a smile, though he imagined it appeared as more of a grimace. She smiled back, tremulous, and took his offered hand.

"Come with me . . ." he trailed off. He had no idea what her name was, or who she was to Marduk.

"I am Aiya," she said. She looked away, and continued, diffident, "The god of war has chosen me to be his consort?"

"Ah," Ahmen said. He turned his attention to the wreckage, to what remained of the flight deck of Marduk's warship wondering why she had presented the information as a question.

"Marduk only cared to protect Ninsunu," she continued, oblivious to Ahmen's unease as she blinked back a sheen of tears. "He left me to die, just like the king and queen of Ikalur. I thought you were Sethi . . ." she looked up at Ahmen, hollow. "How could he have *not* seen us fall?"

"I am sure once he was able to reach you," Ahmen said, pitying her, "he would have come for you."

Aiya nodded and looked away, though a ripple of doubt slid over her features. Half her hair was scorched almost to her scalp, and dozens of cuts seeped blood from all over her body, painting her in rivulets of dark red. He could see beneath the grime and blood, soot and scorched skin, she possessed unparalleled beauty. He wondered what she looked like before—

He got up. He had no time for this. He still needed to find Meresamun. "I must go," he said. "Come with me. You will be safest if you do not remain here, alone."

Aiya followed him out of the wreckage and down the ashlar heap, quiet. They reached the perimeter of the debris. She stared at the shattered, burning remains of Marduk's warship, stricken.

"There is nothing left," she said. "How could anyone survive that? How did I?"

Her words pierced him. Being immortal, Meresamun would have survived, but he didn't look forward to what he would find when he did. He slid a look up to the pyramids to gauge the distance remaining between the capstones. There was still enough space to fit the breadth of Pi-Ramesses in between them, but even as he looked, it diminished. He turned his attention back to the debris, looking for a way in, unwilling to waste another heartbeat of time.

"Look." Aiya pointed toward the pillar.

A shadow flickered against the brilliance of the pillar's light. He could not make out the details apart from the absolute darkness of the shadow. He recalled Marduk's armor in Babylon. The obsidian depths of it. The only thing which could defy the light of the pillar.

"Marduk," he breathed. He took a step toward the pillar, his hand going to the hilt of his blade. He might be sorely equipped to face the one who had brought misery to Elati, but wherever Marduk was, Meresamun would be, too. He would take his chances. There was no time for anything else.

Aiya caught his arm. He looked down. She didn't recoil from the touch of his exposed muscles. "Do not go," she said, tightening her hold. "He will end you."

"I must find her," Ahmen said, unwrapping Aiya's fingers from his flesh. "Do not seek to stop me."

"Ninsunu?"

Ahmen nodded, determination fencing him. He had to try to free her, one last time, before it was too late.

"Then I will come with you." Aiya said. "Perhaps if Marduk knew you saved me . . ."

A ship hurtled over them, its wake hissed behind it, angry, hot.

Ahmen shook his head, already knew the answer. "Can you run?" he bellowed as a volley of explosions peppered the plaza. Gouts of flame erupted into the air. A fierce gust of wind slammed into them, broiling hot, and what remained of Aiya's hair whipped against her face.

She held out her hand.

He took hold of it, and ran toward the light.

※　※　※

Taut with hope and sundered by fear, Meresamun faced the pillar of light. At last. Vindication. She gazed at Zarpanitu's long-sought-after Well. As the reverberation had faded and she and Marduk tumbled back onto the ashlars, the pillar completed its transition from a seething abyss of darkness to a well of translucent wonder, its beauty breathtaking, its perfection humbling. All along, it had been here, hidden behind the tower's infinite walls, though not like this. From within the depths of its infinite haul of utter darkness, something had awakened the pillar's light. It poured up into the heavens toward the pillar of livid darkness which speared it from above, surrounded by an inverted city soaked in eternal night.

The Well of Life. At last she understood. The light was the obverse of the darkness. With Marduk's presence bearing the deepest of darkness in the flesh, balance had been lost, balance Zarpanitu had longed to restore by freeing her consort from the chains which enslaved his soul. Though she knew it would annihilate her, Meresamun longed to step through the wall of stars, to fall into the blistering upwelling of light, to feel the darkness burned from her skin and the taint within her soul scoured by the pure light of Re-Atum, the Creator, the beginning, and the end. She lifted her hand to the pillar's shimmering wall.

Marduk's footfalls approached, slow, cautious. She trailed her fingers along the pillar's sheath. A waterfall of stars trailed in their wake, silent, cold, glorious.

Unlike the dark pillar, which lay enfolded within wrappings of dark ephemeral curtains, the pillar of light's boundary was a single, solid sheath, the thin strip of darkness deep within its core lost in the brilliance of a cascade of a billion streaming stars.

"You are not safe here," Marduk said, his voice harsh in the cocooned perfection of the white light. "I commanded you to wait where I left you." When she said nothing, he stepped closer, his presence baleful, no longer protective, instead, danger sheathed him. She cut a look at him over her shoulder. His visor blossomed with the starlight of the Creator. "I have a battle to finish," he said. "You are wasting my time."

She turned. He stood before her, his armor bathed in the Creator's light, its impenetrable darkness a blot against the sacred threshold of the greatest power imaginable. He held out his gloved hand to her. "Do as you have been commanded. You will remain where I left you. I will not ask again."

"I found it," Meresamun said, ignoring his upturned hand. "Zarpanitu's hidden writing."

Marduk's visor bore into her. He remained utterly still, his hand still held out, a statue, his bearing soaked in rage, carved in darkness, washed in light.

"You let me believe you had shown me all her notes," Meresamun continued. "And you did. All, except one. The one you hid away—the one which completed the rest. The one which after a lifetime of searching, granted me purpose." She gestured at the shimmering pillar. "To think the mirror in my suite led here. To the very place she had searched for all her life—the place *I* was destined to bring you to in her stead."

He lunged at her and caught hold of her arm, his grip biting deep into her seared flesh. "Enough." He tugged her toward him, rough. Her shoulder glanced against the wall of starlight. A flash of white thunder seared her vision and careened down her arm, narrowing into a single point where Marduk's gloved hand gripped her. A jolt slammed out of her into him. He recoiled and backed away from her, wary. Where he had touched her, the black metal of his palm and fingers bore white scorch marks, the demarcation between dark and light, indelible.

"My love." Meresamun stepped closer to him, her soul aching with hope. At last, it would be over. At last, they could be free. No more destroyed cities, no more tyranny. No more gods falling to vile blades crafted of pure evil. Marduk could return to the one he was before he went to Ishev, before he was claimed by the darkness—used by it. "This is the Well of Life. It will cleanse you of the darkness."

Marduk shook his head. Ripples of starlight slid along the surface of his visor. "Have you lost your senses?" he asked, the metallic cut of his derision shearing her heart in two. "I have no wish to be obliterated."

"Nor do I," Meresamun answered. "But I wish to be free of the darkness, and I wish you to be free, too." She took a step back, until the glaring haul of the pillar's power resonated against her spine. "You said you cannot live without me." The heat of the Creator's light scorched her skin, bled into the designs embedded within her skin. She tilted her head at the pillar. "Come with me. Let us end what is in us, forever."

"Ninsunu," Marduk said, low. His fingers went to the latches of his helmet. He pulled it off. His eyes found hers, brilliant gems of carnelian, afire in the pillar's light. "I will not follow you. If you do this thing, you do it alone." He held out his hand to her, coaxed her toward him. "Zarpanitu was wrong. Nothing can cleanse me. I am the darkness personified. Your sacrifice will be for nothing."

Meresamun let her gaze fall from the taut lines of his face to the white scorch marks against his glove. "It will not be for nothing," she said. "It will be for love."

She eased back, the pressure of the pillar calling to the remaining light in her soul, a lodestone. His eyes bore into hers, anguished, ravaged by disbelief.

"Ninsunu," he cried, ragged, lunging after her. "I beg you. Do not do this thing. We are so close. We are destined to rule, together. Forever."

"I cannot be what you want," Meresamun answered. "I can only be who I am—Meresamun—and I will not fall to the darkness. I will not fall to you"

"Please," Marduk said, his hand a mere breath from her. Tears glinted in his eyes, hot with fear, savage with desperation. "Come to me."

"I love you," Meresamun whispered. She stepped back and fell into the blistering embrace of the light.

❋   ❋   ❋

Ahmen staggered to a halt. A nimbus of white light blossomed where Meresamun had just stood, glimmering with stars, a perfect outline of the woman he still loved. The light faded, gradual, the stars merging back into the wall of the streaming pillar, soaring up toward the dark citadel bearing down on them. Meresamun. Guilt rammed the walls of his throat. He had failed her. It had all been for nothing. His attention moved to the one who remained before the pillar, his helmet dangling from his gloved fingers, the rest of him clad in the metallic depths of the abyssal dark, as still as death. Rage shunted through Ahmen. Marduk would pay. Meresamun had obliterated herself to escape him. His hand went to the hilt of his sword. Fury, hot and sharp, sluiced through him. He would sever the monster's head from its shoulders.

Aiya caught his arm. "Wait," she murmured. "Ninsunu is no fool. She would not have sacrificed herself without reason. Allow her this."

Aiya's quiet words, laden with certainty, pierced the walls of Ahmen's wrath. He hauled on the reins of his rage, yanked himself back from the brink of his own annihilation.

"Ninsunu!" Marduk's cry swept past Ahmen, a broken, wounded thing, a prayer, unanswered. The helmet tumbled from his grip, its rough clatter against the ashlars savage against the pillar's eldritch silence. The heavy scrape of metal against stone as Marduk dropped to his knees. "I cannot bear to lose you," he shouted at the implacable light of the pillar. "I cannot bear to go through this again." He stared at the pillar as though expecting her to return. The pillar continued its relentless upwelling of stars, impervious to the chosen one of the dark. He gave an anguished cry and dropped onto all fours, his gloved fists slamming against the ashlars. Defeat bled from him. He remained there, still, alone, vulnerable, the light washing over his armor, bathing his back in brilliance.

Ahmen met Aiya's eyes. She let go of his arm.

"May you find peace, Lord Ahmen."

Ahmen pulled his blade free and strode across the remaining distance, the blistering starlight of the pillar drowning his senses, dulling his hate. Meresamun was in there, nothing more than light, gone, forever. His heart clenched. He would not fail her. He would finish what she had begun. He would end Marduk. At last, the tyrant would fall.

He came to a halt beside Marduk and waited. He would not strike him like this. He would see his face first.

"You seek to finish me," Marduk said, dull. He did not look up. Beneath him, a scattering of fallen tears pockmarked the dust. Marduk shuddered. Another tear fell and joined its brothers. He pushed himself to his knees and lifted his gaze to where Meresamun had just been, her dark-inked form bathed in the pure light of the pillar.

"She found Zarpanitu's hidden words," he said. "The ones my first consort believed would stop what was in me." He shook his head, slow, his jaw tight with grief. "I could have destroyed them, but could not bring myself to do it, to part with anything of hers. I thought she was wrong. I believed nothing could stop me." He fell silent, lost in the endless corridors of his mind. He let out a heavy breath, blinked back the glint of fresh tears. "But

Zarpanitu understood something I did not." He cut a look up at Ahmen. Anguish seeped from him raw, visceral. "She understood she would not be the one to finish me, there would be another, and so she wrote those words I secreted away. Words I could have destroyed but did not. Why?" Muted by the pillar's cocoon of silence, the thin scream of ships tore past. "I think I wanted this," he continued, low. "I wanted to see what I would do if it ever came to this—and here I am, alone, once more." He came to his feet, his gaze returning to where Meresamun had been. "All this time she knew. She did not leave with you because she was determined to do this—to give up herself to set me free." He choked and blinked hard. "Ninsunu. My only love."

"Her name is Meresamun," Ahmen said, his throat aching, the magnitude of her act devastating him. At last, he understood her refusal to leave. The depth of her sacrifice haunted him, humiliated him.

"Meresamun," Marduk repeated, reverent, acknowledging, at last, her true name. He reached up to his chest. Ahmen raised his sword.

"I assure you, you will not need that," Marduk said. He pressed an indentation over his heart. Thin strips of cerulean light streamed away, lighting the channels between the sections of his armor. Piece by piece it loosened with a series of quiet hisses. He pulled the segments away, efficient, determined, dropping them into a jumbled heap against the ashlars. The last piece, his glove—the screen on its wrist still scrolling with symbols—tumbled onto the pile. It rolled away, abandoned, forlorn, lost without its master. He turned toward the pillar, clad in nothing more than a linen cloth over his groin. Across his skin, his inked markings surged along the contours of his muscles, taking the form of streamers and curlicues, reaching toward the pillar. Toward her.

"My demise will not be enough to stop what is to come," Marduk said. "The jihn must be destroyed."

"And Sethi?" Ahmen asked, taut.

Marduk cut a look at Ahmen. "Through the jihn, Sethi belongs to the darkness even more than I." He turned back to face the cascading wall of light. "And so this is the end. At last. Ninsunu, I beg you, let it not be too late. Wait for me."

He stepped forward, the light scouring him as he approached. He clenched his fists, bellowing in torment as streamers of light swept out from the pillar and burned through the markings on his body and cut a path through his flesh. More tendrils delved into him, darting through his torn flesh, scouring through his corruption. He pressed on, step by agonized step, forcing himself toward the punishment of the light as it screamed into him, savaged him, gouged him, shredded him.

At the threshold of the pillar, he cried out her name, and plunged, broken, ruined, bleeding, into the light.

✳   ✳   ✳

His ship still disabled from cloaking, Urhi-Teshub swerved to avoid the glittering annihilation of a cerulean star. He rolled the ship toward the pillar, hit the reverse thrusters and deprived another star of its quarry. He dropped low and cut a burning trail over the boiling wreckage of Marduk's warship.

It took time for the ship-obliterating weapons to recharge and from what he could tell, there were only three of them. He bit back a sour smile. *Only.* Strapped into the seat beside his, Sekhmet eyed the symbols calculating when the next charge would be ready.

"You have the count of thirty left," she said, her slim fingers swiping at the restored readings on the screen. "Get in there and get dirty. At ten, it's time to get out. I'll call it."

He nodded, and cut lower until his ship screamed over the glowing shreds of the shield, their heat lapping against the ship, setting off alarms. He ignored them, his gaze fixed on the heave of oncoming Imarians. Bathed in the pure light of the pillar's white brilliance, Sethi's endless army surged out of the inflamed city up the vast tiers to the plaza, its edge bristling with those who remained of the gods' allies—a wall of mortals, thousands deep—determined to stand with the gods against the greatest manifestation of evil, willing to sacrifice their lives, their souls.

Thousands of dark-armored Imarians beetled the tiers, a swarming, seething onslaught of enhanced power and weaponry. The gods tore back and forth in their ships, raining fire, gouging out bloody swathes, pushing them back. Within heartbeats, hundreds more clambered over the fallen, swarmed in to fill the gaps. A relentless tide.

"I imagine this must have been how Ramesses felt at Kadesh," Urhi-Teshub muttered.

"Who?" Sekhmet asked, not taking her eyes from the screen. Another swipe. "Twenty."

"No one," Urhi-Teshub said, and realized he meant it.

From the center of the Imarian front lines, Sethi strode ahead, undaunted by the resilience of the gods and their allies. An aura of victory sheathed him as he gestured out commands. The jihn's blades streamed with blue-white fire, slavering, relishing the slaughter. Its dark coil skirled through Urhi-Teshub, poisoning his mind with the sting of defeat—of the light within the pillar dying forever and the jihn claiming him, his final fall into the darkness rank with the horror of having failed both Istara and Sekhmet.

Sekhmet's shoulders slumped. Misery drenched her profile.

"Ten," she said, dull.

He released a barrage of golden fire against the deeper lines of the Imarians, far enough from their allies to leave them unscathed and threw full power to the thrusters, cutting a sidewise path away from the tier and the hated jihn toward the bulk of the largest pyramid. The weight of its twin bore down on him, heavy, oppressive, ominous.

They peeled away from the pyramid's wedge. Ahead, the pillar rotated, brilliant, beautiful, its core slivered with a delicate thread of obsidian, its darkness a blight against the light. He eyed it, sensing whatever had changed it had been because of Istara. His heart clenched. She was gone. He was certain of it. He rolled to the side of it, readying for the onslaught of the cerulean stars.

"Incoming," Sekhmet said. "Forty degrees incline, ascending at half a degree per tick." She flashed him a dark smile, her spirit restored. "That's the third shot directed at you in the last six fired. They like you."

He shot her a roguish smile, killed the power and they tumbled down, straight toward the gutted, molten ashlars. The cerulean star skimmed over them, its detonation within the pillar blinding.

In its white heat, his eyes found Sekhmet's. "I love you, too."

Her smile tore through him, radiant, devastating. It carved a blazing path through his heart, blistered it to life. He punched the thrusters and the ship screamed up the face of the pillar toward the inverted, dark city, clad in defiance. They could not fall. Not now. Not when they had only just begun.

✻　✻　✻

Alone in an eternity of dark, Istara slid through the pillar's churning, seething rift. Her light swarmed around her, star-brilliant, granted by the innate power of the Creator's relic—the relic she had left behind to save the one who had once, long ago, saved her. Fetid tendrils of hate lunged after her. Her light sparked against them, a glittering panoply of stars. The tendrils recoiled, their thin cries skidding against the edge of her hearing, blades against bone. They slid back into the morass, shredded by her light.

She looked up. A thin trail of starlight scorched a straight path behind her through the void. In the distance, far below, the faintest prickling of light breached the darkness. She plummeted toward it, its promise of escape brightening with each heartbeat, no longer a pinpoint, but a widening pool, an eddy of hope in a sea of darkness. She fled toward it, gaining speed, her light aflame, scouring a path through the abyss.

At the threshold of the light, she plunged through a scintillating space filled with particles of light and dark locked in an eternal dance. She sped through it, an arrow of starlight hurtling past the last vestiges of the darkness, toward the vortex of stars. The last of the darkness vanished. Light blistered her being, and still she fell, a star within a well of stars, the goddess of healing, drinking of the Creator's light, prepared to face the one who had come for her, alone, and without the relic, cradling the only weapon she still possessed—her heart.

Bathed in the silence of the Creator's light, Istara emerged from the pillar. Beyond its starlit nimbus, the blackened and twisted wreckage of fallen ships smoked and smoldered amongst enormous molten sections of the destroyed shield. Past the complex, across the reach of the city, the incandescence of a thousand fires suffused the darkness. Smuts of ash tumbled through the ruins of the plaza, a storm of black snow caught in the scalding wake of the ships.

She looked up the length of the pillar to its dark root. From its inverted base, an obsidian, upside down copy of the complex and city hung over her in perfect symmetry. Between a wreathing of smoke, the black capstone of the largest pyramid hung a mere breath over Nisu's golden one beneath. One of the ships of the gods scored a searing trail of fire around the pair of capstones and back to the battle, where thousands of the gods' allies seethed in a wall of defiance, their lives the last weapon they possessed to stop the onslaught of darkness.

Starlight trailing after her, she left the pillar's enclave of silence and swept past the broiling debris of fallen ships toward the cries of the wounded and dying. A ship screamed toward her, fast and low, a blinding thing of white-gold, swarming with the reflected stars of the pillar. Horus's golden ship. It curved around the coruscant pillar, its tilted wings granting her a heartbeat of brilliance before it vanished from sight. She faced the rear lines of the allies. The gods would not be here, where Sethi could annihilate them. They would remain in the skies, out of his reach. She would be alone, and unprotected, with only her light and her love to defend her from the one she must face one final time.

Faint with distance, it came to her, the bone-aching, slavering hum of the jihn, raw with hate, its hunger savage, endless. It cut across the ebb and flow of the cries of the commanders, consumed the wails of the fallen, and dulled the crumps of the explosions. Its malignance tasted her light. Malevolence rushed toward her, a starving thing. She braced herself for its onslaught, waited for her will to fail, and her light to retreat. This time Urhi-Teshub would not be able to protect her. She tasted the jihn's contempt, and bled regret for the lost relic. Realization tore through her, saturated with the jihn's taint. Sethi would destroy her in a heartbeat. Her love for him would not protect her, neither would the light the relic had granted her. Nothing would. It was over. The end had come, and she had failed.

She sank to her knees, defeat clawing her soul, baring her to the jihn's poison as it sluiced through her. Her only weapon against the darkness had been sacrificed to save another. It had been a mistake. Everyone would die because she tried to save one. The jihn sensed her thoughts. Its triumph scorched her, mocked her, desiccated her hope.

She endured the onslaught of its brutal evisceration, its precise shattering of her self. Her head lowered, she succumbed to her failure. There was nothing she could do. She would never stop Sethi, without the relic she could never overcome the jihn. The darkness had already won. She closed her eyes, mourning what had been, what was lost, what could never be.

Utter stillness swept through her, the jihn's sudden silence startling her. She opened her eyes. From out of the pillar, an eruption of stars slammed into her, blinded her mind, seared her soul. More stars followed. They crowded into her, bolstered her, empowered her. She lifted her hands. Starlight rushed down her arms and poured from her fingertips. Her power grew, ten, one hundred, a thousand fold.

Brilliance filled her, subsumed her until she became a glittering, star-clad being of pure light. A magnitude of stars surrounded her, shielded her from the brunt of the jihn's malignance. She came to her feet, fierce, afire.

With power like this, she would not fail, could not fail. It was enough. The Creator's light surged through her, its haul beyond anything she could imagine. Awash in the constellation of herself, she continued toward her consort. The force of a million worlds surrounded her, inundated with the power to create life from nothing. It was so much, almost more than she could bear. She walked on, surging with light. Nothing could stop her. Nothing. She had become the Creator's vessel of light just as Sethi had become the darkness's.

In the distance, the sweep of the jihn's blue-white light cut a swathe through the faltering lines of the allies, its feasting distorting the outline of Sethi's dark silhouette. She felt the weight of his gaze on her, the slam of his hatred, his longing to destroy her. Across the expanse separating them, she faced her consort, who had slaughtered Arinna and Thoth and had imprisoned their souls within the bleak walls of the jihn. Barricaded within the light of a thousand universes, she withstood the focus of her consort's weapon as it sought to breach her defenses—tasted its rage, its frustration. Its fury.

She closed her eyes. Soon now.

"Istara."

His voice, warm and resonant, pierced her heart. A memory suffused her, visceral, of the evening warmth of Tarhuntassa's gardens overlaid with the complex scent of leather, soap, and horses. The scent of a warrior—of the prince of an empire. Her protector. He had found her, as he always had. As he always would.

She turned. The jagged blue lightning of the storm god's ax sparked against the wall of her light.

He eyed her brilliance, his golden eyes marked with the fire of the storm god's light. "I promised the Creator I would protect you," he said. "I thought I had failed." He hefted his ax free and turned to face the one making his way toward her. "Never have I been so glad to be wrong."

Horus's ship tore back over them, tipping its wings as it passed. Istara caught a glimpse of Sekhmet at the controls. The goddess of war accelerated and shot up toward the dark city, an arrow of gold.

"We saw your return. She wanted to stand with me. With you." He tilted his head at the cold light of the jihn. "I couldn't risk losing her." Urhi-Teshub followed the ship's spiral back down toward the front lines, the hiss of its released weapons, the explosions peppering the length of the plaza. A wave of disorientation sliced over his features. He blinked and shook his head.

"It has found you," Istara said, recognizing the grinding onslaught of the jihn's misery written on his face. The lies.

Urhi-Teshub nodded, his gaze moved to the jihn. Anguish darkened his features. Defeat crept over him. His shoulders lowered, and his ax blades tilted toward the ground, furrowing the scorched ashlars in the violence of his light. She caught his face in her hands, pressed her forehead to his, and let her light course into him, limning him in a barrier of starlight. He shuddered as the jihn's dark grip faded.

She let him go. The storm god's power surged anew, harsh with fury. It glinted in his eyes, and sparked along the tips of his fingers. Cerulean bolts erupted across his leather-clad chest. Sheathed in vengeance, he hefted his ax, a warrior awakened, a god once more.

"Are you ready?" he asked, his voice dark with the promise of his protection.

"I am."

And she was. She walked on, into the heaving morass of bodies soaked in sweat and blood, a beacon of light in a pit of gore, a place soaked with violence, death, destruction, and fear. Of men killing men, their faces savage. Their cries of anguish tore at the walls of her light, harsh with pleas for her aid. Her light billowing around her, she eyed the devastation, the destruction of life—its carnage ambrosia to the endless appetite of the jihn.

Blood washed against her ankles, and drenched the ashlars. Surrounded by a river of stars, her light washed over the fallen. They rose in her wake, whole, renewed, roaring with triumph as they surged back into the battle, trailing her light, a tide of stars against a storm of metallic dark.

Her consort swept the jihn down and beheaded one of her commanders, the weapon's blades silvering, gorging on his soul. Malevolent triumph devoured his regard. Against his chest, his fractals rotated, perfect, seamless, no longer golden, but obsidian. Her heart shuttered itself against what he had become. Sethi was gone. Hate etched his features, violence and brutality soaked his presence. All that which remained of him was darkness.

She endured the agony of her loss—of the end of their love. He strode through his fallen warriors, treading on their bodies as though they were nothing more than ants, the jihn trailing a blazing path beside him, brightening with each step, the bone saw wails of its desolate, imprisoned souls pinioning her with their anguish. Amongst those cries would be Thoth's and Arinna's, their suffering unspeakable. The jihn's malignant hunger tore at the walls of her light, ravenous, its sharp-cold presence promising her annihilation.

She met Sethi's eyes, withstood the naked abhorrence in his. Once, she had believed she had been a token of men and gods, a piece to be moved upon their game board. But she had been wrong, she had been a piece on the Creator's game board, it had been he who had guided her to this place, to this time—to this final, terrible confrontation. But now none controlled her. She was free. The Creator was powerless now. Via the pillar, he had granted her the last of his power and bequeathed to her the fate of the light—*his* fate. The burden of her responsibility bore down on her. The burden of the light, of life. Of love.

❋ ❋ ❋

Ahmen stood before the heap of Marduk's discarded armor. Silence soaked his heart. Meresamun was gone. Forever. He eyed the barrier, his heart pounding, considering following her, desperate to cleanse his crimes in the light of the pillar as Marduk had done. Without Meresamun, what was left for him? Nothing. There would never be any absolution for his act, he could never know forgiveness, would never be free. It would be his burden to bear, for eternity. No. It was too much. He let go of the sword. It fell, its metallic clatter dulled by the oppressive silence of the pillar. He thought of the day he found in her in the rain at Kadesh. The heartbeat he had felt her again in his arms after those lonely, anguished months spent searching for her. Her vow never to leave him again. Her lips against his. He took a step toward the blistering, pounding wall of light. *Meresamun. Forgive me. I lost myself. I lost you.*

A soft touch against his arm. He turned, startled. Aiya tugged against him, gentle, drew him back, away from the light. Away from Meresamun.

"Please," she breathed. "Stay. Fight. For me. I do not wish to belong to Sethi."

"I—" Ahmen began. He searched for the words. There were none. She recognized the refusal in his eyes. His determination to go. Her hand fell from his arm. She backed away. A sheen of tears coated her eyes.

"Forgive me," she said, tremulous, her green eyes brilliant as malachite. "I should not have asked. I am the enemy after all." A tear slipped free, tracked a path through the soot and blood on her face. "May you find whatever it is you seek." She retreated, desolation shrouding her.

Conflict tore through Ahmen, wedged him in a barren place between the burden of his guilt and the honor of a warrior. He cut a look back at the pillar. Meresamun was gone. Aiya was here, now, and had asked for his aid, a thinly veiled plea for his protection. He could finish this later. He called Aiya's name. She stopped, turned. Hope soaked her.

"I will fight." He collected his sword and slid it back into its scabbard. She waited, vulnerable, bloody, burned. His heart clenched. Shame enveloped him. How could he have considered leaving her alone in the midst of this—to abandon her to Sethi's cruelties? Aching with the magnitude of his dishonor, he lifted his hand to her. She rushed back to him, a drowning thing hauled from the waves of a dark sea, gratitude flooding her, breaking his heart. A shear of white erupted from the pillar, dense, blinding, silent.

Ahmen caught Aiya to him and pulled his sword free. He could see nothing, hear nothing. Frustration clawed at him. For a wild heartbeat he wondered if the pillar had rejected Marduk and thrown him back.

He blinked and bit back a curse. He could not even see Aiya, could only feel her against his chest. A quiet sob, wracked with pain skirted the edge of his hearing. He held still, willing himself not to have imagined it. There. Again. Another shuddering sob.

His heart thudded, blistered with hope. Meresamun. Please. Let the light have returned her to him.

The light faded by degrees, its punishing glare seeping back into the pillar. A little distance past Marduk's heap of armor, a dark-haired woman lay huddled into herself, clad in black and wreathed in light. Bleeding and broken, she shuddered, struggling to bring herself onto all fours—a woman who was not Meresamun. Disappointment scythed Ahmen's soul, raw, harsh. She let out another broken cry, her anguish palpable. He let go of Aiya and went to her. The woman lifted her face to him. He caught his breath. He recognized her, or what remained of her.

"Baalat," Ahmen breathed, taking in the extent of her injuries, even as the light wreathing her sought to piece her back together. "How—"

Baalat pulled her hand out from where she pressed it against her torso. Clutched within her bloody fingers, Istara's relic, swarming with starlight.

"Take me to Istara," she cried. "Before it is too late."

With Aiya beside him, Ahmen gathered up the shattered body of the once-goddess of healing and carried her away from the coursing stars of the pillar, away from its silence, away from Meresamun, and into the flames and darkness of a dying world.

✳   ✳   ✳

Sethi came to a halt a little distance away, the hate in his eyes virulent, devastating. Her consort, the god of war, was no more. He had become another, a vessel of absolute darkness. He slid his gaze over Istara, arrogant, disdainful. She held her ground, barricaded the walls of her heart against him, allowed it no weakness.

His eyes hard, Urhi-Teshub stepped before her, the blades of his ax blistering with the load of his fury. Starlight limned his body, ran along his shoulders. The sickly blue-white wash of the jihn's hunger slid over him, pale, pestilent.

Sethi eyed Urhi-Teshub, unimpressed. His gaze moved to the storm god's ax. His mouth lost its hard edge, slid into a sneer, laden with contempt.

"How pitiful." He stepped closer, the whites of his eyes and his irises gone, glazed by the depths of the darkness. The fractals on his chest rotated in the opposite direction to his golden ones, soaked in obsidian despair. "You think to stop me? Istara is mine." His words cut through the haze of smoke, hate-smeared and cold as death. "Your fate has ever been to watch me take her from you—again, and again, and again." He gestured at Urhi-Teshub with the jihn. Its blades seethed, harsh with anticipation. "I will not use this on you, yet. I want you to see her fall."

A quiver of rage rippled through Urhi-Teshub. Cerulean bolts scythed down his arms and into his weapon. He flexed his grip against the haft of his ax, sparks splintering from his fingertips.

With a scathing look at Urhi-Teshub, Sethi set the jihn onto the ground. Its blades keened, hungry, the song of saws against bone. He rose. "And now—" he rolled his shoulders, the muscles in his arms proud over his clenched fists, "—it will be a fair fight."

Within a nimbus of cerulean lightning, Urhi-Teshub waited, a warrior, a god. The rage of a thousand storms sheathed him. Sethi circled her protector. Scorn seeped from him, as though the storm god's devastating power were no more than a quaint diversion.

Urhi-Teshub slid the length of his storm-laden ax through his fingers. The butt of his weapon smacked the ground. Lightning erupted from its blades and surrounded him, a shield of brutal, elemental power. Sethi rammed his fist into it. Cerulean bolts clawed into his arm and over his torso, staining him in veins of blue fire.

He hauled himself from its talons, his flesh and kilt smoking as he paced before the barrier, black with fury, seeking a way past. Urhi-Teshub lifted his ax and struck the ground again, harder this time. A deep thundering rose from the depths. An ashlar exploded from the plaza, shattered into a thousand pieces and rained its storm on the god of war. From within its brutal onslaught, he lifted his cold eyes to Urhi-Teshub. From within the brutal onslaught of jagged boulders, he lifted his cold eyes to Urhi-Teshub. Scores of deep gashes laced his torso, arms, and face. Blood, black as a starless night, inked his flesh.

He strode back, clad in darkness, his bearing promising a world of suffering. The jihn lay under a pile of debris. He shoved the sharp rocks away, blood coating his hands, soaking the weapon's blades. The jihn's noxious blue-white light licked over him, gorging itself on the essence of its wielder. He hauled the vile thing up, his features harsh in the cerulean light, and drove its blade against the barrier of lightning, his lips twisting into a savage, sadistic grin. Cerulean fire swarmed into the weapon. A scream of anguish came from it. No. Thousands of screams—a wail of unimaginable suffering from beyond the walls of the living, of souls tormented beyond comprehension.

He dragged the jihn against the barrier, first one blade, then the other, alternating them, until both blades blazed with the brutality of the storm god's fury, aware of the tyranny of his act—the cruelty of his method. Urhi-Teshub held his ground, his profile hard, his eyes no longer golden, but cerulean fire, drenched with his power—his rage.

The cries escalated until they drowned out the screams of the ships and the thunder of explosions. The misery of thousands washed over Istara, delving into her until they saturated her soul. Still, Urhi-Teshub held his ground. Stubbornness sheathed him. Her protector glared at Sethi, hate penetrating him, feeding him. He ground the metal-sheathed butt of his ax against the ground, and a renewed surge of his storm's fury erupted from his blades. The cries hollowed, despairing. They tore into Istara. Anguish clogged her heart, filled her soul.

"Urhi-Teshub," she cried. "Cease! Innocents are suffering."

Her protector said nothing. His attention remained fixed on Sethi, laden with vengeance, patient as a crocodile. Istara called to him again, urgent. A command. He did not respond. Sethi cut a look at her, then back at Urhi-Teshub. The storm god remained unmoved. Sethi yanked the jihn away. He came to her, bloodsoaked and malicious, the jihn's decimating lament clawing at her ears.

Istara met his eyes. Her light gathered, surrounded her, a glittering nimbus, pouring with stars. It swarmed over him, swept against the taint of his fractals, glinted against the darkness of his eyes, penetrated the bloody ruins of his flesh. Within the space of a heartbeat he stood before her, whole again. He glanced at himself, then back at her. A flicker of recognition, a mere heartbeat, lost in a breath.

Darkness sluiced through him, leaving her entombed in loss. Movement behind him, hot with trails of cerulean flames. Sethi saw nothing but her, her stars reflected in the abyssal depths of his eyes. His hatred and contempt bore into her, eviscerated her. He lifted the jihn, the muscles of his arm taut against the weight of its tormented souls. Triumph, cold and malignant, stained the planes of his jaw, tainted the curve of his lips. He smiled, dark. His final gift to her.

Istara faced him, wreathed in power, in life, a goddess. Her light stormed around her. It was not over. So long as she bore the Creator's light, it would never be over. She clenched her fists, gathered the force of her light, braced herself for its release.

"You shall not have her!"

Blue fire erupted from Sethi's chest. The once-god of war staggered, roaring in agony. Urhi-Teshub's ax erupted from Sethi's chest, splattering Istara in the stain of her consort's black blood. Her protector twisted his weapon, savage, brutality stamped on the cut of his jaw. Razor-sharp bolts of lightning surged out of the blades into Sethi's torso, clawed into his limbs, sparked against his teeth. Sethi juddered. The jihn slipped from his fingers and slammed against the stained, broken ashlars.

Urhi-Teshub's yanked his ax free, the shorn remains of Sethi's black heart trailing in its grisly wake. Her protector glared at him, his eyes hard as blue ice. "You underestimate my love for her."

Sethi turned, awash in ragged bolts of cerulean fire. "And you, my hate." He drove his fist, fast, sharp, into Urhi-Teshub's skull. Once, twice, three times his blows fell. Istara called to her light as Urhi-Teshub stumbled, bloodied, blinded, his temple crushed. His ax clattered to the ashlars. Another blow and Istara's protector staggered to his knees and slumped onto his side. Her light found him, poured into him.

Sethi rammed his fist into the savage gap in his chest and sank to his knee, his god-light flickered, weak, suppressed by his darkness. Her consort cut a look at Urhi-Teshub, surrounded by the cocoon of her light, healing fast, then up at her from under his brow. Hate lapped over him, slammed into her. Its undertow hauled at her, threatened to pull her under.

"Go on," he taunted as Horus's golden ship sliced over them, seething with acrid heat. "Try to finish me." Poisoned blood dripped from his mouth and nose.

Istara eased toward him. "Your injuries are grievous."

He glared at her and pushed his fist deeper into the gaping hole where his heart had been, grimacing with pain. Blood, dark as ink, smeared his fingers, ran down his forearm, stained his chest, obliterated his fractals.

Istara knelt and caught his face in her hands. He flinched but held still. He glared at her, defiant, proud.

"I can heal you," she said, even as the unutterable distance yawned between them. "I can cleanse you. I can make this stop."

"It is not I who needs cleansing," he grunted as he shifted his weight. A fresh gout of his bleak essence slid over his knuckles. He shot a look at his jihn, then back at her. "It is you."

A thick groan came from behind. The scrape of metal against stone. Istara did not take her eyes from Sethi, waited as Urhi-Teshub dragged his ax back to him. Another groan as her protector pulled himself to his feet. A scorching silence as he took in the scene.

"Istara," he said, harsh. "Whatever you seek to do, do not do it. It will be a mistake."

A savage boom of thunder swallowed her response. It tore through the heated air, eons deep, an epochal death gasp, its resonance escalating until the entire complex reverberated, taut as a skin on a drum. A deafening judder rolled from the largest pyramid. She looked up. The capstones of the largest pyramids kissed. They resisted for a heartbeat, then succumbed to the impossible pull of the other, their thundering oppressive, maddening. A dozen bone-shattering cracks splintered through the capstones, whip-sharp. They sliced through the smoke and fire of the plaza's basin, uncaring of the misery below, their mutual destruction impassive, rank with destiny.

Massive sections of the capstones calved and slid away. They tumbled up the dark pyramid and down the golden one, decimating everything in their paths. A shorn section of the golden capstone hurtled end over end through the far lines of the battle, gouging a bloody path through the warriors of Elati. Horns blared across the length of the plaza. As one, allies and enemies bolted, their enmity forgotten.

Within the pillar's heart, where the darkness met the light, a sphere of utter darkness burst to life, surrounded by a thin sheathe of light. The sphere began to rotate, its size and speed increasing as the pillar shortened. A beacon of harsh white light cut away from the sphere and rotated through the shadows of the darkened city. In the opposite direction, a spear of utter darkness turned against it.

Istara caught Sethi watching her, narrow, his jaw tight, harsh with pain. The pyramids rammed deeper into each other, brutal, sensual, the grind of their obliteration dense with the promise of her own annihilation. She dared a look at the other pyramids. Their golden capstones flickered in the light of the pillar, resigned to the imminent onslaught of their dark counterparts. Soon, they too would be obliterated. Soon, she, Sethi, Urhi-Teshub, the gods, and their warriors would be crushed. It was the end. The end of all things, of time, of worlds, of gods, of life. Sorrow slammed into her. The frigid grip of failure clobbered her. The relic. If only—No. She would not regret her choice. It was too late for that. It was gone. All she had left was the light of the Creator, and her love. There was still something she could do. There was still one she could try to save, before it was too late.

Her heart aching, she turned back to her consort. He hunched into himself, bloody, suffering. Erratic remnants of his light guttered within his sundered chest, useless against the darkness slithering within him.

A fresh thundering slammed into the plaza. The ashlars shuddered, ragged with defeat. She turned just as the second largest pyramid collided with its counterpart. Cracks splintered the capstones, streaked down the sides of the pyramid. A jagged section of the capstone slid down the pyramid's side.

Urhi-Teshub's hand came to her shoulder. He hauled her back, away from Sethi. Her hands slid from her consort's face. Sethi slumped forward, lost to his agonies.

"Leave him." Urhi-Teshub jerked his head toward the sundered capstone cutting a vicious path across the plaza toward them. "It is over. I will return to finish what is left of him."

"No," Istara pulled free of her protector's grip. "You swore to protect me," she tilted her head at the tumbling capstone racing toward them, as vast as a palace. "Do so."

"Have you lost your senses?" Urhi-Teshub bellowed, fury sparking against his eyes. "He is the darkness. He must be destroyed."

"Sethi is not the darkness!" Istara cried. Her light erupted, fierce, defiant. "Protect me," she cried over the thunder of the capstone, "or cease to be my protector."

With a roar of fury, his body crackling with lightning, Urhi-Teshub pointed his ax at the massive shard, its golden skin shorn by obsidian teeth. A storm of blue lightning burst from his blades and slammed into it. Ice-blue bolts streaked over it, living things. It continued to hurtle toward them, trailing cerulean fire. A heartbeat later, a brilliant explosion of blue seared Istara's eyes. She lifted her hand, blinking back tears. The capstone was gone, a fine mist of white, speckled with flickers of cerulean sparks hung in the air. It drifted down, harmless, coating the ground and her protector's shoulders in dusty skeins of gold and white.

His features coated in rage, Urhi-Teshub glared at the empty space, the haft of his ax clenched in his grip. He turned to her, cold. "Your refusal to see what Sethi has become will cost us everything!" He thrust his weapon toward Sethi, its lightning-soaked blades a mere heartbeat from Sethi's neck. "He is gone. He will never come back. He made his choice when he betrayed you." His eyes fell to the jihn, its light sliding toward Sethi, seeking to feed. His face hardened. "When he betrayed Thoth."

He met her look. Revenge bled from him, hot, rank with age. "Let me finish this. Let me end him."

Istara pushed the ax away. "The *only* way to finish this is to overcome the darkness."

"None can overcome the darkness," Urhi-Teshub thundered, violence bleeding from him. He cut a look at the pillar, the blistering white halo of the sphere reflecting in his eyes. "I understand now why the Creator bade me protect you at all costs. The light you carry is the key. *You* must survive for the rest of us to survive whatever *that* is doing." He stepped closer to her. "Do not grant him your light. He will return to what he is and destroy you. Istara!" He caught her arm as she turned back to Sethi, her protector's grip harsh, raw with the ferocity of his power. "You will not do this thing," he bellowed, enraged. "I will not let you."

"Then you leave me no choice," she cried. Hundreds of tendrils of her light swept out from her and captured him in their hold, wrapping him in a sheath of healing light, an unbreakable cocoon.

"Istara!" He rammed his fists against the walls of his confinement. Bursts of light blossomed where he struck. "He will betray you. He will betray all of us. Please," he panted, wild, desperation bleeding from him. "No! I beg you. Istara—"

Istara turned from the one she had once loved to the one she still loved who eyed her from under his brow, raw with malevolence. Amid the thunder of the dying pyramids, the scream of ships overhead, the smoke and fire of Anki's final breaths, she endured the heat of Sethi's malignance and the ragged protests of her protector. At her silent call, her light gathered into a single, blistering stream, enough to raise an army of thousands, millions. Stars swarmed around her, intense, overwhelming, blinding.

"I cannot abandon you to the darkness," she whispered as she reached out to catch his face in her star-clad hands. He resisted for a heartbeat, then relented. An unreadable look slid over the anguish etched into the planes of his jaw. A beat later, it was gone, replaced by contempt.

"Your protector is right," Sethi rasped, bloody, "I will betray you."

"I will not let you," Istara said. "No matter what it costs me."

She closed her eyes and let the light of the Creator pour into him, a flood, a tsunami, soaking him with the purest light of all, closing his wounds, mending his severed heart, scouring the darkness, soaking into the stain of evil. Deep within his soul, her light found the source, lunged after it. Joy skirted the edges of her heart as her light coursed through her into him. It was enough, it would be enough. Soon he would be—

He shoved her away. She opened her eyes, startled, her light streaming back into her—what remained of it. He rose over her, gripping the jihn, whole again, triumphant, his lips curved into a malicious grin. He raised the jihn, its bone-aching hum crescendoing, hot with anticipation. Darkness slayed his eyes.

Deafened by the silence of her consort's hate, she hauled at her protector's prison—sought to undo her mistake. It unraveled, far too slow. She turned back to Sethi, faced her enemy, alone, and unprotected.

She called to her light, sought its defense, pulled it around her. It was not enough. She had given Sethi too much. Just as Urhi-Teshub had warned, her once-consort had soaked up her light, had used her heart against her. A tear slipped free, hot with shame. She met Sethi's eyes, her heart aching, drowning in failure. His eyes flicked over her shoulder. He looked at her again, ragged with brutality. A pair of ships screamed over them, outlined his darkness in fire.

"I love you," she breathed, refusing to let go of who he once was, the one who had sacrificed all for her—who had once loved her beyond reason. He glared at her, lost to her, his hatred tangible, a feast for her soul. The jihn fell, its tormented souls wailing in anguish, soiled with horror.

Wreathed in the starlit remains of the Creator's light, she closed her eyes to what her consort had become and remembered the one had had been. Sethi. Commander of Egypt—his body bloody and ruined, fighting her through that long, cold night at Kadesh. His lips against hers, fierce, as he took her on his bed before facing his execution, their bodies drenched in sunlight. His arrival at the Etemen'anki, having walked across the desert in search of her. The weight of the pillar as it claimed his life. His return as the god of war. His last words before Marduk stole him from her: *I am the one who loves you. The one who will find you again.* Sethi. My love. Another tear slipped free.

The pounding of footsteps. A cry of denial. The dull thump of a blade against flesh. A strangled cry.

Liquid heat splattered Istara, harsh, acrid, metallic. An explosion of light streamed through the backs of her eyes. Silence fell, brutal, immutable. Istara blinked, frantic, desperate to understand, to see. The warmth of blood streaked her arms and chest. Hers? Another's? Whose? Confusion tore a path through her, amplified by the tomb of white light surrounding her, dense as a cocoon. Faint with distance, a low shudder, ragged with sorrow and pain. A single word pierced the silence, a breath.

"Horus."

Aching with dread, Istara felt her way forward. Against the rough surface of the blood-soaked ashlars, the soft material of a silken gown. Her fingers came back, drenched in blood the color of ink. She edged closer, her breaths thin, shallow. Please. Let it not be her. The light thinned, just enough for Istara to make out the shape of a dark-haired woman, slumped on her side, a dark pool of blood beneath her torso.

Her heart taut, Istara turned her onto her back. Baalat's empty eyes met Istara's. Clutched within her hand, a brilliant blister of light. Its starlit tendrils trailed over the once-goddess's sundered torso, her blackened heart, lungs, and organs severed from their lacings—the blow meant for Istara.

Baalat's sacrifice impaled her, devastated her. The one who had granted Istara a second chance to live, and who had sacrificed the last of her light so Istara could become a goddess and pass through Surru had made her final, ultimate sacrifice—had imprisoned her soul in the jihn and forever separated herself from Horus.

Hollow with shame, Istara pulled the relic from Baalat's fingers. At her touch, its light streamed away from her, an awakened star. She rose. No more mistakes. No more would she let her love blind her. Too many had died. Urhi-Teshub had been right all along. Sethi was gone. She had to let him go.

Further away, Sethi's form shimmered and morphed, as though trapped in the heated waves of the desert. In his hand, the jihn's bleak outline stained itself against their cocoon of light.

He turned. Saw her. Strode toward her. His cold gaze fell to the relic. The jihn's light recoiled from it. Its symbols hissed, defensive, wary. Within its heart, its stolen souls fell silent. She sensed their presence, a single, shared breath, held. Within its bleak, hopeless walls: Baalat. Thoth. Arinna. Resolve slammed through her. She would not fail them.

She waited for him to meet her eyes. The darkness in his churned, endless, an abyss. Its evil reached for her, sought to control her, to possess her. She forced herself to hold his gaze, the loathsome sight of tendrils slithering along the surface of his blighted eyes making her flesh crawl.

"I thought I could save you," she said, her words muted in the silence of their isolation. "I thought my love would be enough."

Sethi lifted his brow, reeking disdain. A mocking, derisive smirk tainted the darkness of his mouth. "Whoever you think you love is gone." He shifted the jihn in his grip, though he did not raise it. "I could never love you. You are everything I hate."

His words, said from the mouth which only the night before had possessed hers in a passionate kiss, cut her deep. She let the pain slide through her, let the tide of her broken heart wash it away. She tightened her grip on the relic.

"I was wrong," she continued in the face of his contempt, "you are beyond the redemption of love."

Sardonic amusement touched the curve of his lips. "It must be humiliating to realize the limits of your power." He tilted the jihn, the obsidian depths of his eyes drinking in its aura of malignance. "Unlike you, I face no boundaries. The darkness offers unlimited reach." He cut a heavy look up at her from under his brow. "I tire of your words of love."

"And I, of your hate." She lay the relic against her breast and faced her consort, the sole remaining star in a void of dark.

Sethi hefted the jihn, the muscles of his arm proud against its burden of the dead. She waited for him to hurl a final insult, to spew another barrage of hate. He gave her one last scathing look before he sliced the jihn down, fast, efficient, a clean strike, aimed at her heart.

Calm flooded Istara. She stood before his onslaught, resolute, laced within the billowing halo of the Creator's light, the relic afire. At last, she understood she could not do both—save Sethi and defeat the darkness. To stop the darkness she must destroy the one she loved, a choice she had resisted until this final, anguished heartbeat. Clarity carved a path through her. There could be no greater loss than hers, no greater gain than his. Within the depths of her being, a conduit burst open, drew from the sequestered depths of the Creator's light. It flowed through her, a torrent, breaching her boundaries. Its fire scoured her soul, rendered her mute against its might, magnitudes greater than the power granted from the pillar. Pain screamed. She held on, resisting, as the light shattered her and remade her into an ephemeral being, a living embodiment of the light.

Through her light-laden eyes, the passage of time stalled. The jihn's keening, streaming edge approached the billowing barrier of her light with painstaking slowness. Sethi's eyes followed the fall of it, his features twisted, vicious, brutal, his lips pulled back in a grimace of triumphant, bloodthirsty savagery. The blade cleaved her barrier and smashed into the relic. A blinding, soul-crushing explosion of agony seared Istara's being. Darkness poured into her, poisoned with hate. Locked in her suffering, she met Sethi's eyes as the full brunt of the jihn's evil swarmed through her, sought to consume her.

Her consort clung to the jihn with both hands, his teeth clenched, his look no longer triumphant, but desperate. He hauled at the weapon which hung frozen in place between them, locked in the implacable grip of the relic.

A surge of her starlight roared away from her and swept over the jihn, down his arms and into his torso. It stormed into him, violent, thousands of blades of white fire. They sliced through him and penetrated the darkness in his eyes. He staggered, panting, as her light ripped through him. The fractals on his chest stuttered and flickered, black then gold, then black again.

Inky, dense tendrils of obsidian streamed from his torso, down his arms and into the jihn, where the darkness sought refuge from the relentless pursuit of her light. A million stars erupted from within her breast, a supernova. It streamed into the jihn, eclipsed its malignance, hauled the darkness to her. Against her breast, at the point of crossing between her light and his darkness, a sphere burst into existence, brilliant as a dying star. In its center, utter, impenetrable darkness. Around it, a halo of the purest light. Through the depths of her onslaught, and the unbearable weight of the evil boring into her, she comprehended the totality of her sacrifice. Through the collision between the jihn and the relic, her light and Sethi's darkness were no longer separate, but one.

Together, they suffered. Together, they would be extinguished. Together, they would make right what had become wrong. From the depths of her suffering, she met his eyes. His found hers, no longer black as the darkness fled from him and poured into the sphere. His lips moved. Her name. It bled from him, sacred, beloved, anguished, ravaged with grief.

The sphere spun faster, hauling her light and Sethi's darkness into it, draining them, the jihn, and the relic. From the jihn's heart a stream of souls fled, freed, a silent river of life. They surged into the sphere, slid into its light, sparks against its skin, until it became a glittering, brilliant thing, a world of stars.

The jihn tumbled to the ground, empty, vanquished, a shell. The relic tumbled after it, emptied of its purpose. Only the sphere remained between them, a verdant, perfect, beautiful thing, shimmering with the joy of its liberated souls.

Her consort moved around the sphere and faced her, the darkness within him gone. He remained, nothing more than an ephemeral shell, outlined in gray, his features ragged with remorse for his crimes.

"My love," he breathed, anguished, from within the barricade of his fading existence, "there is almost nothing left of your light."

Istara nodded, mute with grief. Sethi. Her love. Her only love. She drank in the sight of him, whole again, good. A god. Her god. There was so much she longed to say, to share with him. But there would be nothing. Only this brief, dying, shared heartbeat.

The light enclosing them vanished. Time ground to a stop. From within the faint whisper of her remaining light, Istara glimpsed their dying world. One third of the largest pyramid's base still remained, a crumbled ruin, its counterpart pressed against it, locked in their dying embrace. The roof of the dark city hung over them, close enough to see its people cowering and weeping among its shadows. Men, women, and children, riven with horror and fear. Beside one of the children, a dog looked down at them wild-eyed, its mouth open, in the midst of a frantic bark. The ships of the gods hung suspended in the thin space between, one of them on its side, about to curve around what remained of the pillar, collapsed into a massive globe of darkness and light.

Her consort reached out to her, his existence so faint she feared a breath might take him from her. She lifted her hand to his, her own nothing more than a thin outline of light against her near-lightless transparency. It was over. It was done. After all they had suffered, endured, lost, this was all there was left to them, a heartbeat of a reunion. She met his eyes—clear, honest, broken. To save him she had destroyed him—had destroyed herself. She held still, willing just a beat more time. She gazed at him. Memorized him. Soon they would be no more.

He touched her hand. The memory of him shattered the remnants of her soul. His love, eternal, profound, aching with loss, blistered into her.

The sphere shot away and slammed into the globe at the center of the pillar. A scathing wall of light washed over him. His eyes harsh with sorrow, Sethi disintegrated. For a heartbeat he remained, his image cast in ash.

The pillar's sphere spun on, relentless, its revolving beam of light tore through him. His ashes scattered, hurtled away, slaughtered by the light. The dark line of the sphere sliced through her. She exploded into a million stars, vanquished by the darkness. Lost in the chaos of her own destruction, his words found her, his voice intimate, yearning, a promise. She clutched them to her as she plummeted into the abyss of her dying love.

I am the one who loves you. The one who will find you again.

Istara opened her eyes. Speckled rays of early morning sun streamed through the filigreed lattices of her suite and flickered against the wall. For several heartbeats, disorientation clambered over her. Then, it came. The dream. Again. Every morning for the last week it had taunted her—the sensation someone had watched her as she slept.

It lingered at the edge of her awareness, sensual, enticing. She held still, not even daring to breathe. There. A glimpse of starlight over rugged features, eyes of gold, riven with love and longing. Fingers against her lips, tender, worshipful. A kiss, faint, a mere whisper. She clung to it, willing there to be more. The images faded, slid behind the curtain of her mind, elusive once more. In their wake, a wave of yearning, haunted with melancholy.

She lifted herself up onto her elbows and eyed the closed lattices, sensing the one she dreamed of had been here, before, with her, in this suite, in the flesh, and yet, no—it was impossible. She had no consort, nor even a lover. She lived like her confidant and closest friend, Thoth, chaste and alone, her time filled by her duties as the leader of the pantheon of gods.

And yet—frustration prickled. She searched her mind, traversed its lonely corridors. Nothing. She did not recognize the one who had come to her. He was not one of the gods, and neither would any dare use trickery against her, to deceive her into an amorous relationship. A memory of a late night conversation shared with Thoth eons ago tantalized. The god of wisdom had spoken of one who glinted with the power of the stars and resided in a realm far removed from the one of gods and men. The Creator.

Her cheeks warmed, shamed by the arrogance of her thoughts. Of course her visitor was not the Creator. He would never lower himself to take the form of one of his creatures. Or—would he? In the same conversation, Thoth had also mentioned during one of his solitary journeys into the mountains to commune with the Creator, a man—a powerful warrior—had walked out of the evening's shadows and asked to share Thoth's fire. He had carried a pair of fresh-caught fish, which he had prepared and served for their dinner.

They had whiled away the evening, companionable, comfortable, speaking of the stars, and of the vast time which encompassed their slow procession across the heavens. Later, deep in the night, as Thoth fought fatigue and struggled to stay awake, they spoke of beginnings and endings, of the death of eternity, and its rebirth, an endless cycle.

When Thoth woke to the gray light of dawn, his guest was gone, as was all evidence of his having ever been there. It was only as he rubbed his eyes he realized there were no lakes within hundreds of iters of the mountains. Whoever had come to him was no god, neither had he arrived in a ship—

Thoth had stopped there, content to leave the identity of his guest open to speculation. Istara had believed at the time Thoth had merely had a dream. Now, her certainty wavered.

She sat up and pushed the sheets aside, deciding she would ask Thoth more about his fish-carrying visitor, though she would never admit to her dreams, not even to him, with whom she was wont to share most of her thoughts.

Turning her mind to the day ahead, she considered the binding ceremony to come and the celebrations which would follow. She smiled, recalling Urhi-Teshub's joy when he had knelt and requested her blessing. At last, after entertaining the pantheon with their passionate, violent misunderstandings and equally amorous reconciliations, the pair had, at last, succumbed to the other. Both stubborn, both fierce, both alike in so many ways, and yet, they were perfect. It was rumored that atop one of Nisu's *ziqqurati*, Sekhmet had challenged Urhi-Teshub to a duel. Some said she had defeated him with her blades, until he, in turn, conquered her with his love.

Still smiling, Istara reached out to collect her silken robe. A white rose fell from its folds. A glimmer of stars glinted within its heart. It had been no dream after all. The one who had stood over her as she slept, his powerful jaw graced by a shimmer of starlight, had left her a gift.

She lifted the rose, admiring its perfection, the silkiness of its petals, the softness of its kiss against her cheek. Roses were her favorite. Although—white was an odd choice. In Elati, white roses were strewn over the bodies of fallen mortals, a symbol of grief, loss, and sorrow, of the finality of death. Wondering at its meaning, she set it upon her pillow. Despite the day only having just begun, its rich, exotic scent heavy with the warmth of the sun lingered against her soul, a promise.

The clarion peal of horns silvered the morning air. She eyed the rose for another heartbeat, hoping for another shimmer of starlight. It remained innocent of its previous glory, a mere rose once more. Suppressing a shear of disappointment, she left it behind and crossed the marble tiles, surrounded by the whisper of her robe. In the speckled light of the morning's sun, she pulled the nearest pair of shutters open and emerged into the rising warmth of a new day.

She went to the edge of the terrace. The city of Nisu spread away, its valley of white and gold temples, gardens, plazas, libraries, markets, and pools awakening to the steady, stately rise of the sun. The glittering palaces of the gods overlooked the basin of the city, where those who served the gods kept their villas—their indigo, emerald, garnet, and purple awnings rippling in the gentle, jasmine-scented breeze.

Across the sweep of city, nascent bursts of sunlight glinted against the rows of gold-sheathed obelisks lining the plazas and avenues. To the west, caught within the horizon's ribbon of pale pink, Elati's white moon lowered its bulk toward a marble-faced *ziqqurati*, whose tiers overflowed with elegant gardens.

Along the city's palm-lined avenues, movement, as the kings and queens of Elati's kingdoms arrived in their golden chariots and palanquins via the temples housing Thoth's portals. The royals and their guests poured into Nisu from their cities, having crossed vast distances within the space of a heartbeat. In their wake, trains of nobles bearing gifts for the storm god and the goddess of war. They made their way up the tiers to the flower-strewn plaza of the central complex, the buzz of their anticipation sizzling through the morning air.

Istara lifted her eyes past the growing throng clustering around the silken pavilions, past the trio of golden pyramids, which had been there ever since she could remember, to the enormous temple set in the center of the plaza—the temple where Urhi-Teshub and Sekhmet would soon bind their hearts together for eternity. From within the temple's colonnaded depths, an endless pillar of light streamed up into the heavens soaked with the light of stars, an eternal beacon which pierced the darkness beyond the reach of the ships of the gods.

Deep within the pillar's heart, Thoth had perceived a thin, almost imperceptible line of darkness which soaked its core, utter and absolute. Why such a thing was there, amidst the silent pyramids in the center of the city of the gods, or what it did remained a mystery. He had deemed the central complex sacred, an unknowable gift of the Creator and had spent a thousand years constructing the temple around the pillar, a place of mathematical perfection. It became a place for the gods to seek communion with the Creator of all life, though his silence had been deafening.

Istara cut a look over her shoulder, back into her suite, toward her bed where the rose lay, her heart riven between awe and hope. A whisper of the memory of his lips against hers fleeted through her, sending a shiver of pleasure rippling along her spine.

A quiet knock and the doors of her suite opened. Her attendants entered, reverent, quiet, laden with breakfast trays and her finery for the day.

She went to a divan overlooking the city and sat, waiting, as her servants prepared her breakfast platter, her thoughts lingering on the rose, and the one who had left it for her—a glimmer of starlight against his jaw.

※　※　※

Ahmen made his way across the plaza, weaving his way through the crowds toward Serde's pavilion, his heart thudding with anticipation. This would be his chance, perhaps his only chance. Sequestered within the hallowed walls of the queen's palace, he had seen her only twice during his numerous visits to Ikalur, when the queen's court had been present while the king knelt before the *pegagi* Ahmen had escorted from Anki, its liquid eyes enhanced by its affinity with the Creator.

The day he learned her name, the *pegagi*, Amara, had granted Serde's queen its companionship and wisdom for a month. The queen had called her over to greet the *pegagi*. She had lifted her hand to its nose, filled with wonder at its gold-tipped wings folded against its back, ready to take flight within the space of a heartbeat.

Aiya.

Her name sent still ripples through his soul, a gentle rainfall against the yawning ravine of his lonely heart. Since then, he hadn't stopped thinking of her, dreaming of her. He was a wealthy man, as wealthy as most kings, his affinity with the *pegagi* unparalleled, his fortunes enhanced by his friendship with the storm god—though how they had become friends neither of them could quite recall. Urhi-Teshub, having uncovered Ahmen's love interest, had sent a message to Serde's king to ensure Aiya would be in attendance on the day of his binding. In addition, he had requested as a gift to him, that she be released from her duties to the queen for the day.

Ahmen cast a quick look over his attire, ensuring his gold-embroidered kilt hung in its perfect folds, and his golden armbands and gold-embossed belt sat not a hair out of place. His oiled and scented skin gleamed in the light of the mid-morning sun, its nascent heat already warming his flesh. And now, he was only heartbeats from seeing her again, from having to craft a reason to make himself known to her. Within the shade of Serde's blue and white pavilion, he picked up a golden cup of mead from a server's tray and drank, eyeing the beautiful crowd from over the cup's rim. At the far end of the pavilion, atop a raised platform, King Rhewyn and Queen Welyn sat upon their thrones, smiling, happy and relaxed, sipping from jeweled goblets.

The faint scent of gardenias drifted over him, layered with the warmth of the sun, ripe fruits, and sweet spices. He knew that scent. Aiya. His heart thudded. He turned.

She tilted her head at him, a faint smile ghosted her lips. "My lord Ahmen-om-onet, you grace us with your presence." She bowed her head. "It is a pleasure to at last meet the one who communes with the *pegagi*."

Her soft greeting tore through him, unraveled him. He blinked, at a loss, her beauty even more devastating than he remembered. In the heartbeat before she had bowed, her eyes had touched his, brilliant, like emeralds, honest, gentle, good. In all his imaginings of how he would begin a conversation with her, it had never occurred to him she might speak to him first.

She lifted her head, met his eyes, the faint smile at the corners of her lips slaying him. "I am Aiya."

"I know," Ahmen said before he could stop himself. She caught her smile, turned and lifted a cup of mead from a passing server. Sipped. He watched her swallow in an agony of humiliation. Nothing was going as he had planned. Nothing.

"I know you know," she said, quiet, her eyes on the contents of her cup.

Ahmen caught the look she swept up to him from under her lashes, the shy smile, the faint tremor of hope as she caught her lower lip between her teeth, the act both innocent and sensual.

Her vulnerability tore into him, scored a path deep into his heart. To think he had feared she might reject him. He glimpsed the queen eyeing them from over the rim of her cup, her pleasure at their pairing ripe with expectation. He wondered if all this time Aiya had felt the same for him. In time, he would know the truth, but for now, he was content just to be with her, beside her, her heart calling to his.

He bowed, a slave to her perfection. "Lady Aiya," he said, no longer lost, but found, "shall we walk and talk of *pegagi*, and Ikalur, and of the celebrations to come today?"

He lifted his arm to escort her away from the oblique looks of Serde's nobility. The touch of her jeweled fingers against the back of his hand sent a bolt through him. In its wake, an image, sharp, lanced into him, of Aiya trapped within the wreckage of a burning ship, blistered and bloody, looking up at him with terror in her eyes.

He blinked, taken aback, distressed he might have glimpsed their future. No. His heart hardened as he shoved the disturbing image away. There would never be such a future for them as this. He would protect her, always. He looked down into her upturned face, her eyes open and trusting, utterly lacking in the artifice usual among a queen's women.

Under her quiet gaze, the noise of the crowd melted away. The steady thud of his heartbeat filled his senses, alive with the hope of her, and of the end of his fragmented dreams of another, her body laced with dark markings, her sorrowful eyes haunting him long after he woke. He enfolded Aiya's hand in his, and as her fingers laced between his there were no more dark images, only her smile, her light, and her love.

❋   ❋   ❋

In the dead of the night, Urhi-Teshub woke, his mouth dry as dust. His head aching, he rummaged through the detritus of the bedside table in search of something to drink, knocking over empty goblets, half-finished platters of sweets, fruits, cheeses, and savory breads, the riotous clatter unheard by Sekhmet, who slept on her stomach beside him, naked and scented with the love they had made during their first night as consorts. She lay sprawled across the vast bed, lost to the embrace of the gourd of liquor they had emptied on their return from the wedding celebrations, a gift waiting for them from the king of Rzhev.

"*'Friend for life'* the note said," he muttered as another goblet rolled away across the floor and smacked into a table leg. A jagged spear of pain stabbed the backs of his eyes. "Some friend."

He found half a cup of wine abandoned on the floor beside the bed. He emptied it as a shimmer of his light washed through him and dulled the pain in his head. Beside him, sheathed in a faint sheen of perspiration from the heat of the nearby brazier, Sekhmet's eyelids flickered as she roamed the realm of dreams. His heart aching with love, he leaned over and pressed a lingering kiss against her shoulder. Only the afternoon before he had stood with her, clad in white before the pillar of light and opened his heart to her. The heartbeat their hearts fused as one had seared itself into his soul. Their bond, already powerful, had become unbreakable, eternal, blessed by the light of the Creator.

He trailed his fingers along the length of her spine to the curve of her buttocks. Forever they would be one. Pleasure rippled through him. *Sekhmet. My love. My consort. I shall make you happy. So happy.*

At his touch, she roused, turned to face him. Pain tightened her features, dulled her eyes. "Wine," she groaned.

He got up, found an untouched pitcher on one of the side tables, filled a goblet and brought it to her. She took it from him and emptied it. The back of her hand went to her mouth. She wiped it, a warrior, unselfconscious, disarming him anew. He bit back a smile. No other goddess ever did that. He loved it. He loved her, his fierce, wild, warrior goddess.

Her light ignited, rippled over her features, slid through her eyes. A wave of relief shuddered through her. He moved around the bed and sat down beside her, the mattress groaning under the heft of his bulk. She handed him the goblet. He set it on the floor with the others, eyeing the chaos of the room. It had been a good night. Dice lay in the middle of the floor, along with the remains of their garments. He had no memory of having gamed with her, or removing their clothing. He wished he did.

"Better?" he asked.

She lifted her eyes to his, golden, perfect. Her lips curved, slow, seductive. "Almost," she murmured, holding her hand out to him. He pulled her to up him, caught her face in his hands and brushed his thumb over her lips. They parted, ready for his kiss.

"I love you," he murmured. It was the first time he had ever said the words, he had been saving it for this night. He held still, his eyes on her mouth, waiting for her reaction.

A faint smile. Her fingers slid over his pectorals, the closeness of her firm body reawakening his endless hunger for her. Her fingers trailed lower, captured him. "Show me how much."

He caught her against him and carried her down onto the bed. "You wouldn't be able to bear it," he whispered against her ear.

She drew him into her, her eyes burning with the fire of their shared love, and smiled.

※　※　※

His hands folded behind his back, Thoth paced the length of his study to the desk piled high with scrolls and back again to the open doors of the terrace. He paused at the opening, troubled. An anomaly. No. Two.

Lost to his ruminations, he gazed at the potted palms lining the edge of his terrace, granting him the privacy he loved. They stood in the pre-dawn stillness, stark, silent sentinels bathed in the blue light of the full moon, each individual frond outlined in sharp relief.

He turned from the moonlit terrace and the distant glow of the pillar of light, its radiance bathing the abandoned plaza and the silent, debris-strewn pavilions in starlight. On the other side of the room, laid out on a cleared spot on a table, the items which troubled him—items which, on his return from the wedding revelries had manifested before him from out of thin air.

At first he had thought himself far too full of wine, but then, a shimmer of starlight slid over one, and over the other, a ripple of darkness, utter, absolute. A heartbeat later, they lay before him, inert, dead, gray things, shadows from another world, the memory of their searing arrival, and their eclipses of darkness and light, burned upon his mind.

His lips pursed, he ventured to the table and leaned over the strange pair. One appeared to be a pendant the length of his hand. Two snakes entwined each other along the length of a staff. The other item a large weapon, the likes of which he had never seen before. Two crescent blades encircled a central handle. Upon the blades, engraved symbols, the language incomprehensible.

Thoth let out a puff of air, a blanket of vexation saddling him. And it had been such a good night. For the first time in a long time, he had had *fun*. Had even danced with the imperious Ma'at, who had set aside her headdress and let her dark hair fall free. She had smiled for the first time since he could remember, her transformation from severity into a glorious beauty astonishing him. And she had smiled at *him*. No one had ever smiled at him like that before.

He prodded the edge of the weapon's blade, morose. At his touch an image tore into him of a powerful warrior with golden fractals rotating upon his chest, his eyes black as pitch. The fractals juddered, erratic, their torment tangible. The warrior hefted the weapon and sliced it down, its edges keening, slavering with raw hunger, its cold symbols haloed in a desolate, blue-white light. A wall of agony slammed into Thoth's chest riven with darkness and suffering. Beyond the shear of his anguish, a voice called to him, one Thoth had never heard before. Her name blossomed against his mind. Arinna, the taste of it familiar, yet unknown. Together they suffered in a crushing vice of evil, shorn of hope. Time ceased to exist. In the depths of his despair, an eruption of blistering starlight scored the darkness and shattered the chains of his torment. Together with Arinna, he fled their prison into a shimmering well of light.

Thoth snatched his fingers back. He rubbed them against his kilt, seeking to erase the weapon's taint. He eyed it, wary. It had been the one which had been washed with the starlight. He rather thought that the safe one. It was the pendant which had rippled with darkness. He eased back, his fingers against his chin, contemplating the pair anew. Darkness and light, just like the pillar. What could it mean? Why were these items here, now? He rummaged through his scrolls. Perhaps—

Footfalls moved across the terrace, a heavy, confident tread. Startled, Thoth turned. No one could have gained access to his terrace without first coming through the study's door. His flesh crawled. To think someone had been out there, all along. Violation shrieked through him. His heart pounding, he pulled a leather scroll case from the table and brandished it before him.

The intruder strode into the study. The scroll case hit the rug with a quiet thud. It couldn't be. Not again. Not here. Unless—

"You," he breathed.

"Me," the other said, quiet. He walked over to the table. His gaze moved from the weapon to the pendant. A shear of sorrow slid over his features.

"These do not belong here." He cut a look at Thoth. A ripple of starlight washed through his eyes. "A mistake. I have had much to learn, and in a short time."

"Much to learn?" Thoth repeated. He shook his head, to clear it from a rising tide of confusion, realizing belatedly the one who stood before him, who had cooked fish upon the mountains was also the one who had wielded the strange, double-bladed weapon. Had he seen the future or the past? Darkness and light. His orderly world threatened to disintegrate.

"I must know," he stepped nearer to his visitor, memorizing the details of the one whose presence filled the study with light, power, and something . . . other, something unnamable. "Who are you, truly?"

"*What* am I would be a better question," his guest answered, oblique, as he waved his hand over the weapon and it dematerialized in a shimmer of white light. A heartbeat of hesitation, before he did the same to the pendant. He turned. "When I leave you will forget the relic, the jihn, and me. It is better this way." He moved to the terrace. At its opening he stopped and looked back over his shoulder. Thoth held his breath, aching with hope, willing his visitor to grant him something. Anything.

"Ah, you won't remember anyway," his guest relented. "Among other things, I maintain the balance between darkness and light. It is . . . a difficult burden, one to which I am not yet accustomed."

"You *are* the Creator," Thoth breathed. He sank to his knees. "I *knew* it."

"Perhaps one day I will be able to walk among you," the other continued, neither acknowledging nor denying Thoth's statement, "but for now, I have work to do." He looked around the study, out to the terrace, then up at the sky, graced by the globe of the moon lowering its bulk toward the horizon. "Do you like your world?"

Thoth blinked, taken aback by the non-sequitur. "I—yes, I mean, of course, it is beautiful. Quite perfect."

The other nodded, pleased.

"You *are* the Creator?" Thoth asked, diffident, no longer as certain of himself.

His guest shot him an enigmatic smile and vanished in a eruption of stars.

Thoth blinked. What in the Creator's name was he doing on his knees in the middle of his study? The wine must have been stronger than he remembered. With a groan, he pulled himself to his feet, his knee knocking against a scroll case. He bent down to collect it, wondering how it had gotten there. He set it back onto the cluttered table and looked around the room, sensing something was missing. He waited, hoping he might recall what it was, but like the fading of a dream upon waking, it passed.

A wave of fatigue washed over him. He yawned, loud and long. It had been a good night. He wandered toward the door leading to his sleeping room thinking of the pleasant hours he had passed celebrating with the other gods. He had even danced, something he had *never* done before. And Ma'at, she had smiled at *him*. His heart did a little somersault. Perhaps he might ask her to dinner tomorrow. She had an intelligent mind. They could talk about his latest project, the creation of portals to other worlds, though the amount of exotic matter he would need would be enormous—

Absorbed in his thoughts, he went into his sleeping room and closed the door.

❋ ❋ ❋

Teshub drifted, alone, in an endless expanse of light, its existence both as close to the living as a thought and as far from it as a star. Many times he had had the chance to succumb, to let the expanse crush his soul to fragments, granting him the final release of his existence into the light. Each time, he had refused. Not without Arinna.

It came again, the silent thundering wave which swept through the weave of the expanse as heavy as a mountain and as deep as an ocean. Its haul plowed through the souls in its path, crushing them into minuscule pinpoints of light. For what felt like the thousandth time, Teshub tumbled amongst a myriad of explosions. Starlight fragments rained back into the expanse's weave, ready to be remade anew. How long had he waited for her, endured these torrents? It felt like forever. *Arinna. My love. Come to me.*

As he remained where he should not, he had learned distance was irrelevant. He could be both everywhere and nowhere at the same time. This place reminded him of the anomaly inside the tower, of impossibilities—a multitude of dichotomies co-existing as one. He tried not to think about it too much. All he knew was if Arinna were here, he would feel it. He would *know*.

He drifted again, waiting for the light to fill up with more souls, and for the brutal wave to return and disintegrate the influx of new souls: dogs, cats, horses, women, children, men. A massive fish. They slipped past him, asleep, quiet, calm. He would not sleep. Not him. Not yet.

A violent eruption of souls gouted into the weave further away. He willed himself to it, curious. He had never seen anything like it before. Thousands heaved into the expanse, none of them asleep, or calm. They rushed past him, a silent, desperate wash, reminding him of a frantic shoal of fish seeking escape from a net.

A sensation shot through him, as familiar as the beat of his own heart, laden with sorrow. Amongst the chaos of the souls, one called to his, her presence a silvered horn, long awaited. *Arinna.*

He fled to her, found her, broken and weeping. He touched her face, sparks blossomed where their souls met. She looked up. Saw him.

Teshub?

Arinna. My love. I have waited for you.

He let her see what he had done after she fell, his refusal to leave her alone, even in death.

She went to him, his goddess of the sun, bathed in the light. She did not show him her path after she died, only her joy. He held her against him. It was over. At last, they were complete.

In his arms, she slept. He held onto her, cradled her, kissed her, aching with love. He had found her. The wave surged toward him again. This time, its thunder called to him, a reprieve, longed for, welcome. He closed his eyes and pressed his lips against his consort's brow. *I will love you again.*

The light sheared into them. A glimpse of stars, brilliant, beautiful, perfect. He fell with her, his storms at last silenced, into the womb of the light.

❋　❋　❋

The heat of a blazing sun prickled Baalat's skin and painted the backs of her closed eyes in pink and orange. The cry of a sea bird. The crash of a wave. She sat up. The froth of a retreating wave tumbled against the shell-strewn silt of a pale yellow beach.

A gust caught at her hair, rich with the alkaline taste of seaweed and brine. The faint scent of woodsmoke drifted in its wake.

Smoke. A memory tore through her, vivid, bloody, ugly and filled with pain. She lay on the ground in a place of flames, darkness, and death. Ahmen, his face half-gone, carrying her through the heat and violence. Istara, clad in light, about to be struck. Baalat caught her breath. The jihn.

She scrabbled at her gown, opening it to where Sethi had rent her torso almost in two. No. She stared at herself. Her torso lay unblemished. Confusion brutalized her. She should be dead. If not dead, she should be in the dark realm, back with her master. How could she be here on a pristine beach, alone and whole again? It had to be an illusion. She tied her gown back together, her fingers trembling as she awaited her master's return.

The view taunted her. The last time she had been on a beach, Horus had held her in his arms as the waves crashed against them, had kissed her with a ferocity which had taken her breath away. And now, he was gone. Taken from her by her own hands.

Tears swam through her vision, blurred the edges between the ocean and the beach, turned it into a smear. "Horus," she breathed, grief paralyzing her, fragmenting her soul. "My love. Forgive me."

"Forgive you for what?" a voice asked, quiet.

Baalat blinked. She dared not even look up, fearing she would find the dark one disguised as her consort, toying with her once more.

The rustle of a linen kilt as the one who had asked the question sank into a crouch beside her, his forearms coming to rest on his thighs, the movement soaked with familiarity. And yet, the dark one had deceived her before.

"Horus?" she whispered, tremulous, aching with hope.

He nodded, slow. "It is over. We are reprieved. Again." His hand moved to her chin, tilted it up. His eyes met hers, harsh in the brilliant sunlight. "You did everything right," he said, pride shunting through his look. "Everything. There is nothing to forgive."

"But how—"

Horus lowered his hand to her. She took it and followed him as he stood, her flesh prickling from his touch, alive, warm. His sudden presence bored into her, dismantled her walls of grief, sowed fields of hope. Another chance. The Creator had granted them another chance.

"I was there," Horus said. "I saw it all." He reached out and tucked a wind-blown tendril of her hair behind her ear. The act tender, ordinary, at complete odds with the profundity of their re-existence. He looked past her, over the roiling heave of the ocean. She turned, followed his gaze. In the distance, a pod of porpoises leaped from the water in playful arcs, their sleek bodies shimmering in the sun.

"After I fell, the Creator took me into his realm," her consort continued. His jaw tightened. "There was almost nothing left of him, or of his realm." He cut a look at her. "You were gone, too."

"I was there?" Baalat searched her mind. She had no memory of being with the Creator again, apart from the dream she had had in Ikalur. "When?"

"After the jihn took you," Horus answered, quiet, "the Creator brought me to his realm where he sought to protect you from the worst of the darkness." He looked down at his hands, clenched them into fists. "I have missed you so much."

Baalat sensed he was not finished. She waited, gave him time. Through the screen of her lashes she examined him, followed the deep lines around his mouth, the downward curve of his lips. Her consort was not the same as she remembered. A hardness sheathed him, distanced him. His wounds were deep, would take time to heal.

"The disk of the Creator's realm had disintegrated to the size of a courtyard. He took me to the edge and together we watched as you returned to Nisu, and were taken to Istara." His hand came to hers, the backs of his fingers brushed against her own, grief darkened the slant of his jaw. "I saw him kill you," he swallowed and let out an uneven breath. "I watched you fall."

Baalat's throat closed over. A tear escaped and slid down her consort's cheek. She caught his hand in hers. "But I am here now," she said, her words clogged with guilt for what he had witnessed. "My love," she went on, dogged, longing to ease his suffering, "we live again."

Horus nodded, terse. "Because of him."

"The Creator?"

Horus didn't say anything for so long Baalat feared he would not answer.

"No." He brushed the tear away with the back of his hand. "Sethi."

Baalat stilled, the roar of the sea faded, drowned by the thundering of her heart. Dread impaled her. So, their reunion was no reprieve after all but a manifestation of the darkness. She had failed. Istara had fallen. She shrank into herself, once more a hunted animal. Soon, the suffering would begin again.

"Because of your sacrifice," Horus continued, "Istara overcame the darkness." Horus met her eyes, read her disbelief. The muscles in his jaw clenched, he looked again out to the sea, then up to the clear, deep blue sky. "The Creator is gone. Our Creator."

"Gone?" Baalat breathed. She lifted her hand, gestured at the beach, the sea, the wave tops sparkling in the sunlight, all of it drenched in humid, salty air. "Then how is any of this possible?"

Horus fell silent again. His eyes moved along the heave and fall of the ocean's waves as he considered her question. "I doubt I will ever be able to explain, or understand. With the very last fragments of his light, the Creator brought you to his realm and made you whole again, although you did not wake." Horus nodded, as if reassuring himself of his words. "He gave me a look, one of profound pride, a look I will never forget just as the pillar exploded in a blistering wall of light and dark. When it was over, he was gone, and a great, empty void surrounded us. You and I continued to exist where we should not. It felt like an eternity." He shook his head, as if wishing to rid himself of the memory. "Who can say how long it was. Nothing else mattered to me but to hold onto you and never let you go."

Baalat tightened her grip on his hand. "And Sethi?"

Horus lifted his brow. He slid a look back up to the sky.

Baalat caught her breath. "He's—?" she stopped. "No. I cannot believe it."

"Nothing is eternal apart from the darkness and light," Horus said, squinting against the glare of the sun. "All this time I had believed the Creator was the source of all which exists. I was wrong. The Creator is a channel through which the darkness and light are made into all this. His task is to maintain the balance for all of creation."

Baalat sank onto her haunches. The heat of the sand prickled against her skin. Horus joined her.

"Sethi . . . granted us this?"

Horus nodded. He reached out and picked up a handful of sand and let it trickle through his fingers, a fine golden skein.

"What's he like?" Baalat asked as the last of the sand scattered to the wind.

"He is nothing like our Creator. He is . . . different. Stronger."

"And Istara?"

Horus brushed the remnants of the sand from his hand. "He allowed us to remain in his realm while he created our world. She lives again, though with no memory of him. He spared her that, at least."

"So he suffers alone."

Another nod, enigmatic.

Baalat pulled her legs out from under her and leaned back on her elbows. She tilted her face up. The sun kissed her face. She closed her eyes. It was over. At last.

"So it's just us now?" she asked.

The brush of his kilt against her thigh as he joined her. His fingers against her jaw, a caress. His grip tightened. He drew her to him, bathing her in his warmth, his love, his longing to live again, with her.

His lips touched hers, soft, gentle, taking her breath away. He pulled back, pressed his brow against hers.

"It's just us."

❋ ❋ ❋

The warmth of the evening sun on her back, Meresamun wandered along a row of grapevines, trailing her fingers over the ripe purple bunches, ready for the harvest. She smiled, pleased. It had been a good summer, dry and warm, but not too hot. Unlike last year, there would be many jars of wine to take to the market. The storehouse would be full come winter. A ripple of satisfaction washed through her. She enjoyed the life the light had granted her. Although, not a day passed when she did not think of the one who had loved her, his devotion pure, honest, untainted by the darkness.

A memory slid through her mind, of the first time he had taken her into the heavens in his ship and showed her the wonders of the world, of vast swathes of ice and snow, mountains clad in white, and oceans which never seemed to end. She touched her fingers to her lips, recalling his first kisses, as hot as a blacksmith's forge. He had worshiped her, had been enslaved to her. And now, he was gone, the one she still loved, still yearned for—though for all his crimes, for all his violence, she knew she should not.

She lowered her hand and walked on. Over the past two years, since she had woken on the island of Oenone in a sleeping room she did not recognize, and was dressed by her servants in a white gown held at her shoulders with golden clasps in the shape of a wreath, there had been admirers who had sought her hand in marriage—wealthy tradesmen, diplomats from afar, even the second-eldest prince of Knossos had arrived on his ship, its masts clad in ruby-red sails, the renown of her beauty having reached him from across the Great Sea. But she had refused them all. There was only one for whom her heart still beat, there could never be another again. Marduk. Her heart tightened. What had happened to him? To all of them?

From the scrolls she had within her library, she had gleaned much. She lived in a world more than eight hundred years removed from her own. A king with the same name as her father had once reigned in Babylon, preceded by a king with the same name as her grandfather. However, the similarities ended there. Babylon still stood, the destruction she had witnessed had never happened here. Her father's once-kingdom was no longer autonomous, had long been subsumed by one empire after another. Urhi-Teshub's empire of Hatti had vanished soon after they left, lost to famine, disease and the encroachment of other, now long-lost empires. Egypt's might had been reduced to a satrapy of the world's greatest empire, Perses, ruled by Xerxes, a king who reminded Meresamun of Ramesses, driven, ambitious, insatiable.

Only Hellas had remained untouched by Xerxes's grasp, separated from Perses by the walls of the sea. Then, a year ago, he came, his ships carrying more than a hundred thousand warriors to the gates of Thermopylae.

For two days, the Hellenes held them back at a narrow pass until they were betrayed. Forced to retreat, a group of three hundred Spartans had held back the onslaught at the narrow pass for another day, their lives sacrificed to ensure the safe retreat of the Hellenic armies. Then, as the Persiens overran the evacuated city of Athens, and the fires in the city reflected against the Oenone Sea, the tide of the war changed in favor of the Hellenes at the battle of Salamis when Oenone's navy allied itself with its enemy, the Athenians, to stand against the Persiens.

She had watched, along with hundreds of others, atop the highest point of Oenone as the flames and smoke of burning ships darkened the sky, and the thin cries of the war horns drifted to them through the ash. If the Hellenes fell, the Persiens would turn to Oenone, renowned for its mineral wealth and prowess in trade. And, Meresamun, with her vineyards, alone and unprotected, would be taken, enslaved to another king.

In the days before the battle, she had barely eaten, nor could she sleep, impaled by her dread of renewed captivity. Two years. It wasn't enough. She had come to love her freedom and independence, even if its cost came at living alone, in a world almost a millennium removed from her own.

But her fears had come to nothing. Against the savage drums beating their triumph, the Persiens had fled back across the sea, their navy a crippled, broken thing. Hellas was safe. She was safe. That night, she had eaten again, her heart overflowing with gratitude to the brave warriors of Athens and Oenone.

Beyond the vineyard, a sparse forest of fragrant pines clambered up the island's dry slope to the edge of her estate. Their topmost boughs swayed and dipped in the breeze, paying homage to the pink hues of the evening sky. The breeze rippled toward her, along the leaves of the vines, verdant with the sweetness of wild honeysuckle. She breathed in its rich, heady fragrance. Contentment suffused her.

She reached the end of the row of vines and wandered across the dusty earth, dotted with boulders and flowering shrubs toward the lane leading up to her estate from the valley. In the distance, atop another high hill, the newly rebuilt Temple of Aphaia's columns reflected the orange glow of the sunset. Between its two front columns, one, then another brazier flared to life, its flames a beacon to those seeking the solace of the gods in the aftermath of Salamis.

Though they were worshiped in temples across Hellas, no gods lived in this world, and no ships soared overhead, their thunder sundering the skies with flames of fire. Only the cries of birds filled the heavenly expanse. She found she preferred it this way. The time she had spent in Elati had shown her another life, another world soaked in wonder, but her heart longed for simplicity, for the soothing passage of the seasons, her quiet routines and the comfort of her library.

Movement at the bottom of the lane drew her attention from the temple. A warrior approached, a pair of swords strapped to his belt, the shape of his shield marking him as an Athenian. She lifted her brow. A daring man. Oenone and Athens might have stood together at the battle of Salamis, but the two states were bitter enemies, had united only to stop their common enemy.

A mere pair of weeks had passed since then. Perhaps he was making a pilgrimage to the temple, while what little goodwill still remained between the states in the battle's aftermath. She turned and called one of the servants to her, to prepare a platter of olives, bread, and goat's cheese, and to open one of her best jars of wine. Enemy or not, he had ensured her freedom. She would not refuse him a meal.

She waited, watching him work his way up the steep rise, the thick muscles of his chest rising and falling with exertion. Gray flecked his dark hair. An older warrior. She preferred those. Their blood was not so hot, and the stories they told were better. Most had wives and children, and if she refused their suggestion of warming their bed, they accepted her refusal with grace. He breached another turn, the nearest one, and looked up at her, a brief glance.

She caught her breath. Her heart stilled, then jolted back to life, beating so hard, it hurt. He looked so like Marduk—or what Marduk would look like if he had aged twenty years. She hauled her thoughts back, calmed the riot within her breast, remonstrated herself. Of course he was not Marduk. It had been so quick, a glance. The sun had been in her eyes. She had imagined it, her heart seeing what it willed. His head down, the warrior carried on, slow, steady, a limp in his step, betraying an unhealed injury. Now she understood why none had challenged him.

He reached the end of the lane and passed through the opening of the lime-washed boundary wall. He turned and faced her, panting a little from the climb. He walked to her, his blue eyes moving over her, calm, quiet. Meresamun's heart shattered its restraints, its thunder drowning out the gritty tread of the warrior's sandals against the earth. Her breath thinned. She knew she should greet him, but no words would come. His likeness to Marduk bored into her, seared her soul, struck her mute.

He stopped before her.

"You were hard to find," he said, his voice rich, reverent, the hardened, sun-darkened planes of his face softening. "For twenty-two years, I have fought with the armies of Perses, Egypt, and Hellas searching for you. I lived only for the hope of finding you again. At Salamis, I heard of a renowned beauty in Oenone who refused all suitors—even a prince of Knossos. It was said she still loved another . . ."

"Say my name," she breathed.

"Meresamun," he said, low, intimate.

She swayed. He caught her arm, held her steady. His touch scorched her senses, blistered past the long dormancy of her heart, eclipsed the sundered time between them. Memories she had locked away smashed through the walls of her careful confinement. *Marduk.*

He stepped closer. The nearness of him awakened the silence of her soul, filled her with a riot of color, music, life. "My love," he said, earnest. "I am here. I am myself again."

"You followed me," she whispered, her eyes harsh with tears. She blinked them back, unwilling to relinquish the sight of him, afraid he might vanish.

He smiled. Her heart stuttered. It was the same as she remembered but without the taint of cruelty. He was different.

Better. "And now," he said, pulling her toward him, his longing for her visceral, "I have found you."

She succumbed to the pull of his embrace, willing, trembling, aching for his touch. His lips found hers, his passion the same, though richer, sweeter, tinged with sorrow and remorse. He pulled back, stroked her cheeks with his thumbs, his hands rough and callused against her skin. The hands of a warrior. She lifted her hand, put hers over his, savored the warmth of him, the firmness of his sudden existence.

"You called me Meresamun."

He smiled again, easy, confident, the slant of his lips no longer harsh with supremacy, but seasoned with life, with pain. "Meresamun is who you are," he said, his clear blue eyes holding hers, tender. "Who I love."

Euphoria spiraled through her. It swept her away as he drew her against the heat of his scarred chest and kissed her, fierce, possessive, hungry—a prince, a warrior, a man.

❋　❋　❋

Unable to sleep, Istara walked along the sinuous graveled path of her private gardens into the walled maze of the rose arbor, the humid night air laden with the sultry scent of its quiet blooms. She reached out to caress the petals of a red rose, a shaft of longing piercing her. It had been many years since the binding of Urhi-Teshub and Sekhmet. Since that day, there had never again been another rose, or another dream of the one who had visited her, starlight whispering over his features. Each night she had hoped he might return, and each morning she woke, disappointed.

A chill wind swept through the arbor. Wrapping her arms around herself, she cast a look up into the sky. Heavy clouds gathered, their roiling tumult highlighted by the radiant light of the pillar. A distant rumble of thunder strafed the heavens. Istara shivered with anticipation. Thunderstorms were a rarity in Nisu. It would be a pleasure to sit in her suite and listen to the crack of thunder, to wait for the heartbeat the darkness fled from the shear of lightning, and to revel in the rush of rain pounding against her terrace and shutters.

As the wind rose, freeing loose petals from the roses, she began to retrace her steps back through the maze to the palace, her gown whispering against the path, thinking she might infuse a pot of *téy*. Another roll of thunder severed the skies, much closer than the last. Not wishing to be caught out in the rain, she quickened her pace.

A burst of brilliant light erupted behind her. She turned, startled. A faint glow lingered above the center of the arbor's maze. She hurried back through its twists and turns, her heart tight, searching for the rise of smoke over the arbor's walls, dreading the crackle of flames. Please. Not her white roses, not the ones she had cultivated from the one he had left her. Along the last curve of the maze, on the other side of the high wall, within the eye of the arbor—the crunch of heavy footfalls against gravel.

She slowed her steps, wary. Whoever they were, they would have heard her coming. She called to her light and wreathed herself in its protection before pressing on through the arch into the center of the maze. She stopped and turned, slow. The arbor's heart lay quiet, its walls steeped in shadow. Through the screen of her light, she eyed its circumference, followed the familiar shapes of her roses climbing their trellises. There. A blot against the roses. A man. No, a warrior. For a heartbeat a sheet of anger poured through her, how dare a mortal enter her sacred gardens.

A flickering of starlight swept over his body, outlining the shape of him, the power of his build. She caught her breath. Her light faded. Her heart thudded, wild with hope.

A crack of thunder sheared her senses. A bolt of lightning sliced across the top of the sky. He stepped out of the shadows. In his hand, one of her white roses. He came to her, slow, cautious, as though he feared she might flee.

He stopped, no more than an arm span away from her. His presence called to her, ageless, eternal. Another wash of starlight shimmered over his features, highlighting his jaw, the lonely slant of his mouth, the longing in his eyes.

Istara held still, willing it not to be a dream, for him to be real, for these precious heartbeats to never end. He lifted the rose to her. A glimmer of his starlight sparkled against the petals' edges.

She took it, though he was careful not to touch her. She met his eyes, waited, willed him to speak.

"Istara."

Her heart lurched. His voice, she recognized it. Knew it like the contours of her heart. Her name on his lips turned a key to a hidden lock within her soul, opened a door, dragged her back to a forgotten, nameless place of great loss. Raw, jagged peaks of sorrow tossed her from their heights into an ocean of grief.

He gazed at her, gentle, patient, his presence soaked with power far beyond her understanding. "I wish to grant you a gift, though it is one you may wish to refuse."

Istara waited, unable to trust herself to speak. He nodded to a nearby marble bench. She went to it and sat. He sank to his knee before her, his kilt sliding over the slabs of his muscled thigh. His movements called to her, hauled at her like the pull of the ocean's tide. Another wave of sorrow washed through her, poignant, broken. He leaned forward and rested his elbow against his knee, the action intimate, familiar.

"It is the gift of your memories." He waited, watching her from under his brow, his look unreadable.

"My memories?" Istara repeated, at last finding her voice. "But I have my memories."

A shear of sorrow laced through the starlight in his eyes. "Not all of them," he said, quiet. "I spared you those which would have caused you to suffer."

Istara digested his words. Then: "Why would you wish me to suffer?"

"I do not," he answered. "I needed time to become what I am, to control what is within me. I would not have had you suffer for all those years until I could."

She let the question land between them. "Who are you?"

"Will you accept my gift?" he returned, his eyes burning, hot, bright with stars. His look tore into her, harsh with hope.

Thunder slammed through the skies. In the distance, a wall of rain pummeled the palace's roof and terraces, sliced its way toward the gardens, deafening, a roar.

A burst of lightning outlined the planes of his jaw. A shadow of understanding fleeted through her. He did not need to tell her who he was. The truth was buried within her, past the walls of her sorrow. His presence called to the silence within her soul. The answer was within her. The one he would return to her, if she would let him.

"Yes," she said, aching to breach the barrier within her, to open the doors she had not known existed until now. She longed to know him, no matter how much it cost her.

His eyes fierce with pride, he held up his hand to her. She lifted hers to his. Starlight swarmed in his upturned palm. She lowered her hand to his. His warmth tore through her, awakened her. He clasped her hand and rose to his feet, pulling her up after him, enclosing her in the shelter of his arms just as the rain slammed into them.

Locked in his embrace, she clung to him as his starlight poured into her. For a heartbeat, there was only the wonder of him. And then, her memories came in a riot of color, sound, and smell. The siege of Kadesh. Tarhuntassa. Tanu-Hepa. Anash. Urhi-Teshub. The battle of Kadesh. Sethi, fevered and wounded, threatening to kill her. The memories roared on, torrential, carrying her past her death and resurrection, to Sethi's execution and reprieve by Horus. Egypt. Thamud. Babylon. Surru. Elati. The jihn. The relic. Her final sacrifice to save her consort from the darkness. Its cost. Her fall. His promise to find her carved against the walls of her soul.

The rain slowed and pattered against them, soft. Within the shelter of his arms, Istara trembled, overcome. Sethi caught her chin in his hand, tilted her face up to his. She closed her eyes and parted her lips, willing him to go on, to kiss her, to claim her anew, to return them to love they had made before the darkness had stolen him from her.

"My love," he said, his mouth brushing against hers. Shivers raced up her spine, familiar, breathless. "I am yours, if you will still have me."

"How much time do we have?" she whispered, hating the question, but needing to know. He would leave her again. She would be alone. He was the Creator after all. Already her heart ached. Loneliness clawed at her. Sethi.

His arms tightened around her. "Forever," he answered, and carried her to the stars.

ACKNOWLEDGMENTS

All my life, I believed goddesses were female deities with supernatural powers, far removed from us, mere mortals of flesh and bone. But as I worked through the storylines of Istara, Baalat, and Meresamun, and the lesser ones of Sekhmet, Arinna, and Aiya, I realized I was wrong in my understanding. *We* are the goddesses. We are the ones who possess the greatest power: the power to love, to forgive, to sacrifice everything for the greater good. *We* are the light. We have the power to stop the darkness that surrounds us in this world, a world driven by the desires and corruption of the darkness. Of men lost to its decimating thrall.

We live in terrifying, dark times. In many ways, this final book is not only the culmination of the series but an allegory of our fractured society and broken, dying world. But there is hope, so long as we nurture the light within us, and face the darkness of others with strength, love, and perseverance, we will overcome. Without us, the goddesses, there would only be darkness. A world without light.

And so to you, the goddesses who surrounded me with your light when I faced my darkest time, I wish to thank you for bearing me up, for keeping me going, for believing in me, for not letting the darkness overwhelm and destroy me. With all my heart, thank you Irene Oust, Emma Filbey, Alison Wright, Åsa and Lisa

Gunnarsson, Gunilla Pettersson, Jeanine Croft, Scarlett Drake, Deanna Tobin, Antonia Bezinović, Cecilia Peltola, Lisa Buchanan, Tanya Clyde, Angel Mulungi, Melissa Mitchell, Lindsey Clarke, Beth Bowman, Alvida Karlsson, Karen and Sonja Braun, Martha Ross, Julie Gates, Maria Hall, Ana Clements, and Linda Pohl. Each of you held me in your heart, even while facing your own dark times. This book would never have happened without you.

To Michał Karcz, who breathed life into the cover art with each stunning detail. Your mind is a gift, your talent unsurpassed. Only you could have brought to life a world which had long lay hidden in my heart.

To Chris O'Byrne for your professionalism, friendship, and support, and for making this book as beautiful to read as all the others. It was a good day when our paths crossed.

To Debbie O'Byrne who always has time for my questions and projects. Your cheery mails always brighten my day. Thank you for completing the cover design on short notice and for making the map of Elati look just as glorious as all the others. It is such a pleasure to work with you. I still hope to have that Starbucks with you someday.

To Gösta Vedlund, and Philip Oxelbark who were there for me when I needed them most—you have proven the axiom that not all heroes wear capes.

To Kath Stansfield, whose presence both as a friend and an editor during this year gave me the courage to write the most challenging story I have ever told. Your quiet presence, beautifully wrapped gifts and handwritten cards cheered and bolstered my flagging spirits through those long, silent hours at the keyboard. When we first crossed paths in March 2016, you reviewed one of the earliest versions of *The Lost Valor of Love*. Your feedback opened the door to a journey which spanned three books and almost four years of writing. Every step of the way you were there, a gentle presence by my side, watching over me, encouraging me, waiting for this caged songbird to find her wings and fly.

And finally, to Marcelle Snell, my best friend who flew to Sweden to stay with me when my weight plummeted and I had to be fast tracked through the hospital for cancer scans. You held me when I cried, you listened when I ranted, you read my emails when I was too afraid to, you bought me pastries from the bakery, you laughed at my terrible jokes. You consoled me while I fell apart on the stairs late one night. You loved me, my sister, my heart, my friend. I could not live without you. You always believed in me, and in this series. This is for you, my goddess of light. May the darkness at last, end.

The year I spent writing *The Rise of the Goddess* was one of the worst years of my life. It started quietly, like those tremors which rumble months ahead of a devastating magnitude nine earthquake. But that's when it began—when I began to write the final book. If I am honest, I already knew it, I could feel it in my bones. Something awful was coming. I just didn't know what. Now I know.

The first draft of the final book of the series was begun on a broiling hot August day in 2018, during the most severe heat wave and drought in Sweden's history. Fields withered. Trees succumbed. Thousands of livestock were slaughtered because farmers had no food for them. Entire forests burned, so vast they could be seen from space. The acrid stink of smoke was always in the air. Water was rationed. My garden dried up. It was unbearable to watch it die. That was how it began. In the fires of August. The beginning of the end of my world. And with every word I wrote, as though penning my own destruction, my life worsened.

The last word of the first draft was written on another blistering day in August 2019, almost one year later to the day, in a different house to the one where the majority of the series had been written. I sat alone in this house, where I did not feel like I belonged, where I was lonely. Where I did not know anyone. In January

2019, we moved to another house to better accommodate my husband's career and my medical needs. It was the move which triggered the tremors into minor earthquakes, when the windows rattled, and the chandeliers shook. When everything began its brutal descent into the abyss—when I saw what was coming, but fought it with every ounce of my being.

Then, in June 2019, the earthquake struck and its devastating tsunami slammed into me. As I prepared to go out for dinner with him, my husband left. I did not see him again until four weeks later when he informed me he was going to divorce me. After that I never saw him again, the man I had loved for ten years. Gone. Just like that. I wrote this book locked in a vacuum of silence, lost, alone, unloved.

In the end, he was Muwatallis, and I, his unwanted queen, Tanu-Hepa. Wherever he is, I hope he is happy. Even though this year has almost destroyed me, I still have him to thank for having been able to write this series. It was while I was with him I had the freedom to write full time. He supported my writing, was proud of it, was proud of me. Nothing can take that away, not even the sorrow of a broken heart.

Because of what must unfold for each of the characters to complete the story's arc, *The Rise of the Goddess* is perforce the darkest book of the series. Often, I wondered if the pain and sorrow I suffered while writing the book was somehow meant to be, that the strength of the book's narrative lay in the author's anguish. I cannot say. I was driven to write this series years ago. I had planned the final book long before these things unfolded.

And yet. Who can say? Perhaps there is a Creator after all, and I am a piece on *his* game board, and this series was always meant to be written—my heart, happiness, and security its ultimate cost. If so, I would do it again, and again, and again. I could do nothing else but write Istara's story. It is as if I had been destined to write this series. And now, my task is done. Perhaps, for me, at last, a portion of happiness—of love—awaits. Perhaps.

There is very little of historical significance in *The Rise of the Goddess*, since the majority of the book takes place in the fictional world of Elati. However, I could not resist the chance to breathe life into the once-glittering era of an island where I lived for some months in the past. Oenone is the modern day island of Aegina, two hours from Athens by hydrofoil. The Temple of Aphaia is still there, albeit in ruins. Its grandeur still exists in its worn columns and ashlars, and its views over the Saronic Gulf are breathtaking. If you close your eyes, you can imagine falling back into the time when the armies of Athens and Oenone stood together as one, sworn enemies, at the Battle of Salamis and drove Xerxes and the Persians back across the sea, amid the flames and smoke of burning ships and cries of fallen warriors.

E A Carter

ABOUT THE AUTHOR

E A Carter is a Swedish-British-Canadian. She's a drinker of tea, rescuer of cats, fighter of lupus, taker of photographs, and writer of books.

Her debut novel *The Lost Valor of Love* is the first book in the Transcendence series and is the Gold Winner of Adult Fiction in the 2019 Wishing Shelf Book Awards, and a finalist winner in the First Novel and Historical Fiction categories in the 2019 Indie Author Network's Book of the Year Awards.

The Call of Eternity is the second book in the Transcendence series and was shortlisted in the 2020 Page Turner Awards.

The Rise of the Goddess is the third book in the Transcendence series and was a finalist in the 2021 Page Turner Book Award.

The Lost Letters: The Dark World of Narcissistic Abuse was shortlisted in the 2021 Page Turner Book Award, won Highly Commended Non-Fiction Author and a PR campaign from Palamedes PR in London.

In 2021, *I, Cassandra* won Honorable Mention in the 9th Annual Writer's Digest Self-Published eBook Awards.

Find her @ authoreacarter.com

www.ingramcontent.com/pod-product-compliance
Lightning Source LLC
Chambersburg PA
CBHW060606100726
47907CB00006B/1518